Richard Woodman was born in Lo[...] Tall Ships race before becoming a [...] cargo-liners at the age of sixteen. He [...] including weather ships, lighthouse[...]  from apprentice to captain. He is the [...] of fiction and non-fiction, a member of the Royal Historical Society, the Society for Nautical Research, the Navy Records Society and the Square Rigger Club. In his spare time he sails an elderly gaff cutter with his wife and two children.

'This author has quietly stolen the weather-gauge from most of his rivals in the Hornblower stakes' *Observer*

'Packed with exciting incident, worthy of wide appeal to those who love thrilling nautical encounters and the sea' *Nautical Magazine*

'It is in the technical detail of ship handling, sails, rigging and myriad other details that Richard Woodman excels' Philip Wake, *Seaways*

A full list of Richard Woodman's fiction and maritime history titles may be found at www.richardwoodman.com

Distant Gunfire

The Fifth Nathaniel Drinkwater Omnibus

The Shadow of the Eagle
Ebb Tide
The Night Attack
The Steeple Rock
On Nathaniel Drinkwater (essay)

RICHARD WOODMAN

timewarner paperbacks

A *Time Warner* Paperback

This omnibus edition first published in Great Britain by Time Warner Paperbacks in 2003

Distant Gunfire Copyright © Richard Woodman 2003

Previously published separately:
The Shadow of the Eagle
First published in 1997 by John Murray (Publishers) Ltd
Published in paperback by Warner Books in 1998
Reprinted 2000, 2002
Copyright © by Richard Woodman 1997

Ebb Tide
First published in 1998 by John Murray (Publishers) Ltd
Published in paperback by Warner Books in 1999
Reprinted 2000, 2001
Copyright © by Richard Woodman 1998

The Night Attack was first published in *The Mammoth Book of Men o' War Stories*
and *The Steeple Rock* in *The Mammoth Book of Hearts of Oak*,
reproduced with thanks to the editor of the anthologies, Mike Ashley,
and the publishers, Constable & Robinson
On Nathaniel Drinkwater is an original essay specially written for this omnibus
Copyright © by Richard Woodman 2003

A CIP catalogue record for this book is available from the British Library.

ISBN 0 7515 3267 3

Typeset in Palatino by M Rules
Printed and bound in Great Britain by Bookmarque Ltd, Croydon, Surrey

Time Warner Paperbacks
An imprint of
Time Warner Books UK
Brettenham House
Lancaster Place
London WC2E 7EN

www.TimeWarnerBooks.co.uk

The Shadow
of the Eagle

For
Gail Pirkis
with many thanks

Contents

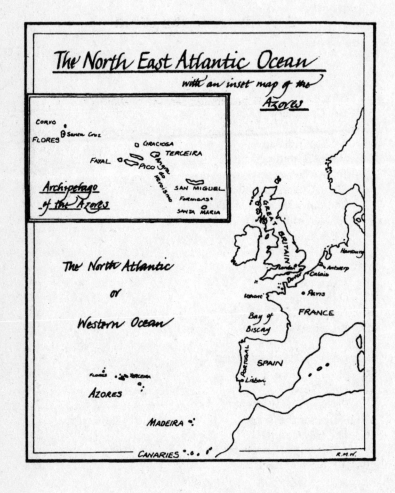

PART ONE
A Whisper in the Wind

'Above all, gentlemen, beware of zeal.'

TALLEYRAND, PRINCE OF BENEVENTO

'Where in the name of the devil, is Montholon?'

The tall officer, wearing the jack-boots and undress uniform of the Horse Grenadiers of the Imperial Guard turned from the overmantel and addressed the newcomer, a young captain of hussars whose lank hair hung in old-fashioned plaits about his fierce, moustachioed features.

'Delaborde, where the hell have you been?' added a colonel of hussars in the sky-blue overalls and brown tunic of the 2nd Regiment, staring round the wing of a shabby chair in which he was seated, puffing at a long-stemmed clay pipe.

'Where *is* Montholon?' the horse grenadier repeated.

'Let the poor devil speak.' The fourth occupant of the room commanded. He was dark of feature, his face recessed in the high collar of his plain blue coat, and he had been sitting in the window, quietly reading, while the impatient cavalry officers fussed and fumed.

'Well, Delaborde, you heard what Admiral Lejeune said . . .'

Colonel Montholon sent me to ask you to wait, gentlemen. He apologizes for keeping you all, but he is not yet free to join us.'

'Why not?' asked the horse grenadier.

'He is waiting upon Talleyrand . . .'

'That pig . . .' A frisson of contempt, mixed with apprehension, seemed to move through the group of officers in the dingy room, enhancing their air of conspiracy.

'It is ironic that it should come to this,' said the colonel of hussars, scratching at the pale weal of a long sabre scar running over the bridge of his nose and down his left cheek. 'Pour yourself a glass Delaborde,' he said, resuming his contemplation of the heavy curls of tobacco smoke that rose from the yellowed bowl of his pipe.

An air of heavy, silent gloom settled on the waiting men, disturbed only by the faint chink of bottle on glass rim and the gurgle of Delaborde's wine. After a few moments Delaborde, prompted by the wine uncoiling in his empty belly, spoke again.

'I am confident Colonel Montholon has the information we want.'

'You mean his sister has the information we want,' sneered the horse grenadier, throwing himself into a spindly chair that stood beside a small, pine table and thrusting out his huge jack-boots so that the rowels of his spurs dug into the meagre square of carpet. The colonel of hussars turned from the wraiths of pipe-smoke and glared at him.

'You may have enjoyed better quarters in the guard, Gaston, but be pleased to respect my landlady's property. This is a palace for a light cavalryman.'

'You aren't thinking of staying,' the horse grenadier remarked sarcastically.

'It looks as though we might have to. Besides it is Paris . . . True I had more princely quarters in Moscow, but they were less congenial . . .'

'For God's sake where the hell *is* Montholon?'

'Delaborde has already told you, Gaston. Now hold your tongue, there's a good man.'

Gaston Duroc expelled his breath in a long and contemptuous exhalation. 'I do not like waiting at the behest of a turd in silk stockings . . .'

'That is no way to refer to the head of the provisional government of France, Gaston,' the colonel of hussars reproved Duroc with a chuckle. 'Talleyrand is not the author of all our misfortunes, merely an agent of destiny. It is we who are going to change that, and if it means waiting until the turd has finished fucking Montholon's sister, then so be it.' Colonel Marbet resumed his pipe.

'Very philosophical, Marbet,' remarked the admiral, looking over his book at Duroc. 'Why don't you join Delaborde in a glass? It seems to have had a good effect upon him.'

They all looked at the young hussar. He had slumped on a carpet-covered chest which stood in a corner of the room, leant his elbow on his shako, and drifted into a doze, the wine glass leaning from his slack fingers.

'Poor devil's hardly had any sleep for a week,' said Marbet, 'he's been escorting Caulaincourt back and forth to Bondy to negotiate with the Tsar. I daresay while Caulaincourt received every courtesy, poor Delaborde was left to sit on his horse.'

Duroc grunted and filled a glass, then the company relapsed again into silence, all of them recalling the tempestuous events of the last few days. Caulaincourt's diplomatic shuttle between the Tsar at the head of the ring of allied armies closing upon Paris, and the beleaguered Emperor of the French at Fontainebleau, had resulted in the allied demand that Napoleon must surrender. A few days earlier, the French senate had cravenly blamed all of France's misfortunes upon the Emperor whom they had formerly fawned upon. Thereafter, Napoleon had abdicated in favour of his young son, but the imperial line was doomed. The British government dug King Louis XVIII out of his comfortable lodgings in Buckinghamshire and prepared to place him on the throne of his fathers. Alone among the crowned heads of Europe who now bayed for the restoration of legitimate monarchy in France, he had never treated with the man they all regarded as a usurper.

To the conspirators in Colonel Marbet's lodgings, the usurper was the elected leader of their country, and the rumours that he had attempted to poison himself gave their intentions a greater urgency.

'Someone's coming!' Duroc's remark galvanized them all. He was on his feet in an instant; Delaborde woke with a start and dropped the glass, caught it on his boot from where it rolled unbroken onto the floor. Colonel Marbet removed the pipe from his mouth and rose slowly, turning in anticipation to the door, while Rear-Admiral Lejeune merely lowered his book.

Colonel Montholon threw open the door and was greeted by the stares of the four men.

'Well?' demanded Duroc.

Montholon closed the door behind him.

'Were you followed?' asked Lejeune.

'I don't think so,' said Montholon.

'Well, where is it to be?' Duroc pressed, fuming with impatience. 'Is the Emperor fit to travel?'

'He'll have to travel, whether he likes it or not,' snarled Duroc. 'The point is where to? You do know, don't you?' The tall man turned on Montholon, 'Or have we got to hang about while your sister . . .'

'Hold your tongue, Duroc!' snapped Lejeune, closing his book, standing up and stepping up to Montholon to place a consoling hand upon his shoulder. 'Take no notice of Gaston, Étienne, he's a boor.'

Duroc grunted again and poured another glass. He also filled a second and handed it to Montholon. 'No offence,' he grumbled.

'He's just a big-booted bastard,' Marbet added genially, smiling conciliatorily, his eyes on Montholon. 'Well, Étienne?'

'It's to be the Azores, gentlemen,' Montholon said, then raised the glass to his lips.

There was a sigh of collective relief, then Lejeune, as though finding the news too good, asked Montholon, 'So it is not to be Elba?'

Montholon shook his handsome head. 'No. I am told there has been much debate. The bastards cannot agree . . .'

'What of the Tsar?' Lejeune pressed.

'He consents. Absolutely,' Montholon replied.

But Lejeune's caution had communicated itself to Duroc. 'He's a damned weathercock. Let us hope he doesn't change his mind.'

Montholon shook his head again. 'No; apparently Talleyrand's stratagem was too seductive.'

'He'd be a damned fool not to consent,' remarked Marbet, 'and your sister had this from Talleyrand himself, eh?'

'Yes,' Montholon nodded, 'the source is impeccable.'

Duroc snorted derisively. 'The source is peccant, you mean . . .'

Montholon's eyes flashed and his hand moved to his sword hilt. 'You've no right . . .!'

'Gentlemen, please!' Lejeune snapped and rose smartly, extinguishing the quarrel. 'I will not tolerate such childish behaviour.'

'Well, Montholon's news settles matters,' added Marbet, recalling them to their duty.

The officers sighed, their strained features relaxed and Marbet ordered Delaborde to refill all their glasses, then turned to Lejeune.

'And your ships, my Admiral . . .?'

'Are ready. They can sail the instant they receive word.'

'And the Azores . . .?'

'The Azores?' repeated Lejeune, a gleam of satisfaction lighting his curiously dark eyes, 'They are perfect!'

Marbet snatched up his glass: 'To the new enterprise!'

'Damnation to the English!'

'Long live the Emperor!'

Chapter One

The Company of Kings

'A pretty sight, sir.'

Captain Nathaniel Drinkwater lowered the glass and looked at the suave young lieutenant resplendent in the blue, white and gilt of full dress, his left fist hitched affectedly on the hilt of his hanger.

'Indeed, Mr Marlowe, very pretty.' Drinkwater replaced the glass to his eye and steadied the long barrel of the telescope against the after starboard mizen backstay.

'Redolent of the blessings of peace,' Marlowe went on.

'Very redolent,' agreed his commander from the corner of his mouth.

Marlowe regarded the rather quaint figure. They were of a height, but there the resemblance ended. Against his own innate polish, Marlowe thought Captain Drinkwater something of a tarpaulin. True, his uniform glittered in the late April sunshine with as much pomp as Lieutenant Marlowe's own, and Captain Drinkwater did indeed sport the double bullion epaulettes of a senior post-captain, but judging by the way they sat upon his shoulders, he looked a little hunchbacked. As for the old-fashioned queue, well, quaint was not the word for it. It was like an old mare's braided tail, done up for a mid-summer horse fair! The irreverent thought caused him to splutter with a half-suppressed laugh. It sounded like a sneeze.

'God bless you, Mr Marlowe.' The glass remained steadfastly horizontal. ''Tis the sun upon the water and all these gilded folderols I expect.'

Drinkwater swung his glass and raked the accompanying ships. To starboard His Britannic Majesty's ship-rigged yacht *Royal Sovereign* drove along under her topsails and a jib. She was ablaze with gilt gingerbread work and gaudy with silken banners. Aloft she bore the fouled anchor of Admiralty at the fore, the Union flag

11

at her mizen with a huge red ensign at her peak, but at her main truck flew the white oriflamme of the Bourbons, its field resplendent with golden lilies. It denoted the presence on board of King Louis XVIII of France, on passage to his restoration as His Most Christian Majesty. Accompanying the king was a suite which included the Prince de Condé, the Duc de Bourbon and the bitter-featured Duchesse d'Angoulême, the Orphan of the Temple, sole surviving child of the guillotined Louis XVI and Queen Marie Antoinette.

Beyond the *Royal Sovereign*, aboard the huge three-decked, first-rate *Impregnable*, flew the standard of Prince William Henry, Duke of Clarence and third son of King George III. As admiral-of-the-fleet, an appointment the prince had held since 1811, he was carrying out this ceremonial duty of escort as an act of political expediency by the British government. He had been removed from the frigate *Andromeda* in 1789, and had not served at sea since then, despite constant petitioning to the Admiralty. Notwithstanding the elevation of his birth, Their Lordships were deaf to his pleading, for he had commanded *Andromeda* with such unnecessary severity that he had earned the Admiralty's disapproval.

As a sop to His Royal Highness's vanity for this short, but auspicious command, His Majesty's Frigate *Andromeda*, lately returned from Norwegian waters with a prize of the Danish frigate *Odin*, was assigned to the Royal Squadron.

Other ships in company were the British frigate *Jason* and the *Polonais*, lately a French 'national frigate', but now sporting the white standard of the restored House of Bourbon, together with a pair of Russian frigates and the cutter-rigged yacht of the Trinity House.

Having scanned this impressive group of allied ships, Drinkwater closed his glass with a snap and turned on his heel, almost knocking Lieutenant Marlowe off his feet.

'God's bones, man . . .!'

'I beg pardon, sir.'

'Have you nothing better to do than hang at my elbow?'

'I was awaiting your orders, sir?'

'Keep an eye on the flagship, then. I imagine the prince will want some evolutions performed before we arrive at Calais.'

The warning was a product of Drinkwater's brief encounter with His Royal Highness and his flag-captain the previous afternoon, when he had joined the squadron off Dover and had reported aboard the *Impregnable*.

The ships had been lying at anchor, awaiting the arrival of King Louis and his entourage from London, whither they had been summoned from Hartwell, a seat of the Duke of Buckingham which had been loaned to the exiled French court. The decision to include *Andromeda* had been taken late at the Admiralty, a result of the interest the prince had taken in the frigate's return from Norway with her Danish prize.

Although his ship was about to pay off at Chatham, Drinkwater had been commanded to remain in commission: His Royal Highness had specifically asked for the 'gallant little' *Andromeda* to be assigned to his fleeting command. Their Lordships had graciously acquiesced and a ridiculous sum of money, sufficient to have fitted out two or three frigates during the late war, had been swiftly squandered on refitting and repainting her. Drinkwater, hurrying down to Chatham, had found the preparations in hand aboard his ship to be quite obscene.

'Good God, Mr Birkbeck,' he had said to the master, 'had I had one quarter of this co-operation from this damned dockyard when I was fitting out the *Virago*, or the *Patrician*, I could have saved myself much anxiety and my people great inconvenience. Why in Heaven's name do they make such a fuss of this business now, eh? I mean where's the sense in it?'

'I imagine the Commissioner sees more profit in pleasing a prince than a post-captain, sir,' Birkbeck remarked drily, and Drinkwater recalled Birkbeck's desire for a dockyard post.

Drinkwater had grunted his agreement. 'Well, it's a damned iniquity.'

' 'Tis victory, sir, victory.'

He found himself muttering the word now, and chid himself for the crazy habit which he deplored as a concomitant of age and, who knew, perhaps infirmity? He recalled, too, the pleasure with which the prince greeted his arrival off Dover. True, His Royal Highness had asked nothing about Nathaniel Drinkwater, scarcely acknowledging him as the victor in the action with the *Odin*, but had continually made remarks about the frigate herself, turning to the suite of officers in attendance, as though he sought their good opinion.

'Who are your officers, Captain?'

Drinkwater had named them, starting with his first lieutenant, 'Frederic Marlowe, sir.'

'Ah yes, I know the fella!' The prince had seized chirpily upon the name. 'Son of Sir Quentin who sits for a pocket borough somewhere in the west country.'

'Ixford, sir, in the county of Somerset,' said a lieutenant helpfully, stepping forward with a sycophantic obeisance of his head.

'Indeed, indeed. Somerset, what . . .'

Only Birkbeck the master and the second lieutenant, Frey, had been in the fight in the Vikkenfiord, and the prince had heard of neither. Drinkwater rather formed the impression that His Royal Highness thought both Marlowe and Lieutenant Ashton, who was known to one of the prince's suite, had both covered themselves with glory in the capture of the *Odin*.

Perhaps it had been sour grapes on his, Drinkwater's part, perhaps it had galled him to be so ignored. He had said as much to the *Impregnable*'s flag-captain Henry Blackwood. Years earlier, in September 1805, it had been Blackwood in the frigate *Euryalus*, who had relieved Drinkwater in the *Antigone*, from the inshore post off Cadiz. A letter in Blackwood's own hand had ordered Drinkwater into Gibraltar and led ultimately to his capture and presence aboard the enemy flagship at Trafalgar.*

'He is a harmless enough fellow,' Blackwood said charitably. 'When he was a midshipman, they used to call him "Pineapple Poll" on account of the shape of his head. Sometimes I'm damned if I think he is capable of a sensible thought, but then he'll surprise you with a shrewd remark and you wonder if he ain't fooling you all the time. The trouble is nobody says "boo" to him and he loves the sound of his own voice. He should have been given something useful to do instead of kicking his heels at Bushy Park with La Belle Jordan. He daren't bungle this little adventure, but at the same time regards it as beneath his real dignity.' Blackwood concluded with a chuckle.

'That must make life difficult for you,' Drinkwater had sympathized.

Blackwood shrugged and smiled. 'Oh, it won't last long. The poor devil hasn't been to sea for so long he scarce knows what to

* See *1805*

14

do, but when he makes his mind up to do something, he thinks he's a second Nelson.' Blackwood had laughed again, his face a curious mixture of exasperation and amusement.

Next morning, the boats of the squadron, each commanded by a lieutenant, had brought off King Louis and his suite from Dover. The reverberations of the saluting cannon had bounced off the white cliffs and the ramparts of the grey castle as flame and clouds of smoke broke from the sides of the allied men-of-war. Simultaneously, the ramparts themselves had sparkled with the fire from a battery of huge 42-pounders, so that the thump and echo of their concussion danced in diminuendo between the wooden sides of the assembled ships. Bunting had fluttered gaily in the light breeze, augmented by the huge white standard which rose to the main truck of the *Royal Sovereign* as the king boarded her. Of imperturbable dignity, King Louis was of vast bulk and still suffering from an attack of gout. Too fat to climb the side, he had been hoisted aboard in a canvas sling, followed by the Duchesse d'Angoulême and other ladies. Meanwhile the seamen in the adjacent ships had manned the yards and cheered lustily, though more at the prospect of shortly being paid off, Drinkwater had suspected, than of respect for the royal personage.

That was undoubtedly true of his own men; what of the French aboard the *Polonais*? After a generation of ferment and opportunity, what were their private feelings? Perhaps they would accept the return of the Bourbon tyranny as the price for peace. As for the Russians, well, who knew what the Russians thought?

The thin rattle of snare drums and the braying of trumpets had floated over the water as the echoes of the guns died away. From the quarterdeck of *Andromeda* the impression given at a distance was of a seething, glittering ants' nest, and Drinkwater had sensed a mood of envy suffusing his own young officers, as though their own presence on the distant yacht would have guaranteed their individual ambitions.

As for himself, was it age that made him relieved that he had not had to pander to the king and his court? He had caught the eye of Lieutenant Frey, the only one of his commissioned officers with whom he had formerly served, and who had recently endured a court-martial from which he had been honourably acquitted. Perhaps the rueful look on Frey's face had spoken for all the foiled aspirations of his young peers; the embarkation of the dropsical and gouty monarch marked the end of the war and thus terminated the gruesome opportunities war presented to them; perhaps, on the other hand, the sensitive Frey was regretting his late commander, James Quilhampton, could not share this moment. The thought pricked Drinkwater with so sharp a pang of conscience that something of it must have shown on his face, for Frey had crossed the deck smartly.

'Are you all right, sir?'

'Yes, perfectly, thank you, Mr Frey,' Drinkwater had said as Marlowe and Ashton turned at the sudden movement. Dizzily, Drinkwater waved aside their concern.

'I thought for a moment, sir,' Frey had observed, lowering his voice, 'you were unwell.'

'No, no.' Drinkwater had smiled at Frey. 'I thought of Mr Q, Frey, and wished he were here to share this moment with us.'

Drinkwater had regretted his confidence the instant he had uttered it, for the shadow had passed over Frey too, and he had shivered, as if it had suddenly turned cold. 'Amen to that, sir.'

For a moment both men had thought of the cutter *Kestrel*, the action she had fought off Norway, and the death of Lieutenant James Quilhampton. It had been the abandonment of her battered hulk for which Frey, as senior surviving officer, had stood trial.

'Come,' Drinkwater had remarked encouragingly, 'let us not debar ourselves from some pleasure on this momentous occasion.'

'I think we have already survived the momentous occasions,' Frey said quietly, his eyes abstracted. 'This has an air of hollow triumph.'

Drinkwater had been moved by this perceptive remark, but his private emotions were cut short by Marlowe's sudden comment that a signal was being run up the *Impregnable's* flag halliards and Birkbeck the master had then hove alongside him, muttering presumptuously that it was the signal to weigh.

Now, in the late afternoon of 24 April, they were well within sight of Calais. To the southward the chalk lump of Cap Gris Nez jutted against the sky; closer the gentler, rounder and more pallid Cap Blanc Nez marked the point at which the French coast turned east, becoming flat and, apart from the church steeples and towers, featureless as it stretched away towards Dunquerque and the distant

Netherlands. The little fishing village of Sangatte was almost abeam as the squadron breasted the first of the ebb tide and carried the breeze which had freshed during the day. An hour, an hour and a half at the most, would see them bringing up to their anchors in Calais Road. Drinkwater examined the roadstead ahead of them, then lowered his glass; he looked once more at the irregular formation of the squadron. It was, as Marlowe had said, a pretty sight.

'Flag's signalling, sir . . .'

Drinkwater's attention was diverted by the necessity of obeying the signals of His Royal Highness. As they came up towards Calais, the cannon of the squadron boomed out in yet another round of salutes, impressing upon the fishermen and townsfolk that the dangerous days of republican experiment and alternative, bourgeois monarchy, were dead.

'Sir, may I formally present Captain Drinkwater?'

Blackwood's introduction had an ironic content, since he had met the Duke of Clarence the previous afternoon, but the scene in the great cabin was stiff with formality and Drinkwater made his obeisance with a well-footed bow. Apart from the *Jason*'s captain, he was the last of the allied commanders to be presented. The prince appeared to notice him as an individual for the first time. Drinkwater was some four years the prince's senior, his long grey-brown hair clubbed at the nape of his neck, the scarred cheek and faint blue powder burns on the lean face with its high forehead marking him as a seasoned officer.

This seemed to surprise Prince William Henry, whose genial, full-lipped and rubicund, pop-eyed features broke into an affable grin as he studied the taller post-captain.

'Well Drinkwater,' he almost shouted, 'what d'ye think of *Andromeda*?'

'She's a fine ship for her class, sir,' Drinkwater remarked.

'She's good enough to have taken the *Odin*, ain't she, eh what?'

'Indeed, sir . . .'

'Drinkwater . . . Drinkwater . . . Ah-hah! I have it! Ain't you the fellow that took a Russian seventy-four in the Pacific?'

'Captain Drinkwater makes a habit of taking superior ships, sir,' Blackwood put in, bending to the royal ear and lowering his voice, 'but it might be tactless to mention it this evening sir.'

'Of course, of course,' boomed the prince, 'I recall, 'twas the

Suvorov, what, what?' Drinkwater caught Blackwood's eye and saw the *Impregnable*'s captain roll his eyes resignedly at the white painted deckbeam over his head. 'Well, well, we're allies now, eh, damn it. And now the war's over, so 'tis all history, eh what?' The prince looked round beaming, as though he had just carried out a major diplomatic coup and Drinkwater was aware of two officers in the dark green full dress of Russian captains, standing stiffly, their bicorne hats tucked beneath their elbows.

'But you didn't do that in *Andromeda*, eh?'

'No sir, the razée *Patrician* . . .'

'So what the devil d'you do in the *Andromeda*, sir? Are you a jobber, or what?'

Despite a supreme effort at self-control, Drinkwater felt himself colouring at the prince's tactless imputation, unaware of the bristling of his fellow officers, manifested by a slight shuffling of feet and a stir as they waited for the presentations to cease and the conversation to become general.

Mercifully, Captain Blackwood was equal to the occasion, 'Captain Drinkwater is a most experienced cruiser commander, sir, he was off Cadiz with me, and Nelson had especially picked him for the *Thunderer*, but he could not get out from Gibraltar before the action.'

'By God, Drinkwater, that was damned bad luck, what? Picked by Nelson, eh? Wish to God I'd been, instead of being left to rot on shore! By Heaven there's no justice in the sea-service, damned if there is, eh, what?'

The moment of embarrassment passed, the insult turned neatly by Blackwood without the need to reveal Drinkwater's long association with special services, by way of an explanation why so senior a post-captain had yet to tread the quarterdeck of a line-of-battle ship, and why he commanded an obsolescent thirty-two gun frigate that should rightfully have been broken up. Drinkwater moved thankfully aside, leaving young Maude of *Jason* to His Royal Highness's mercy. As he moved aside, the bubble broke and conversation rose about him like a tide. Perhaps, he thought, taking a glass from a silver tray borne by a pig-tailed and stripe-shirted steward, it had been simmering all the while.

'We are neighbours at table, Captain Drinkwater,' said an austere, hollow-eyed man in the plain blue coat with the red collar and cuffs of an Elder Brother of the Trinity House. 'May I introduce myself? Captain Joseph Huddart, late of the Honorable Company's service.'

'Nathaniel Drinkwater . . .' The two men shook hands and lapsed into small talk, moving eventually to sit amid the glittering silver and glass of the Duke of Clarence's white-napered table. Drinkwater's other neighbour was a Russian, the captain of the forty-four gun frigate *Gremyashchi*. He spoke a thick English. Try though he might, Drinkwater had difficulty understanding anything beyond three references to the *Suvorov* and these, he deduced, were far from complimentary. After a few moments, the Russian turned to his farther neighbour, the French captain of the *Polonais* who, after a few exchanges, leaned forward and asked Drinkwater in faltering English:

'Capitaine Rakov, he ask if you are English *officier* who capture Russian ship *Suvorov*?'*

Drinkwater looked from the French officer to the Russian. Rakov was watching him closely.

'I am,' he replied, holding the Russian's gaze. Rakov muttered something, then turned pointedly away and settled to natter in French to the Russian on his left. Drinkwater fell into easy conversation with Huddart, whose bald head and wispy side drapes of hair hid an astute and enquiring mind. They talked of many things, discovering mutual acquaintances from Drinkwater's brief period in China, his escort of a convoy of the Company's East Indiamen and from his earlier service aboard Trinity House buoy yachts. In this vein the evening passed very pleasantly until at last, the prince, having called upon Blackwood to propose the first toast to his royal father, initiated a succession of these in which, at least so it seemed, every crowned head in Europe was thus honoured.

Eventually His Royal Highness prevailed and made some general remarks about his sensibility to the honour of commanding an allied squadron at this happy time of peace, alluding to the restoration of legitimate monarchy in France. He related an anecdote of the king, whom he had escorted ashore earlier in the day.

'His Majesty,' said the prince, perspiration and the tears of emotion upon his florid cheek, 'upon landing on the sacred soil of his native land, embraced the Duchess of Angoulême and said, "I hold

* See *In Distant Waters*

again the crown of my ancestors; if it were of roses, I would place it upon your head; as it is of thorns",' and here the sweating prince waved his hand above his head, '"it is for me to wear it." Most moving gentlemen, most moving, what?'

A murmur of loyal assent ran round the table.

'It seems our Billy has learned a thing or two from *La Belle* Jordan,' remarked Huddart drolly, referring to the prince's former mistress who was also a renowned actress.

'Well gentlemen,' resumed their host, 'the merchant and the mariner have now nothing other than the dangers of the elements to encounter, what? And so the prosperity of their pursuits is by consequence more probable, don't you know. What! And therefore I propose a final toast to the sea-services!'

Like the preceding bumpers, they drank this final one sitting down, their faces perspiring from the heat of the candles, the warmth of their conversation and wine. To Drinkwater, chatting amiably to Huddart in the full flush of drunken fellowship, the prospect of peace, of retirement from the demands of active service and all its alarums, risks and hazards, seemed as rosy as the face of Admiral of the Fleet, His Royal Highness, the Prince William Henry, Duke of Clarence and Earl of Munster.

And just as fulsome.

Chapter Two

Nicodemus

Drinkwater could not sleep. He had dined too well and drunk too deeply; moreover he was of an age now that precluded enjoying a full night's sleep and sometime late in the middle watch he irritably entered the starboard quarter-gallery and squatted inelegantly on the privy.

The dark shapes of the anchored squadron were pin-pricked by points of light, where the poop lanterns glowed and ashore a pair of glims marked the entrance to Calais port. Beneath him *Andromeda* lifted to a low ground swell and this motion caused her ageing fabric to creak in a mild protest. She was worn out with service. After the pounding she had taken in the action with the *Odin* she would have been better employed as a hulk, or even broken up. It was ironic that now, at the conclusion of hostilities, and in recognition of her last service attending upon kings and princes, she was fully manned. It was a rare experience for Captain Drinkwater to command one of His Britannic Majesty's cruisers which had a full complement, even after twenty years of war!

He sighed, contemplating the passage of time and feeling not only the ache of his tired body, but a morbid apprehension at his own mortality. He thought often now of death, almost daily since the loss of his friend and sometime lieutenant, James Quilhampton. He felt James's passing acutely and had assumed responsibility for the younger man's widow and child, but the impact upon his own spirit had been severe. He held himself wholly to blame for Quilhampton's death; it was an illogical conclusion. Nathaniel Drinkwater had murdered those whom events cast as enemies of his king and country without remorse, seeing in their deaths the workings of providence, but James's death had been attributable to his following orders, orders that had been given by Nathaniel Drinkwater himself.

'Damn the blue-devils,' he muttered, banishing his gloomy thoughts. He was about to duck through the door into the cabin when he noticed the boat. It was a dark shape and attracted attention by the slight gleam of phosphorescence at its bow and the pallid flashes of the oar-strokes. He thought at first it was a guard-boat, but its movement lacked the casual actions of a bored crew. Moreover, it had curved under the stern of their nearest neighbour, the *Jason*, and was heading directly towards *Andromeda*. Something about the purposeful approach disturbed Drinkwater; his apprehension about death was displaced by something more immediate. Was this another of His Royal Highness's ridiculous jokes? He could not imagine any other reason for the night's tranquillity being disturbed now that His Most Christian Majesty had been landed upon his natal shore to claim the crown restored to him by the grace of Almighty God, the bayonets of the Tsar and the Royal Navy of Great Britain.

From the greater vista of the stern window in the cabin, Drinkwater could see the boat holding unwaveringly to its course towards *Andromeda*.

'Bound to be orders, confound it,' he muttered, unaware that talking to himself was becoming habitual. 'Damn and blast the man!' he swore, pulling the nightshirt over his head and reaching for his breeches. Above his head he heard the faint sound of the marine sentry at the taffrail hail the approaching boat. He kicked his stockinged feet into the pumps he had worn aboard the *Impregnable* earlier that night and peered again through the stern windows. He could see the boat clearly now, the faint gleam of her gunwhale crossed by the moving oar looms. The synchronized swaying of her oarsmen chimed its rhythm with the surge of the phosphorescent bow-wave as the boat dipped and rose slightly under their impetus. He sensed as much as saw these resolved dynamics, a perception born of a lifetime at sea, subconscious in its impact on his intelligence. His conscious mind, compelled to wait for an explanation, briefly diverted itself by a recollection of his wife Elizabeth, whose wonder at first seeing phosphorescence in the breakers running up on the shingle strand of Hollesley Bay had given him a profound pleasure.

'You must have seen so many wonders, Nathaniel,' she had said, 'while I have seen so very little of life.'

'I wish I could have shared more with you,' he had replied

kindly. He tossed the recollection aside as he heard quite clearly the query from the boat.

'*C'est Andromeda?*'

'The devil . . .' He struck flint on steel and had lit a candle when the tap came at the door. Midshipman Paine's disembodied features appeared round the door.

'Captain, sir?'

'I'm awake, Mr Paine, and aware we have a French boat alongside.'

'Aye sir, and a military officer asking to see you, sir.'

Drinkwater frowned. 'To see me? You imply he asked by my name.'

'Asked for Captain Nathaniel Drinkwater, sir, very particularly. Mr Marlowe said I was to emphasize that, sir.'

'Very well, I assume the officer at least was British.'

'Oh no, sir, Mr Marlowe said to tell you he had a lot of plumes on his shako and Mr Marlowe judged him to be either a Russian or a Frenchman.'

Drinkwater was dragging a comb through his hair while this exchange was in progress. It was not in his nature to bait midshipmen, but Drinkwater knew, though the cockpit thought he did not, that Paine had acquired the nickname 'Tom' on account of having the surname of the English revolutionary. He was a solemn but rather prolix lad.

'And what did you make him out to be, Mr Paine?'

'Well, he does have a fantastic shako, sir, but his voice is . . . well, I mean his accent is . . .'

'Is what, Mr Paine?' enquired Drinkwater, pulling on the full dress coat that he had disencumbered himself of when he had returned from the flagship. 'Pray do not keep me in suspense.'

'Well it's English, sir.'

'English?'

'But Mr Marlowe says the shako ain't English, sir . . .'

But Drinkwater was not listening, he was seized by the sudden thought his visitor might be his own brother who had long been a cavalry officer in the Russian service who had now come to pay him a nocturnal visit. He was certain Edward would be serving on the staff of General Vorontzoff who, Drinkwater had heard, was already in Paris. He swallowed the curse that almost escaped his lips and, doubling his queue, ordered the midshipman to bring the stranger down to the cabin. While he waited, Drinkwater lit more candles and washed his mouth out with a half-glass of wine.

Edward's appearance at this time would be damnably embarrassing. A cold and fearful apprehension formed around Drinkwater's heart. Once, long ago, he had helped Edward escape from England and a conviction for murder.* It had been a rash, quixotic act, but Drinkwater had gained the protection of Lord Dungarth and cloaked the affair under the guise of a secret and special service. Now Dungarth was dead, and an untimely resurrection of the usually impecunious Ned would not merely embarrass his older brother. Just when he might retire and enjoy the fruits of his own service, Edward might now ruin him.

Just as this terrible thought brought the sweat out on Drinkwater's brow and caused his blood to run cold, Midshipman Paine's face reappeared.

'Well, bring the fellow in, Mr Paine . . .'

'He won't come, sir. Says he wishes you to wait upon him on the quarterdeck.'

'The devil he does! Well, Mr Paine, what d'you make of the fellow, eh?' The idea the stranger was Edward was swept aside by the conviction that this was one of His Royal Highness's daft pranks. This thought was given greater credibility by Mr Paine's next remark.

'Begging your pardon, sir, I told you the officer was speaking English, but what I didn't say was that I thought the officer,' Paine paused, then went on, 'might be a woman, sir.'

'*You* thought the . . . Well, well, we had better go and see . . .'

If it were so, then at least the stranger was not his brother Edward! The cool freshness of the night air soothed some of Drinkwater's irritation. He braced himself for some piece of royal stupidity, aware of a figure in a cloak standing by the entry, but Lieutenant Marlowe loomed out of the darkness by the mizen mast and waylaid him.

'Beg pardon sir, but have a care. If this fellow's a Russian he may be dangerous, sir.'

Drinkwater frowned. 'Dangerous? Why so?'

'You have a reputation, sir . . .'

* See *The Bomb Vessel*

24

'Reputation?' Drinkwater's tone was edgy. Then he recalled Rakov's hostility.

'You did take the *Suvorov*, sir . . .'

Marlowe's tone was courtly, a touch obsequious, perhaps a trifle admiring. Drinkwater had destroyed a Russian line-of-battle ship in the Pacific, but that had been six years ago, in what? September of the year eight. Good God, the Russians had changed sides since then, when Boney invaded their country and Tsar Alexander had become the French Emperor's most implacable foe.

'Thank you for your concern, Mr Marlowe.' The lieutenant drew back and let his captain past, his head inclined in the merest of acknowledgements. Drinkwater approached the cloaked figure. The bell-topped shako with a tall white plume, a mark of Bourbon sympathy, Drinkwater supposed, stood out against the dark sea beyond.

'Well M'sieur, are you French or Russian?'

'I am French, Captain Drinkwater . . .' The voice seemed oddly familiar, yet artificially deepened. Paine was correct, a clever lad. He knew in the next instant who his visitor was.

'I know you,' Drinkwater said sharply, stifling any further explanation, and raising his voice slightly, so that the eavesdropping Marlowe and any other curious-minded among the listening anchor-watch might hear, added 'and I think I know your business. You are on the staff of the Prince of Condé. Come, we must go below.'

Drinkwater was certain his night-visitor was not on the staff of the Bourbon prince, and with a hammering heart, turned on his heel and led the way, nodding to the marine sentry at his door as the soldier snapped to attention. The French officer had removed the ridiculous shako to pass between decks, but held it in such a way that it masked his face from the marine's inquisitive stare. He was still half hiding his face behind the plume as Drinkwater, closing the door behind them, crossed the cabin and held up the candelabra on his table.

'You come by night like Nicodemus, but you are, if I mistake not, Hortense Santhonax.'

She lowered the shako and shook her head, not in denial of her identity, but to let her hair fall after its constraint beneath the shako. Drinkwater recalled something else about her. In the imperfect illumination, her profusion of hair still reflected auburn lights. She dropped the hat on a chair and unclasped her cloak. For a moment they both stared at one another. She had half-turned her head away from him, though her eyes were focused on his face. Her hair had pulled over her right shoulder, revealing her neck.

It was a quite deliberate ploy and as his eyes wavered towards the disfigurement, Drinkwater saw the twitch of resolution at the corner of her mouth. The scar ran down from under her hair, over the line of her jaw and down her neck. It was not the clean incision of a sword cut, but marked the passage of a gobbet of molten lead.

He took her cloak and without taking his eyes from her, laid it on a chair behind him. It was warm from her body and the scent of her filled the cabin. He reached out his left hand, gently lifting the hair off her right ear. It was missing.

Hortense Santhonax made no protest at this presumption. He let the hair drop back into place. 'I knew of your injury at the Austrian Ambassador's ball, Madame,' Drinkwater said kindly, 'and I am sorry for it.'

'When a woman loses her looks, ' she said in her almost faultless English, 'she loses everything. Thereafter she must live on her wits.'

Drinkwater smiled. 'Then it makes them more nearly men's equals.'

'That is sophistry, Captain.'

'It is debatable, Madame, but you are no less lovely.'

She spurned the gallantry, raising her hand to her neck. 'How did you know . . . about this?'

'Lord Dungarth acquainted me of the fact some time before his death.'

'So, him too.' She paused, and then seemed to pull herself together. 'Men may acquire scars, Captain, and it does nothing but add credit to their reputations,' she remarked, and was about to go on when Drinkwater turned aside and lifted the decanter.

'Is that why you have assumed the character of a man, Madame?' he asked, pouring out two glasses.

She looked at him sharply, seeking any hint of malice in his riposte, but the grey eyes merely looked tired. He saw the suspicious contraction of the eye muscles and again the tightening of the mouth. She accepted the glass.

'Pray sit, Madame; you look exhausted.' He took in her dusty hessian boots, the stained riding breeches and the three-quarter length tunic. There was nothing remotely military about her rig. 'I presume you stole the shako,' he remarked, smiling, handing her a glass.

'There is a deal of convivial drinking in Calais tonight, Captain. A lieutenant of the *Garde du Corps* is going to find himself embarrassed tomorrow morning when the king leaves for Paris.' She returned his smile and he drew up a chair and sat opposite her. He felt the slight contraction of his belly muscles that presaged sexual reaction to her presence. By God, she was still ravishing, perhaps more handsome now than ever!

Was it the wound that, in marring her beauty, somehow made her even more desirable? Or had he become old and goatish?

'That is the first time I have seen you smile, Madame.'

'We have not always met under the happiest of circumstances.'

'Is this then, a happy occasion?'

She lifted the wine to her mouth and shook her head. 'No, I wish it were so, but . . .'

Drinkwater left her a moment to her abstraction. He was in no mood for sleep now and there was something of the extraordinary intimacy that he remembered from their last charged meeting, in the house of the Jew Liepmann, on the outskirts of Hamburg.* But there was something different about her now. He sensed a vulnerability about her, a falling off of her old ferocity. Either he was a fool or about to be hood-winked, but he sensed no scheme on her part to entrap him. Even had she sought to suborn him, she would never have allowed him to lift the hair from her scar in an act that, even now, he could scarcely believe he had accomplished.

She sighed and stirred. 'I have ridden a long way today, Captain Drinkwater, and we are no longer young.'

'That is true. Forgive me; you must have something to eat . . .' He rose and brought her a biscuit barrel, placing it upon the table beside her. She hesitated a moment and he watched her carefully. She was tired, that much was clear, and had undoubtedly lost her former confidence. Was that due to exhaustion, or the consequences of her scars? Had she been abandoned by those friends in high places she had once boasted of: Talleyrand for instance? Even now the *ci-devant* Bishop of Autun, foreign minister and Prince of

---

* See *Under False Colours*

Benevento, was conducting the government of France during the inter-regnum which would shortly end when Louis was restored fully to the throne of his ancestors. In these changed circumstances, a mistress like Hortense Santhonax would be an embarrassment which the calculating Talleyrand would drop like a hot coal.

He watched, fascinated, as she began to eat the biscuits, swallowing the wine with an eagerness that betrayed her hunger. The soft candle-light played on her features and he felt again the urgent twitch in his gut. He recalled the group of fugitives he had rescued off the beach at Carteret years earlier; Hortense and her brother had been among them. Later, at Lord Dungarth's instigation, she had been put back on a French beach once it was known that she had thrown her lot in with a handsome French officer called Edouard Santhonax. Drinkwater remembered, too, the earl's injunction that they should have shot her, not let her go.* Since then she had risen with her husband's star until he was killed, when her name became linked with that of Talleyrand. Such a beauty was not destined for a widowhood of obscurity. Hortense had been present at the Austrian Ambassador's ball, given upon the occasion of the Emperor Napoleon's marriage to the Archduchess Marie-Louise, and this confirmed she was still welcome at the imperial court despite imperial doubts about her husband's loyalty. Now the restoration of the Bourbon monarchy threatened to set her world upside down again, and while the Bourbons could not avenge themselves upon the whole of France, they would undoubtedly visit retribution upon the vulnerable among Napoleon's followers.

'Do you fear the restoration? Surely as a friend of Monsieur Talleyrand, whose position, I believe, has never been stronger, you are safe enough?' She looked up at him, and he saw the effort of will it cost her to set her thoughts in order. 'Or are you seeking my protection and asylum in England?'

She almost laughed. 'Talleyrand . . . Protection . . .? Ah, Captain Drinkwater, I can count on nothing further from the Prince de Benevento, nor would I presume,' she paused for a moment, appearing briefly confused. Then she drew breath and seemed to steel herself, resuming in a harsher tone. 'M'sieur le Prince prefers the Duchesse de Courland these days, but I have not come here to

* See *A King's Cutter*

beg favours, but to warn you. King Louis may have returned, but his presence in France guarantees nothing; France is in turmoil. Three weeks ago the senate which Napoleon had created passed a resolution which blamed the Emperor for all of France's misfortunes. The Prince de Benevento, as head of the provisional government, has himself resolved to have the Emperor exiled. The Iles d'Azores have been suggested, as has your Ile de Sainte Hélène. Caulaincourt has been running back and forth between Talleyrand and the Tsar as an intermediary.'

'And how are you and I involved in this negotiation between the Tsar Alexander and Talleyrand? You did not come here in the middle of the night to tell me what I may read in the newspapers in London? They also mentioned Elba.'

'Pah, d'you think that a likelihood? Why, it is too close to France and too close to Tuscany. Austria will not wish to have the Emperor so close.'

'Your Emperor is the son-in-law of the Austrian Emperor.'

'That counts for nothing. Elba is but a ruse, though the world thinks the matter will rest there . . .'

'And you think otherwise?'

'Captain, I *know* otherwise.' The vehemence in her tone was a warning of something to follow. Drinkwater struggled to clear his tired brain.

'I can think of nowhere better than a more remote island such as you have mentioned if the late Emperor is to maintain some dignity. Otherwise I imagine it is not beyond the wit of your new Bourbon master to find an *oubliette* for him.'

'But Captain Drinkwater, do you think he will remain long on an island? Have not your English newspapers been saying otherwise?'

'He will be guarded by a navy whom he has compelled to master the techniques of blockade duty. I think your Emperor would find it very hard to escape . . .'

'What will your navy employ, Captain,' she broke in, the wine reviving her spirits as she warmed to her argument, 'a brace of frigates?'

The sarcasm in her tone as she guyed the English sporting term was clear. There was a sparkle in the green eyes that suddenly lit her face with the animated and terrible beauty he both admired and feared.

Drinkwater shrugged. *'Peut-être . . .'*

'Perhaps,' Hortense Santhonax scoffed, 'do you think you can cage an eagle, Captain? Come, my friend, you have more imagination than that!'

'Then, Madame,' Drinkwater snapped back, 'speak plainly. You have not come to warn me in so circumlocutory a style without there being something you wish for . . .'

The remark seemed to deflate her. Her shoulders sagged visibly as though the weight they bore was unsupportable. She raised the glass and drained it. 'You are right. I have need of your help . . . There, I acknowledge it!'

Drinkwater leaned over and refilled both their glasses. 'Hortense,' he said in a low voice, 'much has lain between us in the past. We have been enemies for so long, yet you can feel easy addressing me as *friend*. Do you remember when I dug a musket ball out of the shoulder of the Comte de Tocqueville aboard the *Kestrel*? I can see you now, watching me; I felt the depth of your hatred then, though I cannot imagine why you felt thus. Since that time I acknowledge I might have earned your hate, but I think you have come here because you trust me. And, in a strange sense, despite past events, I find myself trusting you.' He reached out and touched her lightly on her shoulder. 'Please do go on.'

She gave so large a sigh that her whole body heaved and when she looked up at him her fine eyes were swimming in tears.

'Yes, I remember the cabin and the wound . . . I remember you drinking brandy as you bent over De Tocqueville with a knife, but I do not remember hating *you*. Perhaps my terror at escaping the mob, of having abandoned everything . . .' She sighed and shrugged, sipping at her glass. 'But I know you to be a man of honour and that you will not abuse the confidence I bear.' She took a gulp of the wine and went on. 'When it was known in Paris that the British ships which would escort the Bourbon back to France included the *Andromeda* commanded by Captain Nathaniel Drinkwater, I knew also that our lives were destined to touch at least once more.' She paused a moment, and then resumed. 'When we last met in Hamburg, I asked you if you believed in providence; do you remember what you said?'

'I imagine I answered in the affirmative.'

'You said the one word, "implicitly".'

'Did I? Pray continue,' he prompted gently.

'I also learned that you had foiled Marshal Murat's plans by stopping the shipping of arms from Hamburg to America . . .'*

'May I ask how?'

'Captain Drinkwater, you are a senior officer in the English navy, yet,' she gestured round her, 'this is only a frigate. And I know it to be an old and ill-used frigate.'

'You are remarkably well informed.'

'It is also known in Paris that you have had much to do with secret and special services. Is that not so?'

'Yes, it is true. It is also true that I took over from Lord Dungarth, but my present command . . .' It was Drinkwater's turn to shrug; he was too keenly aware of the irony to offer a full explanation, and let the matter rest upon implication.

'Your appearance here off Calais is providential not only for myself and for France, but for the peace of Europe.'

Drinkwater was suddenly weary. What had the woman come for? He sensed some mystery but so preposterous a claim seemed to be verging on the hysterical, just when the abdicated Napoleon Bonaparte was to be mewed up on a remote island.

'I see you are growing tired, Captain . . .'

'No, no . . .' he lied.

'I must perforce beg you, as a man of influence, sir, to grant me a small competence if I reveal what I know.'

'Competence? You mean a pension?' So that was what it was all about! Here before him, one of the most beautiful women in Europe was begging. She was one piece of the human flotsam from the wreckage of Bonaparte's empire. He felt meanly disappointed, as though her presence here on this night should have some nobler motive. 'So, you have come to trade.'

'I have almost nothing, Captain, and I must look to the magnanimity of my enemies and the honour of a man I have always thought of as a true spirit, wherever our respective loyalties have led us in these past years. I should hate you for what you did to my husband, but Edouard would have killed you . . .'

'He tried, several times, Hortense . . .'

Ashamed of his meanness, he felt a great pity for her. She would not be the only casualty in the fall of France. Though he had been

* See *Beneath the Aurora*

31

a consistent enemy of his sovereign's enemies, he had often, in the privacy of his own thoughts, admired the establishment of a new order. The regal buffoonery of the preceding day had reminded him of the craziness of the world.

'Pray let us terminate the reminiscences, Hortense, they are painful for both of us. Do I understand you wish me to have you a pensioner of the British government?'

'Please . . .' There was no denying the extremity to which the woman was reduced.

'Sadly, you are unlikely to believe me when I say I am of little influence and certainly quite incapable of finding the support which would gain you such a living . . .'

'I don't ask for very much, Nathaniel; fifty pounds per annum, enough to keep me from the gutter . . . forty even.' She saw him shaking his head and a sudden fire kindled in her eyes. She dropped the intimacy they had fallen into. 'Come Captain, you cannot claim to be of no account. I know you are otherwise; why else are you serving in a squadron commanded by a royal prince? Your Prince William could see to it that I was awarded such a pension! Shall I go and petition him . . .?' She was scornful, her eyes ablaze.

'Madame, Madame, you do not know what you say!' Drinkwater had to laugh. 'His Royal Highness and his brothers are so often in debt that I would counsel you to steer clear of that path. You might find yourself reduced to whoring in his bed in expectation of guineas, only to be paid in florins! England is not France; your Prince of Benevento has far more power than Prince William Henry, and probably a more generous purse, whatever other vices he has.'

'But you can do it, Nathaniel, for God's sake, you must! Do I have to beg? I will . . .' She looked round and saw the cot.

'For God's sake get up! This is too melancholy a drama for such behaviour . . .' Drinkwater was keenly aware that, despite his caution, Hortense Santhonax had boxed him into a corner. 'Forty pounds you say? Well, well, I will see what I can do, though don't depend upon it. Come, come,' he floundered, 'it is not seemly to see you so reduced . . .'

'I have your word?' She had at least the grace to plead.

'You have my word.'

'Thank you, Nathaniel. It gives me no pleasure to be beholden to you.'

'It gives me no pleasure that you are,' Drinkwater replied grimly. He would have to find the woman's pension himself, if he could not obtain funds under some pretext or other. 'So, what is this news that will save Europe?'

To her credit, Hortense Santhonax came straight to the point. 'A group of officers in Paris, unwilling to swear the oath of allegiance to the Bourbon or to take advantage of the dissolution of their vows to the Emperor Napoleon, have already plotted to rescue him from exile.'

She paused a moment, satisfied herself that Drinkwater had taken the bait and went on. 'Talleyrand,' she said, eschewing the former French foreign minister's imperial title, 'is arranging matters so that the Emperor will be exiled on the island of Flores in the Azores. Money has already passed into the hands of certain influential Russians to ensure this, so the decision will be supported by Tsar Alexander. I do not think either the Prince Regent or your government will oppose it. But, having consented not to disturb the peace and tranquillity of France, a deposition to which effect the Emperor has already signed, the Emperor will embark in ships which will convey him from the Azores and transport him to North America. Scarcely will your navy have ordered frigates to watch the islands, than Napoleon will have vanished, as will many of his guard, to join forces with the Americans. Can you not imagine the joy with which Mr Madison will welcome the greatest military genius the world has ever known?'

'I can imagine Mr Madison regretting his eagerness when Mr Madison is no longer Mr President,' Drinkwater remarked drily, but Hortense was quick to dismiss his scepticism.

'Napoleon Bonaparte will have lost Europe, Nathaniel, but he will gain Canada! The Quebecois await him eagerly . . .'

Drinkwater thought of the speculations in the English press and Hortense's earlier reference to them. Napoleon's intended destination of America was at least a speculation. It might be a great deal more. 'And you say the Tsar is complicit in this plot?'

'Absolutely, yes. The matter has been settled between Alexander and Napoleon, thanks to Caulaincourt. I do not believe Napoleon will try and usurp the presidency of the United States, nor that he would again overreach himself, for he too is no longer a young man; but Canada will fall to him, and he will have again an empire the size of Europe! Do you think he cannot beat the British out of the country that was once a possession of France?'

The enormity of the implications came as no surprise to Drinkwater. It was as if the possibility seeped into him, giving form to a deep fear, charged with all the inherent horror of something inevitable. The idea was not new, the thing was perfectly possible and not very difficult. But it marked the base ingratitude of the Tsar, into whose coffers the British had poured thousands of pounds to keep his armies in the field.

'If this is true . . .'

'It is true,' she shook her head as if wishing she could dismiss it. Then she looked up at him, 'And it is worth forty pounds a year.'

But Drinkwater was no longer listening, he had turned away and stared through the stern windows. They had swung to the flood now and the eastern sky was already showing the first glimmer of the dawn. What was proposed was nothing less than the ruin of Great Britain hard upon the heels of the ruin of France. The euphoria of peace would be snatched from an exhausted people, the economy would be wrecked by further war, the troops mutinous if they had to be shipped in great numbers across the Atlantic to confront the resurgent Emperor of the French . . .

It did not bear thinking about. But he could not avoid it. When Britain had lost the Thirteen Colonies of North America, she had still had the vast wealth she derived from India and the sugar islands of the West Indies. Once before India had been threatened by Napoleon, now it was all too clear that it would be the Tsar's patiently obedient and savagely efficient legions who would thrust down towards the sub-continent. Drinkwater had few illusions but that they were capable of such a campaign.

He swung round to find Hortense intently watching him.

'This is not bluff, Madame?' His voice was suddenly hard, his brows knitting above his eyes which glittered fiercely. She felt less sure of herself, saw briefly the man who had killed her husband and who had spent his adult life engaged in a war with the elements as much as her fellow countrymen.

'No, no, if you want proof, you can examine the papers of the port of Antwerp. Three days after the Emperor abdicated, two frigates, new ships just fitted out in that port, sailed for the Atlantic.'

'If true I doubt I have time to examine any papers . . .'

Drinkwater's brain was racing. He, more than anyone else, knew the state of affairs at Antwerp. French money had been building ships on the Scheldt for years. As head of the Admiralty's secret Department he had received regular reports of their progress: no doubt two, three, a dozen frigates and perhaps a seventy-four or an eighty might be in a fit state for sea. And the present time, with the blockade everywhere stood easy, was the most propitious for a quiet departure of two frigates. They could look like Indiamen, by God!

'Do you know the names of these ships?' he asked, his voice rasping.

'I almost forgot,' she said. 'One was to have been called *L'Aigle*, but it has very likely been altered to something more like a Dutch East Indiaman. It was given out that they were bound for the Indies. They wear Dutch colours, but are French, of that you may be certain. Off Breskens they took on arms and men additional to their crews, veterans, men of the Old and the Middle Guard, Chasseurs à Cheval and Empress Dragoons, even Poles of the Lanciers . . .'

'D'you know anything of their passage, Hortense, if they left three days after the Emperor abdicated, then they left on . . .'

'The 9th April, and had weighed anchor from Breskens by the 14th . . .'

'Ten days ago, by God!'

'And they were to go north, to the northwards of Scotland.'

'D'you know who commands them?'

'I do not know the names of the officers who command the ships. The committee in Paris consisted of only a few officers, but one of these will command the *escadron*, how do you say . . .?'

'Squadron.'

'Yes, I had forgotten. It is Lejeune, he is a *contra-amiral, pardon*, a rear-admiral.'

It was too pat; suspicion rose again, clouding Drinkwater's tired mind. 'How are you so well informed? Does Talleyrand have a hand in this?'

Hortense nodded. 'Of course. He presides over everything.' She was unable to conceal her distaste. 'He will accomplish what Napoleon failed to achieve, without lifting a finger . . .'

'But,' Drinkwater repeated, 'how do you know all these details? Talleyrand cannot have discussed . . .' Were these secrets from the intimacy of the bedchamber?

She shook her head. 'No, no, Nathaniel. I know because . . .' She paused and took a different tack, capturing him in the jade gaze of her eyes. 'Do you remember the beach at Carteret, when you came in your little boat and took a frightened *émigrée* off the sand?'

'Yes. It was the first time I saw you.'

'What was the name of your commandant? Griffon . . .?'

'Griffiths.'

'Ah, yes. Do you recall who else came with me in the *barouche*?'

Drinkwater cudgelled his brains. There had been a handful of them, then the light dawned: 'The Comte de Tocqueville, a man called Barrallier who afterwards built ships for the navy and, of course, Étienne Montholon, your brother!'

'Of course. He is now a colonel of chasseurs.'

'And he is privy to this plot?'

'Yes. He has been aide de camp to Caulaincourt and commanded his escort.'

Drinkwater frowned; fatigue and the disagreeable consequences of excess had robbed him of the ability to think through this maze of intrigue. He made an effort to clear his mind and focus his tired eyes upon her, mentally repudiating her obvious allure, so spiced as it was by her propinquity. 'But you are betraying him, Hortense? Are your circumstances so reduced that you would play the traitor to,' he floundered, gathering the catalogue of betrayal, 'to your brother, to Bonaparte, to Talleyrand, to France?'

She was weeping now, shaking and sobbing with tears running down her cheeks and revealing the dust that lay upon them.

'If it had not been you, Nathaniel,' she began in a choked voice, 'I should have taken passage in one of these ships and found my way to England. As it is, I may slip back to Paris unnoticed. Talleyrand is no longer interested in me, I was repudiated by the Emperor and the Bourbon will not want women like me to clutter up his court, nor, would I wish to do so.' She lowered her voice. 'I am a drab, Nathaniel, and like most camp followers, my end will not be an easy one. Your help might at least mitigate my fate.'

She swayed and Drinkwater stooped forward and gently held her by her arms. He was unconvinced, but her hands were on his arms too, and her body touched his, light as a feather, and then with more weight.

'Do not underestimate the risk I have run to tell you these

things,' she breathed, and added as he remained silent, holding her, 'They are like boys, Nathaniel, these conspirators; they would set the world alight again. Is that what you want? Do you not most desire to go home to your wife and children?'

'That is an odd question to ask at a moment like this,' he said, 'or are we two in sudden accord?' He smiled, the twist in his mouth conveying an intense sadness to her, though he spoke to encourage her. 'Come, Hortense, courage. You have lost none of your beauty . . .'

'I have lost an ear!' Her tone was petulant, as though she could betray her world for this disfigurement, and she lowered her face. 'And I am tired of conspiracy and intrigue.'

'Then it makes us the more equal,' Drinkwater said again. It occurred to him that she had received some unbearable humiliation. 'Suppose this plan of Talleyrand's and the Tsar's worked; suppose Napoleon Bonaparte, sent to exile in the Azores, was sprung from his prison and spirited across the Atlantic; suppose your brother commanded a division of trappers and mountain men in the army of New France, eh? Wouldn't you want to be a part of that? A great lady of Quebec, or Montreal, or even Louisbourg if it was rebuilt? Yet you expect me to believe you would hazard all that against a pension of forty pounds per year?'

He was looking down at her hair, the scent of which rose from its auburn profusion. She raised her face and stared up at him. Her yielding body had become rigid.

'I have nothing, nothing!' She hissed, desperation in her tone. 'Why should I come here, tonight, eh?' She pulled away from him, holding him at arm's length as she might have remonstrated with the son she had never had. 'Why should I not sit in Paris and wait for an invitation to become *La Reine de Louisbourg*, eh?' She threw the title at him in French like striking him with a gauntlet. 'I do not owe you anything, and if I come to trade this information it is not to betray France, or my brother . . .'

'What of Talleyrand?' Drinkwater snapped. 'What of Napoleon?'

'Why is it you English men are so *stupid*?' she spat back. 'I am old! It is known what I have been! It is known what I am now! Why is it impossible for men to understand, eh? You never come to terms with the inevitable, do you? Only the clever, men like Napoleon and

Talleyrand, can rise above these petty considerations. It is said in Paris that, despite everything, Napoleon could have rallied the army south of the Loire, but he did nothing. Instead he abdicated in the sure and certain knowledge that only a chapter of his life was over, but not the whole history. He is a Corsican, not a Frenchman. And he believes in fate, just like you.' Hortense paused, to let the point sink in. 'Napoleon has abandoned France just as he abandoned her before and set off for India. Then, when he found his grand design more difficult than he thought, he abandoned his army in Egypt and returned to France. When Admiral Villeneuve failed him at Trafalgar, he abandoned the invasion of England; when he was confronted with difficulties in Spain, he abandoned the war to his marshals; when he was foiled by the Russians, he abandoned his army in the snow . . . Why should he change now? Is fate going to give him another opportunity in Europe?'

'No,' Drinkwater said slowly.

'Certainly, I am being selfish. Perhaps this is a betrayal; perhaps this is saving many lives, perhaps . . .' she shrugged and moved slightly closer to him again, lowering her voice, 'this is fate, Nathaniel . . .'

And she pushed against him unashamed, her head bowed unexpectantly, their roles reversed, as though she was now the child and he the parent. His arms went instinctively around her and though he felt the soft roundness of her breasts it was pity, not lust, which rose and overwhelmed him.

'I think we are both too old,' he murmured into the darkness of the shadows beyond her shoulders, and gently stroked her hair. She seemed to shudder, like a small and terrified animal. 'Shall you want a passage to England?'

She pulled back and looked up at him. 'Where could I go in England?'

He shrugged. Suddenly the reaction of his wife to the arrival of a strange, mysterious and beautiful woman claiming refuge, seemed unlikely to be sympathetic.

'Perhaps one day . . .'

'*Peut-être*, Nathaniel. We shall see . . . I have told you everything . . .'

'I shall see you leave tonight with some money. There will be a ready market for English gold in Calais. I shall also ensure provision is made for you.'

'Is that possible?'

He thought for a moment and then nodded. 'Yes, I can arrange matters . . .'

Her relief was pathetic. The fear left her and he felt her whole body transformed. Lust pricked him as she embraced him once more.

'Hortense . . .'

And then he found himself kissing her as he wished he had kissed her twenty years earlier.

Chapter Three April 1814

A Clear Yard-arm

The eastern sky was lighter by the moment as Drinkwater paced the quarterdeck. The boat had long since vanished in the direction of the Calais breakwater, the Bourbon cockade deceptively jaunty, visible like a rabbit's scut as Hortense bobbed away.

He thought again of the warmth of her body against his and the prickle of lust still galled him. She had been compliant in that moment of mutual weakness, for they both drew back after a moment, almost ashamed, as though their long acquaintance had been supportable only as long as it was above the carnal.

'I am sorry,' he had muttered, even while he still held her, 'but I . . .'

'I am not a drab, Nathaniel.' There were tears in her eyes again, and it was clear she thought his impropriety had been motivated by that presumption.

'Hortense,' he had protested, 'I did not . . . I meant no . . . Damnation I have been bewitched by you for years. Did you not know it? Had I not a wife and children, I should have long ago . . .' He had broken off, seeing the pathetic declaration make her smile.

'Ah, Nathaniel, how,' she had paused, 'how *damnably* English.'

'Do not taunt me. Upon occasions, you have made my life wretched. You have resided in my soul as a dark angel. Tonight you are dispossessed of all the diabolism with which my imagination had invested you. For that I am grateful.'

They had let each other go.

'They you will see that I am provided for?'

'You know I will.'

'Yes . . . Yes I did. To that extent your superstitions were correct.' She smiled again.

'You are returning to Paris?' Seeing her nod, he had gone on, 'There is a bookseller in the rue de la Seine whose name is Michel.

There, in a month, you will find a draft against a London bank. I shall make it out in the name Hortense de Montholon. Should anything go awry, you may send a message through the Jew Liepmann in Hamburg.'

'You are doing this yourself aren't you? This is nothing to do with the British government, is it?'

'Hortense, the British government will not give Nelson's mistress a pension; why should they do anything for you? I know of you and thanks to the fortune of war, I have the means to make a little money available for you.'

'You are very kind, Nathaniel. Had life been different, perhaps . . .'

'Perhaps, perhaps; perhaps in happier times we shall meet again. Let us cage Bonaparte, m'dear, before any of us ordinary mortals think of our own pleasure.'

Hortense had smiled at the remark and, as he held her cloak out for her, she said over her shoulder, 'You and I are no ordinary mortals, Nathaniel.'

He had merely grunted. To so much as acknowledge by the merest acquiescence any agreement with this *braggadocio* seemed to him, filled as he was with apprehension at her news, to be tempting providence most grievously.

Now he was left to his thoughts and they were in a turmoil. He found it difficult to clear his mind of the image of her. On deck, in the chill of the dawn, it was almost possible to believe it had all been a dream, a bilious consequence of dining too well at the royal table. Was that event any more real, he wondered? And then from his breast the faintest, lingering scent of her rose to his nostrils.

Yet the appearance of the curious 'French officer' had far greater importance than the temptation of Nathaniel Drinkwater. He was in little doubt of the truth of her asseveration. Drinkwater had only the sketchiest notions of the military position of the French army at the end of March, but he had gleaned enough in recent days to know that Napoleon's energies seemed little diminished. He had fought a vigorous campaign in the defence of France, only to be overwhelmed by superior numbers against which even his military genius was incapable of resistance. Finally, it was widely rumoured, it had been the defection of members of the marshalate in defence of their own interests which had prompted the Emperor's abdication.

Under the circumstances, Napoleon was an unlikely candidate for a quiescent exile. And across the Atlantic raged a savage war, a repeat of the struggle from which had emerged the independent United States of America. Drinkwater had cause to remember details of that terrible conflict; as a young midshipman he had tramped through the Carolina swamps and pine barrens and had seen atrocities committed on the bodies of the dead.* More recently, he had been involved in the last diplomatic mission intended to prevent a breach between London and Washington, and he knew of the efforts which the young republic was prepared to make to discomfit her old imperial enemy.†

Nor had his foiling of that effort settled the matter. Yankee ambition was like the Hydra; cut one head off and another appeared. Within a few months of destroying a powerful squadron of American privateers, Drinkwater had been made aware of an attempt by the French to supply the Americans with a quantity of arms. The desperate battle fought in the waters of Norway beneath the aurora may have prevented that fateful juncture, but it may not have been the only one; perhaps others, unbeknown to the British Admiralty's Secret Department which Drinkwater had so briefly headed, had taken place successfully. It seemed quite impossible that his individual efforts had entirely eliminated any such conjunction. In short, it seemed entirely likely that some arms had crossed the Atlantic and that Napoleon and devoted members of his Imperial Guard would follow.

In fact, Drinkwater concluded, it was not merely likely, it was a damned certainty! And then the memory of Hortense mimicking his English expletive flooded his memory so that he turned growling upon his heel and came face to face with Lieutenant Marlowe.

'What in damnation . . .?'

'Begging your pardon, sir . . .'

'God's bones, what is it?'

'The French officer, sir . . .'

'Well, sir, what of the French officer?'

* See *An Eye of the Fleet*
† See *The Flying Squadron*

'Are there any orders consequent upon the French officer's visit, sir?'

'Orders? What orders are you expecting Mr Marlowe, eh?'

'I am about to be relieved, sir, and under the circumstances, in company with the Royal Yacht, sir, and His Royal Highness . . .'

Suddenly, just as Drinkwater was about to silence this locquacious young popinjay, the ludicrous pomposity of Prince William's title struck him. Overtired and overwrought he might be, distracted by the weight of Hortense's intelligence as much as that of her voluptuous body, he found the term 'Highness' so great a fatuity that he burst out laughing. And at the same time, as he thought of the coarse, rubicund and farting Clarence, he discovered the answer to the question that had been lurking insolubly in his semi-conscious.

'Indeed, Mr Marlowe, you do right to be expectant. The truth is I have been mulling over the best course of action to take as a consequence of that officer's visit, and now I'm happy to say you have acted very properly, sir.'

'Well, I'm glad of that, sir.'

'And so am I.'

'And the orders, sir . . .?'

Drinkwater looked at the young lieutenant's face. The sun was just rising and the light caught Marlowe's lean features in strong relief. He was a pleasant looking, pale fellow, with a dark beard, and the stubble was almost purple along his jaw. 'What d'you know of, er, His Royal Highness's habits, Mr Marlowe. I saw you hobnobbin' with a couple of the *Impregnable*'s officers last night. One of them was the Prince's flag-luff, wasn't he? What I mean is, did either of the young blades tell you what o'clock the Prince rises?'

Marlowe was somewhat taken aback by his commander's perception. 'I know Bob Colville, sir, but I don't recall our discussing His Royal Highness's habits beyond the fact that he enjoys a bumper or two.'

'Or three, I daresay, but that don't serve.' Drinkwater mused for a moment, then added expansively, 'What I need to know, Mr Marlowe, is what is the earliest time I might see the Prince?'

'In a good humour I daresay too,' added Marlowe, smiling, extrapolating Drinkwater's intentions.

'To be frank, Mr Marlowe,' Drinkwater added, a tone of asperity creeping into his voice, 'I don't much care in what humour His

Royal Highness is, just so long as he is sufficiently awake to understand what I wish to communicate to him.' Marlowe's look of astonishment at this apparent *lèse-majesté* further irritated Drinkwater who was conscious that he had confided too much in his untried subordinate. 'Have my gig ready in an hour, and pass word for my servant.'

As he shaved, Drinkwater turned over the idea he had. It seemed to have formed instantaneously whilst he had been importuned by Marlowe. The young officer had seen little service of an active nature, although his references spoke of several months on blockade duty off Brest. Still, that did not equate with a similar number of weeks in a frigate in a forward position or an independent cruise, though that was not poor Marlowe's fault. Drinkwater wondered if what he was currently meditating would appeal to Marlowe, whose career, at this onset of peace, seemed upon the brink of termination with no opportunity for him to distinguish himself. Perhaps it would not matter to the well-connected Marlowe, but it might to others, for quite different reasons.

And then Drinkwater extinguished the thought with a wince of almost physical pain. How long had he yearned for a cessation of this tedious and debilitating war? How often had he vowed to give it all up? Had he not received with something akin to relief, orders to pay off *Andromeda* and go onshore, to take up half-pay and wait for death or the superannuated status of a yellow-admiral?

God knew he was haunted by the dead, whose shadows waited for his own to join them. The order to pay off had been rescinded and instead, as a mark of respect to Admiral-of-the-Fleet, His Royal Highness, The Prince William Henry, Duke of Clarence and Earl of Munster, *Andromeda* had been ordered to join the Royal Squadron off Dover!

'We're going out with a bang!' Drinkwater had overheard one of the afterguard remark to a mate, and knew the mood of the men was one of willing co-operation in seeing Fat Louis back to France, before finally laying up the frigate and being paid off to go home. And yet despite this imminent end to the ship's commission, Chatham dock-yard had spared no expense and effort to make good the damage *Andromeda* had suffered in the Vikkenfiord.

'You would not believe the difficulties I had to fit out the bomb vessel *Virago* in the year one,' Drinkwater had remarked to

Lieutenant Frey, repeating the wonder he had expressed to Birkbeck, 'and then we were under orders to join the great secret expedition to the Baltic. Now we are off on a merry jape to Calais with His Most Christian Majesty which will last a week at the most, and we are getting more paint than a first-rate at Spithead before a review!' And the two of them had resumed their pacing, shaking their heads at the perverse logic of the naval service, while the ship's company fell to their pointless task with evident enthusiasm.

Now Drinkwater was meditating destroying that almost covenanted expectation. He finished shaving and, waving aside his neck linen, sat at the table and drew a sheet of paper towards him. He began to write as his servant poured coffee, pausing occasionally to gather his wits and couch his words in the most telling manner.

It was only as he completed the fourth missive that it occurred to him that the perversity permeating the naval service also ran through its officers. He himself was not exempt from this duplicity: on the one hand he had just poured out expressions of regret to his wife, yet on the other there was a sense almost of relief that he did not yet have to go home and take off his gold-laced undress uniform coat for the last time.

Why was that? he wondered, sealing the letter to Elizabeth. Because he could not face the obscurity of domesticity, or because he was not yet ready to meet the shades of the dead who awaited him there?

His Royal Highness was not yet awake when Drinkwater presented himself upon the quarterdeck of the *Impregnable*, but Blackwood emerged blear-eyed to greet Drinkwater a little coolly.

'My dear fellow, 'tis a trifle early. Can't you sleep?'

'I beg your pardon, Blackwood, but the matter is important, too important to allow me to sleep.'

'I smell intrigue. I thought you had shaken the dust of the Secret Department off your feet . . .'

'So did I, and I wish to God I had, but it dogs me and last night was no exception.' Drinkwater dropped his voice. 'I had a visit from the shore. An agent of long-standing,' Drinkwater lied, 'has given me disturbing intelligence which, under the circumstances, needs to be communicated to His Royal Highness without further delay.' Tiredness and excitement made him light-headed. He almost choked on the prince's title.

A curious look of doubt and indecision crossed Blackwood's face. 'My dear Drinkwater, is this wise? I mean His Royal Highness may be an admiral-of-the-fleet but he is, how shall I put it . . .?'

'But a fleeting one?' In his elevated state, Drinkwater could not resist the pun. 'I have no doubt His Royal Highness will grasp the import of my news, at least sufficient to give me what I want.'

'Which is?'

'*Carte blanche*, Blackwood, *carte blanche*.'

'To do what, in heaven's name?' asked the mystified Blackwood.

'To chase to the westward. Listen, Blackwood, if I take this news back to Dover and post up to town, I shan't be there before Wednesday and by the time the board have cogitated and informed the Prime Minister and given me my orders it will be too late . . .'

'Well what is this news?' an exasperated Blackwood asked.

'Oh, I beg your pardon. I've been so preoccupied . . . They're going to spring Boney; just when we think we've got him in the bag, he'll be spirited away to America . . .'

'Good heavens! D'you mean Boney will then be free to raise Cain in Canada?'

'Exactly so!'

Blackwood looked straight at Drinkwater. 'By God, Drinkwater, you want discretionary orders over Silly Billy's signature.'

'Yes, I want a clear yard-arm, Blackwood. Two ships have already left Antwerp. I don't have much time. None of us have much time. This American business could drag on for years. If Napoleon is involved . . . well, do I have to spell it out? Surely this whole damned war has to be ended one day.'

'Aye, and the sooner the better . . .' But Blackwood was not so easily impressed and his expression clouded, marked by second thoughts. 'But hold hard. 'Twould not be easy to get Boney out of the Med from Elba . . .'

'But it ain't to be Elba, don't you see; 'tis to be the Azores!'

'But the newspapers . . . I mean they've been talking about Elba . . . The other day the *Courier* mentioned it – there's a copy in my cabin.'

'Blackwood, for pity's sake,' Drinkwater's voice was suddenly hardened by exasperation and conviction, 'I have been up all night, mulling the matter in the wake of this news. You must know the degree to which I have dabbled in intelligence.'

Blackwood stared for a moment at his visitor. 'I've heard you're a shrewd cove, Drinkwater . . .'

'Not really, just grasping at straws in the wind, but experience tells me the wind has a direction and a force.' Drinkwater paused and Blackwood smiled.

'Eloquently put.'

'D'you think Silly Billy knows I have had any connections with the Secret Department?'

'I was indiscreet enough to tell him. He was curious to know why you were so long-toothed and still only had a thirty-two. He recollected you when I mentioned the taking of the *Suvorov*, but that only increased his curiosity. I told him you had been involved in secret operations and that your command of *Andromeda* was temporary and in honour of his own connections with your ship.'

'Well, well. That was a flattering fib.'

'Vanity is the one thing he has in common with Nelson.'

'I shall remember that.'

'Come then,' Blackwood said at last, 'you have convinced me. We should hesitate no longer. Let us go and rouse his Royal Highness from his intemperate slumbers.'

Once persuaded, Blackwood turned on his heel, but the alacrity with which he finally led Drinkwater below, proved a damp and fuming squib. Having passed word, couched with respectful deference, by way of His Royal Highness's flag-lieutenant and thence his valet, that a matter of the utmost urgency had to be communicated to His Royal Highness's person, Blackwood led Drinkwater into his own cabin where they took coffee.

It was clear to Blackwood that Drinkwater had much on his mind and found the wait intolerable; he therefore attempted to calm his visitor, remarking that, 'although the Prince is not himself insistent upon any great ceremony, the damned bootlickers in attendance upon the Royal Personage are confoundedly touchy upon the point. Of course,' Blackwood added, 'in the ordinary circumstances of a ceremonial task of this nature, none of it is of any great moment. Our present prevailing urgency however, is a different matter. But we will carry the day if we do not upset the tranquillity of the Royal Mind.' Blackwood dabbed his mouth with a napkin, as though to purge the sarcasm.

'On last night's showing,' Drinkwater responded, 'I was not aware there was much of the Royal Mind to disturb.'

'La, sir,' Blackwood said, grinning, 'all the more reason for treating it with respect.'

Drinkwater harrumphed and Blackwood forbore to make further small-talk. They were in fact not left kicking their heels for more than an hour. Lieutenant Colville, resplendent in full dress even at the early hour, commanded their presence in the *Impregnable*'s great cabin.

Both officers bowed as the prince stepped from his night cabin, his red cheeks still shining from the ministrations of the razor and his shoulders shaking the heavy bullion epaulettes upon his shoulders.

'So sorry to keep you gentlemen,' the prince greeted them. 'Pray join me to break your fasts,' he added, waving to a table laid with splendidly fresh white linen and a selection of hot dishes. 'The kedgeree is devilish good . . .'

Drinkwater caught Blackwood's eye as he swept his coat-tails aside and sat down. Lieutenant Colville sat next to Drinkwater, a small scribbling tablet and pencil neatly laid beside him.

'Now sir,' the Prince boomed across the table as he spooned the kedgeree onto his plate, 'what's all this urgent nonsense about, eh?' He fixed his popping eyes on Drinkwater and began to shovel the fish and rice into his mouth with a mechanical regularity. 'Surely we all did our duty yesterday, eh what?'

'Your Royal Highness, this is a matter of some delicacy . . .' Drinkwater turned and looked pointedly at Lieutenant Colville. 'The matter I have to discuss with you is confidential.'

The Royal Brow contracted and, with a small explosion of rice grains, His Royal Highness enquired bluntly, 'What's the matter with Lieutenant Colville?'

'Well, nothing, Your Royal Highness,' Drinkwater replied, smiling coldly at the flag-lieutenant whose expression was as outraged as he dared in the presence of two senior captains and an admiral who was also the king's son. 'Except that he is only *Lieutenant* Colville, sir, and therefore cannot, I beg your pardon sir, but *must not* be a party to what I have to say.'

There was a moment's stunned silence. The prince bent forward, fork and spoon poised over the partly ravaged though still substantial pile of food, and looked uncertainly from Drinkwater to Blackwood. Drinkwater noticed again the deference he paid to Blackwood, as though the captain's good opinion mattered.

'If I might say, sir,' Blackwood chipped in quickly, 'Captain Drinkwater's news is properly for the ears of Government . . .' The word was encaptalized in a significant emphasis by the flag-captain and Drinkwater stifled a grin.

'Oh . . . Oh, quite! Quite!' Further rice grains were ejaculated from the Royal Mouth. 'Well Colville, off you go! Off you go! Go and take breakfast in the wardroom!'

There was pointed resentment in the scraping of Colville's chair and he bestowed a look of pure contempt upon Captain Drinkwater as he stooped beneath the deck-beams and left the cabin.

'Well Drinkwater, what's all this nonsense about . . .? Oh damn-and-hell-blast-it, Blackwood, be a good fellow and pass a bottle . . .'

As Colville had risen so had Blackwood, crossing the cabin to close the door communicating with the adjacent pantry and waving out the servant who stood discreetly out of sight but within calling. The Prince's command came as he returned and Blackwood lifted an uncorked bottle of claret from the fiddles atop the sideboard.

'Sir, you are aware of my former duties in connection with the Secret Department, are you not?'

'Yes, yes. Barrow told me all about you, so did Sir Joseph Yorke and Blackwood here did the same. Your stock's pretty damned high, so get on with it, eh? There's a good fellow.'

'Very well, sir. Last night I received intelligence directly from a source well known to me . . .'

'D'you mean a spy?'

'No, I do not. From a person who has had intimate connections with Talleyrand and,' Drinkwater paused just long enough to encourage the prince to look up from his emptying plate, 'Napoleon Bonaparte . . .'

Prince William Henry choked violently and snatched up the glass Blackwood had just filled with claret. Calming himself he wiped his mouth and face with a napkin and rumbled, 'Bonaparte, d'ye say? Go on, sir, pray do go on.'

'This person's attachment to Bonaparte has been severed . . .'

'Ah yes! Didn't I tell you, Blackwood, they'd all come crawling on their damned bellies to save what they've made in the Corsican's service! Didn't I say as much, Blackwood? Didn't I, damn it, eh?'

'You did, sir.'

'Aye. And I said as much to King Louis and the Duchesse d'Angoulême. Told 'em not to trust any damned Bonapartist, well, well.'

'The point is, sir,' Drinkwater broke in, seizing the brief pause in His Royal Highness's self-congratulation, 'we shall have to trust what this person said, because if we don't, we shall rue it.'

Drinkwater had expected further interjections by the prince, but he seemed content to listen and commanded Drinkwater impatiently to 'go on, do go on'.

'I have information that a plot has been matured in Paris that, consequent upon the Emperor Napoleon abdicating . . .'

'Emperor? Emperor, sir? The man is no more than a damned general, General Bonaparte!'

'General Bonaparte, Your Royal Highness, was elected Emperor of the French by plebiscite; he is moreover married to an Austrian Arch-duchess and is therefore still related to the Emperor of Austria. Whatever title he held and whatever title we ascribe to him now matters little, but I lay emphasis upon the point now to,' Drinkwater was about to say 'remind,' but the look in the prince's narrowing eyes, made him change his mind. His sleepless night made him over bold and he came quickly to his senses, 'to acquaint Your Royal Highness of the significance of what Bonaparte has relinquished by his instrument of abdication.'

'He was beaten damn it, Drinkwater! Eh, what?'

'Militarily yes, sir, but his ambition is unbeaten, for he abdicated not in favour of King Louis, but his own son. Moreover, his genius is undiminished.'

'Very well, very well, but what is this to us? He is to be exiled, under guard, locked up as nearly as maybe, what. Yet you come here blathering of plots.'

'Would that it were blathering, sir. The fact is a considerable number of his officers are roaming about disaffected and dissatisfied with the turn events have taken. As we sit here a number are already at sea on passage to rescue their Imperial Master in order to spirit him across the Atlantic to Canada.'

'Canada?' The Royal Brow furrowed again.

'To operate with Yankee support, raise the Quebecois, and re-establish Napoleon's dynasty in Canada with a second empire in the Americas.'

'It ain't possible . . . is it?' The prince wiped his mouth and threw down his napkin. His eyes swivelled in Blackwood's direction. 'Well Blackwood? What the devil do you think?'

'Well sir, ' Blackwood began, 'I must confess I have my doubts.' Drinkwater's heart sank. 'But I'm afraid 'tis not at all impossible, sir, and I share Captain Drinkwater's apprehensions in the strongest manner. An extension of the war in North America under such circumstances with every disaffected Bonapartist taking passage to join the reconstituted eagles on the St Lawrence will cause us no end of havoc. To be candid, sir, we could not withstand a determined onslaught and might lose the whole of the North Americas. I doubt your Royal Father would greet that news with much joy, sir.'

Blackwood's reference to King George III, languishing in Windsor, mentally affected by the ravages of porphyria, was masterly and had the prince nodding agreement.

'There are other factors, sir,' Drinkwater added. 'It is not only the Canadian French in Quebec that should concern us, but the old Acadian families who now live in Nova Scotia would happily revert to a French state, even a Bonapartist one. Moreover, if you consider the matter a stage further, can you not see that it would be no wild conjecture for King Louis to reunite his divided country and wipe out the past five and twenty years by reaching an accommodation with Bonaparte across the Atlantic . . .'

'My God, Drinkwater,' Blackwood muttered, 'that is an appalling prospect . . .'

'I wish it were all; regrettably my information is that Tsar Alexander is not against this scheme and that can mean only that having accepted our gold to keep his armies in the field, he would discomfit us and assume the leadership of Europe.'

'But is all this possible, what?' The prince's pop-eyed face bore the impact of the political possibilities. Drinkwater was reminded of Blackwood's charitable judgement of the previous night and in that moment he could see the prince as a simple and good, if misguided, man. He was clearly having trouble grasping the complexities of the conspiracy.

'The matter can brook no delay, sir,' he said. 'I am asking only for the despatch of my single frigate, and I fear, sir, the future peace of Europe thus rests entirely with you.'

'Me?' Astonishment had transfigured the prince's face a second time. 'Surely the board, Sir Joseph, Melville, Barrow and all the rest of the pack of political jacks . . .'

'Come, sir, with respect, there is no time! These men, these Bonapartists are already at sea and they are desperate. They will wish to spring their Emperor before we have mewed him up too well. I am under your orders and cannot, would not, act without them, but . . .'

'But, thank God, you hold the highest rank, sir!' Blackwood broke in, enthusiastically leaning forward, 'No one would question your probity in instructing Captain Drinkwater here to pursue these two ships in order that we might nip this matter in the bud!'

'D'you think so, gentlemen?'

Blackwood grasped his wine glass and raised it in a half-toast, half-pledge, hissing 'Remember Nelson, sir, remember Nelson!'

The prince looked from one to another, his eyes suddenly alight with enthusiasm. 'Damn-and-hell-blast-it, you are right, what! Drinkwater! Blackwood!' Their names were punctuated by the chink of glass on glass. 'Should we not take the squadron, eh, what?' asked the prince, visibly warming to the idea. 'Why, with the *Impregnable* and *Jason* under my command . . .'

'I think not, sir,' put in Blackwood smoothly, 'we must maintain station to soothe the Russians' suspicions. D'you see?'

'Soothe the Russians? Eh? Oh . . . Quite! Quite!' His Royal Highness erupted in explosions of acquiescence, as though seeing the point a little uncertainly, through powder smoke.

'It would, moreover sir, add some additional glory to *Andromeda*,' Blackwood added.

'Why, damn me yes, it would, wouldn't it, eh?' Prince William Henry beamed pleasantly, thinking of reflected glory. 'To our enterprise then,' he said, raising his glass.

Relieved on more than one count. Drinkwater drained his almost at a gulp.

'Come Drinkwater,' the prince exclaimed, 'I see some of God Almighty's daylight in that glass of yours. Banish it!'

And Drinkwater submitted against his judgement to the refill, while His Royal Highness rattled on about writing Drinkwater's orders and Blackwood leaned back in his chair, a half smile upon his face.

Ten minutes later Drinkwater emerged on to *Impregnable*'s quarter-deck with Blackwood. 'You stuck your neck out a couple of times, Drinkwater. I thought Billy was going to have apoplexy when you insisted on Boney being an Emperor.'

'A sleepless night and a matter of urgency makes one less diplomatic,' Drinkwater said, his eyes gritty in the full glare of daylight.

'Oh, I don't blame you,' Blackwood added dismissively, 'those damned Bourbons have all gone back to France to put the clock back as though nothing has happened there since the outbreak of their damned revolution.' He shook his head. 'D'you think Boney will rest easily anywhere?'

Drinkwater shrugged, 'Who knows? The closer to France the more dangerous he is to the process of restoration; the more distant, then the more amenable to some adventure like this one. Even if I'm wrong and it's Elba, we won't be sleeping that easily in our beds.'

'No, we thought we had peace once before . . .'

'D'you know they've been building ships at Antwerp for the last eight or nine years. These two frigates that have slipped to sea could be just the beginning of a fleet which could get out the minute we lift the blockade. I tell you, Blackwood, just when we think we can go home with our work done, the whole confounded thing could blow up in our faces.'

'Aye, the Russian interference bothers me. The Tsar's interested in Paris and I daresay his bayonets and Cossacks will prop up the Bourbons if there's trouble from the French army.'

'Exactly!' Drinkwater exclaimed. 'And d'you see, the Tsar can't afford to keep an army of occupation in France without our support and while many of Napoleon's satraps will compromise and throw in their lot with the new order, many more of the less privileged French officers and the rank and file will rally to the eagles. Alexander can give equal support to this because it will be in King Louis' interests to be rid of them. Napoleon will lure them with promises of glory, land grants and the hope of a resurrected New France. I know this is possible because, although I do not have the liberty to explain now, it is not new. We have just scotched a transhipment of arms from France to America, resulting from a secret accord between Paris and Washington.'*

'So, with Boney stirring up Canada,' summarized Blackwood gloomily, 'supported by remnants of the Grand Army and a fleet built largely in Antwerp; with France weakened by an exodus of its army and with us rushing about trying to save what we can, Alexander capitalizes on his success at no further exertion to himself because we would be exhausted and bankrupt.'

'Yes. And if you wish to extrapolate further, we know the Americans are building a first-rate. If the ships in Antwerp were made available to them, sold cheaply like Louisiana, with American seamen taking them down the Channel under our noses while we kick our heels here waving bunting at His Most Christian Majesty . . .'

'Pray, Drinkwater, don't go on. Thank heaven you did not extrapolate all this to poor Billy.' The two men laughed grimly and Blackwood added, 'I fully understand, and will make sure there are no problems with Their Lordships.'

'Thank you.'

'Now, is there anything you want? Any way I can help?'

'No, I think if I can work to the westward and lie off the Azores, I might yet prevent this horror.'

'It is as well you were on hand . . . ah, here's Colville.'

The flag-lieutenant was crossing the deck with a sealed packet which he held out for Drinkwater.

'Thank you Mr Colville,' Blackwood said, nodding the young officer away, and then in a lower tone, 'I should have a quick look at them, Drinkwater, to ensure they are what you want.'

Drinkwater broke the seal and scanned the single page. For a moment the two captains stood silently, then Drinkwater looked up, folding the paper and thrusting it into his breast pocket. He held out his hand to Blackwood.

'I declare myself perfectly satisfied, Blackwood, and thank you for your help.'

'*Carte blanche*, eh?' Blackwood smiled.

'*Carte blanche* indeed.' They shook hands warmly.

'Good fortune, Drinkwater,' Blackwood said and turned away. 'Mr Colville! Call Captain Drinkwater's gig alongside.'

* See *Beneath the Aurora*

A few moments later Drinkwater was seated in the boat. Midshipman Dunn stood upright in the stern, anticipating Drinkwater's order to return to *Andromeda*.

'The Trinity Yacht, Mr Dunn,' Drinkwater said, seating himself in the stern-sheets.

'The Trinity Yacht sir,' piped Mr Dunn and turned to Wells the coxswain, and Drinkwater caught the look of incomprehension that he threw at the older man.

'Aye, aye, sir,' Wells responded imperturbably, ordering the bowman to shove the boat's head off, and the vertically wavering oars came down and dipped into the sea. As they came out of the huge flagship's lee, a gust of wind threatened to carry Drinkwater's hat off and he clapped his hand on its crown. A little chop was getting up and the oar-looms, swinging forward before diving into the grey-blue water, sliced the top off the occasional wave. Casting round to orientate himself, Drinkwater realized the wind was from the south-south-west. He was going to have a hard beat to windward.

The Trinity Yacht lay anchored close to the *Royal Sovereign*, the smallest vessel in the squadron, but rivalling the royal yacht in the splendour of her ornamentation. Cutter-rigged, she bore an ornate beak-head beneath her bowsprit, upon which a carved lion bore a short-sword aloft. Her upper wales were a rich blue, decorated with gilded carving, each oval port being surrounded by a wreath of laurel. Her stern windows and tiny quarter galleries were diminutives of a much larger ship. Across the stern these windows were interspersed with pilasters and in the centre were emblazoned the unsupported arms of the Trinity House.

These arms, a red St George's cross quartering four black galleons, were repeated on a large square flag at the cutter's single masthead and in the fly of her large red ensign which fluttered gaily over her elaborately carved taffrail. Drinkwater was familiar with her and the device; many years earlier he had served in several of the Trinity House buoy yachts.

'Boat 'hoy!'

'*Andromeda!*' Dunn's treble rang out, forestalling Wells's response and indicating by the ship's name, the presence of that ship's captain.

The boat ran alongside the yacht's side and a pair of man-ropes covered in green baize and finished with Matthew Walker knots snaked down towards him. Grasping these he scrambled quickly up the side and on to the deck.

'Good morning,' he said dusting his hands and touching the forecock of his hat as an elderly officer in a plain blue coat responded. 'I am Captain Drinkwater of the *Andromeda* . . .'

'You are only a little changed, Captain Drinkwater . . .'

'Mr Poulter?'

'The same, sir, the same, though a little longer in the tooth and almost exhausting my three score and ten.'

'Are you, by God? Well, you seem to thrive . . .'

'Captains Woolmore and Huddart are aboard, sir, but neither have yet put in an appearance on deck.'

'I met them last night and spoke at length to Captain Huddart, but best let the Elder Brethren sleep, Captain Poulter,' Drinkwater said, giving Poulter his courtesy title. 'They dined exceeding well last night. I was sorry not to see you there. You were the only commander not present last night.'

'You know the Brethren, Captain Drinkwater, you know the Brethren,' Poulter said resignedly, as though age had placed him past any resentment at the affront.

'Well, they ought perhaps to know His Royal Highness is already astir.'

'Are we expecting orders?'

'I think not yet for yourselves or the rest of the squadron, but I have to leave you in some haste and that is why I am here. Not seeing you last night led me to hope you might be still in command here, but whomsoever I found, I guessed would be willing to take home private letters for me.'

'Of course, Captain, happy to oblige . . .'

'The truth is I have no idea when the squadron will return to port. I anticipate His Royal Highness may not wish to haul down his flag until he has stretched his orders to the limit, whereas you will be returning immediately to the Thames.'

'You have the advantage of me there, then.'

'Huddart mentioned it last night . . .' Drinkwater drew two letters from his breast pocket, checked the superscriptions and handed them to Poulter. 'I'm obliged to you Mr Poulter.'

'Glad to be of service, Captain Drinkwater. Will you take a glass before you go?'

'Thank you, but no. I have to get underweigh without further delay.'

'Where are you bound?'

'Down Channel to the westward,' Drinkwater held out his hand.

Poulter shook it warmly then sniffed the wind. 'You'll have a beat of it, then.'

'Unfortunately yes.' Drinkwater was already half over the rail, casting a glance down at the boat bobbing below.

'Well, it's fair for the estuary,' said Poulter leaning over to watch him descend, the letters, one to Drinkwater's prize agent, the other to Elizabeth, fluttering in his hand.

'And I daresay the Brethren will be anxious to be off, eh, Mr Poulter?' and grinning complicitly Drinkwater sat heavily in the gig's stern-sheets and allowed Mr Dunn to ferry him back to his frigate.

Out of Soundings

The wind settled in the south-south-west, a steady breeze which wafted fluffy, lambs-wool clouds off the coast of France. Clear of Cap Blanc Nez, Birkbeck had the people haul the fore-tack down to the larboard bumkin, and the main-tack forward to the fore chains. The sheets of the fore and main courses were led aft and hauled taut. *Andromeda* carried sail to her topgallants and heeled to leeward, driving along with the ebb tide setting her south and west through the Dover Strait, and while her bowsprit lay upon a line of bearing with the South Foreland high lighthouse, the tide would set her clear of the English coast.

Periodically a patter of spray rose in a white cloud over her weather bow, hung an instant, then drove across the forecastle and waist, darkening the white planking. The sea still bore the chill of a cold winter, and set anyone in its path a-shiver, but the sunshine was warm and brought the promise of summer along with the faint scent of the land.

'France *smells* all right,' Drinkwater overheard Midshipman Dunn say, 'but it don't mean it *is* all right.'

This incontrovertible adolescent logic diverted Drinkwater's attention from the frigate's fabric, for she would stand her canvas well, to consider the plight of the muscle and brain that made her function.

Under any other circumstances, so fine a day with so fine a breeze would have had the hands as happy as children playing, but there was a petulance in Dunn's voice that seemed to be evidence of a bickering between the young gentlemen. Further forward, Drinkwater watched the men coiling down the ropes and hanging them on the fife-rails. From time to time one of them would look aft, and Drinkwater would catch the full gaze of the man before, seeing the eyes of the captain upon him, he would look quickly away.

Nearer to him, Birkbeck the sailing master checked the course for the twentieth time, nineteen of which had been unnecessary. Marlowe and Ashton were also on deck, conversing in a discreet tête-a-tête, except that their discretion was indiscreet enough to reveal the subject of their deliberations to be Captain Drinkwater himself, at whom they threw occasional, obvious and expectant glances.

Drinkwater knew very well what was on their minds; his dilemma was the extent to which he could explain where they were bound and why they had left the Royal Squadron. Why in fact they were headed, not for the River Medway to lay up their ship, but down Channel. It was a problem he had faced before, and often caused a lack of trust, particularly between a commander and a first lieutenant, but it was made far worse on this occasion because of the source of the intelligence which had precipitated this wild passage to the westward. How could he explain the rationale upon which his conclusions were based? How could he justify the conviction that had led him to obtain his orders? Moreover, he knew it was his conscience that spurred him to justify himself at all, not some obligation laid upon a post-captain in the Royal Navy based on moral grounds, or consideration for his ship's company. In retrospect it all seemed like deception, and as the hours passed, Blackwood's suspicions appeared more justifiable. But to set against this was the reflection that Blackwood had come round to support Drinkwater in the end, and what was the diversion of one frigate, if it could save the peace?

On the other hand, what was it to Blackwood, when all was said and done? The man was almost at the top of the post-captain's list and was virtually beyond any recriminations if things miscarried. In such a light, even the support of Prince William Henry might prove a fickle thing, for His Royal Highness carried no weight at the Admiralty.

Drinkwater shoved the worrying thought aside. He would have to offer some explanation to the ship's company, for the news that peace was concluded and the ship was to have laid up, was too well known to simply pass over it if he wanted his people to exert themselves. As matters stood, it was already common knowledge he had been aboard *Impregnable* earlier that morning; it was also known that even earlier a French staff-officer had come aboard and been in conversation with Captain Drinkwater for a long time.

Most of the night, it was said in some quarters, which added spice to an even more scurrilous rumour that the captain's nocturnal visitor had been a woman!

This was imagined as perfectly possible among the prurient midshipmen, but when it was later postulated in the wardroom, Lieutenant Marlowe pooh-poohed it as ridiculous.

'D'you think I would not know a woman when she came aboard,' Marlowe said dismissively. 'A lot of Frenchmen do not have deep voices.'

This statement divided the wardroom officers into the credulous and the contemptuous, further disturbing the tranquillity of the ship.

'Well, what d'you think, Frey?' Ashton asked as he helped himself to a slice of cold ham. 'You've sailed with the queer old bird before.'

Frey shrugged. 'I really have no idea,' he replied evasively.

'But you must have!'

'Why?' Frey looked up from his own platter.

'Well, I mean does our Drink-water,' Marlowe laboured the name, thinking it witty, 'make a habit of entertaining French whores?'

Frey casually helped himself to coffee. It was painful to hear Drinkwater spoken of in such terms by this crew of johnny-come-latelies, but Frey was too open a character to dissemble. Drinkwater had, he knew, been a party to some odd doings during the late war, but he did not wish to expatiate to his present company. Why should he? These men were not comrades in the true sense of the word; they were merely acquaintances, to be tolerated while the present short commission was got over. Nevertheless he was assailed by a growing sense of anticlimax in all this. Superficially the task of conveying the rightful king of France back to his realm had a comfortably conclusive feeling about it. It was like the end of a fairy story, with the kingdom bisected in favour of the parvenu hero, and the princess given in marriage to cement the plot. Except that that was not what had happened; the parvenu hero had lost, the princess was snatched back by her father and the kingdom was being returned to the ogre.

'Well, Frey? It seems by your silence that you know damned well our Drinkie's a famous libertine, eh?' goaded Ashton.

'What confounded nonsense!' Frey protested. He did not like Ashton, seeing in the third lieutenant a manipulative and unpleasant character, but his introspection had delayed his response and he had left it too late to defend Drinkwater.

'Tut, tut. Now we know why he never hoisted himself up the sides of a two-decker,' said Marlowe pointedly and with such childish delight that a disappointed Frey concluded the man was either superficial, or of limited intelligence.

'You know very well we were only attached to the Royal Squadron in honour of His Royal Highness,' Frey said, trying to recover lost ground.

'I suppose they had to leave Drinkwater in her,' Hyde, the hitherto silent marine officer, put in, looking up briefly from his book. 'After all he has just taken a Danish cruiser . . .'

'I heard he was damned lucky to get away with that,' said Ashton maliciously, 'and I heard he took a fortune in specie.'

'Is that true, Frey?' asked Marlowe, provoking Hyde to abandon his book.

Frey finished his coffee and rose from the table as *Andromeda* hit a wave and shuddered. An explosion of oaths from his brother officers revealed they had yet to acquire their sea-legs while his were perfectly serviceable.

'I expect so, gentlemen. But if you're so damnably curious, why don't you ask him yourself.' And clapping his hat upon his head, Lieutenant Frey left for the quarterdeck.

Later, Lieutenant Marlowe, having plucked up enough courage from the urgings of Lieutenant Ashton, took Frey's advice. He began to cross the deck, colliding with Birkbeck beside the binnacle as he made his way upwards from the lee hance.

'Steady, Mr Marlowe,' Birkbeck growled, 'in more ways than one.'

'What d'you mean by that?' asked Marlowe, reaching a hand out to support himself by the binnacle.

'I mean,' said Birkbeck in as quiet a voice as would carry above the low moan of the wind in the rigging and the surge and rush of the sea alongside, 'I shouldn't go a-bothering the captain just at the moment . . .'

Marlowe looked askance at Birkbeck. The old man had been on deck since *Andromeda* had got under weigh, seeing her clear of the

South Sand Head of the Goodwins and the Varne Bank. He had not been party to the speculation in the wardroom, so how did he know what was in Marlowe's mind? Moreover, he was unshaven and his hair, what there was of it, hung down from the rim of his hat in an untidy and, to Marlowe, offensive manner. Marlowe concluded the ruddy faced old man was an insolent fool. Damn-it, the man was not fit for a quarterdeck!

'I'll trouble you to mind your own business, *Mister* Birkbeck, while I mind mine.'

Birkbeck shrugged. 'Have it your own way, young shaver,' he replied as Marlowe, flushed with the insolence, strove to reach Drinkwater.

The captain had lodged himself securely against the larboard mizen pinrail which, although on the windward side of the ship was, from the effect of the frigate's tumblehome, the least windy place on the quarterdeck. He was staring forward, an abstracted look on his weatherbeaten features against which the line of a sword-scar showed livid.

Just as Lieutenant Marlowe reached the captain, *Andromeda*'s bow thumped into the advancing breast of a wave. She seemed to falter in mid-stride, kicked a little to starboard as the wave sought to divert her from her chosen track, then found her course again. But the sudden increase in heel caught the unsteady Marlowe off-balance. To preserve his dignity and prevent himself from falling ignominiously, Marlowe's hands reached out and scrabbled for the ropes belayed to the mizen pinrail. Instead they encountered Drinkwater's arm.

'What the . . .?'

Drinkwater turned, feeling the young man's vain attempt to seize him, then quickly reacted and seized Marlowe's outstretched hand.

'Come, sir, steady there! What the devil's the matter?'

Marlowe regained his balance, but lost his aplomb. 'I beg pardon, sir,' he gabbled all in a breath, 'but I wondered if you have any orders, sir.'

Had Drinkwater not been so dog-tired and had he not been almost asleep on his feet, he might have been in a better humour and laughed at the young officer's discomfiture. Reluctant to leave the deck, yet content to abandon matters to Birkbeck's competence, he had been languishing in the comfortable compromise of a reverie. As it was, only the helmsmen laughed surreptitiously, while Drinkwater showed a testy exasperation.

'Mr Birkbeck?' he called sharply.

'Sir?' Birkbeck came up the sloping deck with a practised, almost, Marlowe thought, insulting ease.

'What orders d'you have?'

'Why, sir, to keep her full-and-bye and make the best of our way down Channel.'

Drinkwater turned his gaze on Marlowe. 'There, Mr Marlowe, does that satisfy you?'

'Well, not really sir. I had hoped that you might confide in me, sir.'

'Confide in you, sir? If you sought a confidence, should not you have been on deck earlier, Mr Marlowe, when we were getting under weigh? After all, you knew of our visitor last night.'

'Well, sir, you did not condescend to inform me of anything consequent upon your visitor. As you know, under normal circumstances as first lieutenant I should not keep an anchor watch, but having done so since we were engaged upon a special duty, I had turned in and there was nothing in your night orders to suggest . . .'

'That you had to forgo your breakfast, no, of course not; but you are first lieutenant of a frigate on active service.'

'*Active* service, sir?' Marlowe frowned, looking round at Birkbeck who caught his eye and turned away. 'I do not think I quite understand, sir.'

'I am very certain you do not understand, Mr Marlowe.'

'But sir,' Marlowe's tone was increasingly desperate, 'might I not be privy to . . .?'

'No sir, you may not. Not at this moment. If Lieutenant Colville was sent out of hearing while His Royal Highness,' Drinkwater invoked the pompous title with a degree of pleasure, sure that it would silence his tormentor, 'gave me my orders, I do not think it appropriate that I confide in you, do you?'

Crestfallen and confused, Marlowe mumbled a submissive 'No, sir.'

'Very well, Mr Marlowe, then let's hear no more of the matter until we are out of soundings.'

Marlowe's mouth dropped open in foolish incredulity. 'Out of soundings . . .?'

Astonishment lent volume to Marlowe's exclamation Ashton caught it, downwind across the deck, and dropped his jaw in imitation of his senior; Birkbeck caught it and sighed an old man's sigh; Midshipman Dunn caught it and his eyes brightened at the prospect of adventure, and the helmsmen caught it silently, mulling it over in their minds until, relieved of their duty, they would release it like a rat to run rumouring about the berth-deck.

As for Drinkwater, he felt ashamed of his peevishness; this was not how he had hoped to let his ship's company know they were outward bound for the Atlantic Ocean, nor was it how he should have treated his first lieutenant. If he had not been so damned tired . . . He sighed and stared to windward. The comfortable mood eluded him. The little encounter with Marlowe upset him and left his mind a-whirl again.

As soon as *Andromeda* had cleared Dungeness, Drinkwater went below. He was exhausted and, removing his hat, coat and shoes, loosed his stock and tumbled into his swinging cot. He thought for a moment that even now he would be unable to sleep, for his mind was still a confusion of thoughts. The enormity of Hortense's news, the possible consequences of it, the attention to the details of informing Elizabeth and making arrangements for his informant, the influencing of Prince William Henry and now the bother of his ship's company and its officers, all tumbled about in his tired head. Each thought followed hard upon its progenitor, and always at the end of the spiral lay the black abyss of *what if* . . .?

What if they missed the French ships? What if Hortense had lied? What if she told the truth and he miscalculated? What if the Tsar changed his mind? What if . . .? What if . . .? Slowly the thoughts detached themselves, broke up and shrank, slipping away from him so that only the blackness was there, a blackness into which he felt himself fall unresisting, an endless engulfment that seemed to shrink him to nothing, like a trumpet note fading.

Drinkwater woke with a start. Sweat poured from him and his garments were twisted about his body like a torque. He felt bound and breathless. Sweat dried clammily upon him and the latent heat of its evaporation chilled him. There was a dull ache in his jaw. Then he remembered: he had been drowning! He was wet from the sea; gasping from having been dragged beneath something monstrous, but beneath what?

And then the entire dream came back to him: the water, the strange ship, the noise of clanking chains, the white and ghostly figure that had reared above him: Hortense, pallid as a corpse, beautiful and yet ghastly, as though her whole face was riven by scars. Yet the scars were not marks, but the twists of serpents. It was Hortense, but it was also the Medusa which seemed to be borne as a figurehead on the bow of the strange and clattering ship. Then he was under water and fighting for his life as the noise reached a terrifying crescendo from which he knew he must escape, or die.

As he lay mastering his terror, he recognized the old dream. Once, when he was an unhappy midshipman, it had come to him regularly, marking the miserable days of his existence aboard the frigate *Cyclops*. Since then it had visited him occasionally, as a presentient warning of some impending event. But now he felt no such alarm, as though this terror from his youth could only frighten him when he was weak and exhausted. It was just a visitation from the past; a relic. Old men feared death, not the wearying vicissitudes of misfortune. These, experience taught them, were to be confronted and mastered.

In the past, Hortense's image had sometimes occupied the post of what he had come to call the 'white lady'. Perhaps it was because she had again entered his life that the dream had come roaring out of his subconscious. As he lay there, staring up at the deck-head which glowed in the last reflections of daylight coming in through the stern windows, he mastered the lingering fear which was rapidly shrinking to apprehension. His thoughts ordered themselves slowly but surely, returning him to the state of conscious anxiety from which he had escaped in sleep.

Any analysis of his actions must be seen in the light of good faith. The orders the prompted prince had given him cleared his yard-arm as far as the Admiralty were concerned; all his best efforts must now be bent on reaching the Azores and lying in wait for the French ships. If allied warships brought the Emperor Napoleon to the islands before the French ships arrived, so much the better. Drinkwater would be able to persuade their commanders to remain in the vicinity. If, on the other hand, the French ships lay off the islands in waiting for their Emperor, he would attack them and while he could never guarantee success, he was confident he could sufficiently damage them to prevent them rescuing their prize and carrying out their confounded stratagem.

Then an uncomfortable thought struck him. While he had a full crew, most of which had successfully fought in the Vikkenfiord, his officers were largely inexperienced. It would not have mattered if all they had had to do was act as part of Prince William Henry's Royal Squadron. But now, while his elderly frigate was painted to a nicety, she had not refilled her magazines and was woefully short of powder and ball. True, he had a stock of langridge, grape and musket balls, but there was no substitute for good iron shot. And if that were not enough, he was victualled for no more than a month, two at the most, and carried no spare spars. These thoughts brought him from his bed.

The frigate was still close-hauled on the larboard tack well heeled over to starboard, and the rush of water along her sides added its undertone to the monstrous creaking of the hull, the groan of the rudder stock below him and the faint tremulous shudder through the ship's fabric as she twitched and strained to the whim of wind and sea.

Drinkwater reached the quarter-gallery, eased himself and poured water into a basin. It slopped wildly as he scooped it up into his face and brushed his teeth. His servant Frampton had long-since abandoned the captain to his slumbers, and Drinkwater was glad of the lack of fossicking attention which he sometimes found intolerably vexing. He retied his stock, dragged a comb through his hair and clubbed his queue. Finally he eased his wounded shoulder into the comfortable broadcloth of his old, undress uniform coat, pulled his boat-cloak about his shoulders and, picking his hat from the hook beside the door, went on deck.

It was almost dark when he gained the quarterdeck. Low on the western horizon a dull orange break in the overcast showed the last of the daylight. Overhead the clouds seemed to boil above the mast-heads in inky whorls, yet the wind was not cold, but mild.

Seeing the captain emerge on deck and stare aloft, the officer of the watch crossed the deck. It was Frey. 'Good evening, sir. Mr Birkbeck ordered the t'gallants struck an hour past, sir. He also had the main course clewed up.'

Drinkwater nodded then, realizing Frey could not see him

properly, coughed and grunted his acknowledgement. 'Very well, Mr Frey. Thank you.'

Frey was about to withdraw and vacate the weather rail but Drinkwater said, 'A word with you, Mr Frey. There is something I wish to ask you.'

'Sir?'

'Have you any idea what we are up to?'

'No, sir.'

'What about scuttlebutt?' Even in the wind, Drinkwater heard Frey sigh. 'Come on, don't scruple. Tell me.'

'Scuttlebutt has it that we are off somewhere and that it is due to the, er, officer who came on board last night.'

It already seemed an age ago, yet it was not even twenty-four hours. Drinkwater cast aside the distraction. 'And what do they say about this officer then, Mr Frey?'

'Frankly, sir, they say it was a woman, at least, that is, the midshipmen do.'

'Tom Paine is an intelligent imp, Mr Frey,' Drinkwater replied, smiling. 'He noticed straight away.'

'Then it *was* a woman?'

Drinkwater sighed. 'Yes, though you should not attach too much importance to the fact. I'm afraid she brought disturbing intelligence, Mr Frey, not entirely unconnected with that business in the Vikkenfiord.'

Drinkwater could sense Frey's reluctance at coming to terms with this news. 'Then it is not over yet, sir?'

'I fear not, my dear Frey, I fear not.'

A profound silence fell between them, if the deck of a frigate working to windward could provide such an environment. Then Frey said, 'I think you should tell Marlowe, sir. I do not think him a bad fellow, but he feels you do not trust him, and that cannot be good, sir.' Frey hesitated to voice his misgivings about Ashton. 'I don't wish to presume, sir.'

'No, no, you do quite right to presume, Mr Frey, quite right. I fear I used him ill. It was unforgivable.'

'He certainly took it badly, sir, if you'll forgive me for saying so, though I think Ashton made the situation worse.'

'Oh,' said Drinkwater sharply, 'in what way?'

'Well, sir, I think he put Marlowe up to importuning you; made him stand upon his dignity, if you know what I mean.'

'There was a time when a lieutenant had precious little dignity to stand upon.'

'There was much made of it in the wardroom, sir.'

Drinkwater grunted again. 'Well, well, I must put things to rights tomorrow.'

'You don't mind . . .'

'If you speak your mind? No, no. Under the circumstances, not at all.'

'It's just . . .' Frey faltered and Drinkwater saw him look away.

'Go on. Just what?' he prompted.

'Nothing sir,' Frey coughed to clear his throat, adding, 'no, nothing at all.' As Frey moved away, Drinkwater watched him go, wondering what was on his mind.

Chapter Five   *April 1814*

To Weather of the Wight

'Well gentlemen,' Drinkwater looked up from the chart at the two officers before him, 'I think I must confide in you both.'

'Are we out of soundings then?' Marlowe asked, a supercilious expression on his face. Drinkwater had forgotten his earlier remark, made more for the sake of its effect, than as a matter of absolute accuracy, but Marlowe's tone reminded him. He stared at the younger man for a moment, taken aback at Marlowe's attitude, so taken aback that a quick retort eluded him.

'Soundings?' he muttered. 'No, of course not,' then he looked up and glared at Marlowe, though he forbore from snapping at him. 'We have yet to weather the Wight.' He tapped the chart, pausing for a moment. 'What I have to say I shall shortly make known to the people, but for the time being it shall be between ourselves. Once we have resolved those difficulties which we can foresee, and there are several, then having taken what remedial action lies within our compass, we can inform the ship. Is that clear?'

'Perfectly, sir,' responded Birkbeck quickly, shooting his younger colleague a sideways glance.

'I think so, sir.' If Marlowe was being deliberately and sulkily obtuse, Drinkwater let the matter pass. He was resolved to be conciliatory, then Marlowe added, 'But is that wise, sir?'

'Is what wise?' Drinkwater frowned.

'Why, telling the people. Surely that is dangerous.'

'Dangerous, Mr Marlowe? How so?'

'Well, it seems perfectly clear to me. It could act as an incitement. If you make them privy to our thoughts, it would exceed their expectations and we should be guilty of an impropriety. Sir.'

'You think it an impropriety to ask them to go into action without knowing why, do you?'

It was Marlowe's turn to frown. 'Action? What action do you

think we shall be involved in?' The first lieutenant was wearing his arch look again. It was the condescending way one might look at a senile old man, Drinkwater concluded with a mild sense of shock.

'Well, who knows, Mr Marlowe, who knows? Though it occurs to me we might encounter an American cruiser.' It had clearly not occurred to Marlowe. Drinkwater went on. 'Now then, let us be seated in a little comfort. Mr Birkbeck, you have the other chart there, and if you wish to smoke, please do. Mr Marlowe, do be a good fellow and pass the decanter and three glasses . . .'

But Marlowe was not to be so easily pacified. Doing as he was bid, he placed the glasses on the table. 'Look here, sir . . .'

But Drinkwater's fuse had burned through. His voice was suddenly harsh as he turned on the young first lieutenant. 'No sir! Do you look here, and listen too. We are on active service, *very* active service if I ain't mistaken.' Marlowe seemed about to speak, thought better of it and sat in silent resentment. Drinkwater caught Birkbeck's eye and the older man shrugged his shoulders with an almost imperceptible movement, continuing to fill a stained clay pipe.

'Now then, gentlemen, pay attention: what I have to tell you is of the utmost importance. It is a secret of state and I am imparting it to you both because if anything should happen to me, then I am jointly charging you two gentlemen to prosecute this matter to its extremity with the utmost vigour.'

Drinkwater had Marlowe's attention in full now. Birkbeck knew enough of Drinkwater's past to wear an expression of concern. Drinkwater felt he owed Birkbeck more than a mere explanation; as for Marlowe, it would do him no harm to be made aware of the proper preoccupations of experienced sea-officers.

'I am sorry Mr Birkbeck that we have been diverted to this task and I know well that you were promised a dockyard appointment when this commission was over. Well, the promise still stands, it's just that the commission has been extended.' Drinkwater smiled. 'I'm sorry, but there it is . . .'

Birkbeck expelled his breath in a long sigh. Nodding, he said, 'I know sir: a sense of humour is a necessary portion of a sea-officer's character.'

'Just so, Mr Birkbeck,' and Drinkwater smiled his curiously attractive, lopsided grin. 'More wine?'

He waited for them to recharge their glasses. 'We are bound to the Azores gentlemen, to trap Napoleon Bonaparte . . .'

'We are *what*?' exclaimed an incredulous Marlowe.

'So it *was* a woman!'

Mr Marlowe could scarce contain himself, puffed up as he was with a great state secret and half a bottle of blackstrap. Birkbeck gave him a rueful glance as the two officers paced the quarterdeck whence the master had suggested they go to take the air and discuss the matters that now preoccupied the first lieutenant and sailing master of the frigate *Andromeda*.

'May I presume to plead my grey hair and offer you a word of advice, Mr Marlowe,' Birkbeck offered. 'Of course, I would quite understand if you resented my interfering, but we must, perforce, work in amity.'

'No, no, please Birkbeck . . .'

'Well, Captain Drinkwater is not quite the uninfluential tarpaulin you might mistake him for . . .'

'I knew he had fought a Russian ship, but I have to confess I had not heard of him in the Channel Fleet.'

'Perhaps because he has seen extensive foreign and special service. Did you know, for instance, that Nelson sent him from the Med, round Africa and into the Red Sea? He brought a French national frigate home, she was bought into our service and he subsequently commanded her. The captain also served under Nelson and commanded a bomb at Copenhagen. Oh, yes . . .' Birkbeck nodded. 'I see you are surprised. Talk to Mr Frey, he was in the Arctic on special service with Captain Drinkwater in the sloop *Melusine* and I believe Frey was captured with the captain just before Trafalgar. I understand Drinkwater was aboard the French flagship . . .'

'As a prisoner?' asked Marlowe, clearly reassessing his commander.

'Yes, so I understand. Later Drinkwater made up for this and battered a Russian seventy-four to pieces in the Pacific.'

'In the Pacific? I had heard mention of the action, but assumed it to have been in the Baltic.'

'That, if I may say so, is the danger of assumptions.' Birkbeck smiled at Marlowe. 'Anyway, I first met him aboard this ship last autumn when he took *Andromeda* over from Captain Pardoe: not that Pardoe was aboard very often; he spent most of his time in the House of Commons and left the ship to the first luff . . .'

'Who was killed, I believe,' interrupted Marlowe.

'Yes. We had trouble with some of the men – it's a long story.'

'I gathered they were mutineers,' Marlowe said flatly.

'Ah, you've heard that, have you?' Birkbeck looked at the young officer beside him. 'Now I understand why you made that remark about incitement.'

'Well, the temper of the men is a matter I should properly concern myself with.' Marlowe invoked the superior standing of a commissioned officer, as opposed to the responsibilities of the warranted sailing master.

"Indeed it is, Mr Marlowe. But you might also properly concern yourself with the temper of your commanding officer. I fear you may have fallen victim to a misapprehension in misjudging Captain Drinkwater. Consider his late achievement. Last autumn, as soon as he came aboard this ship, which had been kept on guard duties and as a convoy on the coast where her captain could be called to the House of Commons if the government wished for his vote, we went a-chasing Yankee privateers in the Norwegian fiords. We took a big Danish cruiser, the *Odin*. It was scuttlebutt then that Drinkwater had some influence at the Admiralty and was wrapped up in secret goin's on. You heard what he said about that woman who came aboard the other night and that she was mixed up in some such business. I've no doubt the matter we are presently engaged upon is exactly as he told us.'

'I had no idea,' mused Marlowe for a moment, then added, 'So, you consider we might see some action?'

Birkbeck shrugged. 'Who knows? Captain Drinkwater seems to think so. Perhaps just by cruising off the Azores we will prevent all this happening, but if Boney escapes, God help Canada.'

'We are playing for very high stakes . . .'

'Indeed we are.'

'But she's an old ship and lacks powder and shot . . .'

'What d'you think we can do about that?'

'I, er, I don't know. Put into Plymouth?'

'It's a possibility . . .'

'But?'

'Not one he'll consider.'

'Why not?'

'It would delay us too much; we'd be subject to the usual dock-yard prevarications, difficulties with the commissioner, warping in alongside the powder hulk, half the watch running ... No, no, Drinkwater will avoid that trap.'

'Well Gibraltar's too far out of our way,' said Marlowe with a kind of pettish finality, 'so what will Our Father do?'

'Can't you guess?' Birkbeck grinned at the young man.

Irritated, Marlowe snapped, 'No I damn well can't!'

Birkbeck was offended by Marlowe's change of tone. 'Then you'll have to wait and see!' he replied, and left the first lieutenant staring after him as he made his way below.

Lieutenant Hyde of the marines sat in the wardroom reading a novel. It was said to have been written 'by a lady', but, despite this, it rather appealed to him. He was an easy-going man whose lithe body conveyed the impression of youth and agility. In fact he was past thirty-five and conspicuously idle. But whereas military officers were frequently inert, Lieutenant Hyde was fortunate to be able to persuade his subordinates into doing their own duty and a good bit of his own. Moreover, this was accomplished with an enthusiasm that bespoke a keenly active and intelligent commanding officer.

The secret of Hyde's success was very simple; he possessed a sergeant of unusual ability and energy. Sergeant McCann was something of an enigma, even between decks on a British man-of-war which was said to be a refuge for all the world's bad-hats. Sergeant McCann was as unlike any other sergeant in the sea-service as it was possible to be; he was cultured. In fact the novel Lieutenant Hyde was reading was rightfully Sergeant McCann's; moreover the sergeant was diligent, so diligent that it was unnecessary for Lieutenant Hyde to check up on him, and he was well acquainted with the duties required of both a sergeant and an officer. This was because Sergeant McCann had once held a commission of his own.

A lesser man would have let bitterness corrode his soul, but Sergeant McCann had nothing left in the world other than his work. He had been born in Massachusetts where his father had been a cobbler. At the age of sixteen his father had been dragged from their house and tarred and feathered by 'patriot' neighbours for the crime of opposing armed rebellion against the British crown. By morning McCann was the head of his family, his mother had lost her reason and his twelve-year-old sister was in a state of shock. Somehow he got his family into Boston and when that city was evacuated they fled to New York along with a host of loyalist refugees. Young McCann volunteered for service in a provincial regiment, fought at the Brandywine and earned a commission at Germantown. In his absence his mother took to drink and his sister became mistress to a British officer. McCann went south and fought with Patrick Ferguson at King's Mountain, where he was wounded and taken prisoner. After a long and humiliating captivity he found his way back to New York, but no sign of his family. After the peace, in company with other loyalists, he crossed the Atlantic in search of compensation from the British government. In this he was disappointed, and found himself driven to all manner of extremities to keep body and soul together. Finally he entered the service of a moderately wealthy family whose country seat was in Kent. He stuck the subservient existence of an under-footman for three years, then joined the marines of the Chatham division. McCann learned to blot out the past by an intense concentration upon the present. Lieutenant Hyde called him 'my meticulous sergeant' and thus he was known as Meticulous McCann.

Owing to severe losses among the marines during the preceding cruise, Lieutenant Hyde, Sergeant McCann and a dozen additional red-coated lobsters had been sent aboard *Andromeda* at Chatham shortly before the frigate sailed on her escort duties. The combination of the elegantly languid Hyde and the pipeclayed mastery of McCann was thought by the officer commanding the Chatham division to be ideal for such a ceremonial task.

'Is that damned book *so* entertaining, Hyde?' Lieutenant Ashton now asked.

'It is very amusing,' Hyde replied without looking up from the page, adding, 'Shouldn't you be on deck?'

'Frederic has relieved me. He's under the impression I am acting as his clerk. Anyway, old fellow, I hate to disturb you from your intellectual pursuits, but the Meticulous One awaits your attention.'

'Really . . .' Hyde turned a page, chuckled and continued reading.

'Do please come in Sergeant.' Ashton waved the scarlet-clad McCann into the wardroom, then turned to the marine officer.

'Hyde, you infernal layabout, you quite exasperate me! Sergeant McCann is reporting to you.' Ashton rolled his eyes at the deck-head for McCann's benefit.

Skilfully bracing himself against the heel and movement of the ship, McCann crashed his boots and finally attracted the attention of his commanding officer. Hyde affected a startled acknowledge-ment of his presence.

'What the devil . . .? Ah. McCann, men ready for inspection?'

'Sir!'

'Very well.' Hyde put his book, pages downwards, upon the table and got up. He seemed to the watching Ashton not to need to adjust his tight-fitting tunic, but rose immaculate, preened like a sleek bird. He winked at Ashton, picked up his billy-cock hat and preceded McCann from the wardroom. Watching the pair leave, Ashton was shaking his head in wonder at the contrived little scene when a door in the adjacent bulkhead opened and a tousle-haired Frey poked his head out.

'What the deuce is all the noise about?'

'Oh, nothing, Frey, nothing, only Hyde and the Meticulous One.'

'Is that all?' said Frey, preparing to retreat into his hutch of a cabin just as the ship heeled farther over. 'Wind's shifting,' he said, yawning. 'Isn't it your watch?'

'I do wish people wouldn't keep asking me that. The first lieu-tenant has relieved me.'

'What for?'

'He was feeling generous . . . Frey,' Ashton went on, 'you know Our Father, don't you. What's he like, personally, I mean?'

Frey sighed, scratched his head and came out of his cabin in his stockinged feet. Sitting at the table he stretched. 'I'm not sure I can tell you, beyond saying that I have the deepest admiration for him.'

'They say he's an unlucky man to be around,' Ashton remarked. 'Didn't his last first lieutenant get killed, along with that fellow you were with, what was his name?'

'Quilhampton? Yes, James was killed, so was Lieutenant Huke . . .'

'Well?'

'Well what?'

'Well 'tis said we're bound out to the westward in chase of two French ships that have escaped from Antwerp,' expostulated Ashton.

'If that is the scuttlebutt, then it must be true,' said Frey drily, taking a biscuit from the barrel.

'I had it from Marlowe who saw the captain this morning and then heard all about our gallant commander from old Birkbeck.'

'Well then, you know more about it than I do.'

'Oh, Frey, don't be such a confounded dullard . . .'

Andromeda lay down even further to leeward and ran for some moments with her starboard ports awash. Hyde's novel slid across the table and fell on the painted canvas deck covering. Frey bent down, picked it up and gave it a cursory glance.

'Here, put it on the stern settee,' said Ashton. Frey threw it to Ashton who caught it neatly and glanced at the title on the spine. '*Pride and Prejudice*; huh! What a damned apt title for . . .' He looked up quickly at the watching Frey, flushed slightly and pulled the corners of his mouth down. 'Odd cove, Hyde,' he remarked.

Frey stood up; he was about to retire to his cabin and dress for his watch, but paused and said, 'You seem to think most of us are odd, in one way or another.'

Ashton casually spun Miss Austen's novel into a corner of the buttoned settee that ran across the after end of the gloomy wardroom. He stared back at Frey, seemed to consider a moment, then said, 'Do I? Well I never.'

Frey was galled by the evasion. 'What d'you think of Marlowe?'

'Known him for years.' Ashton's tone was dismissive.

'That's not what I asked,' persisted Frey. There was a hardness in his tone which Ashton had not heard before.

'Oh, he's all right.'

'That is what I told the captain,' Frey remarked, watching Ashton, 'though I am not certain I am right.'

'You told the captain?' Ashton frowned, 'and what gives you the right to give him your opinion, or to presume to doubt Mr Marlowe's good name, eh?'

'Something called friendship, Ashton,' Frey retorted.

'Oh yes, old shipmates,' Ashton said sarcastically, 'as if I could forget.'

There was a knock at the wardroom door and Midshipman Dunn's face appeared. 'One bell, Mr Frey,' he said.

'Thank you, Mr Dunn.' Frey shut his cabin door and reached for his neck-linen. There was something indefinably odious about Josiah Ashton and Frey could not put his finger on it. He was too damned thick with Marlowe, Frey concluded, and Marlowe was something of a fool. But it irritated Frey that he could not quite place the source of a profound unease.

As Frey went on deck he passed Hyde's marines parading on the heeling gun deck. They stood like a wavering fence, the instant before it was blown down by a gale. Lieutenant Hyde had almost completed his inspection prior to changing sentries. He caught Frey's eye and winked. For all his intolerable indolence, Frey could not help liking Hyde. One could like a fellow, Frey thought as he grasped the manropes to the upper deck, without either admiring or approving of him.

On deck the watch were shortening sail. The topgallants had already been furled and now the topsails were being reefed. Clapping his hand to his hat and drawing it down hard on his head, Frey stared aloft. The main topsail yard had been clewed down and the slack upper portion of the sail drawn up to the yard-arms by the reefing tackles. The windward topman was astride the extremity of the yard, hauling the second reef earing up as hard as he could, while his fellow yard-men strove to assist by hauling on the reef points as the big sail flogged and billowed.

Lieutenant Marlowe stood forward of the binnacle with a speaking trumpet to his mouth.

'Jump to it, you lubbers!' he was shrieking, though it was clear the men were working as rapidly as was possible. The unnecessary nature of Marlowe's intervention confirmed Frey's revised opinion of the first lieutenant.

Since Frey had last been on deck the weather had taken a turn for the worse. A quick glance over the starboard bow showed the white buttress of the Isle of Wight lying athwart their hawse with a menacing proximity as the backing wind drove them into the bight of Sandown Bay. The reason for Marlowe's anxiety was now clear: he had left the reefing too late, giving insufficient time for the men to complete their task before they must tack the ship. To the north-west, several ships lay at anchor in St Helen's road, while in the distance beyond, a dense clutter of masts and yards showed where the bulk of the Channel Fleet, withdrawn from blockade duties off Ushant, lay once more in the safe anchorage of Spithead. It would be a fine thing, Frey thought, for *Andromeda* to pile herself up at the foot of Culver Cliff within sight of such company!

Frey strode aft, took a quick look at the compass, gauged the wind from the tell-tale streaming above the windward hammock irons, and then stared at the land. Dunnose Head was stretching out on the larboard bow, and Culver Cliff loomed ever closer above the starboard fore chains, its unchanged bearing an ominous and certain precursor of disaster.

Beside Frey the quartermaster and helmsmen were muttering apprehensively and Frey's own pulse began to race. The seamen coming on deck to take over the watch were milling in the waist. The experienced among them quickly sensed something was wrong. The wind note rose suddenly and to windward the sea turned a silver-white as the squall screamed down upon the ship. For a split second Frey's artistic sensibilities compelled him to watch the phenomenon which looked like nothing so much as the devil's claw-marks raking the surface of the sea.

Midshipman Dunn came running up to Marlowe. 'Captain's just coming on deck, sir.'

Marlowe ignored the boy and continued shouting at the men aloft who were now struggling hard to tame the main topsail. Frey could not see the fore-topsail, but presumed the worst. Frey heard Marlowe's next order with disbelief

'Aloft there! Leggo those pendants! Let fly the reeftackles! Standby the yard lifts! Haul away those lifts!' The men stationed at the lifts hesitated and Marlowe leaned forward and screamed at them: 'Haul away, you idle buggers! Haul!' Then the first lieutenant, a curious, pleading expression on his face, turned towards Frey and the men at the wheels, as though explaining his action. 'We'll reef after we've tacked.'

But he received no consoling approval. Aloft they had no such appreciation of Marlowe's intentions. The men at the lifts jerked the yards and they began to slew in the wind. The men on the footropes rocked and three at the bunt of the sail let their reef points go, while someone else started the weather reef-tackle so that the topsail shivered in the squall.

The violent movement of yard and sail was sufficient to unbalance the man astride the larboard main yard-arm. He lost his grip of the reef pendant, which streamed almost horizontally away to leeward; then he slipped sideways and fell. He made a futile grab at the loose pendant, but the wind snatched it from him. The next man on the yard tried to seize him, but it was too late. With a cry, the unfortunate seaman fell with a sickening thud at the feet of Captain Drinkwater as he came on deck.

Frey saw the whole thing happen: saw the topman slip and fall, saw Marlowe seek justification for his action and saw him fail to realize what was happening until the body fell to the deck. He saw, too, the look of horror that passed over Drinkwater's face as he came on deck, then saw the captain suddenly galvanized into action, cross the deck, swing forward and take in the whole shambles in a second. Without a speaking trumpet, Drinkwater roared his orders and took instant command of the deck.

'*All hands!*'

The horrified inertia of the ship's company was swept aside, as Drinkwater called them all to the greater duty of saving the ship.

'*All hands about ship and reef topsails in one!*'

The pipes of the boatswain and his mates shrilled and the order sent men to their stations; those already aloft crowded back along the footropes and into the tops. Drinkwater moved smartly across the deck as the men rushed to their positions; ropes were turned off pin rails; lines of men backed up the leading hands as they prepared to clew down the topsail yards again and man the larboard braces. While others stood ready to cast off the lifts and starboard braces, Hyde's marines tramped up from the gun-deck and cleared away the mizen gear.

'Mr Dunn,' Frey called as he ran to his post. 'Take two men and get that poor fellow below to the surgeon.'

Frey took one last look at Culver Cliff. It seemed to loom as high as the main yard.

'Down helm.' Drinkwater stood beside the wheel as the quartermaster had the helm put over and *Andromeda* turned slowly into the wind. There was a touch less sea running now as they rapidly closed the shore where they were scraping a lee from Dunnose Head at the far and windward end of the bay. As the frigate came head to wind, the sails began to shiver and then come aback.

'*Mains'l haul!*' Drinkwater roared.

'*Clew down! Haul the reef tackles! Haul buntlines!*'

The main and mizen yards, their sails slack and blanketed by the sails on the foremast, were hauled round by their braces, ready for the new tack.

'*Trice up and lay out!*'

With Drinkwater's bellowing acting as a noisy yet curiously

effective tranquillizer imposing order on momentary confusion, the topmen resumed their positions, a new man occupying the larboard main topsail yard-arm. *Andromeda* bucked into the head sea, her rate of turn slowed almost to a stop. Aloft, the frantic activity of the frigate's competent crew paid off. This fruit of hard service off Norway and Their Lordships' solicitude for a foreign king, which had drafted some of Chatham's best seamen into *Andromeda* to replace her losses, had the topsails double reefed in a few minutes. As the ship continued her slow turn, the wind caught the foreyards fully aback, suddenly accelerating the rate of turn. Drinkwater strode along the starboard gangway the better to see the fore-topsail, but Frey had already run forward and pre-empted him, to wave in silent acknowledgement that all was well.

'*Stand by halliards!*' Drinkwater waited for a moment longer, then gave the final command: '*Let go and haul all!*'

Round came the yards on the foremast and the reefed and thundering topsail was trimmed parallel to those already braced on the main and mizen masts. On the forecastle the headsail sheets were shifted, hauled aft and belayed while the braces amidships were turned up and their falls coiled down neatly on the pins.

'*Lay in! Stand by booms! Down booms!*'

Order reasserted itself aloft. The men began to come down.

'*Man the halliards! Tend the braces and hoist away!*'

The yards rose, stretching the canvas and setting the topsails again. 'Belay! That's well!' Drinkwater turned to Birkbeck who had materialized beside the wheel in all the commotion. 'Steady now, Mr Birkbeck. Let's have her full and bye, starboard tack, if you please.'

Andromeda heeled to larboard and a cloud of spray rose above the starboard bow as she shouldered her way through a sea and increased speed. Beyond this brief nebula lay the white rampart of Dunnose Head while on the starboard quarter Culver Cliff drew slowly, but inexorably astern. After the bowlines had been set up and all about the deck made tidy again, the watches changed. Only a small darkening stain of blood on the hallowed white planks marred the organized symmetry of the man-of-war as she stood offshore again.

'We shall work to weather of the Wight now,' said Drinkwater, handing the deck over to Frey.

'Aye, sir.' Both men stared to windward as they emerged from the lee of the headland. The sea was running high and hollow against the strong ebb and the wind again increased in force. Emerging clear of Dunnose Head and some five miles beyond the promontory, St Catherine's Point stood out clear against the horizon. High above the point, on Niton Down where it was already surrounded by wisps of cloud, stood the lighthouse. Forward, eight bells were struck.

'Judging by that cloud and the shift of the wind we're in for a thick night of it.'

'Aye, I fear so, sir,' agreed Frey. For a few moments the two men stood in silence, then Drinkwater asked, 'Did you see what happened?'

'Yes, I did. Marlowe left reefing too late, then feared embayment and lost his nerve.'

'I assumed he countermanded the order and tried to tack the ship first.'

'That is what happened, sir,' said Frey, his voice inexpressive.

'Do you know the name of the man who fell?'

'No sir; Mr Birkbeck will know.' Frey turned and called to the master who hurried across the deck. 'Who was the fellow who fell?'

'Watson. A good topman; been in the ship since he was pressed as a lad.'

'Thank you both,' said Drinkwater turning away. He was deeply affected by the unnecessary loss. 'Another ghost,' he muttered to himself. Moving towards the companionway he left his orders to the officer taking over the watch. 'Keep her full-and-bye, Mr Frey, run our distance out into the Channel. We'll tack again before midnight.'

'Aye, aye, sir.'

It was only when the captain had gone below Frey realized Marlowe had vanished.

Three Cheers for the Ship

Captain Drinkwater looked up at the surgeon. 'Well, Mr Kennedy?'

'He was barely alive when he reached me.' Kennedy's face wore its customary expression of world-weariness. Drinkwater had known the man long enough not to take offence. He invited Kennedy to be seated and offered him a glass of wine.

'Thank you, no, sir.' The surgeon remained standing.

'Then we shall have to bury him.'

'Yes. They're trussing him in his hammock now.' Kennedy paused and appeared to want to say more.

'There is something you wish to say, Mr Kennedy?' Drinkwater asked, half-guessing what was to follow.

'I hear it was Lieutenant Marlowe's fault.'

'Did you now; in what way?'

'That he had begun to reef the topsails while we were running into a bay, that he left it too late, changed his mind and tried to tack with men on the yards.'

'It's not unheard of . . .'

'Don't you care . . . Sir?'

'Sit down, Mr Kennedy.'

'I'd rather . . .'

'Sit down!' Drinkwater moved round the table and Kennedy sat abruptly, as though expecting Drinkwater to shove him into the chair, but the captain lifted a decanter from the fiddles and poured two glasses of dark blackstrap. The drink appeared to live up to its name as twilight descended on the Channel.

'How many men have died while under your knife, Mr Kennedy?'

The surgeon spluttered into his glass. 'That's a damned outrage . . .'

'It's a point of view, Mr Kennedy,' Drinkwater said, his voice level. 'I know you invariably do your utmost, but imagine how matters sometimes seem to others.'

'But Marlowe clearly did not act properly. He should not even have been on deck.'

'Perhaps not, but perhaps he made only an error of judgement, the consequences of which were tragic for Watson. That is not grounds for . . .'

'The people may consider it grounds for . . .' Kennedy baulked at enunciating the fatal word.

'Mutiny?'

'They turned against Pigot when men fell out of the rigging.'

'Things were rather different aboard the *Hermione*, Mr Kennedy. Pigot had been terrorizing his crew and there was no sign of the end of the war. This is an unfortunate accident.'

'You do not seem aware, sir, of the mood of the people. They were anticipating being paid off. As you point out, the war is at an end and their services will no longer be required. Watson might have even now been dandling a nipper on his knees and bussing a fat wife. Instead, he is dead and the rest of the poor devils find themselves beating out of the Channel, bound God knows where . . .'

'I am well aware of the mood of the men, but you are wrong about the war being over. It seems a common misapprehension aboard the ship; in fact we remain at war with the Americans. However, I quite agree with you that Watson's death is a very sad matter; as for the rest, I had intended telling them when the watch changed at eightbells. But for being overtaken by events, they would not have been kept in the dark any longer. That is a pity, but there is nothing I can do now until the morning. We shall have to bury Watson and when I have the company assembled I shall tell them all I can.'

'The ship is already alive with rumour, sir,' said Kennedy, draining his glass.

'I daresay. A ship is always alive with rumour. What do they say?'

'Some nonsense about us stopping Bonaparte from escaping, though why Boney should choose to run off into the Atlantic, I'm damned if I know. I suppose he wants to emigrate to America.' Kennedy rose, holding his glass.

'I should think that a strong possibility, Mr Kennedy.' It was almost dark in the cabin now and the pantry door opened and Drinkwater's servant entered with a lit lantern.

'Oh, I beg pardon, sir . . .'

'Come in, Frampton, come in. Mr Kennedy is just leaving.'

After the surgeon had gone, Drinkwater ate the cold meat and potatoes Frampton set before him. He was far from content with Marlowe's conduct, but at a loss to know what to do about it. He had been preoccupied with considerations of greater moment than the organization of his ship and now berated himself for his folly. He ought to have known Marlowe had precious little between his ears, yet the fellow had seen a fair amount of service. Then it occurred to Drinkwater that his own naval career had been woefully deficient in one important respect; owing to a curious chain of circumstances the only patronage that might have elevated him in the sea-service had actually confined him to frigates. He must, he realized, be one of the most experienced frigate captains in the Royal Navy. The corollary of this was that he had spent no time in a line-of-battle ship. Perhaps the constraints aboard a ship carrying five or six lieutenants and employed on the tedious but regimented duty of blockade gave young officers of a certain disposition no chance to use their initiative or to learn the skills necessary to handle a ship under sail in bad weather. It seemed an odd situation, but if Marlowe, as son of a baronet, was a favoured *élévè* of an admiral, he might never have seen true active service, or ever carried out a manoeuvre without an experienced master's mate at his elbow.

It would have been quite possible for Marlowe to have climbed the seniority list without ever hearing a gun fired in anger! Entry on a ship's books at an early age would have him a lieutenant below the proper age of twenty, with or without an examination, if Marlowe's father could pull the right strings. Drinkwater found the thought incredible, but he forgot how much older than his officers he was. And then it occurred to him that his age and appearance might intimidate those who did not know him; indeed he might intimidate those who *did*!

Did he intimidate Frey?

He must have some sort of reputation: it was impossible not to in the hermetic world of the Royal Navy, and God only knew what lurid tales circulated about him. Then he recalled Marlowe himself making some such reference the night Hortense came aboard, warning him against possible Russian reaction to Drinkwater's presence off Calais. Marlowe knew that much about him. The recollection brought him full circle: Marlowe's initial courtliness could have been a generous interpretation of unctuousness, and although not ingratiating, the man's hauteur in objecting to Drinkwater's proposal to acquaint the ship's company with their task, demonstrated either arrogance or a stupid narrow-mindedness. Or perhaps both, Drinkwater mused.

He had little doubt Marlowe, a man of good birth and social pretensions, was infected with an extreme consciousness of rank and position that coloured all his actions and prevented the slightest exercise of logical thought concerning what he would call his 'inferiors'. There was a growing sensibility to it in the navy, an infection clearly caught from the army, or society generally, and something which Drinkwater heartily reprehended. Men stood out clearly in rank, without the need to resort to arrogance.

Drinkwater grunted irritably. Whatever the cause of Marlowe's disagreeableness, the man was a damned lubber! In tune with this conclusion, Frampton came in to clear the table and Drinkwater leaned back in his chair, toying with the stem of his wine glass.

'There's some fine duff, sir.'

'Thank you, no, Frampton.'

'Very well, sir,' Frampton sniffed.

'Oh, damn it, Frampton, did you prepare it yourself?'

'Of course, sir.'

'Very well then, but only a small slice,' Drinkwater compromised.

Frampton vanished, then brought in a golden pudding liberally covered with treacle. 'God's bones, Frampton, would you have me burst my damned breeches, eh?'

'It'll do you no harm, sir. You should keep your nerves well covered.'

'That's a matter of opinion,' Drinkwater commented drily. He picked up fork and spoon and was about to attack the duff when another thought occurred to him. 'Frampton, would you ask the sentry to pass word for Mr Marlowe.'

'Aye, aye, sir.'

'You sent for me, sir?'

Marlowe swayed in the doorway, the flickering light of the bulkhead glim playing on his features, giving them a demonic cast which somehow emphasized the fact that he was drunk.

'Pray sit down.' Drinkwater considered dismissing him, thought better of it and watched his first lieutenant unsteadily cross the cabin and slump in the seat recently vacated by Kennedy. Drinkwater laid fork and spoon down on the plate, shoved it aside and dabbed his mouth with his napkin, dropping it on the table.

'Please tell me what happened this afternoon, Mr Marlowe.'

'Happened? Why, nothing happened. A damned fool fell from aloft, that's what happened.'

'The damned fool you speak of,' Drinkwater said in a measured voice, 'was an experienced topman. He had been on the ship since she commissioned, since he was a boy, in fact.'

Marlowe shrugged. 'The ship was standing into danger and carrying too much canvas.'

'What were you doing on deck? I thought it was Ashton's watch.'

'It was, but I wished Lieutenant Ashton to undertake another duty and relieved him.'

'What other duty?' Drinkwater pressed, though there was nothing very remarkable about the change of officers.

'Oh, some modifications to the watch-bill.'

Drinkwater had the fleeting impression Marlowe was lying, but the man was cunning enough, and perhaps sober enough to think up an excuse. 'We had the men in special divisions for the royal escort. In view of what you told me, I thought it best to rearrange matters.'

'So you took over the deck in order for Lieutenant Ashton to act as your clerk.'

'I took over the deck with the ship carrying too much canvas. Lieutenant Ashton was concerned about it.'

'But neither of you thought fit to tell me.'

'We thought you would know.'

'So you think it was my fault?' Drinkwater asked quietly. Marlowe shrugged again but held his tongue. 'The fact is, Mr Marlowe, that if the ship was carrying too much canvas, it *was* my fault. Nevertheless, the fact does not exonerate you from the consequences of your own misjudgement. Why did you not complete the reefing before attempting to tack ship?'

'The ship was standing into danger,' Marlowe repeated.

'It is a matter of opinion whether or not you had sufficient time to finish snugging the reef down. I'm inclined to believe you had left it too late. You could have taken in a reef earlier . . .'

'I wanted some shelter from the land.'

'Very well, but a more prudent officer would have tacked and then reefed while the ship lay in the lee of the Wight.'

'A more prudent officer?' Marlowe, emboldened by the drink, affected an expression of wounded pride. 'It was because of my prudence that I took action.'

Drinkwater watched; the man was a fool and he himself was rapidly losing patience, but he had no wish to push Marlowe beyond propriety. Before the first lieutenant could say more Drinkwater stood up. The sudden movement seemed to curb Marlowe. He flinched and frowned.

'Mr Marlowe,' said Drinkwater moving round the table, 'I do wish you to consider this matter. You are the worse for liquor. If one of those men forward, whom you affect to despise, should come on deck in the condition you are now in, I daresay you would have him flogged. Now, sir, do you retire to your cabin and reconsider the matter when you are sober.'

Marlowe looked up at his commander and shook his head. 'Trouble with you, Captain Drinkwater,' Marlowe began, levering himself to his feet, 'is you think you know everything.' Marlowe stood confronting Drinkwater. He swayed so close that Drinkwater could smell the rum on him.

'Have a care, Mr Marlowe. Do please have a care.'

Marlowe stood unsteadily and for a moment Drinkwater thought he was going to raise his hand, but then he concluded a wave of nausea affected the lieutenant and he merely covered his mouth. Whatever his motive, Marlowe managed to stagger from the cabin, leaving Drinkwater alone. Drinkwater let his breath go in a long sigh. In his present circumstances, this was something he could well have done without.

Late morning found them still on the starboard tack, but their course lay more nearly west-south-west, for the wind had continued to veer and was now north-west by north. The thick weather that Drinkwater had predicted had run through during the night. Now the wind was lighter, no more than a fresh breeze. The topgallants had been set again, and *Andromeda* bowled along under an almost cloudless sky. If the tide did not play them up and they maintained no less than the nine knots they had logged at the last streaming, they would clear the Caskets and be free to stand out into the Atlantic before long.

Fulmars and the slender dark shapes of shearwaters swooped above the wake in long, shallow glides. The solitary fulmars rarely touched down into the sea, but the shearwaters would swim in gregarious rafts, lifting by common consent and skating away over the waves as the frigate drove down upon them, disturbing their tranquillity. Away to starboard, in line ahead, a dozen white gannets flew as though on some aerial patrol, graceful and purposeful, with their narrow, black-tipped wings.

'I remember gannets like them having blue feet down in the South Pacific,' Drinkwater remarked to Birkbeck as the two older men took the morning air on the weather side of the quarterdeck.

'Aye, they call 'em boobies, I believe,' replied Birkbeck, 'talking of which, you heard about young Marlowe last night?'

'That he was drunk? Yes, I happened to send for him.'

'It doesn't help, sir, if you don't mind my saying so.

'No, it doesn't.'

' 'Twould be less of a problem if Ashton didn't possess so much influence over him. I can't make Ashton out. He's a clever enough cove, which is something you cannot say for young Marlowe. The two of them shouldn't be on the same ship, but . . .' Birkbeck paused and shrugged, 'oh, damn it, I don't know.'

'Go on, Mr Birkbeck.'

'To be honest, sir, I ain't sure there's anything to add. It's just that when the senior officer in the wardroom is weak, there is usually trouble. Someone tries to take over.'

'Frey doesn't cast himself in that role?'

'Good Lord, no, sir. Poor fellow sensibly keeps himself to himself.'

'And the marine officer, what's his name? Hyde?'

Birkbeck chuckled and shook his head. 'He's impervious to any influence. An idle dog, if ever there was one, but amiable enough. No, I think there's something personal between Ashton and Marlowe, though what it is, the devil alone knows.'

'Do you know what experience Marlowe has had?' Drinkwater asked. 'He was singularly inept yesterday.'

'I don't think there's much to tell, sir. Borne on the books as a servant, then midshipman in the Channel Fleet. Passed for lieutenant under the regulation age, took part in a boat expedition off Brest, his sole taste of action I shouldn't wonder, and the rest of his time on the quarterdeck of a seventy-four, I think. He was invalided ashore for some reason,' Birkbeck paused, 'could have been drink, I suppose, then he came here.'

'Rather as I thought.'

'Well, I couldn't vouch for the details, but the substance is about right.'

'It must be somewhat tiresome for you in the wardroom.'

'Frey and Hyde are pleasant enough, and Ashton and Marlowe are civil when they are separate; 'tis together they begin to smell fishy.'

'Fishy?'

Birkbeck shrugged again. 'Just something I can smell.'

Drinkwater considered the matter as seven bells were struck. 'I think it is time we buried our dead and I spoke to the people. We will pipe up spirits after that, and this afternoon exercise at the guns.'

'Aye, aye, sir.'

By tonight, Birkbeck thought, the ship should have settled down. He felt he could have put money on it if it were not for Mr Marlowe. And Mr Ashton.

They hove-to and buried the dead Watson at noon, when the ship's day changed. The frigate, with her main-topsail and topgallant backed against the mast and her courses up in the bunt and clewlines, dipped to the blue, white-capped seas that rolled down from the west. After Watson's corpse, in its weighted canvas shroud, had slipped from beneath the red ensign and plummeted to the sea-bed, Drinkwater stationed himself at the forward end of the quarterdeck, his officers ranged about him, the red, white and black files of Hyde's marines drawn up in rigid lines on either side, their backs to the hammock nettings. *Andromeda's* midshipmen stood together in a pimply gaggle. Like his officers, they had all been sent aboard by their patrons, even sent by the captains of other ships, as though brief service in the vicinity of a prince of the House of Hanover would admit them to the company of the most august. It gave Drinkwater some grim amusement to consider what patrons and parents would say when it got out that instead of being returned to their comfortable berths after a cross-Channel jaunt, they were stretching out into the Atlantic. On the orders of His Royal Highness, of course!

Amidships, over the boats on the chocks in the waist, along the gangways and in the lower ratlines of the main and fore shrouds, the ship's company waited to hear what he had to say, for scuttle-butt had been circulating since the previous day to the effect that the mystery which preoccupied them all would shortly be resolved.

At the conclusion of the short burial service Drinkwater closed the prayer book and nodded to Marlowe. The first lieutenant looked like death, his naturally pale and gaunt features now con-veyed the impression of a skull, emphasized in its modelling by his dark beard. imperfectly shaved by his shaking hand. He had nicked himself in two places and still bled. At Drinkwater's nod he ordered the ship's company to don hats. Drinkwater watched care-fully, the degree to which this movement achieved near simultaneity was the first indication as to how well his people thought of themselves as a crew. In the prevailing mood immedi-ately following Watson's burial, and in expectation of news from the captain, the result was promising, if not perfect. Drinkwater settled his own hat and stared about him. Every man-jack forward was staring back. He cleared his throat.

'My lads,' he began, using his best masthead-hailing voice, 'the sad loss of Tom Watson is a consequence of the urgency of our situation. We are bound upon a most important service, one that will not, I hope, detain us at sea for more than a month, two at the most . . .' He paused, gauging from the groundswell of the mur-mured reaction, how optimistically this news was received. 'We are under the direct orders of Admiral-of-the-Fleet, His Royal Highness, Prince William Henry, Duke of Clarence and Earl of Munster . . .' Drinkwater rather despised himself for invoking all His Royal Highness's grandiloquent titles. It was a deception, of course, an attempt to mislead, to shift the blame to the inscrutable powers of Admiralty and to defuse any speculation that their mis-sion was no more than Drinkwater's own reaction to a rumour brought aboard by a mysterious nocturnal visitor. The visitor could not escape mention.

'We have been informed by special courier from Paris that after Bonaparte surrendered he intends to escape apprehension and avoid exile by crossing the Atlantic. Arrangements to accomplish this are already in motion. Now, it is not the intention of His Britannic Majesty's government to allow the man who has dis-turbed the peace of Europe these last twenty years to make mischief in America or, for that matter, His Majesty's possessions in Canada . . .'

To what extent all his men understood this, was unclear. But there were enough intelligent and perceptive souls among them to grasp the seriousness and importance of what he was telling them, to allow its weight to permeate the corporate intelligence of the crew in the next few days. He hoped its gravity would divert any doubts as to why the news from Paris arrived aboard *Andromeda*, rather than the *Impregnable* or the *Royal Sovereign*.

'It is our task to run down to a station off the Azores, to where Bonaparte is to be exiled, to guard the islands and to prevent any unauthorized vessels from releasing him. As you know we are only provisioned for a further two months and we shall have to be relieved by the end of that time. If we meet any man-of-war which does not comply with my instructions, we will engage him. If that happens, I shall expect you bold fellows to show the spirit you lately demonstrated in the fiords of Norway. To this end we shall prepare this ship for action. This afternoon we will exercise at the guns. That is all. God save the King!'

There was a moment's silence, then Lieutenant Hyde stepped forward, doffed his hat and swept it above his head: 'Three cheers for the ship, lads: Hip! Hip! Hip . . .!'

Drinkwater went below with the huzzahs ringing improbably in his ears. The last thing he saw, though, was the ghastly expression on the face of Lieutenant Marlowe. It made him think of Watson's corpse settling on the ooze of the sea-bed, already half-forgotten.

Under normal circumstances, Drinkwater would have invited his officers to dine with him that day. It was a good way to get to know new faces and to create the bond among them that might be required to prove itself in action. But he was as reluctant to appear to condone Marlowe's behaviour as he was to further discomfit the young man. Whatever Lieutenant Marlowe's shortcomings, he could not be ignored. On the other hand, Drinkwater wanted to know more about Lieutenant Ashton, who would be in command of the starboard battery if they ever engaged Admiral Lejeune's squadron. Instinct told him he should capitalize upon the mood of the ship, and this lost opportunity was just one more irritation caused by Lieutenant Marlowe.

The gunnery exercise had gone off well enough and Ashton's divisions had acquitted themselves with proficiency, but this was due to the drilling and experience the majority of the men had acquired in the past. Marlowe had been conspicuously inactive on the quarter-deck, though Drinkwater had made nothing of it; he had to give the man time to pull himself together and was eager to put the encounter of the previous night behind them both. He was more concerned with maintaining the gun crews' skill. Anxious not to halt the westward progress interrupted by the necessity of burying Watson, they had not lowered a target, but practised broadside firing with unshotted guns and half charges, for Drinkwater could not afford to be prodigal with his powder and had to conserve all his shot.

Nevertheless the activity had been worthwhile, and the concussions of the guns had satisfied their baser instincts. Hyde had employed the usual expedient of having his marines shoot wine bottles to shivers from the lee main yard-arm. 'Generous of the first luff to provide us with targets,' Drinkwater overheard Hyde remark to Frey and was pleased to see the quick flash of amusement cross Frey's serious features. At least, Drinkwater concluded, those two seemed to be getting along well, though Frey's protracted introspection worried him, bringing back gloomy thoughts of its cause.

Going below after the guns had fallen silent, Drinkwater fought off an incipient onslaught of the blue-devils by writing up his journal, but his words lacked the intensity of his feelings and he abandoned the attempt. He was racked with a score of doubts now about the wisdom of backing Hortense's intelligence, of his folly and presumption in badgering Prince William Henry, of the whole ridiculous idea of seeking two frigates in the vastness of the Atlantic and of the preposterous nature of the notion of Bonaparte escaping Allied custody.

In fact, sitting alone in his cabin, rubbing his jaw where a tooth was beginning to ache, he stared astern and watched the horizon rise and fall with the pitch of the ship. It was quite possible to doubt he had received a visitor at all. The surge of the wake as the water whorled out from under the stern where the rudder bit into it seemed real enough, but it too was remote, a near silent event beyond the shuttering of the crown-glazed windows. Through the sashes he watched a shearwater sweep across the wake, following the ever-changing contours of the sea in its interminable search for food. Though skimming the water, its wings constantly adjusting to maintain this position, it avoided the contact which would have brought it down.

The confidence and poise of the bird struck him as something almost miraculous. How did it learn such a skill? Was it taught, or did the bird acquire it by instinct, as a human child learned to breathe and talk? The power and mystery of instincts capable of forming the conduct of shearwaters and the human young, moved ineluctably through all forms of life. The shearwater did not resist the urge to skim the waves, or doubt its ability to do so faultlessly: it simply did it.

Drinkwater grunted and considered himself a fool. Was it doubt more than knowledge that set men apart from the beasts; doubt which caused them to falter, to intellectualize and rationalize what would be simple if they followed their instincts? Hortense Santhonax had been in this very cabin, not a week earlier. She had communicated urgent news and he had believed her, believed her because between them something strange and almost palpable existed. He felt the skin crawl along his spine at the recollection. Instinct as much as the nature of her news had made him act as he did, and he felt in that solitary moment a surge of inexplicable but powerful self-confidence.

He was so deep in introspection that the knock at the door made him jump. It was the surgeon.

'I beg your pardon, Captain Drinkwater . . .'

'Mr Kennedy, come in, come in. Is something the matter?'

'In a manner of speaking, yes. It's the first lieutenant; he's taken to his bed, claims he's unwell, suffering from a quotidian fever.'

'I gather you do not entirely believe him?' Drinkwater asked, smiling despite himself.

Kennedy pulled a face. 'I tend to be suspicious of self-diagnosis; it has a tendency to be subjective.'

'So what do you recommend?'

'In view of all the circumstances, I think it best to humour him for a day or two. He may be attributing his misjudgements to having been unwell.'

'Yes, that is what I was thinking. It might be an advantage to us all if we were to foster that impression. It would certainly be the best course of action for the ship.'

'D'you want me to cosset him then? Keep him, as it were, out of the way? Just for a little while.'

'Laudanum?'

' 'Tis said to be a very specific febrifuge for some forms of the quotidian ague, Captain Drinkwater,' said Kennedy, rising, his voice dry and a half-smile hovering about the corners of his mouth.

'Don't you have a less drastic paregoric?'

'He has already tried that, sir,' Kennedy flashed back.

Drinkwater sighed. 'Very well, but only a small dose.' Drinkwater had a sudden thought. 'Oh, Mr Kennedy.' The surgeon paused with one hand on the cabin door. 'Would you be so kind as to join me for dinner today?'

'Of course, sir.'

'Then pass my compliments to Mr Hyde and Mr Ashton, oh, and the purser, Birkbeck and two of the midshipmen. Paine and Dunn will do.'

'Of course, sir, with pleasure.'

'Well, well,' Drinkwater muttered to himself, following Kennedy to the door. Opening it, he confronted the marine sentry. 'Pass word for my servant.'

It was only after the surgeon had left, he thought he should have mentioned his incipient toothache.

Chapter Seven April 1814

The Consequences of Toothache

'I am sorry indisposition keeps Marlowe from our company tonight, Mr Ashton,' Drinkwater said, leaning over and filling the third lieutenant's glass. He had been chatting to Ashton for some time, regularly topping his glass up and the lieutenant was already flushed. About them the dinner in Drinkwater's cabin appeared to be cheerfully convivial. As was customary, a small pig had been butchered for the occasion and the rich smell of roast pork filled the cabin.

'Indeed sir, 'tis a pity.'

'I understand you know him well. Have you sailed with him before?'

'Yes. We were midshipmen in the old *Conqueror* and later lieutenants in the *Thunderer*.'

'Really?' remarked Drinkwater, reflecting that had matters turned out differently, Marlowe and Ashton might have served under his command much earlier. He forbore drawing this to Ashton's attention, however, for the wine was working on his tongue.

'As a consequence of our having been shipmates, Frederic, I mean Marlowe, became acquainted with my sister.'

Drinkwater gave his most engaging smile. 'Do I gather that they are now intimate?'

Ashton nodded. 'They became betrothed shortly before we sailed.' There was a distinct air of satisfaction about Ashton. 'I imagine Sarah will take our diversion amiss . . .'

'It will not be unduly long, I hope,' Drinkwater persisted, maintaining his mood of confidentiality, but returning the conversation to the personal. 'I suppose the match is an advantageous one?'

Ashton swallowed a mouthful of wine. 'Sarah's a very handsome young lady,' Ashton said, 'as for Fred, well, he'll inherit his father's title and . . .' Ashton seemed suddenly aware of what he was saying and hesitated, but it was too late, he had already indicated Marlowe stood to inherit some considerable wealth.

'Well,' remarked Drinkwater smoothly, as though not in the least interested in Marlowe's expectations, 'I hope the poor fellow is soon back on his feet again.'

'I am sure he soon will be . . .'

'Tell me something about yourself, Mr Ashton. Have you ever been under fire?' Drinkwater closely watched his victim's face.

'Well no, not exactly under fire in the sense you mean. I took part in some boat operations off the Breton coast. We cut out a *péniche* . . .'

'That was alongside Mr Marlowe, was it not?' hazarded Drinkwater. Ashton nodded. 'But no yard-arm to yard-arm stuff, eh?'

'Well no, not exactly, sir.'

'Pity. Still, we shall have to see what we can do about that, eh, Mr Ashton?'

'Er, yes, sir.' Ashton was visibly perspiring now, though whether owing to the heat of the candles, the fullness of his belly or apprehension, Drinkwater was quite unable to say.

'Well, Mr Ashton, we never know what lies just over the horizon, do we?'

'I suppose not, sir . . .'

The meal proceeded on its course and when the company rose they were in good heart. Left alone in his cabin while his servant cleared away, Drinkwater mused on his conversation with Ashton until Frampton's fossicking distracted him and drove him on deck.

A gibbous moon hung above a black and silver sea and Drinkwater found Frey, an even blacker figure, wrapped in his cloak. At Drinkwater's appearance Frey detached himself from the weather rigging.

'Good evening, sir.'

'Mr Frey, would you take a turn or two with me?'

The two men fell in step beside one another and exchanged some general remarks about the weather. The wind held steadily from the north-west and the pale moonlight threw their shadows across the planking of the quarterdeck to merge with those of the rigging and sails. These moved back and forth as *Andromeda* worked steadily to windward, pitching easily and giving a comfortable, easy roll to leeward.

'It's a beautiful night, Mr Frey.'

'It is, sir.'

'I am sorry that your duty kept you from joining me for dinner, but,' Drinkwater lowered his voice, 'truth to tell, I wanted to sound Ashton about Marlowe. I understand the first lieutenant is betrothed to Ashton's sister . . .'

'Ah, that is not known in the wardroom,' Frey said, reflectively. 'That is unusual.'

'But not,' said Frey with some emphasis, 'if you had a reason for not wanting the matter known publicly.'

'You mean, if neither party wanted it known?' queried Drinkwater, intrigued and wondering what Frey was driving at.

'Neither party would want it generally gossiped about if, on the one hand, one did not want the matter to progress; and, on the other, one feared that it would not come to the desired conclusion.'

'Oh, I see,' chuckled Drinkwater. 'You mean Ashton disapproves and Marlowe wishes it.'

'Quite the opposite,' replied Frey, and Drinkwater found himself realizing that Ashton's behaviour did not square with his own hypothesis. 'Ashton wants it,' said Frey, 'but Marlowe does not.'

'Now I come to think of it,' Drinkwater replied, aware the wine had made him dull-witted, 'Ashton seemed keen enough, but what exactly are you hinting at?'

'I may be incorrect, sir, but I believe Ashton has his claws into Marlowe and whatever part Miss Ashton has to play in all this, it would ultimately be to Ashton's advantage.'

'There was some allusion to wealth . . .'

'A considerable inheritance from his father, and, if one can believe the shrewd lobster,' it took Drinkwater a moment to realize Frey was referring to Hyde, 'there is money on his mother's side too.'

'Well, well, well,' Drinkwater said, lapsing into silence for a while as the two men paced between the carronade just abaft the starboard hance, turned and strode back again towards the taffrail and its motionless marine sentry. 'So how has Ashton achieved this ascendancy?'

'According to Hyde, by the normal manner.'

'You mean the lady has anticipated events?'

'I'd say they had both anticipated events, sir,' Frey remarked drily.

'But if Hyde knows of this scandal, how is the matter not known of in the wardroom?'

'I did not say the scandal was not known about, sir,' said Frey, 'I said the betrothal was not common knowledge.'

'So you did, so you did. I should have been more alert to the subtleties of the affair.' Drinkwater was faintly amused by the matter. 'Now I perceive the effect our diversion into the Atlantic has on all parties,' he remarked, 'not least on poor Miss Ashton.' And in the darkness beside him he heard Frey chuckle.

And as if to chide him for their lack of charity, Drinkwater's tooth twinged excruciatingly.

The frigate settled into her night routine. One watch was turning in, another was already in their hammocks, and the so-called idlers, who had laboured throughout the day, were enjoying a brief period of leisure. The cooks, the carpenter and his mates, many of the marines whose duties varied from those of the seamen, chatted and smoked or engaged in the sailor's pastimes of wood-whittling or knotting.

A few read, and although there were not many books on the berth-deck other than the technical works on navigation which were occasionally perused by the midshipmen, Sergeant McCann was known to have a small box of battered volumes which he had picked up from various sources. His most recent acquisition, Miss Austen's novel, purchased new and which Lieutenant Hyde was so enjoying, was just one of those which he had bought before the ship had sailed. McCann himself, though he had admired the work, had found its reminders of domestic life too painful. At the same time that he had bought *Pride and Prejudice*, he had also acquired a second-hand copy of Stedman's monumental history of the first American War, that struggle for independence which had rendered men like McCann homeless. And although McCann had avoided too often reflecting upon the past, Stedman's partiality for the loyalist cause reopened old wounds.

As a consequence of reading Stedman's book, McCann was unable to avoid the workings of memory and take refuge in his hitherto successful ploy of submerging the past in the present. Moreover, such were McCann's circumstances, that the book shook his sense of loyalty. He had nothing against Lieutenant Hyde, in fact he liked his commanding officer and enjoyed the freedom of action Hyde's inertia allowed him. But it had been officers like Hyde, indolent, careless and selfish, who had degraded his mother and debauched his young sister. He now heartily wished he had not picked up the two heavy volumes of Stedman's works, but having done so, his conscience goaded him unmercifully. Could he not have done more for his mother and sister? He had come to London to seek compensation in order to return to America and rehabilitate his unfortunate dependants, but there had been no money to be gained, and in order to survive he had eventually returned to the only profession war had taught him: soldiering. He had joined the marines with some vague idea that by going to sea he would be the more likely to get back to his native land, though this had proved a nonsense. Year had succeeded year and he had had to abandon hope and find a means to live.

He was no longer a young man; his eyesight was failing and he could not read the pernicious book without a glass. The physical infirmity prompted the thought that time was running out, and while he entertained no doubt that his mother had long since died, he often and guiltily wondered about his sister. But a man who has adopted a mode of acting and made of it the foundation of his existence does not abandon it at once. Indeed, he discovers it is extremely difficult to throw off, so subject to habit does he become. Thus Sergeant McCann at first only indulged in an intellectual rebellion, regarding both Lieutenant Hyde and his own position in relation to his superior officer with a newly jaundiced eye. It was a situation which had, as yet, nothing further to motivate it beyond an underlying discontent. Indeed, McCann was subject to the conflicting emotion of self-contempt, regarding himself as author of his own misery and attributing the abandonment of his sister to base cowardice, ignoring his original motives for leaving North America.

In this he was unfair to himself; but he was unable to seek consolation by discussing the matter with anyone else and consequently endured the misery of the lonely and forlorn. For the time being, therefore, there was no apparent change in the behaviour of Sergeant McCann. But to all this personal turmoil, Drinkwater's explanation of *Andromeda*'s mission came as a providential coincidence. McCann was uncertain as to how this might help him, but the news brought the current war in America much closer, offering his confused and unhappy mind a vague hope upon which he built castles in the air. Some opportunity might present itself by which he might regain his social standing, and perhaps with it his commission. He conveniently forgot he was no longer young; ambition does not necessarily wither with age, particularly under the corrosive if unacknowledged influence of envy and long-suppressed hatred. Nor did it help that in his conclusion to his master-work, Stedman, a British officer who had served from Lexington to the Carolinas, conferred the palm of victory to the Americans because they deserved it; nor that Miss Austen affirmed that lives had satisfactory conclusions.

Drinkwater was interrupted in his shaving the following morning by Mr Paine who brought him the news that the sails of three ships were in sight to the south-west.

'They're coming up hand over fist, sir,' Paine explained enthusiastically, 'running before the wind with everything set to the to'garn stuns'ls!'

'What d'you make of 'em, Mr Paine?'

'Frigates, sir.'

'British frigates, Mr Paine?' Drinkwater asked, stretching his cheek and scraping the razor across the scar a French officer had inflicted upon him when he had been a midshipman just like Paine.

'I should say so, sir!'

'I do so hope you are right, Mr Paine, and if you are not, then they have heard we are at peace.'

'I suppose they could be American . . .' The boy paused reflectively.

'Well, what the deuce does the officer of the watch say about them?'

'N . . . nothing sir; just that I was to tell you that three ships were in sight to the south-west . . .'

'Then do you return to the quarterdeck and present my sincerest compliments to Mr Ashton and inform him I shall be heartily obliged to him if he would condescend to beat to quarters and clear the ship for action.'

Paine's eyes opened wide. 'Beat to quarters and clear for action. Aye, aye, sir!'

It was difficult to resist the boy's enthusiasm, but Drinkwater concluded he could complete dressing properly before the bulkheads to his cabin were torn down. It was quite ten minutes before he appeared on deck, by which time the boatswain and his mates were shrilling their imperious pipes at every companionway and the slap of bare feet competed with the tramp of the marines' boots as *Andromeda*'s thirteen score of officers and men, a few rooted rudely from their slumbers, went to their posts.

On the quarterdeck, Lieutenant Ashton was quizzing the three ships through a long glass. The sun was already climbing the eastern sky, but had yet to acquire sufficient altitude to illuminate indiscriminately. Its rays therefore shone through the breaking wave crests, giving them a translucent beauty, throwing their shadows into the troughs. This interplay of light threw equally long shadows across the deck, but most startling was the effect it had upon the sails of the three approaching ships, lighting them so that their pyramids of straining canvas seemed to glow.

'I have ordered the private signal hoisted, sir,' said Ashton, 'and the ship is clearing for action.' He shut his glass with a snap and offered it to the captain, 'Up from Ushant, I shouldn't wonder,' he added, by way of justifying himself.

Drinkwater ignored the impertinence and declined the loan of the telescope. 'Thank you, no. I have my own,' and he fished in his tail-pocket and drew out his Dollond glass. Steadying it against a stay, he focused it upon the leading ship. She was a frigate of slightly larger class than *Andromeda*, he guessed, but while it was probable that her nationality was British, Drinkwater knew a number of French frigates were at large in the Atlantic, and the matter was by no means certain.

After a few moments scrutiny, Drinkwater lowered his glass. 'Clew up and lay the maintopsail against the mast, Mr Ashton. Let us take the mettle of these fellows.'

'Aye, aye, sir.'

As the order to 'rise tacks and sheets' rang out, the main and fore courses rose in their buntlines and clew garnets while the yards on the main mast were swung so as to bring the breeze on their forward surface and throw them aback. *Andromeda* lay across the wind and sea, almost stopped as she awaited the newcomers, apparently undaunted at their superior numbers.

'Sir,' said Ashton, 'with Lieutenant Marlowe indisposed . . .'

'Do you remain here, Mr Ashton. Frey can handle the gun-deck well enough.'

'Aye, aye, sir.'

Frey's seniority gave him prior claim to the post on the quarter-deck, but Drinkwater was happier if his more experienced lieutenant commanded the batteries, while Ashton would undoubtedly prefer the senior post at his side. Besides, Drinkwater reflected as he raised his glass again, he could keep an eye on Ashton, who was receiving the reports that the ship was cleared for action. He passed them on to Drinkwater.

'Very well,' Drinkwater acknowledged, keeping the glass to his eye. 'Show them our teeth then, Mr Ashton, and run out the guns.'

The dull rumble of the gun trucks made the ship tremble as *Andromeda* bared her iron fangs.

'They're signalling sir,' Paine's voice cracked with excitement, descending into a weird baritone.

'Well, sir, can you read her number?' asked Drinkwater, aware that his own eyesight was not a patch on the lad's, and saying in an aside to Ashton, 'Better hang up our own.'

'In hand, sir.'

'Good . . . Well, Mr Paine?' Drinkwater could see the little squares as flutterings of colour, but needed the midshipman's acuity to differentiate them. The lad fumbled and flustered for a few moments, referring to the code-book, then looked up triumphantly.

'*Menelaus*, sir, Sir Peter Parker commanding.'

'Very well, Mr Paine. Mr Ashton, I shall want a boat . . .'

An hour later, rather damp from a wet transfer, Drinkwater stood in the richly appointed cabin of the thirty-eight gun frigate. Sir Peter Parker was a member of a naval dynasty, an urbane baronet of roughly equal seniority to Drinkwater.

'We've been cruising off the Breton coast,' he said, indicating the other two ships which had followed Parker's example and hove-to. He handed Drinkwater a glass of wine and explained his presence. 'I have received orders to sail for America once I have recruited the ship. I need wood and water, but can spare some powder and shot if we can get it across to you all right.'

'I'm obliged to you, Sir Peter. I confess to the Prince's orders being specific on the matter and, had I not run into you would have had to take my chance without replenishment.'

'So,' Parker frowned, 'Silly Billy insisted you stood directly for the Azores in anticipation of Boney's incarceration there, eh?'

Drinkwater nodded. 'Yes. There seems to be a general anxiety about Boney and his eventual whereabouts. He'll be conveyed to the Azores by a man-o'-war, but His Royal Highness thought it prudent to have a frigate on station there directly. I gained the impression the Prince and Their Lordships don't see eye to eye . . .'

'I suppose Billy wants to let them know he's quite capable of thinking for himself,' Parker remarked, laughing.

'I daresay he had a point in believing the Admiralty Board would take their time in sending out a guardship,' Drinkwater remarked pointedly.

'Well, maybe Billy ain't so silly, eh?' smiled Parker, draining his glass. 'Nor is it inconceivable that Bonapartists would want to spirit their Emperor across the Atlantic. He could make a deal of trouble for us there.'

'Perish the thought,' agreed Drinkwater, 'though it is my constant concern.'

'Well, we shall do what we can.' Parker paused to pass word to his officers to get a quantity of powder and ball across to *Andromeda*, a task which would take some time, and invited Drinkwater to remain aboard the *Menelaus* for a while. The two captains therefore sat on the stern settee reminiscing and idly chatting, while the ships' boats bobbed back and forth.

'So you were part of the squadron that saw Fat Louis back to France then?' Parker asked, and Drinkwater did his best to satisfy Sir Peter's curiosity with a description of the event.

'Seems an odd way to end it all,' he remarked.

'Yes. Somehow inappropriate, in a curious way,' added Drinkwater.

'I presume the Bourbon court will try to put the clock back, while we have to turn our attention to America.'

Drinkwater nodded. 'Though if we bring our full weight to bear upon a blockade of the American coast, we should be able to bring the matter to a swift conclusion.'

'Let us hope so, but I must confess the prospect don't please me and if Boney interferes, we may be occupied for years yet,' Parker said, a worried look on his face, but the conversation was interrupted by a knock at the cabin door and a midshipman entered at Parker's command.

'First lieutenant's compliments, sir, but the wind's freshening. He don't think we can risk sending many more boats across.' The midshipman turned to Drinkwater and added, 'He said to tell you, sir, that we've sent twenty-eight small barrels and a quantity of shot.'

Drinkwater stood up. 'Parker, I'm obliged to you . . .' The two men shook hands and parted with cordial good wishes.

Out of the lee of the *Menelaus*'s side, Drinkwater felt the keen bite of the wind; another gale was on the way, unless he was much mistaken, despite the fact that ashore the blackthorn would be blooming in the hedgerows.

The gale was upon them by nightfall. During the afternoon the sky gradually occluded and the horizon grew indistinct. The air became increasingly damp, the wind backed and a thickening mist transformed the day. The decks darkened imperceptibly with moisture and, although the temperature remained the same, the damp air seemed cooler.

'Backs the winds against the sun, trust it not, for back 'twill run.' Birkbeck recited the old couplet to Mr Midshipman Dunn. 'Remember that, cully, along with the other saws I've already taught you and they'll stand you in good stead.'

'Aye, aye, sir.' Mr Dunn bit his lip; he had failed to learn any of the 'saws' the master had tried to teach him, but dared not admit it and was terrified Birkbeck was about to ask him to recapitulate. Mercifully the cloaked figure of the captain rose up the after companionway, and Dunn took the opportunity to dodge away.

Drinkwater cast a quick glance about. Aloft the second reef was being put into the topsails. The men bent over the yard, their legs splayed on the foot-rope. Drinkwater peered into the binnacle, the boat-cloak billowing around him. From forward, the smoke coiling out of the galley funnel was flattened and drove its fumes along the deck. Above their heads there was a tremulous thundering as the weather leach of the fore-topsail lifted.

'Watch your helm there!' Birkbeck rounded upon the quartermaster, who craned forward and stared aloft, ordering the helmsmen to put the helm up a couple of spokes, allowing *Andromeda* to pay off the wind a little. 'You'll have another man shivered off the yard if you're not more careful,' Birkbeck snapped reprovingly, then turning to Drinkwater he put two fingers to the fore-cock of his hat.

'North of west, sir, I'm afraid,' Birkbeck reported apologetically to Drinkwater.

'It cannot be helped, Mr Birkbeck.'

They would have to endure another miserable night bouncing tiringly up and down, while the grey Atlantic responded to the onslaught of the wind and raised its undulating swells and sharper waves. It would be chilly and damp below decks; the hatches would be closed and the air below become poor and mephitic, a breeding ground for the consumption and an aggravation for the rheumatics, Drinkwater reflected gloomily. He tucked himself into the mizen rigging and sank into a state of misery. His tooth had ceased to equivocate and the infection of its root raged painfully. He had known for days that the thing would only get worse and it chose the deteriorating weather to afflict him fully. He would have to have the tooth drawn and the sooner the better; in fact a man of any sense would go at once to the surgeon and insist the offending tusk was pulled out. But Drinkwater did not feel much like a man of sense; toothache made a man peevishly self-centred; it also made him a coward. Having his lower jaw hauled about by Kennedy who, with a knee on his chest, would wrest the bulk of his pincers around until the tooth submitted, was not a prospect that attracted Drinkwater. As the sun set invisibly behind the now impenetrable barrier of cloud, the fading daylight reflected the captain's lugubrious mood.

He could, of course, insist Kennedy gave him a paregoric. A dose of laudanum would do the trick, at least until the morning. The idea made him think of Marlowe languishing in his bunk and his conscience stung him. Forcing himself to relinquish the clean, if damp, air of the deck, he went reluctantly below.

In the wardroom Lieutenant Hyde had discovered an equilibrium of sorts, having braced his chair so that he might lean back and read with his booted feet on the wardroom table. At the after end of the bare table Lieutenant Ashton sat in a Napoleonic pose, his expression remote, his hands playing with a steel pen, a sheet of paper before him. Neither officer realized who their visitor was until Drinkwater coughed.

'Oh! Beg pardon, sir.' Hyde's boots reached the deck at the same moment as all the legs of his chair, a sudden, noisy movement which snapped Ashton from his abstraction. He too stood up.

'Good evening, gentlemen. Pray pardon the intrusion . . .'

'Lieutenant Frey has turned in, sir,' offered Ashton.

'I came to see Lieutenant Marlowe.'

Hyde indicated the door to the first lieutenant's cabin and Drinkwater nodded his thanks, knocked and ducked inside. Behind him Ashton and Hyde exchanged glances.

The quarters provided for *Andromeda*'s officers were spartan and what embellishments an officer might bring to his hutch of a cabin conferred upon it a personality. Lieutenant Frederic Marlowe had two small portraits, a shelf of books and an elegant travelling portmanteau which, standing in the corner, held in its top a washing basin and mirror.

Of the portraits, one was a striking young woman whom Drinkwater took to be Sarah Ashton, though there was little resemblance to the officer he had just seen in the wardroom; the other was of a man dressed in the scarlet and blue of a royal regiment, the gold crescent of a gorget at his throat.

These appointments were illuminated by a small lantern, the light of which also fell upon the features of Marlowe himself. Drinkwater was shocked by the young man's appearance. Kennedy had led him to believe Marlowe's trouble to be no more than a malingering idleness, but the gaunt face appeared to be that of a man afflicted with a real illness, or at best in some deep distress. Marlowe's eyes were sunk in dark hollows and regarded Drinkwater with an obvious horror.

'Mr Marlowe,' Drinkwater began, 'how is it with you?'

Marlowe's lower lip trembled and he managed to whisper, 'Well enough, sir.'

'What is the matter?'

'Quotidian fever, sir, or so the sawbones says.'

Drinkwater had a rather different perception. He looked round the cabin. A small glass stood in the wash basin, and Drinkwater picked it up and sniffed it. The faint scent of tincture of opium was just discernible. For a moment Drinkwater stood undecided, then he turned back to the invalid, and sat himself down in the single chair that adorned the cabin.

'Mr Marlowe, I do not believe you have a quotidian fever. Pray tell me, to what extent do you owe your present indisposition to the influence of Lieutenant Ashton?' Marlowe's eyes widened as Drinkwater's barb struck home. His eyes glanced at the door to the wardroom, confirming, if confirmation were necessary, the accuracy of Drinkwater's assumption. 'I am aware of your situation *vis-à-vis* Ashton; perhaps, if you wished, you could confide in me. I cannot afford to have my first lieutenant incapacitated; I need you on deck, Mr Marlowe, gaining the confidence of the people . . .'

The shadow of recollection passed across Marlowe's haggard features, then he shook his head vigorously and turned his face away. Drinkwater lingered a moment, then rose, the chair scraping violently on the deck, but even this noise evoked no response from the first lieutenant. 'Damnation,' he muttered under his breath, and stepped back into the wardroom.

Hyde had resumed his reading, though his boots were no longer on the table. Ashton had bent to his writing, but looked up sharply as Drinkwater shut the door behind him and stood before the officers. Realizing their manners, both men made to rise to their feet.

'Please do not trouble yourselves, gentlemen. Good night.'

Rather than returning directly to his own cabin or the deck, Drinkwater descended a further deck in search of the surgeon. He found Kennedy playing bezique with the midshipmen. The intrusion of the captain's features in the stygian gloom of the cockpit produced a remarkable reaction: the midshipmen jumped to their feet, the cards were scattered and Kennedy, who had had his back to Drinkwater, turned slowly around.

'Oh, sir, I er . . . Did you want me?'

'Indeed, Mr Kennedy. I would be obliged if you would pull a tooth for me. At your convenience.'

'There's no time like the present, sir. These young devils have a decided advantage.'

Drinkwater, followed by the surgeon, retired to the half-suppressed sound of sniggering midshipmen.

A few moments later Kennedy joined him in the cabin, producing a small bag from the dark and sinister interior of which gleamed the dull metal of instruments. Drinkwater sat down and braced himself, as much against the motion of the ship as in preparation for Kennedy's ministrations. There was a brief exchange between them, then Drinkwater opened his mouth and allowed Kennedy to probe his lower mandible. It took the surgeon only a few seconds to locate the source of the trouble. He withdrew his probe and searched his bag for another implement. His hand emerged with a pair of steel pincers.

'Humour me and rinse those things in some wine, if you please.'

'It is quite unnecessary . . .'

'Oblige me, if you please . . .'

'Very well.'

Kennedy poured a glass of wine from the stoppered decanter lodged in the fiddles and dipped the closed pincers in it. *Andromeda* groaned mournfully about them as he turned and approached his patient. Drinkwater's knuckles were white on the arms of his chair. Kennedy opened the grim steel tool and bent over Drinkwater, who felt the uncompromising bite of the serrated steel clamp over his own, less robust tooth. There was an excruciating pain which shot like a white hot wire through Drinkwater's brain and he felt the tooth wrenched this way and that as Kennedy bore down on him, twisting his powerful wrist. A faint grinding sound transmitted itself through Drinkwater's skull as Kennedy wrestled with the resisting fang; then it gave way, *Andromeda* lurched and Kennedy almost fell backwards. The pincers struck the teeth in Drinkwater's upper jaw, jarring his whole head. The wine glass fell to the deck and smashed.

A stink filled Drinkwater's nostrils as Kennedy waved the rotting tooth under his wrinkling nose. The surgeon dropped the tooth and pincers, took another glass, filled it and handed it to his spluttering patient.

'God damn and blast it!' Drinkwater bellowed, clapping his hand to his mouth.

'I wouldn't recommend you to swallow, sir. Perhaps the quarter-gallery . . .'

Drinkwater did as he was bid, rinsed his mouth with wine and spat it down the closet. His tongue explored the gaping hole in his teeth as he clambered back into the cabin, a little dizzy and in some pain from the blow to his upper jaw.

Kennedy was clearing away and Drinkwater refilled his glass and filled another for the surgeon.

'Damn me, Kennedy, but you're a confounded brute, and no mistake.'

'I'm sorry,' Kennedy said, smiling, accepting the glass. 'The confounded ship . . .'

'Quite so, but a moment . . .'

'There is something else, sir?'

'Yes. I wish you to cease giving Marlowe laudanum. I am not certain it is having anything other than a deleterious effect.'

'It generally does,' Kennedy observed with that clinical detachment that sounded so cold, 'though Marlowe will not see it that way.'

'I don't much care what way Marlowe sees it. I just want that young man back on the quarterdeck, preferably tomorrow.'

'Tomorrow, d'you say?' Kennedy blew his cheeks out and shook his head. 'I don't believe the man is really ill . . .'

'Well there I disagree with you. I think he is ill, but I don't think his lying in his cot is improving him. I also don't believe his disease is fatal.'

'Well, sir,' responded Kennedy in his touchiest tone, tossing off the contents of his glass with an air of affront, 'what d'you believe his disease is, then? I should be fascinated by your diagnosis.'

Kennedy's irritation amused Drinkwater. 'Oh, his disease is of the heart, Mr Kennedy,' Drinkwater said smiling.

'You mean the man is in love?'

'I mean the man is affected by love, or perhaps I should say infected by love, or at least what passes for love in all its complications.'

'Well, sir,' said Kennedy, putting his glass back in the fiddles, 'I have to confess I hadn't noticed the pox, so I suppose you refer to the disease in its emotional form and there, I think, I must confess to having a somewhat limited expertise in the matter.'

'But you will stop the laudanum?'

'If that is what you wish, Captain Drinkwater.'

'It is, Mr Kennedy, thank you. Oh, and my thanks also for pulling my tooth.'

'Had I not done so you would have been suffering from a quinsy at best and a poisoned gut else, sir.'

'I'm obliged to you.'

'Thank you for the wine.'

''Tis a pleasure,' lisped Drinkwater, withdrawing his tongue from the gap it compulsively sought to explore. And his sibilant farewell seemed echoed as *Andromeda*'s stern sank into the bosom of a wave, then rose as she drove through the swell which seethed, hissing away into the darkness astern.

109

A Patch of Blue Sky

Captain Drinkwater was not the only visitor received by Lieutenant Marlowe that evening, for once word of the captain's interest had reached the wardroom, Lieutenant Ashton determined on showing similar concern for a brother officer.

'Well Frederic, this is a pretty pass, ain't it?' Ashton began, sitting in the chair beside the first lieutenant's cot. 'I do believe Our Father thinks you unwell, which doesn't say much for his intelligence, does it?'

At the last remark Marlowe, who had turned his face away from his visitor, swung back. 'Why in heaven's name d'you have to torment me? Do you not have what you want that you must treat me like this?'

Ashton put a restraining hand upon Marlowe's shoulder and shook his head. ' Fred, Fred, you misunderstand me, damn it,' he said, reassuringly. 'I don't wish you ill; quite the contrary, no man would be happier than to see you up and about again.'

'Damn you, Ashton. You're in league with the captain . . .'

'What?' Ashton's incredulity was unfeigned. 'Why in God's name should I have anything in common with the captain?'

'Because,' said Marlowe, twisting round and propping himself on one elbow, 'he has just been here, not an hour ago, maybe less, telling me he wants me on the quarterdeck tomorrow!'

'Well then, that's fine, Fred, fine,' Ashton said soothingly, 'we all want you back at your duty, why should we not? Aye, and the sooner the better as far as Frey and I are concerned.'

Marlowe peered at his visitor suspiciously. The single lantern threw Ashton's face into shadow. 'What d'you mean as far as Frey and you are concerned?'

'Why, because we are doing duty for you . . .'

'Yes, of course . . .'

'What the devil did you think I meant?'

'Oh, nothing . . .'

'Come on Fred, what?'

'Nothing . . .'

'Come on . . . Was it something the captain said?' Ashton asked shrewdly.

'He thinks you have some influence over me,' Marlowe said in a low, shamed voice.

'What damnable poppycock!'

'It could be said to be true, could it not?'

Ashton lost some of his aplomb, recalling his indiscreet remarks to Drinkwater regarding Marlowe's intended marriage: surely it could derive from nothing more? 'Perhaps he knows of you and Sarah,' he said dismissively.

'Have you said anything?'

'Come to think of it I recall mentioning it when we dined together, but it was nothing.'

'So you told him?' The hint of a smile played about Marlowe's mouth. 'And at dinner.'

'Well, yes, I believe I did,' Ashton confessed, flushing, 'but where's the harm in that?'

'Did you tell him of your sister's condition?'

'No, of course not.'

'Damn you, Ashton, I may be a fool, but I can at least keep my mouth shut!'

'There's no harm in it being known you intend to marry her.' Ashton's temper was fraying, but Marlowe had swung his legs over the edge of his cot and lowered himself unsteadily to his feet. He stood in his night-shirt staring down at his persecutor.

'Oh yes,' he said, holding on to the deck-beams overhead and leaning over Ashton. 'Of course. Now get out, and remember when I appear on deck tomorrow which of us is the senior.'

Thoroughly discomfited, Ashton stood slowly and forced a smile at the first lieutenant. 'Of course, Mr Marlowe,' he said mockingly, 'of course.'

Outside the wardroom Ashton almost bumped into the surgeon. The berth-deck was already settled, the air heavy with the stink and snuffles of over five score of men swaying together in their hammocks. The occasional glims threw fitful shadows, but for the most part it was dark as death. The ship creaked and groaned as she worked in the seaway and both men were cursing as they struggled on the companionway. The area was lit by a lantern and the marine sentry outside the wardroom door was a silent witness to their encounter.

'Ah, Kennedy, a damnable night.'

'I am not disposed to argue, Mr Ashton.'

Ashton was about to pass on when an idea struck him. 'There is a matter about which I might be disposed to argue with you, though. Would you join me for a moment in the wardroom.'

'I am not looking for an argument, Mr Ashton.'

'No, no, but a moment of your time.'

The wardroom was empty, its off-duty occupants had retired behind the thin bulkheads that partitioned either wing of the after end of the berth-deck and conferred privacy and privilege upon the officers. The long table that ran fore and aft had been cleared, and its worn oak surface betrayed years of abuse with wine stains, scratches, cigar-burns and boot-marks showing clearly through the greasy wiping that passed for a polishing. At the after end of the wardroom, the head of the rudder stock poked up from the steer-age below and was covered by a neatly fashioned octagonal drum head table into which were set some tapered drawers. Across the transom a few glasses gleamed dully in their fiddles. Ashton picked two out and splashed some cheap blackstrap out of an adjacent decanter. Kennedy accepted a glass in silence.

'I have just been to see Lieutenant Marlowe,' Ashton said, taking a draught. 'He seems much recovered.'

'I'm glad to hear it,' replied Kennedy. 'Is that what you wished to argue about?'

'Not really to argue over, just to tell you that he is much improved and therefore your diagnosis of quotidian . . .'

'*My* diagnosis,' Kennedy raised an incredulous eyebrow. 'Well, well, so that is how matters stand eh?'

'Well, you know what I mean.'

'No, Mr Ashton, I'm not sure that I do. Tell me,' Kennedy ran on without giving Ashton an opportunity to protest, 'is it mischief you're after making?'

'Mischief? How so?'

'Well, that's what I cannot quite fathom, but up to this minute, solicitude is not what I'd have called an outstanding virtue of yours, Mr Ashton. Unless of course, you wish the first lieutenant back at his turn of duty.'

'Well that would be a decided advantage, to be sure, Mr Kennedy,' said Ashton coolly, 'and to know that he is not only back on duty, but able to sustain the effort. I'm led to believe we may yet see some action, despite the peace. 'Twould be most unfortunate if he were to miss an opportunity through suffering from a quotidian fever, or any other kind of indisposition for that matter.'

'I had presumed,' said Kennedy looking into his glass and swirling the last of the wine round, 'that with the coming of peace, opportunities are scarce nowadays and the prize laws will have been revoked by now. Unless, of course, we come up with a Yankee.' He looked up and it was clear from Ashton's expression that he had not thought about this. 'Well, good night to you, Mr Ashton, and thank you for the wine. I'm certain Mr Marlowe will be back at his post very soon.'

Drinkwater slept badly and woke in a sour mood. His gum was sore and his head ached from the wrenching Kennedy had given it. He rose and shaved, damning and cursing the frigate as *Andromeda* did her best to cause him to cut his throat with her motion. Finally he struggled out on deck into the windswept May morning.

Ashton had the morning watch and gave every appearance of being asleep at his post, but he moved from the weather mizen rigging as Drinkwater appeared, punctiliously touched his fore-cock and paid his respects.

'Morning sir. Another grey one, I'm afraid.'

'So I see . . .' Drinkwater cast about him, staring at the heaving sea, leaden under the lowering overcast. The wind was less vicious and although the waves were still streaked with the white striations of spume, and where the crests broke the spray streamed downwind, there was less energy in the seas as they humped up and drove at the ship.

'Well, Mr Ashton,' remarked Drinkwater, clapping a hand to his hat and staring aloft. ' 'Tis time to shake a reef out of the topsails. This wind will die to a breeze by noon.' Drinkwater looked at Ashton. 'Well, do you see to it, Mr Ashton.'

'Aye, aye, sir.'

Ashton moved away and reached for the speaking trumpet, and Drinkwater fell to an erratic pacing of the quarterdeck, bracing himself constantly against the pitch and roll of the frigate. As he reached the taffrail, the marine sentry stiffened.

'Stand easy, Maggs,' he growled.

'Sir.'

Drinkwater stared astern. The wake was being quartered by birds. The ubiquitous fulmar, the little albatross of the north, skimmed with its usual apparently effortless grace, and there, almost below him, a pair of storm petrels dabbled their tiny feet in the marbled water that streamed out from under *Andromeda*'s stern. Where, he wondered, did those minuscule birds live when the weather was less tempestuous? And how was it that they only showed their frail selves when boisterous conditions prevailed? Did they possess some magic property like the swallow which was said, somewhat improbably, to winter in the mud at the bottom of the ponds they spent the summer skimming for flies?

He grunted to himself, and was then aware of the silent Maggs, so he turned about and walked forward again with as much dignity as rank could induce and the heaving deck permit. To windward the scud was breaking up, looking less smoky and lifting from the *Andromeda*'s mastheads. Aloft, members of the watch shook out a reef and above them he saw the swaying main truck describe its curious hyperbolic arc against the sky.

Out of the recesses of memory he recalled the question old Blackmore used to ask the midshipmen aboard His Britannic Majesty's frigate *Cyclops*. The sailing master would often quiz the young gentlemen to see if they were awake, and Drinkwater chuckled at the recollection as a small, blue patch of sky gleamed for a moment in the wind's eye. He felt his spirits rise.

'Mr Paine!'

The midshipman of the watch ran up, surer-footed than his commander. 'Sir?'

'If a ship circumnavigates the globe, Mr Paine, which part of her travels the farthest?'

Paine's brow creased and he raised his right index finger to his head as though this might aid the processes of intelligence. 'Travels farthest . . .?' The lad hesitated a moment and then light dawned. 'Why, sir, the mastheads!'

'Well done, Mr Paine. Now do you try that out on the other midshipmen.'

'I will, sir,' the boy said brightly, his eyes dancing and his smile wide.

'Carry on then.'

'Aye, aye, sir.' And Paine shifted his finger to his overlarge hat and capered off.

'Was I ever like that?' Drinkwater wondered to himself. The *Cyclops* had been a sister-ship of the *Andromeda* and he remembered how Captain Hope had seemed to him all those years ago an old man who had not gained the preferment he deserved. Sadly Drinkwater concluded he must seem the same to his own midshipmen. He resisted allowing the thought to depress him and his stoicism was swiftly reinforced by a sheet of spray leaping over the weather bow and streaming aft to patter about him. He tasted salt on his lips and felt the sting of the sea-water. The little blue patch had vanished and he wondered if he had not been unduly optimistic in his prediction to Ashton. Nothing, he concluded, would please the young lieutenant more than to recount the captain's misjudgement when he went below at eight bells.

'Sir?'

Drinkwater turned to see Birkbeck hauling himself on deck; it was clear the man was worried. 'What is it, Mr Birkbeck?'

'She's making a deal of water, sir. Three feet in the well in the last three hours.'

Drinkwater frowned. 'Yes, I recall, they were pumping at eight bells in the middle watch. I think that was what woke me . . . Damn it, d'you have any inkling why?'

'Not really, Captain Drinkwater; though I've a theory or two.'

'Caulking?'

'Most likely, with some sheathing come away. The old lady's overdue for a docking, if not worse.'

Drinkwater grunted. 'I was just thinking of the old *Cyclops*; she was broken up some years ago.'

'That doesn't help us much now, sir, if you don't mind my saying so.

'No,' Drinkwater sighed. 'Well, we shall have to pump every two hours.'

'Aye, sir, and I'll have the carpenter have a good look down below. We have so little stores aboard, it might be possible to locate the problem.'

'Very well, Mr Birkbeck, see to it if you please.'

Drinkwater turned away to conceal his irritation. A serious leak, though not without precedent, was a problem he could have done without. There were enough unknown factors in his present mission, but to have to return to port and perhaps prejudice the peace of Europe seemed like too bitter a pill to swallow under the circumstances, however far-fetched it might at first sound. He considered the matter. If the ship was working, and the trouble stemmed from this, it would probably get worse, even if the weather improved. He swore under his breath, when Birkbeck's voice broke into his thoughts. His mind had run through this train in less time than it takes to tell it and the master was still close to him.

'Troubles never come singly,' Birkbeck had muttered, and Drinkwater turned to see Mr Marlowe ascending the companionway.

'Perhaps,' Drinkwater muttered from the corner of his mouth, trying to recapture his earlier brief moment of optimism, 'this isn't trouble.'

'I hope you're right.' Birkbeck turned aside, stared into the binnacle and up at the windward tell-tale.

Drinkwater watched Marlowe as he settled his hat and stared about himself. The first lieutenant's face was drawn, but Drinkwater observed the way he pulled his shoulders back and walked across the deck towards him.

'Good morning, Mr Marlowe. 'Tis good to see you on deck,' Drinkwater called, then lowered his voice as Marlowe approached. 'How is it with you?'

Marlowe threw him a grateful look and Drinkwater felt suddenly sorry for the young man. 'I am well enough, sir, thank you.'

'Good. Then you shall take a turn with me and after that we shall break our fasts. Birkbeck has just reported a leak and the carpenter is to root about in the hold during the forenoon to see if he can discover the cause.'

Drinkwater hoped such gossip would wrench Marlowe's mind from self-obsession to a more demanding preoccupation, but Marlowe was having some trouble keeping his feet.

'Come, come, a steady pace will see to it. Eyes on the horizon . . .'

It took Marlowe four or five turns of the deck to master his queasiness and imbalance. Drinkwater made inconsequential conversation. 'Damned pumps woke me up, then Birkbeck reported the water rising in the well. 'Tis one confounded thing after another, but no doubt we'll weather matters. Saw two petrels astern of us this morning. Odd little birds; I found myself wondering where the deuce they disappear to during moderate weather.'

'I guess they settle on the surface and feed when they're swimming. They only have to take to the air when the waves begin to break and come up under the stern where the sea is smooth.'

'Good heavens, Mr Marlowe, I think you've a point there.' Drinkwater's astonishment was unfeigned. Perhaps Marlowe was not the dullard he had been taken for!

'Perhaps you can help on the matter of the leak. The problem is that I was new into the ship last autumn and Tom Huke, her regular first luff, was killed, so only old Birkbeck and the standing warrant officers know the ship well.'

'That's only to be expected, sir.'

'True, but it don't help us fathom the reason for the leak.'

'She's an old ship.'

'I agree entirely; indeed I suspect she's lost some copper sheathing and maybe some caulking, she's been working enough.'

'How much has she been leaking.'

'Birkbeck reported three feet in three hours.'

'A foot an hour.' Marlowe fell silent for a moment. Drinkwater's sidelong glance suggested he was calculating something, then he said, 'Although she's been working, if she's lost sheathing and caulking, I'd have reckoned on a greater depth in the well.'

Drinkwater considered the matter. He realized Marlowe's logical approach had produced a more realistic assessment than his own sudden apprehension over the *effect* of the leak on *Andromeda*'s task. This had diverted him from any real consideration of its cause. Unless it worsened considerably, additional pumping would contain it; it was no concern of his, he chid himself ruefully, to what extent that simple but irksome drudgery would occupy his hapless crew.

They had reached the taffrail and turned forward again. 'Go on, Mr Marlowe. I scent an hypothesis.'

'I have two actually, sir. A wasted bolt in one of the futtocks . . .'

'Very possible. And two . . .'

'You were in heavy action against the, er . . . Pardon me, I have forgotten the name of the ship you captured . . .'

'The *Odin*.'

'Ah yes, the *Odin*. Well perhaps . . .'

'Shot damage!' Drinkwater broke in.

'Exactly so, sir. Maybe a loose plug. May I ask which side you were engaged?'

'The starboard side.'

'Then I shall start looking there.'

'Mr Marlowe, I congratulate you. That is famously argued; if you can only match reality to theory . . .' Drinkwater left the sentence unfinished and changed tack. 'But not immediately. First you shall breakfast with me.'

'Thank you, sir.'

They had reached the windward hance and Drinkwater paused. 'Is that a patch of blue sky there?'

'Yes, sir. And I think the wind is tending to moderate.'

'D'you know, Mr Marlowe,' Drinkwater said, pleased with the way things had fallen out, 'I believe you are at least right about that.'

As Drinkwater led Marlowe below to eat, he caught Ashton's eye and was quite shocked by the look he saw there.

'I fear we must get used to skillygolee and burgoo if we are to cruise off the Azores for as long as possible,' said Drinkwater, laying his spoon down with a rattle and dabbing his mouth with a napkin.

'I had better take a look at the hold, sir, if you'll excuse me.'

'I will in a moment, Mr Marlowe, but first a moment or two of your time.' Drinkwater waved the hovering Frampton away. 'Mr Marlowe,' he said, fixing the first lieutenant with a steady stare, 'please forgive me, but I was troubled by the accident that occurred off the Isle of Wight . . .'

'Sir, I . . .' Marlowe's face assumed an immediate expression of distress.

'Hear me out.' Drinkwater paused and Marlowe resigned himself to what he anticipated as cross-examination. 'Tell me, have you ever taken a longitude at sea?'

'Of course, sir,' said Marlowe, taken aback. 'Surely you don't think me incapable of that?' he frowned.

'What method do you use?'

'Well I can take lunar observations, but you have a chronometer . . .'

'But you can take lunars?'

'Oh yes. I used to amuse myself on blockade duty aboard *Thunderer* by taking them.'

'Some officers would consider that a tedious amusement, even on blockade duty.'

Marlowe shrugged and the ghost of a smile passed across his features. 'Sir, I am not certain why you are asking me these questions, but I have a certain aptitude for navigation.'

'But not for seamanship?'

Marlowe flushed brick red, caught Drinkwater's eye, looked away, then back again. 'Very well, sir, let me explain. It is true, I do not have a natural aptitude to handle a ship. I find . . . I found it difficult to . . . Damn it! I found it difficult to resolve on the right thing to do first when I found myself in the situation I did the other day.'

'Yet by relieving Ashton, you put yourself in an exposed position,' Drinkwater said, puzzled. Marlowe remained silent and Drinkwater nudged him. 'Come, come, I have seen many officers in my time, Mr Marlowe, and many have made mistakes. Some were foolish, some incompetent and some just made simple miscalculations. You are my first lieutenant and I am seeking an explanation as to why such a thing happened. I do not seek to condemn you, merely to understand.'

Marlowe swallowed and moved uncomfortably in his chair. 'I wished to subject myself to a test, sir.' He produced the words with a faltering diffidence, as if they were torn from him, one by one. Drinkwater watched Marlowe struggle with a detached sympathy, and the complexities inherent in any human being struck him once again.

'You see, sir, I hoped that I might vindicate myself; that I might prove to myself that I was quite as capable as any other officer to tack ship.'

'And prove it perhaps to others, other than myself?' asked Drinkwater shrewdly, the light of perception dawning. 'You have been responsible for some accident, perhaps?'

Marlowe nodded.

'Well, we need not go into that now, but I take it the court-martial acquitted you?'

'There was no court-martial, sir. The matter was not that serious.'

'Not that serious?' Drinkwater queried.

'No ship was lost, sir . . .'

'Go on.'

'Two men were lost overboard.' Marlowe expelled a long breath; the unburdening of confession seemed to release him. 'I was ashamed of myself, sir, robbed of my confidence. I wanted to make amends and then . . . Well, I have another man's life to answer for now.'

'And Mr Ashton was a witness to all this, eh? And is consequently your, how do the French say it? *Bête-noire*?'

Marlowe nodded again.

Drinkwater sighed. Poor Marlowe's superciliousness and his apparent lack of wit and subtlety were the consequences of self-deceit, of attempting to live with failure in the presence of someone who knew all about the cause. And was capable of compounding that knowledge, Drinkwater knew from Frey's scuttlebutt. The unborn bastard was another life to lay to the lieutenant's account. Drinkwater now understood that it was not only Marlowe's conduct which was attributable to his problems; so too was his attitude. Frey's original assessment of him not being such a bad fellow had been accurate. All the damage to his character had been self-inflicted.

'Mr Marlowe, I have no wish to increase your burden, but I think I divine the roots of your misfortunes. Forgive me, but your frankness does you credit and I am aware you are affianced to Ashton's sister.'

'Yes. That is unfortunate.'

'How so? Do you not wish to marry the young lady?'

'Most decidedly, sir, but the ceremony will be delayed by our absence.'

'And the lady is expecting . . .'

'You know!'

'I had heard . . .'

'Damn Ashton!'

'It is unfortunate you do not like your intended brother-in-law . . .'

'Damn it, sir,' Marlowe leant forward, his eyes intense, alive again after the emotional moments of self-revelation, 'the man has designs on my fortune. He seeks to gain an ascendancy over me partly through what he knows of me and also through his sister. That would be bad enough, but this delay . . .' The first lieutenant rose to his feet and ran a hand wildly through his hair.

'Sit down, Frederic, for God's sake,' snapped Drinkwater.

Marlowe turned and stared at Drinkwater, his eyes desperate. 'Sir, I . . .'

'Sit down, there's a good fellow. You are no good to me in this state. We have an important duty to attend to. You are perhaps the last officer in this war to be offered an opportunity.'

'Sir, I am not certain that I am capable . . .'

'Of course you are capable, Frederic! And what is more we shall have you home to marry your Sarah in no time at all.'

'Two months would be too long to avoid a scandal, sir.'

'Well, we shall have to ensure it don't take that long,' said Drinkwater.

'Is that possible?'

'I believe so.'

Drinkwater saw Marlowe relax with relief. 'I hope so, sir, but you just mentioned learning to like burgoo.'

Drinkwater shrugged. 'True. I can't be certain, of course, but I don't believe we shall be kept long on station.' Drinkwater smiled and was rewarded with a reciprocating grin.

'I apologize, sir . . . for my conduct the other night.'

'Let us put the matter behind us; do you just deal with our problems on a day-to-day basis.'

Marlowe rose. 'I shall go and have a look in the hold, sir,' he said, 'and thank you.'

' 'Tis nothing.'

Marlowe nodded over Drinkwater's shoulder and out through the stern windows. 'There's more blue sky showing now, sir.'

'Yes, it may yet prove a fine day.'

Marlowe stood uncertainly, for a moment he strove to speak, then gave up the attempt and made to leave. Drinkwater called him back. 'Mr Marlowe, would you be so kind as to show the midshipmen the method of determining longitude by the chronometer?'

'Yes, of course, sir.'

'And just ignore Ashton.'

Marlowe nodded. 'Yes. Yes, I will.' He paused again, then

blurted out, 'what made you come below and see me last night, sir?'

'I'm not sure,' Drinkwater replied. 'Concern for you, concern for the ship, concern for myself.' He paused and smiled. 'Anyway, why did you come on deck this morning?'

'Because you came to see me last night, sir.'

Chapter Nine *April–May 1814*

A Sea Change

Drinkwater's forecast proved accurate. By noon the wind had again swung into the north-north-west, dropped to a fresh breeze and swept aside the cloud cover, leaving only the benign white fluffs of fair-weather cumulus. The depression moved away to the north and east, following its predecessor into the chops of the Channel. The sea now reflected this change in the atmosphere, losing the forbidding grey of the true Western Ocean, and wearing the kindly blue mantle of more temperate latitudes. And, indeed, when Birkbeck, emerging from the hold, found Captain Drinkwater ready to observe the culmination of the sun on the ship's meridian, their southing was substantial.

Things were less optimistic below decks. The working party in the hold had failed to locate the source of the ingress of water, though some credence was given to Marlowe's hypothesis by evidence of water entering the well from the starboard side. In the wardroom Lieutenant Ashton sulked, much to the annoyance of Hyde, who, when distracted from his amusements sufficiently to notice, began to conclude that Ashton was far from being the amiable fellow he had first assumed. Indeed Hyde inclined towards Mr Frey who, it began to emerge, was an officer of some talent with a paintbrush.

Having endured a degree of persecution from brother officers in the past, Frey was inclined to conceal his love of drawing and watercolour painting, but Hyde caught sight of a small picture he was working on, which showed the *Royal Sovereign* flying the Bourbon standard, accompanied by *Andromeda*, *Impregnable*, *Jason*, *Polonais*, *Gremyashchi* and the Trinity Yacht. Artistic achievement impressed Hyde, and he was driven to confess that he regretted his inability to play an instrument or, indeed, even to sing, let alone draw or paint.

This polite exchange with Frey was overheard by Ashton who

was driven to make some mean sarcasm about Hyde's success at playing being assured, provided he tried to play no more than the fool. Hyde, who had been oblivious to Ashton's presence until that moment, spun round.

'What's that you say?' he demanded.

'That should you decide upon playing anything, my dear Hyde, confine it to being a fool.'

For a moment Frey, fascinated by this encounter, thought Hyde would take the remark lying down, but it seemed the marine officer's indolence extended even to govern the timing of his outbursts of temper. In fact, his momentary silence appeared to discomfit Ashton, judging by the expression on the sea-officer's face as he regarded Hyde.

'The fool, sir?' asked Hyde. 'Did you suggest I might be a suitable candidate to play the fool?' There was a note of controlled menace in Hyde's voice that Frey found quite unnerving, despite the fact that it was not directed at himself

Ashton's face paled. 'A joke, Hyde, a joke.'

And then Hyde had closed the distance between the flimsy door to Frey's cabin and the third lieutenant with a single stride and thrust his face into Ashton's. 'A joke, d'you say, sir? Well, well, a joke . . . A joke to make a fellow laugh, eh? Ain't that what a joke's for, eh Josiah? Well ain't it? Say yay or nay. *You* crack 'em: you should know all about 'em.'

'A joke, yes.' Ashton was cornered, wary. He shot an embarrassed glance at Frey.

'To make us laugh, eh? Eh?' Hyde was relentless; he began to move forward, forcing Ashton backwards.

'Yes.' Ashton appealed mutely to Frey who remained silent.

'Good,' persisted Hyde. 'Since we're agreed on the purpose of a joke, perhaps you'd like to share one with me, Josiah. Listen; if there is a fool hereabouts, it is you. What you hope to achieve by your attitude towards poor Marlowe is your own affair, but whatever it is, or was, you were unwise to make it so public. The man has suffered a humiliation and has, by all the signs this morning, reinvigorated himself. I should scarce have believed it possible had I not seen it for myself. If you have any sense, you will throw yourself on another tack.'

Ashton began to rally under this verbal assault. 'Why you damned impertinent bugger . . .'

'Mr Ashton!' Frey broke in, 'Hold your tongue, sir! I'll not coun-
tenance any further discord.' Frey looked at Hyde and observed
the marine officer had said his piece. He relaxed and turned away,
but Ashton was not prepared to accept advice.

'Oh, you won't, won't you? And what will you do, Frey? Toady
to the captain?'

'What the devil's the matter with you, Ashton?' Frey asked, but
Hyde broke in, sensing a real quarrel in the offing.

'For heaven's sake, Josiah, stow your confounded gab and leave
us in peace.'

'Damn you, and don't "Josiah" me. The pair of you . . .'

'Are what?' snapped Frey, suddenly and ferociously intense.
The gleam in his eye seemed to restrain Ashton who swung away,
muttering, flung open the door of his own cabin and disappeared,
slamming it with such force that the entire bulkhead shuddered.
Frey and Hyde looked at each other.

'What the devil was that all about?' asked Hyde in a low voice.

'Just a squall,' said Frey, subsiding, 'but he wants to watch that
tongue of his, or it'll land him in trouble.'

Both officers, aware that the flimsy partition failed to provide
the conditions for private speculation, let the matter drop. Neither
wanted the discord to persist and both had served long enough to
know the benefits of silent toleration in the confined world of a
frigate's wardroom.

For Drinkwater, the remainder of that day was spent quietly.
Having observed the improvement in the weather and determined
Andromeda's latitude at local noon, he went below to enjoy a nap.
Woken by Frampton at eight bells in the afternoon watch, he sat
and wrote up his journal, indulging himself further with a little
self-congratulation.

It was clear, he wrote, *that Lieutenant Marlowe's indisposition was
some form of self-abasement consequent upon his unfortunate experience
off the Wight, and it occurred to me that his lack of confidence must
spring, not from a general incompetence, but some past event. I have
observed poor Frey much affected by the loss of Jas. Quilhampton and the
subsequent ordeal of his court-martial.*

Drinkwater stopped for a moment and stared into the middle
distance. Poor Frey; the damage to the little cutter *Kestrel* had
resulted in her being abandoned in Norwegian waters. As the

senior surviving officer, Frey had had to be judged by a court-martial to determine the extent of her damage in action and the justification for her loss to the naval service. That it had been Drinkwater himself, supported by a survey by Birkbeck, who had pronounced the cutter in an unfit state to withstand the rigours of a passage across the North Sea and ordered her to be abandoned, ameliorated Frey's situation. Nevertheless, the experience of reliving the events in the Vikkenfiord, from which he had been striving to distance himself, revived those feelings Frey had hoped to forget. Not normally given to outward displays of passion or temperament, Frey had become even more introspective. Drinkwater had blamed himself for much of this. It pained him greatly both to have lost his oldest friend and to see another in such poor spirits. He, himself, bore a deep guilt for Quilhampton's death and Frey's grief. The consolation of knowing that he, and they, had done their duty, wore thin to an officer who had been doing his duty for a lifetime. Frey was no less wounded than had been James Quilhampton, when he had lost a hand at Kosseir.

And yet it had been this concern for Frey which had given him the clue to Marlowe's lack of spirit, and Drinkwater found himself wondering about the circuitous nature of events. He dipped his pen, wiped off the excess ink, and began writing again.

Marlowe's introspection was not dissimilar, and from this I therefore concluded Marlowe was obsessed by some event, and that if he were not, if he possessed no spirit, my appeal to him would prove this by its failure. In the event, matters fell out otherwise and I discovered him more of a man of parts than I would have superficially judged. This gives me some satisfaction, and whatever may come of this chase, we may see Marlowe a better man at the end of it than at its commencement.

Drinkwater waited a moment while the ink dried, then turned the page and resumed writing.

It is, moreover, incontrovertible evidence of the workings of providence that out of the consequences of James's death, should come sulvation to another soul.

For a moment Drinkwater looked at these words then, with a grim, self-deprecating smile he took his penknife from his pocket and neatly excised the page. He had a sailor's horror of tempting providence, especially when it touched him closely. The dream of the white lady had been too vivid for that.

*

'The Atlantic is a vast ocean which extends from pole to pole,' Birkbeck said, regarding the half-circle of midshipmen about him, 'and is divided into that part of it which lies in the northern hemisphere and is consequently known as the North Atlantic Ocean, and that part of it which lies in the southern hemisphere and is named accordingly. However, to seamen it is further subdivided; the Western Ocean is the name commonly applied to that portion of the North Atlantic which lies west of the British Isles and must needs be crossed when a passage is made to America or Canada. There is also that part which is known as the Sargasso, an area of some vagueness, but set generally about the equator. Now what is the equator, Mr Paine?'

Paine produced a satisfactory definition and Birkbeck nodded. 'Indeed, the parallel of zero latitude from which other parallels are taken to the northward, or the southward. Now, Mr Dunn, is the equator a great circle?'

'Er, yes sir.'

'Good. And are the other parallels of latitude therefore great circles?'

Dunn's forehead creased with the effort of recollection. Birkbeck's proposition seemed a reasonable enough one. 'Yes, sir.'

'Not at all, Mr Dunn. Of all the parallels of latitude *only* the equator is a great circle. And why is that, pray? Mr Paine?'

'Because a great circle is defined as a circle on the surface of the earth having the same radius as that of the earth.'

'Very good, Mr Paine. Do you understand, Mr Dunn? One might equally have said it should have the same diameter, or that its centre was coincident with that of the earth. Now Mr Dunn, of all the parallels of latitude, only the equator is a great circle, what would you conclude of the meridians?' Dunn looked even more perplexed. 'You do know what a meridian is, Mr Dunn, do you not?'

'I am not certain, sir,' said the boy hopelessly, adding as he saw an unsympathetic gleam in the master's eye, 'is it, is it . . .?' But the floundering was to no avail and Paine was only too ready to capitalize on his messmate's humiliation.

'A meridian is a great circle passing through the poles by which longitude is measured . . .'

'Very good, Mr Paine.' The midshipmen turned as a body to see Marlowe standing behind them. 'And how do we determine longitude?'

127

'By chronometer, sir . . .'

'By your leave, Mr Birkbeck . . .'

'By all means, Mr Marlowe . . .'

Birkbeck, somewhat discomfited, but in no wise seriously affronted by Marlowe's assumption of the instructor's role, took himself off and, having fortified himself with a nip of rum flip in the wardroom, summoned the carpenter and returned to his painstaking and tedious survey of the hold.

Mr Birkbeck's lecture on the different areas of the Atlantic Ocean seemed borne out in the following days. His Britannic Majesty's frigate *Andromeda*, leaking from her exertions, sailed into sunnier climes. The gale, in its abatement, took with it the uncertain weather of high latitudes and, after almost two days of variable airs, ushered in a north-easterly wind, an unexpected but steady breeze. They were too far north for the trade winds, but the favourable direction augured well for their passage and was no less welcome.

Andromeda's yards were squared and she bore away with a fine bone in her teeth, apparently unconcerned with the problems of her antiquity which preoccupied her senior officers. The ship's company turned the berth-deck inside out, washed clothes and bedding and stummed between decks, sweetening the air. Moreover, the warmer nights and drier weather meant the tarpaulins could be rolled back on the booms, ports opened during the daylight and the entire ship made more habitable. The mood of the people changed in proportion, along with the application of a lick of paint and varnish here and there to brighten up their miserable quarters, no thought having been given to this during the frigate's recent embellishment.

As details of Mr Marlowe's recovery permeated the ends of the ship most distant from the wardroom, they were accompanied by the explanation of illness as causing his temporary loss of control. Alongside this intelligence there went a blasphemous joke that he had been raised from the dead. Lieutenant Ashton's nickname for the captain of 'Our Father' was rather apt in this context and as a consequence the first lieutenant had, quite unbeknown to himself, acquired the soubriquet of Lazarus Marlowe. This, partly generating the changed mood of the ship's company, was yet as much a product of it. In this mild euphoria only Lieutenant Ashton and

Sergeant McCann remained burdened, the one having lost control of his future, the other increasingly obsessed and preoccupied by his past.

Indeed, in the case of McCann, the improved weather only exacerbated his condition. As is common with many, memories of youth and past happiness were associated with sunny days and blue skies such as now dominated the flying frigate. Moreover, the farther west they ran, the nearer they drew to the United States, and the fact that this diminishing distance did not constitute a closing of the American coast, worked insidiously upon poor McCann.

Although they had seen a few ships in the Channel and in the Western Approaches, the wide blue reaches of the Atlantic yielded nothing beyond a pair of Portuguese schooners crossing for the Grand Banks. Captain Drinkwater, sensitive to the mellowing mood of the ship and encouraged by the transformation of Lieutenant Marlowe, ordered several gunnery practices as they romped steadily south and westwards.

In addition to the fulmars, gulls and gannets, the dark, marauding shapes of hawking skuas were to be seen intimidating even the large solan geese; flying fish now darted from either bow, pursued by albacore and occasionally driven on board where they were quickly tossed into frying pans to make impromptu feasts for lucky messes or the midshipmen's berth.

And with the flying fish and the albacore came the bottle-nosed dolphins, lifting easily from *Andromeda*'s bow waves, racing in with seemingly effortless thrusts of their muscular tails, to ride the pressure wave that advanced unseen yet tangible, ahead of the massive bulk of the frigate's driving hull. Attempts to catch them usually failed, but occasionally one would succumb to a harpoon or a lure, to end up, poached slowly in Madeira, as steaks on the wardroom table.

On one such occasion, heady with their success, the officers invited Drinkwater to dinner, and notwithstanding the absence of Lieutenant Ashton on watch, they all enjoyed a jolly evening during which the discussion ranged from the general conduct of the late war and the difficulties of securing the person of Napoleon Bonaparte on a remote island, to the possible causes of *Andromeda*'s leak and the contribution to literature of the unknown 'lady' who had written *Pride and Prejudice*.

Watching Marlowe preside over this pleasant evening, Drinkwater concluded his first lieutenant had made a supreme effort and overcome his unhappiness. Furthermore, Drinkwater began to entertain hopes of high endeavour from him, if things fell out as he hoped they would.

But as the days passed and the reckoning so assiduously calculated by Birkbeck, Marlowe and their coterie of half-willing midshipmen, showed them rapidly closing the Archipelago of the Azores, renewed doubts assailed Drinkwater. And while the pleasant weather drew smiles from his men, he paced the weather side of the quarterdeck for hour after hour, going over and over the interview with Hortense, wondering if he was not a quixotic fool after all, seduced at the last by a face which had haunted him for almost all his adult life. She had sought him out; she knew the role he had played in her husband's death; they had been enemies for a score or so of years; so why in God's name should he trust her now?

He ignored the importance of her news and processed events through the filter of guessed motives, suspicions, old anxieties and even fears. He recalled, with that peculiar insistence that only the lonely can as they chew on introspection, how she had seemed an almost demonic presence at one time; an embodiment of all the restless energies of imperial France. She had loomed in his imagination larger than any metaphor: for *she* alone had represented the enemy, and her beauty had seemed diabolical in its power. He had felt this influence suffocating him, drowning him as he fell flailing beneath the overwhelming power of Hortense as the white lady, so that in the wake of the dream, when the rational world reasserted itself, there always lurked a hint of his own impending madness. He shied away from this like a frightened horse, clinging at logic to prevent the otherwise inevitable overwhelming by the 'blue-devils' of mental depression.

He forced himself to consider again Hortense's motives. Why should she do this? Had she not simply been beggared by the damnable war, as she claimed? And what advantage could she gain by casting one ageing fool of a British naval officer on some ludicrous quest amid the billows of the North Atlantic, if the reason for it were not true? He discarded the morbid, fanciful and faintly ridiculous assumptions of his private thoughts, calming himself with the more rational figurings-out of the ordinary.

As his mother was once fond of saying with the bitterness of premature bereavement playing around the corners of her mouth, there was no fool like an old fool. But to set against that charge he brought the experience of a lifetime in the sea-service and a familiarity with the machinations of secret diplomacy.

Nevertheless, there was also the forbidding spectre of their Lordships' disapprobation, as the stock phrase had it. His departure on his self-appointed quest may well have had the blessing of His Royal Highness, the Prince William Henry, Duke of Clarence and so on and so forth, but their Lordships would be well aware that he was well aware that the whole Royal Navy of Great Britain was well aware that His Royal Highness, the Prince William Henry, and so on and so forth, was a buffoon, if not an incompetent!

On the other hand, what point would there be in him dashing off into the Atlantic on his own initiative if he had no good motive? Everyone knew that although the war in Europe was over, the war in North America was not, and it remained perfectly possible for Bonaparte to cause mayhem in Canada. While that much was possible, if not probable, there was another factor Drinkwater now had to consider. *Andromeda* was officially unfit for further active service; she should have been laid up preparatory to passing to the breakers' yard, and her crew, drafted especially for the Royal Escort duty to France, would almost certainly be dispersed to man more sea-worthy ships refitting for the augmentation of the blockade of the eastern seaboard of the United States. Indeed, at that very moment some of those ships might be eagerly awaiting their draft, and thus delayed by *Andromeda*'s absence.

Amid all his considerations of grand strategy, it was this doubt that remained the most disturbing. Try how he might, Drinkwater was unable to argue his way out of this almost certain error of judgement!

Up and down he paced; not seeing the work of the ship passing all about him, scarcely hearing the bells striking the half-hour, the watch-words of the lookouts or the occasional order passed along. He was oblivious to the break-up of the daily navigation class, made so convenient while the solution to the problem of *Andromeda*'s day's work was so easily reconciled in the north-east wind by the simple application of a plane traverse; nor did he notice the daily quarterdeck parade of Hyde's lobsters, nor remark upon Sergeant McCann's uncharacteristically less-than-perfect turnout. Nor indeed, did Captain Drinkwater observe either the energy of the first lieutenant, or the complementary disinterest of the third. Instead he revolved his wretched arguments in a tediously endless mental circumambulation, locked into the introversion of isolation and independent command.

But whatever these private anxieties might constitute, and whatever paramountcy they might assume in any commander's thoughts, the cares of his ship will always intrude, and on this occasion they took the form of Mr Midshipman 'Tom' Paine over whom the pre-occupied Drinkwater almost fell as the youngster dodged about in front of him to attract his attention.

'God's bones! What in heaven's name is the matter?' Drinkwater finally acknowledged the jumping jack trying to waylay him. 'Why Mr Paine, what the devil d'you want?'

Paine was not a whit discomfited by the difficulties he had experienced in accomplishing his simple errand. Jokes about Old Nat were legion in the cockpit.

'Begging your pardon, sir, but Mr Marlowe's compliments, and he wishes me to inform you that we shall require an alteration of course to make our landfall.'

Drinkwater looked over the boy's shoulder. Marlowe and Birkbeck were exchanging a word or two on the far side of the binnacle.

'An alteration of course, eh? Well sir, to what?'

'Ten degrees to port, sir.'

'To port, eh?' He was about to say that in his day it would have been 'to larboard' but such pedantry would be laughable to the young imp. 'Very well, Mr Paine, kindly see to it.'

'Aye, aye, sir.' The lad touched his fore-cock and made to be off when Drinkwater called him back.

'And when you have attended to the matter and adjusted the yards, pray show me your reckoning of the day's work.'

Paine's face fell. His 'Aye, aye, sir' was less enthusiastic.

Laughing inwardly, Drinkwater crossed the deck and stood on the weather side of the helm while *Andromeda*'s head was swung through ten degrees of arc and settled on her new course. There was a general tweaking of braces, but neither the motion nor the speed of the ship seemed affected and the ageing hull drove forwards through the blue seas with the white wave crests running up almost astern. It seemed quite impossible that this charming scene could ever be otherwise; that the light, straining canvas above their heads could ever turn a rain and spray-sodden grey, as hard on the horniest hands as raw-hide, or that the great bulk of the hurrying ship could be laid over on her beam ends, or tossed about like a cork.

'So, gentlemen,' he said to Marlowe and Birkbeck, who had both been watching the adjusting of the main yards, 'when do you anticipate sighting our landfall?'

'Shortly after first light tomorrow, sir,' Marlowe answered.

Drinkwater looked at Birkbeck. 'Are you two in agreement?'

'Harmoniously so, sir,' Birkbeck replied with a hint of irony.

'Good. I'm decidedly glad to hear it.' Drinkwater smiled at the two men. Marlowe was a transformed figure. 'Well now, we must consider our best course of action when we arrive.'

'Indeed, sir. How far offshore will you cruise?' Marlowe asked.

Drinkwater rubbed his chin and raised an eyebrow. 'Three or four leagues; sufficiently far to be clear of danger, yet not out of sight of the land. According to my reckoning, our friends will come down on the island from the north-north-east.' He waved out on the starboard quarter, as though their sails might appear at any moment.

'D'you think Bonaparte is already there, sir?' asked Birkbeck.

'We shall send a boat in to find out. Do you prepare the launch, stock it for two days and have Frey,' Drinkwater hesitated, 'no, have Ashton command it. Send in half a dozen marines under the sergeant.' Drinkwater paused as Marlowe nodded. 'But to answer your question about Boney, I consider it unlikely, though not impossible, for him to have reached the island yet. I have no knowledge of when he left Paris, nor of his port of embarkation, but he must have been despatched by the time King Louis landed, I'd have thought, and conveyed by express to the west coast; to Brest, or La Rochelle or L'Orient. A fast frigate might, I suppose, have reached the archipelago a little before us.'

'A British frigate?' asked Marlowe.

Drinkwater shrugged. 'I imagine a British frigate or perhaps a small squadron such as we were lately attached to, would accompany him. As for himself, I suppose his dignity as the elected Emperor of the French would be unsupportable in anything but a French man-o'-war.'

'Not if it was the allies' purpose to humiliate him,' put in Marlowe.

'I think a small island humiliation enough after the domination of Europe,' countered Drinkwater. 'Remember what Nelson wrote: "In victory, let the chief characteristic be magnanimity."'

'A very Christian sentiment sir,' responded Birkbeck, 'but not one which I would expect his most serene and culminated, high and God almighty majesty the Tsar of all the Russias to subscribe to where Napoleon Bonaparte is concerned.'

'Perhaps not,' said Drinkwater grinning, 'though you talk like a canting leveller, Mr Birkbeck. I thought your nimble scholar Tom Paine the republican among us.'

And they all laughed companionably, standing in the sunshine enjoying the fellowship of like minds.

PART TWO
A Wild-goose Chase?

'Well, that's the end of it all, though it's throwing the game away with all the trump cards in one's hand.'

TALLEYRAND, PRINCE OF BENEVENTO

Chapter Ten May 1814

The Rock

Shortly before dawn Drinkwater woke with a start. Lying in the darkness he listened intently, but could discern no noise; not even the clanking of the pumps disturbed the night, silent but for the laboured creaking of the ship and above his head the faint, measured tread of one of the watch-keepers. Then his cabin was suddenly lit up, as though someone shone a powerful light in through the stern windows. The spectral illumination startled him. His heart thumped with alarm and he was on his feet in a trice, to stare out through the stern windows. An instant later he had an explanation as the ship drove through bioluminescence and the pale green gleam again lit up the night.

He was unable to sleep after this weird though natural phenomenon, and drew on breeches, shoes and stockings. Winding his boatcloak about himself he went on deck. The pacing footsteps revealed themselves to be those of Lieutenant Frey. They exchanged courtesies and Drinkwater asked the routine question.

'All well?'

'Aye, sir. I have a good man stationed aloft in the foretop, though I doubt we'll sight anything before daylight.'

' 'Tis as well to be on our guard.'

'Yes, of course.'

'The wind is holding fair,' Drinkwater observed. 'One might almost believe we had run into the trades, but our latitude is too high so we must be prepared for our run of luck to end.'

There was a brief pause, then Frey said, 'I believe you're sending the launch ashore, sir.'

'Yes, just to establish whether our friend Boney has been delivered yet.'

'And Lieutenant Ashton's to command her.'

'Yes.'

Frey fell silent. Drinkwater wondered whether he felt himself slighted by the appointment of the junior lieutenant to this task, then Frey asked, 'Will you be going ashore yourself, sir?'

'No.'

For a moment neither man said anything, then Drinkwater remarked, 'I gather there has been something of a sea change in the wardroom, Mr Frey. Things are a little more tolerable, I hope.'

'In a manner of speaking, yes, sir. Where formerly Mr Marlowe seemed to be constantly under the weather, we now have Mr Ashton acting like a spoilt brat. I am of the opinion that acquaintances should not serve together; friendship and duty seem incompatible in the circumstances prevailing in a man-o'-war.'

'Dear me, I hope not,' replied Drinkwater, ruefully.

'Oh, I beg pardon, sir, I didn't mean . . .' The tone of Frey's voice conveyed an embarrassment the darkness hid.

'Think nothing of it,' Drinkwater chuckled, adding more seriously, 'though I have to confess, Marlowe's change of heart seems almost miraculous.'

'That is what they are saying below decks.'

'I don't follow you.'

'That he was raised from the dead. They call him "Lazarus" Marlowe.'

'Lazarus Marlowe . . .?' Drinkwater tested the name and found himself grinning in the gloom.

'I'm afraid you are cast in a more divine role, sir.'

'You mean . . .? Well, 'pon my soul!'

'Seafaring folk have the oddest notions, don't they?'

'Aye, they most certainly do.'

'If I might change the subject, sir . . .'

'Please do, Mr Frey. I am hard-pressed to find anything I can add in support of the Almighty.'

'I'm sure He would be pleased to know that, sir,' Frey added drily, and Drinkwater could just see the smile on his face as the dawn light crept into the eastern sky. 'What I was going to ask, sir, if I might be presumptuous, is what you intend to do? I mean we have no idea of the whereabouts of Napoleon, do we?'

'No, I appreciate that, nor are we likely to learn. My principal, no my *only* concern, is to intercept and if necessary engage the two ships which have been sent from Antwerp to convey Boney and his staff to America. Anything more would be a gross presumption on my part, not something likely to endear me to Lord Castlereagh or any of his cronies.'

'D'you think we shall engage them?'

A horrible thought crossed Drinkwater's mind; was poor Frey a broken man after the terrible encounter with the enemy in the Vikkenfiord? 'Does it worry you if it should come to that?'

'Not at all,' Frey answered without hesitation, 'in fact, I should welcome the event.'

'Not, I hope, because you entertain any foolish notions of covering yourself with . . .'

'Death or glory,' broke in Frey with a short, dismissive laugh. 'No, no, nothing like that. To tell the truth, sir, I should think my active service career the more fulfilled if I had one more crack at the French; that damned affair in Norway was somehow unfinished business.'

'I understand. That is one of the reasons I will not send you out of the ship in any boat expedition, Frey. I want you aboard. All the time; at least until this business is concluded.'

'Thank you, sir.'

'If and when we do encounter the French ships I anticipate they will keep close company and try and overwhelm us. They may be full of soldiers, men willing to fight hand to hand, against which our people would prove inadequate.'

'You would want to hold off and manoeuvre to cripple them, and thereby induce a surrender?'

'Exactly. And while the sea conditions will be lively in these latitudes, and we may have trouble pointing the guns to good effect, the steady breeze should enable us to be nimble.'

'Providing their two against our single ship don't corner us like a dog.'

'We shall have to see . . .'

'Yes.'

It was getting rapidly lighter and already the details of the deck about them were emerging from the shadows of the night. Drinkwater began to feel the pangs of hunger stirring in his belly. He would welcome coffee and some hot, buttered toast. His teeth no longer pained him and the swollen gum had subsided so that the idea of masticating on a slice made his mouth water.

'Might I ask your advice about something?'

'Yes, of course.' Drinkwater thrust his self-indulgent day-dream aside. 'What is it?'

'I have given the matter much thought, sir, but I accept the fact that on our return we will be paid off and I am likely to be compelled to exist on half-pay.'

'I shall do my best for you, Mr Frey,' Drinkwater said. The consideration of another dependant loomed in his imagination, accompanied by the added thought that while some perverse chivalry prompted him to offer support to Hortense Santhonax, he felt a reprehensible resentment at the thought of doing the same for poor, loyal Frey.

'Oh, I know you will, sir, and please do not think I am asking for charity. On the contrary, I have some hopes of supporting myself if I must. No, I have been thinking of James Quilhampton's widow.'

'Catriona . . .?' Drinkwater suppressed his surprise.

'I, er, think she might not be averse to accepting a proposal from me.'

'Pardon the question, Mr Frey, but are you attached to the lady?'

'I think she is fond of me, sir, and she has little means of support. She also has the child . . .'

'Ah yes.'

'I felt . . .'

'Of course. I understand, but a marriage based upon pity may not be for the best, Mr Frey. The lady is a little older than yourself,' Drinkwater said tactfully. 'That may make a difference in time, and while there may be no other person to claim your affections at the moment should you be cast ashore upon your own resources, then you may meet someone other than Mistress Quilhampton for whom, without being ungallant, you may come to feel a greater attachment.'

'That is true, sir . . .'

But Frey got no further, for the cry came down from the foretop that land was in sight.

An hour later two steep-sided islands were visible from the deck as the low sun struck their basalt cliffs conferring upon them a warm, pink colour. To the north-west and perhaps two or three leagues nearer, lay the smaller island of Corvo, while farther off, fine on the port bow, rose Flores.

Drinkwater scrutinized the summit of the island, from which a stream of orographic cloud trailed downwind. Patiently he waited for *Andromeda* to draw near enough for them to see the shoreline, as yet still hidden below the horizon.

'A most appropriate place to cage an eagle,' Drinkwater remarked and Frey, catching the observation, aired a recondite fact: 'The archipelago is named Azores from the Portuguese *açor*, meaning a hawk.'

Among the watch on deck, an air of excitement and expectation animated the men. Word of an impending landfall and a proposed boat expedition had percolated through the ship and the sight of the island, even for those who would approach little closer, nor see more than could be discerned from the frigate's waist, was nevertheless sufficient to break the monotony of their arduous yet dull lives.

'You may close Flores, Mr Frey. We will bring-to off Santa Cruz. I shall want the launch ready then,' Drinkwater ordered, closing his glass with an emphatic snap. 'I am going below for an hour.'

'Aye, aye, sir.'

By the time the watch changed the entire island had risen above the rim of the world and the white breakers of the restless Atlantic could be seen fringing the scree-littered foreshore. Larval cliffs predominated, formed by prehistoric volcanic eruptions, no longer rose-red from the dawn, but grey and forbidding with fresh-water streams cascading into the sea in silver streaks. As they drew closer to Flores they could see clouds of wheeling sea-birds, gulls, petrels and auks, though the officers' glasses were focused not on these aerial denizens, but the few white buildings that formed the port of Santa Cruz. It was something of a disappointment.

'Stap me, but it don't amount to much,' remarked Hyde, voicing the opinion of them all.

Below, Drinkwater completed his preparations. Having washed, shaved and dressed his hair, he eased himself into his undress uniform coat and sat at his desk. Drawing a sheet of paper from his folio, he took up his steel pen, opened the inkwell, inscribed the date and began to write.

To the Governor of Flores,
Santa Cruz.

Sir,

I have the Honour to Command His Britannic Majesty's Frigate Andromeda *presently arrived off this Island under the Express Orders of Admiral of the Fleet, His Royal Highness, Prince William Henry, Duke of Clarence and Earl of Munster.*

Being thus engaged upon a Singular, Special and most Urgent

Service, I call upon the Ancient Amity which has Subsisted between our Two Nations since time immemorial and has been Crowned with Victory in the Late War by the Exertions of the Anglo Portuguese Armies Commanded by His Grace the Marquess Wellington and Marshal Beresford.

To this end, Sir, you will have been informed that Napoleon Bonaparte, lately Emperor of the French, is to be Exiled in the Island of Flores, and kept here until the End of the Term of his Earthly Existence.

However, Information has been made known to His Britannic Majesty's Government that an Expedition has lately been fitted out at Antwerp, and that the Purpose of this Force is to Abduct the Person of Napoleon Bonaparte and to Convey him to America or Canada where his Ambition may yet cause more Misery and Extend a War which His Majesty's Government wish to Terminate as Swiftly as Possible.

This letter comes to you by the Hand of an Officer and I desire you, Sir, having Regard for all the above Circumstances, to inform this Officer whether you have yet taken possession of the Person of General Bonaparte, how he is Accommodated, and whether any Inhabitants of the Island who may have been Fishing Offshore, have reported the Presence of any Men-of-War belonging to any Foreign Power.

I also Request that, upon Receipt of this Despatch, should the said General Bonaparte be already Resident on the Island of Flores, you Undertake to keep a Close Watch upon his Person, his Associates, Staff and Servants. This I Charge you with Under the Terms of the Several Treaties of Mutual Help existing between our two Nations.

Drinkwater paused and re-read his epistle with an amused smile. He had invoked every phrase at his command to alert the Governor of the gravity of the reason for Andromeda's presence off Flores. The long alliance of Great Britain and Portugal, which relied upon several treaties, the first of which dated from as far back as 1373, but the most recent of which was that known as the Methuen Treaty of 1707, had been underwritten by the successes of Wellington's Anglo Portuguese army which had been fighting in the Iberian Peninsula for six years.

He decided he could add little more, other than a courtesy or two, and concluded the letter: .

I Regret that my Duty prevents my Calling upon you in Person at this Time, but Trust that you will Afford the Bearer of this Despatch, Lieutenant Jos. Ashton, every Confidence with which you would Honour me.

I am, Sir, your Obedient Servant,

Nathan'l Drinkwater, Captain, Royal Navy

Ensuring the ink was dry, Drinkwater folded the letter, sealed it and added the superscription. Then he left the cabin, jamming his hat upon his head as he did so.

'Hoist the new colours, if you please,' he ordered as he reached the deck, casting about him. The ship seethed with people; two watches were on deck, as were many of those who might have been below. Upon the quarterdeck the blue and white of the officers contrasted with Hyde's immaculate scarlet, a pretty enough picture with the blue sea and sky as a backdrop astern. Ahead loomed the island, the northern extremity of which, Punta Delgada, was stark against the horizon, while its summit, the Morro Alto, was lost in its streamer of cloud.

Santa Cruz proved a tiny, rock-girt inlet, its few buildings dominated by the baroque tower of the church of São Pedro. The tiny habitation was surrounded by the brilliant green of vegetation which refreshed eyes tired of the ocean. This verdure was interspersed by the brilliant colours of a profusion of flowers, the red and yellow of canna lilies, the orange of montbretia and the blue of agapanthus. Amid this almost pastoral scene, a flagstaff bore the blue and white standard of the House of Bragança, a gallant complement to the new red ensign of the senior squadron of the Royal Navy of Great Britain which streamed from *Andromeda*'s peak.

'I've the saluting guns ready, sir,' offered Marlowe.

'Very good, Mr Marlowe. We shall give the Governor seventeen guns. You may commence as soon as we lay the main tops'l against the mast.'

'Aye, aye, sir.'

Drinkwater nodded to Birkbeck. 'You have the con, Mr Birkbeck?'

'Aye, sir.'

'Bring her to off the mole, if you please.'

'Aye, aye, sir.'

'Have you seen Ashton?'

'Here, sir.' Drinkwater turned to see the third lieutenant hurriedly pulling a tarpaulin around him. Such was the bustling mood of the morning that even Ashton looked a happier man.

'Ah, Mr Ashton, is the launch ready?'

'Yes sir. We have but to bend on the falls when we heave-to.'

'You are victualled for two days?'

'In accordance with your orders, sir.'

'Very well. Now pay attention. I have here a letter to be passed to the *Alcaid*, or Governor of the island. Do you ensure that the man to whom you pass this is the senior civil authority at Santa Cruz, do you understand?'

'Yes, sir.' Ashton frowned, taking the letter.

'Is something the matter, Mr Ashton?'

'Sir, with respect, the letter, is it in English?'

'Of course. Why do you ask?'

'Well, sir, I don't wish to sound impertinent, but will these dagoes understand it? I mean,' Ashton added hurriedly, 'I mean the matter is of considerable importance.'

'These dagoes, as you call 'em, Mr Ashton, are Portuguese, the oldest allies of our Sovereign. They have traded with us for years and if the Governor himself does not speak and read English, which I am confident he does, there will be a British vice-consul who will command the language as well as you or I.'

Ashton nodded. 'Very well, sir.'

'Now, I have asked if Bonaparte has arrived on the island, and whether any strange ships have been seen lying off the island. You should press this point particularly and bring me the answer.'

'Aye, aye, sir.'

'Very well. I have provisioned the boat for two days in case anything should miscarry. I shall lie-to hereabouts until you return, but if for any reason you are delayed, keep your men in the boat and ensure the marine sergeant understands that. I don't want British tars running loose among the women and producing a crop of Andromedas and Perseuses nine months hence!'

'I understand, sir.'

'Very well. Good fortune.' Ashton touched the fore-cock of his hat and turned away. 'Mr Birkbeck!' Drinkwater called. 'You may heave her to!'

'Aye, aye, sir!'

'Mr Marlowe! You may commence the salute!'

His Britannic Majesty's frigate *Andromeda* turned in a lazy circle, her bowsprit describing an arc of some two hundred degrees against the sky as her compass card spun from a heading of south-west by west, through north, to east, her yards swinging in their parrels, as the fore and mizen yards were braced for the port tack and her main mast spars left to fall aback. On the forecastle the battery of stubby carronades barked at precise, five-second intervals, paying respects to the Governor of Flores who, Drinkwater hoped, had been alerted to the presence of a British man-of-war offshore. Each unshotted discharge emitted a grey smoke-ring from which the quick-eyed caught sight of the fragments of wadding whirled into the sea.

As the last gun fell silent, *Andromeda* lay stopped across the wind and sea. To starboard the sea flattened in the lee thus formed and with the yard and stay tackles hooked on, the falls manned and set tight, the heavy white carvel launch lifted from the chocks. She was already manned and, as the men stamped away with the ropes, she began her slow traverse across the deck with her weight taken on the yard tackles and walked back on the stays.

Drinkwater, having given this operation a swift appraisal, had his glass focused once more upon the flagstaff. His expectations were disappointed, for no reciprocating spurt of yellow flame with its lingering cloud of powder-smoke responded to the British salute. Well, he thought, pocketing the glass, he should not complain, perhaps the place was undefended; it certainly amounted to very little. Moreover, *Andromeda* was plainly only a private ship and wore nothing at her mastheads but her pendant, and she was a rather old and worn out one, at that!

Echoing his thoughts, the ship trembled as the mass of the laden boat vibrated the stays. This was transmitted to the masts and thus to the keel itself.

'Interesting to sound the well after this,' Drinkwater said to Birkbeck.

'I'm damned if I can find that leak, sir. I've had the linings out, the ceiling lifted and restowed God knows how many tiers of barrels, barricoes and hogsheads. Damn it, you'd think that with the ship more than three-quarters empty of stores the matter would be easy . . .'

'Nothing in life is easy, Mr Birkbeck, nothing at all,' Drinkwater said soulfully.

'Except begetting brats and earning a woman's bad opinion!' grumbled Birkbeck.

' 'Pon my word, Mr Birkbeck, I thought you more of a philosopher than that,' Drinkwater laughed, thinking of his own orders to Ashton regarding the conduct of the boat's crew.

'After crawling around that confounded hold, I'd challenge Plato himself to philosophize. Hey! Easy there on that main yard tackle, you'll have them all thrown out of the boat! Beg pardon, sir.'

'Not at all. There, they are afloat now.'

Andromeda, which had been listing as the launch reached the outboard extremity of its traverse and hung suspended above the sea, now recoiled from her forsaken burden. The launch had been lowered so that with a resounding smack the sea had embraced its long hull. A moment later her crew had cast off the falls and these had been recovered. Tossing oars, the launch's bowman bore off and the heavy boat was manoeuvred clear of the frigate's tumble-home. Then her oars were being plied energetically, and with Ashton sitting in the stern and Midshipman Paine standing at the tiller, she was headed gallantly for the shore, a red ensign at her stern and the scarlet of Sergeant McCann's marines a bright spot against the velvet blue of the Atlantic.

All hands on deck lingered to watch the launch diminish as it drew off towards the rock-strewn inlet. Beside Drinkwater, Marlowe had come aft and taken up his glass again.

'I can see masts and yards beyond those rocks, sir,' he observed. 'A brig, by the look of her. Certainly no squadron.'

'D'you see an ensign?' asked Drinkwater, fishing for his own glass, extending it and levelling it against a backstay.

'There's some bunting hanging up, but it's blowing away from us. Looks like red and white . . . No, I can't say for sure, sir.'

'Well, no matter, Ashton's almost there now; we'll know soon enough.' Drinkwater closed his glass again. 'Where's Mr Birkbeck?'

'Gone below sir, to check the well,' said Frey. 'I have the ship, sir.'

Drinkwater nodded. 'Very well, Mr Frey. By the bye, have you broken your fast yet?'

Frey shook his head. 'I can wait a little longer.'

'You may have to wait some hours. Here, Mr Marlowe, do you take the deck. Frey, join me for some breakfast.'

Drinkwater looked at the first lieutenant. Marlowe had gone

146

pale. 'Come, come, Mr Marlowe, 'tis nothing. Send for a sextant and subtend the height of the peak and the shore. If the arc grows quickly, you will mark the rate at which the ship drifts inshore. Should you get an increase of say one eighth in an hour, brace up and stand offshore. I shall only be below.'

Marlowe swallowed and nodded. 'Aye, aye, sir,' he acknowledged, glancing anxiously at the white-fringed reefs surrounding Santa Cruz.

Turning, Drinkwater led Frey below. 'How does a man become a first luff with such a nervous disposition?' he asked himself, pitying poor Marlowe and wondering if his confidence might not have been misplaced after all. The last thing he saw of Marlowe was him sending a midshipman below for his sextant.

Breakfast in the cabin was enjoyed in silence. Frey was tired after his long watch and Drinkwater, having relinquished the deck, was now filled with anxiety. However, when the noise of stamping feet and the changed motion of the ship revealed Marlowe had decided to get under weigh, Drinkwater relaxed.

'He'll be all right, sir,' Frey said.

'I hope you are right.'

As Drinkwater poured a second cup of coffee, Marlowe put *Andromeda* on the port tack, standing offshore to the northward.

'There you are, sir. I told you so.'

Drinkwater stared astern out through the stern windows to where Santa Cruz appeared like a picture in a slide show.

'I believe you are right, Mr Frey.'

Frey smiled. 'A pretty sight, don't you think?' he asked, adding 'Flores means the island of flowers.'

Drinkwater smiled. 'You are certainly well informed. I wonder if Bonaparte will find the view so congenial? Will you make a painting of it?'

Frey nodded. 'Perhaps.'

'I admire the skill, but why d'you do it? I mean it's charming and a delight, and something to mark the occasion, but the effort surely out-weighs the advantages.'

Frey grinned. 'To be sure; but it is no rational matter. One is compelled to do it.'

'Compelled? D'you mean to say you are not a rational creature?' Drinkwater asked with a grin.

'If you mean by that question, am I unmoved by reason? No, of

147

course not, but if you mean do I submit upon occasion to some inner prompting? Then yes, I do. We think we are rational beings, attributing our actions to logical thought, but consider sir, we feel first and often act upon our feelings. Our thoughts arise from our feelings . . .'

'You mean our emotions dominate our thinking?'

'Oh, yes, most certainly; but what makes us rational is that we can think about our emotions. It is from this response that the urge to paint or draw comes.'

'Then your artistic achievement is no more than an urge to copy.'

'To record, perhaps to reproduce, but no more. I make no claim to be a great artist.'

Drinkwater felt the conversation touched a raw nerve. Had his own thinking been too much influenced by his emotions? The possibility made him shudder inwardly.

They might have discussed this longer had not a peremptory knock announced the arrival of Midshipman Dunn.

'Yes, Mr Dunn?' asked Drinkwater, wondering what problem Marlowe had conjured up for himself.

'There's a ship, sir, bearing down towards us from the north-east.'

'Colours?'

'Can't see yet, sir.'

Drinkwater shot a quick glance at Frey. 'The Antwerp squadron?'

Frey shrugged. 'No peace for the wicked,' he muttered.

'Very well, Mr Dunn. Have Mr Marlowe clear for action!'

'You fear the worst?' said Frey, hauling himself wearily to his feet.

Drinkwater gave a short laugh. 'I'm just following my feelings, Mr Frey!'

Chapter Eleven

Diplomacy

Mr Ashton lost sight of the ship sooner than those aboard *Andromeda* saw him disappear behind the outer reef of exposed rocks. At sea level, among the tossing wave crests, with his mind cast ahead on the coming hours, apart from a single glance astern to see the frigate's hull behind a rearing sea and only her topsails and upper masts visible, he gave her no thought at all. To say he was puffed up with the importance of his mission would be only a half-truth, for as is common with men of his stamp, it went against the grain to assume even delegated gravity from a man whom one despised. On the other hand, while in the politest society Captain Nathaniel Drinkwater might be regarded as *de trop*, Lieutenant Ashton knew well enough that while at sea, the commander of a British man-of-war possessed a degree of power not given to many. He was, therefore, in something of a quandary, half wishing to inflate himself, yet concerned that since he was not Captain Drinkwater's favourite, he had been sent upon this mission for reasons as yet unclear to him.

However, the effort of the seamen at the oars as they lent forward, then heaved backwards, was testimony enough to the fact that he had been entrusted with an independent task. He cast a quick look at Sergeant McCann and his lobsters, sitting bolt upright, their plumed billycocks foursquare upon their heads and their muskets between their gaitered knees. Then he transferred his attention to Paine. The lad was standing up, leaning on the big tiller as he strove to keep the heavy launch from broaching.

'Take her in beyond the reef, Mr Paine,' Ashton said self-importantly, 'and then we shall find some sort of a landing, I daresay.'

'Aye, aye, sir.'

Ashton felt a little more composed after this brief exchange; he had finally decided that the importance of his mission overrode personal considerations. As if echoing this sentiment, Mr Paine gave a little cough and said, 'May I ask something, sir?'

'What is it?' Ashton responded expansively.

'This island . . .'

'Is Flores, Mr Paine, westernmost of the Azores.'

'I know, sir,' replied Paine, concealing his irritation at being patronized, 'but is it where they are going to keep Boney?'

'Yes,' replied Ashton, looking again at the volcanic mass of the mountainous interior and the vegetation clinging in profusion to its lower slopes. 'Once here, the world will forget him.'

'Wasn't it Prometheus who was chained to a rock, sir?'

Ashton felt this chatty atmosphere was not one to be encouraged, especially as his knowledge of Greek mythology was sketchy. 'I daresay, Mr Paine, it might well have been . . .'

'It was, sir.' The voice was Sergeant McCann's, and he added conversationally, 'And so too was Andromeda, chained to a rock by her mother who was jealous of her beauty – a curious conjunction, seeing as how the ship is so named . . .'

'And it was Perseus who released her,' Paine added enthusiastically, 'then fell in love with her and . . .'

'Hold your damned tongues, the pair of you!' snapped Ashton, aware that matters had got out of hand. The man at stroke oar was grinning. 'And what's the matter with you? Wipe that foolish smile off your face, or I'll see to it with the cat later.' The man's face changed to a dark and sullen anger. 'What's your name?' Ashton asked.

'Shaw,' muttered the stroke oarsman.

'Shaw, eh. Well mind your manners, Shaw.' And Ashton, having established his position, leaned back in the stern of the now silent boat and contemplated the surge of white water about the approaching reef and the little brig beyond it. The hiss and slop of the following sea, the creak of thole pins, the faint grunts of the oarsmen and the splash of the oar-blades were now the only sounds to accompany his contemplation. Fifteen long minutes later, the launch swept inside the reef and into its shelter. The tiny anchorage opened up ahead of them, and beyond a strip of beach, the town, which was no more than a village.

Within the embrace of the rocks lay the brig, moored stem and stern, while some brightly painted fishing craft were drawn up on the beach beyond. Several of these were the slender *canoas* which the Azoreans used to hunt whales offshore. As the launch swept past the brig, a few curious faces stared down at them.

'Look out, boys,' someone aboard the brig shouted, 'the fooking press-gang's here!'

'Damned impertinence,' growled Ashton, while a curious Paine caught the name *Mary Digby* and the port of registry of *Sunderland* upon her stern.

There were a few idlers on the beach, too, some gathered about the fishing boats, others with lines running offshore. They were all watching the launch run in towards the beach. One man shouted something, though their ignorance of Portuguese prevented them from knowing whether it was a greeting or a complaint that Paine had carried away a hook and line.

'We must land on the beach,' Ashton pronounced.

'Aye, aye, sir,' said Paine quickly, leaning on the tiller to head the launch directly for the half-moon of sand.

'Oars.' The men ceased pulling, their oars rising horizontally while they lay on the looms and caught their breath. The momentum of the launch carried it in a final glide towards the beach.

'Toss oars!' The double-banked oars rose unsteadily to the vertical and Paine gave the final order that had them lowered, blades forward, with a dull clatter. A moment later the launch scrunched upon the sharp-smelling volcanic sand. The bowman leaped ashore with the painter. He was followed by the two men at the forward oars and the trio heaved the boat a little higher as a low swell followed her and broke upon the beach.

Lieutenant Ashton looked at them and then at Paine. 'Are you proposing to land me or the boat's crew, Mr Paine?' he asked sarcastically.

'Heave her up a little more,' Paine ordered, blushing.

'No, no, no,' expostulated Ashton, 'there's no need for all that.' The lieutenant rose with the petulant air of a man put out on another's behalf, and stepped up on the aftermost thwart. The two oarsmen seated there drew aside. One of them was Shaw, the sailor whom Ashton had threatened to flog, and he glared up at Ashton, but Ashton did not notice. He clambered forward over successive thwarts, the oarsmen drawing aside for him. Stepping momentarily on the gunwhale, he jumped ashore, but turned and slipped on the bladder-wrack. He half-fell, but caught himself and, while his coat tail dangled in the wet and slithery seaweed that lay on the tideline, he avoided besmirching his white breeches.

'Damnation!' he swore. The boat's crew to a man, looked out across the harbour as though the view was unsurpassable. One or two shoulders shook with what might have been mirth, but Ashton was staring at Paine whose face was almost contorted in the effort of self-control. 'Mr Paine, the boat's crew are to remain aboard. Sergeant McCann, you may land two sentinels.'

Ashton brushed the sand from his hands, turned about and began to ascend the sloping beach. He was met by an officer in the brown tunic of a regiment of *caçadores*.

'Welcome to Flores, sir,' the swarthy officer said pleasantly in good English.

'Er, obliged, I'm sure,' mumbled the astonished Ashton.

The Portuguese officer smiled. 'I am Lieutenant Da Silva. I served in Spain with General Wellesley. At Talavera,' Da Silva added as Ashton appeared even more perplexed, but the penny dropped and Ashton took the proferred hand, aware that it and his right cuff were mucky from contact with the wet wrack on the sand. Serve the dago right, Ashton thought venomously, but he smiled as he responded to the vigorous shake of the Portuguese officer's hand. 'I have a message for the Governor – the *Alcaid*,' he added pompously.

'Yes, of course,' Da Silva replied, indicating the way. 'Please come with me.'

'Can you make out her colours, Mr Frey?' Drinkwater's voice betrayed his anxiety as he fumbled in his tail pocket, extended the Dollond glass and clapped it to his right eye. He swore at the diffi-culty of bringing the strange ship into focus and hoped Frey's sharper eyes would spot the ensign.

'No, sir, hidden behind the tops'ls.'

'Damnation,' Drinkwater hissed under his breath.

'Sir . . .' Frey spoke slowly, 'there's something familiar about her . . .'

For a moment Drinkwater's glass captured the image of the approaching ship which left an impression upon his retina. He instantly agreed with Frey and they simultaneously identified her: 'It's that Russian frigate . . . What's its confounded name?'

'The *Gremyashchi*!'

'What the devil's she doing here?' Drinkwater asked no one in particular, lowering his glass, his heart suddenly hammering in his breast. But he already knew the answer, just as Marlowe ran up, two fingers to the fore-cock of his hat.

'Cleared for action, sir!' he reported, staring over Drinkwater's shoulder at the approaching ship foaming towards them, running before the persisting northeaster. 'That's that Russian we sailed from Dover with!' he said.

'Aye, it is . . . Nevertheless, it's as well to take no chances,' Drinkwater remarked obscurely, trying to think tactically. It was enough that Captain Rakov was here, off the Azores; the reason why could wait. 'Very well, gentlemen. Mr Birkbeck, do you bring the ship onto the larboard taçk, then heave-to athwart her hawse . . .'

'Aye, aye, sir!'

'Mr Frey, you shall run out the starboard battery when I give the word. Load single ball. Mr Marlowe, be so kind as to have the forecastle carronades loaded with powder only. We shall', Drinkwater paused a moment and braced himself as, under Birkbeck's orders, *Andromeda* turned away from her easterly course and swung to the north-north-west, to sail at an approximate right angle to the Russian frigate's course. He turned to Birkbeck: 'Ten minutes should see us close enough . . .'

'Aye, sir,' acknowledged the master.

'We shall', Drinkwater resumed, 'fire the unshotted carronades to bring her to. If she runs down any more I intend to cripple her, Mr Frey, aim high and knock her sticks about.'

'Aye, aye, sir!'

'Sir, I . . .' Marlowe's face wore an expression of grave concern.

'Not now, Mr Marlowe, ' Drinkwater said dismissively. 'To your posts, gentlemen, to your posts,' and seeing Marlowe hesitate, Drinkwater rubbed his hands and added, 'Briskly now, briskly!'

Marlowe shrugged, turned on his heel and ran forward along the starboard gangway. Birkbeck caught Drinkwater's eye and the latter raised his eyebrow; Birkbeck smiled and turned back to watch the approaching ship.

Drinkwater raised his glass again. He could see it was the *Gremyashchi* now, the figurehead of Mars the god of war clearly identified her, and her aspect was opening so that he could just see the white flag with its dark blue diagonal cross fluttering beyond the leech of the main topsail. As *Andromeda* gathered speed on her new tack, the fly of the Russian ensign was again occluded behind the bellying sail. He lowered his telescope a fraction and could just make out a dark gaggle of officers on her quarterdeck.

A flurry of activity could be seen on the *Gremyashchi*'s deck and the straining main course seemed to belly even more, losing its driving power as the sheets were slacked off and then the big sail rose to the yard under the tug of the buntlines and the clew garnets.

Was Rakov clewing up in order to give battle, or merely to exchange pleasantries?

'Now sir?' asked an equally anxious Birkbeck.

'Now is as good a time as ever,' Drinkwater said, coolly, feigning indifference, and Birkbeck's voice rang out with the order to 'clew up both courses and heave her to'. A moment later, *Andromeda*'s main yards were braced round and their sails curved back against the mast, bringing the British frigate to a gently pitching standstill. Drinkwater drew in his breath and hailed the forecastle.

'Mr Marlowe! Fire!'

The carronades forward gave their short, imperative bark. The cloud of powder smoke blew back over the deck, carrying its sharp stench to the quarterdeck. The Russian ship was now some seven or eight cables away, broad on the starboard bow and Drinkwater scrutinized her, eager to see what the Russian commander would do in response.

For several minutes the *Gremyashchi* continued to bear down on them, seemingly contemptuous of the smaller British frigate almost in her track.

'Run out the guns!'

Drinkwater's order was carried to the gun-deck below and he could feel the rumbles of the gun-tracks as their iron-shod wheels carried the black muzzles out through the ports. Drinkwater could imagine the scene below decks with Frey eagerly dancing up and down the line of guns, urging them spiked round on the target; their crews would be straining on tackles, their gun-captains spinning the breech screws to elevate the muzzles. As they completed their exertions, the gasping crews would squat, kneel or crouch beside the monsters they served, the captains kneeling behind the line of guns, squinting along their brute length, the flint-lock lanyards taut in their left hands, their right hands held up so that Frey could see them report their cannon ready.

Less than half a mile now separated the *Gremyashchi* from *Andromeda*. The Russian continued to bear down before the wind under topsails and topgallants, her dark brown sides as yet unbroken by open ports. Then a brief white cloud appeared on her port bow and hung for a moment, running along with the Russian ship and gradually dispersing as the noise of the discharge was blown down towards the waiting *Andromeda*.

The closed gun-ports seemed to signal an acceptance of *Andromeda*'s right to dictate terms, for a moment later she sheered away to starboard, heeling over as her yards were braced sharply round and she settled on a course to the north-north-west, parallel to *Andromeda*'s heading.

'She's making off,' said a surprised Birkbeck. Drinkwater was raking the Russian ship with his telescope. The *Gremyashchi* was broadside onto them now and he could see her mizen mast clearly, with her blue and white colours at the spanker peak.

'By God, do you look at that!' It was Hyde, whose scarlet nonchalance had graced the quarterdeck since clearing for action. All along the *Gremyashchi*'s port side, the gun ports opened and she too bared her fangs, despite the leeward heel. Then, in a ragged attempt at simultaneity, Rakov, whose figure Drinkwater had located standing hat-in-hand upon her rail, discharged his guns. The shots raised a line of splashes ahead of the hove-to *Andromeda*.

'And what is all that about?' Hyde asked.

In the glass Drinkwater saw Rakov wave his hat flamboyantly above his head and jump back down on to his own quarterdeck. 'That, Mr Hyde, is to let us know we did not intimidate him.' Drinkwater pocketed the telescope and called his messenger. 'Mr Dunn! Be so kind as to tell Mr Frey to run in the starboard battery and secure the guns. He will have to draw all charges.'

'Run in the guns and draw all charges, aye, aye, sir.'

'We cannot afford to waste any powder or shot,' he remarked to Birkbeck as the master came across the deck from the binnacle.

'D'you wish to run back towards Santa Cruz, sir?'

Drinkwater cast another look at the *Gremyashchi*. Her stern was square onto them now and there was little sign of her manoeuvring again. A nasty suspicion was forming in Drinkwater's mind. He nodded at the master. 'Yes, if you please.'

Marlowe came aft as the rumbling and vibration in their boot soles told where the 12-pounders below were being run in again.

'He's off after other quarry by the look of it, I'd say, sir.'

'My guess exactly, Frederic,' Drinkwater concurred.

'Looking for what you call the Antwerp squadron, d'you think?'

Drinkwater nodded. 'I cannot think of any other reason for his being here.'

'That rather shortens the odds against us, then.'

'Yes,' said Drinkwater, as the main yards were hauled round parallel with those on the fore and mizen masts and *Andromeda* began to gather headway again. 'Yes, it may well do if he has orders to engage us. He certainly wasn't about to hang about and parley.'

For a moment both men stood side by side, watching the exertions of the men at the braces, trimming the yards almost square across the ship as *Andromeda* answered her helm and swung to port, to run downwind again, heading for Flores which loomed five miles away.

'On the other hand,' mused Drinkwater, 'we are supposed to be allies.'

'Those shots across our bow didn't look very friendly,' laughed Marlowe ruefully.

'No, they didn't, but Rakov might have been trying to cow us.'

'Why should he do that, sir?'

'Oh, I don't know,' Drinkwater replied wearily, unwilling to explain to Marlowe the hostility he had felt from the Russian when Rakov discovered he was the British officer responsible for the destruction of the *Suvorov*. 'It's just a feeling I have,' he added conciliatorily, seeing Frey come up from the gun-deck. 'Perhaps another time, Mr Frey.'

'I rather hope not, sir: they were 18-pounders at least.'

The knot of officers laughed a trifle uneasily. 'Poor old Ashton,' remarked Hyde. 'He's missed all the fun.'

Lieutenant Da Silva had conducted Ashton to the Governor's undistinguished residence where the British officer was received with every courtesy including a glass of wine. Da Silva introduced the Governor, Dom Miguel Gaspar Viera Batata, his secretary, whose name appeared to be Soares, and a tall thin man in a black worsted suit, silver buckled shoes and the elegant affectations of an English fop.

The Englishman introduced himself. 'I am Edmund Gilbert, Mr Ashton, British consul at Angra. By good fortune I am visiting

Dom Batata at this time.' Ashton had no idea where Angra was, but his bow was elegant enough and it took them all in.

'Your servant, gentlemen. Lieutenant Josiah Ashton of His Britannic Majesty's frigate *Andromeda*, gentlemen, Captain Nathaniel Drinkwater commanding.' He took Drinkwater's letter from his breast and handed it to Batata.

'Thank you, Lieutenant.' Batata took the letter, slit the wafer and began to read while Soares served the wine. When he had finished reading, Batata passed the letter to Gilbert who blew his gaunt cheeks out and expelled his breath slowly, as if this was an essential accompaniment to the process.

'Well, well, well,' he concluded, refolding the letter and returning it to Batata who passed it directly to Soares.

'May I . . .?' Gilbert sought the Governor's permission which was granted by a grave nod of Batata's head. 'Do I gather from this missive, Lieutenant . . . I beg your pardon, sir, I have forgotten . . .'

'Ashton, Mr Gilbert,' Ashton prompted quickly, colouring uncertainly.

'Yes, yes. Well, Mr Ashton, do I infer your commander, Nathaniel What's-his-name, believes Napoleon Bonaparte is to be exiled here, on the island of Flores?'

'Yes, sir,' replied Ashton, slightly mollified by Gilbert's inability to remember Drinkwater's name and accepting a refill of his glass from Soares, 'if he ain't here already.'

'Here? Already? 'Pon my soul, Mr Ashton, this is the first hint we've heard that Napoleon Bonaparte *ain't*, as you say, Emperor of the French!'

'He has abdicated, gentlemen,' Ashton explained, inflated by his assumption of the role of harbinger.

'You are our winged Mercury.' Gilbert echoed Ashton's thoughts with a thin smile.

'King Louis has returned to France.'

'Then the war is over?' asked Batata.

'Indeed yes, sir. In Europe, at least.'

'Ah yes, your country is still at war with the Americans. Now these other ships, Lieutenant, we have no knowledge of them, have we?' Gilbert shrugged and a query to his secretary by Batata produced a negative shrug from Soares. Batata turned back to Ashton. 'We have no knowledge of any other ships other than merchantmen . . .'

'And is there no news at all in the archipelago, of preparations for the reception of Bonaparte, gentlemen?' Ashton asked as Soares bent over his glass again.

Batata shrugged and shook his head. Gilbert was more emphatic. 'I have heard nothing on Terceira and am certain we should have done by now, if such a thing was meditated.'

'Very well,' Ashton bowed, 'thank you for your time, gentlemen. I am sorry to have troubled you.'

'It is no trouble, Lieutenant,' Dom Batata said.

Gilbert addressed the Governor in fluent Portuguese and Batata nodded in agreement, then Gilbert turned to Ashton. 'Mr Ashton, I have been here for ten days attending to some business with the master of the brig *Mary Digby* of Sunderland. If your Captain Drinkwater would condescend to convey me back to Angra, we could quickly ascertain if the packet from Lisbon has brought orders relevant to the fate of Bonaparte.'

'Well, sir, I suppose Captain Drinkwater will have no objection . . .'

'Good, then the matter is settled. Give me a quarter of an hour, and I shall be with you.'

Da Silva accompanied Ashton and Gilbert back to the beach, with two servants bearing between them Mr Gilbert's portmanteau. As they approached the boat, Ashton noticed two of the launch's seamen sauntering ahead of them, each carrying a canvas bag.

'If you will excuse me, Mr Gilbert, I will just get on ahead and prepare the boat for you.' Ashton proferred the excuse and, without waiting for a reply, walked briskly on. A moment later he overtook the two seamen, one of whom he recognized as the launch's stroke oarsmen.

'Shaw!' he called and the man turned round as Ashton hurried up. 'Shaw, what the bloody hell d'you think you are doing out of the boat?'

'We was sent up by, er . . .'

'Went to get fresh bread, sir,' the other man said, holding up one of the canvas bags.

'Who the devil said you could leave the boat?'

'Well, sir, we only sent to get bread, sir, had a tarpaulin muster and reckoned we could afford a few loaves . . .'

'Let me see in those bags.'

'It's only bread, sir . . .'

'Let me see, damn you!' Furious, Ashton pulled the loaves out and hurled them into the water.

'Sir! We paid for them!'

'Aye and you paid for these too, I daresay!' Ashton triumphantly drew two bottles from the bottom of the bag and turned to Shaw. 'Empty yours too,' he commanded.

'Sir!' Shaw protested.

'Empty it, damn you and be quick!' Ashton was aware of Gilbert approaching as Shaw upended the bag. Four richly smelling and warm loaves fell out and two green bottles followed. One hit a stone and smashed with a tinkle, staining the sand with wine. Ashton kicked both loaves and broken glass into the water where screaming gulls were already congregating round the floating debris of the first lot of bread. He hurled the two remaining bottles after them while the fishermen tending an adjacent *canoa*, watched in astonished silence.

'Now get back to the boat and be damned quick about it!' Ashton hissed. He turned as nonchalantly as he could as Gilbert came up to him.

'Trouble, Lieutenant?'

'Not really, Mr Gilbert. Not what I'd call trouble . . .'

'And what would you call trouble, Lieutenant Ashton?' asked Gilbert, spurning the broken neck of one of the bottles with his foot, and looking at the ravenous gulls tearing the loaves apart, their wings beating with the fury of their assault on the abandoned bread.

'Oh, I don't know,' Ashton said, utterly discomfited.

'I suppose finding Bonaparte sitting on Terceira would be trouble of a real nature, don't you think?' offered Gilbert.

'I suppose it would, yes.'

They had reached the boat by then, and Shaw and his mate were resuming their places as oarsmen. Midshipman Paine who had obviously been dozing in the stern-sheets with his hat over his eyes, stirred himself at the commotion in the boat, for Shaw was clearly explaining what had happened, and the boat's crew were staring over their shoulders, sullen and resentful.

'Mr Paine, let us have a hand here, to get this gear aboard.' The two marines posted as sentries came forward. One was Sergeant McCann. As two seamen came out of the boat to pass Gilbert's portmanteau along, Ashton drew McCann aside. 'Sergeant, I thought I made it quite clear that the boat's crew were not permitted to leave the launch?' he asked furiously.

McCann looked down at the lieutenant's hand on his arm and remained silent. 'Sergeant, don't you trifle with me, damn you. You heard what I said.' He shook McCann's arm, barely able to control himself.

'You ordered the boat's crew to remain with the boat, sir, but Mr Paine gave permission for two delegates to nip ashore for some food. The men had brought a little money, d'you see, sir.'

'Sergeant,' insisted Ashton, hissing into McCann's face, 'they had purchased liquor . . .'

'They were not alone, then, Mr Ashton,' McCann snarled, his temper fraying to match the sea-officer's, as he caught the whiff of Ashton's breath.

'I shall have you flogged for your impudence, McCann, when I get you back aboard! Now get in the boat, you damned Yankee bugger.'

McCann coloured; for a moment he contemplated responding, thought better of it and shut his mouth. Then he turned on his heel, nodded to the private soldier to precede him and clambered over the gunwhale.

'All sorted out now?' asked Gilbert matter-off-factly, with his thin, supercilious smile.

'Do mind yourself on the thwarts, Mr Gilbert,' Ashton replied equivocally, waving the consul into the boat.

'After you, my dear fellow.'

'Convention demands you go first, Mr Gilbert.'

'Does it now. Well we had better not flout convention then, had we?'

Five minutes later, the launch was pulling clear of the reef, leaving the harbour in comparative peace, for the gulls had destroyed the loaves and only a few continued to quarrel over the last remnants. As for the watching fishermen, they shook their heads in incredulous wonder and resumed their work.

A Matter of Discipline

The recovery of the launch proved a tediously tricky business in the lively sea running off Flores, despite the lee made by the ship. While Marlowe and Birkbeck struggled with the heavy boat, Drinkwater surveyed his unexpected passenger who had scrambled up the ship's side after Ashton. Clearly Mr Gilbert, whatever else he was, was a nimble fellow, not unfamiliar with ships.

'You wish for a passage to Terceira, Mr Gilbert?' Drinkwater asked, after the ritual of introduction.

Gilbert nodded. 'In case word has arrived there concerning Bonaparte,' the British consul tersely replied.

'Yes, yes, I understand, sir, but my orders indicate he will be brought to Flores,' said Drinkwater, stretching the truth to buttress his argument, 'and I fear if I abandon this station,' he paused and shrugged, 'well, who knows?'

Gilbert frowned. 'But you are here to guard him, are you not?' and then Gilbert's quick intellect grasped the import of Ashton's questions about other men-of-war in the offing. 'Ah, you are expecting other ships, ships which might interfere with arrangements for the accommodation of Boney.'

It was said as a statement of fact and Drinkwater nodded. 'There is, I understand,' he replied, 'a conspiracy afoot in France to have him taken to Canada . . .'

Gilbert's eyebrows rose in comprehension. 'Dear God!' he murmured.

'I see you are as apprehensive as I am.'

'Quite so . . .'

Both men remained a moment in silence, then Drinkwater suggested, 'I can have you put ashore again here.'

Gilbert shook his head. 'I should really return to Angra.' He paused, then added, 'May I take your boat? She will make the passage under sail, I daresay?' he looked at the launch somewhat dubiously.

'It must be upwards of forty leagues . . .'

'No matter, your boat is up to it.' Drinkwater looked askance at Gilbert; he was clearly a man of resilience and resolution. In the waist the launch was swinging slowly across the ship to its chocks on the booms. 'Very well,' Drinkwater agreed, 'she is provisioned for two days, perhaps you will be kind enough to replenish her when you arrive; we are precious short of stores. Some fruit would be most welcome,' he said, and raising his voice he called, 'Mr Marlowe! Have the launch put back in the water!' Drinkwater ignored the moment's hesitation and the sudden irritated stares of the labouring seamen who were quickly ordered to reverse their efforts; he summoned Ashton.

'Mr Ashton, run down to my cabin and take a look at the chart on my desk. A course for Terceira; you may take Mr Gilbert back to Angra in the launch.'

'Sir, if I might suggest something.'

'Well, what is it?'

Ashton edged round to attempt to exclude Gilbert from his remark to the captain. 'I should like to lay a formal charge against Sergeant McCann.'

'Oh, for heaven's sake, Mr Ashton, now is hardly the moment. What has Sergeant McCann done?'

'Disobeyed my orders, sir,' Ashton hissed intensely.

Drinkwater felt a great weariness overcome him; he was tired of these minor problems, tired of Ashton and the whole confounded pack of these contentious and troublesome men. He was tempted to consign Ashton to the devil, but mastered this intemperate and dangerous instinct; instead he caught sight of Lieutenant Hyde and called him over.

'Mr Hyde, Mr Ashton here says that Sergeant McCann disobeyed his orders.' He turned to Ashton. 'Perhaps you would tell us how this occurred.'

'I left orders that no one was to leave the boat while I waited upon the Governor. Upon my return I found two men had defied me and been into the town . . .'

'*Two* men, d'you say?' Drinkwater asked.

'Yes, and . . .'

162

'To what purpose did these two men go into town?' Drinkwater persisted.

'That is the point, sir, they had been into town and purchased liquor.'

'What liquor?' Hyde asked.

'What does it matter what liquor? They had disobeyed my orders and left the boat . . .'

'Were sentries posted?' Hyde pressed.

'Yes, of course, under your Sergeant McCann . . .'

'But Sergeant McCann was only in charge of the marines. Who commanded the boat?'

'Well, Midshipman Paine.'

'Then why isn't he in the soup?'

'I think we should have a word with Midshipman Paine,' broke in Drinkwater. 'Be so kind as to send for him.'

It took a few moments to fish Paine back out of the launch which was now bobbing alongside again. He reported to the trio of grave-faced officers on the quarterdeck and was asked for an explanation.

'Whilst you lay in Santa Cruz, Mr Paine, were you not aware that Mr Ashton had given orders to the effect that no one should go ashore?' Drinkwater asked.

'Well, sir,' Paine replied, 'yes and no . . .'

'What the devil . . .?' began Ashton, but Drinkwater put out a hand to stop him going further.

'That is too equivocating, sir,' Drinkwater said, his voice hard and level. 'Kindly explain yourself.'

'Well, sir, I understood Mr Ashton to have said that the boat's crew were not to go ashore. When Shaw asked me if, on behalf of the men, he and Ticknell might not run up to the town to buy some fresh bread, I consulted Sergeant McCann and he felt that it would not be contrary to the spirit of your orders if just two men went. The boat's crew had a tarpaulin muster . . .'

'What d'you mean "would not be contrary to the spirit of my orders"?' demanded Ashton, 'you knew damned well I meant no one could go ashore.'

Paine stood his ground. 'I understood you did not want shore-leave granted, sir, but the men could not desert and had taken money on trust from their ship-mates. I did not see the harm . . .'

'Very well, gentlemen.' Drinkwater silenced the midshipman and strove to keep the exasperation out of his voice. 'It is clear this

163

matter cannot be resolved quickly. It is also clear that we cannot hang about here dithering. Have the launch swung inboard again; we will take Mr Gilbert to Angra ourselves, and the sooner the better. Do you pass word to Mr Marlowe, Mr Ashton; Mr Paine, I shall speak to you later. Mr Hyde, thank you.'

Ashton seemed to hesitate a moment, but then the officers broke away and Drinkwater crossed the deck to where Gilbert awaited his departure, masking his curiosity in a thinly veiled attempt at indifference.

'My apologies, Mr Gilbert, I have changed my mind; we shall run you to Terceira in the ship.'

'Thank you, Captain,' Gilbert replied, smiling, 'I cannot pretend that a long passage in an open boat is much to my liking, though I did not wish to inconvenience you.'

'That was most considerate of you.' Drinkwater returned the smile. 'My chief anxiety is that I do not miss any rendezvous of enemy ships by being absent from my station. The whole thing,' he confessed, 'is something of a hazard.'

'Is such a rendezvous likely now the war is over?'

'Is the war over, Mr Gilbert? I wish I was so sure. Anyway, the die is cast.'

Both men watched while the tackles were hooked on to the launch again. Drinkwater intensely disliked giving orders and counter-orders, for nothing created distrust between officers and men more than such obvious uncertainty in the former.

'I beg your pardon, Captain Drinkwater,' said Gilbert, 'but does your change of heart have anything to do with the little incident ashore?'

'What incident?'

'Well, it is none of my affair, but I observed some breach of discipline which gave rise to your Lieutenant Ashton remonstrating with two of your sailors. They appeared to have offended in some way by purchasing bread . . .'

'Bread?'

'Yes, they had a bag apiece, which Lieutenant Ashton kicked into the harbour. He seems a rather headstrong and intemperate young man.'

'Was there no liquor involved?' Drinkwater asked.

'There may have been a few bottles of wine,' Gilbert replied, 'but my chief impression was of a quantity of bread.'

'Thank you, Mr Gilbert. Perhaps you would like to make yourself as comfortable as possible in my cabin.'

'That is most kind of you, Captain. I can assure you that your cabin will be luxurious compared with the bilges of your launch,' Gilbert said, smiling.

The overnight passage east-south-east towards Terceira cost Drinkwater the remains of his equanimity. Already consumed by anxiety and speculation about the sudden appearance of the *Gremyashchi*, this unwanted diversion of almost two hundred miles to the eastward was a sore trial. Had he not so desperately wanted news of the whereabouts of Bonaparte, he would have returned Gilbert to Santa Cruz, but at least providence had ensured that *Andromeda* had arrived off Flores at the same time that the English consul had been visiting the island, and they had not had to resort to communicating with a Portuguese vice-consul who, whatever assurance Drinkwater had given Ashton, while perfectly reliable, would not have been so capable of supporting an informed, speculative debate.

However, the presence of the *Gremyashchi* confirmed the veracity of Hortense's intelligence, and the action of Rakov had clearly been as intimidatory as his orders allowed him. But while the appearance of the Russian frigate removed a major doubt in Drinkwater's mind, it caused another: Rakov's purposeful withdrawal to the north and west suggested he too was to rendezvous with the 'Antwerp squadron', and while he was doing this, *Andromeda* was waltzing off to the eastwards with a passenger!

As night shrouded the ship, Drinkwater paced the quarterdeck angry and frustrated, feeling the advantage he had so assiduously cultivated being thrown away with every cable *Andromeda* sailed towards the eastern Azores. In his heart he was doubly annoyed with Lieutenant Ashton.

It was, Drinkwater concluded, a mean thought to ascribe his current woes to the young officer, but he was meanly inclined that evening, reluctant to go down to his cabin which he would have to share with Gilbert, yet irritated by his tumbling thoughts which kept him pacing and fidgeting about the quarterdeck. What was he to make of this damnable business at Santa Cruz? It would have been a silly incident, he had no doubt, but on the one hand lay the argument for order and discipline, and upon the other that for toleration and humanity. And he, as commander, amid his other preoccupations, was obliged to reconcile the essentially irreconcilable.

He paced up and down, only vaguely aware that the watch was about to change with a flurry of activity, the flitting of dark shapes about the quarterdeck, a shuffle of figures around the helm partially lit by the dim glow from the binnacle. He sensed, rather than saw Marlowe on deck, engaged in discussing something with the shorter, slightly stooped figure of Birkbeck. It was then that the idea struck Drinkwater.

He stopped pacing, turned to windward and barked a short, monosyllabic laugh. Coming on deck late, just as eight bells struck, Midshipman Dunn caught sight of the captain and heard the odd sound, stored it away to add to the cockpit's fund of stories about the eccentricity of Old Nat. As for Drinkwater, he turned on his heel, crossed the deck and confronted the first lieutenant. It was too dark by now to see the expression of satisfaction upon his face.

'Mr Marlowe, may I have a word with you?'

'Of course, sir. As a matter of fact, I wanted to speak with you.'

'Oh, what about?'

'I have just been telling the master here, I think I have located the leak.'

'That is very satisfactory, at least I hope it is. Is the matter serious?'

'Serious enough: it's a dockyard job, but we may be able to do something to reduce it.'

'Does it compromise our present situation?'

'Not as long as we have men to man pumps, no, sir, but it is likely to get worse. I'm afraid the leak is caused by devil-bolts.'

'God's bones,' Drinkwater swore quietly. The dockyard practice of making repairs with short and inadequate screw-bolts had once been common. It was a mark of the corruption of a great public service, the indolence of its overseers who grew fat on the myriad minor economies they practised widely, and their indifference to the fate of the ships of war placed in their hands for refitting. It was widely believed in the sea-service that ships had foundered in heavy weather owing to their working in a seaway, their planking springing because it was not properly secured to the framework of the ribs.

The loss of HMS *Blenheim* in the Indian Ocean, homeward bound from the Hooghly with Admiral Sir Thomas Troubridge on board, was attributed to this cause and the resulting scandal had, it was generally thought, ended this particular dockyard malpractice. Of course, it was impossible to say when the bolts now causing *Andromeda*'s leak had been fitted. Probably some time ago. The slow decomposition of the iron and its infection of the surrounding oak progressively weakened any fastening, even when payed and covered with sheets of anti-fouling copper, but a short bolt, with insufficient of its screwed shank penetrating the futtock behind the planking, would deteriorate and spring within a few years, and such bolts were cheaper and more easily fitted substitutes than the effective oak trenails or heavy copper bolts.

The news somewhat dimmed Drinkwater's satisfaction in having resolved his earlier problem, but it was at least satisfactory to know the cause, and neither problem would vanish unless something were to be done about each of them.

'Well gentlemen, better the devil you know, I suppose.' This little witticism was greeted by respectful chuckles. 'Perhaps you will have a look at the area tomorrow, Mr Birkbeck?'

'Aye, aye, sir.'

'There is another matter though, Mr Marlowe,' Drinkwater went on, 'one that I'd be obliged to you for a moment of your time to discuss.'

'Yes, of course, sir.'

'I'll take my leave then, sir,' said Birkbeck.

'Yes. Goodnight, Mr Birkbeck.'

Drinkwater led Marlowe across the deck to the weather rail where they stood staring to windward, out of earshot of the men at the helm.

'I don't know if you are aware of it, but there was some sort of incident at Santa Cruz today. I gather Ashton left orders that no one was to go ashore, then two men went into the town for provisions and Ashton accused Sergeant McCann of disobedience.'

'I had heard something of the matter. Hyde was rather inflamed about it; he had heard McCann's side of things and said Paine was in command of the boat.'

'Yes, I had gathered that too. Ashton seems to have regarded his instruction as explicit and all-embracing, which is undoubtedly what was intended. Nevertheless, McCann seems to be implicated and Ashton is demanding a flogging for him. I expect Mr Paine was prevailed upon to release two men to get some fresh bread on the grounds that two men did not constitute a boat's crew.'

'And the two men brought back some bottles of wine as well as bread,' added Marlowe.

'Yes, I think you have the scene in your mind's eye. Ashton, of course, painted the picture of a foraging expedition intent on acquiring liquor. The fault, of course, lies with Paine, which is unfortunate, and Ashton no doubt put fuel on the flames with his eagerness to punish the defiance to his order. This, I imagine, is where McCann got involved.'

'I heard from Hyde that Ashton called McCann, a "Yankee bugger".'

'A Yankee bugger?'

'McCann's from Loyalist American stock, sir,' Marlowe explained, 'like Admiral Hallowell.'

'Was McCann provoked?' Drinkwater asked quickly.

'I don't know,' Marlowe replied. 'Knowing Ashton,' he paused, 'well, who knows? Probably.'

'That is what I want you to find out, Frederic. I want you to hold an enquiry tomorrow. We can send Frey in with the boat taking Gilbert ashore and you shall gather evidence in the wardroom. Report to me when you have concluded . . . by tomorrow evening at the latest, by which time we shall, I hope, be resuming our station off Flores. Do you understand?'

'Yes,' said Marlowe.

'It's another chance, Frederic, to rid yourself of this man's influence.'

'He may see it as something else.'

'He may see it how he likes; I am instructing you to carry out this duty and you are the first lieutenant of the ship. Whatever complexion Mr Ashton may wish to put upon the case is quite irrelevant, but it will do you no harm either way. Oh, and by the bye, either way I want the matter examined with scrupulous fairness.'

'Of course, sir,' said Marlowe.

'That way any opinion Ashton may have to the contrary will be conscionably groundless.'

The wardroom presented an untypical appearance next morning, for Marlowe had ordered the table cleared completely and all personal items, which in the usual run of events would have cluttered the place, removed into the cabins of the individual officers. The announcement of this requirement was made at breakfast to which all, except for Frey, the officer of the watch, were summoned. The usually degenerately homely room now took on a forbidding appearance.

'What's afoot?' Hyde asked, aware that some sort of effort was required on his part and that his entire day was being set awry at an early moment by this disruption of routine.

'I am charged with examining the circumstances surrounding the incident which occurred on the mole at Santa Cruz yesterday . . .' began Marlowe, only to be interrupted by an incredulous Ashton who rose and asked:

'You are *what*?'

'Oh do sit down Ashton,' said Hyde laconically, 'and pray don't be too tiresome, I have other things to do.'

'The day you actually accomplish them will be witness to a damned miracle,' Ashton snapped unpleasantly. 'I asked a question and I demand an answer.'

'I think, Josiah,' Marlowe cut in quickly, 'you should heed the advice you have just been given. You shall demand nothing, and sit down at once.' Marlowe took no further interest in Ashton and turned to Hyde. 'I wish you to sit with me, Hyde. We will commence our examination at two bells; Mr Birkbeck, I should be obliged if you would relieve Ashton of his watch this forenoon, in order that we can carry out this duty without delay. He may substitute for you after noon.'

'Very well, Mr Marlowe.' Birkbeck drew his watch from his pocket and stared at it a moment, then he rose, went briefly into his cabin, reappeared and went on deck.

As soon as he had gone, Ashton began to expostulate. 'Look here, Freddy, is this some kind of a joke, because if it is . . .'

'It's no joke, Josiah. I'd be obliged if you would clear that boat-cloak and bundle of papers and remain in your cabin until called.'

'By God, I'll . . .!'

Ashton stood up again with such force that he cracked his head on the deck-beams above and ducked in reaction with a further torrent of oaths. Then, seeing he was cornered, he snatched up his cloak and papers and withdrew into his cabin, shutting the door with a bang.

169

'Knocked some sense into himself at last,' remarked Hyde with a grin as Frey entered the wardroom, his hair tousled.

'Hullo, I hope you lubbers haven't done with breakfast yet; I'm ravenous. Sam!' The messman having been summoned, Frey was soon spooning up a quantity of burgoo and molasses, drinking coffee and pronouncing himself a new man, whereupon Marlowe opened the proceedings by summoning Ashton from his cabin. The third lieutenant was quizzed as to the exact nature of his orders and Hyde noted down his reply. He was then told to cool his heels in his cabin, to which order he resentfully complied, giving Marlowe a malevolent glare.

Midshipman Paine was then called and permitted to sit at the table. He admitted having been asked by the boat's crew if they could nominate two of their number to obtain some fresh bread.

'Why do you suppose the boat's crew wished to purchase bread, Mr Paine?' Marlowe asked.

'Because they were hungry, sir, and could smell fresh-baked bread from a bakery across the harbour.'

'And how did you think they were going to pay for this bread, the scent of which so fortuitously wafted across the harbour?' queried Hyde.

'Why sir, from money which they had brought with them.'

'Isn't that a little unusual?' asked Marlowe.

'That they had money, sir?'

'Yes.'

Paine shrugged, 'I didn't think so, sir. I believe it was no more than a few pence.'

'Did any of the marines contribute?'

'I'm not sure, sir. I don't think so.'

'Where was Sergeant McCann at this time?'

'He had posted himself on the beach as one of the sentinels, sir.'

'So he was not party to any of the discussion in the boat.'

Paine shook his head. 'No, sir, though it wasn't really a discussion.'

'Did you think there was any ulterior motive in the men's request, Mr Paine?'

'You mean . . .?'

'I mean, did it, or did it not occur to you that the men might have come ashore with ready money in order to buy liquor?' Marlowe asked.

Paine flushed. 'Well, sir, yes, it did occur to me, but the smell of the bread persuaded me that . . .' The midshipman's voice tailed off into silence.

'How many men contributed money towards this bread?' Marlowe enquired.

'I can't be absolutely certain, sir, but about a dozen.'

There was a brief pause while Hyde made his notes and then he looked up and asked, 'Did you make a contribution towards the bread, Mr Paine?'

Paine coughed with embarrassment and his Adam's apple bobbed uncomfortably. 'Yes,' he murmured.

'Speak up, damn it,' prompted Hyde, dipping his pen.

Paine coughed again and answered in a clearer voice, 'Yes sir.'

'And it *was* bread you were investing in, I take it?'

'Oh yes, sir.'

'Why?'

'I was hungry, sir.' A thought appeared to occur to the midshipman and he added, 'I was jolly hungry, and I thought the men must be, too, since they had had a long hard pull from the ship, sir.'

'So you thought that justified disobeying Mr Ashton's order?'

Paine's mouth twisted with unhappiness. 'No, not exactly, sir . . .'

'Then do enlighten us, Mr Paine,' pressed Marlowe, 'what *exactly* you did think.'

Paine relinquished the role of martyr and confessed: 'I thought if only two men went, they would soon be back.'

'Soon be back . . .?' prompted Marlowe, his face expectant.

'You know . . . before Mr Ashton returned.'

Both officers sat back and exchanged glances. 'So you deliberately disobeyed Mr Ashton's order?'

'In a manner of speaking, yes, sir.'

'Why?'

Having placed himself at the mercy of his interrogators, Paine's attitude hardened and he fought his corner. 'I thought no harm would come of it.'

'But harm has come of it, Mr Paine,' argued Marlowe.

'Yes, sir, and I regret that and I take full responsibility for it. As a matter of fact, sir, I thought Mr Ashton's order unreasonable. The men could not desert, for the place is an island and for two men out

171

of sixteen to run ashore for some bread, seemed, in my opinion, reasonable enough.'

Marlowe pressed his finger tips together before his face, sat back and regarded the midshipman in silence. Hyde pursed his lips and made a soft blowing sound.

'I had no idea Mr Ashton would make an issue of the matter with McCann, sir. I cannot allow the sergeant of marines to be involved. The truth is that having let Shaw and Ticknell go, I confess I made myself comfortable in the stern-sheets and was roused by the kerfuffle when Mr Ashton returned with the passenger.' Paine finally fell silent and looked down at his threadbare knees.

'Well,' began Marlowe, 'it seems Mr Ashton's wrath was misdirected. You realize what this means, Mr Paine?'

'The gunner's daughter, sir?' Paine's face twisted with apprehension.

'At the very least, my lad.'

Paine drew himself up in his seat. 'Very well, sir.'

'You may carry on. The matter will be referred to the Captain with our recommendations.'

Paine got to his feet. 'Aye, aye, sir.'

When he had retired, Marlowe turned to Hyde and said, 'That would seem to wrap the matter up then.'

'No, Mr Marlowe,' said Hyde, stirring himself, 'it won't do at all. Of course Paine must be punished, but Ashton's treatment of McCann remains reprehensible.'

'That's as may be, Hyde, but the crime was disobedience to Ashton's order and it was Paine, not McCann who was culpable. Ashton's intemperate conduct was unfortunate, but McCann is only a non-commissioned officer of marines.'

Hyde drew in his breath sharply. 'Mr Marlowe, that non-commissioned officer of marines once held a commission in a Provincial regiment and fought for King and Country as, I suspect, Lieutenant Ashton has only dreamed of. He was insulted, called a Yankee bugger, neither of which accusations can be substantiated and for which, had they been used to me, I would have demanded satisfaction!'

'I daresay you would,' observed Marlowe drily, 'but they weren't addressed to you. Anyway, what do you suppose we can do about it?'

'Get Ashton to apologize,' said Hyde in a voice loud enough to be heard on the far side of the flimsy bulkhead dividing the dining area of the officers' accommodation from their personal sleeping quarters. It proved too much for the eavesdropping Ashton, who wrenched the door open and made his appearance at this moment.

'Damn you, Hyde!' he snarled, 'You heard my orders and you've found your culprit. What more d'you want?'

'Well, old fellow,' said Hyde leaning back in his chair, 'since you ask, an apology to McCann.'

'I'll be damned first!'

'Very likely, but Ashton am I correct in thinking you flung the bread, not to mention four miserable bottles of wine – four, mark you, about the number you would drink in a good evening at Spithead, to be shared between at least a dozen men – that you flung this bread into the harbour?'

'Of course.'

'Why "of course"?' persisted Hyde.

'Because they had no business buying it.'

'Ashton, have you never drunk French brandy?'

'Why yes, but . . .'

'Which you had no business buying, I daresay . . .' Hyde sneered and Ashton coloured, realizing he had taken the bait. Beside Hyde, Marlowe smiled.

'And which you would have defended as your own, no doubt,' Marlowe added, whereupon Ashton shot the first lieutenant a look of such pure venom that Hyde was certain Marlowe had hit upon some incident in their mutual past.

'So you will not apologize to McCann?' Hyde pressed.

'The devil I will!'

Hyde completed his note. Marlowe sat forward and closed the proceedings. 'I believe we asked Sergeant McCann to hold himself ready for questioning. I do not think that will be necessary at this juncture.'

'I shall go and tell him so,' said Hyde, rising and fixing his eyes on Ashton. 'You are a lesser man than I had hitherto thought, Josiah. McCann would have forgiven you a momentary loss of temper. By refusing to withdraw your remark, you not only affirm it, you make him an inferior, and I am not persuaded he is. Certainly not now.'

Hyde swept from the wardroom without a backward glance, leaving Marlowe with a fuming and humiliated Ashton. For a moment the two officers sat in silence then Ashton rose and leaned over Marlowe.

'I wish,' he said menacingly, 'I had words adequate to describe what I feel for you, Frederic, and I wish I could express the pity I feel for Sarah!'

But if Ashton thought the contempt in his voice could intimidate Marlowe, mention of his sister was a sad miscalculation. Marlowe's spirit was no longer cowed, and he stood slowly and with a new-found dignity to confront his future brother-in-law. 'I pity her too, Josiah, but I have at least the consolation Sarah chose me.'

And with this Parthian shot Marlowe left the wardroom to report to Drinkwater. As for Ashton, he turned to find Frey standing in the open doorway to his cabin regarding him with a cold stare.

Chapter Thirteen

A Long Wait

'Angra do Heroismo,' observed Birkbeck, staring through his glass at the principal port on the island of Terceira. Once again *Andromeda* was hove-to and awaiting one of her boats, the port quarter-boat commonly called the red cutter, which had been sent in under the command of Lieutenant Frey to convey Mr Gilbert ashore. It was anticipated that it would be absent for some time and in the interim Captain Drinkwater was in his cabin, dining early with Mr Marlowe and discussing the fate of Mr Midshipman Paine, who slouched disconsolately about the quarterdeck, awaiting the captain's verdict.

Although relieved as officer of the watch by Lieutenant Ashton, Birkbeck remained on deck, watching the red cutter as it swooped over the wave crests and vanished in each succeeding trough. Its worn lugsails were only a shade lighter than the grey of the sea, which had forsaken its kindly blue colour after the wind had swung back into the south-west again. Although only a moderate breeze, this had first veiled the sun, then at noon brought in a layer of thickening overcast which presaged rain and turned the sea a sullen hue.

Finally, Birkbeck could see the cutter no more as it passed into Angra. He shut his glass with a decisive snap and made his way below.

In the cabin, Drinkwater toyed with his wine glass as Marlowe concluded his report.

'So, sir, the nub of the matter is that Paine disobeyed Mr Ashton's explicit order and while Ashton may have acted in an intemperate manner, falsely accusing Sergeant McCann of being the culprit, it is Paine who must be punished.'

Drinkwater grunted. 'Yes, I suppose so. What have you in mind?'

Marlowe considered the matter for a moment and said, 'A dozen strokes, sir.'

'A pity. I thought the boy had promise. This will be a humiliation for him.'

'I had thought of that, sir. It doesn't have to be done over a gun. I can turn the midshipmen out of the cockpit . . .'

'Or the officers out of the wardroom. But the purpose of the punishment is as much to deter others as to strike at the guilty.'

'The others will all know, sir.'

'Yes, that is true. Very well then,' Drinkwater concluded with a sigh, 'you must do as you see fit.'

'There remains the problem of Ashton. Hyde thinks he should apologize to McCann for calling him a Yankee bugger.'

'I must say I rather agree. Notwithstanding the fact that Ashton set this whole thing off by demanding a flogging for McCann.'

'Well, in the light of our findings that would be outrageous.'

'I agree entirely. Ashton's claim is indefensible and I won't have officers abusing the privilege rank gives them no matter how high and mighty they consider themselves.'

Marlowe held his peace and waited while Drinkwater came to his own verdict. 'Very well; if Ashton will not withdraw his remark to McCann, I shall make my disapproval known by other means.' Drinkwater paused, then went on, 'You may tell Mr Ashton that for his intransigent insistence on misusing his rank, he may enjoy the privilege of standing watch-and-watch until further notice.' Drinkwater looked at Marlowe, 'Well, d'you have something to say?'

'No, sir.'

'Good. Well go and put Paine out of his misery and then inform Ashton of my decision.'

'Aye, aye, sir.'

Lieutenant Hyde had found Sergeant McCann in the gunner's store, making up cartridges as a means of seeking privacy. Hyde thrust his head through the woollen safety curtain and McCann looked up apprehensively.

'You are not to be flogged,' Hyde said with a grin, and the gentle sag of McCann's shoulders told of his relief. 'It would have been unpardonable to have done so,' Hyde expatiated.

'I have very little faith in the equity of British justice, sir,' said McCann, 'particularly in a man-o'-war.'

'Oh ye of little faith,' Hyde, 'as a matter of fact, you should have.'

'Why so, sir? Is Lieutenant Ashton prepared to retract his insult?'

Hyde pulled a face. 'Regrettably, no. I would not have thought him a man of mean spirit on first acquaintance,' Hyde went on conversationally, 'just as I would not have thought of the first lieutenant as a man with any backbone, but,' Hyde shrugged, 'ship-board life reveals much.'

'Usually more than one bargained for,' observed McCann. 'But in what way should I be grateful?'

The edge of bitterness in McCann's voice did not escape Hyde, who smiled and said, 'Marlowe has just told me old Drinkwater has put Ashton on watch-and-watch.'

'Ah . . .' An incipient smile twitched the corners of McCann's mouth. 'What about the disobedience to Ashton's order, sir?'

'Ah, that. You are exculpated. Poor Mr Paine is likely to live up to his name.'

'It's a pity Ashton didn't look to his own when handing out the insults, sir,' McCann said, ignoring the joke.

'Now hold your tongue, Sergeant,' Hyde advised. 'Your native forthrightness may be a virtue in America, but it don't serve too well in a man-o'-war.'

'It never serves well in England,' McCann said to himself after Lieutenant Hyde had gone.

In the wardroom, Lieutenant Marlowe regarded the errant midshipman. Mr Paine had been brought before the first lieutenant by the boatswain and Mr Kennedy, the surgeon. Birkbeck had returned to the hold to harry the carpenter and his mates, while Hyde was occupied inspecting his marines on the gun-deck.

'Mr Paine, you are to be given a dozen strokes of the cane for wilful neglect of an order given to you by Mr Ashton when you were lately left in charge of the ship's launch in the harbour of Santa Cruz. Do you understand?'

'Yes, sir.' Paine's voice was a dry croak.

'And have you anything to say?'

'Only that I am sorry for it, sir.'

'Very well. Let us proceed. The boatswain will carry the punishment out and the surgeon will ensure you not abused. Please remove your coat.'

Paine did as he was bid and, looking round for somewhere to lay it, saw Kennedy's outstretched hand.

'Thank you, sir,' he whispered, giving Kennedy his garment.

Then Marlowe resumed. 'I shall not ask you to remove your breeches, but you shall bend over this chair.' Marlowe indicated a chair at the forward end of the wardroom table.

Paine swallowed hard, stepped forward and bent over the chair, his hands holding the back, the knuckles already white with fear.

'Very well.' Marlowe nodded at the boatswain, who moved forward, revealing the long, flexible twisted rattan cane of his office. The polished silver head nestled familiarly inside his powerful right wrist, the end tentatively touched Paine's buttocks as the midshipman screwed up his eyes.

'Do you wish for something to bite on?' Kennedy enquired. Eyes closed and teeth gritted, Paine shook his head emphatically, eager only to get his ordeal over.

'Carry on, Bosun,' Marlowe commanded, and the petty officer drew back the cane until it struck the deck-head above. Had the punishment been administered in the open air over a quarterdeck carronade as was customary, the swipe of the rattan would have had more momentum. Watching, both Marlowe and Kennedy wondered if Drinkwater had knowingly limited the scope of the boatswain's viciousness by ordering the matter carried out between decks. Paine, however, was not in a position to appreciate the captain's clemency, witting, or otherwise. The rattan's descent whistled in a brief and terrible acceleration then struck him with such violence that the impact provoked a muscular spasm which in turn moved the rickety chair across the wardroom deck with a squeak. Paine himself made no such sound; for a second his whole body seemed impervious to the blow beyond its sharp, physical reaction. The second stroke was already on its way by the time the agony filled his whole being with its sting. To this, the successive strikes felt only as an increase of the first, terrible violation, like the roll of a drumbeat after the first loud percussive beating of the sticks.

Wave after wave of nausea seemed to press up from the pit of his stomach; it seemed the seat of the chair was forcing itself through his chest, that he would break off the legs by the tension in his arms. As the strokes followed, he tasted salt and knew he was sobbing. He knew too that he was not crying; the sobbing was the only way he could breathe, great gasps of air, sucked in by some reflexive action of his jaw as his lungs demanded it to fill his tensed muscles with oxygenated blood. He had no idea at the time that this gasping successively clamped his teeth upon his tongue.

Even to those watching, the dozen strokes seemed to last forever. Marlowe was reminded of lying awake unsleeping in his family home, listening to the long-case clock strike midnight. Kennedy watched in disgust; the evident relish with which the boatswain acquitted himself of his duty revolted him, and the humiliation of the young man bent double before them, compounded this revulsion. Marlowe averted his eyes for fear of passing out.

'That's enough!' snapped Kennedy the instant the last stroke had been laid on, earning himself a glare from the boatswain.

'I know my duty,' the petty officer grumbled.

'Thank you, Mister,' Marlowe muttered dismissively, wiping the back of his hand over his mouth. Kennedy bent over Paine.

'You all right, younker?'

Paine's back rose and fell as the midshipman took short, shallow breaths. He nodded his head, his hair damp with perspiration. Kennedy looked at Paine's buttocks. Blood and plasma oozed through the cotton drill of his trousers. 'I shall have to deal with that,' he remarked accusingly.

'You may attend to it here, if you wish,' said Marlowe.

'Well, now, that's very kind of you, Mr Marlowe,' Kennedy replied sarcastically.

'Pass word for someone to bring a clean pair of pants and breeches from Mr Paine's chest when you leave,' Marlowe instructed the boatswain, ignoring Kennedy.

'Aye, aye, sir,' replied the boatswain as he put on his hat and, ducking, left the wardroom to the officers.

'Can you move?' Kennedy asked, as Paine slowly pulled and pushed himself upright. Tears streamed down his sweat-sodden face and blood trickled from his mouth. He finally stood, slightly bent, supported by the wardroom table. His eyes remained closed as he mastered the pain, and as though he refused to open them on the scene of his humbling.

'There, Mr Marlowe,' said Kennedy with heavy sarcasm, 'justice has been done!'

'I'll thank you to hold your tongue, Kennedy,' Marlowe

snapped, his own face pale as he fought a rising gorge and turned to the decanter. He paused a moment and then filled a glass.

'Here, Mr Paine,' said Marlowe, holding out the bumper of blackstrap, 'drink this up.'

'Beg pardon, sir, but the boat's returning.'

The midshipman's puckish face, appearing disembodied round the door, had more than the usual impish look about it as Drinkwater woke from his nap with a start accompanied by an undignified grunt.

'The boat's returning, sir.' There was a hint of impudence about the young man's repetition which irritated Drinkwater who considered himself taken for a somnolent old fool.

'Very well, damn it, I heard you the first time!'

The querulous tone of the captain's voice sent the lad into full retreat. He had seen poor Paine return to the cockpit. Drinkwater was left alone to gather his wits. He could not imagine why he felt so tired, and rose stiffly, bracing himself against the lurch of the ship. Rinsing his mouth and donning hat and coat, he went on deck.

On the quarterdeck he forced himself to wait with an outward appearance of disinterest as *Andromeda* was hove-to and the red cutter brought in under the swinging davit falls. He forbore staring over the side while the fumbling snatches of the bow and stern-sheetsman captured the wildly oscillating blocks and caught the hooks in the lifting chains, whereupon the two lines of seamen tailing on to the falls ran smartly along the gangway at the boatswain's holloa to 'hoist away!'

With the boat swinging at the mizen channels and the griping lines being passed, Drinkwater could see Frey attending to the boat, giving no thought to the anxiety of his commander's mind. But as Frey climbed over the rail and jumped to the deck, he could contain himself no longer.

'Well, Mr Frey?' he asked eagerly, consumed with impatience to learn what intelligence Frey had gleaned ashore. Drinkwater had convinced himself that at Angra the Portuguese Captain-General, overlord of the Azores, would have by now received specific instructions to prepare to receive 'General Bonaparte'. He was not to be disappointed; immediately Frey confronted him, Drinkwater felt the flood of relief sweat itself out of his body, betraying the extent of his inner anxiety.

'The Portuguese Governor received me with every courtesy and said that he had received a despatch brought by Captain Count Rakov to the effect that preparations were to be made to receive Boney and to have him held under open arrest at some villa or other in the country outside Santa Cruz. He also protested that he had received no instructions from Lisbon as to whether he was supposed to cede an island, or to regard Boney as a prisoner. There were some other details about the size of Boney's suite and personal staff which I have to confess I didn't hoist in.'

'No matter . . .' Drinkwater ruminated for a moment then asked Frey, 'And did you learn when Bonaparte was expected?'

Frey shook his head. 'No, sir, not really. Gilbert asked but His Excellency did not know and could offer no clues himself. He let Gilbert read the despatch, which was in French, and all Gilbert could conclude was the tone of the language suggested the matter was imminent and that no further information would precede the arrival of Napoleon.'

'Well, that is something,' Drinkwater said.

'But is that sufficient, sir? I mean, it was no more than an intimation.'

'By a shrewd man who, I think, knows his business.' Drinkwater smiled and added, 'I think this enough to act upon.'

'Then we did not labour in vain,' Frey said, pleased that Drinkwater regarded the niggardly news with such relish.

'Not at all. Short of actually running into Boney and his entourage, I think we can pronounce ourselves satisfied.'

'May I ask, then, why we don't simply await the arrival of Boney at Santa Cruz?' Frey asked.

'Because, my dear fellow, we have no real business with Boney; our task is to prevent him being spirited to the United States and to intercept those ships sent by his followers to accomplish this. To do otherwise would be to exceed our instructions,' Drinkwater said, concluding, 'We do not want to be the cause of an incident which might rupture the peace.' He suppressed a shudder at the thought. Exceeding an instruction that was largely self-wrought would have his name earn eternal odium by their Lordships if this affair miscarried.

'I see.' Frey nodded, unaware of the turmoil concealed by his commander's apparently worldly wisdom. 'It could be a long wait then.'

'Perhaps,' Drinkwater replied, and, thus dismissed, Frey disappeared below to divest himself of his boat-cloak and wet breeches while his commander fell to a slow pacing of the quarterdeck, nodding permission for Birkbeck to get the ship under weigh again as soon as the quarter-boat was hoisted.

Despite his misgivings, Drinkwater was clearer in his mind now. There seemed to him little doubt Rakov had brought the news to Angra in pursuit of Tsar Alexander's policy. But was finding *Andromeda* on station off Flores a shock to Rakov, particularly as Rakov had last seen her in Calais Road? In order to implement his master's policy, if he knew about it in detail, Rakov must have realized that the Antwerp ships would profit by his escort, and while Drinkwater might commit *Andromeda* to an action with two men-of-war acting illegally under an outlawed flag, the presence of a powerful Russian frigate would dissuade even a zealous British officer from compromising his own country's honour by firing into an ally!

As for the degree to which Captain Count Rakov was privy to Tsar Alexander's secret intentions, Drinkwater could only conclude however Rakov saw the presence of *Andromeda*, that of *Gremyashchi* was more revealing to himself. There seemed a strong possibility that Rakov's task in conveying the despatch to Angra might be subsidiary to that of pursuing and outwitting Captain Nathaniel Drinkwater of His Britannic Majesty's frigate *Andromeda*. Quite apart from anything else, it would be a small but personal revenge for Captain Drinkwater's destruction of the *Suvorov*.

And then it occurred to Drinkwater that something must have happened to Hortense, for how else could Rakov have followed so swiftly in their own wake? It seemed that while the war was over, the old game of cat and mouse would go on, though who was now the cat and who the mouse, remained anyone's guess.

For Sergeant McCann the fact that Lieutenant Ashton was compelled to stand watch-and-watch held no more satisfaction for him than the beating of Mr Paine. Ashton's double insult had wounded him deeply, vulnerable as he was, reinforcing his feelings of inadequacy as well as affronting his sensibility. These feelings were exacerbated by Ashton's unrepentant attitude, manifested by the lieutenant's haughtiness as he nursed his own wounded pride through the tedious extra duties imposed upon him by Captain Drinkwater.

Under such stress, the predominant aspects of the temperaments of both men dominated their behaviour; the sergeant of marines nursed his grievance, the lieutenant cultivated his touchily arrogant sense of honour. And such was the indifference to private woe aboard the frigate, each man in his personal isolation formed dark schemes of revenge. Under the foreseeable circumstances, such imagined and impractical fantasies were no more than simple, cathartic chimeras.

These disaffections were set against the burgeoning of Mr Marlowe who, under Drinkwater's kindly eye and with the tacit support of Frey, seemed to grow in confidence and stature in the following few days. Frey rather liked Marlowe, whose dark visage held a certain attraction, and had engaged to execute a small portrait of the first lieutenant, a departure for Frey, whose subjects were more usually small watercolour paintings or pencil drawings of the ship and the landmarks which she passed in her wanderings. As for Marlowe, his contribution to the relative success of Birkbeck and the carpenter in partially staunching the inflow of water by caulking and doubling the inner ceiling of the hull, had lent substance of a practical nature to his increased stature. It was thus easier for his fellow ship-mates to attribute his former behaviour to indisposition, and for him to gain confidence in proportion.

With these small ups and downs mirrored throughout the ship's company as the men rubbed along from day to day, *Andromeda* lay to, or cruised under easy sail to the north of Corvo, never losing sight of this outpost of the Azores, yet ever questing for the appearance of strange sails approaching from the north.

But all they saw were the cockbilled spoutings of an occasional sperm whale and, at the southern end of their beat, the hardy Azoreans out in their *canoas* in pursuit of their great game, chasing the mighty cetaceans with harpoon and lance, so that the watching Drinkwater was reminded of the corvette *Melusine* and the ice of the distant Arctic.* Along with this reminiscence, came gloomy thoughts of the inexorable passing of time and the tedious waste of war.

For a dismal week, under grey skies alleviated occasionally by

* See *The Corvette*

promising patches of blue which yielded nothing but disappointment, *Andromeda* haunted the waters north of Corvo and Flores.

'We haul up and down like a worn-out trollop on Portsmouth hard, draggling her shawl in the mud,' Hyde observed laconically, yet with a certain metaphorical aptness, leaning back in his chair, both boots on the table.

'Indeed,' agreed Marlowe, sighing sadly, thinking of Sarah and his child growing inside her, 'my only consolation is that our diminishing stores will compel Our Father to head for Plymouth Sound very soon.'

'I think,' warned Frey, 'that he will hang on until the very last moment.'

'Well, that's as maybe, but the last moment will arrive eventually,' said the flexible Hyde philosophically.

'I do not think,' Frey said with a wry smile, 'you quite understand how Captain Drinkwater's luck has a habit of running.'

'You mean you think we shall encounter these ships?' Marlowe asked.

Frey nodded. 'Oh yes; I have no doubt of it. They cannot long be delayed now and the presence of that Russian almost guarantees it. Why else did she turn up like a bad penny?'

Marlowe shrugged and twisted his mouth in a curious grimace of helpless resignation. 'Perhaps you'll prove to be right, perhaps not.'

'Well, if you ask me,' put in Hyde, 'I think it is a wild-goose chase. All right, the Russkie turns up and his appearance ain't coincidence, but neither is ours as he is concerned and my money is on his intercepting these so-called Antwerp ships and turning them back.'

'That would mean *they* had had the wild-goose chase,' laughed Marlowe.

'Or that's what we have all been engaged on,' added Frey, pulling out his pencil and sketch block.

'Well, let's drink to the damnation of His Majesty's enemies, damnation to Boney, wherever he is, damnation to the Tsar of all the Russians, damnation to despair and depression and anything else which irks you,' Hyde said, his boots crashing on the deck as he rose to pour three glasses of blackstrap and pass them to his messmates.

'I do wish you would move with a little more grace and a little less noise, Hyde,' complained Marlowe good-naturedly.

'Sudden decisive action, Freddie, is the hallmark of the accomplished military tactician.'

'Or a lazy oaf,' Marlowe riposted, grinning as he accepted the proffered glass.

'Steady, or I'll be demanding satisfaction,' joked Hyde.

Marlowe pulled another face. 'One touchy sense of honour in a wardroom is enough, thank you,' he said.

'Don't forget Sergeant McCann,' prompted Hyde.

'Oh, he don't count . . .'

'Don't be too sure,' warned Hyde. 'He is no ordinary man.' And Frey looked up from his drawing with a shudder, catching Hyde's eye. 'You all right?' Hyde asked.

'Yes. Just a grey goose flying over my grave,' Frey said quietly.

'More likely a wild goose,' Marlowe added with a short laugh.

'Perhaps,' said Frey in a detached tone of voice that made Hyde and Marlowe exchange glances.

PART THREE.
Caging the Eagle

'Napoleon in the Isle of Elba has . . . only to be patient, his enemies will be his best champions.'

GENERAL SIR ROBERT WILSON

Chapter Fourteen   *May 1814*

St Elmo's Fire

Drinkwater had experienced no such premonition as Lieutenant Frey. The appearance of the *Gremyashchi* had finally laid to rest the vacillating anxieties and uncertainties of the preceding days, replacing them with a firm conviction that Hortense's report was about to be fulfilled. Nor did he consider Captain Count Rakov would divert the Antwerp ships from their purpose, as was the opinion of Lieutenant Hyde in the wardroom below. Drinkwater's assessment was quite otherwise: Rakov was on the scene to guarantee the matter. There would be no bloodshed, no international incident, Bonaparte would simply be removed from the Bourbon French ship bringing him to Flores, transferred to one of the Antwerp squadron and conducted to the United States.

It was quite clear that the only certain rendezvous where this could be accomplished without attracting undue attention was off the Azores, and the fact that no proper arrangements had been concluded with the Portuguese captain-general at Angra do Heroismo, was evidence none was necessary, for there had never been any real intention of landing Bonaparte in the first place. And to guarantee the Tsar's plan, revealing the sly hand of Talleyrand, the Bourbon commander of the French naval ship carrying the former Emperor into exile would not be accosted by a couple of Bonapartist pirates, but a squadron operating under the ensign of Imperial Russia.

It was a cleverly conceived plan, but, concluded Drinkwater, this embellishment made his own task acutely difficult. It was he alone who would have to assume responsibility for thwarting the Tsar's intention. Not that he entertained any personal doubts as to the rightness of this challenge. It was clearly not in British interests to have the foremost soldier in the world free to command troops in the United States. A successful invasion of Canada would be a disaster for Great Britain, and Drinkwater did not need the protection of Prince William Henry's orders to buttress his own moral doubts, only to afford protection from those in the establishment who might regard his action as intolerably high-handed.

What now nagged him was the impossibility of the task. At least two well-armed ships had sailed under the command of this Admiral Lejeune, and while Drinkwater might have had a chance to out-manoeuvre them, they were now reinforced by the *Gremyashchi*, a powerful frigate in her own right, which alone would be more than a match for *Andromeda*. He was conscious that the action his zeal had now made inevitable could end only in defeat. If any premonition disturbed the tranquillity of Nathaniel Drinkwater during those tedious days in late May, it was that death would take him at the moment of his country's hard-won victory.

In the circumstances such a death would not be without dishonour, but he doubted much credit would be to his actions to warm his widow's heart. Poor Elizabeth; she did not deserve such a fate. To be left alone to manage his small estate, not to mention the dependants he had foisted upon her, would be a terrible legacy. His death would, moreover, burden her with the promised annuity to Hortense!

The thought appalled him. In his headlong dash into the Atlantic, thoughts of an early death had not really occurred to him, for he had lived with risk for so long, and while he had intimated in the letter he had sent to his wife by the Trinity Yacht that complications had been introduced into their lives by recent events, meaning those at Calais, he had withheld details as being best dealt with face-to-face. Now he could not even leave her a second letter, for the chances of its being discovered after a bloody action were next to nothing.

He slumped at his desk as behind him a pale, watery sun set over a heaving grey sea. All about him *Andromeda* creaked mournfully, echoing his dismal thoughts and ushering in an attack of the blue-devils. As the daylight leached out of the sky and the twilight gloom increased, he fell into a doze. Hortense and Elizabeth were in the cabin with him, both were restored to the beauty they had possessed when he had first set eyes upon them and both improbably held bands like sisters, and smiled at him approvingly. He woke with a start, his heart beating furiously, possessed with a terrible fear of the unknown.

The cabin was completely dark. During his brief sleep and unknown to Drinkwater, Frampton had entered the cabin but seeing his commander asleep had beat a tactful retreat. Waking thus, Drinkwater was overcome with the feeling that the cabin was haunted by ghosts In an instant, he had rammed his hat on his head and fled to the quarterdeck wrapped in his cloak.

He almost instantly regretted this precipitate action. The quarterdeck was scarcely less congenial than the cabin; in fact it was a good deal less so. Night had fallen under a curtain of rain which knocked the sea down, hissed alongside as it struck the surface of the water and sharply reduced the temperature of the air. Ashton had the watch, his extra duty relieving Birkbeck of the task, and so the emotional air was even chillier than the atmospheric, though Drinkwater himself took little notice of this and, in his own way, only added to it by his presence.

His cloak was soon sodden, but he paced the windward quarter, his stride and balance adjusting to the swoop and roll of the ship as, with her yards braced up sharply, she stood northwards under easy sail, steering full-and-bye with the wind in the west-north-west. It was a dying breeze and about four bells the rain stopped abruptly as the wind veered a point or two. Drinkwater was vaguely aware of Lieutenant Ashton adjusting the course to the north-eastwards, maintaining the trim of the yards in accordance with the provision of Drinkwater's night orders for cruising stations. Within fifteen minutes the sky was clearing rapidly as the overcast rolled away to leeward and the stars shone out in all their glory.

If the air had been chilly before, it was positively cold now, or so it seemed to Drinkwater as the dramatic change woke him from his reverie and he found shivering. He was about to go below and seek the warm comfort of his cot, when something stopped him. He stood like a pointing hound, tingling with instinctive premonition. He looked anxiously aloft. The pale parallelograms of the topsails and topgallants were pale against the sky; the main course was loose in its buntlines, but the fore course was braced sharp up, its tack hauled down to the port bumkin. Behind him the quadrilateral spanker curved gracefully under the pressure of the wind. As he watched, it flogged easily, the failing wind easing and then filling it again, causing a fitful ripple to pass across the sail, from throat to clew. The lines of reef points pitter-patted against the tough canvas. Despite this apparently peaceful scene, something struck him as wrong. Something in the air which made his scalp creep.

'Mr Ashton!'

'Sir?' Ashton stirred from the starboard mizen rigging.

'Get the t'gallants off her!'

'The t'gallants, sir?'

'The t'gallants sir! And at once, d'you hear me?'

Drinkwater could almost hear Ashton's brain turning over the captain's lunatic order, but then the word was passed and the watch stirred out of its hiding places, hunkered down about the decks, and the shapes of men moved about the pin rails and prepared to go aloft. There was little urgency in their demeanour, obvious to Drinkwater's acute and experienced eye, even in the dark.

'Look lively there!' he cried, injecting a sharp urgency into the night. Ashton began to cross the deck towards him and Drinkwater turned away in silent rebuff, staring to windward, watching to see what would happen. Then he saw the cloud as it loomed into the night sky, rapidly blotting out the stars to the north-westwards. He could feel its presence as the air suddenly crackled with the dull menace of the thing, revealing the source of his premonition. It was odd, he thought, as he watched the vast boiling mass of it rear up and up into the heavens, how such a gigantic manifestation of energy could almost creep up on one unawares.

The cumulo-nimbus cloud moved towards them like a mythological creature; potent and awe-inspiring. Drinkwater had no idea of its altitude, indeed he was unable to see the distant anvil-shaped thunder head which was torn from its summit by the strong winds of the upper-atmosphere; nor did he know of the movement of air and moisture within it that made of it a cauldron seething at the temperature ice formed. What concerned him was the wind he knew it would generate at sea level, and the hail that might, in the next quarter of an hour, hit them with the force of buckshot.

Then, as if to signal an intelligence of its own, the thundercloud gave notice of its presence to the less observant men on *Andromeda*'s deck. It was riven from top to bottom by a great flash as the differences in electrical charge within the cloud sought resolution. The sudden, instantaneous illumination galvanized the men into sudden, furious action and within minutes *Andromeda*'s topgallants were off her before the first erratic gusts of the squall arrived; then it was upon them in unremitting fury, producing a high-pitched whine in the rigging as the full force of the wind struck them.

'Steady there,' Drinkwater said, striding across the deck to brace himself alongside the helmsmen, 'ease her if you have to, Quartermaster.'

The frigate heeled to the onslaught and began to accelerate rapidly through the water which foamed along her lee rail. The sea was almost flat; the earlier rain had done its work and now hailstones beat its surface with a roar. *Andromeda* raced through the water so that even Ashton was moved to comment.

'My God, sir,' he said, coming up to Drinkwater, 'she's reeling off the knots as if pursued by all the devils in hell!' He laughed wildly, caught up in the excitement of the moment as, with a tremendous thunderclap, lightning darted all about them and the retina was left with a stark impression of wet and drawn faces about the wheel, sodden ropes and the lines of caulking in the blanched planking. Even the streaks of a million hailstones as they drummed a furious tattoo on the deck remained, it seemed, indelibly impressed upon the brain. So vivid was this brief vision that the quarterdeck seemed inhabited by more ghosts, and Drinkwater shivered as much from the supernatural moment as the cold drenching he was undergoing.

Circumstances remained thus for some twenty minutes, with the ship driving to the north-east, her helm having been eased up to let her run off before the wind a little and ease the strain on the gear aloft, for she still carried her full topsails, fore topmast staysail and spanker. Periodically illuminated by lightning and assaulted by thunder, *Andromeda* ran headlong. After the first moments of apprehension, the glee infecting Ashton had spread to the men at the helm and a quiet chuckling madness gripped them all. The excitement of their speed was undeniable and their spirits rose as the hail eased and then stopped.

As the huge cloud passed over them, it took the wind with it. The first sign of this moderation was a slow righting of the ship, so that while she still heeled over, the angle at which the deck canted eased imperceptibly back towards the horizontal. And it was at this moment that the frigate was visited by the corposant.

It began imperceptibly, so that the watchers thought they were imagining it and made no comment lest their mates thought they had taken leave of their senses; then, as it grew brighter they looked at each other, and saw their faces lit by the strange glow. Out along the yards and up the topgallant masts the greenish luminescence grew, stretching down towards the deck along the stays and lying along the iron cranes of the hammock nettings so that *Andromeda* assumed, in the wastes of the North Atlantic Ocean, the appearance of some faery ship.

The weird glow had about it an unearthly quality which was almost numinous in its effect upon those who observed it, silencing the brief outburst of loquacious wonder which it had initially prompted. Here was something no man could explain, though some had seen it before and knew it for St Elmo's fire. Some it touched personally, sending crackling sensations up the napes of their necks, making their hair stand on end and in a few cases glow with the pale fire of embryonic haloes. All smelt the dry, sharp stink of electrical charge, and as the display slowly faded, a babble of comment broke from the watching men, officers and ratings alike, an indiscriminate wonder at what they had all seen.

Ashton seemed to throw off his peevishness and was unable to resist the temptation to discuss the phenomenon with Midshipman Dunn, while the men at the wheel, kept usually silent by the quarter-master in charge of them, chattered like monkeys. The remainder of the watch, settling down again after their exertions, speculated and marvelled amongst themselves in a ground-swell of conversation.

Isolated by rank and precedent, Drinkwater found himself refreshed as though by a long sleep. Afterwards, he attributed this invigoration to the electrical charge in the air which had been palpable. More significant, however, was the effect it had upon his mental processes. Hardly had the wonder passed and the quiet nocturnal routine settled itself again upon the ship, than his racing mind had latched on to something new.

Gone were the morbid preoccupations of earlier; gone were the complex doubts about the propriety of his course of action, of his conniving to get Prince William Henry to sanction it. Gone, too, was the gloomy, fateful conviction of his own impending doom. He shook off the weight of the dead ghosts he had borne with him for so long. James Quilhampton's was not a vengeful spirit, and the earlier manifestations of Elizabeth and Hortense were exhortations to greater endeavours, not the harbingers of doom!

This train of thought passed through his mind in a second. Having settled in his mind the eventual, anticipated arrival of *Gremyashchi* and the Antwerp squadron, he was now stimulated by a strange optimism. He found himself already considering how, when he met Count Rakov and his unholy allies, he might handle *Andromeda* to the best advantage and perhaps inflict sufficient damage before surrendering, to prevent them accomplishing their fell intent.

He was still on deck at dawn, though he had been fast asleep for three hours, caught by a turn of the mizen topgallant clewline around his waist, a dark, bedraggled figure whose hat was tip-tilted down over one shut eye, who yet commanded in this dishevelled state the distant respect of those who came and went upon the quarterdeck of His Britannic Majesty's frigate *Andromeda* as she cruised to the north of the islands of Flores and Corvo.

Nor did he wake when the daylight lit the eastern horizon and the cry went through the ship that three sails were in sight to leeward.

Chapter Fifteen   *May 1814*

First Blood

Sergeant McCann was woken as *Andromeda* heeled violently under the onslaught of the squall. He had turned in early, eschewing the company of the corporals, increasingly isolated by his obsessions. His messmates and privates, gaming or yarning about him, reacted to the sudden list of the ship by putting up an outcry, taken up by the adjacent midshipmen so that the orlop bore a brief resemblance to a bear-pit until word came down from the upper-deck that the ship had been struck by a heavy gust of wind and the noise gradually subsided. It had, however, been sufficient to wake McCann from the deep sleep into which he had fallen shortly before.

Now he lay wide awake, the edge taken off his tiredness, his heart beating, staring into the stygian gloom. Like Captain Drinkwater's cabin two decks above him, Sergeant McCann's accommodation was inhabited by ghosts, but unlike his commander's visitation, which had been on the edge of consciousness, McCann could summon his mother and sister almost at will; and unlike Captain Drinkwater he could not pace the quarterdeck to escape his delusions. Instead he embraced himself in his hammock and once again let the sensation of waste and failure flood his entire being.

In the days they had lain off the Azores, Sergeant McCann's self-loathing had eclipsed the affront he had felt at Ashton's double insult. Instead he had convinced himself that if he were neither a Yankee nor a bugger, he was something worse: he was a coward. Looking back upon his worthless life, he saw that he had always taken the path of least resistance, a path the politics of his parents had set him on. He realized his loyalism had not been based on any personal conviction but was an inherited condition, and while he had given his oath to the king as a provincial officer, it had been as much to revenge himself upon those who had despoiled him of his natural inheritance, rather than out of any principle towards the crown and parliament on the far side of the Atlantic Ocean. Recalling the homespun battalions confronting the British regular and provincial troops across the Brandywine, he realized he had always had more in common with them than the rough infantrymen and their haughty officers, or the poor benighted Hessian peasants and their red-faced and drunken *junkers*.

In contrast, on the exposed deck above the unhappy McCann, his tormentor, Lieutenant Ashton, was undergoing a transformation. The wild schemes born out of his anger were washed out of him by the squall and the visitation of St Elmo's fire. But Sergeant McCann enjoyed no such liberation. His preoccupations were deeper rooted and the springs of his being were wound tighter and tighter by his misery. Having set it aside for so long he found he was no longer able to forsake his past, unable to detach it from the present, and subconsciously ensured it was to influence the future.

Eventually, in common with all those in the gloomy orlop, Sergeant McCann fell asleep, awaiting the events of the dawn.

Lieutenant Frey woke Drinkwater who was stiff and uncomprehending for a moment or two, until the import of Frey's news struck him.

'Do you lend me your glass,' Drinkwater urged, holding out his hand. Grasping the telescope Drinkwater hauled himself up into the mizen rigging, the mauled muscles of his shoulder aching rheumatically after the exposure of the night. Drinkwater's hands were shaking as he focused the glass, as much from apprehension as from cold and cramp, but there was no denying the three sails that were, as yet, hull-down to the eastward. And while it was too early to distinguish one of them as the *Gremyashchi*, he already knew in his chilled bones that among them was the Russian frigate.

For a long moment Drinkwater hung in the rigging studying the three ships, estimating their course and guessing their speed. He was computing a course for *Andromeda*, by which he might intercept the 'enemy' in conformity with the idea he had hatched during the night. He could not call it a plan, for to lay a plan depended upon some certainties, and there were no certainties in his present situation. He doubted if *Andromeda*, against the darker western sky, had yet been seen by the strangers, but it would not be long before she was, for Rakov would have warned *Contre-Amiral* Lejeune of the presence of the British ship. Drinkwater turned, Frey's face was uplifted in anticipation.

'Wear ship, Mr Frey, and lay her on a course of south-east; set all plain sail and the weather stun's'ls. Be so kind as to turn up all hands and have them sent to break their fasts. We will clear for action at eight bells, after the ship's company have been fed.'

'Aye, aye, sir!'

Drinkwater was almost ashamed of the gleam his words kindled in Frey's eyes. He jumped down on to the deck and, leaving Frey to handle *Andromeda*, went in search of Frampton, some hot water and his razor. Meanwhile the word of impending action passed rapidly through the ship. Between decks she sizzled with a sudden stirring as the watches below were turned out, to dress, bundle up their hammocks and stow them in the nettings on the upper deck while the complaining cook flashed up the galley range and cauldrons of water went on for burgoo. In the wardroom the officers rummaged in their chests for clean linen, the better to ward off infection if they were wounded; in the cockpit the midshipmen unhooked their toy dirks from the hooks on the deck-beams above their heads, and chattered excitedly. Even Mr Paine, for whom the last few days had been a humiliating ordeal, livened at the prospect of being able to prove himself a man in the changed circumstances of an action. In the marine's mess, the private soldiers quietly donned cross-belts and gaiters, while a corporal checked the musket flints in the arms racks; Sergeant McCann dressed with particular care, and sent the messman forward to the carpenter with his sword and the instruction to hone it to a fine edge. He also carefully checked the pair of pistols which were his private property and the last vestige of his former employment as a provincial officer.

As the watches below assembled at the tables on gun-deck to receive their hot burgoo, a black, gallows humour was evident, containing less wit than obscenity, more readily endured by those at whom it was aimed than would normally have been the case under ordinary circumstances, for by such means was courage invoked.

'Jemmy,' one wag shouted across the deck, 'you'll get your pox cured today, if you're lucky!'

To which the rotting Jemmy swiftly replied, 'Aye, you cherry, an'

you may never get the chance to catch it!' This grim exchange provoked a general mirth, broken only by the order to relieve the
watch on deck and the subsequent pipe of 'Up spirits!'

After this necessary ritual, the marine drummer ruffled his snare
and beat them all to quarters, at which the bulkheads came down
aft, and Drinkwater's insubstantial private quarters metamorphosed into an extension of the gun-deck. All along the deck, the
tables had vanished, whisked away like a conjuring trick, giving a
prominence to the bulky black guns. The breechings were cast off
and the cannon moved inboard from their secure, stowed positions with their muzzles lashed hard up against the lintels of the
gun-ports. Their crews ministered to them, clearing the train-
tackles, worming the barrels and checking the firing-lanyards and
flints of the gun-locks. On the upper deck the carronades and chase
guns were cleared away; Hyde held a swift parade of his marines
and sent them to their posts. Then Drinkwater called all the officers
to the port hance from where he was watching the three strange sails.

They were hull-up by now and one was plainly identified as the
Gremyashchi. Although unable to see any name, Drinkwater
remembered Hortense had said one of the ships from Antwerp
was called *L'Aigle* and had speculatively concluded that she was
the nearer of the trio, a frigate of at least equal, and probably
superior force to *Andromeda*, if only in the calibre and weight of
metal of her guns. On her port quarter lay the second Bonapartist
ship, while the Russian was ahead of and slightly more distant
than the others. Drinkwater marked this disposition with some
satisfaction: Captain Count Rakov had made his first mistake.

Andromeda was running down towards the three ships with the
wind almost dead astern. They lay on her port bow and, if both she
and her quarry remained on their present courses, they would be
in long cannon shot in about an hour. Drinkwater relished the time
in hand, though he knew it would play on his nerves, for it would
play on the enemy's too. With her studding sails set and the morning light full on her spread of canvas, *Andromeda* would look a
resolute sight from the Franco-Russian squadron as she bore down
upon them. The morning was bright with promise; the blue sea
reflected an almost cloudless sky, washed clean by the passage of
the cold-front in the night. A small school of dolphins gambolled
innocently between *Andromeda* and her objectives which continued
to stand southward apparently unmoved by the headlong

approach of the British frigate. Drinkwater was gambling on Rakov and Lejeune assuming he was running down to quiz them, not to open fire, and this seemed borne out by the lack of colours at the peaks of the strange ships.

Drinkwater was aware of the restless gathering behind him. As *Andromeda* ran with the wind, even the coughs and foot-shufflings of the waiting assembly of officers were audible. He turned around and caught Marlowe's eye.

'You have the weather gauge, sir,' the first lieutenant remarked nervously.

'*We* have the weather gauge, gentlemen,' Drinkwater corrected with a smile, 'and perhaps we shall not have it for long . . .' He looked round the crescent of faces. Marlowe was clearly apprehensive, while Hyde remained as impassively calm as ever; Birkbeck showed resignation and Ashton a new eagerness. As for Frey, well Frey was an enigma; best known of them all and much liked, he had become a more difficult man to read, for there was an eagerness there to match Ashton and yet a wariness comparable with Birkbeck's and perhaps, remembering his friend James Quilhampton, a fear akin to Marlowe's. But there was also a touch of Hyde's veneer, Drinkwater thought in that appraising instant, and yet of them all, Frey's complexity most appealed to him. Frey was a good man to have alongside one in a tight corner. Drinkwater smiled again, as confidently and reassuringly as he could; he was being unfair because he knew Frey of old. They would all acquit themselves well enough when push came to shove.

'Well gentlemen,' he said, indicating the other ships, 'this is what we have been waiting for. Now pay careful attention to what I have to say, for we are grievously outnumbered and outgunned and, if we are to achieve our objective, we have to strike first, fast and very hard, before we are brought to close action and lose any initiative we may be able to gain by engaging on our terms.

'It is my intention that we do all we can to avoid a close-quarters action. If my information is correct the two Bonapartist ships will not only have sufficient gunners, but they will be full of sharp-shooters and soldiers, enough to make mince-meat of our thirteen score of jacks. I shall therefore be using the ship's ability to manoeuvre and will attempt to disable them first. They will almost certainly attempt the same trick, so I am counting on the accuracy of our shot. Frey and Ashton, your respective batteries must be fought with the utmost energy and economy. We must have no wasted powder or shot; we cannot afford it. I am not so much concerned with the precision of broadsides, rather that every shot tells. Make certain, *certain* mark you, every gun-captain comprehends this. D'you understand? Ashton?'

'Yes, sir.'

'Frey?'

'Aye, sir.'

'Very well. Now mark something else: when I order you to be prepared to stand-to I want everything at maximum readiness except that the guns are to be kept concealed behind closed ports. The order to open ports will be automatic when I order the commencement of fire and I will endeavour to allow enough time for the guns to be laid. D'you follow?'

'I'm not sure I do, sir,' said Ashton.

'I don't want *Andromeda* to be the first to show her teeth, Mr Ashton, though I hope we shall draw first blood.' Drinkwater paused, then added for Ashton's benefit, 'If we are to fire into a Russian ship, I need the pretext of self-defence . . .'

'Ah, I see, I beg pardon . . .'

'Very well. Mr Marlowe,' Drinkwater turned to the first lieutenant, 'I leave the upper deck guns in your hands, but the same procedure is to be followed.'

'I understand, sir.'

'Mr Hyde,' Drinkwater swung round on the marine officer, 'your men are to do their best to pick off anyone foolish enough to show himself, but particularly any officers. Pray do not permit any of your men to anticipate my order to open fire.'

'Very good, sir.'

'Mr Birkbeck, I shall want the ship handled with all your skill. I shall feint several times at their bows and if you can oblige me, bear up and rake, preferably across their sterns.' Drinkwater turned back to the lieutenants, 'So you gentlemen in the gun-deck must be aware that if we ain't standing off and knocking the sticks out of them, I shall want the elevation dropped and shot sent down the length of their decks. Such treatment may demoralize the soldiers among 'em. We shall see.

'As for the Russian, well Rakov is our greatest threat, the more so because we don't know his orders or his intentions. We do know he ain't here on a picnic and I am convinced he followed us from Calais suspecting our intention and determined to stop us. It all depends upon the mettle of the man and when and where he chooses to engage us. My guess is he may try and overwhelm us when we are otherwise occupied, but at least he has to work his way up from the lee station first . . .'

'He appears to be doing that already,' interrupted Ashton, indicating the ships over Drinkwater's shoulder.

'Indeed he does, Mr Ashton, replied Drinkwater, who had observed the *Gremyashchi*'s converging course some moments earlier, 'but then I should have been surprised if he hadn't, eh?' Drinkwater paused and looked round them all. 'Well now, are there any questions?' He paused as the officers shook their heads. 'No? Good. Well, let us hope providence gives us at least a chance, gentlemen. Good fortune to you all. Now, if you please, be so kind as to take post.'

He turned and levelled his glass as they moved away. He would have liked to say something to Frey, but that would not have been fair on the others. Anyhow, what could he say? That they had a couple of hours before they would be prisoners, and while they might not be prisoners for long, the humiliation of defeat was a risk that lay beyond the greater hurdle of death itself? Such thoughts lay uneasily alongside the affirmations of duty. He sniffed as he strove to focus on the *Gremyashchi*, but had to wipe his eye before he accomplished this simple task. Beside him someone coughed. He kept the telescope firmly clamped to his eye socket and spoke from the corner of his mouth.

'Ah, Mr Marlowe, I did not deliberately keep you out of my orders; yours might be the most difficult task and I would ask you to steel yourself. If I should fall, you are to strike at once, the only proviso being that the ship has endured some enemy shot. I would not have an unnecessary effusion of blood . . .'

'If I do that, sir, and do not prosecute the action with some energy, I may be taken for a coward.'

'You may indeed, Mr Marlowe, but that is preferable to death and will at least legitimize your offspring. Believe me, sir, this damned war has gone on long enough and there are men aboard the ship deserving of a better fate.'

'But, sir, by your own persuasion, if we do not stop this migration of Boney, the war may drag on.'

'I like "migration", Mr Marlowe; it implies Boney is a sum of greater proportion than one man, but you are to obey my orders, do you hear, sir?'

'I hear you, sir . . .'

Drinkwater suppressed a smile. Marlowe's intention to disobey was as clear as the sunlight now dancing upon the blue waves of the ocean. He was truly steeled and his self-doubt had been banished by his sense of honour. It was a mean trick, Drinkwater concluded, and might yet add a bastard to the Ashton clan! Unconsciously, Drinkwater too resorted to the crude gallows humour of men preparing themselves for the possibility of death or wounding.

'There's a good fellow,' he said, closing the telescope and turning to smile at the first lieutenant. 'Now, will you have a string of bunting run up to the lee fore-tops'l yard-arm. Anything will do, just to confuse them.' He jerked his head at the three ships. 'They're all flying Russian colours. I suspected they might.'

'They're trying to intimidate us,' Marlowe asserted. 'Damned cheek!'

'Well, let's return the compliment. And let us discharge a chase gun to draw attention to the hoist.'

Drinkwater paid little attention to the sequence of flags that was run aloft a few minutes later beyond noting the gay colours were brilliant in the spring morning. Truth to tell, Mr Paine, to whom this duty had fallen, had paid little attention either, but the dull report of the gun gave a spurious authority to the fluttering bunting, investing it with an importance it did not have and perhaps buying *Andromeda* a further few minutes of respite as she bore down upon what must now be conceived as the enemy.

For Drinkwater, patiently watching the range of the three ships decrease, the flaunting of Russian ensigns by all three ships suggested at the very least a malign intent and the connivance of the Tsar's officers. He imagined Count Rakov must have boarded the two French ships at sea and held council with Lejeune. In fact the possibility of French and Russian ships enjoying a rendezvous to the north of the Azores seemed most likely now, accounting for the delay in the Antwerp ships appearing off the archipelago. Such an argument, ominous though it was, was but further confirmation of the factual content of what had once been a mere whisper upon the wind.

Or upon the lips of Hortense Santhonax.

Drinkwater paid particular attention to the *Gremyashchi*. Idly, as he studied the Russian ship working back to windward, he wondered what her name signified. It was no matter, and he was more interested in observing how Rakov handled her and how swiftly she answered his intentions. It was difficult to judge; at the moment she was simply close hauled and sailing harder on the wind than the two Bonapartist ships, losing a little speed by comparison, but closing with them so that if *Andromeda* stood on, the interception would be as near coincidental as human heart could contrive, if human heart wished for it.

While this might be Captain Count Rakov's desire, it was not Nathaniel Drinkwater's, for it would be a trap from which escape would be impossible and he was aware that once he had been engaged by all three ships, or even only two, he would find it impossible to extricate himself. He therefore called the master and, without taking the glass from his eye, said, 'Mr Birkbeck, take the stun's'ls in if you please. After which you may clew up the main course. We will let the fore course draw a little longer.'

'Aye, aye, sir.'

Birkbeck picked up the speaking trumpet and within a minute or two the studding sails bellied, fluttered and then collapsed inwards, drawn into the adjacent tops to be stowed away. After this the booms were struck inboard, running into the round irons above the upper yards on the fore and main masts, until they were next required.

'Main mast there!' bellowed Birkbeck, 'Clew garnets there! Rise tacks and sheets!'

Without the driving power of the studding sails and main course, *Andromeda* slowed perceptibly. While the *Gremyashchi* continued to haul up to windward, closing her consorts, the common bearing of the three ships began to draw ahead.

'Bring her round two points to starboard, Mr Birkbeck.'

'Two points to starboard, sir, aye, aye.'

Remaining to windward, *Andromeda* drew on to a parallel course, slightly increasing her speed as she came on to a reach so that, after a few moments, the relative bearings of the enemy steadied again.

'Mr Marlowe, another gun, I think, to draw attention to our signal.'

The forecastle 9-pounder barked again, but prompted no response. Drinkwater began to feel an elation in his spirits. The squadron was standing on and in this apparent steadfast holding of their course, Drinkwater read a degree of irresolution on their part. Were they waiting for Rakov to act first, perhaps, in the capacity of senior officer? He was, however, acutely aware that pride always preceded a fall and his glass was most often focused on the *Gremyashchi* which was now slightly to windward of the French ships, though still to leeward of *Andromeda*, and a little less than a mile ahead, on her port bow.

'Rakov dare not wear, for it would cast him too far to loo'ard and he dare-not tack for fear of missing stays . . .'

'By God, sir! You're wrong! He's going about!' Marlowe's voice cracked with excitement as ahead of them the Russian frigate turned into the wind and prepared to come round to pass closely between the French ships and *Andromeda*. It was a bold move and while it would mask the gunfire of her consorts, a broadside from the *Gremyashchi* could well serve to incapacitate the British frigate and thereby deliver her to the guns of the combined squadron.

'Mr Paine!'

'Sir?'

'Run up a different hoist. Make us look a little desperate.'

'A little desperate, sir. Aye, aye.'

For a brief, distracted moment Drinkwater thought there might have been a hint of sarcastic emphasis on the diminutive adjective, but then he was passing word to the gun deck: 'Larboard battery make ready langridge and round shot if you please.'

Drinkwater heard the order taken up and passed below. With the angle of heel the elevating screws would need winding down. He would have to lessen the angle of heel to assist the gunners.

'Mr Birkbeck! Clew up the fore-course!'

He levelled his glass on the *Gremyashchi* again. She was passing through the wind now, hauling her main yards. White water streamed from her bow as she plunged into the head sea as she turned. Then she had swung and her sails rippled and filled on the port tack. She began gathering speed towards *Andromeda* on a reciprocal course to leeward. Instantly Drinkwater saw his opportunity. He felt the surge of excitement in his blood, felt his heartbeat increase with the audacity of it. Bold though Rakov had been, Drinkwater might out-Herod Herod.

'Starboard battery make ready!'

'Chain shot ready loaded sir!' It was Frey's voice, Frey at the quarterdeck companionway, ducking below at the same moment.

'Mr Birkbeck, I want the ship taken across his bow . . .'

'Sir?'

'At the last moment, d'you hear?'

'You'll rake from ahead sir?'

'Exactly. Will you do it?'

'Aye, sir!'

'At the last moment . . .'

'We risk taking her bowsprit with us.'

'No time to worry about that, just carry us clear. Man the braces and square the yards as we come round. Mr Hyde, some target practice for you lobsters!'

'Can't wait, sir!' Hyde called gaily back.

No one on the upper deck was unaware of Drinkwater's intentions and, thanks to Frey, most men on the gun-deck understood. Those that did not knew something was about to happen and both batteries waited tensely for the opportunity to open fire.

Drinkwater cast a quick look at Marlowe He was so pale that his beard looked blue against his skin. 'Remember what I said, Mr Marlowe,' Drinkwater reminded his first lieutenant in a low voice, 'if I should fall.'

Marlowe looked at him with a blank stare, into which comprehension dawned slowly. 'Oh yes, yes, sir.' Drinkwater smiled reassuringly. Marlowe smiled bravely back. 'I shall not let you down, sir,' he said resolutely.

'I'm sure you won't, Mr Marlowe,' Drinkwater replied, raising his glass again and laying it upon the fast-approaching Russian.

Andromeda remained the windward vessel and Drinkwater knew at once that Rakov intended to use his heel to enable his guns to fire higher, aiming to cripple the British frigate, cross her stern with a raking fire and then take his time destroying her. It was always a weakness of the weather gauge that although one could dominate the manoeuvring, when it came to a duel, the leeward guns were frequently difficult to point.

Rakov was clewing up his courses, confident that Andromeda was running into the trap with her futilely flying signals and every gunport tight shut.

'D'you wish me to try another hoist, sir?' asked Paine.

'Good idea, Mr Paine,' responded Drinkwater, adding, 'and a gun to windward, Mr Marlowe, to add to the effect.'

'Aye, aye, sir.'

Details were standing out clearly now on the *Gremyashchi*. Her dark hull with its single, broad buff was foreshortened, but the scrollwork about her head, her knightheads and bowsprit were clear, so clear in the Dollond glass that Drinkwater could see an officer forward, studying his own ship through a huge glass.

'Keep the guns' crews' head down, Mr Marlowe, we're being studied with interest.' A moment later the unshotted starboard bow chaser blew its wadding to windward with a thump. In an unfeigned tangle of bunting and halliards which trailed out to leeward in a huge bight, Mr Paine was the very picture of the inept greenhorn struggling to get a flag hoist aloft in blustery weather; the matter could not have been better contrived if it had been deliberate!

Beside Drinkwater, Birkbeck was sucking his teeth, a nervous habit Drinkwater had not noticed before. 'Shall I edge her down to loo'ard, sir?'

'A trifle, if you please . . .'

Drinkwater's heart was thumping painfully in his breast. What he was about to attempt was no ruse, but a huge risk. If *Andromeda* turned too slowly, or the men at the braces did not let the yards swing, the wind in the sails would tend to hold the ship on her original course. If he turned too early, he would give Rakov time to respond and if too late all that might result was a collision, and that would spell the end for Drinkwater and his ship.

'Stand by, Mr Birkbeck!'

Drinkwater's voice was unnaturally loud, but it carried, and Birkbeck was beside the wheel in an instant. If only Rakov would show his intentions . . .

'Make ready on the gun-deck!'

Drinkwater was conscious that in another full minute it would be too late. The two frigates were racing towards each other, larboard to larboard at a combined speed of twenty knots. *Gremyashchi*, having the wind forward of the beam, was heeling a little more than *Andromeda*, exposing her port copper which gleamed dully in the sunshine. *Andromeda*'s heel was less, but sufficient to require almost full elevation in her port guns. Not, Drinkwater thought in those last seconds, that she would be using them first.

The time had come for Drinkwater to commit himself and his ship to a raking swing by passing *Andromeda* across *Gremyashchi*'s bow, come hell or high water. Just as he opened his mouth to shout the order to Birkbeck the *Gremyashchi*'s larboard ports opened and her black gun muzzles appeared, somewhat jerkily as their crews hauled them uphill against the angle of heel.

'Now Birkbeck! Up helm!' Birkbeck had the helm over in a trice, but Drinkwater's heart thundered in his breast and his skin crawled with apprehension as he watched *Andromeda*'s bowsprit hesitate, then start to move across the rapidly closing *Gremyashchi*, accelerating as the frigate responded to her rudder.

'Braces there!' Birkbeck shouted.

'Starboard battery, open fire when you bear!'

Marlowe was running aft along the starboard gangway and beneath their feet the faint tremble of gun trucks running outboard sent a tremor through the ship. Along the upper deck the warrant and petty officers at the masts and pin rails were tending the trim of the yards driving *Andromeda* at her maximum speed as she swung to port, right under the bows of the *Gremyashchi*.

Drinkwater saw the officer with the long glass lower it and look directly at the British ship, as though unable to believe what he had first observed in detail through his lenses; he saw the man turn and shout aft, but *Gremyashchi* stood on, and even fired a gun in the excitement, a shotted gun, for Hyde cried out he had spotted the plume of water it threw up, yards on their starboard beam. As *Andromeda* turned to port, the component of her forward speed was removed from the equation. The approach slowed, allowing *Andromeda* time to cover the distance of the offset from her windward station.

Then the forwardmost gun of Frey's starboard battery fired, followed by its neighbours. The concussion rolled aft as each successive gun-captain laid his barrel on the brief sight of the Russian's bow as it flashed past his open port, like a pot shot at a magic lantern show. And on the upper deck, first the chase gun, then the short, ugly barks of the carronades as they recoiled back up their slides, followed the same sequence, the gun crews leaping round with sponges and rammers, to get in a second shot where they were able. As for Hyde's marines, they afterwards called it a pigeon shoot, for they claimed to have picked off every visible Russian in the fleeting moments they were in a position to do so, though whether this amounted to four or seven men remained a matter of dispute for long afterwards.

Andromeda's rolling fire was more impressive than a broadside; there was a deliberation about it that might have been coincidence, or the fruits of twenty years of war, or the sheer bloody love of destruction enjoyed by men kept mewed up in a wooden prison for months at a time, year-in, year-out, denied the things even the meanest, most indigent men ashore enjoyed as their natural rights. And if the liveliness of the sea deprived Drinkwater of the full effect of a slow raking, the destruction wrought seemed bad enough to allow him to coolly pass his ship clear to leeward of the faltering Russian as, obedient to her helm, *Andromeda* swung back on to her original course and swept past the *Gremyashchi*, starboard to starboard. So confident had Rakov been that Drinkwater would hang on to the weather gauge that hardly a starboard gun opposed her.

'Run down towards those French ships, Mr Birkbeck then we will tack and come up with the *Gremyashchi* again . . .'

'Drive a wedge between 'em, eh sir?' It was Marlowe, darkened by powder smoke and the close supervision of the upper deck carronades, who ranged up alongside Drinkwater and suddenly added, 'By God, you're unarmed, sir!'

Drinkwater looked down at his unencumbered waist. Neither sword nor pistol hung there. 'God's bones, I had quite forgot . . .'

'I'll get 'em for you sir.' And like a willing midshipman, Marlowe was gone.

Drinkwater turned and looked at the *Gremyashchi*, already dropping astern on the starboard quarter. Her starboard ports were open now, and several shots flew at *Andromeda*, but there was no evidence of a concerted effort and it was clear Rakov had been completely outwitted and had had all his men up to windward to assist hauling his cannon quickly out against his ship's heel.

'How far from her were we, sir?' Birkbeck asked conversationally. 'I was rather too busy to notice.'

'I'm not sure, Drinkwater replied, 'thirty or forty yards, maybe; perhaps less; long pistol shot anyway.'

Both men spared a last look at the *Gremyashchi*. It was impossible to say what damage they had done; none of her spars had gone by the board and only two holes were visible in the foot of her fore-topsail, but they were fast approaching the two French ships, the nearer of which had the appearance of an Indiaman and was clearly frigate built. It was oddly satisfying for Drinkwater to read the name *L'Aigle* on her stern, beneath the stern windows. Hortense and her intelligence seemed a world away from this!

Beyond *L'Aigle*, lay the smaller French ship, a corvette by the look of her, and both had their guns run out.

'Not too close, I don't want to risk them hitting our sticks, but would like a shot at theirs.'

'Aye, aye, sir.' Birkbeck replied, impassive to his commander's paradoxical demand.

'Down helm, my lads, nice and easy.' Birkbeck conned the ship round and Drinkwater walked forward and bellowed down beneath the booms, 'Now's your chance, Mr Ashton; larbowlines make ready and fire at will when you bear!' He turned, 'Ah, Marlowe, you're just in time . . . Thank you.'

Drinkwater took the sword and belt from Marlowe who laid the brace of pistols on the binnacle and hurried off. Drinkwater caught Birkbeck's eye and raised an eyebrow.

Then Ashton's guns fired by division, the forward six first, then the midships group and finally the aftermost cannon, by which time the forward guns were ready again, and for fifteen minutes, as *Andromeda* ran parallel to *L'Aigle*, they kept up this rolling fire. It was returned with vigour by *L'Aigle*, but the corvette scarcely fired a shot, being masked by her consort.

Drinkwater could see the spurts of yellow flame and the puffs of white smoke from which came the spinning projectiles, clearly visible to the quick eye.

'Have a care Birkbeck, they're using bar shot . . .'

A loud rent sounded aloft and the main-topsail was horizontally ripped across three cloths and half the windward topmast shrouds were shot away, but the mast stood. A few innocuous holes appeared in *L'Aigle*'s sails and even the corvette suffered from some wild shot but there appeared to be little other damage until Hyde called out there was something wrong amidships and that he had seen a cloud of splinters explode from a heavy impact.

Drinkwater was far more concerned with the conduct of *Andromeda* herself As long as he struck without being hit, he was having at least a moral effect upon his enemy. He raised his glass and could see the blue and white of infantrymen on the deck of *L'Aigle*.

'Pass word to Mr Frey, I am going to rake to starboard!' he called, turning to Birkbeck, but the master was ahead of his commander.

'Let fly the maintops'l sheet . . . !'

Andromeda began to slow as the driving power of the big sail was lost; *L'Aigle* and the corvette appeared to accelerate as they drew ahead, and then Birkbeck put the helm up and again *Andromeda* swung to port, but instead of passing under the bow of an enemy, she cut across the sterns of L'Aigle and then the corvette, whose name was now revealed as *Arbeille*.

They were, however, moving away, and although having achieved his aim in allowing them to pass ahead before turning, Birkbeck's swing to port was a little later than the copybook manoeuvre. Nevertheless, it was clear who was dominating events as *Andromeda* drove across the sterns of both French ships, cutting through their wakes as Frey's guns thundered again. Nor was there any mistaking the damage inflicted, for the shattering of glass and the stoving in of the neatly carved wooden columns, the caryatids and mermaids adorning their sterns, was obvious. Staring through the Dollond glass, Drinkwater could clearly see a flurry of activity within the smashed interior of *L'Aigle*. By a fluke, the Russian ensign worn by the *Arbeille* had been shot away and a replacement was quickly hoisted in the mizen rigging: it was the *tricolore*.

'Shall I wear her now, sir?' Birkbeck was asking, and Drinkwater swung round, snatched a quick look at the *Gremyashchi*, almost two miles away by now, but still holding on to her original course. She had either sustained some damage, or was breaking off the action.

'If you please, Birkbeck, let us give chase to the Russian and see what he does.'

'Now they're discarding pretence and showing their true colours, sir,' remarked Marlowe as he returned to the quarterdeck, gesturing to the French ships. *L'Aigle* had joined her consort in sporting the ensign of the Revolution and Empire and both were also turning in *Andromeda*'s wake.

'Well, sir,' Marlowe remarked cheerfully, 'at least we drew first blood.'

'Indeed we did, Mr Marlowe,' Drinkwater replied, 'indeed we did.'

Chapter Sixteen   *May 1814*

Rules of Engagement

'Mr Frey, sir!'

'Ah, Mr Paine . . .'

'Message from the captain, sir.' Paine paused to catch his breath and caught Ashton's eye. Smoke still lingered on the gun-deck and the atmosphere was acrid with the stink of burnt powder and the sweat of well over a hundred men. Having reloaded, most of the guns' crews had squatted down and were awaiting events. Some chewed tobacco, others mopped their heads and a low, buzzing chatter filled the close air. Frey, standing upright between the beams of the deck above, stretched. His face was already grimy, but his expression was one of cheerful expectation.

'Well,' he prompted, 'what's the news?'

Ashton joined them. He ran a grubby finger round the inside of his stock. Paine noticed he had yet to shave.

'Captain's compliments, gentlemen,' Paine said diplomatically, 'and to say the gun crews acquitted themselves very well. He don't know how much damage we've done, but we ain't, beg pardon, we haven't suffered anything bar a few holes aloft. We're in chase of the Russian again and Captain Drinkwater says to keep it up. He'll do his utmost to continue manoeuvring and hitting from a distance. He says to be certain sure I tell you not to waste powder and shot and to make every discharge count.'

Frey looked from Paine to Ashton with a smile. 'That seems perfectly explicit, eh Josh?'

'Yes,' said Ashton, yawning. By rights the third lieutenant should have been turned in after standing his watch; he was beginning to feel the cumulative effects of his punitive regime of watch-and-watch.

'So round one's to us, eh young shaver?' Frey said light-heartedly.

'How long before we've caught up with the *Gremyashchi*? We can't see her from down here.'

'About an hour, may be a little more. We've reset the courses.'

'We can see that from the waist,' Ashton said with a cocky air, indicating the open space amidships and the bottoms of the boats on the booms. Sunlight shone obliquely through the interstices, the shafts prominent in the lingering gunsmoke, oscillating gently with the motion of *Andromeda*.

'Very well, Mr Paine,' said Frey, 'pass our respects to Captain Drinkwater . . .'

'And tell him we've suffered no casualties down here and are none the worse for the experience,' added Ashton.

'Except for a crushed foot,' Frey corrected reprovingly. 'Poor little Paddy Burns tried to stop a recoiling 12-pounder.'

Thinking of the bare-legged powder-monkeys, Paine grimaced and Ashton said callously, 'The damned little fool got in the way.' Frey pointedly ignored Ashton and nodded dismissal to the midshipman before he turned to cross the deck and peer out of a gun-port to see if he could catch a glimpse of the pursued *Gremyashchi*. As Paine made off, Ashton called him back.

'Mr Marlowe all right, Mr Paine?'

'Mr Marlowe, sir? Why yes . . .'

'Good, good.' Ashton paused, but Paine waited, puzzled at the question. Ashton realized the need of an explanation was both superfluous and demeaning, especially to a midshipman, and waved Paine away, but Paine's own solicitude had been awakened.

'Sir!' He arrested Ashton's turn forward and Frey looked up from his position crouched by the gunport.

Ashton swung round and stared at the importunate midshipman.

'What happened to Burns, sir?' Paine asked

'Kennedy's taking his foot off now,' Ashton said coldly and, turning on his heel, resumed his walk forward.

Paine ran back up to the quarterdeck where he caught Drinkwater's eye. 'Beg pardon, sir, both Mr Frey and Mr Ashton send their respects and perfectly understand your orders.'

'Very well.'

'And they've had one casualty.'

'Oh? Who is it?'

'A powder-boy, sir,' Paine said, recalling just in time Captain Drinkwater's proscription of the term 'powder-monkey', especially by the young gentlemen.

'Which one?' Drinkwater asked.

'Burns, sir.'

Drinkwater frowned. 'Oh, yes, I know the lad; dark hair and a squint. Was he killed?'

'No, sir, a recoiling gun-truck crushed his foot. He's in the surgeon's hands at the moment.'

'Thank you, Mr Paine. And you, are you all right?'

'Perfectly, sir, thank you.'

Drinkwater nodded and then resumed his scrutiny of the *Gremyashchi* on their port bow; the Russian frigate was nearer now and Paine was aware he had been absent from the quarterdeck for some time, so much had they shortened the distance. They would be in action again soon and a moment of panic seized him and he blurted out, 'Beg pardon again, sir, but I'm very sorry . . .'

Drinkwater turned and looked at the youngster in some surprise. 'What on earth for, Mr Paine?'

'For making such a mess of getting that flag hoist aloft, sir.'

Drinkwater's smile cracked into a brief laugh and he patted the midshipman on the shoulder. 'My dear Mr Paine, think nothing of it. As far as the enemy was concerned, I think you managed the business most ably. As a *ruse-de-guerre* I imagine it achieved its objective.'

Paine's incomprehension was plain, but he did not question Drinkwater's reply. On any other occasion he would have been dressed down by one of the officers for making so abysmal a hash of the simple task. Action, it seemed, was played to different rules, those of engagement he supposed, so he resumed his station, puzzled but happier. He had survived what Mr Frey had called the first round; perhaps he would be lucky and survive the second.

Lieutenant Hyde took advantage of the hiatus to look to his men. Instructing his two corporals to issue more cartridges and ball, he ordered Sergeant McCann to make his rounds of the sentries posted throughout the frigate.

'See the boys are all right, Sergeant, and make sure they don't feel left out of things.'

McCann ignored the deck sentinels at the after end of the quarterdeck. They were always stationed there, action or not, to maintain a guard and to throw the life-preservers over the side if any unfortunate jack fell overboard.

Below, on the gun-deck, there was a sentry at the forward and after companionways to ensure no one ran below without authority. By this means the cowardly or nervously disposed were kept at their stations and prevented from seeking the shelter of the orlop deck. Only stretcher parties, officers or midshipmen carrying messages were permitted to pass the companionways, along with the powder-boys like Paddy Burns, who carried ammunition up from the magazines and shot lockers to satisfy the demands of the gun-captains.

McCann ascertained there had been no problems with either of his men at these posts and went below where, in the berth-deck and the orlop, other solitary marines did their duty despite the mayhem raging on the decks above. Spirit room, outer magazine, the stores and the hatchways to the holds, each had its guard and every man professed all was well, one asking to be relieved for a moment while he in turn eased himself. McCann obliged then left the comforted soldier to his miserable, ill-lit duty in the mephitic air of the hold.

McCann returned up the forward companionway and walked aft along the gun-deck, exchanging the odd remark with several of the gun crews.

'Cheer up, Sergeant,' one man chaffed, 'what've you got to be glum about up there in all that sunshine and iron rain!'

'Mind your manners,' McCann responded morosely and then found himself confronted by Lieutenant Ashton.

'Silence there!' Ashton ordered, obstructing the marine. 'Well, McCann, what the deuce are you doing down here?'

McCann recognized provocation in Ashton's voice. 'Checking the sentries, sir, on the orders of Lieutenant Hyde.'

'Are you, indeed . . .?'

'If you'll excuse me, sir . . .'

Ashton drew aside with deliberate slowness. 'Off you go, Sergeant Yankee.'

McCann paused and confronted the urbane Ashton. With difficulty he mastered his flaring anger, though his eyes betrayed him, allowing Ashton to add insolently, 'Have a care, Yankee, have a care.'

McCann turned and almost ran aft up the companionway, gasping in the sunlight and fresh air, as if he had escaped the contagion of a plague-pit. He had no idea why Ashton had staged the unpleasant little scene, but it crystallized all the pent up venom in McCann's tortured soul. As for Ashton, idling away the time before *Andromeda* resumed the action, he felt little beyond a petty amusement that might have been nothing more than the result of mere high spirits and the elation of a man carried away by the excitement of the morning, if it had not had such fatal consequences.

As *Andromeda* slowly overhauled the *Gremyashchi*, Drinkwater strove to make some sense out of the situation. Astern of the British frigate, *L'Aigle* and *Arbeille* were coming up hand over fist, though they would not reach *Andromeda* before she herself was in range of the Russian. It was clear Rakov, who could have brought Drinkwater to battle within a few moments by reducing sail, was content to trail his coat, drawing the British after him, in the hope that he could pin *Andromeda* long enough for the two French ships to come up and overwhelm her.

In short, it seemed to the anxious Drinkwater that, having won a brief advantage, he was now allowing himself to be drawn into a trap which could have only one consequence. His alternative was to put the wind a point abaft the beam and escape on *Andromeda*'s fastest point of sailing. Within this tactical debate there lurked a small political imperative. Rather than run, Drinkwater considered whether to back his hunch, or not. If he proved right, then he might yet extricate his ship from what otherwise seemed her inevitable humiliation. There was something about Rakov's trailing away to the north that did not quite square with the setting of a trap. Drinkwater could not quite put his finger on his reason for thinking thus, beyond an intuition; perhaps that first raking broadside of *Andromeda*'s had had an effect, and perhaps the damage had been more moral than physical.

Captain Count Rakov had been sent with his ship to prevent Drinkwater from thwarting the Tsar's plan. That much was obvious; but what were Rakov's rules of engagement? It was inconceivable that having chased *Andromeda* out to the Azores, he did not have any! But was Rakov empowered to destroy a British man-of-war? Such an event would at the very least cause a rupture between London and St Petersburg and might be a *casus belli*, touching off a new European war. As matters stood, the exchange of fire between *Gremyashchi* and *Andromeda* could be written off as

216

'accidental', an unfortunate misunderstanding which both governments regretted profoundly.

Drinkwater lowered his glass, his mind made up. He was lucky, damned lucky. As things stood at that precise moment, he had enough room to call Rakov's bluff.

'Mr Birkbeck!'

'Sir?'

'Wear ship! I want to pass between those two Frenchmen. Mr Marlowe! Mr Hyde! D'you hear?'

'Aye, aye, sir!'

'Mr Paine, be so kind as to let the officers on the gun-deck know my intentions.'

The cries of acknowledgement were followed by a flurry of activity as *Andromeda* gave up her chase and prepared to turn to bite her own pursuers. While his action with *Gremyashchi* could be dressed up as a regrettable incident, *L'Aigle* and *Arbeille* both now flew an outlawed flag. 'Mr Protheroe,' he called to an elderly master's mate who ran up and touched his fore-cock. 'Be so kind as to make a log entry to the effect that the frigate of which we are in pursuit has been determined to be unequivocally Russian, we have broken off the chase and intend to proceed to compel the two privateers formerly in company with her and sheltering under her colours, to strike the former French tricolour which they promptly hoisted when the Russian frigate stood away from them.' Poor Protheroe looked confused and nodded uncomprehendingly. 'Write it down, man, quickly now . . .'

Flustered, Protheroe finally complied and Drinkwater repeated his formal explanation. If he fell in the next two or three hours, posterity would have that much 'fact' to chew upon.

'I have it, sir,' Protheroe acknowledged. Such a veneer of legality would suffice. But if Rakov followed him round to close the trap, Drinkwater would know the worst. Birkbeck was looking at him expectantly.

'Ready, Mr Birkbeck?'

'Aye, sir.'

'Very well. Carry on.'

'Up helm!' Birkbeck sang out, and the shadows of the masts, sails and stays once more waltzed across the white planking as *Andromeda* answered her rudder and turned about.

*

All four ships were now reaching across the north-westerly wind, the Russian heading north-north-east with the *Arbeille* and *L'Aigle* on a similar course, but some three miles to the southward of the *Gremyashchi*. Between them *Andromeda* now headed back to the south, her course laid for the gap between the two French ships. At the same moment Drinkwater saw the folly of this move Birkbeck made the suggestion to pass downwind of the leeward ship, the weaker corvette *Arbeille*, a suggestion Drinkwater instantly sanctioned, it having occurred to him simultaneously.

'You know my mind, Mr Birkbeck, but feint at the gap and make them think they have us.' Drinkwater could hardly believe his luck. On a reciprocal course it was not unreasonable for an arrogant British officer to take his ship between two of the enemy and while it exposed her to two broadsides, it allowed the single ship the opportunity to fire into both enemy ships at the same time and thus double her chances of inflicting damage. But by suddenly slipping across the bow of the leeward ship, he would place the *Arbeille* in the field of fire of *L'Aigle* and thus deprive *Contre-Amiral* Lejeune of the heavier guns of the bigger vessel.

Drinkwater ran forward to the waist and bellowed below. Frey's face appeared, then that of Ashton. 'Starboard guns, Mr Frey: double shot 'em and lay them horizontally; zero elevation!'

'Aye, aye, sir! '

Ashton looked crestfallen. 'You'll get your turn in a moment or two. Mr Ashton, don't you worry.'

They were rushing down towards the enemy now and Drinkwater resumed his station, casting a look astern at the *Gremyashchi*; she remained standing northwards. Rakov was detaching himself. At least for the time being. A sudden, sanguine elation seized Drinkwater, the excitement of the gambler whose hunch is that if he stakes everything upon the next throw of the dice, all will be well. It was a flawed, illogical and misplaced confidence, he knew, but he dare not deny himself its comfort in that moment of anxious decision.

But then he felt the unavoidable, reactive visceral gripe of fear and foreboding. There were no certainties in a sea-battle, and providence was not so easily seduced.

Sauce for the Goose

'Fire!'

The French corvette lay to starboard, so close it seemed one could count the froggings on the scarlet dolmans of a dozen hussars standing on the *Arbeille's* deck with their carbines presented, yet so detached one scarcely noticed the storm of shot which responded to the thunder of *Andromeda's* broadside.

Drinkwater felt the rush of a passing ball and gasped involuntarily as it spun him around and drew the air from his lungs. Beside him Protheroe fell with a cry, slumping against Drinkwater's legs, causing him to stumble. One of the helmsmen took the full impact of a second round-shot, his shoulder reduced to a bloody pulp as he too swung round and was thrown against the mizen fife-rail so that his brains were mercifully dashed out at the same fatal moment.

As Drinkwater recovered his balance, a small calibre shot shattered his left arm. One of the hussars had hit him with a horse pistol. The blow struck him with such violence his teeth shut with a painful, head-jarring snap and a second later he felt the surge of pain, which made him gasp as his head swam. For moment he stood swaying uncertainly, submitting to an overwhelming desire to lie down and to give up. What the hell did it matter? What the hell did any of it matter . . .?

'Are you all right, sir?'

What was the point of this action? They were little men whose lives had been lived under the shadow of the eagle. Rakov and Lejeune and Captain Nathaniel Drinkwater were mere pawns in the uncaring games of the men of power and destiny. Why, he could feel the chill in the shadow of the eagle's wings even now, and see the beguiling curve of Hortense's smile seducing him towards his own miserable fate. What would the omnipotent Tsar

Alexander care for the fate of Count Rakov and his frigate? Or would the great Napoleon, whose ambition had contributed to the deaths of a million men, concern himself over the fate of a few fanatics who could not settle themselves under a fat, indolent monarch?

'Are you all right, sir?'

The British contented themselves under a fat, indolent monarch; or at least a fat, indolent regent. Why could these troublesome Frenchmen not see the sense playing the same game . . . God's bones, but it was cold, so confoundedly cold . . .

'Sir! Are you all right?'

He saw Marlowe peering at him as though through a tunnel. He could not quite understand why Marlowe was there, and then his mind began to clear and the nausea and desire to faint receded He was left with the pain in his arm. 'I fear,' Drinkwater said through clenched teeth, mastering his sweating and fearful body, 'I fear I am hit, Marlowe . . .'

'But, sir . . .'

'Send . . . for . . . laudanum, Marlowe . . . Pass word . . . to Kennedy . . . to send me . . . laudanum.' He breathed in quick and shallow gasps which somehow eased him.

'At once.' Marlowe saw with a look of horror the bloody wound just above Drinkwater's elbow.

Drinkwater's perception of the action was seen through a red mist; it cleared gradually though his being seemed dominated by the roaring throb of his broken arm. He was dimly aware the guns had fallen silent, that the shadows of the masts and sails once again traversed the deck which pitched for a few moments as *Andromeda* was luffed up into the wind. Then the guns thundered out again, adding to the throbbing in his head. Somewhere to starboard, he perceived the shallow curve of the *Arbeille*'s taffrail lined with shakoed infantry-men, and the sight roused him. By an effort of will he commanded himself again.

A fusillade of musketry swept *Andromeda*'s quarterdeck. Drinkwater felt a second ball strike him, like a whiplash across the thigh, then someone was beside him, holding a small glass phial.

'Here sir, quick!'

He swallowed the contents and for a moment more stood confused, trying to focus upon Hyde's marines whose backs were to him as they lined the hammock nettings, returning fire. Then

Arbeille drew away out of range and *Andromeda*, having raked her, fell back to port, making a stern board.

Drinkwater felt the opiate spread warmth and contentment through him; the pain ebbed, becoming a faint sensation, like the vague memory of something unpleasant that lay just beyond one's precise recollection. He was aware that *Andromeda* had come up into the wind under the stern of the French corvette and he was aware of Kennedy blinking in the sunlight, hovering at his elbow.

'Hold still, sir, while I dress your wound.' Kennedy clucked irritably. 'Hold still, damn it, sir.' Drinkwater stood and supinely allowed the surgeon to cut away his coat and bind his arm. 'You have a compound fracture, sir, and I shall have to see to it later.' Kennedy grunted as a musket ball passed close. 'Luckily the ball must have been near spent; 'tis a mess, but no major blood vessels have been severed. I may save it if it don't mortify.'

'Thank you for your encouraging prognosis, Mr Kennedy,' Drinkwater said, his teeth clenched as Kennedy finished pulling him about with what seemed unnecessary brutality. He turned back to the handling of the ship as Kennedy grabbed his bag of field dressings and scuttled back to the orlop. It must have been the first time the surgeon had been so exposed to fire, he thought idly.

'Who gave orders to rake?' he asked no one in particular.

'You did, sir,' a hatless Birkbeck reassured him.

'What are our casualties?'

'I've no idea, though a good few fellows have fallen, we knocked that corvette about . . .'

'Where's Marlowe?'

'Here, sir.'

Under the laudanum, Drinkwater's mind finally cleared. The elation he had felt earlier returned imbuing him with confidence. The wound in his thigh was no more than a scratch, his broken arm no more than a damnable inconvenience, already accommodated by shoving his left hand into his waistcoat. He strode to the rail. The marines withdrew to make room for him and he stared to starboard. The sterns of both French ships were now eight or nine cables away: the *Arbeille* trailed a tangle of wreckage over her port side and *L'Aigle* had shortened sail to keep pace with her. Their stern chase guns barked and a brace of shot skipped across the water and thudded ineffectually into *Andromeda*'s hull.

'Where's that damned Russian?'

'Somewhere beyond the Frogs, sir,' Marlowe volunteered.

Drinkwater cast his eyes aloft. All the topsails and topgallants were aback. Intact, they were nevertheless peppered with holes, and severed ropes hung in bights. Men were already aloft splicing.

'Throw the helm over, Mr Birkbeck!' Drinkwater ordered, 'Let's have her in pursuit again and bring that lot to book!'

Contre-Amiral Lejeune lay board to board with his wounded consort only as long as it took him to appraise the damage. A moment later L'Aigle's yards were braced sharp up and the frigate detached herself on the port tack, moving away from the corvette preparatory to rounding on the British frigate. As Andromeda also gained headway and began to come up with the almost supine Arbeille, L'Aigle tacked smartly and began to run back towards the British frigate. This time being caught in the cross-fire was inevitable. By using the Arbeille to mask L'Aigle's guns, Drinkwater had also ensured the French frigate's preservation and fed her company with the desire to avenge her weaker consort. Undamaged, L'Aigle bore down to finish off the perfidious Englishman. Lejeune was staking his own mission on a final gamble.

'We are the bully cornered, I fancy,' Drinkwater remarked lightheartedly. He was aware that he had the initiative and was now about to surrender it. But he was thinking clearly again; in fact his mind seemed superior to the situation, detached and almost divine in its ability to reason, untrammelled by doubts or uncertainties. He gave his orders coolly, as the first of Arbeille's renewed fire struck Andromeda, in passing the corvette to engage her larger and more formidable sister.

Frey's battery fired into the Arbeille. Drinkwater could see the boats smashed on her booms and the wreck of her main topgallant and her mizen topmast; he saw men toiling on her deck to free her from the encumbrance while the brilliant tunics of her complement of soldiers fired small arms, augmenting her main armament of 8-pounders. It puzzled Drinkwater that shots from Andromeda had flown high enough to knock down so much tophamper, but they were soon past the Arbeille and preparing to engage L'Aigle.

'Mr Ashton! Now's your chance! Fire into the frig sir!'

'Aye, aye, sir!'

'Stand by to tack ship!'

Then Ashton's port battery crashed out in a concussive broadside, only to be answered by the guns of *L'Aigle*. Within a few moments, Drinkwater knew he had met an opponent worthy of his steel. Whatever the history of *Contre-Amiral* Lejeune, here was no half-sailor who had spent the greater part of the last decade mewed up in Brest Road, living ashore and only occasionally venturing out beyond the Black Rocks. Nor had his crew found the greatest test of their seamanship to be the hoisting and lowering of topgallant masts while their ship rotted at her moorings. Lejeune and his men had been active in French cruisers, national frigates which had made a nuisance of themselves by harrying British trade.

As they passed each other and exchanged broadsides, both commanders attempted to swing under their opponent's sterns and rake. *L'Aigle*, by wearing, retained the greater speed while *Andromeda*, turning into and through the wind to tack, slowed perceptibly. The guns were now firing at will, leaping eagerly in their trucks as they recoiled, their barrels heated to a nicety, their crews not yet exhausted, but caught up in the manic exertions of men attending a dangerous business upon which they must expend an absolute concentration, or perish.

Aboard both frigates the enemy shot wreaked havoc and although the smoke from the action did not linger, but was wafted away to leeward by the persistent breeze, to shroud the *Arbeille* as she too drifted to the south-eastward, it concealed much of the damage each was inflicting upon the other.

Having tacked, and having not yet lost any spars, Drinkwater temporarily broke off the action by holding his course to the southward in an attempt to draw Lejeune away from Rakov, who still stood northwards but who had, significantly, reduced sail. Lejeune bore round without hesitation.

'He's damned confident,' said Marlowe, studying *L'Aigle* through his telescope.

'Of reinforcement by the Russian?' mooted Drinkwater, levelling his own glass with his single right hand, then giving up the attempt.

'Are we to resume the action, sir?' asked Birkbeck.

'Very definitely, Mr Birkbeck. Now we are going to lay board to board on the same tack. That will decide the issue, and we have at least reduced the opposition to one.'

'For the time being, sir,' Birkbeck said, looking askance at Drinkwater.

'I am not insensible to the facts, Mr Birkbeck,' Drinkwater said brusquely, 'but if we can but cripple *L'Aigle*, she will not be in a fit state to take Bonaparte to the United States, and if we can but take her, well the matter's closed.'

'You are considering isolating and boarding her then, sir?' asked Marlowe.

'I am considering it, Mr Marlowe, yes. Please shorten down, Mr Birkbeck. We will allow this fellow to catch up.'

'Very well, sir.' Birkbeck turned away.

'The master ain't happy, Marlowe,' Drinkwater remarked, raising his glass again,

'I think,' Marlowe said slowly, '*he* is not insensible to the fact that *you* have taken an opiate, sir.'

Drinkwater looked hard at the first lieutenant. 'He thinks I am foolhardy, does he?'

'He wishes to survive to take up that dockyard post you promised him.'

'I had forgotten that. And what of you, Mr Marlowe? Do you think me foolhardy?'

Drinkwater saw the jump of Marlowe's Adam's apple. 'No sir. I think you are merely doing your duty as you see it.'

'Which is not as you see it, eh?'

'I did not say so, sir.'

'No. Thank you, Mr Marlowe.' Then a thought occurred to Drinkwater. 'By the bye, Mr Marlowe, pipe up spirits.'

The helmsmen heard the order and Drinkwater was aware of a shuffling anticipation of pleasure among them. It would do no harm. 'Sauce for the goose,' he muttered to himself, 'is sauce for the gander.'

The respite thus gained lasted for only some twenty minutes. The forenoon was almost over, but the day was unchanged, the sea sparkled in the sunshine and the steady breeze came out of the northwest quarter. The four ships were spread out over a large right-angled triangle upon the ocean. At the northern end of the hypotenuse lay the *Gremyashchi*, now hove-to; at the point of the right-angle, the battered *Arbeille* continued to lick her wounds and drift slowly down to leeward. Both vessels were awaiting the outcome of events at the far end of the hypotenuse, where *Andromeda* lay, and astern of her, swiftly catching her up, *L'Aigle* followed.

Despite the scepticism of his sailing master, Drinkwater was confident of having almost achieved his objective. If the *Arbeille* was commanded by an officer of similar resolution to that of *L'Aigle*, and it seemed impossible that he should not be, the fact the corvette had dropped out of the action suggested she had sustained a disabling proportion of damage. He clung on to these thoughts, arguing them slowly, interspersed with waves of pain from his arm which gradually became more assertive as the effect of the laudanum wore off.

Under her topsails, Andromeda stood on and her crew awaited the enemy. As *L'Aigle* approached, Drinkwater skilfully maintained the weather gauge by edging *Andromeda* to starboard every time he observed Lejeune attempt the same manoeuvre with *L'Aigle*. On the upper-deck the marines and the gunners relaxed in the sunshine, going off a pair at a time to receive their rum ration on the gun-deck. This hiatus was soon over.

His head throbbing with the beat of his pulse, Drinkwater strode forward and bellowed down into the waist, 'Stand-to, my lads. The Frenchman is closing us fast; there's hot work yet to do.'

Lieutenant Ashton had not given a second thought to Sergeant McCann after the marine had departed from the gun-deck. His baiting was the vice of a man who habitually used a horse roughly, sawed at the reins and galled his mount with a crop, a man who was given to mindless and petty acts of cruelty simply because fate had placed him in a station which nurtured such weaknesses. Since his schooldays, Ashton had learned that small facts gleaned about others could be put to entertaining use, and McCann had been a trivial source of such amusement. Yet he was not a truly vicious man, merely a thoughtless and unimaginative one. His solicitude for Marlowe, expressed in his question to young Paine, had been out of concern more for his sister and her unborn child than for the actual well-being of the man responsible for impregnating her. Blood-ties, if they were inevitable, should not be reprehensible, and it mattered much to Josiah Ashton that Marlowe acquitted himself well, perhaps more than to Frederic Marlowe himself. It would not have mattered much to Ashton had Marlowe been killed, provided only that his death was honourable, or appeared so, even if some stain upon his sister's good character was then unavoidable.

As he waited in the gun-deck for the action to resume, Ashton, having dispensed with Marlowe, was calculating his chances of advancement if matters fell out to his advantage. Down below he was relatively safe, unless they were boarded, and even then he was confident that his own skill with a small sword and a pistol would keep him out of real trouble. Marlowe, he judged, might attempt some quixotic act and was as likely to get his come-uppance in a fight, assuming he survived the next hour. Word had already come down to the gun-deck that Captain Drinkwater had a shattered arm. If he did not fall it was quite likely that gangrene would carry him off later. On the other hand, perhaps some opportunity for Ashton to distinguish himself would emerge during the forthcoming hours.

Ashton looked across the deck to where Frey, ever diligent, peered out of a gun-port, striving to see the enemy frigate coming up from astern. Frey was senior to him, but who knew? Perhaps he too would stop a ball before the day was over.

'I can't see a damned thing,' Frey complained, crossing the deck and passing close to Ashton as he bent to stare out of one of his own larboard battery gun-ports. 'Ah, here she comes. Looks as though it's your turn for it first.' Frey smiled and patted him on the shoulder. 'Good luck.'

'Good luck,' Ashton replied with more duty than true sincerity.

A moment later one of the gun-captains called out, 'Here she comes, me lads!' and a ripple of expectation ran through the waiting men, like a breeze through dry grass.

'Lay your guns,' Ashton commanded. He waited until, like statues, the crews stood back from their loaded and primed pieces, their captains behind the breeches, lanyards in hand. Eventually, all along the deck the bare arms were raised in readiness.

'Fire!' Ashton yelled, and the gun captains jerked the lanyards and jumped aside as the still-warm guns leaped inboard with their recoil, and their crews fussed round them again.

On the deck above, Sergeant McCann had ensured each marine checked his flint and filled his cartouche box. Worn flints would cause misfires, and most of his men had fired profligately.

'Make every shot count,' McCann warned them, 'and every bullet find its mark.'

His men muttered about grandmamas and the sucking of eggs,

but they tolerated Meticulous McCann. He was a thoughtfully provident man and though few knew him enough to like him, for he had too many of the ways of an officer to enjoy popular appeal, they all respected him.

When the captain's warning to stand-to and prepare to receive fire came, Hyde merely nodded to McCann, who repeated the order. It was then, in the idle, fearful moment before action, McCann thought of Ashton and as he lowered his weapon and lined foresight and backsight on a small cluster of gilt just forward of L'Aigle's mizen mast, it was Josiah Ashton's image that his imagination conjured up beyond the muzzle of his Tower musket.

It was almost three bells when Ashton's guns barked again, beating the enemy by a few seconds. Although the range was short, Drinkwater had Birkbeck edge Andromeda away from L'Aigle, to prevent Lejeune running up too close and attempting to board and exploit his greater numbers. Even so, the storm of enemy musketry was prodigious, and the rows of hammocks were destroyed by lead shot ripping into them, fraying the barricade they made, so that the shredded canvas fluttered in the breeze. Those balls which passed over the hammocks in their nettings, either buzzed harmlessly overhead, or found a target. Most passed by, but a few struck the masts, or the boats, and a few knocked men down.

As for the enemy's round shot, they thudded into the hull or struck the lighter bulwarks, sending up an explosion of splinters. Occasionally a ball came in through a port, struck a carronade and ricocheted away with a strident whine. Others flew higher, aimed to bring down Andromeda's upper spars, discommode those on the upper deck and rob the British frigate of the ability to manoeuvre which she had thus far so brilliantly exploited to avoid such a fate. The cries of the dying and the wounded filled the air again, and a large pool of blood formed at the base of the mizen mast, pouring in a brief torrent from the shattered body of a topman lying across the trestletree boards of the mizen top high above.

The action had reached its crisis, and Drinkwater, increasingly assailed by the agony of his wounded arm, knew it. He fought the excruciating ache and the desire to capitulate to its demand to lie down and rest; his mouth was dry as dust and his voice was growing hoarse from shouting, though he could not recall much of what he had said in exhorting his men.

He knew too, that whatever the shortcomings of his ship and her company, they could not have fought her with more skill and vigour. From Birkbeck masterfully conning her, to the men who put the master's orders into practice; from the solicitous and grateful Marlowe running about the upper-deck directing the carronades, to the lieutenants and gunners below, he could not have asked for more. Nor should he forget Kennedy and his mates, labouring in the festering stink of the orlop, plying scalpel and saw, curette and pledget to save what was left of the brutalized bodies of the wounded. His own mortality irked him: he would have to submit to the surgeon's ministrations if he survived the next hour, for his bandaged arm oozed blood.

The thunder of their own guns bespoke a furious cannonade; the decks trembled with the almost constant rumblings of recoil and running out of the 12-pounders of the main armament, and it was clear to Drinkwater's experienced ear that Frey's unengaged gunners had crossed the deck to help fight the larboard battery. In fact Frey had assumed command of the forward division, an order Ashton had not liked receiving though he could not avoid obeying it, for to do so would have been to have transgressed the Articles of War in refusing to do his utmost in battle.

But Ashton could not deny the effectiveness of the reinforcement, and so furious did the gunfire become that not even the brisk breeze could now clear the smoke and the gap between the two ships became obscure. Neither the officers in the gun-deck nor those upon the quarterdeck could now see very much. L'Aigle was marked by her lines of flashing muzzles and the tops of her masts above the cloud of powder-smoke. Then they heard a cheer ripple along the upperdeck and watched as, in an almost elegant collapse, L'Aigle's main topmast went by the board. Within a quarter of an hour, however, Andromeda had lost her own mizen mast and the wreckage brought down her main topgallant. Two carronades on the quarterdeck were also dismounted in the general destruction of her bulwarks adjacent to the mizen channels. A moment later she had lost her wheel and all those who manned it as her upper-deck was swept by a hail of grapeshot.

Marlowe was nowhere to be seen in the confusion as Drinkwater summoned a hatless and dishevelled Birkbeck who seemed otherwise unscathed. 'She'll get alongside us now, by God!' the sailing master bellowed above the din.

'We must have given as good as we've got!' Drinkwater roared back.

For a few moments there was utter confusion, then *L'Aigle* loomed close alongside and through the clearing smoke they could hear cries of '*Vive L'Empereur!*' and '*Mort à l'Anglais!*' as the French soldiers whipped themselves into a frenzy.

'Prepare to repel boarders!' Drinkwater shouted, his voice cracking with the effort as his head reeled, and then the two ships came together with a sudden lurching thud and a long, tortured grinding. Above their heads on the quarterdeck, *L'Aigle's* mainyard thrust itself like a fencer's extended and questing *épée*, wavering as the two ships moved in the seaway. Shapes like ghosts appeared over the rail as veterans of Austerlitz and Borodino, of Eylau, Friedland, Jena and Wagram prepared to launch themselves across the gap between the two frigates, on to *Andromeda's* deck.

Lower down, beneath the pall of smoke that lay in the gulf between the two ships, Frey had seen the approach of *L'Aigle* and heard the excited shouting of the battle-mad troops. The cry to repel boarders came down through the thick air in the gun-deck and passed along the lines of cannon in shouted warnings.

Frey withdrew from his observation post and hurried aft to where Ashton was scurrying up and down his guns, half bent as he squinted along first one and then another as they jumped inboard for reloading. Steam sizzled as the wet sponges went in, adding a warm stickiness to the choking atmosphere. Frey tapped him on the shoulder.

'Josh!' Frey bellowed until he had attracted his colleague's attention. 'Josh! I'm taking my fellows to reinforce the upper-deck.'

'What?' Ashton was almost deaf from the concussion of the cannon and Frey had to shout in his filthy ear before Ashton understood.

'No, let me. You fight the guns.' The words were uttered before Ashton realized the implications: he had given voice to his thoughts and wavered briefly, half-hoping Frey would contradict the suggestion.

'If you want to go fire-eating good luck to you.' Frey nodded assent, straightened up and hastened back up the deck, half bent to avoid collisions with the beams. 'Starbowlines!' he bellowed, 'Small arms from the racks and follow Mr Ashton on deck! D'ye hear there? Starbowlines with Mr Ashton to the upper-deck! We're about to be boarded!' Men came away from the guns and helped themselves to cutlasses, withdrawing across the deck to where Ashton hurriedly mustered them while Frey turned back to invigorate the now flagging port gun-crews.

'Bear up, my boys, we can still blow their bloody ship to Old Harry!'

As Ashton led his men off, Frey's guns continued to engage L'Aigle's cannon muzzle to muzzle.

On the quarterdeck Hyde came into his own. In a few seconds, he had concentrated his lobsters into a double line of men behind which Drinkwater and Birkbeck could gather their wits and attempt to avert disaster. By passing messages to the steering flat, Andromeda might yet break free of L'Aigle's deadly embrace, but they had first to clear away the wreckage of fallen masts and throw back the wave of invaders.

Birkbeck's gaze ran aft and he clutched with thoughtless violence at Drinkwater's wounded arm. 'By God, sir! Look! There's the Russian!'

He pointed and Drinkwater, shaking from the pain of Birkbeck's unconscious gesture, turned to see above their stern the taut canvas of the Gremyashchi as she bore down into the action.

Chapter Eighteen   *May 1814*

The Last Candle

Drinkwater felt the chill of foreboding seize him. The game was up.

He was conscious of having fought with all the skill he could muster, of having done his duty, but the end was not now far off. He saw little point in delaying matters further, for it would only result in a further effusion of blood, and he had done everything the honour of his country's flag demanded. Besides, he was wounded and the effect of the laudanum was working off; spent ball or not, it had done for his left arm and he could no longer concentrate on the business in hand. He was overwhelmed with pain and a weariness that went far beyond the urgent promptings of his agonizing wound. He was tired of this eternal business of murder, exhausted by the effort to outmanoeuvre other equally intelligent men in this grim game of action and counter-action The effort to do more was too much for him and he felt the deck sway beneath his unsteady feet.

'Here the bastards come!'

It was Marlowe waving his sword and roaring a warning beside him. The first lieutenant had lost his hat like Birkbeck, and his sudden appearance seemed magical, like a *djinn* in a story, but it was a Marlowe afire with a fighting madness. Both his amazing presence and his words brought about a transformation in Drinkwater.

To strike at that moment would have resulted in utter confusion: Napoleon's veterans were after a revenge greater than the mere capture of a British frigate and the thought, flashing through Drinkwater's brain in an instant, compelled him to a final effort.

'God's bones! The game is worth a last candle . . .'

But his words were lost as, with a roar, the boarders poured in a flood over the hammock nettings and aboard *Andromeda*. They were answered by a volley from Hyde's rear rank of marines who promptly reloaded their muskets in accordance with their drill. Beside Drinkwater, Birkbeck drew his sword in the brief quiet. The rasp of the blade made Drinkwater turn as the front rank of marines discharged their pieces from their kneeling position.

'Stand fast, Birkbeck! I promised you a dockyard post. Hyde, forward with your bayonets!'

Drinkwater had his own hanger drawn now and advanced through the marines with Marlowe at his side. He distinctly heard Marlowe say 'Excuse me,' as he shouldered his way through the rigid ranks, and then they were shuffling forward over the resultant shambles of the marines' volleys.

Only the officers had been protected by Hyde's men; as the Frenchmen scrambled over the hammock nettings and down upon *Andromeda*, they had encountered the upper-deck gunners, topmen and waisters, the afterguard and those men whose duties required them to be abroad on the quarterdeck, forecastle and the port gangway. At Drinkwater's cry to repel boarders, most of these had seized boarding pikes, or drawn their cutlasses if they bore them.

L'Aigle's party had not been unopposed, but they outnumbered the defenders and while some were killed or remained detained in the hand-to-hand fighting, more swept past and were darting like ferrets in their quest for an enemy to overcome, in order to seize the frigate in the name of their accursed Emperor. Hyde's marines had fired indiscriminately into the mass of men coming aboard, hitting friend and foe alike, aided by discharges of langridge from the swivel guns in the tops that now swept *L'Aigle*'s rail and inhibited further reinforcement of the first wave of boarders.

All this had taken less than a minute, and then, after their third volley, Hyde's men were stamping their way across the deck, their bright, gleaming steel bayonets soon bloodied and their ranks wavering as they stabbed, twisted and withdrew, butted and broke the men of the Grand Army who had the audacity to challenge them at sea, on their own deck. They were all slithering in blood and the slime that once constituted the bodies of men; the stink of it was in their nostrils, rousing them to a primitive madness which fed upon itself and was compounded into a frenzied outpouring of violent energy.

White-faced, Drinkwater advanced with them, his left shoulder withdrawn, his right thrown forward. With shortened sword arm, he stabbed and hacked at anything in his way. He was vaguely conscious of the jar of his blade on bone, then the point of a curved and bloody sabre flashed into his field of view and he had parried it and cut savagely at the brown dolman which bore it. A man's face, a thin, lined and handsome face, as weather-beaten as that of any seaman, a face disfigured with a scar and sporting moustachios of opulent proportions and framed by tails of plaited hair, grimaced and opened a red mouth with teeth like a horse. Drinkwater could hear nothing from the hussar whose snarl was lost in the foul cacophony to which, hurt and hurting, they all contributed in their contrived and vicious hate.

The hussar fell and was shoved aside as he slumped across the breech of a carronade. The enemy were checked and thrust back. Men were pinioned to the bulwarks, crucified by bayonets, their guts shot out point-blank by pistol shot, or clubbed with butts or pike-staves, and then with a reinforcing roar Ashton's gun crews came up from the waist, eager to get to closer grips with an enemy they had shortly before been blowing to Kingdom Come with their brutal artillery.

Drinkwater sensed rather than saw them. It was all that was needed to sweep the remaining able-bodied French, soldiers and seamen alike, back over the side of *Andromeda* and across the grinding gap between the two heaving ships. Drinkwater was up on the carronade slide himself, trying to get over the rail one-handed. Frustrated, he put the *forte* of his hanger in his mouth, afterwards recalling a brief glimpse of dark water swirling between the tumble-home of *L'Aigle* and *Andromeda*. He leaned outwards and seized an iron crane of *L'Aigle's* hammock nettings as Ashton's men joined Hyde's marines and their combined momentum bore the counter-attack onward.

Sergeant McCann had been the right-hand marker as Lieutenant Hyde ordered the marines to advance. They had only to move a matter of feet; less than half the frigate's beam, but every foot-shuffling step had been fiercely contested, and McCann felt his boots crunch unmercifully down upon the writhings of the wounded and dying. The pistols in his belt felt uncomfortable as he twisted and thrust, edging forward all the time, but they reminded him of his resolve.

Suddenly he was aware of movement on his extreme right. As the flanker, he turned instinctively and saw Lieutenant Ashton lead the gunners up out of the gun-deck. He grinned as his heart-beat quickened and Ashton, casting about him to establish his bearings and the tactical situation, caught sight of Sergeant McCann appearing in the smoke to his left.

'Forward Sergeant!' he cried exuberantly, engaging the first Frenchman he came across, a dragoon officer who had shed his cumbersome helmet and fought in a forage cap and a short stable coat. The dragoon slashed wildly, but Ashton was supported by two sailors and the three of them cut the man to his knees in a second. The dragoon fell, bleeding copiously. Lieutenant Ashton felt a surge of confidence as he swept his men forward.

Smoke enveloped them and Ashton half turned, again shouting 'Come on, Sergeant!' his voice full of exasperation. Unable to see the full fury of the action on the quarterdeck, Ashton hacked a path forward and then, as the pressure eased, McCann advanced at a quickening pace. The line of marines began to gain momentum as the column of gunners continued to emerge from the gloom of the gun-deck. Below, their remaining colleagues carried on adding their remorseless thunder to the air as they fired indiscriminately without aiming, into the wooden wall that heaved and surged alongside.

Sergeant McCann followed Lieutenant Ashton as he clambered over the bulwark amidships, and stretched out for the fore chains of *L'Aigle*. He could have killed Ashton at that moment, stabbed him ignominiously in the arse as he had sworn to do, but he faltered and then Ashton had gone, and with him the opportunity.

Further aft Lieutenant Marlowe had reached *L'Aigle*'s mizen chains and was hacking his way down upon the quarterdeck of the French frigate. Between the two British officers, the line of defenders bowed back, but it had already transformed itself as the French attack was repulsed and the tide turned. As Marlowe struck a French aspirant's extended arm and deflected the pistol ball so that it merely grazed his cheek, the whole line began to scramble aboard *L'Aigle*.

Carried forward by this madness, Drinkwater felt his ankle twist as he landed on the enemy deck, and he fell full length, cushioned by the corpse of a half-naked French gunner who lay headless beside his gun. The stink of blood, dried sweat and garlic struck him and he dragged himself to his feet as a fellow boarder knocked him over again. The seaman paused, saw whom he had hit and gave Drinkwater a hand to rise.

'Beg pardon, sir, but 'ere, let me . . .'

'Obliged . . .'

It seemed quieter now and Drinkwater took stock. There were fewer of the enemy, which seemed strange since they were now aboard *L'Aigle*. The wave of men he had led aboard dissipated, like a real wave upon a beach, running faster and faster as it shallowed, until, extended to its limit, it stopped and ran back. Bloody little fights took place everywhere, but the numbers of men already slaughtered had robbed *L'Aigle* of all her advantage, and it now became apparent to what extent *Andromeda*'s cannon-fire had damaged the French ship.

About the helm lay a heap of bodies and Drinkwater caught the gleam of sunlight on bullion lace. Was one of the ungainly dead *Contre-Amiral* Lejeune? The boats on *L'Aigle*'s booms were filled with holes, her main fife-rails were smashed to matchwood, releasing halliards and lifts. Parted ropes lay like inert serpents about the decks, drawing lines over and about the corpses, like some delineation of the expiring lives which had left an indelible impression upon the carnage.

About the broken boats on the booms amidships and at the opening of the after hatchway, Hyde's marines were clustered, firing down into the gun-deck below, thus preventing any reinforcement of the upper-deck such as Ashton had managed, and which had turned the tide of the battle. Elsewhere a handful of British jacks chased solitary Frenchmen to their deaths, and it seemed in that short, contemplative moment that they had achieved the impossible and seized *L'Aigle*. Drinkwater thought he ought perhaps to order his own guns to cease fire, but when he stopped to think about anything the pain of his broken arm came back to him and he wanted to give in to it. Surely providence was satisfied: surely he had done enough. Then, as if from a great distance, Drinkwater heard a cry.

'Look to your front, sir!' There was something urgent and familiar about the voice. Slowly he turned about and saw through the smoke, the hazy figure of Birkbeck standing above *Andromeda*'s rail and gesturing. 'Look to your front!'

'What the deuce are you talking about?' Drinkwater called, unaware that the terrible noise of battle had partially deafened him and he had been shouting his head off so that his voice was a feeble croak.

'The Russian! The *Gremyashchi!*' Birkbeck waved over Drinkwater's head, gesturing at something and Drinkwater turned again. Looming above the port bulwark of *L'Aigle*, unscathed and perhaps a foot higher in her freeboard, the big Russian frigate appeared. Drinkwater could see her bulwarks lined with men, many of them fiercely bearded, like the Russians he had seen on the coast of California many, many years ago . . .

And then he suddenly felt the naked exposure of his person.

'Take your men below, Sergeant!'

Ashton shoved a marine aside and pointed down into *L'Aigle*'s gundeck.

'Sir?'

'You heard me! Lead your men below and clear the gun-deck.'

McCann hesitated; Ashton was ordering him to a certain death.

'Are you a coward?'

'The hell I am . . .'

'Then do as you are ordered! I'll take my men down from forward.'

Furious, McCann ported his musket and began to descend into the smoke-filled hell. 'Catten,' he instructed one marine, 'run back aboard and let the master know we're going below before that stupid bastard has us all shot by our own gunners. The rest of you, follow me!' he cried.

Ashton was right: he, McCann, *was* a coward. Only a coward would have submitted to the thrall of soldiering; only a coward would have passively acquiesced to this madness and only a coward would have let slip the opportunity to rid the world of Ashton. Almost weeping with rage, McCann charged below.

What confronted the invaders when they spread out across *L'Aigle*'s gun-deck was horrifying. The planking was ploughed up by shot. In places, splinters stood like petrified grass. Stanchions were broken and guns were dismounted. Sunlight slanted into the fume-filled gloom through the frigate's gun-ports. *Andromeda*'s 12-pound shot at short range had beaten in the ship's side in one place, while the grape and langridge she had poured into *L'Aigle* had piled the dead about their guns in heaps.

*

On *Andromeda*'s gun-deck, Lieutenant Frey received the message to cease fire from Mr Paine who also added the request for the larboard guns to be withdrawn and the ports shut.

'What's amiss?' asked Frey, unable to do more than shout to hear his own voice.

'We need your men on deck, sir. Most of our fellows are aboard the Frenchman and that bloody Russian's just coming up on her disengaged side!'

'Where's the captain?' Frey asked.

'I last saw him going over the side with his hanger in his teeth.'

'Good God!'

Frey turned and began bellowing at his men.

As McCann shuffled forward in the oppressive gloom of *L'Aigle*'s gun-deck, resistance became increasingly fierce. It was clear that some of the soldiers had either retreated to the shelter of the guns amidships, or had been held in reserve there. A volley met the marines and several men fell. McCann took shelter behind the round bulk of the main capstan and prepared to return fire as if in his native woods, sheltering behind the bole of a hickory tree.

As his eyes became accustomed to the semi-darkness McCann began to select targets and fire with more precision. A small group of marines took cover either with him or behind adjacent guns. He was conscious of an exchange of fire at the far end of the deck where Ashton was attacking down through a pale shaft of sunlight lancing in by way of the forward companionway. It was clear that there, too, resistance was disciplined and effective. Then above the shots and yells, McCann heard Ashton's voice.

'McCann! Where the devil are you? Come and support me you damned Yankee blackguard!'

Ashton's intemperate and ill-considered plea took no account of McCann's own predicament, but was a reaction to the situation Ashton's headstrong action had landed him in. But its insulting unreasonableness struck a chord in McCann's psyche, and his spirit, loosened by the heat of battle, broke in hatred, remorse and the final bitter explosion of his reason.

And then McCann saw Ashton standing halfway down the forward companionway, illuminated by the shaft of light that lanced down from the clear blue sky above. He presented even an indifferent marksman a perfect target, and the fact that no Frenchman amidships had yet hit him confirmed McCann in his belief that Ashton had been providentially delivered to his own prowess. He knew the moment was fleeting and his Tower musket was discharged: McCann drew a pistol from his belt, on Ashton's silhouetted head, and fired. As the smoke from the frizzen and muzzle cleared Ashton vanished. McCann's triumph was short-lived; a second later he heard Ashton's voice: 'McCann, give fire, damn you!'

Alone, his bayonet fixed and his musket horizontal, Sergeant McCann forsook the shelter of the capstan and, with a crash of boots and an Indian yell, ran forward. Four balls hit him before he had advanced five paces, but his momentum carried him along the deck and he could see, kneeling and levelling a carbine at him, a big man whose bulk seemed to fill the low space.

'Sergeant McCann . . .!' Ashton's plaintive cry was lost in the noise of further musketry. McCann saw the yellow flash of the big horse-grenadier's carbine. The blow of the ball stopped him in his tracks, but it had missed his heart and such was his speed that it failed to knock him over. He shuffled forward again and in his last, despairing act as he fell to his knees, he thrust with his bayonet. Gaston Duroc of the Imperial Horse Grenadiers parried the feeble lunge of the British marine with his bare hand.

'Sergeant McCann, damn you to hell!' cried Lieutenant Ashton, retreating back up the forward companionway and calling his men to prevent the counter-attacking French from following and regaining the upper-deck.

Captain Drinkwater was aware of men about him, though there were few enough of them.

'My lads . . .' he began, but he was quite out of breath and, besides, could think of nothing to say. It would be only a moment or two before the Russians stormed into L'Aigle and wrested the French ship back from his exhausted men. He closed his eyes to stop the world swaying about him.

'Are you all right sir?'

He had no idea who was asking. 'Perfectly fine,' he answered, thanking the unknown man for his concern. And it was true; he felt quite well now, the pain had gone completely and someone seemed to be taking his sword from his hand. Well, if it meant surrender, at least it did not mean dishonour. If they survived, Marlowe and Birkbeck would manage matters, and Frey . . .

The bed was wondrously comfortable; he could sleep and sleep and sleep . . .

He could hear Charlotte Amelia in the next room. She was playing the harpsichord; something by Mozart, he thought, though he was never certain where music was concerned. And there was Elizabeth's voice. It was not Mozart any more, but a song of which Elizabeth was inordinately fond. He wished he could remember its name . . .

'Congratulations, Lieutenant.'

Frey bowed. 'Thank you, sir, but here is our first lieutenant, Mr Marlowe.' Frey gestured as an officer almost as dishevelled and grubby as himself came up. A broken hanger dangled by its martingale from his right wrist. In his hands he bore the lowered colours of *L'Aigle*.

'What's all this?' Marlowe demanded, his face drawn and a wild look in his eye. His cheek was gouged by a black scabbing clot. The appearance of the Russian had surprised him too, for he had been occupied with the business of securing the French frigate upon whose deck the three men now met.

'Captain Count Rakov, Marlowe, ' Frey muttered and, lowering his voice, added 'executing a smart *volte-face* in the circumstances, I think.'

'I don't understand . . .'

'For God's sake bow and pretend you do.' Frey bowed again and repeated the introduction. 'Captain Count Rakov . . . Lieutenant Marlowe.'

'Where is Captain Drinkwater?' asked the Russian in a thick, faltering accent. 'I see him on the quarterdeck and then he go. You,' Rakov looked at Marlowe, 'strike ensign.'

'I, er, I don't know where Captain Drinkwater is . . .' Marlowe looked at Frey.

'He is dead?' Rakov asked.

'Frey?'

'Captain Drinkwater has been wounded, sir,' Frey advised.

'And die?'

'I do not believe the wound to be mortal, sir.' Frey was by no means certain of this, but the Russian's predatory interest and the circumstances of his intervention made Frey cautious. Rakov's motives were as murky as ditchwater and they were a long way from home in a half-wrecked ship. Frey was not about to surrender the initiative to a man who had apparently changed sides and might yet reverse the procedure if he thought Captain Drinkwater's wound was serious.

'In fact, Mr Marlowe,' Frey lied boldly, 'he left orders to proceed to Angra without delay.' Frey turned to Rakov and decided to bluff the Russian and hoist him with his own petard. 'And he asked that you, Count Rakov, would assist us to bring our joint prizes to an anchorage there. He regretted the misunderstanding that occasioned us to fire into each other. I believe there was some confusion about which ensigns these ships were flying.'

Rakov regarded Frey with a calculating and shrewd eye, then turned to Marlowe. 'You command, yes?' he broke the sentence off expectantly.

'Yes, yes, of course,' Marlowe temporized. 'If that is what Captain Drinkwater said . . .'

'He was quite specific about the matter, gentlemen,' said Frey with a growing confidence.

'You British . . .' said the Russian and turned on his heel, leaving the *non sequitur* hanging in the air.

'Whew,' exhaled Frey when Rakov was out of earshot.

'D'you mind telling me what all that was about, damn it?' Marlowe asked.

'I think we won the action, Frederic, in every sense. Now, you had better see whether we have enough men to get this bloody ship to Terceira.'

'Have you seen Ashton?'

'Ashton? No, I haven't, but I suspect the worst.'

'Oh God . . .' Marlowe stood uncertainly shaking his head. Then he looked up at Frey, a frown on his face. 'I've a curious ringing in my ears, Frey . . .'

'Count yourself lucky that's all you've got,' said Frey. 'Now let us take stock of matters, shall we.' It was a gentle hint more than a question, and Marlowe dumbly nodded his agreement.

Chapter Nineteen   *May–June 1814*

A Burying of Hatchets

'Mr Gilbert, please forgive me for not coming ashore . . .'

'My dear Captain Drinkwater, pray do not concern yourself. It is you who have been put to the greater exertion, I do assure you.' Gilbert smiled urbanely. 'As for the Captain-General, why, he perfectly understands your situation and joins me in wishing you a speedy recovery.'

'Please convey my thanks to His Excellency and, pray, do take a seat.'

Gilbert sat in the cabin chair opposite Drinkwater whose left arm was doubled in a splint and sling. He observed the sea-officer's pallid complexion as Drinkwater moved uneasily in his chair, evidence of the pain he was in.

'Frampton, a glass for Mr Gilbert.'

'Thank you.'

Frampton offered a glass from a small silver tray and Gilbert raised it in a toast. 'To the squadron that never was,' he said, indicating the view from the stern windows of the cabin. Lying at anchor between the commanding guns of His Britannic Majesty's frigate *Andromeda* and His Imperial Majesty's frigate *Gremyashchi*, lay the *Arbeille* and *L'Aigle*.

'Your fellow Marlowe gave a vivid account of the action,' Gilbert said, sipping his wine. 'It seems a pity it will go unrecorded, but . . .' he shrugged, *'c'est la guerre.'*

Drinkwater raised his own glass and half-turned to contemplate the view. The sheltered anchorage of Angra lay between low, *maquis*-covered slopes, and the subtle, poignant scent of the land permeated the open sash. The ships presented a curious appearance, the regularity of their masts cut down by the action and now undergoing repair. The shortfall of spare spars occasioned by *Andromeda*'s hurried departure for escort duties was being made good from the stock aboard the French ships, so that it was estimated that within three or four days all would be sufficiently sea-worthy to attempt the passage to a home port. And therein lay complications.

'That is where you are wrong,' Drinkwater said, swinging round to Gilbert. 'Unfortunately it is not war; unfortunately it is a mess, though you are correct it will go unrecorded. Poor Marlowe will be disappointed if he expects to get a step in rank or even to take a prize home. We have taken no prizes . . .'

'I entirely agree, Captain, and the situation is the more complicated since we received news from Lisbon only yesterday that Napoleon Bonaparte has for some time been installed as King of Elba . . .'

'Elba?' Drinkwater frowned. 'I know only of one island of Elba and it is off the Tuscan coast, a dog's watch distance from France, not far from Naples . . .'

'Your incredulity is unsurprising, but it is the same Elba.'

'Good God!'

'I have no idea why the place was selected; it seems the height of stupidity to me.'

'So all the endeavours of these poor benighted devils would have been wasted, which consideration begs the question of my own . . .'

'And Rakov's,' added Gilbert.

'I suppose that is some consolation.'

'I understand from young Marlowe that Rakov played a double-game.'

Drinkwater nodded. 'It would seem that having offered the Bonapartists his protection, he abandoned them when it became obvious that to do so meant a full-scale engagement with a British frigate. I don't know how much discretion Rakov was permitted in the interpretation of his own orders, but he can scarcely have been sleeping easily since our confrontation.'

'It was just as well that he did have a change of heart,' said Gilbert. 'According to Marlowe, he was in a position to retake L'Aigle . . .'

'Ah, yes, but he came alongside the French ship on the opposite side to ourselves; had he meant mischief to the last, he would have ranged alongside our unengaged, starboard side.' Drinkwater paused a moment, then added, 'We were a sitting duck.'

'I see,' said Gilbert contemplatively, adding, 'Well, the interpretation of your own orders cannot have been easy.'

The remark brought a rueful smile to Drinkwater's face. 'I enjoyed far greater latitude than Count Rakov,' he said, then cutting off any further comment which might have been indiscreet and let too much slip to a stranger, Drinkwater said, 'As matters stand now, Rakov's action has fortuitously compromised no one.'

'Indeed not. In fact, quite the contrary, for if the Lisbon papers are to be believed, and I have one here,' Gilbert put down his wine glass and fished in a large black-leather wallet, ' 'twas the Tsar himself who approved Elba.'

'The Tsar?' queried Drinkwater, 'But that makes no sense.'

'Unless His Imperial Majesty had second thoughts.' Gilbert held out the newspaper.

'I don't read Portuguese,' said Drinkwater drily.

'Of course not, I do beg your pardon . . .'

'It occurs to me that if you were able to read that to Rakov, we might defuse any further problems.'

'Why not read it to them all? Boney's partisans should know this too. It diverts their attention from America back to Europe . . .'

'And will ensure we can send both ships in to a French port,' added Drinkwater enthusiastically.

'Who commands the French?'

'As far as I can determine, their original leader was a Rear-Admiral Lejeune but he was mortally wounded and it would seem that a military officer is now the senior.'

Gilbert uncrossed his legs and sat up, placing his half-empty glass on the table 'Captain, may I presume to make a suggestion to which I am also able to make a modest contribution?'

'By all means.'

'Would you be prepared to host a dinner here, this afternoon? I shall send off a porker and some fresh vegetables, together with some tolerable wine. If you invited, say, three French officers, Rakov and two of his own men together with some of your own, we might stop any further unpleasantness and thereby offer all the other poor devils an explanation.'

'Would you act as interpreter of the newspaper?'

'Yes, why? Oh, you are thinking the French or the Russians might not trust us?'

' 'Tis a possibility.'

'You are quite right; I will bring one of the Portuguese customs officers.'

Drinkwater nodded and Gilbert, pulling out a gold hunter, said, 'At three of the clock?'

'What time have you now . . .?' Drinkwater confirmed Gilbert's Azorean time coincided with *Andromeda*'s own ship's time and nodded. 'We shall expect you then. I will arrange to have invitations delivered.'

Gilbert rose, his manner suddenly brisk. 'We both have work to do, Captain, so I shall take my leave for the nonce and look forward to seeing you later.' He smiled. 'An event like this: certainly livens up a dull, if pleasant place.'

'I should have thought,' replied Drinkwater, walking with Gilbert to the cabin door, 'that this was almost lotus-eating.'

'Almost,' Gilbert said with a laugh, 'but a man can choke, even on lotuses.'

When he had seen Gilbert's boat off, Drinkwater returned to the cabin and stood for a moment looking out through the stern windows. The atmosphere aboard the two French ships must be wretched in the extreme with half of Hyde's marines doing duty as guards, just as disarmed French *grognards* did duty as donkeys aboard *Andromeda*, assisting with the business of re-rigging and labouring under duress. Matters can have been no happier aboard the *Gremyashchi*. Rakov had studiously avoided personal contact with Drinkwater and conducted all intercourse through the medium of his son, a lieutenant who spoke better English than his father. Drinkwater turned and his eye was caught by Gilbert's abandoned, half-full glass. He recalled the consul's offer of some 'tolerable wine'.

His own was obviously intolerable. Well, so be it; lotus-eating clearly had its drawbacks. Drinkwater eased himself into his chair, reached for pen, ink and paper and called his servant.

'Frampton, pass word for a midshipman to report in a quarter of an hour. I shall be entertaining at six bells in the afternoon watch. Dinner for,' he paused and made a quick calculation, 'for seventeen. Yes, I know, we shall have to borrow some of the wardroom silver and their table. A pig and some vegetables will sent off this morning from the shore.'

'Aye, aye, sir.' Frampton's tone bore the dull acquiescent tone of the hopeless servitor. He began his shuffling retreat to his pantry with a sigh when Drinkwater, who already had bent to his writing, looked up.

'Oh and, Frampton, the consul will also be sending off a quantity of tolerable wine.'

'Very good, sir.'

The unusual nature of the gathering aboard HMS *Andromeda* that sunlit afternoon precluded any real sociability. Two thirds of those present had recently been, as the colloquialism had it, at hammer and tongs with each other, while the motives of the other third were highly suspect. A jolly, convivial dinner being out of the question, Drinkwater had decided that the proceedings would be formal and the serving of the meal incidental to the real business in hand. To this end, Drinkwater instructed Hyde to parade those of his marines left aboard *Andromeda*, and two files lined the quarterdeck as a guard of honour, commanded by Hyde, resplendent in scarlet, with his gorget glittering at his throat and a drawn sword in his white-gloved hand. The turnout of the marines owed much to the assiduous training of the late and lamented Sergeant McCann who lay, with over a score of his ship-mates buried off the western cape of the island of Graciosa.

Drinkwater had also turned out in full dress, as had his three lieutenants, the master and the surgeon, though Drinkwater suspected the latter resented the flummery of the occasion. All the British officers wore their hangers and, in accordance with Drinkwater's instructions, each had his assigned group of foreign officers to look after. In his written invitations, Drinkwater had stated *Andromeda*'s boats would pick up the French officers, and his midshipmen had been given explicit orders to allow the barge from the *Gremyashchi* to arrive alongside ahead of them. Gilbert and the Portuguese customs officer, however, came off first.

'Captain Drinkwater, may I introduce Senhor Bensaude,' Gilbert said, smiling.

'Welcome aboard, sir, I understand you have a good command of English and will translate the news for us.'

'It will be my pleasure, Captain.'

'I have acquainted Senhor Bensaude with the delicacies of the situation,' Gilbert added.

'Indeed, I understand quite perfectly,' Bensaude added, his accent curiously muted.

'Your English is flawless, Senhor,' Drinkwater replied, impressed.

'I formerly worked in a Lisbon house exporting wine to England. It was run by an English family by the name of Co'burn.'

'Ah, that explains matters.' Drinkwater turned to Gilbert. 'And thank you for your pigs; as you can smell, they will be ready shortly.'

Marlowe approached with the news that the *Gremyashchi*'s boat was coming alongside, and a few moments later Captain Count Vladimir Ivanovich Rakov and his son were engaged in conversation with Gilbert and Lieutenants Ashton and Frey, while Drinkwater welcomed the party from the French ships.

He recognized their leader immediately. The thin, ascetic, sun-burnt features with the dependent moustaches, the pigtails and queue were that of the hussar officer Drinkwater had cut down and he had last seen slumped against a carronade slide. Beneath the burnished complexion, the hussar's skin bore a ghastly pallor. Like Drinkwater, he wore a sling, but he concealed this beneath his brown, silverfrogged pelisse which he wore, contrary to common practice, over his sword-arm. A large sabretache dangled from his hip, vying for the attention of any onlookers with his sky-blue overalls, but he wore no sword.

The hussar officer carried an extravagantly plumed busby under his left arm. His hessian boots were of scarlet leather and bore gold tassels. Apart from regimental differences, he reminded Drinkwater, in his dress, of Lieutenant Dieudonné, whom he had fought on the ice at the edge of the Elbe.*

'I am Colonel Marbet,' the hussar officer said in halting English, inclining his head in a curt bow. Then, having established his precedence, he stood back and a naval officer came forward.

'I am Capitaine de Frégate Duhesme.' Drinkwater had a vague recollection of seeing this man before after he had suffered the ministrations of debridement and bone-setting by Kennedy, when he accepted the formal surrender of *L'Aigle* and relinquished the details to Marlowe and Frey, with the sole instruction to return her commander's sword to him.

'Welcome aboard, Capitaine. I understand Capitaine Friant of the *Arbeille* is too indisposed to join us.'

* See *Under False Colours*

'He is badly wounded,' answered Duhesme in good English. 'Colonel Marbet of the Second Hussars is the senior of us, but this is Capitaine Duroc of the Imperial Horse Grenadiers . . .'

The big man in the blue and white coat held a huge bearskin under the crook of his left arm and wore ungainly jack-boots and spurs. These had been buffed for the occasion, and judging by the gleam in his eyes, there was fight still left in Duroc.

Drinkwater coughed to gain their collective attention. 'Gentlemen, there is much to discuss and it would be the better done over dinner. Please be so kind as to follow me into the cabin.' And without further preamble he led the way below.

As soon as the company was seated and their glasses filled, and while the lieutenants each carved a joint of pork, Drinkwater rose and addressed them all.

Gentlemen, welcome aboard His Britannic Majesty's frigate *Andromeda*. For those of you who do not already know it, I am Nathaniel Drinkwater, a post-captain in the Royal Navy of Great Britain.' He spoke slowly, allowing Duhesme to translate for Marbet and Duroc. 'The unfortunate circumstances that led to the actions between our several vessels,' Drinkwater paused a moment, laying emphasis on the point and staring at Rakov, 'have been overtaken by events. Mr Gilbert here, the British consul at Angra do Heroismo, has informed me that news has arrived from Lisbon which affects us all, one way or another.

'Capitaine Duhesme, would you be kind enough to translate what I have said for the benefit of Count Rakov . . .'

'Not necessary,' Rakov said. 'I understand . . .'

'I beg your pardon, Count, I did not know you spoke English very well.'

'I serve with Admiral Hanikov's squadron in North Sea. You not know . . .'

'On the contrary, Count, I am perfectly acquainted with Admiral Hanikov's movements in the North Sea. Now I shall proceed . . .'

Drinkwater ignored Rakov's glare and continued while the plates were passed and vegetables served. Frampton and the ward-room messmen fussed about the fringes of the tables and Drinkwater noted Gilbert's wine was tolerable enough to be swallowed in considerable quantities.

'Mr Gilbert has solicitously brought off Senhor Bensaude, an officer of the Portuguese customs service, to impartially translate this news to us. Drinkwater turned to Bensaude. 'Senhor, if you would be so kind . . .'

Bensaude rose and the crackle of the newspaper filled the expectant cabin as he held it up to read. He was not a tall man, but the broadsheet's top touched the deck-beams above his head.

'The despatch is dated Paris, 2nd May, and the date of this newspaper is Lisbon, 14th May. The despatch states that: "It is reported from Frejus that Napoleon Bonaparte arrived at that place and embarked in the British Frigate *Undaunted*, Captain Ussher commanding, on the evening of 28th April. Bonaparte landed at Portoferraio on the morning of 4th May and assumed the title of King of Elba . . .'

But Bensaude got no further, the succulent pork and its steaming accompaniment of cabbage and aubergines went ignored for three full minutes, while the assembly digested the fact of an Elban exile and its implications for them all. Drinkwater's attempt to break the parties by interspersing his own officers among his guests only added to the babel, for Rakov leaned across Frey and Duroc to speak to his son, at first in French and then in Russian, while Duroc, his face dark with anger, almost bellowed at Marbet across Hyde, Marlowe and the interval between the two tables. For Drinkwater himself, the thought that a mere four days difference would have saved them all the necessity of the tragic adventure that now drew to its conclusion, ate like acid into his soul. He thought again of the urgency of Hortense's news, of the awful consequences should the thing come to pass, and of the needless dead who had been sacrificed to prevent something that would, as matters turned out, never have happened anyway.

Thought of the dead made him look at Marbet. The hussar was trying to listen to Duroc, who boomed at him passionately, but the fight with pain and sickness was obvious to a fellow sufferer. Drinkwater felt a sudden presentiment that Marbet would not see France again. The guilty certainty diverted him and he wondered if the French conspirators knew Hortense Santhonax, then dismissed from his mind any intention to ask. If they agreed to what he was about to propose, he did want another, vengeful death laid to his account. Let Hortense prosper, even though he must himself support her. The thought of this brought Drinkwater to himself. He waited a moment for things to quieten down and when there seemed no prospect of this, he thumped on the table until the cutlery and the glasses rang, simultaneously calling them all to order with a commanding, 'Gentlemen! Gentlemen! Please do not neglect your victuals!'

He paused just long enough for those translating to effect a silence. Like guilty schoolboys they picked up knife and fork. He took advantage of their awkwardness and resumed his speech. 'I appreciate this news excites us all. Colonel Marbet and Capitaine Duhesme, I trust that you will return to a French port. If I may suggest it, flying the Bourbon lilies to ease matters. I am sure Count Rakov would join me in signing a document saying that you were lately on a cruise and learned about the fate of the Emperor from us . . .' Drinkwater smiled as Marbet looked at Duhesme and Duroc, exchanging quick, low remarks with both officers. While this public, if muted conference took place, Drinkwater caught Rakov's eye.

'As for you and the *Gremyashchi*, Count Rakov, I consider the unfortunate matter of our exchange of fire should be regarded as accidental.' Drinkwater watched Rakov's expression, ramming his point home: 'Unless of course you wish me to report your opening fire upon the British flag . . . It was doubtless an error, probably attributable to one of your officers . . .' Drinkwater picked up his glass and smiled over it. 'Well, then, it seems a pity that the French national cruisers *L'Aigle* and *Arbeille* had not heard of the abdication of the Emperor Napoleon and the restoration of King Louis, and engaged this ship before Capitaine Duhesme could be acquainted with the facts . . .'

Drinkwater looked round the table. The French were disconsolate; not only had they suffered defeat, they now knew the fate of their Emperor was no glorious resurrection in Canada, but that of a petty king, on an arid and near worthless island off the Italian coast. Count Rakov seemed sunk in gloom, alternating deep draughts of wine with short bursts of conversation with his son who seemed to be arguing some point of cogency.

Drinkwater raised an eyebrow at Gilbert who gave an almost imperceptible nod of satisfaction, before addressing a remark to Bensaude. Drinkwater decided to avail himself of the pork before him, which had been carved in small slices for him to eat one-handed. It was almost cold, but the flavour remained delicious, and with Gilbert's wine to wash it down Drinkwater began to relax.

'Capitaine Drinkwater . . .'

Drinkwater looked up. Duhesme was addressing him from the far table. 'Colonel Marbet . . .' Duhesme looked at Marbet who nodded with an exhausted resignation, then at Duroc whose face looked more drawn than ever. Duhesme began again. 'We agree your idea and accept your proposal.'

'That is good news, Colonel.' Drinkwater turned to Rakov. 'Count, it remains for you to agree . . .'

Rakov coughed and put his wine glass down with a heavy nod. 'Ver' well. I agree.'

Drinkwater looked round the table and raised his own glass high. 'Gentlemen, we have all lived our lives under the shadow of the eagle and the eagle is now caged. Let us drink to peace, gentlemen.' He looked round the table. Duroc's face was full of the rage of humiliation and mutilated pride and Drinkwater added, 'At least for the time being.'

A full belly dimmed the pain of his arm and Drinkwater felt the burden of responsibility lifted from his shoulders. It was the first time he had felt relief since his fateful meeting with Hortense Santhonax. He spoke to several of his departing guests as they went over the side.

'I hope you recover fully from your wound, Colonel,' he said to Marbet as the French officer prepared to be helped over the side into Midshipman Paine's cutter. 'And I am sorry that I was the means by which you suffered it.'

Duhesme was at Marbet's elbow, assisting him and acting as interpreter. The hussar looked at Drinkwater, shrugged and muttered something which Duhesme translated as, 'Per'aps the war is not yet over, Capitaine, and peace may be short. The eagle, as you call the Emperor, is not caged, but perched upon a little rock. If he raises himself, he can see France.'

'I fear you are right. This may be *au revoir* then.'

Duhesme translated and Marbet, fixing his eyes upon Drinkwater, muttered a comment which Duhesme duly interpreted.

'For me, Capitaine, the Colonel says, it is good-bye . . .' And Drinkwater saw death quite clearly in Marbet's deep-set eyes.

'He is a brave man, Capitaine,' Duhesme added.

'That is the tragedy of war, M'sieur,' Drinkwater replied. 'Tell him I honour his courage and that his Emperor was gallantly served.'

Moved by the incongruous sight of the curiously attired hussars as they somehow descended to the boat despite their tasselled boots, pelisses and wounds, Drinkwater turned aside.

Rakov's barge left after *Andromeda*'s cutter had swept the French away. Saying his farewells, Drinkwater asked, 'What does the name *Gremyashchi* signify, Count Rakov?'

The Russian officer consulted his son and replied, 'It means "thunderer".'

'Well I'm damned! I was appointed to command a British ship of that name. Well Count, it seems we have always been allies. May I say that I hope we part friends.' Drinkwater held out his hand and, after a moment's hesitation, Rakov took it.

Gilbert and Bensaude were the last to leave and both shook Drinkwater's hand warmly. 'I am obliged to you both,' Drinkwater said, 'and can only express my sincere thanks.'

'It has been a pleasure Captain,' said Gilbert, 'and I consider you have rendered these islands a signal service. Bonaparte's presence here would have been disastrous for us; his presence elsewhere beyond these islands would have been far worse. You have moreover buried hatchets with commendable diplomacy.'

'I agree absolutely with Mr Gilbert,' Bensaude said, and then they were gone and Drinkwater swept his officers back into the cabin, refilled their glasses and addressed them as they stood there in an untidy, expectant knot.

'There will be several unanswered questions occurring to you, gentlemen, not least among them what the events of recent days have been about. Perhaps I can best explain them by saying that it is more important to remember what they have not been about. They have not been about the prolongation of the war in Europe; more importantly, they have not been about the triumph of the Americans, of Canadian rebels and perhaps the establishment of a second Napoleonic empire in the North Americas.

'I have offered the French a means by which they may return to France with honour, allowing them to go back to their homes and families. I have also offered the Russians a means by which they too can return to the Baltic without discredit.

'In these conclusions I believe we have done our duty and

upheld the dignity of the British crown. Now I wish only to drink to your healths.'

Drinkwater swallowed his wine and put the glass on the nearest table. A moment's silence filled the cabin and then Marlowe raised his own glass and looked round.

'I give you Captain Drinkwater, gentlemen!'

And they raised their glasses to him, men who seemed still to be no more than mere boys, but with whom he had gone through the testing time, and who had not let him down. As they filed out, he turned away and surreptitiously wiped the tears from his eyes.

'Any orders sir?' Marlowe asked from the door. He was the last to leave.

'Let me know when the ship is ready for sea, Mr Marlowe.'

'Aye, aye, sir.'

After they had all gone and Frampton had cleared away, Drinkwater sat at the table and, spreading a sheet of paper, began to write his report of proceedings. He penned the superscription, thinking of John Barrow, the Second Secretary, who would read his words to the assembled Board of Admiralty. He had much to say and began with the well-rehearsed formula: *Sir, I have the honour to report* . . . Then he paused in thought and laid down his pen. A moment later he had fallen asleep, smudging the wet ink.

'Well, Ashton, it's homeward bound as soon as we're ready for sea,' Marlowe announced, and Hyde, who was disrobing himself from the tight constraints of his sash, reappeared in the doorway of his cabin.

'That's damned good news,' he said.

'I'm not certain I relish existing on half-pay,' Ashton grumbled, throwing himself into a chair.

'I shouldn't think you'll have to,' remarked Frey acidly.

Hyde chuckled, then added soberly, 'Well at least you ain't dead, like poor McCann. I still don't understand why he ran out of cover like that. It was so unlike McCann, who was always so strict and disciplined in everything he did.' No one offered an opinion and Hyde yawned and stretched. 'A full belly always makes me sleepy,' he observed, yawning.

'Most things make you sleepy,' Ashton jibed.

'Aren't you supposed to be on deck, Josiah?' Marlowe asked.

'When I have changed into undress garb,' Ashton mumbled, sighing and half rising.

'You have a sleep too,' Frey said, emerging from his cabin in the plain coat of working rig, 'I'll tend the deck.'

'Damned lick-spittle,' Ashton said.

'Don't be so bloody offensive, Ashton,' Hyde called from his cabin, and Marlowe looked pointedly at the third lieutenant.

'Hyde's right, Josiah . . .'

'Oh, damn the lot of you,' Ashton said, and getting up he retired to his cabin, slamming the door so that the whole flimsy bulkhead shook and Hyde reappeared in the doorway of his hutch.

'You know,' he remarked conversationally to Marlowe, 'when I first met him, I rather liked him. It's remarkable how a sea-passage can change things, ain't it?'

'Yes,' replied Marlowe, 'it is.'

'It was a moonlit night when we engaged the *Sybille*, d'you remember?'*

'I was in the gun-deck, sir,' Frey replied. 'It is invariably near dark there . . .'

Drinkwater chuckled; 'I'm sorry, I had forgot. I sometimes think I have been too long upon a quarterdeck. In fact,' he said with a sigh, 'I fear I am fit for precious little else.'

So bright was the moonlight that it cast the shadow of the ship on the heaving black sea beyond them and the undulating movement of the water made the shadow run ahead of *Andromeda*, adding an illusory component to the frigate's apparent speed as she ran to the north and east, bound for the chops of the Channel. Above their heads the ensign cracked in the wind which lumped the sea up on the starboard quarter, and *Andromeda* scended with alternating rushes forward on the advancing crests, and a slowing as she fell back into the following crests.

The two officers stood for a moment at the windward hance and watched the sea.

' 'Tis beautiful though,' Drinkwater observed wistfully.

'You are thinking you will not long be able to stand here and

---

* See *The Flying Squadron*

admire it.' Frey made it a statement, not a question and Drinkwater took their conjoint thoughts forward.

'Could you paint such a scene?'

'I could try. I should like to attempt it in oils.'

'I commissioned Nick Pocock to paint the moonlit action with the *Sybille*. The canvas hung in my miserable office in the Admiralty. If you could do it, I should like a painting of *Andromeda* coming home . . .'

'At the end of it all,' said Frey.

'D'you think so?' asked Drinkwater. 'While I certainly hope so, I doubt Napoleon will sit on his Tuscan rock sulk for ever. '

'I suppose we must put our trust in God, then,' Frey said wryly.

'I have to confess, I do not believe in God,' said Drinkwater, staring astern where a faint phosphorescence in the sea drew the line of the wake on the vastness of the ocean. 'But I believe in Providence,' he added, 'by which I mean that power that argues for order and harmony in the universe and which, I am certain, guides and chastises us.'

He turned to the younger man by his side whose face was a pale oval in the gloom of the night and sighed. 'You only have to look at the stars,' he said, and both officers glanced up at the mighty arch of the cloudless sky. The myriad stars sparkled brilliantly in the depths of the heavens; several they knew by name, especially those by which they had traced their path across the Atlantic, but there were many, many more beyond their knowledge. The light, following breeze ruffled their hair as they stared upwards, then abruptly Drinkwater turned and began to walk forward, along the length of *Andromeda*'s quarterdeck. The planking gleamed faintly in the starlight.

'Have you noticed,' Drinkwater remarked as they fell into step beside each other, 'there is always a little light to see by.'

'Yes,' agreed his companion.

After a pause, Drinkwater asked, 'Who is the midshipman of the watch?'

'Paine.'

'Pass word for him, will you.'

Paine reported to the two officers, apprehensive in the darkness. 'Mr Paine,' said Drinkwater, 'I wished to say how well you acquitted yourself in the action.'

'Thank you, sir.'

'Now cut along.'

'Aye, aye, sir.'

'Well,' Drinkwater yawned and stretched as the midshipman ran off, 'it's time I turned in.' He gave a final glance at the binnacle and the illuminated compass card within. 'You have the ship, sir,' he said formally, adding 'Keep her heading for home, Mr Frey.'

And even in the gloom, Frey saw Drinkwater smiling to himself as he finally went below.

Chapter Twenty

June 1814

A Laying of Keels

The wedding party emerged from St James's in Piccadilly and turned west, bound for Lothian's Hotel and the wedding breakfast. It was a perfect summer's day and Drinkwater felt the sun hot on his back after the cool of the church. He creaked in the heavy blue cloth and gilt lace of full-dress and his sword tapped his thigh as he walked. His left sleeve was pinned across his breast and within it his arm was still bound in a splint while the bone knitted, but beyond a dull ache, he hardly noticed it. Drinkwater cast a look sideways at Elizabeth and marvelled at how beautiful she looked, handsomer now, he thought gallantly, than in the bloom of youth when he had first laid eyes upon her gathering apples in her apron. She felt his glance and turned her head, her wide mouth smiling affectionately.

Thinking of her protestations that she was unacquainted with either the bride or groom when Drinkwater had written from Chatham that she should come up to town and meet him at their London house, he asked, 'Are you glad to be here, Bess?'

'I am glad that you are here,' she said, 'and almost in one piece.'

He drew her closer and lowered his voice, 'And I am glad you brought Catriona.'

James Quilhampton's widow walked behind them on the arm of Lieutenant Frey, who looked, to Drinkwater's surprise, as sunny as the morning.

'Do you think we shall hear more wedding bells?' he began, when Elizabeth silenced him with a sharp elbow in his ribs.

'You shout, sir,' she teased, her voice low. 'You are not upon your quarterdeck now.'

Drinkwater smiled ruefully. No, he was not, nor likely to be again . . .

'I should have liked *you* to have brought your surgeon, so that I might thank him for saving your arm.' Elizabeth had been uncharacteristically angry when she had learned of her husband's wound, remonstrating with him that he had doubtless exposed himself unnecessarily, just as the war was over and she might reasonably expect to have him home permanently. Drinkwater had not argued; in essence she was quite right and he understood her fear of widowhood.

'Oh,' chuckled Drinkwater, 'Mr Kennedy is not a man for this sort of social occasion.'

'I shall write to him, nevertheless.'

'He would appreciate that very much.'

Ahead of them the bride and groom, now Lieutenant and Mrs Frederic Marlowe, turned into Albemarle Street, followed by the best man and brother-in-law to the groom, Lieutenant Josiah Ashton. Only a very sharp-eyed and uncharitable observer would have remarked the bride's condition as expectant, or her white silk dress as a trifle reprehensible in the circumstances.

Sarah looked round and smiled at the little column behind her and her husband. A gallant, pausing on the corner, raised his beaver as a compliment.

'Damned pretty girl,' Drinkwater remarked.

'And I don't mean you to turn into a country squire with an eye to every comely young woman,' Elizabeth chid him.

'I doubt that I shall turn into anything other than what you wish, my dear,' Drinkwater said smoothly, then watched apprehensively as a small dog ran up and down the party, yapping with excitement.

They had just turned into and crossed Albemarle Street when a man stepped out of a doorway in the act of putting on his hat. He almost bumped into Drinkwater and recoiled with an apology.

'I do beg your pardon sir.' The gleam of recognition kindled in his eye. 'Ah, it is Captain Drinkwater, is it not? Good morning to you.'

Drinkwater recognized him at once and stopped. Behind them Frey and Catriona Quilhampton were forced to follow suit.

'Why Mr Barrow!' He turned to his wife. 'Elizabeth, may I present Mr Barrow, Second Secretary to their Lordships at the Admiralty. Mr Barrow, my wife . . .'

Barrow removed his hat and bent over Elizabeth's extended hand.

'I am delighted to make your acquaintance, Mrs Drinkwater. I have long esteemed your husband.'

'Thank you, sir. So have I.'

'Mr Barrow,' Drinkwater said hurriedly, 'may I present Lieutenant Frey, a most able officer and an accomplished artist and surveyor, and Mrs Catriona Quilhampton, widow of the late Lieutenant James Quilhampton, a most deserving officer . . .'

'Madam, my sympathies. I recall your husband died in the Vikkenfiord.' Barrow displayed his prodigious memory with a courtly smile and turned to Frey. 'I have just called on Murray the publisher, Mr Frey perhaps you should offer some of your watercolours for engraving; I presume you do watercolours . . .'

'Indeed, sir, yes, often at sea of conspicuous features, islands and the like.' Frey was conscious of being put on the spot.

'Well perhaps Mr Murray might consider them for publication; could you supply some text? The observations and jottings of a naval officer during the late war, perhaps? Now I should think the public might take a great liking to that, such is their thirst for glory at the moment.'

'I, er, I am not certain, sir . . .'

'Well,' said Barrow briskly, 'nothing ventured, nothing gained. I must get on and you have fallen far behind your party.'

They drew apart and then Barrow swung back. 'Oh, Captain, I almost forgot, I have a letter for you from Bushey Park. Are you staying in Lord North Street?'

'Indeed.'

'Very well, I shall have it sent round; it will be there by the time you have concluded your present business . . .' Barrow looked up the street at the retreating wedding party. 'The Marlowe wedding I presume.'

'Yes.'

'Well, I wish them joy. Mesdames, gentlemen, good day.' And raising his hat again, Barrow was gone.

'What an extraordinary man,' observed Elizabeth.

'Yes, he is, and a remarkable one as well. Frey, I hope you did not mind my mentioning your talent.'

'You flattered me over much, sir.'

'Not at all, Frey, not at all. Mr Barrow is an influential body and not one you can afford to ignore.' Drinkwater nodded at the brass plate on the door from which Barrow had just emerged, adding, 'And he is a man of diverse parts. He contributes to *The Quarterly Review* for Mr Murray, I understand. Now we must step out, or be lost to our hosts.'

'What is the significance of a letter from Bushey Park, Nathaniel?' Elizabeth asked as they hurried on.

'It is the residence of Prince William Henry, my dear.'

'The Duke of Clarence?'

'The same. And admiral-of-the-fleet to boot.'

'Lord, lord,' remarked Elizabeth smiling mockingly, 'I wonder what so august a prince has to say to my husband?'

'I haven't the remotest idea,' Drinkwater replied, but the news cast a shadow over the proceedings, ending the period of carefree irresponsibility Drinkwater had enjoyed since leaving Angra and replacing it with a niggle of worry.

'One would think,' he muttered to himself, 'that a cracked arm would be sufficient to trouble a man.'

'I did not quite catch you,' Elizabeth said as they reached Lothian's Hotel.

'Nothing, m'dear, nothing at all.'

'Congratulations, Frederic; she is a most beautiful young woman and you are a fortunate man.' Drinkwater raised his glass.

'I owe you a great deal, sir,' said Marlowe, looking round at the glittering assembly.

'Think nothing of it, my dear fellow.'

'There was a time when the prospect of this day seemed as remote as meeting the Great Chan.'

'Or Napoleon himself!' Drinkwater jested.

'Indeed, sir.'

'It is a curious fact about the sea-officer's life,' Drinkwater expanded, warmed by the wine and the cordiality of the occasion, 'that it is almost impossible to imagine yourself in a situation you knew yourself to have been in a sennight past.'

'I know exactly what you mean, sir.'

'The past is often meaningless; enjoy the present, it is all we have.' Drinkwater ignored the insidious promptings of ghosts and smiled.

'That is very true.' Marlowe sipped at his wine.

'How is Ashton?' Drinkwater asked, looking at the young

officer across the room where he was in polite conversation with an elderly couple.

'As decent a fellow as can be imagined. Shall I forgive him the past too?'

'If you have a mind to. It is sometimes best; though I should keep him at arm's length and not be eager to confide over much in him.'

'No, no, of course not.' Marlowe paused and smiled at a passing guest.

'I am keeping you from your duties.'

'Not at all, sir. I should consider it an honour to meet your wife, sir.'

'Oh, good heavens, forgive me . . .'

They walked over to where Elizabeth was in conversation with Lieutenant Hyde and a young woman whose name Drinkwater did not know but who seemed much attached to the handsome marine officer.

'Excuse me,' he interjected, 'Elizabeth, may I present Frederic Marlowe . . .'

Marlowe bowed over Elizabeth's hand. 'I wished to meet you properly, ma'am. Receiving guests at the door is scarcely decent . . .'

'I'm honoured, Mr Marlowe. You are to be congratulated upon your bride's loveliness.'

'Thank you ma'am. I should like to say . . .' Marlowe shot an imploring glance at Drinkwater who tactfully turned to Hyde and his young belle.

'You have the advantage of me, Mr Hyde . . .'

'I have indeed, sir. May I present Miss Cassandra Wilcox . . .'

Drinkwater looked into a pair of fine blue eyes which were surrounded by long lashes and topped by an intricate pile of blonde hair. 'I fear I am out of practice for such becoming company, Miss Wilcox, you will have to forgive an old man.'

'Tush, Captain, you are not old . . .'

'Oh, old enough for Mr Hyde and his fellows to refer to me as Our Father,' said Drinkwater laughing and catching Hyde's eye.

'How the devil did you know, sir?' queried Hyde, eyebrows raised in unaffected surprise.

'Oh, the wisdom of the omnipotent, Mr Hyde. It was my business to know.' Drinkwater smiled at Miss Wilcox. 'Have you known Mr Hyde long, Miss Wilcox?'

'No sir, we met at Sir Quentin's two nights ago.'

'We sang a duet, sir . . . at Marlowe's father's,' Hyde added, seeing Drinkwater's puzzlement.

'Ah yes, of course, he is the gentleman in plum velvet.'

'The rather *large* gentleman in plum velvet,' added Miss Wilcox mischievously, leaning forward confidentially and treating Drinkwater to a view of her ample bosom. She seemed an ideal companion for the flashy Hyde.

'Would you oblige me by introducing me, Hyde?'

'Of course, sir.'

'Miss Wilcox, it has been a pleasure. I shall detain Hyde but a moment.' Drinkwater bowed and Cassandra Wilcox curtseyed.

'Is Frey about to strangle himself in the noose of matrimony, sir?' Hyde asked as they crossed the carpet to where Sir Quentin, a large, florid man as unlike his heir as could be imagined, guffawed contentedly amid a trio of admiring ladies.

'It very much looks like it, don't it.' Drinkwater looked askance at Hyde. 'You do not approve?'

'She is his senior, I'd say,' Hyde said with a shrug, 'by a margin.'

'But a deserving soul and Frey is a man of great compassion. What about yourself and Miss Wilcox?'

'A man must have a reason for staying in town, sir, or at this season for visiting in the country . . . Excuse me, ladies; Sir Quentin, may I introduce Captain Nathaniel Drinkwater?'

It was a pleasant stroll across St James's Park towards the abbey. They walked in silence for a while and then Elizabeth, casting a quick look over her shoulder at Frey and Catriona Quilhampton who lingered behind them, remarked, 'You seem to have made an impression on young Frederic Marlowe, my dear.'

Drinkwater grunted. 'What did he have to say?'

'Rather a lot. He said you saved him from a fate worse than death.'

'I'd say that was rather overstating matters. He was simply in some distress, both personally and professionally. He was concerned at the unexpected delay in our return to London . . .'

'Ah,' observed Elizabeth perceptively, 'then the lady *was* expecting.'

'Good heavens, Bess, do you miss nothing!'

'And professionally?' Elizabeth prompted.

'Oh he had had some experience that had not passed off well. He was unsure of himself.'

'A bit like Humpty-Dumpty? Only in this case the king's men did put him back together again?'

'Yes,' laughed Drinkwater, looking at his wife. 'Damn it, Elizabeth, but you are a lovely woman.'

The letter from Bushey was waiting for them when they arrived at the house in Lord North Street. Williams handed it to Drinkwater on a salver and, after he had struggled for a moment one-handed, Elizabeth rescued him from his embarrassment just as Catriona and Frey entered the room.

'Some tea, Williams, I think,' Elizabeth ordered as the company sat.

'How is the arm, sir?' Frey asked.

'Oh, pretty well. Not for the first time Kennedy saved me, though I suspect he rather wished I had got my just desserts.'

'Nathaniel! That's an ungrateful thing to say!' Elizabeth was profoundly shocked.

'Oh, you don't know Kennedy, m'dear.' Drinkwater flicked open the letter, read it while the company waited – all by now aware of the writer – expectantly watching Drinkwater's face.

'Well?' Elizabeth asked, as, expressionless, Drinkwater laid the letter in his lap.

'Well what?'

'What news? What does His Royal Highness write to you about? Or is it more secrets?'

'No, no.' Drinkwater took a deep breath. 'He has promised Birkbeck, who was my especial concern, a dockyard post.'

'That is good news, sir,' commented Frey approvingly.

'Yes.'

'And . . .?' Elizabeth prompted and then, when Drinkwater sat silently, fisted her hands and beat them into her lap. 'Oh, Nathaniel, why do you have to be so tiresome? Either tell us, or say you cannot!'

Drinkwater looked up with a familiar, wry smile upon his face. 'Well, my dear, His Royal Highness,' he said the words with sonorous and deferential dignity, 'has been so impressed with the actions of *Andromeda* and, though modesty prevents me from laying undue emphasis upon the point, with my services . . .'

262

'Oh, Nathaniel, please go on, you are submitting us to the most excruciating torture.'

'Please do tell us,' put in Frey.

'Catriona, m'dear,' Drinkwater appealed to his red-haired guest, 'surely you don't want to hear this nonsense?'

'Oh, but I surely do,' Catriona replied in her soft burr.

'Very well,' Drinkwater sighed. 'His Royal Highness has been graciously pleased to suggest I am made a knight-commander of the Bath . . .'

'Why, sir,' exclaimed Frey leaping up from his chair, 'that is wonderful news!'

Drinkwater looked at his wife. She had gone quite pale and held both hands in front of her face while Catriona looked concernedly at her friend.

'You had better hear me out,' Drinkwater went on. 'His Royal Highness also says that since hauling down his flag, he is not presently in a position to recommend me, but that he,' Drinkwater unscrewed the letter and read aloud, '"will ever be completely sensible of the great service rendered to the nation by His Majesty's frigate *Andromeda* in the late action off the Azores and, should His Royal Highness be in a future position to honour Captain Drinkwater, His Royal Highness will be the first to acknowledge that debt in the aforementioned manner . . ."'

Drinkwater crushed the letter with a rueful laugh amid a perfect silence.

'I think it is time for bed. It has been a long and eventful day.' Drinkwater stretched and Frey tossed off his glass of *oporto*.

'Sir, before we retire I should like to acquaint you of my, of our, decision.'

'Of course, Frey. Pray go on.'

'You will have guessed, Frey said, smiling, 'my proposal has been accepted.'

Drinkwater stood and held out his hand. 'Congratulations, my dear fellow.' They shook hands and Drinkwater said, 'I am glad you don't share Hyde's opinion of marriage.'

'What was that?'

'That it was a noose.'

'Doubtless Hyde would find it so.' Frey paused, adding, 'I know the lady to be . . .'

'Please say no more, my dear fellow. The lady has much to commend her and James would be pleased to know you care for Catriona, for her existence has not been easy. I am delighted; we shall be neighbours. Come, a last glass to drink to all our futures now that the war is at an end.'

'If not to your knighthood.'

'Ah, that . . .' Drinkwater shrugged. 'There is many a slip 'twixt the cup and the lip.'

Both men smiled across their glasses, then Drinkwater said, 'You know, in all the years I have been married, I have never been at home longer than a few months. Perhaps my permanent presence may not be an unalloyed joy to my wife.'

'That does not constitute a noose.'

'No, but I would not want it to be even a lanyard . . .' Drinkwater paused reflectively and Frey waited, knowing the sign of a germinating idea from the sudden abstraction. 'You will live at Woodbridge when you have spliced yourself with Catriona?' he asked at last.

'That is our intention, yes. I shall have only my half-pay and intend trying my hand at painting. Portraits perhaps.'

'That is a capital idea; portraits will be all the vogue now the war is over, but I too have an idea which might prevent any talk of nooses or the like.'

'I guessed you were hatching something.'

'What I am hatching is a little cutter. It occurs to me that the coming of peace and the decision of Their Lordships to break up the *Andromeda* leaves us without a ship. We could have a little cutter built at Woodbridge and I daresay for fifty pounds one could get a tolerable yacht knocked up . . .'

'*We*, sir?' Frey frowned.

'I daresay you'd ship occasionally as first luff with me, wouldn't you?'

'Oh,' said Frey grinning hugely, 'I daresay I might.'

Drinkwater nodded with satisfaction. 'Then the matter's settled.'

Author's Note

At the time of Napoleon's abdication, negotiations between Talleyrand and Tsar Alexander, who was then resident at the château of Bondy, were conducted by Caulaincourt and Count Mikhail Orlov. Among the subjects discussed was the most suitable place to exile Napoleon. St Helena and the Azores were suggested. In the event Elba was chosen, with the inevitable consequence that discontent at the resumption of Bourbon rule allowed Napoleon to return and seize power again, only to suffer final defeat at Waterloo in June 1815. Although it was to be Alexander who approved Elba in the teeth of opposition from the British and the Austrians, Alexander's complex but essentially vacillating, capricious and quixotic nature was such that so clement and generous a decision may easily have contradicted an earlier, harsh and extreme one. As the most charismatic sovereign among the crowned heads, the role of allied leader fell to Alexander almost by default. He had been captivated by the spell of Napoleon's personality and suborned by the insidious influence of Talleyrand. Alexander nevertheless saw himself as the implacable enemy of Napoleon, the usurper, who challenged the concept of legitimate monarchy with a new, unorthodox and dangerous creed.

From Alexander's meeting with Talleyrand at Erfurt in 1808, the wily Frenchman had begun manipulating the Tsar, insisting the peace of Europe rested with him, not to mention the future of France. Alexander's own position rested almost entirely upon two props; the weight of his armies, with their patient, peasant soldiery, an the British gold which kept them in the field. And along with the implicit expectations of Britain, he had to balance the demands of Austria. Both countries were represented by brilliant statesmen, Castlereagh and Metternich, whose intellects far surpassed Alexander's own. Among them all, however, Talleyrand must be regarded as the most able. He was careful to distance himself from the more disreputable goings-on, but we know he was distantly party to a number of stratagems which he doubtless encouraged as a means of distracting attention from his own plans. There was, for instance, a group who wished to assassinate Napoleon, so the humbling of Britain in the wake of the humiliation of Napoleon is a not improbable option considered during the negotiations between Bondy and Paris in the uncertain spring of 1814.

The atmosphere was thus ripe for plots by officers loyal to Napoleon, and there existed a number of these groups pledged to restore the Emperor. A growing Bonapartist faction laboured under the impositions of the first Bourbon restoration, increased the discontent among the middle classes and ensured Napoleon received a rapturous reception when he finally returned from his Elban exile. Most significant was the loyalty of the French army in its entirety. It is said that when the former Imperial Guard paraded for Louis XVIII, they had murder in their eyes.

As for Louis, I have taken few liberties with the sparse accounts of his Channel crossing. Prince William Henry had formerly commanded the frigate *Andromeda* and while accounts vary as to whether he was aboard the *Royal Sovereign*, the *Impregnable* or the *Jason* at the time of the return of the Bourbon king, I have followed Admiral Byam Martin's recollections, which seemed the most credible, as he knew the Prince well and had a low opinion of him. In a letter to his son, George FitzClarence, Prince William Henry himself boasted he commanded 'our fleet' off Calais. The squadron under his flag did, however, include French and Russian warships as well as the principal Trinity House yacht. A painting of the event was exhibited by Nicholas Pocock at the Royal Academy in 1815. HMS *Impregnable* was commanded by Henry Blackwood who had been captain of the *Euryalus* at Trafalgar. Blackwood had been created a baronet and hoisted his flag as an admiral before the end of 1814. Sir Peter Parker of the *Menelaus* was less fortunate; he was killed later that year in the United States near Baltimore, where he had landed to create a diversion during operations against the Americans.

During the period of Napoleon's exile on Elba, the allied plenipotentiaries assembled at Vienna to determine the future shape of Europe after the fall of Napoleon and break-up of the

First French Empire. The congress was characterized by its dances more than its debates and the former allies nearly came to a renewed war, with Britain and Russia leading opposite factions. Napoleon's father-in-law, the Emperor Francis of Austria, was vigorously opposed to the deposed Emperor's presence so close to his own possessions in northern Italy, as well as against any further intimacy between Napoleon and his daughter, Marie-Louise. To effect the latter policy he appointed Count Neipperg to her entourage with instructions to seduce the Archduchess. Neipperg's successful debauchery ensured the intellectually dull Marie-Louise forgot her husband and, after Napoleon's death, married the one-eyed, but dashing count.

During the tortuous negotiations in Vienna and Napoleon's occupation of the Elban throne, his ultimate fate continued to be discussed, and both the Azores and St Helena were again suggested as possible final solutions to the problem of what to do with the quondam Emperor. At one point the purchase of an Azorean island from the Portuguese was considered. In the event, the dilatory nature of the debates, the increasing discontent in France and the refusal of Louis XVIII to pay Napoleon his pension, guaranteed a brief, heady success for Napoleon as he returned to France for what history knows as 'The Hundred Days'. The action however, immediately united the congress, which unanimously declared Napoleon an outlaw with the consequence of ultimate defeat for his cause at Waterloo, and his final exile on St Helena.

Taking advantage of the wranglings and intrigues at Vienna, Talleyrand skilfully rehabilitated France among the first rank of European powers. Indeed at one point when a new war seemed inevitable, the idea was mooted that Napoleon himself be brought home from exile in order to command French armies in the field against the Russian faction!

Thus was the eagle finally caged, though Captain Nathaniel Drinkwater was to play one last part in the drama during the Hundred Days.

Ebb Tide

For
Jane and Vernon Hite

Contents

There is a tide in the affairs of men,
Which taken at the flood leads on to fortune;
Omitted, all the voyage of their life
Is bound in shallows and in miseries.

Shakespeare, *Julius Caesar*, IV, iii

Mr Martin Forester was growing anxious. He pulled out his watch
and looked at it, then glanced up at the sky before turning his gaze
impatiently towards the shoreline. It was getting late and wanted
only six minutes to sunset, but an advancing overcast had obscured
the setting sun to cause a premature darkness. He did not like the
look of the weather. The ship, although anchored in the lee of the
high land half a mile to the south of her, lifted to a low swell rolling
along the coast, and the wind was strong enough, even here, to set
up a mournful moan in the rigging. Beyond Bull Point to the westward the Atlantic was brewing an unseasonal gale. He felt the
vessel, lying with her head to the west, snub to her cable as the
flood tide surged past her hull and fought for mastery of her with
the wind in her rigging. If the wind got up any more, he knew she
would see-saw back and forth, her cable occasionally jumping
against the whelps on the windlass gypsy with a judder, until the
tide turned and she lay betwixt wind and tide, rolling to the swell.
It was not going to be a pleasant night. Not for mid-July, anyway,
he concluded, giving vent to his feelings.

'Damn it!' he muttered.

Sensing rather than hearing the mate's agitation, the quartermaster on the port side of the bridge above the paddle-box lowered
the long watch-glass and announced helpfully, 'No sign of the boat
yet, sir.'

'No,' responded Forester irritably. 'Damned nuisance.' He
sighed resignedly and walked across to where Quartermaster Potts
stood. 'She won't be back before sunset, so we'll make colours first.
Pipe the hands to stand by.'

'Aye, aye, sir.' Potts replaced the telescope in its rack and moved
to the centre of the bridge where the wheel and binnacle stood,
relinquishing his post to Forester. The mate was not a bad fellow,

275

Potts thought, but always wanted things to run smoothly, and when there was a delay, as there was this evening, he was apt to become irritable. Potts had been the victim of Mr Forester's short fuse on several occasions and had learned to live with it. He put the call to his lips and blew the piercing summons that would bring the watch on deck.

Standing out over the paddle-box, Forester took another quick glance at his watch and then, composing himself for the few minutes he had yet to wait until the obscured sun dipped below the western horizon, he looked about himself. Being the steamer's mate and a conscientious seaman, he cast an experienced eye over her from his vantage point. The paddle-box that rose over the sponson was not only high above the water but was also outside the line of the ship's rail. With his back outboard he could, in a single sweep, take in the whole ship from her bowsprit to her counter stern.

A seaman emerged from the forward companionway and walked up to stand by the jackstaff. The jack, a curious device of St George's cross quartering four ancient ships whose broadside cannon belched fire, flapped vigorously in the southwesterly breeze that came off the Devon coast, carrying with it the scent of grass and wood-smoke. The foremast yards with their close-furled sails were neatly squared to Mr Forester's exacting standards. The sails on the mainmast astern of the narrow bridge that spanned the vessel from paddle-box to paddle-box were equally tidily stowed. But rising above and dominating the whole after part of the ship was the great black column of the funnel.

Mr Forester hated that funnel. Even now a sulphurous shimmer from its top told of the banked boiler hidden down below and, if he looked across on the starboard quarter, he could see the faint but unmistakable pall of its smoke laid on the grey surface of the sea. With the boiler fires banked, the funnel was quiescent, a malevolent threat which, it seemed to Forester in his more irritable moments, possessed a secret hatred for the mate, for he was engaged in a ceaseless war with the thing. Mr Forester had been bred in a tough school and had spent most of his life under sail. He had, moreover, seen service in the Royal Navy as master's mate and had been in Codrington's flagship, the *Asia*, at Navarino. He was therefore accustomed to decks being white, not besmirched by soot and smuts. Steam, whatever its advocates might claim, seemed to Forester to have introduced as many problems as it had solved. He sighed and let his gaze roll aft again. Beyond the long after deck with its saloon skylight and the glazed lights which illuminated the staterooms below, rose the huge ensign staff. A seaman stood alongside it, the halliards of the large defaced red ensign ready in his hands. Its snapping fly bore the same device as formed the jack and it was repeated yet again in the flag which stood out like a board from the mainmast truck high above his head, indicating the presence on board the steamer of an Elder Brother of the Trinity House.

Satisfied, Forester turned forward again, distracted by the noise of voices almost immediately below him on the foredeck where the crew closed up round the polished brass barrel of the short six-pounder, one of four carriage-mounted guns borne on the long deck of the Trinity House Steam Vessel *Vestal*.

'Colour party mustered, sir,' Potts reported, as the gun-captain below the bridge knelt behind his gun's breech, one hand upraised.

'Aye, aye.'

Forester withdrew his watch again. One and a half minutes. He wished the boat had returned and that he could have had the whole deck snugged down with the cutter in her davits before embarking on this ritual. If the wind veered and caught them on a lee shore, they would have to get under weigh, so he wanted to make sure the ship would be fit for the eventuality sooner rather than later.

He stared out over the leaden water with its froth of white caps and watched a fulmar cut its shallow, sweeping dive across the very surface of the waves, its wings immobile. The absolute confidence with which the bird made so close an approach to the turbulent surface never failed to amaze him. Beyond lay the high coast. Lights were appearing in the town of Ilfracombe which nestled beneath the moor in the seclusion of its rocky bay. The strong tide which flooded east offshore would be scarcely felt within the compass of those rocks, he reflected. Then he saw the boat.

It came clear of Chapel Hill, its oars moving in perfect precision, and headed out towards *Vestal*, the diminutive flag at its bow showing grey in the gathering gloom. As the coxswain cleared the land he applied his helm to offset the eastward sweep of the flood and the cutter began to crab across the tide, exposing her starboard side, though making for the steamer in a direct line, judged to a nicety.

277

'Damned good coxswain, that Thomas,' Forester murmured approvingly before glancing at his watch again. He nodded at Potts, turned aft, drew himself up and raised two fingers to the forecock of his hat.

The pipe shrilled its high, imperative note and Forester saw the ensign start its slow descent. Behind and below him on the boat-deck the gun-captain applied his match, and the sudden boom of the gun, with its sharp stink of burnt powder, echoed round the bay, reverberating from the cliffs and sending into the air scores of roosting auks and kittiwakes. The smoke swept past Forester as he stood immobile, atop the paddle-box, until, giving an almost imperceptible nod to Potts, the quartermaster blew the descending notes of the 'carry-on'.

Forester relaxed and walked inboard to where the bridge widened on the ship's centreline to provide the compass platform and steering position, behind which stood the handsomely var-nished teak charthouse. 'Very well, Potts. Pipe the watch to stand by the boat falls.'

Potts blew the pipe yet again and both men waited as the hands turned up from below. A steam-ship provided power for hoisting the boats, so the job could be accomplished with the deck-watch alone. Now that they worked the three-watch system, it made life much easier for the seamen, though Forester, in his blacker moments, was certain all this ease was not good for any of them. He had a remorseless belief in the imperatives of duty.

'No need for another flag, Potts,' he remarked to the quarter-master, 'now that Cap'n Drew's is up.' Forester nodded at the main truck where the Elder Brother's flag still flew, unstruck at sunset since it was a command flag and remained aloft as long as the offi-cer so honoured was on board.

'There's Drew now, sir,' said Potts as a gold-braided figure appeared on deck below.

'Come up to meet the new fellow,' Forester added conversa-tionally, mellowing now the cutter was almost back.

'Who is 'e, sir, this new fellow?' Potts inquired.

'Captain Sir Nathaniel Drinkwater KCB,' explained Forester, who made it his business to know such things. 'Newly elected to the Court of Trinity House, but a distinguished sea-officer.'

' 'Ow is 'e distinguished, then, sir? Were 'e at Navarin?' asked

Potts mischievously, knowing Mr Forester enjoyed reminding them of his presence at the battle.

'No, he was well known as a frigate captain in the war. I don't think he ever commanded a ship-of-the-line, though. Spent a lot of time on special service, I believe . . .' A cough interrupted this cosy chat and Forester turned. 'Ah, Cap'n Poulter, sir, red cutter's approaching, Captain Drew's on deck, and the wind's tending to freshen.'

'Very well, Mr Forester. I had better go down and join Captain Drew.'

Poulter settled his hat and made for the ladder, hesitating at the top and turning his head as though sniffing the air. 'You're right about the wind, Martin,' he added informally, then disappeared to the deck below.

Captain Sir Nathaniel Drinkwater drew his boat cloak more closely round him as the cutter pulled out from the shelter of the bay. He could sense the damp in the air as it made the old wound in his shoulder ache, and there was a discouraging bite to the wind as they came out from under the shelter of the land. He cast an eye over the men at the oars. They were all kitted out in ducks and pea-jackets, long ribbons blowing in the wind from their round hats as they bent in synchronized effort to their oars. Beside him the *Vestal*'s second mate, a young man who had introduced himself as William Quier, directed the coxswain's attention to the influence of the tide.

'Mind the force of the flood now, Thomas,' he said with quiet authority, catching Drinkwater's eye, then looking hurriedly away again towards the ship. Drinkwater followed his gaze. She was an ungainly brute, he thought, her great funnel and huge, grey paddle-boxes dominating the black hull. He supposed by her two masts that she was, technically at least, a brigantine, but the presence of the funnel gave so great a spread to them that she lacked all pretence at the symmetry and elegance he thought of as characterizing the rig. He recalled the brig-rigged *Hellebore* and her handiness, and could find no indication that *Vestal* might be manoeuvred with such facility. He grunted, and Quier shot him a quick glance, to be recalled by the boom of the gun at which the young man jumped involuntarily while the men at the oars grinned.

'Sunset gun, sir,' Quier observed unnecessarily.

'Yes, indeed.'

Drinkwater smiled to himself; poor Quier seemed a rather nervous young man and he himself was a damned old fool. He had forgotten the ship ahead of them had a steam engine, even though the confounded thing proclaimed itself by that hideous black column!

'How does she handle, Mr Quier?' Drinkwater asked, nodding at the *Vestal*. 'I presume you can back one paddle and pull or', he added with a self-deprecating shrug, abandoning the metaphor familiar to men used to pulling boats, 'put it astern, eh?'

'Indeed yes, sir. She handles very well in smooth water. She can be turned in her own length.'

Drinkwater regarded the younger man. 'You can turn a brig in her own length, you know. I suppose a brigantine is not so handy.'

'Not quite, sir, but for either you need a wind.'

'Of course . . .' The folly of old age assailed Drinkwater again and he smiled ruefully to himself. There was no point in feeling foolish; one simply had to endure it with the consolation that it would come even to this young man one day. He reassessed Quier. The young man was shy, not nervous. It occurred to Drinkwater that he might be a rather intimidating figure, sitting stiffly in the *Vestal*'s cutter.

But Quier was overcoming his diffidence and was not going to let Drinkwater escape so easily. 'Is this the first steam-ship you have been aboard, sir?'

'No, I made a short passage on the sloop *Rhadamanthus* – oh, I suppose eight or nine years ago, just after Evans brought her back across the Atlantic, but I'm afraid I don't recall how well we manoeuvred.' Drinkwater paused, recollecting something the second officer had said. 'You mentioned *Vestal* manoeuvred well in fine weather . . .'

'In a smooth sea, yes, sir. She isn't so handy when a chop is running. '

'Oh?'

'It's the paddles, d'you see,' Quier explained, his pleasant face betraying his enthusiasm. 'They function best at a particular draught; if the ship rolls heavily, the deeper paddle has greater effect than the shallower one. When steering a course the inequities tend to cancel each other out, but when manoeuvring, matters aren't so predictable.'

'I see. D'you use the sails to help?'

'You can, sir, but we don't usually have sufficient men to do all that if we are manoeuvring to lift a buoy.'

'No, of course not . . .'

'And when we set our sails to assist the steam engine, the steady heel, though more comfortable, tends to hold one paddle down all the time.'

'Yes,' Drinkwater nodded, 'yes, I comprehend that.'

'You see, it doesn't usually matter too much, sir, because we can only pick up buoys in reasonably good weather . . .'

'Yes, of course,' Drinkwater broke in. Then, seeing Quier's crestfallen look at the interruption, he added, 'A long time ago, Mr Quier, I myself served in the buoy-yachts.

Quier looked at his passenger in some astonishment. The old man's face was shadowed by the collar of his cloak and the forecock of his hat, but Quier could see that the watery grey eyes were shrewd, despite one curious drooping lid with what looked like a random tattoo mark upon it. The deeply lined mouth curved into a smile, revealing by a slight asymmetry that one at least of the furrows seaming Sir Nathaniel's cheeks was due not to the passage of time, but a sword-cut.

'You are surprised, I believe.'

'Only that I supposed you had always been a naval officer, sir.'

'I was unemployed after the American War.' Drinkwater saw the young man frown. 'Not the recent affair,' he explained, referring to the war which had ended twenty-eight years earlier and during which Mr Quier might just have been born, 'the *first* American War.' He paused again, adding, 'in which the United States gained its independence.'

Quier's mouth hung open and when he realized his astonishment was as rude as it was obvious, he said hurriedly, 'I see, sir.'

'It was', Drinkwater agreed ruefully, 'a very long time ago.'

'Comin' alongside, sir,' the coxswain muttered, and, as the *Vestal* suddenly loomed huge and menacing, her stilled paddles ahead of them like the blades of an enormous water-wheel, Quier was obliged to attend to the business of hooking on to the falls.

Helped out of the boat as she swung in the falls and was griped in to the rail, and creaking with what he called 'his rheumaticks',

Drinkwater retrieved his cane from Quier and acknowledged the salute of his fellow Elder Brother, Captain Richard Drew.

'Good to have you aboard, Sir Nathaniel, how was your journey?'

'Good to be aboard, Drew. I've been two days on the road from Taunton, damn it, so the ship's a welcome sight.'

'May I introduce Captain Poulter, the vessel's master . . .'

'Sir Nathaniel . . .'

'Captain Poulter, how d'ye do? I knew your father; served under him for a while after the first American War. I met him last in 'fourteen when we both served under the late king when he was, as he was pleased to term it, "Admiral of the British fleet".'

'It's good to have you aboard, sir.'

'I understand we're taking a look at the light at Hartland Point tomorrow if the weather serves?'

'That's right,' Drew interrupted, 'I've told Poulter we should be off the point at about half tide to gain the best conditions. There's a small breakwater at the foot of the cliffs. We shall land there.'

'All being well,' Drinkwater added, smiling, sensitive to Poulter's resentment at Drew's authoritarianism.

As if to confirm this perception, Poulter nodded. 'Quite so,' he said.

Quier arrived and informed Poulter that Sir Nathaniel's effects had been placed in the second state-cabin, whereupon the gathering on the deck broke up.

'Come and take a glass, Sir Nathaniel,' Drew invited, 'there's no need for *us* to keep the deck, eh?' and the Elder Brother led the way below chuckling.

It was now almost dark as Forester chivvied the hands about the deck, and the overcast covered the sky.

Drinkwater was floundering and he beat vainly for air as though his flailing arms could provide what he gasped for if he strove hard enough. He was curiously aware that he was drowning, yet equally convinced that he was dry, and that if he kept his arms moving he would survive. Yet the sensation filled him with terror. Somehow his subconscious mind registered the fact that this was not real, that the drowning was purely a vehicle for fear, and that it was only the fear which could touch him now.

As he grasped this and felt his heart hammer with increasing apprehension, he caught sight of something he dreaded with all the primeval fear of which his imagination was capable. She came upon him with ferocious speed, at first a faint glow in the distance, then with the velocity of recognition. Now she loomed over him and he felt the chill of her presence and her cold ethereal fist reaching for his lurching heart.

He would fain have averted his eyes, but her face, at once as beautiful as it was hideous, compelled his attention. And with her came the noise, a noise of roaring and clattering, of the scream of wind and of things – what things he did not know – tumbling in such confusion that it seemed the whole world had lost its moorings and only the ghastly white lady maintained her terrifying equilibrium, poised above him. Then she descended upon him like a gigantic succubus. He felt his body submit to her in a painful yet oddly delicious sensation while his soul fought for life.

Drinkwater woke in a muck sweat, the perspiration streaming from him and his heart thundering with such violence that he thought it must burst from his body. He imagined he had screamed out in his fright, yet around him all seemed quiet as he recollected his circumstances, making out the unfamiliar shapes of the state-cabin's furniture. As his heartbeat subsided, the last images of the dream faded. He could still conjure into his mind's eye the white lady, but she was receding, like the dying image of a sunlit window on the closed eyelid, identifiable only as an afterglow of perception.

For a moment he thought he had suffered a seizure, such had been the violence of his heartbeat, but it had only been a dream, and an old, almost familiar one. He tried to recall how many times he had had the recurring dream during his long life and remembered only that it had often served as a premonition.

The thought worried him more than the dream's inherent, terrifying images. They were so contradictory as to be easily dismissed, mere eldritch phantasms inhabiting the fearful hours of the lonely night when extraordinary, illogical contradictions possessed the power to frighten. But if it were premonition, what did that signify?

He lay back and felt his mortality. He was an old man. How many summers had he seen? Eighty? Yes, that was it, eighty summers and this his eighty-first . . .

He sighed. His heart, which had hammered with such insistence, would not beat forever and he had lived longer than so many of his friends. Poor Tregembo, for instance, whom he himself had dispatched with a pistol ball fired out of mercy to end the poor man's fearful suffering; and James Quilhampton, killed in a storm of shot as his cutter, *Kestrel*, had been raked in the Vikkenfiord . . .

How he mourned Quilhampton. Better that Drinkwater himself should have died than poor James, so newly wed after so long a betrothal . . .

Drinkwater pulled himself together and shook off the last vestiges of the dream. He was no stranger to wakefulness in the night and knew its promptings were more substantial than a damned dream! Wearily he threw his legs clear of the bunk and fumbled for the jordan.

But even after relieving himself he could not sleep. The ship was rolling now, the tide having turned and the wind grown stronger. She hung in equilibrium, tethered to the sea-bed by her anchor and cable which would now be stretched out to the eastward, but with the strong wind in her top-hamper canting her round against its powerful stream.

'Some things', Drinkwater mused, thinking of *Vestal*'s steam-powered sophistication, 'remain always the same.'

The rolling was persistently irritating. He was unused to the fixed mattress in the bunk and found the way his body-weight was pressed first on one side and then on the other a most disconcerting experience. He lay and thought fondly of his wife, knowing now, as he tossed irritably, that she had been correct in thinking him a fool for wanting to go back to sea.

'There is, my dear,' he could hear her saying, 'no fool quite like an old fool. Every dog has his day and surely you have had yours, but I suppose I shall let you have your way.'

It had been no good protesting that, as an Elder Brother of the Trinity House, it was his duty to ensure that the lighthouses, buoys and light-vessels around the coast were properly maintained for the benefit of mariners.

'If you had never sent in that report about the deficiencies of the lighthouse on Helgoland they would never have heard of Nathaniel Drinkwater and never have elected you to their blessed fraternity,' Elizabeth had berated him. 'Either that or they wanted your knighthood to adorn their Court . . .'

'Thank you, Lady Drinkwater,' he had said, aware that her head for all its customary good sense, had been turned a trifle by the title. God knew, it was little enough by way of compensation for all the loneliness she had suffered over the years, but perhaps, he thought, imagining her lying abed on the opposite side of the country listening to the rising gale, he should have spared her this last anxiety.

When at last he fell asleep it was almost dawn. He stirred briefly as the ship weighed her cable and her paddle-wheels thrashed the sea until they drove her along at nine knots. Then, acknowledging that the responsibility of command was not his, he rolled over and settled himself again. It was a supreme luxury to leave matters in the hands of another.

He woke fully an hour later as *Vestal* met a particularly heavy sea and shouldered it aside, her hull shuddering with the impact. A moment later the steward appeared, deferentially producing a coffee pot and the news that they had doubled Bull Point and that he might break his fast in the saloon in half an hour.

Drinkwater rose and shaved, bracing himself against the heave of the ship with the reflection that he had never, in three score years, proceeded directly to windward like this. He sipped the strong coffee as he dressed, cursing the need to perch spectacles on his nose in order to settle his neck-linen. Though never a dandy, Drinkwater had always tied his stock with a certain fastidious-ness, and the one concession he made to fashion now that in his private life he rarely wore uniform, was a neat cravat. Satisfied, he pulled on a plain blue undress coat over the white pantaloons that he habitually wore, and walked through to the saloon.

Drew looked up and half rose from the table where he was hack-ing at cold mutton. 'Give you good day, sir.'

'And you, Richard . . .' The two men shook hands and Drinkwater joined Drew at the table.

'Did you sleep well?'

'Well enough,' Drinkwater replied. He was at least thirty-five years Drew's senior and had no wish to arouse the younger man's impatience with tedious references to a weakening bladder and those damned rheumaticks! Instead he would test the mettle of the man, for he knew Drew had made his name and a competent fortune in the West India trade before he was forty, and had been a member of the fraternity for some years. He was, therefore,

285

Drinkwater's senior aboard *Vestal*. 'What d'you make of the weather?'

Drew pulled a face. 'Well, it ain't ideal, to be sure, but the worst of it went through during the night and it was short-lived. The swell will soon drop away. We've a good chance of making a landing.' Drew smiled blandly and Drinkwater hid his scepticism. The situation reminded him of a terrible day . . . but then so many situations reminded him of something these days. He dismissed the memory and forbore from alluding to it lest Drew consider him among those men whose present consists of boasts about their past.

'Of course,' Drew expatiated, laying down his knife and fork and sitting back as *Vestal* gave a lurch, 'if we cannot scramble ashore we shall have to steam across to Lundy and anchor in the lee until there's a moderation.'

When they had finished breakfast, they repaired to the bridge. *Vestal*'s long, elegant bow and bowsprit pointed directly into the wind's eye as she rose and fell, meeting the advancing ridges of water with her powerful forward impetus. Her engine was remarkably quiet, though the splashing of her paddles as they thrashed the water and drove the ship along made a counterpoint to the wind soughing in the rigging. The decks were wet with spray and recent rain, and the sky remained heavily clouded, though there was some break in the overcast to the south-westward.

Mr Quier was studying a pair of luggers on the port bow and clearly had the watch, but Poulter too was on the bridge and crossed to greet them. 'Good morning, gentlemen.'

'Mornin' Poulter,' Drew said, acknowledging his salute.

'Good morning, Captain,' said Drinkwater. 'Not the best of 'em I fear.'

'Alas no, Sir Nathaniel . . .'

'What d'you give for our chances?'

Poulter pulled the corners of his mouth down and was about to speak when Drew interrupted him. 'Oh, we've a good chance of it. We may have to lie off in the boat and pick our moment, but we shall have a shot at it, eh Sir Nat? You're game for it, ain't you?'

Drinkwater disliked being called 'Nat' by anyone not a close friend, and Drew's overbearing familiarity was as irritating as it might be dangerous. He looked at Poulter and replied, 'Of course I'm game, Drew, though I'd not want to risk the boat's crew contrary to Captain Poulter's judgement.'

The gratitude on Poulter's face was plain and Drinkwater sensed that these men had been at odds before he came aboard. Poulter's task was no easy one and Drew's presence on board was analogous to that of a fractious admiral, for while he must carry out the wishes, instructions and orders of the members of the Trinity Board embarked, the safety of the ship and her people remained the master's responsibility. Drinkwater recalled the dilemma with startling clarity, remembering Poulter's father in the same position many years earlier when he himself had held young Quier's post.

'Yes, yes, of course,' Drew was saying testily, 'of course, we'll see. But we can prepare the boat, nonetheless,' and he stumped off across the bridge. 'Here, sir! Mr Quier, sir! The loan of your glass if you please!'

Quier spun round and offered the glass with a hasty gesture, and Drinkwater met Poulter's gaze. Propriety would keep Poulter's mouth shut as it ought to secure Drinkwater's, but he was an old man and age had its privileges. 'You have been having a difficult time I think, Captain, have you not?'

Poulter nodded resignedly. 'There is an assumption, Sir Nathaniel,' he said with ill-concealed obliquity and bending to Drinkwater's ear, 'that we know all about the lighthouse service. For myself, I'm used to it, but poor Quier has suffered rather.'

Drinkwater nodded. 'I gathered as much. He seemed a little nervous of me last evening.'

Poulter smiled. 'You come with a formidable reputation, Sir Nathaniel. Quier's a fine seaman, but unfortunately he was over-ridden in the boat at Flatholm a day or two ago . . . It serves ill in front of the men.'

'Of course. I shall endeavour to take advantage of my grey hairs, though he seems determined to have a shot at the landing.'

'Yes. The business at Flatholm was unfortunate in that Captain Drew was proved right . . .'

'And thus considers himself a greater expert than formerly, while Quier feels a touch humiliated, eh?'

Poulter nodded. 'Indeed. Quier was not at fault, merely a trifle cautious . . .'

'Because, no doubt, Captain Drew was in the boat beside him?'
'Exactly so.'

'Well, we shall have to see what we can do to moderate matters,' Drinkwater said.

'I hope you won't mistake my meaning, Sir Nathaniel, but . . .'

'Think no more of it, Poulter,' Drinkwater replied reassuringly and then, seeing Drew lower the glass and turn towards them again, he called out, 'Well, what d'you make of it?'

'It's not so bad,' Drew answered, leaning against the cant of the deck and waving the telescope at the headland that lay like a grey dragon sprawling along the southern horizon on their port bow. Its extremity dipped to the sea, and just above the declivity stood the squat lighthouse of Hartland Point, revealed in a sudden patch of brightness that banished the monotone and threw up the fissured rock, patches of vegetation and the white structure of the lighthouse and its dwellings.

'See, the sun's coming out!' Drew threw the remark out with a flourish.

A few moments later sunlight spread across the sea, transforming the grey waste into a sparkling vista of tumbling waves through which, it suddenly seemed, *Vestal*'s passage was an exuberant progress. As if to emphasize the change of atmosphere, a school of bottle-nosed dolphins appeared on the starboard bow, racing in to close the plunging steam-ship and gambol about her bow under the dipping white figurehead.

'And the wind is dropping,' added Poulter with a rueful nod.

'I believe you may be right, Captain Poulter,' Drinkwater agreed, turning to judge the matter from the snap and flutter of the flag at the masthead. 'And let us hope it continues to do so.'

They had lowered the boat in the *Vestal*'s lee. Poulter had set the foretopsail to ease the roll of the ship as she fell off the wind, and the slowed revolution of the paddles kept a little headway on the ship, laying a trail of smooth water alongside her after hull, beneath the davits.

The boat had been skilfully lowered and they had swiftly drawn away from the ship, the men bending to their oars with a will. Once clear of the protection of the *Vestal*'s hull, both wind and sea drove at their stern as they pulled in towards the land. Hartland Point rose massive above them as they approached, and Drinkwater stared at the surge of the sea as it spent itself against the great buttress of rock. He sought the breakwater and saw a short length of hewn stone forming a small enclosure, but it seemed that the turmoil of the sea within it was no better than outside, and this was worsening.

Off the intrusion of the headland, the tide sped up and they felt the force of it oppose the wind to throw up a vicious sea, dangerous to *Vestal's* cutter. Drinkwater could see that this sudden steepening of the waves surprised Drew. He caught his fellow Elder Brother's eye.

'There's an ebb tide in here,' Drew called, raising his voice in some wonder above the sound of the wind and the sea which was no longer making a regular, subdued hiss, but fell in a noisily slopping roar of unstable water.

'It's an eddy under the headland,' Drinkwater replied, 'it's not uncommon.'

'Sir, I think . . .' Quier began, catching Drinkwater's eye.

'I agree, Mr Quier,' he nodded and looked again at Drew, 'there's no chance of a landing. We should put about.'

Drew was clearly reluctant and turned to stare again at the towering mass of rock. They could see two lighthouse keepers and one of their wives standing on the path that wound tortuously down the cliff face. One of the men was waving his arms to and fro across his breast in a gesture of warning and the apron of the woman fluttered in the wind.

'I suppose', said Drew offensively, 'you ain't as handy on your legs as you might once have been.'

'If that is put forward as a reason for abandoning our attempt, Captain Drew, I shall overlook the impropriety of the remark . . .' Drinkwater retorted, aware of a sharp intake of breath from an incredulous Quier beside him. 'I prefer, however, to consider that common prudence dictates our actions.' He gave Drew a withering glance and turned to Quier. 'Put up the helm, Mr Quier, and let us return to the ship.' Quier turned to the coxswain and, the relief plain on both their faces, the boat began to turn as the coxswain called, 'Put yer backs into it now, me lads!'

Drinkwater ignored Drew's spluttering protest and turned to cast one last glance at the forbidding cliffs, only to feel an imperious tap upon his knee. Drew was leaning forward. 'Sir, I am the senior!' he hissed, his face red with fury. 'I shall give the order!'

'Sir,' Drinkwater replied in a low voice, ' 'tis seniority in a Pizzy Club, pray do not make too much of it, I beg you.'

Drew's mouth twisted with anger and he reluctantly sat upright, visibly fuming, his sensibilities outraged. Drinkwater, incredulous at the man's stupidity, turned his attention to the now distant *Vestal*. The men at the oars were going to have to work hard to regain the safety of her, for she alternately dipped into the trough of the seas so that only the trucks of her masts and the pall of her funnel smoke were visible, then rose and sat on the elevated horizon like an elaborate toy.

The boat's bow dropped into a trough and threw up a sheet of spray that whipped aft. 'God blast it!' snarled Drew. Then the stern fell while the bow climbed into the sky and breasted the tumbling wave. The men grunted unconsciously as the man at stroke oar set the pace. Drinkwater could see the oar-looms bowing with their effort.

He shivered. It had grown suddenly chilly. He looked up to see that the sun had once more disappeared behind a thickening cloud, and the joy went out of the day.

Aboard *Vestal* Forester, peering attentively through the long glass, had seen the boat turn. He lowered the large telescope and reported the fact to Poulter.

'Thank the Lord for small mercies,' Poulter said, relieved. 'D'you keep an eye upon it if you please, Mr Forester, while I run down towards them.'

'Aye, aye, sir.'

Poulter leaned over the forward rail and called to some seamen on the foredeck. 'D'you hear there! I'm running off before the wind for a few moments. Hands to the braces and square the foreyards!'

The hail of acknowledgement came back to them as Poulter rang for half speed ahead on the telegraph, ordered Potts to put the helm up, and watched as *Vestal* paid off before the wind.

Forester's glass described a slow traverse as the ship swung and then he was staring ahead. A moment later Poulter called, 'Very well, Mr Forester, I can see the boat perfectly now, thank you.' Forester lowered the glass and glanced forward as the men on the foredeck belayed the swung braces.

'Harrison!' he shouted. 'Pass word for the hands to stand by the boat falls!'

'Usual drill, Mr Forester.' Poulter's tone was abstracted as he concentrated on closing the cutter.

'Aye, aye, sir.' The *Vestal*'s mate shipped the telescope on its rack. Casting a final look at the boat ahead, he dropped smartly down the port ladder to the main deck to muster the men at the boat falls and supervise her recovery.

Drinkwater saw *Vestal* swing and head towards them. Here was a real facility, he thought admiringly, the quick response of the steam propulsion to the will of the vessel's commander; a minimum of effort, hardly a hand disturbed in the process, and while his hypothetical brig could as easily have swung and run downwind, it could not have been accomplished without the co-ordinated presence of at least a score of men. Drinkwater, who had hitherto considered the new-fangled steam engine best left to young men, felt a faint, inquiring interest in the thing. Perhaps, he thought, he ought to have a proper look round the engine-room. There was a Mr Jones on board who rejoiced in the rank of 'first engineer' and who was to be infrequently glimpsed on deck in his overalls, like an old-fashioned gunner in a man-of-war whose felt slippers and pallid complexion betrayed his normal habitat far below in the powder magazine.

Captain Poulter watched the boat breast a wave and dive into the trough where he lost sight of it for a moment. *Vestal* was running before the wind, her paddles thrashing as her hull scended to the succession of seas passing under her, yawing slightly in her course.

'Watch your helm now, Quartermaster,' he said, and Potts mumbled the automatic 'Aye, aye' as he struggled to hold the ship steady on her course.

Poulter stood watching the boat and the sea, gauging the shortening distance. In a few moments he would turn *Vestal* smartly to starboard, reversing the starboard paddle and bringing the ship round to a heading of south-south-east, off the wind but not quite across it, to reduce the rolling effect of the seas. He was aware that as the ship moved closer inshore, the state of the sea worsened, for the cumulative effect of the presence of the land, throwing back the advancing waves which met their inward-bound successors, created a nasty chop.

If he judged the matter to a nicety, he could tuck the plunging boat neatly under his lee and almost pluck her out of the water. Forester and his men were well practised at hooking on the falls, while Quier and Coxswain Thomas were a competent pair. All in all, it ought to impress the objectionable Captain Richard Drew! As for poor Sir Nathaniel, Poulter marvelled at the old man's pluck.

He looked at the foredeck. Forester, being the good mate he was, had a few hands on the foredeck ready to tend the topsail braces as the ship was brought to. Poulter looked again at the boat, missed her, then saw her much closer and right ahead.

He moved smartly to the engine telegraph and rang for the paddles to be stopped. The jangle of bells seemed oddly short, as though First Engineer Jones had had his hand on the thing. Perhaps he had, Poulter thought, pleased with his ship and her personnel. A man could take pride in such things. He took two steps to the bridge rail and peered over the dodger. He had lost sight of the boat again, then she appeared almost under the bow and Poulter's self-satisfaction vanished. *Vestal*'s paddles were still thrashing round, the wash of them now hideously loud in Poulter's receptive ears. His mouth was dry and his heart hammered painfully as he jumped for the telegraph and swung the handle in the violent double-ring of an emergency order. The heavy brass lever offered him no resistance. Instantly Poulter knew what had gone wrong: the long chain connecting the bridge instrument with the repeater in the engine-room had broken somewhere in the narrow pipe that connected him with the first engineer down below.

Just as the realization struck him, Poulter heard the cry of alarm from the foredeck.

'Hard a-starboard!' he roared at the quartermaster, then rushed to the rail. The two men posted forward to handle the braces were pointing and shouting, looking back up at the bridge, their faces white with alarm.

'Oh, my God!'

It was then that Poulter realized he had compounded matters, that he was in part author of the disaster he was now powerless to avert. In his moment's inattention, Poulter had not noticed the ship slew to port, nor observed Potts' frantic attempt to counter the violent skewing effect of a large sea which had run up under *Vestal*'s port quarter with fatal timing. As a result, as the ship's head had fallen off to port, she had brought the boat across to her starboard bow. Poulter's attempt to throw her unstoppable bulk away from the boat consequently resulted in the exact contrary.

Even as he watched, too late to do anything, Poulter's ship ran down her own boat.

Drinkwater had seen *Vestal*'s head fall to port and thought the sheer deliberate, perhaps the first indication of a turn. But the sudden steadying of her aspect, growing in apparent size with the speed of her approach, turned her from a welcome haven to a terrifying threat. For a few seconds those in the stern staring forward processed the implications of the evidence before their eyes. Drinkwater heard Quier swear under his breath, joined by the coxswain in a louder tone.

'Bloody hell!'

Drew's cry completed this crescendo of comprehension while his look of stark fear caused the oarsmen to break stroke as each man jerked round to stare over their shoulders. Quier leant for the tiller even as Thomas hauled it over. But it was too late, and in those last few attenuated seconds men thought only of themselves and began to dive over the port side of the boat in a terrified attempt to escape the huge, dark mass approaching them.

Only Drinkwater sat immobile. In that second of understanding and nervous reaction, as the combined weight of all those in the boat moving to escape destruction from that terrible, overwhelming bow caused her to capsize, he knew the meaning of his dream. The presentiment of death was confirmed, for he saw above him, in the pallid shape of the *Vestal*'s figurehead, the white lady of his recurrent nightmare. Hers was not the petrifying face of Medusa, nor the fearsome image of a terrifying harpy; she bore instead the implacable expression of indifference.

As he was pitched out of the boat into the sudden, shocking chill of the sea, Drinkwater felt the utter numbness of the inevitable. For a ghastly moment of piteous regret, he thought of his wife. He heard her cry and then a figure loomed briefly near him, open-mouthed in a rictus of terror, and was as suddenly gone. He glimpsed the sky, pitiless in its lowering overcast, as his body was swept aside by the moving mass of the ship. As suddenly he was tugged back again. The ship's black side with its copper sheathing rushed past him.

Suddenly loud in his ears, he heard the familiar clanking of the dream, a crescendo of noise which filled him with fear and abruptly resolved itself into the thrash of the great starboard paddle-wheel and the adjusting of its floats by the eccentric drive-rods radiating from its centre.

Then he was trampled beneath it.

It battered him.

It shoved him down until his whole head ached from the pressure and he bled from the lacerations of its indifferent mechanism.

Finally, it hurled him astern, three fathoms below the surface of the sea, as his bursting lungs reacted and his terrified mind thought that he would never see Elizabeth again.

PART ONE
Flood Tide

It is commonly held, though upon what authority I am uncertain, that a drowning man clutches at a straw, that he rises three times before the fatal immersion and that his life passes before him in a flash.

Chapter One

Elizabeth

It was end of November 1781 when His Britannic Majesty's frigate *Cyclops* rejoined the Grand Fleet at Spithead. In the grey half-light of a squally winter afternoon her cable rumbled through the hawse and she brought up to her anchor amidst the huge assembly of ships and vessels. Since frigates were constantly coming and going, her return from the Carolinas was unremarkable, but Captain Hope called upon Rear-Admiral Kempenfelt with some misgivings, for *Cyclops*'s mission had been unsuccessful.

Having seen Hope down into his gig, Acting Lieutenant Nathaniel Drinkwater, a captured French sword at his hip, crossed the quarterdeck to where Lieutenant Devaux was levelling a telescope on the flagship. Kempenfelt commanded the rear division of the Grand Fleet from which Hope's frigate had been detached for special service some months earlier, flying his flag in the huge first-rate *Royal George* which lay some three miles away.

Drinkwater halted at the first lieutenant's elbow, coughed discreetly and said, 'Captain's compliments, sir, but would you be good enough to ensure no boats come alongside until he returns.'

Devaux lowered the glass a little and turned his gaze on the steel-grey waters of Spithead which were being churned by the vicious breeze into a nasty chop.

'D'you see any boats, Mr Drinkwater?'

'Er, no sir.'

'Er,' Devaux mimicked, replacing the telescope to his eye, 'no sir. Neither do I.'

'Except for the Captain's gig, that is, sir.'

'But no boats containing pedlars, usurers, tailors, cobblers, whores or whoremasters, eh?'

'None whatsoever, sir.'

'Then, Mr Drinkwater,' said Devaux with an ironic smile, turning his hazel eyes on the younger man, 'do you ensure that not one of them gets alongside. We must keep all manner of wickedness away from our fair ship, don't you know.' Devaux allowed a crease to furrow his equable brow and asked conversationally, 'Now, Nathaniel, do you suppose this sudden concern for the moral welfare of our people has anything to do with the fact that Rear-Admiral Richard Kempenfelt is a religious man?'

'I suppose it might, sir.'

'I suppose it might, too,' responded the first lieutenant with a heavily exaggerated smile, replacing the telescope to his eye and returning his attention to Kempenfelt's flagship.

Drinkwater smiled to himself. Lieutenant the Honourable John Devaux was a man whom Drinkwater both admired and liked. He cautiously hoped that Devaux held Drinkwater himself in some esteem, for the nineteen-year-old enjoyed no patronage beyond the initial recommendation of his parish priest. Although this had secured him a midshipman's berth aboard *Cyclops*, nothing more could be expected from it. His acting rank was merely a convenient expedient for the ship, detached on special service as she had been. He expected to be returned to the midshipmen's mephitic berth in the next few days, as soon as a replacement could be found from the admiral's numerous *élèves* who inhabited this vast concourse of ships. Drinkwater sighed as he thought of his consignment to the orlop. His previous experiences of it had been far from happy. Hearing the sigh, Devaux turned upon him, lowering the glass and closing it with a sharp snick.

'Well, sir? How the deuce d'you intend to shoo the damned bum-boats off our side if you just stand there sniffing like an impregnated milkmaid?'

'I'm sorry, sir.' Drinkwater was about to turn away, aware that he had tested the first lieutenant's patience, when Devaux, staring around the ship, said with an ironic smile, 'Ah, but I see you *have* seen them all off.'

'I haven't seen a single one throughout the anchorage.'

'No, no one in his right mind would be out in a boat on an afternoon like this unless they had to be. 'Tis almost cold enough for snow, don't you think, or is it just because we hail from warmer climes?'

'Well, 'tis certainly chilly enough.'

'And I suppose you're concerned about your future, eh?'

'A little, I must confess.'

'You damned hypocrite, Nathaniel!' Devaux laughed. 'But don't expect a thing, cully. There'll be enough young gentlemen hereabouts', he went on, waving a hand expansively round the crowded anchorage, dark as it was with the masts of the fleet, 'to ensure we aren't without warm admirers. When word gets about that we've a berth empty in the gunroom, they'll all be writing to Howe or Kempenfelt or . . .'

'But there isn't an empty berth in the gunroom,' Drinkwater protested.

'A prophet is never credited in his own land, is he, eh?' Devaux remarked ironically. 'Resign yourself to the fact that by nightfall you will be back in the orlop.'

'I already have, but I cannot say I relish the prospect.'

Devaux looked seriously at Drinkwater. 'I shouldn't be surprised, Nathaniel, if we were not to be here for some time. If you would profit from my advice, I should recommend you to seek examination at the Trinity House and secure for yourself a warrant as master. You cannot afford to kick your heels in a midshipmite's mess until someone notices you. Unless I am completely out of tune with the times, there will be fewer opportunities to make your name as this war drags to its unhappy conclusion. At least with a master's warrant, your chances of finding some employment in a peace are much enhanced.'

'I shall mind what you say, sir, and thank you for your advice.'

' 'Tis no matter. I should not entirely like to see your abilities wasted, though my own influence is too small to afford you any advantage.'

'I had not meant . . .' Drinkwater protested, but Devaux cut him short with a brief, barked laugh.

'You've no need to be ashamed of either ambition or the need to make your way in the world.'

'But I had not meant to solicit interest, sir. I think, however, that I want experience to be considered for examination.'

'Don't be so damned modest.' Devaux turned away and raised the glass again.

Drinkwater had relinquished the deck when Hope returned. A cold and windy night had set in, with the great ships tugging at their cables, their officers anxious that they should not drag their anchors. The chill struck the gunroom, and those officers not on duty were considering the benefit to be derived from the blankets of their cots when Midshipman White's head peeped round the door.

'Mr Drinkwater,' he called, 'Mr Devaux's compliments and would you join him in the captain's cabin, sir.'

Ignoring the taunts of the other officers, Drinkwater pulled on his coat, picked up his hat and made for the companionway to the gundeck. He halted outside the captain's cabin, ran a finger round his stock, tucked his hat neatly under his arm and, as the marine sentry stood to attention, knocked upon the door.

'Come!'

Captain Hope clasped a steaming tankard of rum flip, his shivering body hunched in the attitude of a man chilled half to death as he sat in his chair while his servant chafed his stockinged feet. The flickering candles showed his gaunt face pale with the cold and his eyes reddened by the wind. Devaux sat, elegantly cross-legged, on the settee that ran athwart the ship under the stern windows over which the sashes had been drawn, so the glass reflected the light of the candelabra.

'Ah, Drinkwater, my boy. I have some news for you.'

'Sir?'

'We are to have a new third lieutenant, I'm afraid.'

Drinkwater looked for a second at Devaux, but the first lieutenant's attention was elsewhere. 'I understand, sir . . .'

'No you don't,' said Hope so sharply that Drinkwater coloured, thinking himself impertinent. 'Lieutenant Wallace will join tomorrow,' Hope went on, 'but since the establishment of the ship has been increased by one lieutenant, I have persuaded the Admiral to allow you to retain your acting commission.'

'I am much obliged to you, sir.' Drinkwater shot a second glance at Devaux and saw the merest flicker of a smile pass across his face.

'I have recommended that your commission be confirmed without further examination. I can make no pledges on Admiral Kempenfelt's behalf, but he has promised to consider the matter.'

'That is most kind of you, sir.'

'Well, well. We shall see. That is all.'

In the succeeding weeks *Cyclops* languished at Spithead, turning to the tide every six hours, but otherwise idle. Her people were active enough, hoisting in stores, water, powder and shot, and in due course other transactions began to take place. Though unpaid, since the present commission was of less than four years' standing, the frigate's people had received their accumulated prize money. Hardly had this been doled out by Captain Hope's prize agent's clerk than *Cyclops* was surrounded by bum-boats and invaded by a colourful and noisy mob whose trades and skills could provide both officers and ratings with their every want. A host of tricksters, fortune-tellers, tooth-pullers, pedlars, cobblers, vendors of every manner of knick-nack, traders' runners (advertising the expertise of their principals as sword-cutlers, tailors, pawn-brokers and portrait artists), Jewish usurers, gypsy-fiddlers and two score or so of whores infested the ship.

Amid this babel, the routine duties of the ship went on. Captain Hope absented himself for three weeks and Lieutenant Devaux took a fortnight's furlough. The ship underwent a superficial survey by the master shipwright of the dockyard, and her upper masts and yards were lowered and new standing rigging set up and rattled down. Five spars were renewed and Midshipman White spent three miserable days in the launch towing out replacements from the mast-pond in Portsmouth Dockyard.

Lieutenant Wallace arrived and was revealed as a protégé of the Elliot family to whom he was distantly related. His claim on their favour was small, it seemed, and it was acknowledged that he could have been a great deal worse. Life in the gunroom was thus tolerable enough. Drinkwater enjoyed the society of his fellow-officers, particularly the amusing banter between Devaux, when he was present, and the serious-minded but pleasant Lieutenant Wheeler of the marines. The sonorous gravity of the surgeon, Mr Appleby, often verged on the pompous, but his lengthy perorations could fill the gloom of an otherwise tedious evening with amusing targets for what passed for wit. Drinkwater exercised regularly with foils, and Wheeler and he recruited White and three other midshipmen into their *salle d'escrime*, as Wheeler, with light-hearted pretentiousness, insisted on calling the starboard gangway. As the junior lieutenant, Drinkwater was responsible for training the hands in the use of small arms, holding regular cutlass drills and target practices when, in the wake of the marines, they would shoot at bottles slung at the main yardarm.

In the midst of this activity Drinkwater received a letter, an answer to one he had sent off almost as soon as *Cyclops* had dropped her anchor, and he was soon afterwards anxious to obtain a few days' leave himself. The letter was from Miss Elizabeth Bower, whom he had met when last in England and to whom he had formed a strong attachment. She, it seemed, felt similarly attracted to him and they had exchanged correspondence, but he was uncertain of her whereabouts since her widowed father, with whom she lived, had moved from the Cornish parish of which he had briefly been inter-regnant. Now, having hardly dared hope that his letter would reach her, for he had sent it by way of the Bishop of Winchester, he found that her father had been inducted as incumbent in the parish of Warnford, which lay in the upper valley of the Meon, not many miles north of Portsmouth.

. . . It is so Comforting to hear from You, Elizabeth had written, *for Poor Father Exhausts himself in his Exertions to help the Unfortunate and Deserving Poor hereabouts . . . We have a Pleasant House with more Chambers than we can Sensibly use and Father joins me in Extending a Warm Invitation to you for Christmas, should You be Fortunate to Gain Your Freedom . . .*

Keen both to justify Hope's faith in him and to oblige Devaux in the hope that in due course the first lieutenant would indulge his request for leave, Drinkwater penned a cautious note of acceptance hedged about by riders explaining his predicament, then threw himself into his duties. Occasionally these took him out of the ship, as when he acted for Hope on some business with the captain's prize agent, carrying papers ashore to the lawyer's chambers at Southsea. On this occasion, and in confident anticipation of his request being granted, Drinkwater spent two guineas of his prize money on a present for Elizabeth and was in high good humour as he returned from his expedition.

At the Sally Port he hired a wherry to take him back to the ship. It was a fine, cold winter's afternoon, with a brisk wind out of the northeast. A low sun laid a sparkling path upon the sea and threw long, complex shadows from the spars of the fleet. The wherryman set a scrap of lugsail as the boat cleared Southsea beach and they swooped and ducked over the choppy water in the lively but remarkably dry little craft as it fought the contrary tide. The panoply of naval might lay all about them in the brilliant sunshine. Curiously Drinkwater regarded each of the great ships as they lay with their heads to the westward, stemming the flood tide but canted slightly athwart its stream by the brisk wind. As they passed each of the ships-of-the-line, though his passenger could perfectly well read them, the boatman volunteered their names as if this additional service would ensure a large gratuity.

'*Edgar*, sir, seventy-four guns . . . *Monarch*, seventy-four . . . *Glenelg*, transport . . . *Bedford* . . .'

Drinkwater stared up at each as they struggled past; occasionally someone stared back and once a midshipman in a bucking cutter alongside a frigate waved cheerfully. With their yard and stay tackles manned, the ships were taking in stores from hoys and ketches bouncing and ranging alongside them. One vessel was landing a defective gun – Drinkwater could see a trunnion missing from it – and several ships were working on their top-hamper, sending down their upper spars. And above every stern the squadronal ensigns of red, white or blue snapped in the breeze.

'*Royal George*, sir, first-rate. Tallest masts in the navy an' 'er main yard's the longest.'

Drinkwater stared at the great ship with her ascending tiers of stern galleries and her lofty rig. Above the ornate decoration of her taffrail, a huge blue ensign bowed the staff as it strained at its halliards.

'Dick Kempenfelt's flag, sir . . .'

'Yes,' Drinkwater replied, glancing up at the blue rectangle at the mizen truck, wondering if, at that moment, Kempenfelt was sitting at his desk mulling over the wisdom of recommending confirmation of the acting commission of the young man whose hired wherry even then bounced over a wave under his flagship's transom.

'Bin the flagship of Anson, 'Awke, Rodney an' Boscawen,' obliged the loquacious and informative wherryman. Then he leaned forward and gave Drinkwater a nudge with the air of a conspirator. Drinkwater turned, caught sight of a quid of tobacco as it rolled between caried teeth, and received a waft of foul breath.

'But she'm rotten, sir, fair rotten, they tell me.' He nodded, adding with malicious relish, 'They were to dock her way back, but it got put off.' He grinned again. 'Bit of luck you're on *Cyclops*, eh?' and the boatman laughed.

'I thought she was well built,' Drinkwater said, looking up at the great ship, for anything else seemed inconceivable. Upon her quarterdeck high above him, an officer was studying him through a telescope and Drinkwater thought him bored with his anchor watch. 'Didn't I hear she took ten years to build?'

'That's right, sir,' the boatman agreed enthusiastically, 'an' what 'appens to timber what's left out ten year?'

'Well, it weathers.'

'That's bollocks, sir, if you'll pardon me lingo,' and the man spat to leeward as if adding to the contempt of his dismissal. 'Beggin' your pardon, sir, but if that's what they teaches you young officers nowadays, then 'tis no wonder the fleet's rotten. Look sir, what happens wiv a fence when you puts it up, eh?'

Drinkwater had never in his life put up a fence, but he supposed the task might not be beyond him. 'Well you tar it, I imagine,' he ventured.

'You're a bright 'un, sir,' the boatman said. 'Of course you does. You tars it. You don't leave it out for ten year for the rain to soak it and the sun to split it, do you? No. But that's what they done wiv the *Royal George*!'

A week before Christmas, young Dicky White informed Drinkwater that his father had written and asked that his son be allowed to come home for Christmas. Drinkwater and White had become close friends and though Drinkwater's acting commission had distanced them, it had not destroyed their friendship. Even so, he knew that White possessed family interest and that his father's request would receive a favourable reply. The knowledge irked Drinkwater for he had no equivalent clout and, whatever his position *via-à-vis* the midshipmen, he was the most junior officer in the gunroom. He felt a sudden certainty that the duty of Christmas would fall upon him. He stared for a moment out across Spithead to the grey shore of the Isle of Wight.

'I should like you to come with me and I have asked the first lieutenant,' White confided with a smile. 'You'll be glad to know he has no objection. Wallace has volunteered to remain on board.' White dropped his voice and added, 'There's a skeleton in the third lieutenant's locker, Nat. I've heard 'tis a gambling debt. I think he dare not set foot ashore. Either that, or an angry husband has a pair of pistols ready primed!'

The expression on White's face made Drinkwater laugh. 'I've heard nothing of the kind, Chalky. You have too much time in that mess of yours to let your imaginations run wild.' He grew serious,

'Look, my dear fellow, I'm vastly obliged to you for securing my release,' he paused, 'but . . . oh dear, this is deuced awkward . . .'

'You do not wish to accompany me to Norfolk?'

'I would dearly like to do so, but I have . . . Damn it, Chalky, I have an invitation from . . .'

'A lady!' White slapped his thigh in a highly precocious manner, his face broadening to a smile. 'Let me not stand in the way of love, Nat! I shall not say a word. I am so glad that I was the means of your furthering your suit! We shall leave together and we shall return to tell the first luff what a jolly time we had bagging pheasants!'

'Do you think we should go that far?' Drinkwater asked, laughing.

'Do you think we should not?' White retorted.

'Well, stap me, Chalky, if you aren't a veritable Cupid!'

Christmas of 1781 saw the streets of Portsmouth under snow. Even the warren of brothels and grog-shops that they passed through were lent an ethereal beauty by the dazzling whiteness of the snow. Set against an even tone of pearl-grey sky, the tumbled roofs, crooked chimneys and black windows seemed a haven of humanity rather than a nursery of vice and disease. The thin coils of smoke rising from fires of wood and sea-coal lent an air of happy domesticity to this illusion.

Soon they had left Portsmouth behind and found the road passable as it ascended the downs on the way towards Petersfield. White, with the air of a conspirator, had insisted he and Drinkwater leave the ship together. The conveyance Sir Robert White had provided for his son now departed from the post road sufficiently to put Drinkwater down within sight of the church tower of Farehurst. It was with a beating heart that he lugged his small portmanteau towards the vicarage, but anti-climax met him in the person of a small, careworn woman who opened the door and motioned him inside. She ushered him into what he took to be Mr Bower's study, for an ancient writing-table and a battered chair from which the majority of the stuffing had long since escaped, stood in the middle of the room. A litter of papers covered the table and two bookcases flanked the fireplace. An unlit fire was laid in the grate. Three odd upright chairs were set about the room, the pine boards of which were bare, and the windows were half-shuttered.

The woman opened these and waved him to a chair with a grunt. She avoided his eyes and pulled a grey shawl about her shoulders as if to emphasize the cold penury of the house. He did not sit, but moved to look at an engraving of Wells Cathedral above the overmantel, chafing his hands to stimulate circulation. Several books lay on the mantelshelf; idly he picked one up. It was a little anthology of poetry. On the flyleaf it bore the name *Eliz. Bower, her Book*. He flicked the pages over until the name *Kempenfelt* caught his eye and he had just started reading the admiral's poem 'Burst, ye Emerald Gates' when the door opened.

Elizabeth stood just inside the room, her dark hair bound up in a ribbon, her brown eyes wide with surprise. 'Nathaniel!'

She took a half-step towards him and then faltered; he felt her eyes on his face and remembered his scar.

'You have been hurt!'

In a sudden, embarrassed reflex he touched it with his fingers. ' 'Tis nothing but a scratch. I had forgot it. I hope . . .'

She stepped closer and he clasped her outstretched hands. 'Oh, but it does,' she said smiling, 'it utterly ruins your looks. I am pleased to say no sensible woman will ever look at you again.'

'You guy me.'

'La, sir, you are clever too!'

'And you, Elizabeth, how are you?'

She sighed and her gaze fell away for a second, but then she brightened and looked at him, her face alive with that infectious animation that he sometimes thought he had almost imagined. 'Much the better for seeing you . . .'

'And your father?'

'Is old and worn out. He takes no thought for himself and is unwell, but he refuses to listen to my entreaties.' She paused, then tossed her head with a sniff. He drew her to him and felt her arms about him and smelt the fragrance of her hair as he brushed the top of her head with his lips. 'I am so very glad to have found you again,' he said.

She drew back and looked up at him, tears in her eyes. 'All I asked was that you should come back. How long do you have?'

'A sennight . . .'

After Mattins on Christmas morning, dinner in the vicarage was a merry meal. Having Drinkwater as a guest seemed to have given the Reverend Bower a new lease of life and his emaciated features bore a cheerful expression, notwithstanding the fact that he gently chided his house-keeper for failing to attend divine service.

'She doesn't understand,' he said resignedly, 'but when God has made you mute from birth, much must be incomprehensible. Nathaniel, my boy, do an old man a favour, slip out in about ten minutes with a glass of claret for her. She needs cheering, poor soul.'

After the modest meal of roast beef and oysters had been cleared away they exchanged gifts. Elizabeth had bought her father a book of sermons written by some divine of whom Drinkwater had never heard but who was, judging by old Bower's enthusiasm, a man of some theological consequence. So keen an appreciation of an intellectual present made Drinkwater's offering to old Bower seem insignificant, for he had been unable to think of anything other than a bottle of madeira he had bought from Lieutenant Wheeler. For his daughter, Bower had purchased a square of silk. It was the colour of flame and seemed to burst into the dingy room as she withdrew it from its wrapping. Elizabeth flung it about her shoulders and kissed her father, ruffling his white sidelocks with pleasure.

As unobtrusively as possible, Drinkwater slid Elizabeth's small parcel across the table. As she folded back the paper and opened the cardboard box it contained, her eyes widened with delight.

'Oh, my dear, it's beautiful!' She lifted the cameo out, held it in the palm of her hand and stared at the white marble profile of the Greek goddess on its field of pink coral. She looked up at him, her eyes shining, and it occurred to him that, though inadequate, his gift was sufficient to illuminate her dull existence. 'Look, Father . . .'

Elizabeth secured the vermilion silk with the cameo, leaned across and kissed him chastely on the cheek. 'Thank you, Nathaniel,' she said softly in his ear.

Drinkwater sat back and raised his glass. He was astonished when Elizabeth placed two parcels before him. 'I have no right to expect hospitality and generosity like this.'

'Tush, Nathaniel,' Elizabeth scolded mischievously, 'do you open them and save your speeches until you see what you have been saddled with.'

He opened the first. It contained a watch from the vicar. 'My dear sir! I am overwhelmed . . . I . . . I cannot . . .'

'I find the passage of time far too rapid to be reminded of it by a device that will outlive me. 'Tis a good time-keeper and I shall not long have need of such things.'

'Oh, Father, don't speak so!'

'Come, come, Elizabeth, I have white hairs beyond my term and I am not feared of death.'

'Sir, I am most grateful,' Drinkwater broke in, 'I do not deserve it . . .'

'Rubbish, my boy.' The old man waved aside Drinkwater's protest with a laugh. 'Let's have no more maudlin sentiment. I give you joy of the watch and wish you a happy Christmas. I shall find the madeira of considerably more consolation than a time-piece this winter.'

Drinkwater turned his attention to the second parcel. 'Is this from you, Elizabeth?'

She had clasped her lower lip between her teeth in apprehension and merely nodded. He opened the flat package. Inside, set in a framed border, was a water-colour painting. It showed a sheet of water enclosed by green shores which were surmounted by the grey bastion of a castle. In the foreground was a rakish schooner with British over Yankee colours. He recognized her with a jubilant exclamation. 'It's *Algonquin*, *Algonquin* off St Mawes! Elizabeth, it's truly lovely, and you did it?'

She nodded, delighted at his obvious pleasure.

'It's utterly delightful.' He looked at Bower. 'Sir, may I kiss your daughter?'

Bower nodded and clapped his hands with delight. 'Of course, my boy, of course!'

And afterwards he sat, warmed by wine, food and affection, regarding the skilfully executed painting of the American privateer schooner *Algonquin* lying in Falmouth harbour. He had been prize-master of her, and the occasion of her arrival in Falmouth had been that of his first meeting with Elizabeth.

Chapter Two

A Commission as Lieutenant

Cyclops cruised in the Channel from early January until the end of April and was back in Spithead by mid-May when news came in of Admiral Rodney's victory over De Grasse off the West Indian islets called Les Saintes. Guns were fired and church bells rocked their steeples; peace, it was said, could not now be far away, for the country was weary of a war it could not win. It seemed the fleet would spend the final months of hostilities at anchor, but at the end of the month orders were passed to prepare for sea.

Admiral Lord Howe thrust into the North Sea with a dozen sail-of-the-line and attendant frigates to waylay the Dutch. The Dutch in their turn were at sea to raid the homeward Baltic convoy, but news of Howe's approach compelled them to abort their plans and Lord Howe had the satisfaction of bottling up the enemy in the Texelstroom. At the end of June he returned down Channel and his fleet was reinforced from Spithead. Twenty-one line-of-battle ships and a cloud of frigates stood on to the westwards, led by Vice-Admiral Barrington's squadron in the van and with Kempenfelt's blue squadron bringing up the rear. Rumour was rife that the combined fleets of France and Spain were at sea, as they had been three years earlier, but this time there would be no repeat of the débâcle that had occurred under the senile Hardy when the enemy fleets had swept up the Channel unchallenged. The Grand Fleet had the satisfaction of covering the Jamaica trade coming in under the escort of Sir Peter Parker and then stood south in anticipation of falling in with the enemy's main body. But the British were running short of water and reports were coming in that Cordoba, the Spanish admiral, had turned south to bring Gibraltar finally to its knees. Lord Howe therefore ordered the Grand Fleet back to Spithead to take on water and provisions. At the end of August the great ships came into the lee of the Isle of Wight under a cloud of sail.

Some three hundred vessels lay between Portsmouth and Ryde, attended by the ubiquitous and numerous bum-boats, water-hoys, dockyard victualling craft, lighters, barges, wherries and punts, as well as the boats of the fleet. Despite the demands of the cruise and the sense of more work to be done as soon as the fleet was ready, the return to the anchorage brought a dulling to the keen edge of endeavour. The sense of urgency faded as day succeeded day and then the first week drifted into a fortnight.

Drinkwater had heard nothing of his commission being confirmed and began to despair of it, recalling Devaux's advice to petition the Trinity House for an examination for master. It was increasingly clear that he would receive no advancement without distinguishing himself, and since any opportunity of doing this seemed increasingly remote, his future looked decidedly bleak. His only consolation was a letter from Elizabeth, but even this irked him, for he had resolved to propose marriage to her when his affairs were on a better footing, and a lieutenant's commission would at least secure him half-pay if the war ended. Poor as it was, half-pay would be an improvement on her father's miserable stipend. His anxiety for her grew with the reflection that upon the old man's death she would not only be penniless but also roofless. He had almost lost her once before and could not face the prospect of doing so again, perhaps this time forever.

In the dreary days that followed, he fretted, unsettled by the proximity of the shore yet daily reminded of its blandishments; rooted by duty, but made restless by the lack of activity. This corrosive mood of embitterment settled on him as *Cyclops* swung at the extremity of her cable, and even the odd task that took him ashore failed to lighten his mood, since to go ashore but to be denied the freedom to go where he wished was simply an irksome imposition. Robbed of real liberty, Drinkwater had already acquired the true sailor's preference for his ship.

On a morning in late August, Drinkwater was returning from Portsmouth town whither he had been sent on behalf of the mess to make some purchases of wine, a decent cheese and some fat poultry. He was approaching the Sally Port and looking for Tregembo, the able seaman he had ordered to take back one load of mess stores, when a portly clerk bustled up to him.

'Excuse me, young sir . . .' The man attached himself to Drinkwater's sleeve.

'Yes? What is it?'

The clerk was breathless and anxious, wiped his face with a none-too-clean handkerchief and gaspingly explained his predicament. 'Oh sir, I just missed Acting Lieutenant Durham, sir, he's aide to Rear-Admiral Kempenfelt . . . There's his boat, confound it . . .' The little man pointed at a smart gig just then pulling offshore. Plunging his handkerchief back in his pocket, he drew a letter from his breast. It was sealed with the dockyard wafer.

'I wonder, sir, if I might trouble you to deliver this to the admiral aboard the *Royal George*. He is most urgently awaiting it.' Drinkwater's hesitation was momentary, but the clerk rushed on in explanation. 'There's a leak in the flagship, d'you see? The admiral and Captain Waghorne are very concerned about it. This is the order to dry-dock her and I was, I confess, supposed to have it ready for Mr Durham but . . .' The clerk wiped his hand across his mouth and Drinkwater sensed some awesome and official retribution awaiting this unfortunate drone of Admiralty. Suddenly his own lot did not seem so bad.

'But,' the clerk ran on, 'he is a most precipitate young man and had left before I had completed the copying . . .'

'Please don't concern yourself further,' Drinkwater interrupted impatiently. 'The flagship lies in my way. I only hesitate because I am waiting for some provisions and it may be ten or twenty minutes before I am ready to leave.'

Relief flushed the clerk's face and he pawed at Drinkwater in an effusion of gratitude. 'Oh, my dear sir, I require only your assurance that you will deliver the letter this afternoon, otherwise in your own good time, sir, in your own good time, to be sure.'

'Well you may rest assured of that.'

'And pray to whom am I indebted, sir?'

'Drinkwater, fourth of the *Cyclops* frigate.'

'Ah yes, Captain Hope. A most tenacious officer. Thank you, sir, thank you. I am vastly obliged to you, vastly obliged.' And the curious fellow backed away into the crowd, half bowing as he retreated. Drinkwater was left pondering the aptness of the adjective 'tenacious' as it applied to Hope.

A quarter of an hour later, *Cyclops*'s port cutter drew away from the beach and began the long pull to windward. Drinkwater settled himself in the stern-sheets, resting his feet on a large cheese. Compared to the clerk, he was indeed fortunate, and it occurred to him that the encounter might be fortuitous, if not providential. The order in his pocket offered him an opportunity to present himself before Kempenfelt. The thought gave him a private satisfaction and his mind ran on to the order in his pocket, recollecting that other boat trip he had made in the chilling winter wind when the wherryman had given him lessons on ship-building and the erection of fences.

When they arrived alongside the flagship, Drinkwater ordered the cutter to lie off and wait, then scrambled up the huge ship's tumblehome and stepped into the gloom of the entry. The marine sentry came to attention at the sight of his blue coat whence the white collar patches had been removed but which betrayed their recent presence, and the duty midshipman, a young boy of perhaps eleven years of age, accosted him.

'May I enquire your ship and business?' the boy asked in a falsetto pipe that seemed incongruous against the dark and heaving background of the gun-deck.

'Drinkwater, fourth lieutenant of the *Cyclops*. I have a letter for Admiral Kempenfelt,' Drinkwater explained, adding, lest the boy take it from him and rob him of his opportunity, 'please be kind enough to conduct me to His Excellency's quarters.'

Drinkwater was shown into Kempenfelt's dining quarters which served, betwixt dinners, as an ante-room. At the table sat a man in a plain civilian coat. His pen moved industriously across a sheet of paper, stopping occasionally to recharge itself with ink from the well. Drinkwater observed that this action was so familiar to the admiral's secretary that he did not have to look up, but dipped his pen with unerring accuracy. Completing his task, the secretary sanded the paper, shook it and looked up over the top of a pair of half-moon spectacles. He had a shrewd face and his eyes did not miss the betraying patches of unweathered broadcloth on Drinkwater's lapels.

'Well, sir? State your business.'

'I bear a letter from the dockyard for His Excellency. I believe it was not ready when Lieutenant Durham left.' Without a word, the secretary held out his hand. Anxious to secure at least a glimpse of Kempenfelt, Drinkwater added conversationally, 'I understand the admiral is most anxiously awaiting it . . .'

'Then give it here, sir, and remove the anxiety from your mind,' the clerk retorted, his outstretched fingers making an impatient little flutter. At that moment the door to the great cabin opened and the light from the stern windows shone through, silhouetting a tall figure.

'Is Durham back with that order to dock yet, Scratch?'

'No, Sir Richard, but this young man has it.' Drinkwater relinquished the letter and the secretary applied his paper-knife while Kempenfelt regarded the stranger.

'Have I seen you before?' he asked, stepping out of the doorway so that Drinkwater could see his face properly.

'I think not, Sir Richard,' Drinkwater bowed, 'Drinkwater, acting fourth of the *Cyclops*.'

'Ah yes, Hope's hopeful.' Kempenfelt smiled. 'You've been wounded.'

'In the taking of *La Créole*, sir, in the Carolinas.'

'The Carolinas?' Kempenfelt's brow furrowed in recollection. 'Ah yes, I recall the business. A privateer, eh? A murderous skirmish, no doubt. Now Scratch,' went on the admiral, turning to his secretary who had read the note, 'what d'ye have there? Good news, I hope.' Kempenfelt held out his hand. 'Good day to you, Mr Drinkwater.'

Drinkwater retired crest-fallen, once again disappointed in the high aspirations of impatient youth.

'Our number, sir,' Midshipman White reported formally to Drinkwater, 'send a boat.'

Drinkwater raised the long watch glass and studied the *Royal George* and the flutter of bunting at her mizen yardarm. It was three days since he had taken aboard the order to dock and the great ship had remained stationary in her anchorage.

'Very well, Chalky, do you take the starboard cutter and see what they want, and while you're over there, try and find out why she hasn't been taken to dock. I took aboard an order for it and they seemed anxious to get her in.'

White obeyed the order with evident reluctance. The seductive smell of coffee and something elusive wafting up from below reminded them both that they had been on deck for some hours and were eager to break their fasts. A trip to the *Royal George* might delay White's breakfast indefinitely. Drinkwater watched amused as his young friend slouched off and called the duty boat's crew away. It was a fine, sunny morning and, were it not the latest of a now numberless succession of such days, Drinkwater might have taken more pleasure in it. He could not understand why the relief of the fortress of Gibraltar had lost its urgency and supposed Admiral Cordoba had himself retired to Cadiz. Such matters had been much discussed in the gunroom of late and all concluded depressingly that the war was as good as over and that they sat at Spithead as mere bargaining counters for the diplomats.

Drinkwater fell to pacing the deck. Along the starboard gangway the sergeant of marines was parading his men for Lieutenant Wheeler's routine morning inspection prior to changing the sentries. Below, in the waist, the sail-maker had half the watch with needles and palms stitching a new main topsail. Hanks of sailtwine and lumps of beeswax were in evidence as the heavy canvas was stretched by means of hooks and lanyards to facilitate the difficult job of creating the sail. Old 'Sails' wandered round, looking over the shoulders of the seamen as they laboured, chatting quietly among themselves. Woe betide any man who drew less than ten stitches per needle-length, for he would receive a mouthful of abuse from the sail-maker. 'Such neat work would put a seamstress to envy,' Drinkwater recollected being told by Mr Blackmore, the sailing master, 'and so it should, for what seamstress has to build a dress capable of withstanding the forces aloft in a gale?' This seemed to clinch the superiority of a man-o'-war's sails over a duchess's gown, for though much reputation might ride on the latter, far more might rely on the even strength of those seams when worn aloft in a man-of-war.

Drinkwater smiled and looked forward. On the forecastle a party of men squatted on the deck, plying dark fids of *lignum vitae* as they spliced a large rope. Drinkwater had no idea where it was intended that the heavy hemp should go, for the work was endless, presided over by Blackmore and Devaux, whose men laboured away at the ceaseless task of maintaining the frigate's fabric. More men were scattered in the rigging, worming and parcelling, tarring and slushing.

Idly Drinkwater wondered at the cost of it all in terms of material. If such activity was going on in every one of the ships gathered together in that crowded roadstead, the financial resources behind them must be unimaginable: five, seven, perhaps ten or a dozen millions of sterling!

'Cutter's returning, sir,' the duty quartermaster reported, rescuing Drinkwater from his abstraction. White scrambled up the side and touched his hat-brim to the quarterdeck. 'Message for the captain,' he said, waving a letter, 'be back in a moment.'

White reappeared a few minutes later. 'The Commander-in-Chief wants a status report. Defects, powder, shot, victuals and water. Looks like we at least might be under sailing orders very soon. We've an hour to get it ready. The captain's to wait on Admiral Kempenfelt at nine.'

'I see.' Drinkwater greeted the news with mixed emotions. If they really were going to sea again, he resolved to write to Elizabeth immediately. It was pointless to prevaricate further. If she dismissed his suit he would no longer toss so aimlessly from horn to horn of this confoundedly disturbing dilemma!

'As for the other matter,' White rattled on, 'I had a long chat with a young shaver in her launch.' Drinkwater smiled inwardly. The 'young shaver' was probably a year or so younger than White himself who had matured marvellously since the mess bully Morris had been turned out of the ship. Perhaps it was the eleven-year-old that Drinkwater himself had met the other day. 'Apparently she *was* to dock and then a couple of dockyard officers came aboard and located a leak in the larboard side of the hold. They put the work in hand to caulk the seam from the inside and afterwards declared her fit for sea.'

'Did your young shaver venture an opinion as to how the ship's people felt about that?'

White frowned at the question. 'Well, he said that in his opinion the dockyard officers were a laggardly pair of old hens, but the ship was the finest in the Service. I considered challenging him on that, but declined on grounds of his youthful inexperience!'

'Very wise of you, Mr White,' Drinkwater observed drily. 'Besides, to maintain the honour of our thirty-six guns against his hundred-and-something would be to push matters to extreme measures.' Drinkwater stared across the water at the distant flagship which he could see in the interval between two third-rates. 'Your informant's opinion of the dockyard officers sounds like the repetition of someone else's, though. I've heard the ship is decayed, though what proportion is rumour and what is rot, is rather hard to judge.'

'Ah but that's not all, sir,' said White, enjoying being the bearer of scuttlebutt. 'Yesterday evening the *Royal George*'s carpenter reported another leak, this time on the starboard side where the inlet valve draws water for the washdeck pumps!'

'What's that, d'ye say?' The master came on deck to catch part of discussion. 'A leaking inlet valve, eh? Where d'ye say? Starboard side? If it ain't enough to be pressed for another damned inventory of stores at short notice . . .'

'Morning, Mr Blackmore,' Drinkwater greeted the protesting master as he sought to tuck his unruly white locks under his hat. 'Rest easy. We were talking of the *Royal George.*'

'Well,' replied Blackmore, glancing at the flagship with relief, 'at the best it means the grommet sealing the valve's flange has become porous, but at worst the spirketting may be rotten, in which case the compression of the bolts will be ineffective and she'll leak.'

'Then she'll *have to* dock,' Drinkwater observed.

Blackmore shook his head. 'I doubt the inlet is more than half a fathom below the waterline. If we're in so confounded a hurry to sail, it's my guess they'll careen her. Now, I've work to do. If you've nothing better for this young imp, Mr Drinkwater, I've a host of errands for him!'

Drinkwater grinned at the expression of despair on White's face. It was the lot of a midshipman to tread the deck of a flagship one moment and rummage in the stygian gloom of a frigate's hold the next. 'You may have him, Mr Blackmore, and with my compliments.'

'Obliged, Drinkwater. Now, young shaver, you come with me . . .'

Smiling, Drinkwater watched the two of them go below. White's breakfast remained in doubt.

Lieutenant Wallace relieved Drinkwater at eight bells and he hurried below after colours. Lieutenant Devaux was lingering over his coffee and poured Drinkwater a cup as the messman brought in some toast and devilled kidneys.

'Compliments of the first lieutenant, sir,' the man mumbled in his ear.

'Thank you, sir,' said Drinkwater, catching Devaux's eye. His mouth watered in anticipation as he fisted knife and fork. 'This is a surprise. I thought I smelt something tasty, but I couldn't identify it and in any case assumed it to be for Captain Hope's table.'

'The single joy of our situation, Nathaniel, is the occasional ame-lioration of our tedious diet. Sometimes I think it worth it, but at others I do not. This morning is no exception, for the kidneys come with . . .', Devaux paused to sip his coffee, 'well, you will know about it.'

'The stores inventory?'

'I wish to God that's all it was, but dear old Kempenfelt wants to know how many musket balls the esteemed Wheeler has. "Enough", replies Wheeler, "to kill every Frenchman to be found in Spithead!"' Devaux paused, laying down his empty cup and refill-ing it. 'In the absence of any true wit, one is constrained to laugh,' he added.

Drinkwater smiled as he chewed the kidneys. 'I had better lend a hand then. I gather Captain Hope has to see the admiral at nine, so there is little time.'

'Indeed not, but you had better shave and dress your hair. You must go with the captain.'

'I must?' Drinkwater asked, his mouth full.

'I shall not tempt fate, Nathaniel, but consider how you might clear a foul hawse, or send down the t'gallants, or get the mainyard a-port-last.'

'I am to be examined?' Drinkwater asked in astonishment, his eyes wide.

'You cannot expect a proficiency with that damned French skewer of yours to entitle you automatically to a commission in His Majesty's navy. '

'No, I suppose not.'

'So good luck. Eat up all those kidneys and prove yourself a devil to boot!' Devaux rose, smiling at his own wit, took his hat from the peg by the gunroom door and turned, suddenly serious. 'Don't forget to take your journals.' The door closed behind him and Drinkwater was abandoned to a lather of anxiety.

By a quarter to nine on the morning of 29 August 1782, Spithead was already crowded with the movement of boats and small craft. Among them coasting vessels worked through the congested road-stead. One of them, the fifty-ton *Lark*, laid herself neatly alongside the larboard waist of the *Royal George* and soon afterwards began to discharge hogsheads of rum into the first-rate, a task made some-what easier for those hauling on the tackles by a slight larboard list.

A few moments later a dockyard launch went alongside and the Master Plumber of the Dockyard seized the vertical manropes and laboriously hauled his bulk up the flagship's tumblehome. As soon as the yard boat had laid off, *Cyclops*'s gig ran in under the entry, just astern of the *Lark*, and Captain Hope, in undress uniform, went up the side to the screech of the side-party's pipes. He was followed by Acting Lieutenant Drinkwater, whose bundle of journals went up after him on a line.

As he trailed behind Hope through the gun-decks, leaning against the flagship's increasing list, Drinkwater observed men coiling down the larboard batteries' gun tackles, for all the guns on that side had been run out through the opened ports. It was clear the *Royal George*'s company were in the process of careening her, as Blackmore had said they would. He also noted that the decks were even more crowded and noisy than those of *Cyclops*, the *Royal George* being similarly infested with what Blackmore collectively referred to as 'beach-vermin', but Drinkwater's anxious mind was dominated by the imminent and summary examination he must undergo and he thought no more of these facts.

Outside the admiral's cabin Hope paused and turned, bracing himself as if the ship were on the wind. 'Wait on the quarterdeck, Mr Drinkwater. You may be kicking your heels for some time. Be patient and muse on your profession. The admiral is a fast friend to those he knows, and particularly to men of merit. I have commended you most warmly, but I doubt not that he will want some confirmation of my opinion.'

'I understand, sir. And thank you.'

'Report to the officer of the watch then. Good luck. I shall send the gig back for you in due course.'

'Aye, aye, sir.'

Drinkwater touched his hat to Hope and turned for the companionway to the quarterdeck. The upper gun-deck which stretched forward from where he stood was a scene of utter chaos. The dutymen had crossed the deck from securing the larboard batteries and were running in the starboard guns to the extent of their breechings to induce an even greater list, upsetting the cosy nests that wives and families had established between the cannon. In consequence, there were squeals, shouts, oaths and every combination of noise that flustered women, exasperated men and miserable children could make.

As Drinkwater came up into the sunshine of the quarterdeck, he saw the officer of the watch and a warrant officer just in front of him.

'She's listed far enough, sir,' he heard the warrant officer say, presuming he must be the flagship's carpenter, 'and the water's just lapping the lower-deck gun-port sills.'

'Well get on with your work then, damn it,' the lieutenant responded tartly, 'and start the pumps.' He turned and caught sight of Drinkwater. 'Who the deuce are you?'

'Drinkwater, Acting Lieutenant of *Cyclops*, sir. I'm waiting on Admiral Kempenfelt.'

'Oh are you.' The lieutenant stared at the journals tucked under Drinkwater's arm and, seeming to sum up his situation, expelled his breath contemptuously. 'Well, keep out of the confounded way! I could do without a lot of snot-nosed infants hanging around my coat-tails this morning.'

'I shall of course keep out of your way, sir.' Drinkwater had no wish to further acquaint himself with the objectionable officer. He acknowledged the man had his own problems this morning and soon forgot him as he turned over in his own mind the answers to those questions he thought he might be asked. He presumed a small board of examination had been convened, for there were enough senior officers hereabouts to form a score of such boards, and the thought led him to wonder if he were not the only candidate. The lieutenant's comments seemed to indicate there might be others.

Drinkwater struggled uphill to the high starboard side and peered over in the vain hope of catching sight of the work that was causing all the trouble. The marine sentries on either quarter muttered an exchange and, as Drinkwater turned to cross the quarterdeck to the low side, a man wearing the plain blue coat of *Royal George*'s master came up from below and looked briefly about him. His face wore an expression of extreme apprehension and he too was muttering. He caught sight of the officer of the watch.

'Mr Hollingbury! Damn it, Mr Hollingbury . . .'

Lieutenant Hollingbury turned. 'What the devil do *you* want?'

'I must insist that you right the ship as I asked some moments ago. Right the ship upon the instant, sir! I insist upon it.'

'Insist? What the deuce d'you mean by insisting, Mister? *I* insist that you finish work on the damned cock. Have you finished work on the cock?'

'No, but . . .'

'Then attend to the matter. It is not pleasant standing here with such a heel . . .'

'Get the ship upright, you damned fool, there's water coming in over the lower-deck sills . . .'

'*What* did you say?' Hollingbury's face was suffused with anger and he advanced on the warrant officer. 'We haven't got her over this far to jack in before the task's done. I've ordered the pumps to be manned. Just attend to that damned cock, or I'll have the warrant off you, you impudent old bugger!'

The master turned away, his face white. He hesitated at the top of the companionway and his eyes met Drinkwater's. At that instant they both felt a slight trembling from below. 'She'll go over,' the master said, looking away from Drinkwater and down the companionway as though terrified of descending.

A sudden cold apprehension took possession of Drinkwater's guts. The master's prophecy was not an idle one. Instinctively he felt there was something very wrong with the great ship, though he could not rationalize the conviction of his sudden fear. For a moment he thought he might be succumbing to the panic that held the master rooted to the top of the companionway. Then he knew. The list was no greater than if the *Royal George* had been heeled to a squall of wind, but there was something unambiguously dead about the feel of her beneath his feet.

Then from below there came an ominous rumbling, followed by a series of thunderous crashes accompanied by cries of alarm, screams of pain and the high-pitched arsis of human terror.

Drinkwater ran across the deck and leaned out over the rail to catch sight of *Cyclops*'s boat.

'Gig, hoy!' he roared. '*Cyclops*, hoy!' He saw the face of Midshipman Catchpole in the stern look up at him. Drinkwater waved his arm. 'Stand clear of us astern! Stand clear!' He saw the boy wave in acknowledgement and then thought of Hope down below in the admiral's cabin. He made a dash for the companionway. The master had gone, but now an indiscriminate horde of men and women, seamen, marines, petty officers and officers poured up from below, all shouting and screaming in abject panic. Then Hollingbury, his face distorted by fury at the rank disorder, barred his way. It occurred to Drinkwater that Hollingbury was one of those men who, even in the face of enormity, either deceive themselves as to their part in it or are too stupid to acknowledge that a crisis is occurring

'The ship is capsizing, sir!' Drinkwater hurled the words into the lieutenant's face. 'Capsizing! D'you understand?'

Hollingbury's expression changed as the import of Drinkwater's statement dawned upon him, though it seemed the concept still eluded him, as though it was beyond belief that the almost routine careening of a mighty man-of-war could so abruptly change to something beyond control. But the pandemonium emerging from below finally confirmed that the warning shouted in his very face by this insolent stranger might be true. Comprehension struck Hollingbury like a blow. The colour drained from the lieutenant's face and he spun round. 'My God!' His eyes fell upon the hogsheads of rum hauled out of *Lark* and lying on the deck. In a wild moment of misguided inspiration, he sought to extricate the ship. The only weights he could move rapidly on the low side of the *Royal George* were those rum barrels. 'Get those casks over the side! Heave 'em overboard! Look lively there, damn your eyes!'

A boatswain's mate saw the logic of the order and, driven by habit, wielded his starter. The men on deck and those who were pouring up from below, themselves habituated to obedience, did as they were bidden and rushed across the deck in a mass. But it was too late; their very movement contributed to disaster. The ship's lower deck ports were now pressed well down below the level of the sea. Water cascaded into the ship, settling her lower in the water, deadening her as Drinkwater had divined, drowning those still caught on the orlop and in the hold spaces, and adding the torrential roar of its flooding to the chaos below.

Drinkwater failed to reach the companionway. His momentary confrontation with Hollingbury had delayed him, but even had he succeeded, he would have been quite unable to defy the press of terrified people trying to reach the upper deck. Instead he lost his footing and fell as a gust of wind fluttered across Spithead to strike the high, exposed bilge and the top-hamper of her lofty rig. The gust laid the *Royal George* on her beam ends.

No longer able to support the weight of the remaining starboard guns, the rest of the breechings parted. On the lower gun-deck the huge thirty-two-pounders broke free and hurled their combined tonnage across the lower deck, joined on the decks above by the twenty-four- and twelve-pounders. Lying full length, Drinkwater felt the death throes of the great ship as she shook to a mounting succession of shudderings. He cast about for his journals as they slid down the deck, his heart beating with the onset of panic, abandoned them and clutched at a handhold.

Throughout the *Royal George*'s entire fabric a vast disintegration was taking place. It had started as the first guns broke adrift, careered across the decks and carried all before them, weakening stanchions, colliding with their twins on the opposite side of the gun-decks and knocking out the sills and lintels of the gun-ports piercing the larboard side. The increasing influx of water only settled the *Royal George* deeper. Had her capsizing moment been arrested, she might yet have righted herself sufficiently to be saved, but the rush of men to the larboard waist was just enough to further increase the flow of water and, augmented by that fatal gust of wind, took her past the point of no return.

Finally, the parting breechings of the majority of the guns loosed an avalanche of cast iron in a precipitous descent. Gun after gun crashed into the ship's side, embedding themselves in softening timber, dislodging futtocks and transmitting tremulous shocks throughout the fabric of the hull. Such dislocations sprung more leaks far below, where the upward pressure of the water bore unnaturally upon her heavily listing hull and found the weaknesses of rot. The roundness of her underwater body caved inwards in a slow, unseen implosion that those far above, in terror of their lives, felt only as a great cataclysmic juddering.

Drinkwater, clinging to a train tackle ring-bolt, felt the tremor. Almost, it seemed, directly above his head, one of the half-dozen six-pounder guns that had lined the starboard rail of the quarter-deck strained at its breeching. He watched the strands of the heavy rope unravel ominously. The sight of it galvanized him with the reactive urgency of self-preservation. He began to scrabble upwards, fascinated by the fraying rope-yarns, as though they counted out the remaining seconds of his existence. He did not dare catch hold of the gun-carriage lest his weight accelerate the rope's parting, and stretched instead for the gun-tackle on the left-hand side of the carriage, the hauling part of which now dangled untidily downwards. Somewhere in the back of his mind was the image of the ship's starboard side at which he had glanced out of idle curiosity only a few moments earlier. If he could make the rail and get over it, he might yet escape!

His fingers closed on the gun-tackle, worked at it as his right foot, lodged on the eyebolt, raised him an inch, his fingers scrabbling for a better grip. Then he caught and grasped it and was about to grab it with his other hand when the gun breeching failed. The six-pounder ran away and he found himself pulled the last few feet up the violently canted deck as the descending gun unrove the gun-tackle. The truck hit his foot and he kicked at it just as his eyes caught sight of the proximity of the standing block to his fingers. He let go of the rope, kicked again, found a momentary foothold on the slewing and falling gun-carriage, and grabbed another rope which had dropped from a pin on the mizen rail. He slid back as it ran slack, then drew tight; he began to climb, frantic in his movements, gasping for breath, his objective in sight. With a final effort dredged from the inner resource of pure terror, he hauled himself up to the pinrail. Here there was no lack of handholds and, almost exhausted with the effort, his heart beating in his breast and his breath rasping painfully in his throat, he threw himself over it. Panting and shaking, he glanced back, almost vertically downwards. The mainyard, its extremity already in the water, had stabbed down across the deck of the *Lark*. What had happened to the crowd of people he had seen in the coasting vessel's waist a few moments ago, he had no idea, for only a few heads bobbed in the water, and he thought it unnaturally quiet.

He turned away, shuddering too much from exertion and visceral fear to be able to stand. Instead he crawled past the open ports of the starboard side whence came the loud sibilance of compressed air roaring upwards with columns of debris. He understood now why he could not hear anyone shouting or screaming. Every unsecured port on the starboard side stood open, venting a furious mist in which unidentifiable items flew upwards, to flutter down beside the ship. What had once been a woman's shawl or a baby's diaper, a book, a shoe or a man's hat, fell into the surrounding sea as flotsam. Drinkwater pulled himself together as he realized that, shallow though the water was, it was deep enough to swallow whole the vast bulk of the *Royal George*. He began to crawl aft.

Perhaps ten other men and a solitary woman who screamed

and rent her hair in despair were visible on the starboard side. Another man, a marine by his tunic, was hauling himself out of an open port on the middle gun-deck, the water running off him. Drinkwater scrambled towards the woman, but she turned on him in a fury, her eyes wild with dementia, a torrent of abuse pouring from her. He turned aft, thinking again of Hope below in the admiral's state-cabin. Perhaps he could free the stern windows before it was too late, but the wreck beneath his feet trembled again and suddenly the venting roar died away and the circle of water about him approached.

He was on his feet now, running aft in search of *Cyclops*'s gig. He could see boats laying off, their oars immobile, the faces of their crews pale ovals as they watched the awesome sight of the *Royal George* foundering in the midst of the Grand Fleet, within sight of over three hundred vessels and the shore.

He had survived the immersion, being dragged painfully over the gig's transom and surrendered to the solicitous Appleby who had chafed his naked and bruised body with brandy. He had been touched by the anxious concern of White and Devaux, and later mourned the loss of his journals.

He was never to know, though he might afterwards have guessed, that a few days later a sabre-winged fulmar, sweeping low over the wave crests somewhere to the westward, in the overfalls that run off St Alban's Head, had its roving eye caught by a patch of white. It banked steeply and rolled almost vertically as it made its curving turn, keeping the white patch in view as it swooped back on its interminably hungry reconnaissance. But the white paper was of no nutritional value to the fulmar and it levelled off and skimmed on westwards towards Portland Bill, its wings motionless as they had been all the time it had surveyed the sheet of paper.

The secretary's ink had run by then and no one could have read Kempenfelt's last signature, nor that the paper was a commission made out in the King's name for a certain insignificant Nathaniel Drinkwater.

Chapter Three Winter 1782

The Flogging

The North Sea was a heaving mass of grey crests which broke in profusion, the pallid spume of their dissolution driving down-wind. Under close-reefed topsails and the clew of the foretopmast staysail, *Cyclops* fought the inevitable drift to leeward, towards the shoals off the inhospitable Dutch coast. Beneath the lowering sky, from which neither sun nor moon obliged the patient Blackmore and his quadrant, the frigate lay battered by the fourth day of the gale. It was the third day of cold rations, since it had proved impos-sible to maintain the galley fire, and the only consolation to the shivering ship's company was that they had loaded a fresh stock of beer at Sheerness.

Everything below decks was its usual compound of stink and damp. Sea water squirted through the interstices of closed gun-ports as the lee side buried itself, and the crew were employed at the pumps for an hour and a half every watch. Men barely spoke to each other; nothing beyond the barest detail of duty was discussed and every man, irrespective of his station, sought only the meagre comfort of his hammock or cot as he came below from the greater misery of the deck.

Relieved by White, Midshipman Drinkwater made his bruised and buffeted way below and clambered wearily into his hammock. The dark of the orlop deck was punctured by the swaying lanterns which imparted their weird and monstrous shadows as they oscil-lated at different rates to the laden hammocks. From below came the swirl and effluvia of the bilge, counterpoint to the creaks and groans of the frigate's hull and the faint thrum of the gale roaring above through the mast and rigging.

Despite his exhaustion, Drinkwater was unable to sleep. His active brain rebelled against the fatigue of his body. Dulled by the monotony of the gale and the necessity of ignoring his protesting and empty stomach, it now refused to let him drift into the seaman's one palliative for misery, the balm of exhausted sleep.

It hardly seemed possible that *Cyclops* was the same frigate that had fought under Rodney in the Moonlight Battle, or that the sullen faces of the seamen were those that had followed the young Midshipman Drinkwater through the bilge of the Yankee schooner *Algonquin* in a bid to avert confinement in a French fortress. But it was not the weather or the duty of a winter cruise in the North Sea which had induced this sleepless anxiety, it was the misery which prevailed aboard, so reminiscent of his first months in the frigate when the very cockpit to which an unkind fate had now returned him had been dominated by the vicious presence of the bugger Morris. Far from obtaining a commission, Drinkwater had found himself deprived of the privacy and privileges of the acting rank to which he had grown accustomed.

It was a cruel blow, made worse by the departure of Devaux. After the tragic loss of Captain Hope aboard the *Royal George*, Lieutenant Devaux had briefly commanded the ship for the passage to Sheerness. On arrival there, Devaux, whose eldest brother had blown out his own brains over a gambling debt, now learned the news, already months old, that his second brother had died in the trenches before Yorktown. Devaux thus found himself the 6th Earl of Dungarth in the Irish peerage, and this change in his circumstances induced Miss Charlotte Dixon, a young woman outstanding for her beauty and intelligence, to consent to become his countess. As Miss Dixon was not merely lovely and clever but also the sole daughter of a nabob, Dungarth was in some hopes of repairing his family's fortunes and swiftly relinquished the profession of a naval officer. To Drinkwater, Devaux's departure seemed like a double desertion, for the first lieutenant, poor though he might be, left to make an advantageous marriage, abandoning his lieutenant's commission without a second thought. Drinkwater, for whom such a qualification seemed an impossible attainment, was left to muse upon the inequities of life, with only the thin consolation of his correspondence with Elizabeth to help him come to terms with his return to the midshipmen's mess.

'I am sorry, my dear fellow,' Devaux had said on their last night in the gunroom as *Cyclops* lay within half a mile of the light-vessel at the Nore. 'I should have liked to help you but my naval service is over. Perhaps we shall meet again, perhaps when there is peace you will come and stay with us . . .'

Perhaps . . . perhaps . . . How full of pathos that word seemed, and how Drinkwater envied Devaux the use of that plural pronoun.

Under orders though they were, their brief halt at Sheerness saw changes in the cockpit, as well as in the gunroom, but most of all a new commander read his commission to the ship's company.

Captain Smetherley, whose father supported the new government of Lord Rockingham, was twenty-six years old. Pleasant in disposition, he possessed an easy manner of command but had little practical experience to his name. He had been entered on a ship's books as a boy, had dodged the regulations and had been commissioned at sixteen with neither achievement nor examination to testify to his suitability. During his six months as a commander, he had been in charge of a sloop which had spent half that time at anchor in the Humber. With Captain Smetherley came an elderly first lieutenant named Callowell, a hard-drinking tarpaulin of the old school sent by a considerate Admiralty to offset the professional shortcomings of the new post-captain. Callowell was a man from the other end of the navy's social spectrum. Twice the age of his commander, a man with neither influence nor the dash that might have earned him merited promotion, he offered no threat to Smetherley in the matter of glory, but he was well known as a highly competent seaman and a tough sea-officer. Unfortunately, Callowell was also a harsh man. Cruelty and faultfinding were visited on all, irrespective of rank. Moreover, fellow-officers more favourably placed than himself who were disposed to assist the advancement of a competent, if disadvantaged officer, were turned away by Callowell's spite.

Within a few days, Drinkwater reflected, Callowell had made enemies of Appleby the surgeon, Lieutenant Wheeler of the marines and poor Lieutenant Wallace, and it was borne in upon Drinkwater how fine an influence Devaux had been on the frigate as a whole. He was greatly missed and, Drinkwater felt certain, he himself would not have been turned so precipitately out of the gunroom had Devaux remained aboard.

Smetherley's arrival had also, in Callowell's phrase, 'cleaned out the midshipmites' cockpit'. Only White and Drinkwater remained of the original midshipmen, and they were now joined by four young kill-devils to whose families Smetherley owed some obligation or who had solicited his favour. Both White and Drinkwater viewed this invasion with disquiet. It was clear that the four all knew each other, and while seasickness had demoralized them for the first few days, it was obvious from their slovenly indiscipline, their abuse of Jacob the messman, and their noise that they were going to prove troublesome.

Had they remained a week longer at anchor at Spithead, Drinkwater knew that White would have been able to leave the frigate, for he was daily in expectation of the order, but within a few days of the foundering of the *Royal George*, *Cyclops* had sailed for Sheerness. Rodney's defeat of De Grasse had revenged Graves's disgrace off the Virginia Capes, though it did not restore the Thirteen Colonies, and even as they tossed in the fury of the northern gale, Lord Howe and the Grand Fleet were relieving Gibraltar for the third and final time. As the unpopular conflict spluttered to its close, *Cyclops* had to maintain her vigil to see that neither Dutch nor French cruisers stole a march on the exhausted British nor tipped the delicate balance of negotiations in the peace talks that all seemed certain were about to bring matters to a conclusion. Perhaps, Drinkwater thought as he resolutely composed himself to grab a few hours' sleep, the war would at last be truly over. Providence had saved him from plunging to his death with all those other poor souls trapped aboard the *Royal George*; it must surely have preserved him for some purpose, and what purpose could there possibly be other than to allow him to return to Elizabeth?

Lieutenants Callowell and Wallace stood on the weather quarterdeck staring to windward. Callowell, his feet well spread and both hands gripping the rail against the heel of the frigate, was speaking to Wallace, his cloak beating about him in a sinister manner – like a bat's wings, Drinkwater thought, approaching them. He touched his hat to the two officers as he made his way aft to the taffrail to heave the log which the two quartermasters were preparing. It was almost eight bells, the end of the morning watch, and Drinkwater was tired and hungry. He nodded to the two petty officers, and the log-ship went over the side, drawing the knotted line off the spinning reel while Drinkwater regarded old Bower's watch.

'Now!' he called, and the line was nipped. 'Five knots?'

'And a half.'

'Very good. And how much leeway d'you reckon?' Drinkwater shouted above the roar of the gale, cocking an eye at the older quartermaster. The man had served as mate in a merchantman and knew his business.

' 'Bout eight degrees, I'd say.' Drinkwater and the second quartermaster nodded their assent.

'Very well. We'll make it so. You may hand the log.' And leaving them to wind in the hemp line, Drinkwater walked forward to move the pegs on the traverse board. The glass was turned, eight bells were struck and the forenoon took over from the morning watch. On deck men in sodden tarpaulins were stamping about, eager to be dismissed below, and those just emerged from the foetid berth-deck huddled in miserable groups in what shelter they could find, trying to delay the inevitable moment of a sousing for as long as possible. The petty officers made their reports and Drinkwater went aft to where Wallace and Callowell were still in conversation, staring out over the grey waste to windward.

'Beg pardon, sir . . .' Drinkwater shouted. The two officers looked over their shoulders, Callowell raising an interrogative eyebrow, though it was Wallace who was about to be relieved.

'Starboard watch mustered on deck. Permission for the larbowlines to go below, sir.'

Callowell looked at Drinkwater. From Wallace's look of embarrassment, Drinkwater knew trouble was brewing. He repeated his report and Callowell said in a voice raised above the wind, 'Mr Drinkwater, we are waiting . . .'

'Sir?'

'Waiting, damn you . . .'

'I'm sorry, Mr Callowell, but . . .'

'Mr Callowell is waiting for the courtesy of a "good morning",' Wallace said hurriedly.

Drinkwater had thought himself absolved from such an absurdity by the violence of the weather, the fact that he and Wallace had been on deck since four o'clock in the morning, and the salute he had given the two officers as he made his way aft to heave the log. He was about to swallow his pride, aware that to provoke Callowell with any form of justification was a waste of time, when Callowell denied him this small amelioration.

'As first lieutenant of this frigate, I expect my midshipmen to demonstrate the respect due to the senior officer below the commander. You, sir, can disabuse yourself of any advantages your late acting rank gave you, or any that might have been conferred by your friendship with the last first lieutenant or the late Captain Hope. The fresh air of the foretopmasthead will do you the world of good, will it not, Mr Wallace?'

Wallace mumbled uncomfortably, but Callowell was not yet satisfied. 'But you shall first heave the log again and be pleased to use the glass, not your damned watch. She makes six knots.'

It was growing dark when Drinkwater was brought down from the masthead. The topgallant masts had been struck and he had lashed himself into the shelter available, passing the afternoon in a miserable, semi-conscious state, wracked by cold, cramps and hunger. He had been incapable of descending the mast unaided, and Tregembo and another seaman had sent him down on a gantline.

'There, zur,' the Cornishman had muttered, 'that bastard'll get a boarding-pike in his arse if ever we zees action.'

'Poor bugger can't hear you,' his companion said.

'Maybe not,' Tregembo said philosophically, 'but when he wakes up, he'll agree with me.'

On deck the pain of returning circulation woke Drinkwater to a full and agonizing consciousness that was too self-centred to admit even a single thought of revenge. He gasped with the pain, involuntary tears starting from his eyes, as poor White brought orders that were to further prolong his distress. From this state of half-recovery, Callowell demanded his immediate presence on the quarterdeck where, Drinkwater was told, it was time for him to stand his next watch. Had not Drinkwater been able to rely upon the loyal White to smuggle him victuals on deck and had he not eaten them equally unobserved, his collapse from cold and hunger would have proved fatal. As it was, he endured the ordeal.

Drinkwater was not the only victim of Callowell's harsh malice. Before the gale finally abated, several floggings of undue severity had been ordered out to the hands for trivial offences. Several of these would normally have been summarily dealt with by the frigate's regulating system, minor punishments being meted out by the boatswain and his mates. Devaux, had he even bothered to notice them, would have disdained to act. Callowell, on the other hand, possessed a knack of always observing these small incidents so that it seemed his presence actually caused them, and men shrank from him. The first lieutenant appeared indifferent to this shunning. Appleby named him *Ubique* Callowell, to the amusement of Wheeler, but it was Appleby who first warned of serious discontent among the hands. His position as surgeon enabled him to divine more of the frigate's undercurrents than any gunroom officer and, as his business chiefly occupied him below decks, he was particularly sensitive to the moods of the people. In fact Callowell's behaviour only exacerbated a deteriorating situation. The ship's company had largely been aboard *Cyclops* since October 1779 and in all that time had not enjoyed a single day of liberty ashore. Nor had these long-suffering men been paid their wages. They had, however, had women aboard and had revelled in the excesses of unbridled lust, a pleasure paid for by their share of prize money but now requiring Appleby's mercurial specific against the lues. Some prize money, however, remained, and this excited an envious greed among those intemperate spendthrifts who were now paying painfully for past pleasures.

To compound matters, before leaving Spithead *Cyclops* had been obliged to pass twenty men to the *Bedford*, then under sailing orders, and had made up the deficiency from a draft embarked at the Nore where her new captain joined before she sailed to her cruising ground on the Broad Fourteens. The new crew members were duly taken aboard from the *Conquistador*, guardship at the Nore, the majority being 'Lord Mayor's men', those who made up the deficiencies in the parish quotas by the simple expedient of being released from the confinement ordered by the petty sessions.

Among the men from *Conquistador* were some skilled petty felons, men who owed neither His Britannic Majesty's Royal Navy in general nor their shipmates in the frigate *Cyclops* in particular any shred of loyal forbearance. Even before they had weighed from the anchorage off Sheerness, thieving had broken out on the berth-deck, but it was after the abatement of the gale that these men revealed the full extent of the two unsought contributions they had brought aboard.

The thieving was bad enough, but far worse was the gaol fever. The outbreak of typhus, a disease harboured in the parasites inhabiting these men's filthy garments, caused Appleby much labour and anxiety. The surgeon found the purser unwilling to issue slop-clothing until Callowell approved it and this the first lieutenant declined to do. Thus both thieving and disease permeated the ship, causing infinite distress and disorder among the men. The knowledge of a deadly infection striking indiscriminately only fuelled the pathetic desperation with which the miserable hands sought other diversions. With silver florins unspent upon the berth-deck, every form of card-sharping, knavery, pilfering and coercion flourished. Nor was this moral disintegration the sole province of the newly drafted men; on the contrary they were but the catalyst. Men who had been messmates, even friends, when confronted with sudden personal losses, turned on their equals to redeem them. As if this witches' cauldron were not enough, there were among the drafted men two devil-may-care light dragoons sentenced by a court martial to be dismissed from their regiment and sent as common seamen into the Royal Navy. They had received a flogging and had come to *Cyclops* with the notion that, since service in the navy was of a punitive nature, it was little deserving of respect. In their former corps, the 7th Queen's Own Light Dragoons, both men had been non-commissioned officers and they resented the treatment meted out to them by the boatswain's mates and, in particular, the midshipmen.

In the choice of his new midshipmen, Captain Smetherley had been unfortunate. Of the four who had come in his train, all were ignorant and incompetent, while the example of Callowell encouraged a viciousness sometimes natural in young men. Despite their youth they were usually more drunk than sober and they had discovered a means of amusing themselves by bullying and taunting the men until, answered back, they ordered the boatswain's mates to start the alleged offenders.

Such was the sorry state of affairs aboard *Cyclops*, and it augured ill after the fair and relatively humane regime of Hope and Devaux. The effect of the gale only exacerbated the deterioration in morale. What occurred in a few short days might have taken longer in a better climate or a pleasanter season, but it came as no surprise to those who regarded the new regime with distaste when trouble arose.

Two days after the gale had blown itself out and patches of watery sunshine and blue skies had replaced the grey wrack that had streamed above the very mast trucks, a sail was made out to the northward. The change in the weather had brought most of the officers on to the quarterdeck and the mood lightened still further as this news broke the monotony of their existence. The ship was standing to the northward, close-hauled on the larboard tack and carrying sails to the topgallants.

'Royals, sir?' Callowell asked Smetherley as he came on deck.

'As you see fit, Mr Callowell,' Smetherley said, falling to pacing the weather planking, hands clasped behind his back. Callowell turned to bawl his orders. *Cyclops* set her kites flying, the yards being run up when required and the sheets rove through the top-gallant yardarms by the upper topmen. The pipes shrilled and the seamen leapt aloft, poking fun at the fumbling landsmen who were preparing to heave the halliards.

'A glass at the foremasthead, sir?' prompted Callowell.

'If you please, Mr Callowell,' assented Captain Smetherley with urbane assurance. Callowell turned to find Midshipman Baskerville at his elbow.

'Take a glass aloft and see what you make of him,' Callowell growled, and the midshipman passed Drinkwater with a smirk. He was the most loathsome of the captain's toadies, the leader of the quartet, related by blood to Smetherley and therefore unassailable. To Baskerville, Drinkwater was a passed-over nonentity, and while he was cautious of White, for he recognized him as one of his own, he did not scruple to use a high and usually insolent tone with Drinkwater. As Baskerville hauled himself into the foremast rigging, Drinkwater walked over to the lee rail where Blackmore was peering through his battered perspective glass, trying to gain a glimpse of the strange sail.

'Can you make him out yet, Mr Blackmore?'

'Not yet, but I'm thinking he'll be British, and sailing without convoy. Out of Hamburg at this season.' Blackmore was apt to be inscrutable at such moments and Drinkwater recollected that he had commanded a Baltic trader until ruined by war and knew the North Sea trade better than any other man on board. As the two men waited for the sail to be visible from the deck, neither witnessed the incident that provoked the coming trouble.

Amongst the men ordered into the lower rigging to see the royal yards run clear aloft was Roach. He had been rated landsman, as was customary, but as a former troop corporal of light dragoons, he was an active and an intelligent man. Whatever the shortcomings of their fellow landsmen, neither Roach nor his fellow-cavalryman Hollins lacked courage. Contemptuous of their new Service, they flung themselves into the rigging as though charging an enemy, disdaining to be associated with the drabber, duller men of the Sheerness draft. They were not yet of much use aloft but were clearly the raw material of which upper topmen were made, and their dare-devilment had already earned a grudging admiration from *Cyclops*'s people, especially those who had observed the state of their backs.

In descending the foremast rigging Roach, aware that to go through the lubber's-hole was considered the coward's path, was about to fling himself over the edge of the top and into the futtock shrouds. The heels of his hessian boots, which he had found an indispensable weapon on the lower deck, trod on the up-reaching fingers of Midshipman Baskerville just then ascending the mast with his telescope. Hearing the youth's shout, Roach drew back into the top and, as the midshipman came over the edge, muttered a half-hearted apology. But he was grinning and this, combined with the sharp pain, provoked Baskerville.

'You bloody fool! You've made me drop the glass! What the devil d'you mean by wearing those festerin' boots, damn your eyes?'

'Doin' my duty, *sir*.' The dragoon drew out the last syllable so that it oozed from him like a sneer and he did it with the studied insolence of twenty years of barrack-room experience, deeply resenting the authority of the young oaf. Roach pressed his advantage. 'I apologized to you, *Mr* Baskerville.' Again there was that sibilant distortion in the title which set Baskerville fuming while Roach persisted in his grinning. But then another figure appeared in the top. It was a boatswain's mate.

'Mr Jackson,' Baskerville asked quickly, 'd'you see that man's grin?'

'Aye, I do.'

'Then mark it well, Jackson, mark it well and take the bugger's name!'

'Very well, sir. Here's your glass. You were fortunate I caught it.'

Baskerville almost snatched the telescope from Jackson's outstretched hand, then, without another word, swung himself into the topmast shrouds and scrambled upwards.

'And what have you done to upset Mr Baskerville, Roach?' the boatswain's mate asked.

'I trod on his fingers, Mr Jackson, and I apologized.'

Jackson shook his head. 'Tch, tch, tch. There's no fucking justice, is there? I wish you'd trodden on his fucking head, but you'll get a checked shirt for this, my lad, or my name's not Harry Jackson.'

Blackmore's prediction turned out to be accurate and the sail revealed herself as the brig *Margaret* of Newcastle, bound from Hamburg to London with timber and flax. At the frigate's signal she hove to and *Cyclops* rounded up under her lee quarter, backing her own maintopsail. Alongside Drinkwater, Blackmore muttered, 'Damn, you can smell the turpentine from here!'

Callowell leapt up on to the rail and raised a speaking-trumpet to his mouth. 'You're not in convoy, Mister. Any sign of enemy ships?'

'Aye,' responded a stout figure at the *Margaret's* rail in the unmistakable accents of the Tyne, 'convoy dispersed by a ship-rigged Frenchman. He took twa vessels oot of tha ten of us. Be aboot twenty guns.'

'What of your escort?'

'A bomb-vessel. She couldn't work to windward before the Frenchman made off.'

'Where away?'

'Norderney!'

'Thank you, Captain! *Bon voyage!*' The patrician accent of Captain Smetherley replaced the abrupt Callowell. For once he had the situation in hand. 'Haul your maintopsail, Mr Callowell. Mr Blackmore, lay me a course for Norderney, if you please. Let's see if we can catch this damned Frog.'

'Lay *me*, be damned,' Blackmore muttered to Drinkwater and then, raising his voice, called out, 'Aye, aye, sir.'

Summary justice was a principle upon which Jonas Callowell dealt with all matters of discipline and good order. If an offence was committed, it was swiftly punished. When he received Baskerville's complaint he reported to Smetherley who lounged in his cabin, a glass of port in one hand.

'Damned rascal was insolent to the midshipman, insolence witnessed by Jackson, sir.'

'Jackson, Mr Callowell?'

'Bosun's mate.'

'Ahhh.' Smetherley took a mouthful of port and rolled it around his tongue, swallowed and smacked his lips. He looked up at Callowell with a frown. 'And you demand punishment?'

'Of course, sir. For the maintenance of discipline. Absolutely indispensable,' Callowell replied, a little astonished.

'Naturally, Mr Callowell, but the principle of mercy . . . does it enter into the particulars of this case?'

'Not to my mind, sir,' said Callowell, who had never heard anything so damned stupid.

'Will two dozen suffice for insolence to a midshipman?'

'As you see fit, sir,' responded Callowell drily, but Smetherley, pouring another glass of port, needed to maintain the fiction of command and enjoyed a little light-hearted baiting of his first lieutenant.

'What, if you were in my position, would you give the man, Mr Callowell?'

'I'd smother the bugger with the captain's cloak, sir.'

'Three dozen, eh? Isn't that a trifle hard?'

'Not in my view, sir.'

'Mr Baskerville is a somewhat forward young man. His only redeeming feature, as far as I can see, is a rather lovely sister.' Smetherley pulled a face over the rim of his glass. 'But that would not concern you, Mr Callowell. Two dozen will suffice, I think.'

'As you see fit, sir,' Callowell repeated, leaving the cabin.

Roach was confined to the bilboes until the watch changed. When Appleby heard, he hurried to the gunroom where the first lieutenant was tossing off a pot of blackstrap.

'You cannot mean this, Mr Callowell?'

'Mean what?' asked Callowell, whose contempt for the surgeon's humanity was only exceeded by his dislike of the man himself whom he regarded as a meddling old wind-bag.

'Why flogging Roach, of course!'

'And why, pray, should I not flog Roach?' asked Callowell, lowering his tankard and staring at Appleby. 'Is he not guilty of insolence to an officer?'

'A very junior, inexperienced *under* officer,' Appleby expostulated testily, 'a mere insolent aspirant himself, without skill and wanting common manners to boot, but that is not the point . . .'

'Then for God's sake get to your damned point, Appleby!'

'How many's he getting?'

'Two dozen.'

'Two dozen! But that's twice the permitted limit for a post-captain to award!'

'Are you questioning the captain's authority, Mr Appleby? My word, you'd make a fine sight at the gratings yourself!'

'Damn it, Mr Callowell, you have no right . . .'

'Is that your point, Appleby?' Callowell broke in impatiently.

'No, no it isn't.' Appleby collected himself. 'Mr Callowell, Roach was given two hundred and fifty lashes after his court martial. I am empowered to prevent . . .'

'I've no doubt but that he deserved them,' broke in Callowell. 'As for your being empowered to do anything, Mr Appleby, I believe it is limited to advice. Well, thank you for your advice. It was my advice to Captain Smetherley that Roach be given *three* dozen . . .'

'I daresay it was, but heed me. The man's back is in no state to suffer further punishment. You'll kill the fellow.'

'So much the better. The man is no good to us, he will be nothing but trouble.'

'But . . .'

Callowell's emptied tankard crashed down upon the table and he rose to his feet, leaned across it and thrust his face into that of the surgeon. 'Listen, Appleby, do you cure the pox, the gaol fever, the itch, button scurvy and the clap, and when you can do all that you may come back here and teach me *my* duty. Now take your damnable cant back to where you belong and keep your fat arse out of the gunroom. It's for the commissioned officers, not bloody tradesmen. Get out!'

Appleby departed with what dignity he could muster, but word of the encounter percolated rapidly through the ship. The surgeon himself was far from capitulating. He approached Captain Smetherley and obtained a stay of execution of two days, until the Sunday following. It was unlikely to achieve anything other than to compel the inexperienced Smetherley to think again and, in the event, Appleby's compassion misfired badly. The delay only served to fuel resentment at Roach's sentence. Strict discipline made the life of the decent majority of the ship's company bearable, saving them from the predatory conduct of the worst elements of their own kind. But a virtual death sentence on a grown man of proven courage for insolence to a boy whose authority far exceeded his abilities and who had yet to prove his mettle to the hands, was a different matter.

Drinkwater was more aware of the state of things than the feckless wastrels who pounded Baskerville's back in congratulation as though he had won a great victory. He wished he had known of the matter before Baskerville had reported it to Callowell. Watching the scene, he determined matters could not go on and, now that they all appeared recovered from their seasickness, the moment seemed opportune. White was absent on deck and Drinkwater laid down the book he had been trying to read by the guttering illumination of the purser's dip.

'You sicken me, you really do.'

Silence fell on the rabble and the four faces turned towards him. 'Whom are you addressing?' Baskerville asked superciliously.

'All of you,' replied Drinkwater, staring up at their half-lit faces. In the gloom they possessed a diabolical appearance. 'You are a scandalous disgrace. It is likely that Roach will die, if not under punishment then as a consequence of it. If you had a shred of decency, Baskerville, you would go at once and withdraw the charge, say it was a mistake and apologize.'

'Why you contemptuous shit, Drinkwater,' said Baskerville, looking round at his friends. 'He needs a licking . . .'

'If one of you so much as lays a finger on me,' Drinkwater said, reaching up to where his French sword was slung by its scabbard rings on the deck beam overhead, 'I'll slit his gizzard.' He drew the blade with a rasp. 'Four to one is Frenchmen's odds, my fine bantam cocks, and you've yet to see action. Please, don't give me the excuse.' He paused. Irresolution was already visible in one or two faces and the light played on the wicked blade of the French sword. 'No, don't give me the excuse to defend myself, or I might take singular pleasure in it. '

Drinkwater rose. 'Brooke,' he said quietly, addressing the youngest of the midshipmen before him, 'go and fetch Jacob.' The boy hesitated and looked at Baskerville for permission, whereupon Drinkwater commanded, 'Go boy!' and Brooke scampered off in search of the messman. While he was gone, Drinkwater dragged his chest out, opened it and threw his belongings into it. A moment later the messman appeared, rubbing sleep from his eyes. 'Jacob, move my chest and hammock forrard. I shall sleep with the marines.'

'Aye, aye, sir.'

Drinkwater paused at the canvas curtain that served to screen off that portion of the orlop known as the cockpit. 'The stink of puppy-dogs in here is overpowering!'

By Sunday morning *Cyclops* had passed Norderney without sighting any enemy cruiser. The wind had dropped and there was a mist which persisted into the forenoon, resisting the sun's heat.

'Dense fog by nightfall,' Blackmore remarked.

After divine service the hands remained mustered to witness the punishment. The officers gathered about the captain; the marines lined the hammock nettings, their bayonets fixed. In the waist, over two hundred men were assembled. They murmured softly, like a swarm of bees. Triced up in the main shrouds, the grating awaited the prisoner.

Roach was escorted on deck by two boatswain's mates. He walked upright between them, his shirt loose and his breeches tucked into the offending boots. At the grating he took off his shirt, revealing the scabbed welts and blue bruising of his former punishment. The murmuring was replaced by a low rumbling.

'Silence!' commanded Callowell.

Smetherley stepped forward. 'Landsman Roach, I tolerate no insolence to my officers, commissioned or otherwise, aboard any ship under my command. You will receive two dozen lashes. Bosun's mates, do your duty!'

'Trice him up!' Callowell ordered, and Roach was thrust forward and his wrists seized and strapped to the grating. One of the men grabbed his hair and jerked his head back to shove a leather wad into his mouth.

'Shame!' called a voice from forward. It was answered by a chorus of anonymous 'Ayes!' from the crowd amidships. Wheeler drew his sword and commanded the marine drummer to beat his snare. Callowell bawled, 'Lay on!'

The two boatswain's mates, each with a cat-o'-nine-tails, began to administer the punishment, six lashes each in succession, while the drummer manfully maintained his roll and the men mouthed their disapproval. Roach spat the leather wad from his mouth and roared defiant curses until, at about the nineteenth stroke, he fell silent.

Drinkwater felt an utter revulsion at the spectacle. He sought distraction by observing the other officers. Appleby stood rigid, his portly frame wracked by sobs, the sheen of angry tears upon his ruddy cheeks. Blackmore gazed out over the heads of the crew, sure that the foremast catharpings could do with some attention. Wheeler stood like a statue, his drawn sword across his breast, his eyes flickering restlessly over the ship's company, waiting for the first sign of trouble. Callowell too watched the men, but with less apprehension than the marine officer. Blinded by the insensitivity of a life circumscribed by duty, he possessed no imagination, no compassion and few feelings for others. *Cyclops* was a man-of-war and sentiment of any kind was out of place upon her decks. To a man of Callowell's stamp, the emergence of personality among the people was an affront, and his cruelty stemmed from this conviction rather than any sadistic impulse. It was his lot to administer, and theirs to endure.

But next to Drinkwater, White stood stock still. 'Christ Almighty, I can see his ribs,' he whispered.

Servants of the Night

The fog Blackmore had predicted closed down during the after-noon. All day the becalmed *Cyclops* had drifted with the tide and, as the visibility deteriorated, the rattling blocks, slack cordage, slatting canvas and black hempen stays dripped moisture on to the wet decks. Below, the damp permeated everything. Shortly after sunset, when the light went out of the vapour surrounding them, Appleby reported the death of Roach. The news surprised nobody and *Cyclops*, shut in her world of sodden misery, seemed to hold her breath in anticipation.

Drinkwater was late being relieved at midnight. White rushed on deck breathless with apologies and anxious to avoid trouble.

'Couldn't sleep, Nat. Kept thinking of that poor devil's bones, then I must have dropped off . . .'

'Best not to think too much, Chalky,' Drinkwater put a hand on the younger midshipman's shoulder, 'you'll get over it.'

As he passed through the gun-deck on his way below, Drinkwater was half aware of movement forward. He hesitated. If trouble was brewing, he ought not to let it pass, but when he looked he could see nothing untoward and so passed on, bone-weary and eager for the small comfort of sleep. A light still showed through Appleby's door and Drinkwater went forward, ducking under the swaying hammocks, to wish him goodnight, for he knew the surgeon had been upset by the death of Roach. Drinkwater knocked. There was no reply and he cocked his ears. In the creaking darkness, assailed by the thousand sounds of the ship and of men snoring, he thought he heard an insistent grunt. Another, more identifiable, followed. He turned the handle, found it locked against him and forced the flimsy door with his shoulder. Appleby was trussed and gagged. His face was an unpleasant colour and his eyes started from their sockets.

Bending, Drinkwater released the gag and Appleby gasped for air while his rescuer turned his attention to the light-line binding wrists and ankles. Catching his breath, Appleby spat out, 'Mutiny, Nat! They meant me no harm. Wanted to know if I'd said Roach was unfit . . . to receive punishment. That's my duty. My privilege . . .'

'Who's their leader? The other dragoon?'

Appleby nodded. 'Yes. Hollins, his name is. I told them to desist.' Appleby rubbed his wrists, his face contorted with pain. 'I told 'em what'd been done to Roach was chicken-feed compared with what'd be done to them if they persisted, but they'd have none of it. So they trussed me. Apologized, but trussed me . . . They're after Callowell. We've got to stop them, for they'll take Smetherley and Baskerville too! Before you know it, we'll all be involved!'

'Very well!' snapped Drinkwater, getting Appleby's ankles clear and rubbing them himself. 'Do you get Wheeler. Now!' He stood, remembering the noise in the gun-deck. 'There's no time to be lost,' he added, helping the surgeon get to his unsteady feet, then he turned and scrambled aft under the hammocks to the marines' berth. Grabbing his sword he savagely elbowed the hammock next to him. A grunt emanated from it.

'What the fuck . . .?'

'Get your men up, Sergeant! Quietly!' he hissed insistently. 'Bayonets! And hurry! We've trouble!'

'Oh shit!' Waiting only for the appearance of the pale form of Sergeant Hagan's emerging limb, Drinkwater moved swiftly to the companionway leading to the berth-deck above. As he passed the cockpit, the light of the lantern at the foot of the companionway caught a face peering round the canvas curtain. 'Is something amiss?' It was Baskerville.

'No. Turn in! Keep out of the way!'

'Why've you got your sword?'

'Turn in!' Drinkwater could brook no delay for explanations. Crouching, he turned his back on Baskerville and cautiously ascended the companionway ladder. He could see no movement under the hammocks of the berth-deck and swung round the stanchion, heading for the gun-deck. As he poked his head above the upper coaming he realized he was not a second too soon. A pale, almost spectral group of barefooted men, perhaps a dozen of them, in shirts and breeches, each clutching some form of weapon in their hands, were approaching the doors to the officers' cabins. Turning his head slowly, Drinkwater saw in the light of the after lantern that the marine sentry outside Captain Smetherley's door was nodding at his post.

There was no doubt that he was witnessing a combination of men bent on mutinous conduct, whatever the limitations of their intentions. Should he raise a general alarm or seek to defuse an explosive situation himself? He had no time to ponder and took consolation from the thought that Sergeant Hagan was behind him, for Appleby would not reach Wheeler in time. The men merged with the deep shadows round the guns, almost concealed behind the few hammocks that were slung in the gun-deck. To a casual observer the place was normal, a dark space the after end of which, abaft the companionway below, was lined with the cabins of the lieutenants and master, and which terminated with the captain's accommodation across the stern.

With sudden resolve Drinkwater flung himself over the hatch coaming and drew the hanger from its scabbard. The hiss of the steel rasped against the brass mounting, abruptly arresting the progress of the mutineers.

'Stand where you are!' His voice was low, yet carried through the gloom. 'Get forrard and out of my sight before I set eyes on one of you.'

'They killed Roach, Mister.' Hollins's voice came out of the darkness.

'And you've assaulted the surgeon. That's mutiny and you'll hang for it unless you obey me! Get forrard! Now!'

Drinkwater heard rather than saw the men behind him, smelt their presence and, glancing round, saw the dull gleam of drawn bayonets. 'We're right behind 'e, sir.' Sergeant Hagan's voice added to the menace of the stalemate.

'You don't frighten us with your boot-necked bullies . . .' Hollins began, but Hagan cut him short.

'Shut your fuckin' mouth, Hollins, or you're a dead man.'

Drinkwater was aware of someone else puffing up on his left. 'What the devil's going on here?' asked Lieutenant Wheeler, a drawn hanger in his right hand.

'These men are being recalled to their duty, Mr Wheeler.'

'Is this a damned combination?'

'No, no,' Drinkwater said quickly, lowering his sword point, 'they were gambling, Mr Wheeler. A foolish occupation at this time of night,' Drinkwater jerked his head aft, 'but not as reprehensible as being asleep on sentry.'

Wheeler looked round at the nodding marine posted outside the captain's door. 'Sergeant Hagan!' he said in a low voice, pointing at the offending sentry.

'Now what about . . . Stap me, they've gone!' In the few seconds allowed them, Hollins's men had melted away forward.

'Yes.' Much relieved, Drinkwater lowered his sword. Had they dispersed for the time being, or would they recombine? Perhaps tomorrow, or the next night? Would that something would happen, Drinkwater prayed, to distract them from the bloody death of their comrade.

'And what, Nathaniel,' Wheeler asked pointedly, after he had sent all his men except the sergeant below again, 'was all that about?'

'As far as I know, Mr Wheeler, those men were gambling dangerously.'

'With their lives, I gather, from what Appleby said,' Wheeler observed.

'With someone's,' Drinkwater replied.

'Make damned certain it ain't yours, my lad.'

'Or yours, sir.'

Drinkwater heard Wheeler sigh in the darkness. 'Damn you, Drinkwater,' he muttered, but even though he could not see the marine officer's face, Drinkwater knew there was no malice in Wheeler's voice. As if to confirm the matter, he felt a pat on the back. 'Better put that sword up.'

'Where's Appleby?' Drinkwater asked as he ran the French blade into its scabbard.

'In my cabin, recovering his wind. I gather the buggers . . .'

Wheeler broke off and turned to the contrite marine whom the sergeant brought forward into the circle of lantern light at the head of the companionway. 'How in Hades' name did you sleep through all this?' he asked the unfortunate man.

'Dunno, sir. I'm very sorry, sir . . .' The marine was trembling.

'You stink. Were you drinking before you were posted?'

'No, sir.'

An insistent cough came from Sergeant Hagan and the man admitted, 'Yes, sir.'

'You know what this means?'

'Aye, sir.'

'Post another sentinel, Sergeant, and put this ass in the bilboes. We'll deal with him later.'

He had just finished berating the sentry when Callowell's door suddenly opened. 'What's all this damned racket?'

In his hand Callowell held up a lantern. He peered about him, catching sight of the odd assembly of Wheeler, Drinkwater, Sergeant Hagan and the wretched marine at the head of the companionway. In the euphoria of his relief, Drinkwater almost burst out laughing at the ludicrous figure the first lieutenant cut in his night-shirt and tasselled night-cap. The spectacle clearly amused Wheeler also, for Drinkwater detected the catch in his voice as he replied, 'Damned sentry was dozing, Mr Callowell. Thanks to Mr Drinkwater's vigilance, he'll be punished.'

'What's that?' Wheeler repeated the explanation while Drinkwater caught the marine's eye. It was unfortunate that the marine should suffer the inevitable cat, but he had been asleep deeply enough not to be woken by the confrontation further forward.

'Damned certain he will be!' Callowell snorted, staring round him again. Appearing satisfied, he grunted and retired within his cabin. Wheeler and Drinkwater stood uncertainly for a moment, then Wheeler expelled his breath in a long, relieved sigh. 'Very well, Sergeant, carry on.'

'Aye, aye, sir.'

'Well,' said Wheeler in a low voice, 'as I said, poor old Appleby's hiding in my cabin where I've the remains of a bottle to crack.' Wheeler led aft, then paused, turned and giggled in Drinkwater's ear, 'Damn me if old Callowell don't remind me of Wee Willie Winkie! '

Neither of them saw the pale face of Baskerville retreat into the darkness of the berth-deck below.

Two days later, as *Cyclops* remained inert in the foggy calm, Drinkwater discovered a scrap of paper laid inside the lid of his sea-chest. On it were crudely spelt the words:

Yr Honor Mr Drinkwater,
Yr humble Servants of the Night present ther Duty and
Thank You fr yr indulgence.
       Ever yr Faithfull Friends.

In the days that followed, Drinkwater was more content and the incident appeared to have relieved the tension in the frigate. He felt an occasional anxiety when he thought of Baskerville's face peering from the cockpit, but with Lieutenant Wheeler's support and every appearance of the suppression of mutinous sentiments, this lessened as time passed.

The fog persisted for several days, but eventually a cold breeze sprang up from the north-east and, under easy sail, *Cyclops* cast about between Helgoland and Borkum, still in search of an enemy sail. For her people, the wearying routine of the ship ground inexorably on. Occasional lighter moments were engineered when the weather served, and on the first afternoon of pallid sunshine, as the decks gradually dried after the fog, Lieutenant Wheeler determined to encourage some proficiency in fencing

'How many times do I have to tell you, Nat? The merest pronation and pressure with the thumb and forefinger are all that are required. Look.' Wheeler removed his mask and demonstrated the point with his own foil.

Drinkwater and the marine officer occupied the starboard gangway during the afternoon watch. Both were stripped to shirt and breeches, despite the season, and their exertions had attracted a small crowd of off-duty sailors who sat on the forecastle guns or boats, or in the lower forward rigging, watching the two officers recommence the opening gambits of their bout.

Wheeler advanced, changing his line. Then, with a quick shift of footing, he executed a *balestra* and lunged at the midshipman. Drinkwater was not so easily fooled. He parried Wheeler's blade and riposted, catching the marine officer's shoulder. The hit was acknowledged and they came *en garde* again and resumed, with Wheeler quickly advancing. Drinkwater retreated, disengaged and drew his blade, then swiftly cut over Wheeler's *pointe*, dropped his own and lunged low at Wheeler's stomach.

Wheeler unmasked. 'By heaven, Nat, that was damnably good. To tell you the truth, I doubt there's much more I can teach you now you've digested my late point.'

Drinkwater tugged his own mask off. He was grinning as the two shook their left hands.

'Beg pardon, sir . . .' The former light dragoon Hollins approached Wheeler.

'What is it?' Wheeler ran his hand over his damp hair.

'Begging your pardon, sir, but have you ever considered introducing sabre parries for hand-to-hand fighting?'

'Well, cutlass drill incorporates some elements . . .' Wheeler blustered, but Hollins could barely stifle a snort. He had seen the jolly tars exercising. It scarcely compared with the precise sabre drill of the Queen's Own Light Dragoons.

'May I, sir?' Hollins held out his hands to Drinkwater who relinquished foil and mask. Hollins flexed the blade, donned the mask, flicked a salute at Wheeler and came on to his guard. 'Cut at me, Mr Wheeler,' he said through the mesh of the mask, 'any point or direction.'

Wheeler advanced and cut at Hollins's head and the dragoon parried with his own blade held horizontally above his head. Wheeler cut swiftly at his flank and again the dragoon's blade interposed. For four breathless minutes, closely observed by the watchers, Wheeler whirled the foil from every conceivable direction. Hollins always met it steel to steel. Then, as the marine lieutenant flagged, Hollins counter-attacked and cut at Wheeler's cheek so that the mask flew off. The watching seamen burst into a spontaneous cheer until a voice cut them short.

'You there! With the mask!' It was Callowell who had come on deck. Disapproving of these sporting bouts, though unable to prevent them, Callowell had sought such an opportunity to curtail his subordinates' pleasure. He knew very well who the masked swordsman was, for the boots and cavalryman's breeches betrayed Roach's companion.

Hollins drew off his mask. Callowell strode over to him, wrenched the foil from his grip and rounded on Wheeler. 'Is this yours?'

'You know damned well it is. I lend it to Drinkwater,' Wheeler replied in a low, angry voice, darting glances at the surrounding seamen. Callowell was blind to the hint.

'Did you give this to this man?' Callowell asked Drinkwater, gesturing at Hollins.

'In a manner of speaking, sir.'

'You gave this weapon to a man serving His Majesty under sentence of a court martial? A known and convicted criminal?'

'It's only a practice foil . . .'

'Never mind that, did you *give* it to him?' Callowell laid an implacable insistence upon the verb.

'Well, I lent it to him, sir. We were only practising . . .'

'What is the trouble, Mr Callowell?' The captain's reedy voice interrupted Callowell's interrogation of the midshipman. He stood at the head of the companionway, pulling his cloak about him in the chill. Callowell stumped aft to report.

'Get forrard, Hollins, and keep out of sight,' Wheeler muttered, gathering up the fencing equipment and nodding to Drinkwater to precede him below.

'Mr Drinkwater!' Reluctantly Drinkwater laid aft to where Smetherley and Callowell stood beside the binnacle.

'Sir?' After the events and responsibilities of the last few days, Captain Smetherley's self-assured youth struck Drinkwater with peculiar force.

'Is it true that you gave a weapon to a seaman under punishment?'

'I lent a practice foil to a man for the purpose of a demonstration . . .'

'Did you, or did you not, give your weapon to this man . . . er . . .'

'Hollins, sir,' offered Callowell helpfully.

Drinkwater knew he had been boxed into a corner. 'I lent the foil I borrow from Lieutenant Wheeler to Hollins, yes, sir.'

'Well, Mr Drinkwater, that is a serious misjudgement on your part. I cannot see why the late Captain Hope had such faith in you. Such behaviour is as irresponsible as it is reprehensible and I shall consider what measures I shall take. As for this habit of appearing on the quarterdeck improperly dressed', Smetherley indicated Drinkwater's shirt, 'and uncovered,' the captain gestured at Drinkwater's bare head, 'I shall cure that immediately. What is our latitude, Mr Callowell?'

'Fifty-four degrees north, sir.'

'Fifty-four north and November. Fore t'gallant masthead, Mr Drinkwater. Perhaps that will teach you to behave properly.'

The hours he spent aloft in this second mastheading were of almost unendurable agony. After the perspiration of the bout and the climb, the light wind quickly began to chill him and his nose, ears, fingers and feet were soon numbed, while his body went into uncontrollable fits of shivering He had, as before, lashed himself securely out of a sense of self-preservation, but it was not long before he could not have cared less whether he lived or died, and then he was walking with Elizabeth through knee-length grass and would have been happy had there not been the anxiety that the fields through which they wandered hand-in-hand were limitless. The disquiet grew and grew, robbing him of any comfort until, looking at her, he found Elizabeth had gone and he held the frozen hand of a pallid and terrible Medusa and recognized the hideous pale succubus of his recurring dream.

But it was in fact Midshipman White, shaking him and calling him to wake up and wrap himself in the greygoe and tarpaulin he had hauled aloft. From that point, Drinkwater drifted in and out of semi-consciousness until Captain Smetherley ordered him on deck at midnight to stand his watch. The agony of returning movement wakened him and when he finally went below to his hammock a further four hours later, he was exhausted and fell asleep immediately.

The following morning, Appleby averred it was a miracle that he had survived, but Wheeler remarked that Drinkwater was 'an individual of considerable inner resource', a remark deliberately made in Callowell's hearing, though in the course of a half-private conversation between the marine officer and the surgeon.

At four bells in the forenoon watch, Captain Smetherley sent for Drinkwater. As he entered the cabin from the gloom of the orlop, his head and body still wracked by aches and pains from the previous evening, Drinkwater could see little of Smetherley but the captain's bust silhouetted against the stern windows. Beyond a watery sunlight danced wanly upon the wavetops and the bubbling wake as it drew out from under the hull. On the captain's left sat Lieutenant Callowell and also present, but standing, was Lieutenant Wheeler. The marine officer was in the panoply of full dress and his gorget reflected the light off the sea. As he entered the cabin, Drinkwater was aware that Wheeler was concluding an account of the fencing bout, prolonging it for Drinkwater's own benefit, that he might divine how matters lay. It seemed to Drinkwater that Smetherley might be beginning to perceive he was in danger of being made a fool of, for in his conclusion Wheeler was astute enough to placate Smetherley and to offer the captain some way out of his dilemma, without unduly arousing Callowell's further hostility.

'And so, sir, my excess of enthusiasm for the sport led to foolishness on my part, compromising Midshipman Drinkwater. Mr

Callowell misunderstood the situation but, as a zealous officer, sought to prevent a, er . . .', Wheeler strove to find the means of explaining himself, '. . . a *contretemps*.'

Smetherley shifted uncomfortably in his seat and turned his attention to Callowell. 'Well, Mr Callowell?'

'The offence was committed, sir. A weapon was deliberately given to a man under punishment . . . Mr Drinkwater's part in the affair is uncontestable: he admitted culpability in your hearing.'

'It was a foil, Callowell,' an exasperated Wheeler broke in, but Smetherley silenced him and Callowell pressed doggedly onwards.

'The weapon was deliberately given to a man under punishment by a man . . .', Callowell paused and fastened his eyes upon Drinkwater who felt an instinctive fear of what the first lieutenant was about to say, 'by a man, sir, who has been seen engaged in conduct of a mutinous nature.'

Drinkwater felt himself go light-headed. Weakened as he was, his whole being fought the desire to faint and he clutched at the back of an adjacent chair while Wheeler took a half-step towards him out of concern before voicing his protest, but Smetherley's hand again restrained him.

'You talk in riddles, Mr Callowell.'

'Aye, sir, because I am unsure of the exact nature of the facts, not being a witness to the entire event, and I was apt to put a more charitable explanation upon matters until this present incident persuaded me that I had failed in my duty and should have reported my misgivings earlier.'

'Sir,' interjected Wheeler, ' this is a preposterous notion . . .'

'Mr Wheeler, your partiality to a former messmate does you some credit, but let us hear what Mr Callowell has to say.' Smetherley was watching Drinkwater as the accused young man fought to master himself. 'I am marking the reaction of Mr Drinkwater with interest, and I wish to hear of what this event consisted. Mr Callowell, pray continue.'

'Well, sir, 'tis simple enough. The midshipman was outside my cabin the other night at the head of a number of other scum, known trouble-makers, sir, Hollins among 'em. Had not Lieutenant Wheeler arrived in the nick of time, at which this jackanapes put up his sword and whispered to the conspirators to disperse, you and I might not be sitting here now . . .'

Drinkwater had mastered his nausea now and was filling with a contrary sense of burning outrage. He recalled Baskerville's face and knew for a certainty that the younger midshipman had concocted some malicious tale and let it be known to Callowell. He had little doubt that to Callowell, Drinkwater could be represented as a man nurturing an embitterment, though why that should act as incitement to mutiny seemed so perverse a sequence of cause and effect that it begged the motive of jealousy. Drinkwater's analysis was more accurate than he knew; it was also a shrewd summation of Callowell's own bitterness. Deprived of patronage himself, he habitually clipped the wings of any young rooster who seemed likely to get on. As for Baskerville, he was a nasty little toady, a boy for whom survival had been a matter of constant currying of favour and at which he had become expert. Baskerville was quite unable to see that, sooner or later, Callowell would select him for similar treatment.

For a moment there was silence in the cabin, then Drinkwater said in a low voice, 'That is a damned lie, Lieutenant Callowell, and since you have made it so publicly, I shall ask you to retract it, or I shall . . .'

'The only part of your statement that bears the slightest shred of truth, Callowell, is the fact that I arrived in time,' Wheeler broke in before Drinkwater could fling himself into deeper trouble. 'Mr Drinkwater had sent for me since he had the notion there was some trouble brewing after the death of Roach.'

'And was there?' Smetherley asked sharply.

'Oh yes,' Wheeler replied with cool assurance, 'and I, sir, was not surprised, neither in an emotional nor a practical sense . . .'

'Are you implying . . .?'

'I am implying nothing, sir,' Wheeler said with more force, 'I am merely stating that both Mr Drinkwater and myself in particular, as the officer commanding the marines, did our duty with an assiduity of which even Mr Callowell should have approved.'

'And you would have concealed this . . . this evident combination from me?'

Wheeler shook his head. 'I do not know where you received the idea of a mutinous combination, sir. Had it been such a thing, I doubt Mr Drinkwater would have survived his ordeal, since he confronted the disaffected men alone, and by the time I arrived he had cooled their ardour.'

351

'Well, what in God's name d'you think a party of men wanderin' around in the middle of the night is about, if it ain't murdering their officers?'

'Had they been intent on so doing, sir, Mr Drinkwater would not be here. He turned aside their anger very quickly . . .'

'What the devil d'you mean, "anger"?'

Wheeler sighed. 'Sir, in my opinion, and since you press me on the matter, it was unwise to have flogged Roach on the word of Midshipman Baskerville.' Wheeler paused for a second and then an idea seemed to strike him, for he suddenly asked, 'Mr Callowell, did you see Mr Drinkwater with a drawn sword?'

'I knew he had drawn his sword . . .'

'But did you see him?'

'Well, I, er . . .' Callowell scratched his head.

'Or did Midshipman Baskerville tell you he had seen Mr Drinkwater with a drawn sword?'

'What the devil has Baskerville got to do with all this?' Smetherley asked, signs of boredom evident in the captain's face.

'He's a veritable imp of Satan, Captain Smetherley. I'm surprised you didn't know that . . .'

'But you lied to me, Wheeler,' Callowell said, 'you told me Drinkwater had called your attention to that marine we flogged for being asleep at his post.'

'That was not a lie, Mr Callowell, that was the perfect truth.'

'It wasn't all . . .'

But before Callowell had completed his new explanation or Smetherley had gathered his wits, a peremptory knock at the cabin door ushered in Midshipman White. 'Mr Wallace's compliments, sir, but we've a frigate under our lee and Mr Wallace thinks it's the man-o'-war we've been looking for!'

There was a moment's hiatus in the cabin, then Captain Smetherley shoved his chair back and rose to his feet. 'I shall have to give this matter further consideration, gentlemen. It seems we have more pressin' matters to hand. We shall resolve this later.'

The strange sail lay to until *Cyclops*, foaming downwind towards her, bared her iron teeth and broke out British colours at her peak. Having expected a friend and now realizing his rashness, the stranger crowded on sail and a chase began.

As they had left the captain's cabin with Smetherley's 'we shall resolve this later' ringing ominously in his ears, Drinkwater had expressed his gratitude to Wheeler.

'We are not yet off the lee shore, Nat, but by heaven I'll not see you ruined by that little bugger Baskerville, nor that oaf Callowell, neither. Just thank providential intervention for this fellow.' Wheeler jerked his head as though at the strange sail. 'Who, or whatever he is, he is a *deus ex machina*!'

Drinkwater's only shred of comfort was that his action station was now on the quarterdeck as signals midshipman and the captain's aide, a position that seemed to offer at least the opportunity of demonstrating his loyalty if an action resulted in the forthcoming hours. A cold resolution grew on him as time passed and the autumn day drew towards its close. He entertained little hope for the future, and the memory of his more recent mastheading filled him with a wild contempt for life itself.

A gibbous moon shone fitfully from behind the clouds, the pale shape of the stranger's towering canvas now dimming to a distant faintness, now revealed as a dramatic image. The two ships were close enough to remain in sight of each other throughout the night as both ran on to the northwards but, though *Cyclops* held her ground, she was unable to overhaul her quarry.

At about three o'clock in the morning the enemy attempted a ruse to throw off *Cyclops* and catch her pursuer at a disadvantage. Still some three points to starboard and about two miles distant, the enemy ship abruptly came to the wind, tacked and stood across *Cyclop*'s bow.

'Stand to your guns! Stand to your guns!' Callowell roared through his speaking-trumpet. The crew of the *Cyclops*, who had been clustered half-awake at their action stations for hours, were now summoned to full consciousness.

'What is it, Mr Callowell?' Smetherley asked, staggering forward and peering into the gloom. Quite unaware that the enemy was athwart his own hawse with his larboard broadside trained on *Cyclops* as she bore down upon his guns, like a bull upon the matador's sword, Smetherley rubbed the sleep from his eyes and relinquished the slight shelter and support of the mizen rigging.

'Up helm!' Callowell roared again. 'Up helm or we'll be raked!'

Callowell's order was too late. The flicker of the enemy cannon showed close ahead, just as the helmsmen began to drag the great tiller across the steerage below.

'Larboard battery! Fire as you bear!' Smetherley's voice cracked the night in its imperious shrillness. As the enemy shot tore into *Cyclops*, there was a brief pause and then a desultory fire was returned. The strange ship continued to turn off the wind to larboard and the two frigates ran down each other's sides on opposite courses, with *Cyclops* herself beginning her swing off the wind.

'Belay that order!' Smetherley now shouted, confusing the issue. 'Put your helm *down*, sir! *Down*!'

As the British frigate turned, she increasingly presented her vulnerable stern to the enemy, inviting further raking fire. Smetherley now sought to cross the enemy's rear, but the matter had been left far too late. The reversing helm dragged speed off the British frigate's progress and the brief moment in which *Cyclops* had her quarry at a disadvantage was lost. The larboard guns had yet to be reloaded, and the raking shots fired were far too few to achieve anything of significance. Then, as the enemy extended the range, the opportunity was lost.

Drinkwater reported his sighting of the enemy's ensign. 'French colours, sir.'

Smetherley's attention, however, was swiftly diverted to a more immediate concern.

'She'll not stay, sir,' Drinkwater heard Blackmore shout as *Cyclops* came up in the wind with a sluggish feel to her.

'God damn!' Smetherley swore as the ship steadied, heading into the wind's eye. With a crack and a kind of roaring noise that was compounded of parting ropes, flapping canvas and wood and iron descending in slow motion, the foretopmast went by the board. The extra pressure of the wind had parted forestays damaged by the enemy's opening shots and now, as *Cyclops* emerged into a patch of moonlight, the foredeck was littered with fallen spars and festooned with rigging and canvas from aloft. Some hung over the side, to tear at the frigate's forechains where men were already cutting away the wreckage.

Drinkwater dutifully returned his attention to the progress of the enemy. He thought the Frenchman would now escape entirely, but the enemy commander, having seen the predicament of the British frigate in the sudden moonlight, was not about to let an opportunity slip through his fingers.

'Enemy's wearing ship, sir!' Drinkwater reported.

'What's that?' Smetherley spun round, distracted from the mess on the forecastle and in the waist by Drinkwater's shout.

'He's wearing ship, sir.'

The patch of moonlight spread and they could plainly see the enemy cruiser's larboard broadside as she turned her stern through the wind.

'He's going to re-engage, sir,' Drinkwater remarked. Smetherley raised his glass and Drinkwater could hear him muttering. 'Call the master,' he said audibly after a moment.

Drinkwater went forward in search of Blackmore whom he found directing the work of clearing the mess forward and bringing the ship under command again.

'Captain wants you, Mr Blackmore,' he said.

Blackmore grunted, gave a final instruction and walked aft. 'Carpenter's reporting water in the well, sir,' he stated. 'That Frenchman's hulled us.'

'And he's coming back to finish off what he started, Mr Blackmore,' Smetherley said, pointing astern just as the moon disappeared again and they seemed suddenly plunged into an impenetrable gloom.

'Well, we're making a fine stern board at the moment, sir, he may misjudge matters.'

'I wish to re-engage,' Smetherley replied. Then, turning to Drinkwater, he ordered, 'Let the officers on the gun-decks know they're to open fire when their guns bear, the unengaged side to assist the other. D'you understand, Drinkwater?'

'Perfectly, sir.' Drinkwater ran off to find Wallace and cannoned into Callowell at the head of the companionway.

'Where's the master?'

'On the quarterdeck, sir, with Captain Smetherley. The Frenchman's running back towards us and I'm to let the officers on the gun-deck know.'

Callowell made off as Drinkwater descended into the greater darkness of the gun-deck. In contrast to the chaos above, a sinister order reigned below. Almost on the very spot where Drinkwater had turned aside the mutiny, all had changed. Gone were the grey lumps of the hammocks and the neat row of officers' cabins; gone were the white painted bulkheads shutting off the after end of the ship for the privacy of her commander and officers. Now a long, almost open space, intersected by stanchions, gratings, half-empty shot-garlands and the massive bulk of the two capstans, was lined by the gleaming black barrels of the frigate's main armament of guns. The fitful light of the protected battle-lanterns threw long shadows and conferred an ominous movement upon what was largely a motionless scene, with the gun-crews in readiness about their pieces and only the scampering of the ship's boys making any significant noise in the expectant gloom. It struck Drinkwater with peculiar force that these men had almost no knowledge of what was going on above their heads. He ran forward in search of Wallace and found him peering out of a gunport.

'Mr Wallace, sir.'

Wallace turned and straightened himself up as far as the deck-beams would allow. 'Ah, what news do you bring?'

'We've lost the foretopmast . . .'

'We thought something must have given way . . .'

'And the enemy's worn ship. You're to re-engage with whatever battery bears, the other side to assist.'

'Short range?'

'I would think so, sir.'

'Shot?'

'Whatever you think fit, sir,' said Drinkwater, only afterwards noting the significance of the phrase.

'Ball on ball, then. That should do for a start. ' Wallace turned and shouted, 'Double-shot your guns, my lads! They're coming back for a taste of rusty iron!'

Suddenly the gun-deck was alive with movement, like a nest of rats stirred from their sleep, the gun-trucks rumbling on the planking and sending a trembling throughout the frigate.

'Good luck, sir.' Drinkwater hurried aft in search of the companionway and the upper-deck. Here too all had changed, for the distance between the two ships had closed and the enemy seemed to tower over them as he drove across their bows for a second time. But this was a more ponderous manoeuvre in contrast with the quick-witted desperation of the first. The enemy ship had shortened sail and, while *Cyclops*'s stern board had robbed the Frenchman of the chance to attack from leeward and rake the vulnerable stern of his quarry by throwing her maintopsail aback at the right moment, he might still inflict severe punishment on his former pursuer by lying to athwart *Cyclops*'s hawse.

However, now that the French ship was committed to raking from ahead, *Cyclops*'s stern could be thrown round so that her larboard broadside bore upon the Frenchman. Callowell and Blackmore were urging this on Smetherley who gave the impression of dithering before agreeing. By hauling the main braces and putting over the helm, *Cyclops* was now brought round by degrees so that as the enemy guns reopened fire, the British frigate's larboard guns roared out in reply.

But the French commander was a bold man and backed his own maintopsail, drifting slowly down on to *Cyclops* and fighting his opponent gun for gun, matching discharge for discharge. A slow cloud of acrid powder-smoke rolled down upon them, musketry swept the deck like hail and, while heavy shot thumped into *Cyclops*'s hull, the lighter calibre ball from the Frenchman's quarterdeck guns, mixed with deadly canister and langridge, blasted holes through the hammock nettings and knocked men down like bloody ninepins in the cold light of the growing dawn.

The view each man had of the fight became obscured in the smoke. Drinkwater, obliged to be always at the captain's elbow, kept his eyes on the dull gleam of Smetherley's figure. The din of the guns and the sharp crack of musketry rendered him partially deaf so that he felt rather than heard the almost simultaneous discharge of a French broadside. It struck him as a wave of hot, stinking gas, accompanied by the whirring roar of a passing ball and the involuntary gasp as the thing winded him.

Two more such devastating detonations followed, acts calculated to have maximum effect before boarding, for Drinkwater heard Callowell, as if at a great distance although he could be seen through the smoke, screaming to repel boarders.

Drinkwater saw Smetherley draw his sword and, as he drew his own, he caught a glimpse beyond the captain of a looming hedge of cutlasses and boarding-pikes a moment before there came to him the jarring impact as the two frigates ground together. A moment later he was fighting for his life.

He thrust his right shoulder forward and parried a pike, recovered and hacked at the arm that held it. He missed, but the man was past him and lunging to the left where, out of the corner of his eye, Drinkwater saw a marine jabbing a bayonet. He was confronted next by an officer with fiercely gleaming eyes. Drinkwater beat the man's extended blade and, in something akin to disbelief, watched the blade drop from the officer's fingers. Dully he realized the man's wrist had been shattered and that the ferocity in the poor fellow's eyes was the shock of pain. A cutlass blade seemed to appear from nowhere, being drawn back to hack at him. Drinkwater swept his arm in a cutting arc which Hollins would have approved of and felt his blade bite into the cutlass-bearer's side as the weapon in turn slashed down. Somehow it missed him as the man dropped, knocking into Drinkwater with considerable force. Twisting away, Drinkwater slithered and fell. He felt a foot on his back and gasped for breath, filled with the vague idea that he would now be in further trouble for having deserted the captain. Then, the next instant, he was overcome by a desire to stay where he was, to give up this madness and succumb to the aching of his muscles. Who would notice? He might lie like a dog while the world took its course without him. It cared not for him; why should he care for it? He looked round and saw, twenty feet abaft him at the frigate's taffrail, a French officer fiddling with the ensign halliards. *Cyclops* was taken!

The thought filled him with an odd contentment. Smetherley and Callowell could go to hell, along with Baskerville and his miserable crew of insufferable cronies. But then he thought of poor White and of the things he had done for Drinkwater in tending him while he was enduring his two mastheadings; and Wheeler, who had helped him the previous morning; and poor old Blackmore and Appleby. Then the thought of captivity suddenly burst upon him as the French officer seemed to clear the halliards and begin to take down the British ensign. A second later Drinkwater was on his feet and rushing aft. The man looked round just as Drinkwater ran him through. Ice had settled in his heart now and his mind was strangely clear. He drew his blade from the dead weight of the fallen body, belayed the halliards and swung round. Looking forward he saw Captain Smetherley surrounded by three French seamen who were jabbing at him with pikes. Taking them in the rear, Drinkwater had dispatched two of them before the third fled and he confronted Smetherley who drew his breath in gasps.

'Recall, sir,' Drinkwater shouted, 'my loyalty's in question!' He was lightheaded now, not with the fainting fit which had almost overwhelmed him in Smetherley's cabin, but with a mad yet calculating coolness. Smetherley had regained his breath and, imbued with a bloody fighting lust and scarcely recognizing Drinkwater, flung himself at the rear of more Frenchmen who were pressing Wheeler's marines amid the heaving mass of men who struggled for possession of the forward quarterdeck. Drinkwater was left in sole possession of the space abaft the mizen and someone on the French frigate had noticed. A musket ball scored Drinkwater's shoulder, opening the seam of his coat and half turning him round with the force of its impact. As he stumbled, another French officer came over the rail, obviously intent on sweeping Drinkwater out of the way and finally hauling down the British colours.

Drinkwater met him with a savage swipe. The officer parried, but only partially, and such was the force of Drinkwater's blow that his blade slid down the French officer's sword, cutting in to the man's thigh, severing a tendon and causing him to drop to one knee. As his head slipped forward, Drinkwater thumped at the back of the man's skull with the pommel of his sword, felling him completely.

A moment later another man slumped at his feet and Drinkwater recognized the bloody wreck of Smetherley who had been cut down by three or four Frenchmen intent on taking him prisoner and securing the surrender of the frigate. 'Drinkwater!' Smetherley cried.

Drinkwater stepped across the captain's body and stood over him, slashing wildly left and right, holding off the attackers. Beyond his immediate surroundings, he was quite oblivious of anything else. Down below, the gunners still plied their deadly trade, the gunfire unabating as the guns' barrels warmed up and the great pieces fairly leapt with eagerness at each discharge.

He could not tell that the fire from the French frigate had slowed and then almost stopped as the battering of the British guns gradually overcame their opposition. Thus, as the French boarders gained ground on the upper deck of *Cyclops*, the fierce tenacity of the British gunnery from the deck below was pounding their ship to pieces. Drinkwater drove off those of the enemy immediately intent on securing Captain Smetherley, unaware that he himself had received several light flesh wounds.

As the French withdrew, Drinkwater regained his breath, aware of a general retreat and of an increasingly panic-stricken scrambling backwards of desperate men, pricked by Wheeler's marines' bayonets and hounded by British seamen. He had no idea what had caused this retrograde movement, but once started it seemed irreversible and soon Drinkwater saw the backs of the marines stabbing their way over the rail. Looking down, Drinkwater caught sight of Smetherley staring up at him, his eyes fixed and already clouding. The captain's white waistcoat was dark with blood and a great pool of it spread out round Drinkwater's feet. Then something splattered the pool of blood. Looking up, Drinkwater saw the French sharp-shooter still in the mizen top. Without a pistol Drinkwater relinquished his charge and stepped to the larboard rail, put his foot on the truck of a quarterdeck gun and hoisted himself into the mizen rigging.

The French seamen were fighting like demons, contesting every inch of their own deck, but Wheeler was screaming at his marines, the majority of whom had ceased their advance or withdrawn to stand elevated in the *Cyclops*'s larboard hammock netting.

'Call off your men, Callowell!' Wheeler shouted at the top of his voice. 'I'll clear the deck!'

The marines discharged a volley at Wheeler's command. The musket balls were indiscriminate in finding their marks and several of the more advanced British seamen were caught in the fire, but the general effect threw the defenders back and into the brief interval the British poured, Drinkwater jumping down among them, unsatiated and eager for the appalling excitement of action.

A boy ran under his guard and stabbed a seaman next to him, then turned and made to jab at Drinkwater. Drinkwater drove the guard of his hanger into the boy's shoulder and knocked him down. Then he pronated his blade and lunged at a pig-tailed quartermaster defending the binnacle with a cutlass. Drinkwater's point drove through the quartermaster's windpipe and the wretched man died with a curious gasping whistle, clutching at his throat as he fell.

A tall, dark officer lay against the binnacle, his high collar decorated with gold, his broad shoulders bearing the bullion embellishments of epaulettes. A younger officer knelt by his side, then, sensing the looming presence of an enemy as the quartermaster crashed to the deck, stood and confronted Drinkwater, his hand holding a broken sword.

'Do you surrender, sir?' Drinkwater asked. To his astonishment the younger man nodded, dropped the broken weapon, bent and took from the feeble grasp of the fallen captain that officer's sword and offered it hilt foremost to Drinkwater.

'*Merci, M'sieur,*' Drinkwater managed, mercilessly adding with a jerking motion to the great white ensign overhead, '*et votre drapeau, s'il vous plaît.*'

The younger man looked down at the pallid face of his commander. The mortally wounded French captain opened his eyes, looked at Drinkwater, then closed them with a nod. A few moments later the oriflamme of Bourbon lilies fluttered to the deck just as the sun lifted over the lip of cloud that veiled the eastern horizon and flooded the scene with a sudden, dazzling light.

Peace

They had been cheated of their prize, for within moments of her striking her colours, the French frigate *L'Arcadienne* took fire. It was necessary for *Cyclops* to be worked clear of her and to lie to and lick her own wounds while *L'Arcadienne* burned furiously, until, about an hour after noon, she exploded with a thunderous roar, flinging debris high into the air. This fell back into a circle of sea flattened by the detonation, over which hung a pall of smoke. When the smoke cleared, the French ship and most of her company had disappeared.

Among their own dead and wounded was old Blackmore. He took six days to die of a musket ball in the bowels, begging Drinkwater to take his belongings home to his wife and giving him his folio volumes of carefully observed notes and sketches, the fruit of a lifetime's interest. After the action, Lieutenant Callowell had taken command and was driven to the expedient of reappointing Mr Drinkwater to a temporary berth in the gunroom. Callowell remained indifferent to him, but no more was ever said of Drinkwater's participation in any mutiny and he suspected Wheeler's intervention. At all events, the incident was apparently closed and the shadow of it gradually passed.

After the terror of an action in which he had not distinguished himself but had been knocked unconscious, Midshipman Baskerville seemed less inclined to tell tales. Though he would not admit it, he was privately glad that Drinkwater never afterwards referred to the incident, though Wheeler spoke to him, leaving Baskerville in no doubt but that there were several officers who knew of his mendacity. After *Cyclops* was laid up in the Medway, Baskerville went ashore, never to return to sea, though in later years he spoke knowledgeably of naval affairs in the House of Commons, being returned as one of two members for a pocket borough. Captain Smetherley was granted an encomium in the *Intelligencer*, having died, it was stated, 'at his moment of triumph'. Moreover, the *Intelligencer* informed its readers, 'the Royal Navy had been thereby deprived of a gallant officer in the flower of his youth, and the Nation of a meritorious officer of whom it might otherwise have entertained expectations of long, gallant and distinguished service'.

The last weeks of the commission were strangely melancholic for all the officers, coloured by the dolorous prospect of half-pay. By contrast the hands were far more cheerful. The pressed men especially could scarcely refrain from desertion as they lay at the buoys in the Medway, with the smoking chimneys of Chatham a mere stone's throw distant. Only the promise of their pay, in some cases of four years' arrears, kept them at their duty as they sent down spars and ferried stores, guns, ammunition and sundry other items ashore. By the time they had finished, *Cyclops* was only a vestige of her former self, a dark and hollow hulk, stripped to her lower masts and with her jib-boom removed. She seemed much larger, for her thirty-two twelve-pounders and the chase and quarter guns had been laboriously hauled ashore, so lightening her considerably and causing her to ride high out of the water. Gone were the iron shot and powder, the cheese and butter, the kegs of beer and spirits, the hogsheads of salt pork, barricoes of water, bags of dried peas, sacks of hard grey flour, bales of wadding and oakum, blocks of pitch and barrels of tar. She bore little cordage, for most had been removed, from her huge spare cable to the reels of thin spun yarn. Only the lingering smell of these commodities served as a reminder of the warlike machine she had once been. All the myriad odds and ends that had made her existence possible, whose supply and issue had occupied the book-keeping skills of a small company of officers and petty officers over the long months of the commission, were removed for storage ashore. Shorewards went her anchors, lowered on to the mooring lighters from the dockyard by means of the only spar left crossed for the purpose, the maintopsail yard hoisted on the foremast in place of the foreyard. When the final load had gone, the large blocks were sent down and small whips left at the yard-arms. As almost the last task, the yard was cockbilled out of the way, leaving room for the next ship alongside.

In those last days, Lieutenant Callowell had received his promotion to commander, though he refused to leave the ship until she was reduced to the condition known as 'in ordinary'. He finally announced his decision to quit on the morning following the removal of the anchors. Early that forenoon, the marines were paraded for the penultimate time. Sergeant Hagan assembled his men with his usual precision, ensuring their appearance was immaculate. Their white cross-belts had been pipe-clayed to perfection, their breeches were like snow and their gaiters black as pitch. The older seamen watched with delight, knowing that the marines' imminent departure meant their own pay and discharge were soon to be forthcoming. As Hagan satisfied himself, the captain's gig was piped away and the sergeant fell out the entry guard who now joined the side-boys in *Cyclops*'s last show of pomp in the present commission.

A grey sky lowered over the river and a keen easterly wind brought the odour of saltmarsh across the ruffled surface of the Medway. The lieutenants and warrant officers assembled in undress uniforms, their swords hitched to their hips; the midshipmen fell in behind them. Wheeler, having inspected his men in Hagan's wake, placed himself at their head and, drawing his hanger, called them to attention. A deathly hush fell upon the upper deck. A moment later, Commander Callowell ascended the companionway. He wore a boat cloak over his uniform and as the wind whipped it about him, Wheeler threw out the order for his men to present arms.

The clatter of muskets and simultaneous stamp of feet were accompanied by the wicked gleam of pale sunlight upon bayonets. Wheeler's hanger went up to his lips and then swept downwards in the graceful arc of the salute. The assembled lieutenants brought their fingers up to the cocks of their hats.

'Gentlemen . . .' Callowell remained a moment looking forward and responded to the salutes of his officers and the guard. Then, without another word, he walked to the rail and went over the side to the shrilling pipes of the boatswain's mates.

The silence lasted a moment more, then someone forward shouted out, 'Three cheers for "Bloody-Back" Callowell!' The air was split by a thunderous bellow. It was a cheer such as they had given *Resolution* in the gathering gloom at the beginning of Rodney's Moonlight Battle three years earlier. Drinkwater remembered the disquieting power of the noise and he watched now as they cheered and cheered, not for Callowell, but for themselves. They cheered for what they had made of *Cyclops*, for their collective triumphs and disappointments; they cheered at the alluring prospect of that spirit of unity being broken into the individual delights of discharge, grog shops and brothels.

As the gig pulled out clear of the ship's side, they could see the figure of Callowell humped in the stern-sheets. He did not look back.

That evening the gunroom held a valedictory dinner in the vacated captain's cabin. Wallace, as acting first lieutenant, presided in name only, for in reality it was Wheeler's evening. The midshipmen were guests, as were the senior warrant officers and senior mates, and the intention was to drink off the remaining wine in the possession of the gunroom officers, a quantity of the former having been taken out of *L'Arcadienne* before the fire had driven back the looters. Once the eating was dispensed with, the serious business of the evening commenced. Amidst the wreckage of chicken bones and suet dumplings, bumpers of increasing extravagance were drunk to toasts of increasing dubiety.

The whole evening was a marked contrast to Drinkwater's first formal dinner on board when Captain Hope had dined with Admiral Kempenfelt and he had been compelled to toast the company. He was a very different person from the ingenuous and inebriated youth who had risen unsteadily to his feet on that occasion. The harsh path of duty had matured him and his capacity for wine had much improved. Now he joined lustily in the singing of 'Spanish Ladies' and 'Hearts of Oak', and clapped enthusiastically when O'Malley, the Irish cook and the ship's fiddler, scraped the air of 'Nancy Dawson' on his ancient violin.

Finally Wheeler rose unsteadily to his feet. His handsome face was flushed, but his cravat remained neatly tied under his perspiring chin as he called the lubberly company to order.

'Gennelmen,' he began, 'gennelmen, we are gathered here tonight in the sight of Almighty God, the Devil and Mr Surgeon Appleby, to conclude a commission memorable for its being in an infamous war in which I believe all of us here executed our duty with honour, as behoves all true Britons.' He paused for the cheers that this peroration called forth from the company to die down.

'Tomorrow . . . tomorrow we will be penniless beggars, but tonight we are as fit as fighting cocks to thrash Frenchmen, Dons and Yankees . . .'

Wheeler paused again while more cheers accompanied Midshipman White's disappearance as he slid slowly beneath the table, his face sinking behind the cloth like a diminutive setting sun, to lie unheeded by his fellows whose upturned faces awaited more of Wheeler's pomposities. 'Gennelmen, I give you a toast: A short peace and a long war!'

The company cheered yet again and some staggered to their feet. They gulped their wine and thumped the table, calling for more.

'Silence! Silence!'

Hisses were taken up and some sort of order was re-established. 'It has been brought to my notice by the purser,' continued Wheeler, 'as Christian a gennelman as ever sat on a purser's stool mark you, that we are down to our last case of wine, which is . . . which is . . . which is what, m'dear fella?'

'Madeira.'

'Madeira, gennelmen, madeira . . .'

Wheeler collapsed into his chair amidst more cheers. The vacuum was filled by the last bottles being set out and the ponderous figure of Appleby rising to his feet. An attempt was made to shout him down. 'No speeches from the surgeon!'

'You're a guest! Sit down!'

But Appleby stood his ground. 'I shall not make a speech, gentlemen . . .' His voice was drowned in further cheers, but he remained standing when they died away. 'I shall simply ask you to raise your glasses to fallen comrades . . .'

A hush fell on the company and a scraping of chairs indicated a lugubrious assent to Appleby's sentiment. A shamefaced mumbling emanated from bowed heads as they recalled those who had started the commission and had not survived it – Hope, Blackmore and many others.

'And now . . .', resumed Appleby, and the mood lightened immediately.

'No speeches, damn your eyes!'

'Appleby, you farting old windbag, sit down!'

'And now,' Appleby went on, 'I ask you to raise your glasses in another toast . . .'

'For God's sake, Appleby, we've drunk to everything under heaven except your mother and father!'

'Gentlemen, gentlemen!' roared the surgeon, 'We have forgotten the most important after His Majesty's health . . .' Silence, apart from White's brutish snoring under the table, again permeated the cabin. 'I prithee charge your glasses . . . Now, gentlemen, I ask you to drink to this one-eyed frigate, gentlemen, this Cyclopean eye-of-the-fleet. Just as you are closing both of your limpid orbs in stupor, she is closing her noble eye on war. Gentlemen, be upstanding and drink to the ship! I give you "An eye of the fleet, His Britannic Majesty's frigate *Cyclops*!"'

There were punning shouts of 'Aye, aye!', much nudging of neighbours' ribs and more loud cheers which finally subsided into gurgling, dyspeptic mumblings and an involuntary fart from Wheeler. Suddenly the cabin door flew open and Sergeant Hagan entered wearing full dress uniform. Wheeler looked up blearily as the sergeant's boots crashed irreverently upon the deck and his right hand executed an extravagant salute circumscribed only by the deck beams above.

'Sah!'

'Eh? Whassa matter, ser'nt?' Wheeler struggled upright in his chair, affronted by the intrusion and vaguely aware that the sergeant's presence in parade dress augured some disagreeable occurrence elsewhere. Wheeler fixed the man with what he took to be a baleful stare, the vague disquiet of a summons to duty intruding upon his bemused brain.

'I have the honour to escort the officers' cheese, sah!' Hagan replied, looking straight into his commanding officer's single focused eye.

'Cheesh, ser'nt? Whadya mean cheesh?'

'Mr Dale's orders, sah!'

'Dale? You mean the carpenter?' Wheeler shook his head in incomprehension. 'You don't make yourself clear, ser'nt.'

'Permission to bring in the officers' cheese, sah!' Hagan persisted patiently in pursuance of his instructions, holding himself at rigid attention throughout this inane exchange.

Wheeler looked round the company and asked, 'We've had cheesh, haven't we, gennelmen? I'm certain we had cheesh . . .'

But his query went unheeded, for there were more table thumpings and cries of 'Cheese! Cheese! We want cheese!'

Wheeler shook his head, shrugged and slumped back in his chair, waving his assent. 'Very well, Ser'nt Hagan. Please escort in the cheese!'

'Sah!' acknowledged Hagan and drew smartly aside. Two of the carpenter's mates entered bearing a salver on which reposed the cheese, daintily covered by a white damask napkin. At the lower end of the table, midshipmen drew apart to allow the worthy tarpaulins to deposit their load. They were grinning as they withdrew and Wheeler's numbed brain was beginning to sense a breach of propriety. He rose very unsteadily, leaning heavily upon the table. 'Sergeant!'

'Sah?'

'Whass that?' Wheeler nodded at the napkin-covered lump.

'The officers' cheese, sah!' repeated Hagan in the reasonable tone one uses to children, and executing another smart salute he retreated from the cabin, closing the door behind him.

Wheeler's misgivings were not shared by his fellow-diners who had just discovered that the remaining stock of wine amounted to at least one glass each. The demands for cheese were revived and with a flourish Drinkwater leaned forward and whipped off the napkin.

'God bless my soul!'

'Stap me vittals!'

'Rot me cods!'

'God's bones!'

'It's the festering main truck!'

'The what?'

'It's the god-damned truck from the mainmasthead!'

And there, amid the wreckage of what had passed for a banquet, sat the cap of the mainmast, pierced and fitted with its two sheaves for the flag halliards.

'Well, of all the confounded nerve . . .'

'I'm damned if I understand . . .' Wheeler passed a hand over his furrowed brow. Next to him Wallace had begun a slow *dégringolade* beneath the table.

'Hang on for your cheese, Wallace,' someone said.

'Dale's right,' Drinkwater said, 'I remember not believing him when he swore he had told me the truth back in seventy-nine.'

'Whadya mean?' Wheeler asked.

A chorus of slurred voices demanded an explanation. 'Mr Dale made it out of pusser's cheese,' Drinkwater explained. 'He carved it out of a cheese which had been supplied for the hands to eat . . . it's cheese, d'you see? Cheese; it really is cheese!'

'Well I'm damned.' Wheeler sat back in his chair, looking fixedly at the object before him. 'Well, I'll be damned . . .' and with that he slid slowly downwards, to join the company assembling beneath the table.

'Well, Nathaniel,' Appleby said, raising his glass and holding it up to the stumps of the candles in the candelabra, 'there are only a few of us worthy of remaining above the salt, it seems. Your health, sir.'

'And yours, Mr Appleby, and yours.'

'You don't care for any cheese, I take it?'

'Thank you, no.'

The next morning the marines turned out in order of route. Pulled ashore in the launch, bound for their billets at Chatham barracks, they left to ribald farewells from the high-spirited boats' crews. Wheeler departed with them, his pale face evidence of an aching head. Before he went down into the boat, he shook his fellow-officers' hands in farewell. To Drinkwater he said, 'Good luck, young shaver. Always remember what I have taught you: never flinch when you parry and always *riposte*.'

During the forenoon other officers left. Midshipman Baskerville and his gang were seen off without regret, but White, hung-over and emotional, took his departure with a catch in his voice.

'Damn it, Nat,' he said, wringing Drinkwater's hand, 'I'm deuced glad to be leaving, but sorry that we must part. You shall come and see us, eh? There's good shooting in Norfolk and there's always a bed at the Hall.'

'Of course, Chalky. We shall remain friends and I shall write as soon as I have determined what to do. You won't forget to deliver Blackmore's dunnage?'

'No, no. His house lies almost upon my direct route. I shall lodge at Colchester and make the detour to Harwich without undue delay.'

'Please pass my condolences to his widow. You have my letter.'

'Of course.'

'Well goodbye, old fellow. Good fortune and thank you for your solicitude when I was aloft. Appleby considered you saved my life.'

'Then we are quits,' White said, following his sea-chest over the rail with a gallant smile that seemed to cause him some agony. Drinkwater, suffering himself, grinned unsympathetically.

After the departure of the officers and their dunnage of sea-chests, bundles, portmanteaux, sword-cases, hat-boxes and quadrant-boxes, the frigate's remaining boats were sent in to the boat-pond and she was left with a dockyard punt of uncertain antiquity to attend her. At noon the ship was boarded by the pay-master and his clerks who brought with them an iron-bound chest with its escort of marines from the dockyard detachment. The men were mustered to the shrilling of the pipes in an excited crowd under the final authority of the boatswain and his mates. They turned out in all the splendid finery of their best shore-going out-fits, sporting ribboned hats, decorated pea-jackets, elaborately worked belts of white sennet and trousers with extravagantly flared legs. Many held their shoes in their hands and those who had donned theirs walked with the exaggerated awkwardness of men quite unused to such things. As each man received his due reward, signing or marking the purser's and the surgeon's ledgers for the deductions he had accrued over the commission, he turned away with a wide grin, picked up his ditty-bag and went to the rail in quest of transport. Word had passed along the river, and boats and wherries arrived to lie expectantly off *Cyclops*'s quarters from where the unfortunate crew were confronted with the first joy of the shore, being subjected to the ravages of landsharks who were demanding exorbitant charges to ferry them ashore.

In the wake of this exodus, the ship sank into a state of suspension, the silence along her decks eerie to those who had known them crowded with men and full of the buzz of human occupation.

Responsibility for the ship now fell upon the standing warrant officers, for Drinkwater's acting commission ceased the day *Cyclops* decommissioned, and in the absence of a master, the gunner was the senior. Drinkwater remained on board unofficially, his sole purpose in lingering to augment his knowledge and study, for he had received word from the Trinity House that he could attend for examination in a little over a fortnight and he was deter-mined to secure at the very least a certificate as master as soon as possible. With the approval of the gunner, he therefore remained in the gunroom, and in that now echoing space once loud with Devaux and Wheeler's discourse, he unrolled Blackmore's charts and studied the legacy the old man had left him. Apart from a treatise on navigation, Drinkwater had found a dictionary and, to his surprise, some works of poetry. Somehow the memory of the sailing master and his didactic lectures on the mysteries of lunar distances did not square with the love-poems of Herrick and Rochester. Oddly, though, there seemed a strange, almost sinister message from beyond the grave implicit in a slim anthology which contained a work by Richard Kempenfelt. He read a couplet out loud:

> Worlds and worlds round suns most distant roll,
> And thought perplexes, but uplifts the soul . . .

This discovery briefly diverted his thoughts to Elizabeth and the book of hers that he had found containing a hymn of the admiral's. But it was the manuscript books which most fascinated Drinkwater for, from his first appointment as second mate of a merchantman, Blackmore had kept notebooks containing details of anchorages and ports and the dangers of their approaches, of landfalls, conspicuous features, leads through swatchways and gatways, and the exhibited lights and daymarks of lighthouses and alarm vessels. Interspersed with the carefully scribed text were exquisite drawings, some washed in with water-colours, which turned these compendiums into private rutters of sailing directions. It was a double surprise to find these talents in the old man, filling Drinkwater with a profound regret that he had not done so earlier, that he had in some way failed the dead man. The discovery of these things after Blackmore's death laid a poignant burden upon him, a feeling of lost opportunity.

To the inhabitants of the cockpit as a whole, Blackmore had been a fussy old woman whose interest in versines, Napier's logarithms and plane sailing were as obsessive as they were boring. Fortunately Drinkwater had not found them so, and as a result had benefited from Blackmore's patiently shared experience. He was too young to know that such enthusiasm was enough for Blackmore and had decided the dying man to leave his professional papers to his aptest pupil.

Drinkwater turned the pages of Blackmore's rutters. They charted the dead man's life from the Gulf of Riga to the Dardanelles. There were notes on anchorages on the coasts of

Kurland and Corsica, on ice in the Baltic and on the currents in the Strait of Gibraltar. There were notes of the approaches to Stralsund and some complex clearing marks off Ushant. There were observations on Blackmore's native Harwich Harbour, and on the Rivers Humber and Mersey, together with a neat chartlet of the Galuda River in South Carolina. Drinkwater shuddered. He remembered the Galuda too well, its mosquitoes, its dead and the manner of their dying. He did not care to think of such things and dismissed them from his mind. In an effort to concentrate, he wrote to Elizabeth, then bent himself to his studies.

Trinity House was an impressive building, situated on the rising ground of Tower Hill. Iron railings provided a forecourt to the stone facade, the ground floor of which comprised an arched entrance with Ionic columns supporting a plain entablature pierced by tall windows. These in turn were interspersed with ornate embellishments comprising the Corporation's arms and the medallions of King George III and Queen Charlotte, together with representations of nautical instruments and lighthouses. The Elder Brethren who formed the ruling court of this ancient body, as well as licensing pilots and buoying out the Thames Estuary, the Downs and Yarmouth Roads, and generally overseeing their own and private lighthouses, also examined the proficiency of candidates seeking warrants as masters or mates in the Royal Navy.

It was a contentious matter, for to command a brig-sloop or unrated ship of less than twenty guns, a lieutenant or commander was supposed to have passed an examination before the Elder Brethren of the Trinity House. Indeed, implicit in the very rank 'Master and Commander' was lodged an acknowledgement of navigational skill, allowing the holder the courtesy title of 'Captain', without the confirmed and irreversible rights attaching to that of 'Post-Captain'. Therein lay the rub. Despite the fact that the Brethren were mariners of experience, all having commanded ships, and in spite of the Corporation being empowered by Royal Charter, they were themselves merchant masters. Officers holding commissions from the King considered that to submit to such examination was an affront to their dignity. Thus the exigencies of service at sea and abroad, and the expediences of special cases, combined with the more powerful influences of blood and interest almost to negate the wise provision of this regulation. It was, therefore, unfortunately observed mostly in the breach. The resulting ineptitude of many commissioned officers as navigators had frequently caused danger to naval ships and ensured continuing employment for those men brought up in merchantmen, whose humbler path led them into the navy as masters and mates. These men had their certificates from the Trinity House and their warrants from the Navy Board but, competent though they might be, commissioned they were not.

Strictly according to regulation, a midshipman was not permitted to act as prize-master unless he had passed for master's mate and thus demonstrated his competence to bring his prize safely into port. A mixture of luck and expedience had secured Drinkwater his own warrant as master's mate when he had served briefly in the Corporation's yacht under Captain Poulter. At the time she had been flying the flag of Captain Anthony Calvert, an Elder Brother on his way to the westward from Plymouth, and Calvert had obtained a certificate for the young Midshipman Drinkwater. Despite this brief service in the Corporation's buoy-yacht, this was the first time Drinkwater had visited the elegant headquarters on Tower Hill, built by Samuel Wyatt.

Drinkwater was shown to a seat in an ante-room by a dark-suited clerk. An Indian carpet deadened all sound except the measured and mesmeric ticking of a tall long-case clock which showed the phases of the moon. On one wall a magnificently wrought painting by Thomas Butterworth depicted a ship being broken to pieces under beetling cliffs. Drinkwater rose and studied the picture more closely. It was of the *Ramillies* whose wrecking, Drinkwater recalled being told, was due to the errors made by her sailing master. The thought was uncomfortable and he turned, only to gaze into the forbidding stare of a pendulous bellied master-mariner whose portrait glared from under a full peruke wig. The mariner pointed to a chart on an adjacent table upon which were also a telescope and a quadrant. Beyond lay a distant view of an old ship, leaning to a gale.

'This way, sir.' The clerk's appearance made Drinkwater jump. Nervously gathering up his papers, he followed the man into an adjacent but larger chamber. Here more ancient sea-captains stared down at him, and a seductive view of a British factory somewhere, Drinkwater guessed, on the coast of India, occupied one entire wall. In the background, surrounded by green palm trees and some native huts, lay the grim embrasures of a dun-coloured fort above which British colours lifted languidly. In the foreground three Indiamen lay at anchor, with a fourth in the process of getting under weigh, while native boats plied between them. Between Drinkwater and the painting there was a long table upon which lay some books, charts, rules and dividers. Gingerly Drinkwater laid his papers alongside them on the gleaming mahogany.

A moment later a man in a plain blue coat with red cuffs, white breeches and hose, his hair powdered and tied in a queue, strode briskly into the room. Drinkwater recognized him as Captain Calvert.

'Mr Drinkwater, good morning. I recall our previous meeting. You caused me a deal of trouble.'

'I did sir?' Drinkwater's surprise was unfeigned. Such a beginning was unfortunate.

'The Navy Board wished you to sit a proper examination before they granted your warrant and referred the matter back to this House. I said you had passed a better examination than most of your ilk and the matter became a shuttlecock until they relented and issued you your warrant.'

'I had no idea, sir,' Drinkwater said. 'You must think me an ingrate for not thanking you properly.'

'Not at all. It was a point of principle between us and the gentlemen in the Strand.' Calvert waved Drinkwater's embarrassment aside and asked for his journals.

'I do not have them, sir,' he began as Calvert looked up sharply and withdrew his expectant hand. 'I was ordered to present myself for examination as lieutenant aboard the *Royal George* on the fatal morning she capsized, sir . . .' He paused and passed across the table a slim volume of manuscript. 'This is what I have done subsequently.'

'So you were one of the few to escape?'

'Yes, sir.'

'And would have passed for lieutenant otherwise?'

'I entertained that hope, yes, sir.'

'We are more exacting here, Mr Drinkwater. A master's certificate is not so easily come by.'

Calvert drew the book towards him and turned its pages with maddening slowness while Drinkwater sat, endeavouring to mask his nervousness. When he had finished, Calvert closed the book and looked up. 'Well, sir, you seem to have committed some knowledge to paper, let us determine to what extent you have retained it elsewhere.'

Drinkwater's mouth felt dry.

'How many methods are there to determine longitude?'

'Two, sir. By chronometer and by lunar distances.'

'And which would you employ?'

'The former, sir, though I have tried the latter.'

'And on what grounds do you favour the former method?'

'It is less complex and better suited to shipboard observations now that the necessary ephemerides are available.'

Calvert nodded 'Very well. Pray, explain the principle of observation by chronometer.' Drinkwater launched himself into an explanation of the hour-angle problem, discoursing on polar distances and right ascensions. He had hardly finished before Calvert threw him a simple query about latitude. Drinkwater hesitated, sensing a trap, but then answered.

Without reacting, Calvert continued: 'You are asked by your commander to advise him of the best time for a cutting-out operation. On what would you base your response?'

Drinkwater's mind went obligingly blank. He had survived one such attempt by a French ship when *Cyclops* had been anchored in the Galuda. He remembered it only as a wild night of gun flashes, sword thrusts, shouts and mayhem.

'Come, come, Mr Drinkwater, this is not so difficult, surely?' Calvert prompted impatiently. 'Employ your imagination a little before you are dead with indecision.'

'I er, I should require a dark night . . . I should, er, make a study of any dangers to navigation and endeavour to supply sufficient details of these and any clearing marks which might aid the passage of boats . . . Oh, and I should seek to make such an attempt when the tides were most favourable, particularly for bringing the prize out.'

'Very well.' Calvert unfolded a chart and, turning it, pushed it across the table. He also indicated an almanac, a sheet of paper and a pencil. 'I wish to make such an attempt on a vessel lying in Camaret Road within the next week. When should I carry it out?'

Drinkwater bent to his task. Calvert presumed he knew the location of Camaret Road which was unfortunate, because he was not certain, but he soon found it near Brest and began the calculation that would give him a moonless night with the most favourable tide. It took him fifteen minutes to resolve the problem satisfactorily. An ebb tide out of the Iroise and a dark night gave him three possibilities and he chose the first on the grounds that if the operation failed or the weather was inclement, he would have two alternatives. Calvert expressed his approval and went on to ask him more questions, questions concerned with anchoring and sail-handling.

After further calculations, Calvert asked to be 'conducted verbally in a frigate from Plymouth Sound to St Mary's Road, Scilly'. It was a chink of daylight, for both men knew Drinkwater had made such a passage in the Trinity yacht all those months earlier. Drinkwater expatiated on the manoeuvre of weighing from Plymouth and standing out clear of the Draystone, of avoiding the Eddystone and the lethal, unmarked danger of the Wolf Rock, which he cleared by a bearing on the twin lights of the Lizard. Finally he recalled the leading marks for entering the shelter of St Mary's Road, keeping clear of the Spanish and Bartholomew Ledges.

Some questions followed about the stowage and storage of stores and cordage, an area of unfamiliarity to the candidate. Calvert asked, 'How would you stow kegs of spirits, Mr Drinkwater?'

Drinkwater havered. Did the significance of the question lie in the fact that the commodity concerned was spirituous? Or that it was in kegs? Clearly Calvert, a merchant master by trade, regarded it with some importance, as if a trick lay in its apparent simplicity. Then a magic formula occurred to Drinkwater, one he had heard Blackmore use frequently. Though he had never thought to employ it himself, being unsure of its precise meaning, its purpose struck him now. He ventured it in a blaze of comprehension. 'I should ensure they were wedged bung-up and bilge-free, sir.'

'Excellent. That will do very well, Mr Drinkwater. I desire you to wait in the ante-room. I shall fill out your certificate and you may present it to the Comptroller's clerks at Somerset House. I would not be too sanguine of an immediate appointment in a sixth-rate with the war ending, though.' Calvert smiled and held out his hand.

'I am not anticipating any such luck, Captain Calvert,' Drinkwater replied, taking Calvert's hand. 'I shall seek a berth in a merchant ship. I am anxious to marry and have been advised that opportunities in Liverpool are more likely.'

Calvert nodded. 'A fellow like you would be of considerable use in a slaver, no doubt of it. Well, good day to you. Pray wait a moment next door and I shall have my clerk bring you your paper.'

Drinkwater gathered up his documents as Calvert left the room. He returned to the ante-room and picked up his hat. He would go home to Barnet tonight, and see his mother and brother, then write again to Elizabeth with the news. He could afford to visit her before he went to Liverpool in search of a ship. Though greatly tempted, he forbore from winking at the pot-bellied mariner still gazing sternly down into the room. He was well pleased with himself and promised that before he made for Barnet, he would indulge himself with a meat-pie and a bottle in one of the eating houses nearby.

The clock ticked and the minutes drew into a quarter of an hour. He supposed Calvert had been distracted on some important matter and settled himself to wait. After another quarter of an hour, he found himself incapable of sitting still and instead rose and began to study the wreck of the *Ramillies* under Bolt Head, but even this did not absorb him and he started to pace the carpet with mounting impatience.

At last, after what seemed an interminable delay, the clerk reappeared, but he bore no paper, only a summons that Drinkwater should wait a few moments more. After a further interval of ten minutes, Calvert reappeared.

'Mr Drinkwater,' Calvert said solemnly, so that Drinkwater imagined the very worst, 'the damndest coincidence, don't ye know . . .'

'You have the advantage of me, sir.'

'I have kept you kicking your heels, Mr Drinkwater, because news has just come in from Gravesend that the Buoy Warden requires the services of a mate in the *Argus*. It occurred to me that, were you so inclined and bearing in mind your intention to marry, the post might have fallen vacant at a providential moment.' Calvert paused, allowing Drinkwater to digest the fact that he was being made an offer of employment.

'The inordinate delay, I'm afraid, was occasioned by the urgent necessity to establish whether or not another officer, who had been half promised the next vacancy, still wished to take up our earlier offer. Happily, in view of the Peace, he has declined, and sails a week hence in a West Indiaman.' Calvert smiled. 'So there, sir. What d'ye say, eh?'

Drinkwater stammered his delighted acceptance.

Nathaniel Drinkwater and Elizabeth Bower were married in her father's parish church on a warm, late autumn day in 1783 during a short furlough taken by the groom. The Peace of Paris had been concluded two months earlier in September, and Drinkwater settled to his work in the service of the Trinity House, rising rapidly to mate. His wife stayed with her father for the first eighteen months of their marriage until his death in 1785. She then removed to London and took rooms in Whitechapel where she interested herself in a charitable institution. Drinkwater maintained a correspondence with Richard White, whose promotion to lieutenant and appointment to a frigate on the Halifax station he learned of in the summer of the following year.

Drinkwater also remained in contact with Lord Dungarth who on several occasions asked Drinkwater to dine with him in his modest town house. The two men were both interested in hydrographical surveying and Lord Dungarth had been asked by the Royal Society to evaluate the quality of charts then available to the Royal Navy and British merchant ships.

His Lordship moved in illustrious circles compared with the indigent and struggling Drinkwater, but he entertained his guest without condescension, increasingly appreciating his judgement and acknowledging his professional skills. As for Drinkwater himself, he gradually forgot his naval aspirations.

PART TWO
High Water

Without careful and patient observation, the culmination of the tide is a moment so fleeting that it is soon gone, leaving only the mark of its passing as it falls.

The White Lady

The passing of the *Vestal*'s paddles had thrust Drinkwater astern, tumbling him in the pitiless whirling of the water so that the pressure in his ears seemed like lances thrust into his skull, and the ache of his held breath had translated itself into a mighty agony in his lungs. Within the strange compass of this pain appeared to teem a plague of memories, each passing in such swift succession that they seemed agents of his destruction, tormenting him to stop holding his breath and let his lungs inhale . . .

There was a vague lightening in the darkness and as it grew the memories faded. As his ribs faltered and could no longer contain the desire to breathe in, he struck upwards and the light was suddenly all about him. He was overwhelmed by it and gasped with the shock. The pain in his lungs seemed far worse now, as he broke the sea's surface and sucked in great gulps of air.

As mate of the *Vestal*, Mr Forester had run up from the boat-deck to the bridge the moment he heard the cries of alarm and knew something was wrong. Poulter turned from the bridge wing above the starboard sponson, his face ashen.

'I have run over the boat . . . The telegraph failed . . . The engines could not answer . . .' Poulter's voice barely carried over the noise of the wind and the thrashing of the paddles.

'I will clear away the other boat,' said Forester, casting a quick look in their wake where, for a brief second, he thought he could see something bobbing, but then the counter lifted and a wave intervened.

'I could not stop the ship . . .', Poulter went on as Forester turned and saw Potts staring at the captain. It was clear neither man could quite believe what had just happened. Forester hesitated for a moment, then said, 'We must stop, sir. Stop and turn round.'

'Yes . . . Yes, of course.' Poulter made a visible effort to shake off the effects of shock and Forester moved swiftly to the charthouse and, quickly opening the log-slate, scribbled against the time: *Telegraph failure. Unable to stop engines. Ran down port cutter.*

Then he leapt for the bridge ladder, shouting orders as he went. 'Call away the starboard cutter!' he yelled. 'Boatswain, post a man in the foretop with orders to keep a lookout! We've run the port boat down!'

Notwithstanding the badly shaken Captain Poulter, Forester consoled himself with the thought that they had successfully rescued men from the water before. As for Captain Poulter, the *Vestal*'s master pulled himself together with the need to react to the emergency. He quickly passed word that the men on the foredeck should remain as additional lookouts. Then he ordered a chain of men to pass his orders verbally to the first engineer. Having slowed his ship, Poulter began to turn her, to comb her wayward wake and relocate his lost boat, all the time hoping that the people in her had clung together and had not been the victims of *Vestal*'s huge and lethal paddles.

Such arrangements took time to effect, but within fifteen minutes Poulter had brought his ship's head round and had closed the estimated location of the disaster. Calling down for dead slow speed, he scanned the sea ahead of the ship. Up at the base of the bowsprit and aloft in the rigging, his men were doing likewise. One of the men at the knightheads called out and pointed at the very instant he saw something himself. He was joined by the seaman in the foretop. Poulter focused on the object as *Vestal* neared it.

It was a dark, hard-edged shape, like a porpoise's fin, which he recognized instantly as a section of the boat, the bow he thought, where the gunwales and the stem were joined with a knee. Then he saw a head bobbing near it, and another . . . Poulter's spirits rose in proportion. It was always damnably difficult to see men in the water and, he thought, the men in the boat could not have been dispersed very much. If only Captain Drinkwater had not been so old and the boat had not run under the ship. Perhaps they would be lucky . . .

Drinkwater was reduced to a terrified primal being, intent only on staying afloat and aware of the feebleness of his body. He was wounded and hurt, wracked with agonies whose location and origins were confused but which seemed in their combined burden to be preventing him from swimming. The realization overwhelmed him with anxiety. He had a strong desire to live, to see his wife and children again. He was shivering with cold, weighed down by his waterlogged clothes but, energized by the air he now drew raspingly into his lungs, he renewed his fight to live.

In terror he found he could no longer swim. His body seemed leaden, unable to obey the urgent impulses of his brain. He went under again, swallowing mouthfuls of water as he floundered, before panic brought him thrashing back to the surface, his arms flailing in a sudden reflexive flurry of energy. Then, quite suddenly, both ending the panic and bringing to his conscious mind a simultaneous sensation of sharp pain and a glorious relief, his right arm struck an oar. A second later he had the thing under his armpits and was hanging over it, gasping for breath and vomiting sea water and bile from a burning throat.

The sensation of relief was all too brief, swept aside by a more sobering, conscious and logical thought. They would never recover him. He was going to die and he recalled the presentient feeling of doom he had experienced when lost once before in a boat in an Arctic fog. It had been cold, bone-numbingly cold so that he had shivered uncontrollably then as he shivered now. He had no right to live, not any more. He was an old and wicked man. He had killed his friends and betrayed Elizabeth. He had lain with Arabella Stuart in that brief liaison that had drawn from him an intense but guilty passion. Why had Arabella so affected him and turned his head? Was it because it had always been turned since he had set eyes on Hortense, whose haunting beauty had plagued him throughout his life, an exciting alternative to Elizabeth's loyal constancy? And what was love? And why was it that what he had was not enough? Was it ever enough, or were men just wicked, inevitably, innately evil? But he had not loved Arabella, not as he loved Elizabeth. Their parting had not affected him beyond causing him a brief, if poignant regret. Yet his hunger for her at the time had been irresistible. Was that all? Was the sole purpose of their encounter nothing more than that? The waywardness of it struck at the certainties he had clung to all his life. Surely, surely . . .

And as he sucked the air into his aching lungs he recalled

Elizabeth and tried to seize her image, as if holding it in his mind's eye would revive hope and lead him to understand what was happening to him. Were all men left to die and obliged to relinquish life in this terrible desolation? Was it not therefore better to be cut in two by an iron shot and to be snuffed out like a candle? And then he knew, and felt the conviction with the absolute certainty of profound insight. He had been tempted, and had succumbed to the flirtatious loveliness of the American beauty, because the remorse he had afterwards suffered had saved him from the greater, irreversible sin of insensate entanglement with Hortense.

It made sense with a simplicity directly attributable to providential intervention, and in the moment that he realized it, he felt a great burden lifting from him. This relief came with an easing of his breathing and the final eructation of his cramped and aching stomach. He raised his head as he lay wallowing over the oar, and looked up. He could see the ship again! She had turned round and grew larger as she came towards him. As she drew near, he could see a man up in the knightheads pointing ahead of the ship.

Drinkwater raised an arm and waved. He tried to shout, but nothing came from his mouth except a feeble croak. It would be all right! They could see him. He was not going to drown. He was redeemed, forgiven. He began to laugh with a feeble, manic sound through chattering teeth.

The forward lookouts aboard *Vestal* had not seen Captain Drinkwater. They had caught sight of two of the oarsmen and Captain Drew, who clung to the bow section of the port cutter in which was lashed an empty barricoe for added buoyancy. They lay some two hundred yards beyond Captain Drinkwater, who again passed unseen beneath the plunging bow of the *Vestal*.

Drinkwater looked up again. *Vestal*'s bowsprit rose over him like a great lance. He saw the rigging supporting it, the twin shrouds, the white painted chain bobstay which angled down to the iron spike of the dolphin-striker that passed half a fathom above his head. Then came the white lady who, following the iron spike as the ship drove her bow into a wave, seemed to sweep down towards him with malevolent intent. A cold terror seized his heart as the ship breasted the wave and rose, lifting the figurehead so that the white lady seemed suddenly to fly above him higher and higher, retreating as she did in the dream.

Then the forefoot of the *Vestal*'s bow thrust itself at him, striking the oar and wrenching it from his grasp. The foaming bow wave separated him from it and swept him down the ship's port side. He tried to shout again but suddenly the sponson threw its shadow and the paddle-wheel drove him down and he was fighting for his life with Edouard Santhonax in an alley in Sheerness, breathless after his run, and aware that he had allowed himself to be caught at a disadvantage, the consequences of which were as inevitable as they were dreadful. As the Frenchman's sword blade struck down in the *molinello*, he felt the thing bite into his shoulder with the same awful finality as he had experienced all those years ago.

Two paddle floats hit him in succession in passing and sent him deeper into the swirling depths of the turbulent sea. The roaring in his ears was the thunder of a great battle, the endless, ear-splitting concussion of hundreds of guns. It was inconceivable, terrible, awful. He glimpsed Camperdown and Copenhagen and Trafalgar. He glimpsed the darkness of a night action and saw, as he came near the surface in the swirling water of the paddle race, the pallid faces of the dead.

There were so many of them! Faces he had forgotten, faces of men he had never known though he had had a hand in their killing – of a French privateer officer, of a Danish captain called Dahlgaard, of an American named Tucker, of an anonymous officer of the French hussars, of Edouard Santhonax, of old Tregembo whom he had dispatched with a pistol shot, of James Quilhampton whose death he had mourned more than all the others. They seemed to mock him as he felt his body spin over and over, and the constriction in his breast seemed now to be worse than ever and somehow attached to the laughter of these fiends who trailed behind the white lady and struck with the cold, deep into his soul.

Chapter Six

Tales of the Dead

'Nathaniel, what is it?'

Elizabeth looked up from her needlework as she sat by the fire. Her husband was staring through the half-opened shutter, out across the lawn in front of Gantley Hall where, judging by the draught that whirled about her feet and the noise in the chimney, a biting easterly wind was blowing. The rising moon cast a pale glow on his face, a chilling contrast to the warm candle-light and the glow of the fire. She watched his abstracted profile over her spectacles for a moment, then bent to her work with a sigh. He was not with her in the warm security of their home; his restless spirit was still at sea and his poor, divided heart revealed itself in these long intervals of abstraction. Then she heard the chink of decanter on glass and the low gurgle of poured wine.

'You drink too much,' she said without looking up.

'Eh? What's that?'

'I said, you drink too much. That is the fourth glass you have had since dinner. It does not improve your conversation,' she added drily.

'You are becoming a scold,' he retorted.

She ignored the provocation and looked up at him. 'What is troubling you?'

'Troubling me? Why nothing, of course.'

'Why then are you looking out of that window as though expecting to see something? Is the garden full of ghosts?'

'How did you know?' he asked, and their eyes met.

'There is something troubling you, isn't there?'

He shook his head. 'Only the weather, my dear,' he said dismissively, closing the shutter and crossing the room to sit opposite her. He stretched his legs out towards the fire.

'And the ghosts?'

He sighed. 'Oh, at moments like this I recall Quilhampton . . . And one or two others . . .'

'Why at moments like this?' she asked, lowering her needle-point and looking at him directly over her spectacles. She saw him shrug.

'I don't know. They say old men forget, and 'tis largely true to be sure, but there are some memories one cannot erase. Nor perhaps should you when you have borne responsibility.'

Elizabeth smiled. 'It is the burden of that responsibility that prevents you from accepting things as they are, my dear,' she said gently. 'If, as you say you believe, Providence guides us in our lives, then Providence must bear the burden of what it creates. After all, you yourself are what you are only partly by your own making.'

Drinkwater smiled over his glass. 'Yes, you are right.' He leaned forward and patted her knee. 'You are always a fount of good sense, Elizabeth.'

'And you drink too much.'

'Do I?' Drinkwater looked at his empty glass. He placed it on an adjacent table. 'Perhaps I do. A little.'

'What o'clock is it?' Elizabeth asked.

Drinkwater lugged out his watch and consulted it. 'Almost ten,' he said, looking up at her. 'What is it?'

'Oh nothing. I was just thinking you have had that watch a long time.'

He gave a short laugh. 'Yes, so long that I forget it was your father's.'

'It was, I think, the only thing of any real value he had.'

'Except yourself,' he said.

'Thank you, kind sir.' Elizabeth stifled a yawn. 'I shall not linger tonight,' she said, laying down her work. 'Susan will have put the bedpan in an hour since.'

'Then I shall not make up the fire . . .'

Drinkwater was interrupted by a loud and urgent knocking at the door. 'What the devil . . .?' Their eyes met.

'Were you expecting someone?' Elizabeth asked, a sudden suspicion kindled in her.

'No, not at all,' Drinkwater answered, shaking his head and rising stiffly. He hobbled awkwardly towards the hall door muttering about his 'damned rheumaticks'.

Elizabeth sat and listened. She heard the front door open and felt the sudden in-draught of cold air that sent the dying fire leaping into a brief, flaring activity. She heard, too, a man's insistent voice and her husband's lower response. Cold air ceased to run into the room and she heard the door close. The exchange of voices continued and then her husband came back into the room.

'What is it, Nathaniel?'

'There's a vessel in trouble in the bay. I have Mr Vane in the hall. He has his trap outside. I shall have to go and see what can be done.'

Elizabeth sighed. 'Very well. But please ask poor Mr Vane in for a glass while you put on something suitable for such a night.'

Drinkwater turned back to open the door and waved for the visitor to enter. 'Remiss of me, Vane, come in. My wife will look after you while I fetch a coat.'

'My boots, Captain . . .'

'Oh, damn your boots, man. Come you in.'

'Thank you, sir.' Vane was a large man who always looked uncomfortable indoors, despite the quality of his coat and cravat. He entered the drawing-room with his customary awkwardness. 'Mistress Drinkwater.' He bowed his head, turning his low beaver in his hands.

'I should like to say it was pleasant to see you, Mr Vane, and in a sense it is,' Elizabeth said, as she rose smiling, 'but at this hour and in such circumstances . . .'

'Aye, ma'am. There's a ship in trouble. I saw the rockets go off just as I was going up with Ruth and, as you know, the Captain likes to know . . .'

'Oh, yes,' Elizabeth said, handing a glass to her unexpected visitor, 'the Captain likes to know. Here, take this for your trouble.'

'I didn't ought to . . .'

'You may need it before the night's out.'

Vane's huge fist closed round the glass and he smiled shyly at his benefactress, for Elizabeth had established him as the tenant in Gantley Hall's only farm. Vane had been driven off land that his family had worked for years by an extension of the Enclosures Act. He had come to Elizabeth's notice while eking out a living as a groom in Woodbridge where, for a while, she and Louise Quilhampton, the dead James's mother, had run a small school. Louise had heard of his plight and the incumbent of Lower Ufford had stood as guarantor of his character when Elizabeth, in the absence of her husband at sea, had come to grips with the management of the small farm they had bought with the estate. She had liked his slow patience and the ability the man possessed to accomplish an enormous amount without apparent effort. It was in such stark contrast to her own erratic attempts to accomplish matters that she had regarded the arrival of Mr and Mrs Vane as providential, an opinion shared by her fatalistic husband. Vane was supported by his energetic wife. Ruth Vane was a plain woman of sound good sense who managed a brood of children with the same efficiency as her geese and hens. On his rare visits to Home Farm, 'The Captain' as Drinkwater was always referred to between them, voiced his approval. 'Mistress Vane runs as tight an establishment as the boatswain of a flag-ship, and that bear of a husband of hers puts me in mind of a lieutenant I once knew . . .' Elizabeth smiled at him now.

'Please sit down. Do you know what manner of ship is in distress, Mr Vane?'

'No, ma'am. But I've the trap outside. We can soon run down to the shingle and take a look.'

A moment later Drinkwater re-entered the room in his hessian boots and cloak. He bore in his hands his cocked hat.

'You will need gloves, my dear.'

'I have them, and my glass.' Drinkwater patted his hip. 'Come, Vane. Let's be off.'

Vane put his glass down and a moment later Elizabeth stood alone in the room. She turned, made up the fire and resumed her needlework.

'Can't see a damned thing!'

Drinkwater spoke above the roar of the wind which blew directly onshore and was much stronger than he had anticipated. They stood on the low shingle escarpment which stretched away to the north-east and south-west in a pale crescent under the full moon, its successive ridges marking the recent high tides. The shallow indentation of Hollesley Bay, 'Ho'sley' to the local people, was an anchorage in westerly winds, but in the present south-easterly gale, washed as it was at this time in the moon's life by strong tides, it could become a deathtrap.

'Well, Vane, there are no more rockets going up . . .'

'No, sir.'

'And that's all you saw?'

'Aye. I didn't waste time coming down to take a look, remembering your orders, like.'

'Quite right.' Drinkwater swept the desolate tumbling waters of the bay with his glass once more, then shut it with a snap. 'Well, 'tis possible she was farther out and may have got into Harwich.' He waved his glass to the southward.

'Aye, Captain, that may well be the case.'

Drinkwater remained a moment longer, his cloak flapping round him like a dark flag, and then he turned to Vane. 'Well, Harry, we've done our best. If any poor devil is out there, there's precious little we can do for 'em. Let's to bed!'

'Right, Captain.'

And with that the two men turned and stumped up the shingle beach towards the waiting trap, the stones crunching under their boots.

Susan Tregembo woke them the next morning with the news. There had been a wreck in the night, a lugger, it was thought, though not much of her had been washed up and rumour said she had knocked her bottom out on the Cutler shoal in the dark, though how anyone knew this only compounded the mystery. This conjecture had been brought by Michael Howland who worked for Henry Vane and whom Vane had sent down on one of the plough horses to ride the tide-line between Shingle Street and Bawdsey soon after dawn.

'Have they found any of the poor devils?' asked Drinkwater, sitting up in bed, eyeing the coffee pot that Susan seemed reluctant to settle in its usual station.

'Yes, Captain, and there's a note for you.' She set the tray down and handed Drinkwater a folded paper. He reached for his spectacles and recognized Vane's rounded hand.

> *Home Farm*
> *About 6*
>
> *Sir,*
>
> *I have had from my Lad Howland some Sad News that Four Bodies came Ashore between the Towers at Shingle Street. He is much Frighted, but I am gone to get Them. One he says is of a Woman. Will you send to the Justices or What ought I to Do?*
>
> *Yr Serv't*
> *Hen. Vane.*

Having dismissed Susan with orders for his horse to be saddled, Drinkwater pulled on his breeches, dressed and drank his coffee. Twenty minutes later, after a quick breakfast, he was in the saddle, urging the horse past the gaunt ruins of the old priory which rose, ivy-covered, in the grounds to the rear of the Hall. He had no time for such antiquities this morning, for on horseback Drinkwater was as awkward as Vane in a drawing-room. He loathed riding, not merely because at his age the posture of sitting astride pained 'his rheumaticks' sorely, but because he had no expertise in the saddle. A passion for horses had killed his father, and his brother Edward had loved the damned beasts, but Nathaniel had disappointed his parent in having no natural aptitude for them, and an early fall had so knocked him about that his mother had insisted that Ned might ride because he enjoyed it, but Nat should not if he did not wish to. Nat had never wanted to since, but there had been a wild and tempestuous ride from Tilsit to Memel . . .

'By God!' he muttered, bobbing up and down as his nag trotted and his hat threatened to go by the board, and remembering how Edouard Santhonax had tried to prevent Drinkwater bringing *Patrician* back from the Baltic with the news of the secret treaty between Tsar Alexander and Napoleon, and how he had fought Santhonax in the Dutch frigate *Zaandam*. 'That mad dash all ended here in Ho'sley Bay!'

He had killed Santhonax in the fight, revenging himself upon the Frenchman who had so savagely mauled his shoulder ten years before in an alley in Sheerness. And he had thereby widowed Santhonax's wife, Hortense . . .

But enough of that. Such thoughts plagued younger men than himself, though he had seen Hortense a year ago when she had come to him like Nicodemus, by night. Damn the woman for a witch! She had inveigled out of him a pension on the grounds that she had performed a service to the British government. Drinkwater had been obliged to pay the thing himself. One day Elizabeth must find out and then there would be the devil to pay and no pitch hot enough, by God!

He found Vane and his two men with a small cart from the farm. They had already loaded two of the bodies and were handling the third as Drinkwater approached. Drinkwater forced his horse down the shingle towards the breakers that still crashed with a mighty roar. But the wind had dropped, and although the air was full of the salty tang of spray, it was now no more than a strong breeze.

A few pieces of black painted wood were strewn about the beach, and a large grating around which some small kegs had been quickly lashed told how the four had come ashore.

'When Michael found 'em, they were all tied to that,' Vane explained, coming up to Drinkwater's horse and pointing to the extemporized life-saver.

'They are all dead, I presume,' Drinkwater queried.

'Come and see, Captain.'

Drinkwater dismounted and Vane took his horse's reins as they walked across the shingle. The third body had just been put on to the cart and the men were returning for the fourth. By the feet, he could see it was that of a woman, though a shawl had been thrown over her face. Drinkwater bent and drew back the shroud.

Underneath, the vacant face of Hortense Santhonax stared unseeing at the sky. She was as white as the lady in his dream.

'Why do they have to come here?' Elizabeth asked, as she watched Vane's men carry the corpses into the lower barn.

'We shall bury them in the priory,' Drinkwater said shortly, his face grim.

'It is very sad . . .'

'I can only think they must have been trying to run into the Ore, though to do so in a south-easterly wind would have been sheer foolhardiness . . .' He was thinking out loud and Elizabeth held her peace. If she was bewildered by her husband's idea of burying the victims of the storm within the grounds, his next remark astonished her.

'I want the woman brought up to the house. Susan shall lay her out . . .'

'But I have sent for old Mrs Farrell. She always . . .'

'No,' Drinkwater said sharply, 'Farrell may do the men, but Susan shall see to the woman.'

'But why . . .?'

'Because I say so.'

Elizabeth looked sharply at her husband and was about to remonstrate when she caught sight of the expression on his face as he turned away. On rare occasions, he still considered himself upon a quarterdeck and she was usually quick to disabuse him of the idea, but there was something different about this.

Elizabeth held her peace until the late morning, when the woman's body had been brought up to the Hall. Vane's men were busy sawing up planks for the coffins and Drinkwater was drafting a statement to send into Woodbridge after it had been attested to by Vane. Elizabeth went into the parlour where Susan was laying out the wretched woman.

'Oh, ma'am, you didn't ought to . . .'

'It's all right, Susan, I'm no stranger to death. I had to do this for my father . . .'

Susan seemed about to say more but held her peace and worked at loosening the woman's clothes.

'She was very beautiful,' Elizabeth remarked sadly.

'But for this,' said Susan, lifting a heavy tress of hair which had once been a glorious auburn but which now contained strands of grey. She exposed the right side of the dead woman's head.

'Dear God!' A coarse scar ran in heavy seams of fused flesh from under the profusion of hair, over the line of the jaw and down her neck. The right ear was missing 'The poor woman.'

'Looks like a burn,' said Susan, rolling a pledget into the mouth and forcing the jaw closed. 'Mistress, I have to move her to reach her lower parts.'

'Let me help.'

' 'Tisn't necessary, Mistress, really 'tisn't.'

'It is quite all right . . .'

Elizabeth sensed Susan's resentment at her interference. It was unlike the woman, with whom she had enjoyed a long and amicable relationship. Elizabeth began to sense something odd about the whole business and said, 'I wonder who she is? She is well dressed for travelling. This habit is exquisite . . .'

'Mistress, I . . .'

'What on earth is the matter, Susan?'

' 'Tis the Captain, Mistress . . .'

'The Captain?' quizzed Elizabeth, frowning. 'What on earth has he to do with this matter?'

Susan shook her head and said, 'If you wish to help, Mistress, take her camisole off. 'Twill be there if 'tis anywhere.'

'Susan! What in heaven's name are you talking about? What will be there?'

'It would have been better had you not known, my dear.'

Elizabeth spun round to see her husband standing just inside the parlour door. Both she and Susan sought to interpose themselves between Drinkwater and the pale form lying half exposed upon the table.

'Well, Susan?' Drinkwater addressed the housekeeper.

'Nothing yet, sir, but I haven't had time to . . .'

'Nathaniel, what is all this about?'

'*Who* is all this about, my dear, would be more correct.'

'You know her, do you not?' Elizabeth's question was suddenly sharply charged with horrible suspicions.

'I do, yes. Or rather, I knew her. Once.'

'Shall I go, sir?' Susan asked anxiously, aware of the gleam in her mistress's eyes.

'That is not necessary,' Drinkwater said flatly. 'I have entrusted you to search her and you know enough to have your curiosity aroused. Such titillation only causes gossip. You would be prudent not to make too much of what you hear, and to speak about it only between yourselves.' He smiled, a thin, wan smile, so that Elizabeth's initial suspicion was at once confirmed. Yet she also felt strangely moved. There was much about the life her husband had led that she knew nothing of, but she sensed that if he had deceived her with this once lovely creature, there would have been more than common infidelity about it.

'She is, or was until last night, a sort of spy,' Drinkwater began, addressing Elizabeth. 'She peddled information and acted as a go-between. Her presence aboard a wrecked lugger in Ho'sley Bay argues strongly that she intended coming here . . .'

'Here? To see you?' Elizabeth asked.

'Yes.' Drinkwater sighed. 'It is a long and complicated story, but many, many years ago she was among a group of *émigrés* we rescued off a beach in western France. Some time afterwards, while resident in England, she turned her coat and married a dashing French officer named Edouard Santhonax. It was he who gave me the sword-cut in the shoulder.' Drinkwater touched the place, and Elizabeth opened her mouth in astonishment.

'Later, he was sent out to the Red Sea where, by chance, I was party to the seizure of his frigate which I afterwards commanded . . .'

'The *Melusine*?' asked Elizabeth, recalling the sequence of her husband's ships.

Drinkwater shook his head. 'No, it was some time after that . . .'

'The *Antigone*?'

Drinkwater nodded. 'But her husband and I were to cross paths again. It is odd, but I fought him not far . . . no perhaps', he said wonderingly, 'on the very spot where she drowned. Just offshore here, some few miles off the Ness at Orford. I killed him in the fight . . .'

'Then you made a widow of her.' Elizabeth looked at the face now bound up with a bandage.

'Yes.'

'That is terrible.'

'I do not deny it. But had I not done so, there is little doubt but that he would have made a widow of you.'

Elizabeth considered the matter. 'How very strange.'

'That is not all.'

'You mean you . . .'

'I have seen her since,' Drinkwater broke in, 'the last time less than a year ago, in April . . .'

'Nathaniel!'

'She came aboard *Andromeda* while we were anchored off Calais. She laid before me information concerning the intention of some French officers to liberate Napoleon after he was sent into exile.' He paused and gave a wry smile. 'It may sound extraordinary, but one might say the world owes the present peace, at least in part, to Hortense Santhonax . . .'

They looked at the corpse with a curious fascination, the silence broken suddenly by a faint escape of gas from the body which moved slightly, startling them.

'Oh, Lord!' giggled Susan nervously, pressing a hand to her breast.

Drinkwater's expression remained grim. 'Come, Susan, search the lining of her habit.'

'Do you look for papers, Nathaniel?' Elizabeth asked.

'It occurs to me that she might have been carrying them, yes.'

'But the war is over.'

'Yet she intended to come here. Unless she came on her own account, she must have had a purpose.'

'Why should she come upon her own account?'

'My dear, this is neither the time nor the place . . .'

'Then let us discuss it elsewhere.' Elizabeth was suddenly brusque. 'Susan is busy and we should leave her to her task.'

Drinkwater shrugged and let his wife hustle him out of the parlour and into the drawing-room.

'Well, sir,' she said sharply, turning on him. 'You have something to tell me, I think. If she was coming here on her own account, and I cannot think, with the war over, that any other reason would move her, I wish to know it. Besides, you said just now that the last time you saw her was in April last. How many times had you seen her previous to that? Do you expect me to believe all this was related to Lord Dungarth's department? Tell me the truth, Nathaniel. And now, before you have a drink, sir.'

'Sit down, Bess, and rest easy.' Drinkwater smiled and eased himself into a chair, leaning forward to rake the fire and throw some billets of wood on it. 'I met her before our encounter last April in the house of a Jew named Liepmann, near Hamburg, and yes, it was all in some way connected with Lord Dungarth and the business of his Secret Department. After his death it fell to me, as you know, to carry on some of his work. Hortense had moved in high places. It was said she was the mistress of Talleyrand, until the Prince of Benevento ousted her in favour of the Duchess of Courland. Did you see her scar? She was badly burned at the great ball given by the Austrian Ambassador in Paris on the occasion of the marriage of the Archduchess Marie-Louise to Napoleon. There was a fire, d'you see . . .'

'The poor woman.'

'Yes, she was much to be pitied.'

'And you pitied her?'

'A little, yes.'

'To the extent of . . .' Elizabeth faltered.

'Of what? Come, say it . . . You cannot, eh?' Drinkwater was smiling and stood up, crossing the room to pour two glasses of madeira as he spoke. 'Yes, I pitied her but not as you imagine. It would not be true to say I did not consider lying with her, she was extraordinarily beautiful and possessed a very great power over men.' Drinkwater handed Elizabeth a glass. 'I shall tell you frankly that I once embraced her.'

Drinkwater paused, sipping his wine as his wife held hers untouched, regarding him with a curious, suspended look, as if both fearful and eager to hear what he had to say.

'I pitied her certainly, for when I saw her last, she was much reduced in her circumstances. She asked me to arrange a pension, but', he shrugged, 'it was impossible that any minister would listen to me and I did not possess the influence of John Devaux.'

'So you made her a grant yourself of fifty pounds per annum.'

'You know!'

'I knew you were supporting someone. We have the wreckage of others here, Susan and Billie Cue . . . I knew from an irregularity in our accounts that you had provided for someone else. It never occurred to me that it was a Frenchwoman.'

Drinkwater sighed. 'I had not wished you to know, lest the explanation be too painful, but I give you my word that nothing beyond that embrace ever passed between us.'

'Your bankers are indiscreet, Nathaniel,' Elizabeth said with a smile. 'But', she went on, her face sobering, 'she cannot surely have been coming here to see you about that, unless she wished for more. D'you think that was it?'

Drinkwater shook his head emphatically. 'No. She would never have asked for more. She wanted the means to live quietly, that is all. No,' Drinkwater frowned, 'it is very odd, but I was thinking of her only last night, wondering how she was surviving under the restored Bourbons . . .'

'She was your ghost?'

Drinkwater nodded. 'Yes, damned odd. She had, like almost all of her generation, sided with Bonaparte. Obscurity would have been best for her, but that may not have been possible for such a creature under the restored Bourbons. It strikes me therefore that there must have been two possible reasons for her coming here now. One might have been to solicit accommodation hereabouts, to appeal to our charity. The other, to bring me some intelligence.'

'And to sell it, perhaps?'

Drinkwater shrugged. 'Perhaps. Perhaps it was to do both, to sell the latter to gain the former. She would have been safe enough in England, heaven knows . . .' He frowned. 'But . . .'

'But?'

'I don't know, but neither seems quite in keeping with so hazardous an undertaking as making passage in a lugger in such unpropitious circumstances . . . And yet . . .'

'Go on.'

'It is just possible that news of sufficient importance might make the game worth the candle, and it would be entirely in keeping with her character to persuade the commander of an unemployed lugger-privateer to make the attempt.' He stood and refilled his glass.

'I see.' Elizabeth held out her own glass. 'She was an uncommon woman.'

Drinkwater nodded and poured more madeira. 'Not as uncommon as you, my darling, but remarkable, none the less.'

'Then we had better let her turbulent spirit go, and put her earthly remains within the old sanctuary.'

Drinkwater bent and kissed his wife's head. 'I ought to see if Susan has found anything'

But all Susan had found were twenty golden sovereigns sewn into the lining of Hortense's skirt. Drinkwater gave five to Susan, three each to Vane's men who had helped recover the bodies, five to Vane for the elm boards and his own trouble, and the remaining four to the clergyman who buried her under the great flint arch of the ancient priory.

In the days that followed, it occurred to Drinkwater that Hortense might have been motivated by some intrigue involving the delegates at the Congress of Vienna. But the idea of his being able to influence anything of such consequence was ridiculous. He was now no more than an ageing post-captain, superannuated on the half-pay of his rank, one of hundreds of such officers. The notion that he might cut any ice with the government was preposterous!

There was, nevertheless, something that still troubled him, and it seemed to offer the most likely explanation for Hortense taking so great a risk as to try and contact him in such weather. And ten days later it was Elizabeth herself who confirmed his worst fears. Vane had just ridden in from Woodbridge and had seen the mail go through with the news being shouted from the box.

Napoleon had escaped from Elba on 26 February. Hortense's body had been washed ashore on the 21st.

Chapter Seven   *April 1815*

The Letter

Drinkwater, in common with every other superannuated officer in the British navy that spring, wrote to the Admiralty offering his services. He ended his letter with a *postscriptum*.

If Their Lordships have no immediate Command for me, I would be Honoured to act in a Voluntary Capacity to Facilitate the Embarkation of the Army destined for Flanders from Harwich, if that was the Government's Purpose, or in any Other Capacity having regard for the Urgency of the Occasion. Should such Employment not be Consonant with the Board's wishes, I desire that Their Lordships consider that my Cutter-Yacht, Manned at my Private Expense, be made available for any Service which may Arise out of the Present Emergency. She would Prove suitable for a Dispatch Vessel, could mount Four Swivel Guns and is in Commission, in Perfect Readiness for Sea. I should be Happy to provide a Berth for Lieutenant G.F.C. Frey if Their Lordships so wished and that Officer could be placed upon Full Pay.

Drinkwater had acquired his cutter-yacht from a builder at Woodbridge who had laid her down as a 'speculation'. Drinkwater was certain this so-called speculation might have proved profitable had not the war ended the previous year and with it the immediate conditions favouring prosperous 'free trade'. Though in the event the peace was to prove but a temporary hiatus, the cessation of smuggling meant that the cutter was up for sale, and Captain Drinkwater's arrival in search of a pleasure yacht was regarded by the builders as providential. She was bought in the late summer of 1814 for the sum of seventy guineas, which amounted to the interest paid on some investments Drinkwater had made with the house of Solomon and Dyer. Drinkwater and his friend Lieutenant

Frey had commissioned her in a short cruise out to the Sunk alarm vessel that autumn. Thereafter, they had contented themselves with a single pleasant jaunt upon the River Ore, entertaining their wives and making poor Harry Vane hopelessly sick, though they had ventured no further than the extremity of the river's bar.

Throughout the winter, the cutter had lain on a mooring in a creek which ran inland from the mouth of the Ore, a short ride from Gantley Hall. After his experience 'at sea', Vane refused to ship in her a second time, but he used her as a static gun-punt and, with the help of his cocker spaniel, loaded all their tables with succulent waterfowl for Christmas.

Notwithstanding the superstitious notion that to use the name again might bring bad luck, Drinkwater had named the cutter *Kestrel* as a tribute to his old friend James Quilhampton who, like Drinkwater himself years before, had commanded a man-o'-war cutter of the same name. Lieutenant Frey, who had served with both Drinkwater and Quilhampton, had acquiesced, for he had married Quilhampton's widow Catriona. Frey, reduced to genteel penury on a lieutenant's half-pay, now occupied himself as a portraitist and had within a short time earned himself a reputation in the locality, being much in demand and receiving commissions from officers of both the sea and land services, many of whom wanted their exploits at sea or in the peninsula recorded with their likenesses. He therefore executed battle scenes as well as formal portraits. As a consequence of his assiduous industry, he had a busy studio and had rescued both himself and his wife from the threat of poverty.

Despite this activity, Frey was not averse to joining Drinkwater in offering his own services to the Admiralty, and when Drinkwater received a letter *requesting and requiring* him to submit his cutter for survey at Harwich *as soon as may be convenient*, he sent word to Frey. Their Lordships had fallen in with Drinkwater's suggestion that, provided he gave his services as a volunteer, Lieutenant Frey should notionally command the cutter, which would be taken up for hire provided she satisfied the surveyor resident at the naval yard at Harwich.

Neither Catriona nor Elizabeth greeted the news with enthusiasm, but Drinkwater's explanation that he doubted *Kestrel* would do much more than act as tender to the transports slightly mollified his own wife. Catriona, having lost her first husband, was less easily consoled, for she had conceived the notion that she might as certainly lose her second husband as she had the first in a vessel of the same name. Poor Frey, who was devoted to her, was clearly torn between the prospect of playing a part in the new campaign with the inducement of professional preferment or of continuing his work as a provincial artist. However, during March, a string of sittings were cancelled due to the flood of army officers returning to the colours, and this recession in trade and the prospect of full pay overcame Catriona's misgivings with the potent argument, traditionally attractive to a MacEwan, of sound economic sense.

Drinkwater took on two unemployed seamen at his own expense and, having laid in some stores, wood and water, sailed from the Ore to arrive at Harwich on 6 April. He presented himself the following morning to the naval commissioner of transports at the Three Cups, a local public house, where his deposition that the vessel was newly built dispensed with the inconvenience of a survey. Captain Scanderbeg, the commissioner, though senior to Drinkwater, had previously been employed ashore and was too hard-pressed to make an issue of such matters.

'Sir,' he had agreed civilly, 'if you say she is new-built and sound, I shall not detain you. The documents for a demise charter will be prepared by this evening.'

At sunset on 7 April 1815, the yacht *Kestrel* became a hired cutter on government service. However, the matter of an armament proved more difficult until the eager Frey discovered eight swivel guns which had been taken out of a merchantman then undergoing repairs at the naval yard. With a little judicious lubrication of palms and throats, he inveigled four of the small pieces out of the hands of the vessel's master, along with a supply of powder and shot. More powder and some additional bird-shot were a matter of requisition, to be supplied by the artillery officer in the Harwich Redoubt, a place already known to Drinkwater.

'Were we here at any other time, in any other circumstances, Frey, we should have found our path strewn with every obstacle known to the ingenious mind of man, but this', Drinkwater gestured at the bustle of the port as they stood on *Kestrel*'s deck, 'almost beggars belief!'

Harwich Harbour was largely a roadstead with no wharfage beyond the slips of the naval yard. The town, dominated by the spire of its church of St Nicholas, the patron of sailors, stood upon a small, low peninsula, surrounded by river, sea and saltmarsh, and commanded the entrance to the haven formed by the confluence of the rivers Stour and Orwell with the guns of its newly built redoubt. A notable battle had been fought in the town's narrow streets in 1803 when the Impress Service decided to round up the greater part of its male population for His Majesty's service. The local inhabitants were, however, versed almost to a man in the ways of the sea, and the over-eager regulating officers soon discovered that they had miscalculated and found themselves imprisoned with their prisoners, while the doughty wives of their victims waved their gutting knives in the streets outside. In fear of their lives, the press-gang eventually released their unwilling recruits and retreated with a few 'volunteers', men whose absence from the town meant they avoided unplanned matrimony or a summoning before the misnamed justices for the illegal acquisition of game. It was after this, known locally as 'the Battle of Harwich', that Scanderbeg had arrived to tighten up the public service.

Though for long a packet station, whose inn-keepers and publicans were notorious for fleecing travellers for the bare necessities of a night's lodging and whose civil officers understood that a certain necessary urgency might prevail in matters of official communication, the little town was unused to coping with the unprecedented military influx which now assailed it. Every inn and every lodging-house seemed stuffed with redcoats. Stands of arms littered the paved walkways of the narrow streets, horses were tethered in lines upon the green, and an ancillary village of canvas tents lay between the old gatehouse of Harwich and the adjacent twin town of Dovercourt. The remnants of the hospital, used for the accommodation of thousands of soldiers dying of the Walcheren fever but six years earlier, had been revived to harbour battalions of infantry, troops of cavalry and batteries of artillery.

The only consistent military organization obvious to a casual observer was a determined effort on the part of officers and men alike to assume attitudes of ease as close as possible to a source of liquor. True, the occasional horseman rode in from Colchester on a lathering horse, calling out for directions to the adjutant of a regiment of foot, or desiring to be directed immediately to the lodgings of Colonel So-and-so, but soon afterwards, a shrewd observer might have noted, the immediacy had gone out of the young aide's quest and he would be seen quaffing a glass or two, or attempting the intimate, if temporary, acquaintance of an absent fisherman's wife or daughter. And all this inactive activity was accompanied by a vast and querulous noise which spilled into the streets from open doors, and accompanied everyone abroad in the narrow lanes and narrower alleyways which divided up the town.

As for Colonel So-and-so, he had gone to ground in a room in the Three Cups or the Drum and Monkey, with or without a local moll, but assuredly clasping a bottle or two. The only industry clearly under weigh was that of the seamen, whom the soldiers had temporarily displaced from the role of the town's habitual drunks. These men laboured off the beach which flanked the eastern side of the town, ferrying a steady dribble of infantrymen and their equipment in flat lighters out to the transports waiting at anchor on the Shelf whose blue pendants lifted languidly in the light airs from the west.

'The army embarks,' intoned Frey, getting out his sketching block. ''Tis odd that the gentlemen who wish for their likenesses to be shown against great sieges never ask me to paint such confusion, yet it seems to be the means by which the army goes to war.'

'Indeed it is and I find it rather frightening,' Drinkwater added. 'Do you suppose the French proceed in the same way?'

'I suppose', Frey said, laughing, 'that they do it with a good deal more noise, better food and more humour . . .'

'Why more humour?' Drinkwater asked, mildly puzzled.

'They must be more inured to it than our fellows,' Frey answered, with that simple logic which so characterized his level-headed good sense. 'If you do something idiotic many times, you must laugh at it in due course, surely?'

Drinkwater shrugged. 'It is a point of view I had not considered before. Perhaps you are right.'

'Men laugh in action, at the point of death, and men laugh on the gallows, so I suppose it is quite natural, some sort of reflex to ease the mind.'

'Or mask it from common sense,' Drinkwater added.

'Yes, probably. I confess I should not like to be landed on a foreign beach and march to meet an enemy who might kill me. At least if I die on a ship, I am among friends.'

'I suppose these lobsters consider their battalions constituted of friends.'

'I still pity them,' said Frey, finishing off his rapid sketch of the

Harwich waterfront. He looked up at Drinkwater. 'Do we have any orders, sir?'

'Well, I have received nothing, Mr Frey, but as lieutenant-in-command, perhaps you should solicit some from the commissioner, Captain Scanderbeg. He has his office in the Three Cups, in Church Street, adjacent to the church.'

'There is one other thing, sir.'

'What is that?'

'We need a small-arms chest. You and I have our swords and I have a single pistol . . .'

'I have a brace of them, but certainly we have nothing for the men. Do you ask Scanderbeg.'

'Very well.' Frey picked up his hat and called for the boat.

Drinkwater was certain that the reopening of hostilities would in due course result in the speedy recommissioning of many frigates and ships-of-the-line and the resumption of the blockade of French ports. It was possible, though by no means probable, that he would be called upon to take command of one of the latter, but he could not sit idly at home while events on the Continent took so exciting a turn in the hope that Their Lordships might remember him. They knew where he was if they required him.

The news of Napoleon's escape had been accompanied by several wild rumours, not the least of which was his sudden death, but the appearance of the quondam Emperor at the head of his troops in Paris and that of Louis XVIII in Ghent put paid to all wishful thinking. The Bourbons had returned to France and behaved as though the Revolution had never occurred, and the French populace had welcomed their Emperor back again. Misgivings they might have had, but the lesser of two evils was clearly preferred. King Louis had wisely removed himself over the frontier.

The hurried reassembly of the Allied armies was put in hand. The delegates at Vienna declared Napoleon Bonaparte to be outside all laws, broke up their conferences, balls and assignations, and returned to their chancelleries, palaces or headquarters. Everywhere Europe was astir again, jerked out of its euphoric assumption of peace, for the devil rode out once more at the head of his legions. It was impossible for a man of Drinkwater's character and history to sit idly by while the world teetered on such uncertainties. Until such time as Their Lordships had a ship for him, the proximity of Gantley Hall to the natural harbour of Harwich compelled him to take part in the urgent movement of the army across to the Belgian coast. Serving as a volunteer was a time-honoured course of action, and placing Frey in command of *Kestrel* gave the younger man the chance, if the war dragged on, of attaining the rank of commander and perhaps post-captain, thus securing a comfortable living for the remainder of his days.

For Drinkwater, in the fifty-third year of his life, the status of volunteer aboard his own yacht was most congenial. Frey delighted in the notion of command, and Drinkwater could relax, as he did now, watching with some amusement the movement of the flat lighters shipping out the horses of a regiment of light dragoons. The seamen assigned to the duty clearly had some difficulty in making the troopers understand the necessity of the animals remaining tranquil on the short passage across the shallows to the transports, and even more in communicating this requirement to the horses themselves. A good deal of shouting seemed essential to the task, which made the horses more nervous, and Drinkwater saw two seamen knocked into the sea and one wretched horse go overboard, to swim wild-eyed in the frothing tide that ebbed to seaward, pursued by a boat whose coxswain failed to understand that the more he holloaed and whistled at it, the more determined the horse became to escape. Drinkwater had some sympathy with the poor beast when its hooves found the bottom and it dragged itself up the beach by the Angel Battery, to be caught at last by some infantrymen lounging about there.

Drinkwater was surrounded by such vignettes and totally absorbed in them, so that he started as Frey, returning in the yacht's boat, ran alongside, almost under his nose. He was even more astonished to see Elizabeth sitting in the stern alongside the lieutenant.

'Elizabeth! What on earth brings you here? Not bad news, I hope?'

He helped her over the side and kissed her, and as he did so, she whispered, 'I have something very private for you,' with such insistence and so significant a stare of her brown eyes, that he took alarm. 'How did you get here?' he asked, frowning.

'We lashed poor Billy Cue on the box of the barouche . . . I left him at the Three Cups where a young woman promised to help him.' Poor Billy had had both legs shot off and, while immensely strong in the trunk and arms, was otherwise like a baby. Drinkwater had provided for him years earlier, and he had proved a useful member of the household, propelling himself about on a low board mounted on castors. Dismissing Billy from his thoughts, Drinkwater tried to gloss over Elizabeth's intrusion.

Turning to Frey he asked, 'Did you find any orders for us?'

'No, sir, but remarkably, I have been told that we are to receive a draft of six seamen and that we are to draw stores and victuals from the Victualling Board officers at the Duke's Head. And I am to bring off an arms chest. Apparently the Impress Service maintain extra arms here in the Redoubt, ever since there was some trouble with the local populace. I've the matter in hand.'

'Good Lord, Captain Scanderbeg has not been idle. We shall be remarkably tight then. See to it, if you please. I daresay orders will follow . . .' But Elizabeth was plucking with annoying urgency at his sleeve. He turned and ushered her below.

'What the devil is it, Elizabeth?' he asked as soon as they were in the saloon. Putting her finger to her lips, she drew him aside into the small cabin Drinkwater had had partitioned off.

'Nathaniel, I have been out of my wits hoping you had not precipitately sailed off to glory,' she said hurriedly in a low, mocking tone. 'Something remarkable and rather macabre has occurred.'

'Go on,' he said with growing impatience, as she appeared to fumble with her riding habit.

'You recall that when we buried Hortense, we laid her out in her small clothes?'

'Yes.' Drinkwater frowned as Elizabeth held out a pair of fine kid gauntlets.

'After you had gone, a sheepish Susan came to see me, to say that she had not disposed of Hortense's outer garments but had cleaned them and put them aside. I suppose she had some idea of retaining them herself, for they were very fine, or of disposing of them at some pecuniary advantage . . .'

'Yes, yes, I understand, but what has this . . .?'

'Please be silent a moment,' Elizabeth retorted sharply. 'She had been considering what to do, I think, probably troubled by her conscience, and, in drawing these beautiful gloves through her hands thus,' Elizabeth demonstrated the abstracted action, running the long cuffs of soft grey leather through her fingers, 'she encountered a stiffness which aroused her curiosity.'

Elizabeth took one glove and turned the cuff. A satin lining of pale blue had been snipped open, revealing a secret hiding-place.

'And inside she found what? Nothing?' Drinkwater asked.

'On the contrary. She found this.' Elizabeth now drew from her breast, with something of the air of a conjuror, a tightly folded and sealed letter. 'It has your name upon it.'

Drinkwater took the letter and turned it over. It bore his name without title in a hand he did not know.

'In view of what you had told us both when Hortense was being laid out, Susan came to see me and made a clean breast of the matter. I made light of it, thanked her, and told her that of course she might have what she wished of Madame Santhonax's effects. I promised her the gloves when I returned. I brought them merely to make you understand why the letter took so long to find. I suppose it was fortunate that we did find it . . . Nathaniel, are you quite well?'

Drinkwater looked up. He had broken the seal of the letter and had read its contents. A cold fear clutched at his heart. On his face, now grown pale, beads of perspiration stood out. Before he had gathered his wits, he murmured, 'My God Bess, this could ruin us.'

Elizabeth frowned. 'What do you mean?' she asked, both her husband's fright and his ghastly expression alarming her. Drinkwater laid the letter down on the shelf formed by a stringer and reached inside a locker for a bottle and two glasses. Elizabeth picked up the letter and read it. Drinkwater filled the glasses and turned to hold one out to Elizabeth. 'I don't understand,' she said, looking up from the letter. 'What is there in this to so alarm you?'

'She would have explained, of course,' Drinkwater said, half to himself, 'that was her purpose in coming and in such circumstances.' He drank deeply, adding, 'the damned fool'.

'That is hardly fair . . .'

'No, no,' he said, shaking his head, 'not her. *Him.*'

'Him? What *him*? Nathaniel, if you are going to speak of ruin, please don't use riddles . . .'

Drinkwater shook himself out of his introspection. 'I am sorry, Bess, it's something of a shock. This', he took the letter gently from her unresisting hand and folded it, 'is from my brother Edward. You know a little of his circumstances. He left this country many, many years ago and, after some time, obtained a position along with many other foreigners in the Russian Army. I had some dealings with him during my service in the Baltic . . .'

407

'Was he connected in some way with Lord Dungarth's Secret Department?'

'Yes, loosely. Certainly he sought to gain credit by assisting me and, by implication, Lord Dungarth. I suppose, from what this says,' he tapped the letter, 'he reached Paris when the Allies occupied the city last year. I would judge that there he met the ever-resourceful Hortense, and at some stage in what I deduce to be an *affaire*, he may have revealed his true identity.' Drinkwater paused. 'Indeed,' he went on with a profound sigh, looking at Elizabeth directly, 'it seems only too probable that he revealed everything.'

'And that everything constitutes our ruin, I assume?'

'Yes.'

'But why?'

'Because when he left this country, he was wanted for murder.'

'*Murder*?' Elizabeth faltered, her face draining of colour and an edge entering her voice. 'And you, of course, being you, helped him escape.'

'I was a damned fool . . .'

'But she is dead and this letter . . . I wish I had never opened the glove, but I thought it something important, that you should know of it and that . . .' Elizabeth faltered, and then added with sudden conviction, 'It doesn't matter though, does it? The letter asks that you should go to Calais to meet the person who signs himself "O". You have merely to ignore it, to pretend it never arrived . . . I mean, how are you so sure that it is from Edward?' And with that Elizabeth snatched the offending paper back and tore it swiftly into pieces. Drinkwater looked on with a chillingly wan smile.

'But it did arrive, Bess. You know it, I know it, Susan Tregembo knows it. Even Frey must be aware that something is up.'

'But you don't *know* it was from Edward. You are guessing, aren't you?' Elizabeth pressed. 'It is signed O. Of what significance is that?'

'Only that Edward's assumed name, the name by which Lord Dungarth knew him, was *Ostroff*. In Russian it means island, a small piece of land surrounded by a hostile sea.'

'You are certain?'

'I am as certain as I can be. In fact I think I recognize the hand now', he added, 'from the way my, no, *our* surname is formed.'

408

There was a brief silence as they regarded the fragments of paper littering the cabin deck. It was broken by Elizabeth. 'Well, you are surely not suggesting you go to Calais?'

'If my brother is in Calais now, then he is stranded there, a Russian officer in a French port which has become Bonapartist again. He might be murdered there, which would be retribution of a sort, but otherwise there is nothing to stop him crossing the Channel by hiring a boat or bribing a fisherman. If I can at least try to reach him, I may discover his intentions. Perhaps, after all these years, we have nothing to fear, but I cannot live the rest of my life knowing that I abandoned my brother, feckless devil though he is and possessing as he does the power to ruin us all.'

'And what shall you do if you do meet him? Shoot him?'

Drinkwater laughed. 'Would you prefer I drowned him?'

'I wish to God you had never had anything to do with him . . .'

'And what would you have done when your own kith and kin came to you in the extremity of desperation . . .?'

Elizabeth bit her lower lip and shook her head. 'I don't know. But murder . . .'

'Well, I am not exculpating him,' Drinkwater said with a sigh, 'but he caught his mistress in bed with another man. You yourself found the merest suspicion of such conduct betwixt Hortense and myself a thing deeply disturbing. An intemperate man like Ned, in the high, indulgent passion of his youth, was scarcely to be expected to react other than as he did.'

Elizabeth considered the matter for a moment, then it seemed that she braced herself as she made up her mind. 'You shall go to Calais. And I shall come with you. '

'No. I shall go to Calais,' Drinkwater said with sudden decisiveness. 'Edward, through Hortense, knows where we reside. You shall go home and stand guard. If Edward comes to you, send Vane to leave word at the Three Cups in Harwich. The letter shall state that the mare has produced a fine black foal and you thought I should know. Remember that. Occupy Ned, and I will return as soon as possible. Mercifully, I can leave Frey in command and absent myself without occasioning any trouble. My only concern at this moment is to detach myself from this place. Come, we must go ashore at once. Take those damned gloves to Susan. I wish her joy of them. Let us lay this confounded ghost once and for all!' And taking his wife in his arms, he crushed her to him. 'Now, put on a

happy smile and look as if you are pleased to see me while I escort
you ashore.'

Having seen Elizabeth off, with a smiling Billie Cue lashed happily
upon the box, Drinkwater ducked into the Three Cups. He had
met Lieutenant Sparkman in its taproom some eighteen months
before when Sparkman, an inspector of Sea-Fencibles, had reported
the arrival of a strange Neapolitan officer on the Essex coast and lit
a train of powder that had led to the fight with the *Odin* and the
death of James Quilhampton in the Vikkenfiord. A woman bobbed
in front of him, her stays open to reveal her breasts, offering him a
drink. He did not remember Annie Davis, though she had
delighted Sparkman all those months ago and, more recently, had
put a smile on Billie Cue's face, though it had cost him a small fortune. Now Drinkwater swept past her and made for the back room
where Captain Scanderbeg held court.

'Ah, Captain Drinkwater, pray do sit down.' Scanderbeg sat
back in his chair and lifted a pewter mug interrogatively. 'A drink?'

Drinkwater shook his head. 'Thank you, no.'

Scanderbeg was in his shirt-sleeves, the table before him littered
with papers, some of which had found their way unintentionally to
the floor while others were more purposefully arranged in a wicker
basket at his feet next to which was coiled a small spaniel. A ravaged quill pen stuck out of a large ink-well and a pen-knife lay
beside them.

'I have ordered a small draft of men for you . . .'

'So I hear and thank you for that, but it is not the cause of my
visit. Captain Scanderbeg, I can see you are a busy and, if I mistake
not, a harassed man . . .'

'By God, sir, I have never known such a thing as this damnable
embarkation. I was Regulating Captain here a year ago and was
resurrected for the present emergency in *this* blasted incarnation.'
Scanderbeg tapped his breast as though this revealed his change of
status. 'I tell you, sir, governments know not what they do when
they declare war with such alacrity! Would you believe that I had
a pipsqueak captain of light dragoons in here this very forenoon
complaining, *complaining* mark you, that my men, the seamen that
is, were taking insufficient care of his blasted horses. When I asked
to which ship they were assigned, the *Adventure*, *Philarea* or *Salus*,
he said he did not know, so I asked which troop he meant, the first

410

or second and so forth, that I might divine the men responsible. He said, "Oh, I don't mean troop horses, damme! I mean me own chargers, sir!" I asked how many of these festering chargers he had and he said four, two of which had cost him four hundred guineas. Four hundred guineas! God, sir, I hope the poxy French shoot the fucking things out from under his arse! I told him that if he had nothing better to do than complain, he had time enough to see to the matter himself and that a couple of hundred guineas to the tars embarking the cavalry mounts would see each of his damned chargers piggy-backed out on the backs of a score of mermaids! Bloody popinjay!'

Drinkwater could not help but grin at Scanderbeg's predicament, despite the urgency of his business, and wondered if the horse he had seen in the water earlier had been one of the importunate young dragoon officer's mounts.

'He threatened to report me to General Vandeleur,' Scanderbeg railed on, 'and I said he might do as he damned well pleased. When the regiment had all embarked, I discovered their field forge and farriers still sitting in the horse lines out by the barrack field. No one had passed word to them to mount up, or whatever the festering cavalry do when they want to move off! I tell you, Drinkwater, the French will make mince-meat of 'em! Thank God for the North Sea and the Channel. Aye and the navy!' And with that Scanderbeg tossed off the contents of his pot and slammed it down on the table. He shook his head and blew through his cheeks. 'I beg your pardon, Captain, but . . .' he shrugged. 'What can I do for you?'

'I think, Captain Scanderbeg, 'tis more what I can do for you. I can relieve you of one anxiety at least.'

'That, sir, would be the first word of co-operation I have received a sennight since!' Scanderbeg brightened visibly. 'You are going to tell me you have some orders.'

'Indeed I am. How did you know?'

'Too long in the tooth, Captain Drinkwater, not to know that I would be the last to be told. Well?'

'I am pushing over to reconnoitre Calais and Boulogne. If the French have any of their corvettes ready for sea, they might wreak havoc among our transports . . .'

'By heaven, sir, you're right! Well, well, go to it, sir, and if there is anything further you require, I shall do my limited best.'

'Thank you. I hope your post don't become too irksome.'

'I could *almost* wish for a frigate with her bowsprit struck over the Black Rocks,' Scanderbeg riposted with a smile, and Drinkwater left with the impression of an indomitable man who would, despite the odds and to the discomfiture of many, get the army embarked in time.

Walking back down Church Street he encountered a troop of horse artillery. The five field-guns and single howitzer gleamed in the sunshine. The bay horses that pulled them were handsome in their harness, and the soldiers that rode postillion were sitting chatting, while the young officer commanding them, having made a few remarks to his bombardier, turned in his saddle, caught sight of Drinkwater and saluted.

'Good day, sir. Captain Mercer of G Troop Royal Horse Artiller at your service. Are you perhaps the naval commissioner?'

Drinkwater returned the salute and shook his head. 'Alas, no, Captain Mercer, the officer you want is Captain Scanderbeg. He is quartered next to the church in the Three Cups.'

'Thank you, sir.'

'Captain Mercer . . .'

'Sir?'

'Make sure you don't leave anything behind . . . the odd gun or limber, for example. I fancy your colleagues in the light cavalry have sorely tried his patience this morning.'

Mercer grinned. 'What would you expect of Vandeleur's brigade, sir?' he remarked.

'I have no idea, Captain, but a little more than they appear capable of, it seems. I just hope the French are as accommodating as Captain Scanderbeg. Good day to you.'

Drinkwater passed on, quite ridiculously light-headed. He had Scanderbeg to thank for bringing the problem of Edward into a more reasonable perspective. Moreover, he had released himself from any obligation to the commissioner. And he would be going to sea. Suddenly that, at least, was compensation enough. And with the thought buoying him up, he hailed the boat.

Chapter Eight   *April 1815*

Calais

The following morning proved foggy and while it delayed the transports from leaving port, the hired cutter *Kestrel* lay wallowing damply off the Head of the Falls, having slipped out of Harwich the previous evening. Hardly had Frey's men lugged the stores and arms chest aboard than Drinkwater passed orders to sail. Once her mainsail was hoisted, and provided the weather remained reasonable, she was an easy vessel to handle. Though Drinkwater and Frey stood watch and watch, it was possible to divide their crew into idlers, available throughout the daytime, with the pressed men in three watches. It was scarcely a punishing regime and, superficially at least, bore a resemblance to the yachting excursions Drinkwater and Frey had indolently planned during their winter evenings together.

Drinkwater's notion of reconnoitring Calais was a sound one; indeed he expected to encounter at least a gun-brig from Chatham keeping an eye on the port. More difficult would be penetrating the place, not an easy task for a British naval officer during so uncertain a political period, but the greatest problem he confronted lay in the means by which he might locate Edward. The letter had given him few clues, and Elizabeth had screwed it up and torn it into so many pieces that his attempt to reconstruct it proved futile. It did not matter. It was intended merely to validate Hortense's appearance. He recalled it as a simple enough message, to the effect that *an old friend* who was *now very intimate with the bearer* wished to be *embarked at Calais and looked forward to renewing a close acquaintanceship*. There were key words containing a hidden significance which Drinkwater, with his eye for such things combined with a conscientious anxiety, had soon noticed. The *old friend* gave away a little, but in truth there were few now left in the world who could claim an 'old' friendship with him. Besides, this relationship was emphasized by the words *close acquaintanceship*. As to intimacy with the bearer, Drinkwater did not need to read between the lines there: Hortense, though mutilated by boiling lead, had still been beautiful, and Ned was past fifty. The only real mystery was how the two had met, and he had no way of divining that fact without asking directly. Of one thing he was certain, Hortense had risked a great deal in her attempt to contact her benefactor. He recalled Lord Dungarth's prophetic remark when they had let her go years earlier, that they would save themselves a deal of trouble if they had shot her. Well, well, Drinkwater mused, they had not shot her, and their combined infirmity of purpose had led to his present predicament. The fact that brother Edward had become Hortense's lover was an exquisitely painful irony, he thought, turning his mind back to the problem of contacting a fugitive Russian officer in a hostile port.

It did not suit Drinkwater to leave matters to fall out as they might. That something would turn up was a maxim that in his experience rarely functioned, except for other people, of course. It seemed he had but two choices, to do the thing himself or to get someone else to do it, and neither recommended itself. He did not wish to go ashore and if he did, what could he achieve? He could hardly wander round Calais in his uniform and to do so in his civilian garb invited arrest and a firing squad. And even if he were to risk going ashore, he could scarcely knock on doors and ask, in his barbaric and imperfect French, if a Russian officer who was really an Englishman had been seen hanging about. The whole matter bordered on the preposterous!

The alternative was to contact a fishing-boat. French fishermen were no different from their English counterparts and would do anything for money. Fortunately he had sufficient funds with him and could buy access to the network of gossip that would exist among the drinking dens, *cafés* and *bistros* that these men frequented when ashore. The fishermen of the Dover Strait, irrespective of nationality, had been carrying odd persons back and forth across the Channel for a generation, and they would almost certainly know of anyone who was seeking a passage. Besides, by now Edward might well have bitten the bullet and arranged his own passage. In fact, it was more likely that he would turn up at Gantley Hall to alarm Elizabeth than that he would be standing obligingly on the beach at Calais. Too long a period had elapsed since Hortense had left in her lugger for an impatient man such as Edward to remain long in idle impotence.

For the whole of 10 April, *Kestrel* lay inert, washing up and down in the tide, her decks wet with the condensation that dripped from her sails and rigging. Drinkwater took the opportunity of calling his tiny crew aft. He had appointed his own two paid hands as boatswain and carpenter, and they had some notion of who they were working for, but the half-dozen pressed men had no idea.

'My lads,' Drinkwater began, looking over the smallest crew he had ever commanded, smaller even than that allocated to him when, as a midshipman, he had been sent away as prize-master of the Yankee schooner *Algonquin*. 'For those of you just shipped aboard, I am Captain Nathaniel Drinkwater. I am the owner of this cutter and she is on charter to the Government for special service. She is commanded by Lieutenant Frey here and he is acting under my orders, both of us being in His Majesty's service. Our orders in the first instance require us to take a look into Calais. Much will depend thereafter on what we discover. What I shall rely upon you for is a prompt and willing response to orders. That is all.'

He watched them disperse. The pressed men were quite clearly seamen and did not seem unduly resentful at their billet. Perhaps they were meditating desertion at the first opportunity. Oddly, Drinkwater did not find the thought particularly uncomfortable. At a pinch he and Frey could sail *Kestrel* home themselves.

On the morning of the 11th, a breeze sprang up out of the northwest quarter and, though it soon dropped again, there was sufficient to keep steerage way on the cutter as she ghosted southeast towards Calais. It was Drinkwater's first real passage in her and it was clear she had been built for speed, for with the quartering wind and her long boom guyed out to port, she ran down wind with ease. Frey seemed content to lean against the long tiller as the white wake ran out from under the counter, leaving Drinkwater to pace along the windward side, from the heavy sister-blocks of the lower running backstay to the starboard channel. The small swivel guns, one of which was mounted on either bow, with the second pair aft covering the cutter's short waist, pointed skywards. Their iron crutches could be lodged in the same holes drilled for belaying pins, and Drinkwater mentally selected three other positions which might prove useful if they ran into any trouble. Of one thing he was relatively certain: if there was any kind of wind, even a light air, he judged they had an excellent chance of out-running even a French *chasse marée*.

None the less, considerations of this kind were mere temporary distractions and, when the French coast hove in sight, Drinkwater realized he was no nearer a solution as to how to contact Edward than he had been when they had sailed. Contacting fishermen seemed the best option, though how he might guarantee that remained an unresolved problem. For some minutes he stood amidships, his glass steadied against the heavy shrouds, watching the low white cliffs fall away as the coast stretched eastwards towards Calais. A strong tide ran along the shore and it would carry them up to the jetties. Drinkwater decided to progress by degrees, and the first of these would be to determine the state of the port. He closed his Dollond glass with a snap, pocketed it and walked aft.

'Now, Mr Frey,' he said formally, looking upwards, 'we have British colours at the peak.'

'Aye, sir.'

'I mean to run up along the coast and approach Calais from the west. The tide will be in our favour and I want to push up between the jetties. Make as though you intend to enter the port. Load all the guns with well-wadded powder. No shot. Be prepared for the French to fire on us, but I want a demonstration made.'

'You're going to tempt anyone bold enough to try their luck against us, are you, sir?'

'I think we might have the legs of even a French corvette, don't you?' Drinkwater replied, dissembling with a grin.

'I'd be damned disappointed if we didn't, to be honest, sir,' Frey replied, smiling back.

'Very well. We will then haul off for the night and heave to offshore. Tomorrow morning we shall do the same again. After that I shall decide what further we can achieve.'

'Very well, sir, I understand.'

Drinkwater was tempted to say, 'No you don't', but confined his reaction to a confirming nod. 'I gather from the smell that you have found one among the pressed men capable of acting as cook,' Drinkwater remarked, sniffing appreciatively, for their table thus far had been unappealing.

Frey nodded. 'One of 'em volunteered, sir. Name of Jago.'

'Well that's fortunate. Let's hope we deserve such luck.'

It was early evening and the wind had steadied to a light breeze as they wore ship off Cap Blanc Nez and began to run along the coast towards the spires of Calais. The cutter heeled a little, slipping through the water with astonishing grace and speed. Had Drinkwater not been so preoccupied, he might have appreciated the sublimity of the moment, but he was denied that consolation, and it was left to Frey's sensibilities as he leaned against the tiller, his eye occasionally wandering upwards to the peak of the gaff where the large red ensign lifted in the breeze. The flooding tide added to their speed and this augmentation made them appear to scud along the shoreline, persuading Frey that the subject would make a delightful painting.

Drinkwater, for his part, watched the approaching port with unease. Just inshore and slightly ahead of *Kestrel* a pair of small luggers were running parallel with them, making for home. They appeared unconcerned by the proximity of the British cutter, so fluid was the political situation. Drinkwater wondered if they might not provide the contacts he required. He turned and walked aft.

'I assume the swivels are ready?' Drinkwater asked.

'Aye, sir. As you required.'

'Very well. Now edge down on those fishermen, Mr Frey, if you please. I want them to get a clear look at us.'

'Aye, aye, sir.' Frey leaned on the tiller and *Kestrel*'s bowsprit swung round as she turned a point to starboard, lining itself up on a church spire.

'Friendly waves to the Frogs now, lads, if you please,' Drinkwater said as they caught up with the rearmost lugger. The two French boats were trailed by screeching gulls who dipped and fought over the scraps of entrails lobbed overboard by the men industriously cleaning their catch before they reached port. The heavily treated brown canvas of their sails and the festoons of nets half-hanging over their rails gave them a raffish appearance, and the low sunlight flashed on the gutting knives and the silver skins of the fish as the fishermen worked with deft and practised ease. Aft, the skippers stood at their tillers, with a boy to trim the sheets, regarding the overtaking British cutter with little more than a mild curiosity as she surged alongside them.

Drinkwater stood beside the lower running backstay and raised his hat. Along the deck his crew waved. Impulsively the lad alongside the aftermost lugger responded, but the skipper merely jerked his head and those of the fishermen amidships who looked up did so only for a second, before bending to their task again.

'Happy-looking lot,' someone remarked as the first lugger dropped astern and they overtook the second. She was closer and Frey altered to port again to avoid actually running her down. Drinkwater read the name across her transom: *Trois Frères*. They received a similar reception from her. 'Very fraternal,' Frey remarked.

'Never mind, Mr Frey. Word of an insolent British cutter in the offing will circulate the waterfront before dark and they have at least saved us from the attentions of those gentlemen.'

Drinkwater indicated a small hill which overlooked the final approach to the entrance. It mounted a battery, and at least two officers, conspicuous in their bell-topped shakos, could be seen regarding them through telescopes.

'Stand by those swivels then,' Drinkwater said, and Frey called to his men to blow on their matches.

'I want you to tack in the very entrance and fire both guns to loo'ard as you do so.'

Frey called his men to stand by the sheets and runners. They were drawing close to the jetties now, and were being watched by at least one man who stood at the extremity of the seaward jetty beneath the lighthouse.

The stream of the tide bypassed the entrance itself but ran fast across it, swirling dangerously round the abutment of the seaward jetty now opening on their port bow. 'Watch the tidal set on that jetty, Mr Frey.'

'Aye sir, I have it . . .' Frey grunted with the effort.

'Ready about and down helm!' Frey called, and *Kestrel* turned on her heel and came up into the wind with a great shaking of her sails. The wind was getting up as the men ran away with the starboard runner falls and let fly those to port. The two crumps of the swivel guns echoed back from the wooden piles of the jetty, then *Kestrel* lay over on the starboard tack and stood to the westward. On *Kestrel's* port quarter the two French luggers sailed blithely into Calais and on her starboard beam the piles of the extremity of the seaward jetty suddenly loomed above them. Drinkwater looked up. The man was still there, staring at them, with the lighthouse rising behind him.

Drinkwater raised his hat again and, with a grin, called out *'Bonsoir, M'sieur!'* But the man made no move of acknowledgement beyond spitting to leeward. 'An expectorating Bonapartist,' Drinkwater remarked, jamming his hat back on his head.

Frey gave a laugh of nervous relief. He had nearly been caught out by the tide carrying him against the jetty-head. Panache was one thing, but it had seemed for one anxious moment dangerously close to disaster!

As if to chastise them for their impudence, two shot plunged into the sea off their port beam. Looking astern, Frey and Drinkwater caught sight of the smoke dispersing from the muzzles of the cannon in the battery.

'Well, I think we have made our presence known, Mr Frey,' Drinkwater said.

They stood away to the north-west as darkness closed in and when they had hauled sufficiently offshore, Frey hove to. Leaving the deck to the boatswain, the two officers went below to dine.

'Well, I don't know what we will achieve tomorrow, but I think we should be off Blanc Nez again by about five o'clock . . .'

'That will give us the tide in our favour again,' Frey added enthusiastically, sipping at his wine as Jago came in with a steaming suet pudding. 'By God, Jago, that looks good!'

'Bon appetit, they says hereabouts I think, sir.'

Drinkwater looked up sharply. 'You don't speak French do you, Jago?'

'Mais oui, M'sieur. I speak it well enough to pass among the French without their suspecting I am English.'

'And how did you acquire that skill, may I ask?'

'Well, sir, 'tis how I learned to cook, too. You see, sir, I was a boy shippin' out of Maldon in ninety-eight with my old pa. We was, er, fishin' like,' he winked, looking at Drinkwater and then at Frey, 'if you gets my meanin', sir . . .'

'You mean you were smuggling?'

'Good God, no sir. I was a mere lad . . .'

'Then your father was smuggling.'

'Not quite, sir. We was actually fishing off the Kentish Knock when up comes this big cutter, flying British colours, and lies to just upwind and floats a boat down to us. Imagine our surprise when over the side comes this Frog officer, all beplumed and covered in gold. He wants the skipper, that's me dad, to take a packet into Maldon and to hand it over to a man at an address he gave him. I think he gave Pa some fancy passwords and such like. To make sure of it, he took me out of the boat and carried me off with him . . .' Jago shrugged. 'Sommat happened to the boat, I remember she was leakin' awful and there was some bad weather blew up next day. Anyway there I was dumped on a small farm near Abbeville. The farmer was an invalid soldier and I learned the place was often used by strange men who were passin' back and forth across the Channel. They avoided bein' seen in Calais or Boulogne but weren't far away when the time came for 'em to ship out. That's how I speak French, sir.'

'Fascinating, Jago. You must have been released at the Peace then.'

'That's right, sir. One day I was put aboard the Dover packet with three golden sovereigns in me pocket and told to go home. Me old widdered mother thought me the answer to her prayers.'

'You seem to be the answer to ours,' Frey said, picking up knife and fork.

'Oh yes, sorry, sirs. Don't you let me spoil your suppers.'

'What an odd tale,' Frey said with his mouth full.

'Yes, indeed.'

They were off Blanc Nez at dawn, and to the southward, running up from Boulogne, was a brig-sloop. 'British or French, I wonder?' Drinkwater asked as he came on deck in answer to Frey's summons.

'It doesn't much matter, sir, since we don't have the signal book aboard. If you've no objection, I suggest we run straight up and keep ahead of him.'

'Very well. With the wind the way it is this morning, if he's French we can escape to windward,' Drinkwater replied, for the breeze had veered a point or two into the north-north-west. 'We should have the legs of him.'

A few moments later it was clear that the brig-sloop had seen them and had decided to give chase, for she was setting studding sails with a speed that bespoke British nationality. However, they were already running along the sandy shore to the west of Calais, impelled by the hurrying tide, the hands busy loading the swivels and joking amongst themselves. A few moments later, as the sun rose above a low bank of cloud over the fields of France, the red ensign went aloft once more.

This morning there were no fishing-boats to mask them, nor did the earliness of the hour render them invisible to the vigilant eyes of the French gunners. As they ranged up towards the entrance of Calais harbour, shot plunged into the sea around them, raising tall columns of water on either beam.

But the speed of the tide under them combined with the swiftness of the cutter to frustrate the French artillery. The nearest they got to hitting *Kestrel* was to soak her decks with water. There were some early morning net fishermen on the seaward jetty whose gear dropped over into the water, but they took scant notice of the British cutter. Years of war and blockade had inured them to such things and they were quite indifferent to the presence of a British ship so close to home.

When they had tacked off the breakwaters and stood back to the westwards, they found that the French gunners in the battery had shifted their attention to the brig-sloop. As they went about, the commander of the brig-sloop, seeing that the cutter was not French and running for shelter in to Calais, also tacked, frustrating the French gunners. Both vessels now stood clear of the coast, with *Kestrel* overhauling the brig.

Drinkwater closed his glass with a snap. '*Adder*, mounting eighteen guns,' he announced. As they surged up under the brig's quarter, Drinkwater saw her young commander at the starboard hance raise his speaking-trumpet.

'Cutter, 'hoy, what ship? You are not answering the private signal!'

Frey looked at Drinkwater and Drinkwater said simply, 'You are in command, Mr Frey.'

Frey handed the tiller over to the boatswain and went to the rail, cupping his hands about his mouth.

'Hired cutter *Kestrel*, Lieutenant Frey commanding, under special orders. We have no signal books but I have Captain Drinkwater aboard,' Frey added, to avoid being taken under the sloop-commander's orders. 'Have you seen any French men-of-war?'

'Who d'ye say is on board?'

'Captain Nathaniel Drinkwater . . .'

'Ask him who his commander is,' Drinkwater prompted.

'. . . Who desires to know who commands the *Adder*.'

'I am John Wykeham. As to your question, there are three corvettes in Boulogne, but heave to, if you please, I have something to communicate to Captain Drinkwater.'

'You had better do as he asks, Mr Frey.'

'Very well, Captain Wykeham. I shall come to the wind in your lee.'

Half an hour later the young Commander Wykeham clambered aboard *Kestrel* and looked curiously about him. Frey met him with a salute. The two men were of an age.

'May I introduce you to Captain Drinkwater, sir . . .'

The two men shook hands. 'I thought I was to be the only cruiser on the station, sir,' Wykeham said.

'Is that what you came to say?' Drinkwater asked.

'Not at all, it is just that your presence is something of a surprise, sir. And, forgive me for saying so, but your cutter is somewhat lightly armed for so advanced a post.'

Drinkwater smiled. 'She is a private yacht, sir, on hire for Government service, but come below, Commander Wykeham, and let us discuss what troubles you over a glass.'

Once in the tiny cabin with charged glasses, Wykeham asked, 'Your special Government service, sir . . .'

'Yes?'

'Does it have anything to do with a Russian officer?'

Drinkwater was quite unable to disguise his astonishment. After mastering his surprise he replied, 'Well, as a matter of fact, yes. Do you know of such a person?'

'I have a Russian officer on board. He came off to me by fishing-boat the day before yesterday. Speaks broken English, but excellent French, a language in which I have some ability. I gather he was caught in Paris by the return of Bonaparte and failed to get out in time. *Cherchez la femme*, I think. How did you know about him?'

'I had a message about him,' Drinkwater said obscurely, adding to mollify the obvious curiosity in the young commander's eyes, 'I have long had dealings of this sort with the enemy coast.'

'Ah, I see.'

Drinkwater smiled. 'I doubt whether you do, but your discretion does you credit. What is this fellow's name?'

'He claims to be a colonel, Colonel Ostroff. An officer of cossacks, or irregular horse. Is he your man?'

'I rather think he might be,' Drinkwater replied, his heart beating uncomfortably, 'but tell me something of the circumstances by which he made contact with you.'

Wykeham shrugged. 'I have been poking my nose in and out of Calais and Boulogne this past fortnight. My orders are to ensure no French men-o'-war escape to harry our shipping crossing to Ostend and if anything of force emerges either to engage or, if of superior force, to run across to Deal, make a signal to that effect, then chase until help arrives. Well, the evening before last, we were approached by a fishing-boat with which we had had some contact a few days earlier. Actually we paid good English gold for some *langoustines*, and I thought the avaricious buggers had come back for more, until, that is, they fished this Russkie lobster out of the hold. Green as grass he was,' Wykeham recollected, laughing. 'He asked for a passage to England, said he would pay his way and that he had been cut off in Paris and had only escaped to the coast by the skin of his teeth. Muttered something about bearing diplomatic papers.' Wykeham shrugged. 'I had no reason not to rescue the poor devil, so I took him aboard. He was anxious to be landed, but I told him he would have to wait. He was most indignant, but now fortunately you have arrived. '

'Well,' said Drinkwater, 'I can take him off your hands and leave the station to you. '

'That would be very satisfactory,' said Wykeham, rising, 'I shall send him over directly.'

Drinkwater followed Wykeham on deck and stood apprehensively as the brig's boat bobbed back over the waves and ran alongside. Fishing out his glass he levelled it and watched a figure, dressed in a sober coat and beaver, clamber down into it, whereupon the boat shoved off and headed back towards them. Drinkwater's heart thumped uncomfortably in his breast. He had a dreadful feeling of chickens coming home to roost, and his knees knocked, making him foolishly vulnerable to an indiscretion. He made an effort to pull himself together, but found himself in the grip of a visceral terror he had never before experienced.

Chapter Nine   *April 1815*

Colonel Ostroff

Paralysis gripped Drinkwater as he watched the boat approach. He was robbed of the capacity to think, and stood like a loon, as though his brother's return automatically meant the ruin he had so greatly feared. He might, he thought afterwards, have acted in such a way as to bring ruin upon himself had not he recalled, quite inconsequentially to begin with, that this supposed stranger allegedly spoke poor English. He did, however, speak good French and that fact called for an interpreter. The presence of Jago would act as a brake upon any precipitate action the impetuous Edward might take. Drinkwater turned and called forward, 'Pass word for Jago to lay aft!'

Then he said to Frey, 'Send this man below with Jago, I'll interview him in the cabin. You may set course for Harwich.'

'Aye, aye, sir.'

Drinkwater hurried below, seated himself in the cabin and endeavoured to compose himself. A few moments later, with a clattering of feet on the narrow companionway, Jago led the newcomer into the cabin.

'Pray sit down, sir,' Drinkwater said coldly, waving to the bench settee that ran along the forward bulkhead as Jago rendered the invitation into French. Time had not been entirely kind to his brother and there was a moment when Drinkwater thought they might have got the wrong man. A wide scar ran across his cheek and bit deep into the left side of the nose. Unlike his elder brother, Edward seemed to have lost much hair.

'Ask him his name, Jago.' The exchange revealed the stranger to be Colonel the Count d'Ostroff, of the Guard Cossacks, lately in Paris on the staff of Prince Vorontzoff.

'He asks for a pail, sir. Feeling sick.'

'You'd better get one.'

The gloom of the cabin after the daylight on deck clearly caused 'Ostroff' some difficulty in seeing his interlocutor, but the moment Jago had gone, he leaned forward and peered into Drinkwater's face. 'It is Captain Drinkwater, isn't it?' he asked with a low urgency.

'I am Captain Nathaniel Drinkwater, yes.'

'Don't you recognize me?' A touch of alarm infected the man's voice, which betrayed a trace of accent.

'Yes . . .'

'Nat, I must talk to you.' 'Ostroff' swallowed hard, his face pallid, his eyes intense.

'Help me at least by maintaining this fiction until we reach Harwich,' Drinkwater said coolly.

'No! You cannot leave the French coast . . .'

'I understand', Drinkwater said in a loud voice, overriding his brother as Jago and the bucket noisily descended the companion-way, 'that you speak a little English.'

But the Colonel had no time to confirm or deny this. Instead he grabbed the bucket from Jago's hand and vomited copiously into it. As his head emerged he turned it to one side and, between gasps for breath, let out a stream of French. The only words Drinkwater recognized, and which seemed to be repeated with emphasis, were *tres important*.

'He says, sir, that it is very important that you do not leave the coast. He says there are three people ashore who must be taken aboard before they are killed.'

'Did he ask Commander Wykeham of the *Adder* to bring them off?' The question was relayed and the Colonel nodded his head. 'And what did Commander Wykeham say?'

Drinkwater waited. It was a foolish question, he realized, but Edward was equal to the occasion, even though he was suffering. 'He, that's Commander Wykeham, did not seem to understand, he says, sir. That's why he, the Colonel here . . . Do I call him the Colonel or the Count, sir?'

'Let's stick to Colonel, Jago.'

'Very good, sir. Well, that's why the Colonel came across to us so obligingly, sir. Thought we'd be an easier touch.'

'Yes, thank you, Jago.' Drinkwater caught Edward's eye and sighed. 'Who are these three fugitives? Victims of the change of government?'

The Colonel nodded and set the bucket down beside him. 'I speak good English,' he said, looking at Jago, 'I can speak directly to your captain, thank you.'

Jago turned from one officer to the other with an astonished expression on his face. 'Well, God bless my soul,' Drinkwater said hurriedly. 'I think you may go then, Jago. I'm obliged for your help.'

'Will you be all right, sir?' asked Jago, looking suspiciously at the Colonel.

'I think even I can defend myself against a seasick man, Jago, thank you.'

Jago withdrew with an obvious and extravagant reluctance. As he disappeared, Drinkwater held up his hand. 'The rules of engagement', he said in a low voice, 'are that you call me "Captain" and I refer to you as "Colonel". Now, I have news for you, your mistress is dead.' Edward's mouth fell open, then he retched again, a pitiful picture of personal misery of the most intense kind. Drinkwater felt a sudden wave of sympathy for his visitor, that instinct of protection of the older for the younger. Averting his face, he pressed on. 'It is only by the greatest good fortune for you that she died almost on my doorstep, otherwise you would have had to consign yourself to the ministrations of Commander Wykeham . . .'

'*Mon Dieu* . . . *La pauvre* Hortense . . . How did it . . .? I mean . . .' Edward raised his unhappy, sweating face from the wooden bucket, all thoughts of Commander Wykeham far from his mind. A pathetic tear ran down his furrowed cheek and Drinkwater guessed he was near the end of his tether.

'You sent her off at a terrible risk . . .'

'No! It was she who insisted on sailing in that damned *chasse marée*; insisted it would be all right, that she could contact you . . . The bloody skipper promised he knew the English coast like the back of his hand.'

'Well, that's as may be. The lugger was dashed to pieces upon a shoal,' Drinkwater persisted. 'Hortense was washed up dead on the beach not far from my home, between the Martello towers at Shingle Street. We found her the next morning. She has been buried . . . Well, never mind about that now. I am sorry, I had no idea you knew her.'

Edward shook his head and wiped his eyes. 'Damnation, Nat . . .'

'Stop that!' Drinkwater snapped, 'Don't let your damned guard down! Not yet!' He veered away from the personal. There would be time to rake over their respective lives later. 'These confounded fugitives, I have no wish to appear inhuman, but what the devil have they to do with me?'

'If the Bonapartists get hold of them they will probably be shot.'

Drinkwater sighed. 'A lot of people have been shot in the last twenty-odd years, Colonel. I had the dubious honour of escorting King Louis back to his country a year ago. It seems our labours were in vain. From what I hear, the Bourbons did little to endear themselves to their subjects and those who support them deserve little sympathy . . .'

'These are not Bourbon courtiers, Captain,' Edward said, pulling himself together and speaking rapidly. 'They are the Baroness de Sarrasin and her two children, aged nine and ten. The Baroness was born into a liberal but impoverished noble family. She was very young during the worst excesses of the Revolution and, being a woman living in the remote countryside, escaped the worst. Later she married an officer in the army. He too was of noble blood, an *émigré* who returned when Napoleon invited the nobility back to France to join the army. He served Bonaparte with distinction and was created a Baron of the Empire, but last year he was on Marshal Marmont's staff and . . .' Edward shrugged.

'And?' Drinkwater prompted.

'You do not know what Marmont did?'

'Should I?'

'Marmont surrendered his entire Army Corps before Paris, pre-cipitating the fall of Napoleon. The Baroness's husband was implicated in the capitulation and she is consequentially tainted as a result of *his* involvement. The loyalties of all members of the family have, as I believe you know, been confused and inconstant.'

'As *I* know?' Drinkwater queried with a frown. 'How should I know about this Baroness de Sarrasin and her family?'

'Since her husband's disgrace she has reverted to using her maiden name. The officer she married was named Montholon . . .'

Drinkwater frowned. 'Montholon! But that was Hortense's maiden name. So, he is Hortense's brother?'

'*Was* her brother. He was mysteriously killed while out riding soon after Napoleon reached Paris. The Baroness and her children were hidden by friends. You have to help her!'

427

'*Have to?* Is she your lifeline now?'

Edward shook his head. 'For God's sake,' he said, dropping his voice still further, 'I am neither an ingrate nor a monster. I have the chance to make some sort of reparation for the past. I need your help. If you cannot do it for me, pray do it for Hortense's sake. She said you were fond of her, that you had duelled with each other for years . . .'

'Did she?' Drinkwater said flatly. 'Duelled, eh? Is that how she put it? Well, I suppose 'tis as good a metaphor as any. Tell me how you met her. That strikes me as the oddest coincidence of all.'

'It is easily explained. Hortense was a friend of Madame Ney's. The Marshal had made something of a reputation in Russia and Prince Vorontzoff wished to meet him. I was on the Prince's staff and we attended one of Madame Ney's *soirées* . . .'

'Where you met Hortense, and thereafter matters took their natural course.' Drinkwater's tone was rueful.

'Quite so.'

'But how', Drinkwater went on, 'did you make the connection with me?'

'It was our intention to marry . . .'

'You and Hortense proposed to marry!'

Edward nodded. 'Yes. Does that surprise you?'

Drinkwater shook his head. 'No,' he said, giving a low, ironic laugh, 'no, not in the least. Pray continue.'

Edward shrugged. 'The war was over and I obtained my discharge from the Russian army. Paris was most congenial, and my long acquaintanceship and service with the Russian *ton* had taught me French. I thought in French and now hardly ever utter a word in English, though Prince Vorontozoff knew me to speak it and, as I was in his confidence, he occasionally conversed in it with me.'

'Did he know you to be an Englishman?'

Edward nodded. 'Yes, there are many foreign officers in the Russian service, though most are Germans. I gave out that I came from a family of merchants who had lived abroad for some time.'

'And by the time you met Hortense, you had proved yourself to the Russians.'

'It was difficult after Tilsit, but Prince Vorontzoff was wholly opposed to the alliance with Napoleon. He retired to the country and I went with him. He had Arab bloodstock and you will recall my interest in horses.'

Drinkwater nodded. 'But you have not told me how you linked Hortense with me.'

'Well, I wished to marry her and settle in Paris. I had provided for myself quite well.' Edward grinned. 'There were some rich pickings between Moscow and Paris, but that is by the by. Hortense struck me as being alone, despite her intimacy with Madame Ney. Baroness de Sarrasin was suspicious of her, due to the disgrace of her first husband, and it was clear she was the recipient of charity. The fall of Napoleon did not divide France, it fragmented the country. Many of the Marshals accepted the restoration of the Bourbons in return for the retention of their positions, titles and fortunes. Be that as it may, Hortense accepted me. In confidence, she told me she received a small competence from a source in England for services to the British government. I assumed this was to prove to me that her loyalties were sound. I also assumed she meant a pension and she might have lied, but she didn't, she said no, it was from a man she held in the highest esteem, though fate had made him an enemy. I thought, of course, that she had been this mysterious benefactor's mistress and that the enmity had grown up after some intimacy, but she denied this vehemently. Sheer curiosity led me to ask the name of her benefactor and sheer innocence led her to reply with our . . . your surname.'

'God's bones, I had no idea . . .'

'You see, the fact that she was an intimate of the Neys, and I knew she was the widow of a disgraced officer, Edouard Santhonax, yet had a pension for services to Great Britain, led me to conclude that her past was as complex as my own, beset by divided loyalties and so forth.' Edward rubbed a hand over his sweating chin. 'I suppose it gave us something in common; we were both what used to be called, with disparagement, "adventurers".'

'So you told her you were my brother?' Drinkwater asked, frowning.

'Yes, eventually. When Napoleon escaped from Elba and Paris was in an uproar. Friendships that seemed to cement the new order of the restored Bourbons dissolved overnight. Everyone seemed compromised, some more than others. There will have been no shortage of informers to jostle the petitioners at Napoleon's new court. Ney rode south to bring back Bonaparte in an iron cage and promptly went over to his old master. As for me, I was now a

Russian living in a city which was set fair to turn hostile, and Hortense was among the tainted. In addition the Baroness arrived, her husband dead, her own fortunes overturned. She was now in the same position as her once despised sister-in-law. Hortense was fond of her brother's children. She had had none of her own . . .'

'I never thought of her as a matron . . .'

'She was not all ambition, you know, but she was brave and resourceful.'

'She suggested you contacted me, I suppose.'

Edward nodded. 'Yes. She regarded you as a person of some influence. I had no idea whether you were an admiral, but from our last meeting I recalled you were engaged in matters usually outside the competence of a common captain in the Royal Navy. Hortense knew that you and a certain peer were involved in clandestine activities, so naturally you seemed the only person we could turn to. This was as clear to me as to her, but over this fortuitous circumstance lay the foolish actions of my youth. I had compromised you fatally. I had to tell her we were related, and why I could not come directly. She was astonished, of course,' he said with a wan smile, 'and at first refused to believe that I could possibly be your brother. I think she thought the claim an extravagant attempt on my part to impress her, but she eventually saw the folly of that and I was able to persuade her by revealing the few facts I knew about you.' He sighed, then added, 'She knew you a long time ago, I gather.'

'I rescued her from the revolutionaries – oh, years ago – just as it appears I must do again with this Baroness of yours.'

'Nat . . .' Edward leaned forward, his face earnest, his voice very low. Grasping his brother's wrist he said, 'I have not forgotten the great debt I owe you for helping me escape the gallows . . .'

'You escaped justice, by God!'

'Maybe. But the rescue of the Baroness and her children is something in reparation.'

'A noble expiation', Drinkwater said with heavy irony, 'which you have already alluded to, but somewhat dependent upon the charity of your over-burdened kin.'

'And I have lost Hortense . . .'

'Perhaps we have both lost her.'

Edward frowned. 'You were never her lover . . .'

'Is that a question or a statement? But no, I never was,'

Drinkwater said hurriedly. He paused a moment, then asked, 'Hortense was not the only woman in your life. Have you not left a wife in Russia?'

Edward shook his head. 'A mistress, yes, in fact two, both married. But I am not the complete smell-smock you think me.'

Drinkwater smiled. '"Smell-smock", now there's an expression that betrays how long it is since you spoke English.' He sighed. 'Well, it is good to see you again. Our last meeting in Tilsit was, you will recall, dangerous enough . . .'

'Look, Nat . . .'

'For God's sake, do not relax your guard! Stop calling me that, or 'twill slip out!' Drinkwater snapped. 'I have a great deal . . .'

'I realize what you have done . . . Look, I have no intention of being anything other than a Russian officer. I can arrive in England as a Russian officer protecting the Baroness. I can spend the rest of my life speaking French. I can retire as the Baroness's protector, if she wishes, and live somewhere quietly. God knows I've endured my own share of frozen bivouacs! This might not quite equate to your cumulative privations, but I do not think there is a soul alive who would recognize Ned Drinkwater, do you?'

Drinkwater looked at his brother. 'How did you get that?' he asked, indicating his own nose. 'A sabre cut?'

Edward nodded. 'On the field of Borodino. A cuirassier of the 9th Regiment. They carried the Raevsky redoubt at the point of the sword. It was my misfortune to have borne a message into the place about thirty seconds before they arrived!'

Drinkwater rose and drew out a bottle and glasses from the locker. 'You will not know that it was Hortense's husband who tried to frustrate my return from Tilsit with the intelligence you obtained for us.'

'That is not possible!'

'And I killed him,' Drinkwater added.

'*Mon Dieu!*' Edward sat back, clearly astonished.

'I think', Drinkwater said slowly, handing Edward a glass, 'that your services at Tilsit might buy you immunity for your crime.'

Edward shrugged. 'Perhaps, but I should not wish to put the matter to the test. It would still cloud your own reputation. Aiding and abetting . . .'

'Yes, yes,' Drinkwater interrupted testily, 'those two words haunt me to this day.' He tossed off his own glass and rose to stand swaying in the cabin as *Kestrel* stood out to sea.

'I can stay Russian,' Edward almost pleaded. Drinkwater paused and the two men stared at each other in the shadowy cabin. 'What damned curious lives we have led,' Edward added reflectively.

'What damned curious times we have lived through,' Drinkwater replied.

'D'you remember what Mother used to say?'

'No, what in particular?'

'That "a friend is a friend at all times, but a brother is born for adversity".'

'Am I supposed to find that consoling? If so I find it confoundedly cold comfort. We are about to stick our heads into a noose, Colonel. By demonstrating so conspicuously outside Calais last night and this morning, in order that somehow you should be made aware of our presence, we have alerted the authorities very effectively. Now we must turn back and make a landing. I presume this Baroness and her children are in Calais itself?'

'No, at a small farm outside. You will need to get ashore to the east of the port if you don't wish to pass through Calais itself.'

'I certainly have no wish to do that. On an open beach, in an onshore wind, with a single small boat. You certainly were born for adversity, Colonel.' And with that Drinkwater left his brother with the bottle, the bucket and his thoughts, making his way on deck to try to put his own in order.

Chapter Ten

The Landing

Kestrel stood offshore until the coast of France had dropped over the horizon astern, then they altered course to the east-north-east and ran parallel with the shoreline before turning south again. Just as twilight occluded the day, they saw the faint glim of light at Calais and, allowing for the set of the tide, laid their course for a point some five miles east of the town. In the interim, Drinkwater had told Frey the bare essentials of the operation. The Russian officer, Colonel Ostroff, was responsible for aiding the escape of a French baroness and her two children. They were currently in a farmhouse outside Calais and a small party was to be landed on the beach that night. Frey's orders were to haul offshore and to wait. Ostroff had assured Drinkwater that they could reach the farmhouse, withdraw the fugitives and escape to the beach before daylight. The shore party was to consist of Drinkwater, Ostroff and Jago, for the latter's knowledge of the local dialect might prove useful.

Both Drinkwater and Frey knew that the operation hinged entirely upon their getting safely ashore and pulling the much larger party out again. It was one thing to land three men through the surf, men who might flounder ashore wet but in reasonable safety, but quite another to re-embark those three men after a night's march with the added encumbrance of a woman and two children. However, any alternative plan seemed too risky, and it was a business Drinkwater had some knowledge of. He therefore gave Frey careful instructions, and the entire crew of the cutter were made aware of the night's business.

As they ran in towards the coast again, they all ate a hearty meal of boiled ham, onions and carrots, accompanied by the last of the fresh bread. Ostroff and Drinkwater prepared a brace of pistols each which, with their swords, were neatly parcelled up with powder, ball and shot, and wrapped in oil-cloth. Drinkwater pulled grey trousers on over his boots but wore his old undress uniform coat and a plain bicorne hat. Ostroff remained in his dark civilian habit and Jago was loaned a blue coat.

There would be a quarter moon after midnight, though the night sky was cloudy and the blustery northerly breeze was chilly enough to drive people indoors after dark. The breeze would, however, also create a heavy surf on the beach, and Drinkwater tried to warn his brother of the problems they might encounter. It was an hour after dark before they finally closed with the coast, the boatswain plying the lead amidships. The proximity of the shore was announced by a steepening of the sea and the appearance of the pale strand with its fringe of rollers above which the spray smoked pallidly in the fitful starlight. Frey brought the cutter to, the boat was launched and the three men tumbled into it, Drinkwater amidships at the oars, Jago forward and Ostroff aft. Each man carried his oil-cloth bundle over his back on a line. The two oars were secured by lanyards so that they should not be lost, and in Jago's charge the boat's painter was secured to a long length of line flaked out on the cutter's deck, a line made up of several lengths which the cutter had provided and which included the unrove halliards from the main and jib topsails.

As soon as the boat had shoved off, Frey dropped the cutter's headsails, scandalized her mainsail and let go her anchor, to hold *Kestrel* just long enough to let the boat, under the impetus of wind and sea, drift and be paddled towards the beach. Drinkwater gently backwatered, keeping the boat's head to sea, while Jago watched the line as the men on board *Kestrel* paid it out. The boat bobbed into the surf where it fell first one way and then the other, the drag on the line and a deft working of the oars by Drinkwater amidships keeping her from completely broaching to, though she rolled abominably and Edward shifted awkwardly, clearly unhappy with the violent motion and the occasional slop of water into her.

'Sit still, damn it!' Drinkwater commanded sharply. Suddenly, some twenty yards from the thundering surf, the boat jerked. The line was not long enough. Then, after a few moments, the vessel fell violently into the trough of a wave, evidence that a further length had been bent aboard *Kestrel* and was being paid out. Now

434

they entered the last and most dangerous phase of their uncomfortable transit.

Drinkwater leaned back and turned his head. 'Be ready, Jago.' He had to shout to make himself heard as the waves now peaked and fell in breakers all about them. Rising high, the boat suddenly dropped and Drinkwater anticipated a bone-jarring crash as the keel struck the sand, but the next second, at a steep angle and lurching to one side as she went, she seemed to climb like a rocket as a roller ran ashore under her.

'Now!'

Jago jerked the boat's painter with all his might and they felt the bow tugged round as those aboard *Kestrel* ceased paying out and belayed the long line. They shot up and down, the spray filling the air about them, their hands, gripping the gunwales, soaked by water splashing into the boat.

'Over you go!' Drinkwater shouted at Edward, who sat hunched and immobile in the stern. The violent movement of the boat almost threw them out of its own accord, then he was gone, suddenly leaping and turning all at the same moment, so that a few seconds later Drinkwater saw the dark shape of him floundering ashore against the pale sand and the final wash of the breakers as they surged exhausted up the beach.

Now it was his turn. He shipped the oars and moved aft, taking his weight and bracing himself with his hands on the gunwales. He crouched on the stern thwart, facing the beach. In fact he felt his muscles cracking with the effort; he was too damned old for this sort of thing! In fact he was a bloody fool! He looked up. Edward was standing not thirty yards away, watching the boat as it sawed at the painter and rose up and crashed down in the very midst of the breakers. Drinkwater cleared his head and concentrated, seeking a moment as the boat descended when he should not have too much water beneath him. Sensing the time was right, he jumped over the stern, landed heavily up to his knees in water and ran forward as fast as he could, almost toppling as he went. He felt his brother grab him and he paused, panting.

'Damn you and your confounded Baroness,' he gasped without rancour. Edward chuckled and both men turned and watched for Jago to follow. 'You managed that very well,' Drinkwater said.

'It is just as well that I learned a few Cossack riding tricks,' Edward muttered shortly. 'Ah, here he comes.' Jago was caught by an incoming breaker which washed up around him, soaking him to the waist, but now they were ashore, their bundles dry and none of them much the worse for the experience.

'It'll be a damned sight more difficult leaving,' Drinkwater remarked, as they turned and walked directly up the wide slope of the beach. Half way up the sand they stopped and stood in a group. Drinkwater reckoned that with the night-glass, Frey would be able to see that they had made it and, sure enough, the boat was suddenly gone, plucked back to *Kestrel* by the long line. Before they struck inland Drinkwater took a last look seaward. He could just make out the dark shape where the cutter's scandalized mainsail stood out against the sky. The tide was making and had two hours yet to rise.

'Come on,' he said, and turned inland. They needed to find the coast road and a landmark to which they could return and which would lead them back to the right part of the vast beach which ran for miles, from Calais to Ostend and beyond, to Breskens and the great estuary of the Schelde, away to the east-north-east.

They found some pollarded willows which would serve their purpose, then Edward went ahead to discover the road. He said something in French which Jago repeated to Drinkwater. 'He says, sir, that it is as well he is an officer of light cavalry. An officer of light cavalry has to have an eye for the country.'

'I see,' said Drinkwater as, after employing this instinct for a few moments, Edward led them towards the track. Soon afterwards, with the sea lying to their right, they were tramping along the paved coast road in silence, with only the sound of the wind rustling the grass and brushwood in counterpoint to the deeper thunder of the surf on the shore.

They walked thus for about an hour. A few cows in meadows to the left of the *chaussée* looked up at them and lowed in mild surprise, but they might otherwise have been traversing an uninhabited country. Finally, however, they came upon a cluster of low buildings which revealed themselves as a small village strung out along the road and through which they walked as quietly as possible. They had almost succeeded when, at the far end, they disturbed a dog which began to bark insistently, straining at the extremity of its retaining chain. As they hurried on, the dog was joined by a clamorous honking of alarmed geese.

Ahead of him, Drinkwater heard Edward swear in French, then a window went up and behind him, with commendable presence of mind, Jago shouted something. It cannot have been very complimentary, for the disturbed villager yelled a reply to which Edward quickly responded. The riposte made the window slam with a bang. Drinkwater forbore to enquire the nature of the exchange and hurried on. Once clear of the village the deserted *chaussée* stretched ahead of them again until it disappeared in a low stand of trees.

When they were well away from the village, Edward turned and made a remark to Jago. The seaman laughed and Drinkwater recognized Jago's response of '*Merci, M'sieur*'. They were the only words he had been able to interpret for himself.

'What did you say to that fellow, Jago?' Drinkwater asked.

'Only that he should strangle his fucking dog before I did, beggin' yer pardon, sir. Then he said honest folk should be in bed and the Colonel replied that honest folk should be marching to join the Emperor's eagles, not lying in bed next to their fat wives.'

'That was well done,' Drinkwater said admiringly. Such an exchange was scarcely going to arouse suspicions that foreigners were abroad.

'There is a turning somewhere ahead,' Edward said quietly in English. 'I am relying upon our finding it, for it leads directly to the farm we want, though it may still be some way off, for I never went east of it before.'

They marched on in silence and less than half an hour later discovered the turning, no more than a track joining the paved road. However, if Drinkwater had anticipated that the location of the track would bring them near their goal, he was mistaken, for they seemed to tramp inland for miles over slowly rising ground. Drinkwater began to tire. Like most seamen, while he could do without sleep for many hours and endure conditions of extreme discomfort, walking was anathema to him. The sodden state of his boots and stockings, the chafing of wet trousers and the chill of the spring night only compounded his discomfort, and already blisters were forming on his feet. Added to these multiple inconveniences, Edward set a fast pace, moving with such heartening confidence that, though Drinkwater was content to let him lead on, privately he cursed him. He began, too, to feel a mounting concern at the length of the return journey. The night was already far advanced

437

and he fretted over the state of the tide and the conditions they would find on the beach when they returned to it.

At last, however, the shape of a building hardened ahead of them. As an enormous orange quarter moon lifted above a low bank of cloud to the east, they arrived on the outskirts of the farm within which the mysterious Baroness had taken refuge.

Edward left Drinkwater and Jago in the lee of a stone wall and proceeded alone to give notice of their arrival. As he vanished, another dog began to bark. The noise, unnaturally loud, seemed to fill the night with its alarum, but both men hunkered down and closed their eyes, speaking not a word but bearing their aches and pains in silence. It occurred to Drinkwater that he had got ashore almost dry-shod compared with Jago. The poor man must be in an extremity of discomfort.

'Are you all right, Jago?' he whispered.

'A little damp, sir, but nothing to moan about.'

'Very well,' Drinkwater replied, marvelling at the virtue of English understatement and settling himself to wait. He almost drifted off to sleep, but a few minutes later Edward returned and called them in. Drinkwater rose with excruciating pains in his legs and back. The warm sickly smell of cattle assailed them as they clambered over the wall and then passed through a gate in a second wall. Crossing a yard slimy with mud and cattle excrement, they entered the large kitchen of a low-ceilinged stone house. The room was warmed by a banked fire and dominated by a large, scrubbed table. Edward was speaking rapidly to an elderly man who wore a nightgown and a cap whose tassel bobbed as he nodded. Behind him, similarly attired, was a buxom woman pouring warm buttermilk into three stoneware mugs. To this she added a dash of spirits before shoving them across the table. Drinkwater muttered his formal '*Merci*', but Jago was more loquacious and the farmer's wife nodded appreciatively while her husband continued to engage Edward in what appeared to be a violent argument.

'A little bargaining and complaining, sir,' explained Jago over the rim of his steaming mug, divining Drinkwater's incomprehension. Suddenly the door behind them opened. The sharp inrush of cold night air was accompanied by the terrifying appearance of a large bearded figure, wrapped about in a coat and wearing oversize boots. Turning at this intrusion, Drinkwater's tired brain registered extreme alarm, and he was about to reach for a pistol when Edward's response persuaded him it was unnecessary.

'Ah, Khudoznik, there you are . . .' Edward caught his brother's eye. 'My man Khudoznik. He is a Cossack.'

Drinkwater recognized the type, and the faint smell that came with him, from his time at Tilsit. 'You might have mentioned him,' Drinkwater retorted, looking at the Russian who stared back. Then they were distracted by the swish of skirts. The Baroness, a pretty but pale and frightened blonde woman with her two children, all in cloaks, appeared from the door guarding the stairs and seemed to fill the kitchen with a nervous fluster. She looked anxiously at the strangers, darted an even more suspicious glance at the silent Cossack and, though Edward stepped forward to embrace her and reassure her, continued to regard them all with deep concern.

Edward briefly indicated Drinkwater, referring to him as '*Le Capitaine Anglais*'. The woman half acknowledged Drinkwater's bow, then swung round and gabbled at Edward, but he was up to the occasion.

'*Silence, Juliette!*' *He* turned to the children. '*Allons, mes petits! Allons!*' He passed a handful of coins to the farmer and indicated the door. Drinkwater emerged into the stink of the yard once more. Five minutes later they were heading north along the track which was now bathed in pale moonlight.

Inevitably, the return journey took longer. Neither the Baroness nor her children were capable of moving at the speed of the four men. The girl whimpered incessantly until, without a word, Edward took her hand from her mother's and, clasping it in his own, led her on. After a few hundred yards she tripped over a flint in the track, pitched to her knees and began to wail.

Edward's palm covered her mouth as he picked her up. Whispering into her ear, he scarcely slackened his pace, giving the Baroness no time to commiserate with her unhappy daughter. The girl clung to his neck. The boy tramped doggedly on. Drinkwater had heard Edward say something encouraging to him in which the words '*soldat*' and '*marche*' were accompanied by '*mon brave*'. After a while Jago fell in alongside the lad and, from time to time, spoke briefly in French. The boy responded, and Drinkwater judged from his tone of voice that the lad was not uninfluenced by the adventure of the night. He himself was left to offer the Baroness his arm.

She accepted at first, but they had dropped somewhat behind when the girl fell and, having relinquished it in order to catch up, she did not seek his support again, politely declining further assistance. Despite this she made a greater effort to keep up, though Drinkwater thought she found the plodding presence of the Cossack at the rear of the little column intimidating.

Drinkwater now began to consider how on earth they were going to get the frightened trio and the Russian into the boat and soon decided that the method he had chosen would prove inadequate. He had mentioned this possibility to Frey who, with the change of tide, would have his own work cut out in remaining as near as possible to the landing place without dragging his anchor. The tide would be on the ebb now and, if they were much delayed, Frey might have to haul *Kestrel* off into deeper water. Drinkwater tried to console himself with the thought that they were making quite good progress, all things considered, though he wondered how long Edward could carry the girl. The wind had dropped a little too, he thought, and that was all to the good.

When they gained the *chaussée*, they turned right and, reaching the low stand of trees, they paused for a short break. Something seemed to be bothering Edward, for while the others caught their breath under the trees, he went out into the middle of the road, scuffing the dust with his right boot. Drinkwater pushed himself off from the tree trunk against which he had been leaning and approached his brother.

'Is something amiss?' he asked in a low voice.

'Yes,' said Edward, pointing at the ground. 'Since we were here last, some horses have passed through.'

'Cavalry horses?'

'Yes. Quite a lot of them too, I would say.'

'Going which way?'

'East. The wrong way for us.'

'God's bones!' Drinkwater considered the matter a moment. 'We shall be all right if we remain behind them, though, surely?'

'Let us hope so,' Edward responded grimly, 'but if I were you, I'd get your arms ready before we move off.'

'I'll tell Jago, but we don't want to alarm our friends.'

'They're alarmed already.'

'Your Cossack might prove useful. Is he armed?'

'He has a pistol.'

'How long has he been in your service?'

'Some seven years now. He attached himself to me after the battle of Eylau. Khudoznik is a nick-name meaning "artist". 'Tis a tribute to his abilities at foraging.'

'He will be quite unfamiliar with the sea, I imagine.'

'That, brother, is why I did not tell you of him before.'

Chapter Eleven   *April 1815*

The Fugitives

Before they set off again, Edward warned them to walk at the edge of the *chaussée* in single file and to drop into the grass beside the road at his signal. If they hesitated, he emphasized, they would be lost. Drinkwater was aware that he impressed this point upon the Baroness and that she nodded in acknowledgement, her face clear in the moonlight.

Drinkwater looked up at the sky. The cloud had almost gone, leaving only low banks gathered on the horizon. 'Of all the damnedest luck,' he muttered to himself. Then they set off again.

It seemed to the anxious and weary Drinkwater that they marched in a dream. The ribbon of road, set for the most part along a raised eminence and flooded by moonlight, appeared to make them hugely conspicuous and quite unavoidable. Their gait was tired and they stumbled frequently, the Baroness immediately in front of Drinkwater falling full length at one point. He helped her up, but she shook him off and, as their eyes met, he could see by the line of her mouth that she was biting back tears of hurt, rage and humiliation.

They walked like automata, their brains numbed by fear and exhaustion. Robbed of all professional instinct ashore, Drinkwater had abdicated responsibility to Edward whose military experience was, he realized with something of a shock, clearly extensive. Watching their rear, his brother would also, from time to time, run on ahead on some private reconnaissance. Once he stopped them and they crouched in the grass, unaware of what had troubled their leader, but after a few terrifying minutes which woke them all from their personal catalepsies with thundering hearts, Edward waved them on again and they resumed the bone-wearying plod-plod of the march. In a curious sense the return appeared to be both longer and shorter than the outward journey. Though they seemed to have been traversing the high-road for half a lifetime, quite suddenly they were approaching the huddle of buildings that formed the farm on the outskirts of the village and where the exchange of repartee had amused them earlier. Matters seemed less risible now.

Looking anxiously ahead, with apprehensions about the geese and dog uppermost in their minds, they had almost forgotten their rear when the Cossack suddenly ran forward to join Edward. The two men abruptly crouched down. At the peremptory wave of Edward's arm, the rest of the party dropped into the grass again, sliding down the shallow embankment into the damp shadows. Raising his head, Drinkwater caught a glimpse of his brother staring back the way they had come. Then he heard a whisper in French, loosely translated by Jago. 'Keep absolutely still, sir. There's someone coming up astern.'

As he lay down and closed his eyes, Drinkwater felt the beat of the horse's hooves through the ground. He remained motionless as the noise peaked. The regular snort of the horse, the jingle of harness and the clatter of accoutrements seemed almost on top of them. Then the odorous wind of the passing of man and beast swept over them and was gone. Drinkwater looked up. The single horseman had not noticed them.

Edward wormed his way back down the line to where Drinkwater lay. 'That was a hussar orderly,' he whispered. 'My guess is that he had orders for the body of horse which passed along this road earlier. They may be in the village ahead or they may have passed on, but we cannot take any chances. I am going forward to have a look. You remain here with Khudoznik.'

'Very well, but remember we do not have much time. The tide . . .' But Edward was gone and Drinkwater felt a sudden deep misgiving. He turned and wriggled forward to warn the Baroness through Jago. 'Explain to her that our ship is not far away.'

'Aye, aye, sir.' Jago did as he was bid, then came back to Drinkwater.

'Beg pardon, sir.'

'What is it?'

'The lady says, "nor is the dawn", sir.'

'No.'

They must all have slept or dozed. Drinkwater was vaguely aware of the girl and the Baroness moving away at one point. Realizing the personal nature of their intended isolation, he made no move to remonstrate. He was too stiff and chilled. The next thing he knew, it was growing light. Seized by a sudden alarm, he realized they could wait no longer. It was clear that the village was full of French cavalry and that, presumably, Edward had remained concealed somewhere to keep them under observation and watch for when they moved on. But suppose something had happened to Edward? Suppose he had been taken prisoner?

Drinkwater was now fully awake, his mind racing, his concern for Frey's predicament paramount. Edward was a plausible bugger, he spoke excellent French and would probably come to little harm. As for himself, the Baroness and her children, their soiled presence on a coastal road in northern France would be far less easily accounted for. As for the Cossack, what reasonable explanation would any French officer accept on *his* score? After all, Drinkwater himself wore a sword, had a pair of pistols stuck uncomfortably in his belt and wore the uniform coat of a British post-captain. Cautiously he wriggled up the slope. The road remained empty as far as he could see, but the roofs of the village seemed much nearer now and there were wisps of smoke rising above them. People were on the move, and whether they were villagers stoking their stoves or hussars lighting bivouac fires was immaterial. They effectively blocked Drinkwater's escape route.

Where the hell was Edward? Drinkwater cast aside the peevish reliance on his brother. Whatever had happened to him, it was clear that Drinkwater himself must now take matters into his own hands. There was only one thing to do.

'Jago!' he hissed. There was a movement in the grass and the seaman's bleary-eyed face appeared, looked round and realized it was daylight. 'We are going to have to go down to the beach and walk along it, below the line of this road. There's no other way of getting round the village. The Colonel seems to have disappeared. Tell the Baroness to get ready to move. And be quick about it.'

'Aye, aye, sir.'

Drinkwater rose to his feet and jerked his head at the Cossack. The man understood, looked round and peered in the direction of the village. Then he shook his head. Drinkwater shrugged with massive exaggeration, though it understated his irritation at finding himself saddled with the man. The Russian indicated the village and Drinkwater turned away. If the damned fool went into the village it might distract the French cavalry, but it might also precipitate a search for more odd characters wandering about the roads.

Drinkwater's head was just below the level of the *chaussée*. He raised it cautiously and stared north. The rough scrub gave way to sand dunes about half a mile away. They would have to move quickly, before the whole damned world and his wife were awake! '*Allons!*' he said, breaking cover.

Despite the danger of leaving their place of concealment, he felt better once they began to move. Their cramped and chilled bodies protested at the demands of walking, but by degrees the activity proved beneficial. Low willows broke the landscape and periodic halts in their shadows revealed that they were free from pursuit. The first stop also revealed the lonely figure of Khudoznik following them. Once they had passed the dunes, Drinkwater considered they would be relatively safe and he tried to pick a route which would place an intervening dune between themselves and the village, regretting, in a brief and bitter moment of irony, that he did not have a light cavalry officer's eye for the country. He would have removed much anxiety from his mind had he done so, for in fact the village was already hidden behind a shallow rise, protected from the icy blasts off the North Sea. Obscured by this low undulation, they reached the dunes without being detected.

Their going slowed as they dragged through the fine sand and Drinkwater ordered a halt, turning back for fifty yards to see if he could observe anything of Edward. The line of the road formed the horizon and was clear against the lightening sky, hard-edged and quite empty. It promised to be a fine spring day and the air was already full of the multiple scents of the earth. Of Edward there was no sign but when he reached the others it was clear the Baroness was in a frenzy of anxiety.

'The lady wants to know where Colonel Ostroff is, sir. She says she won't move without him.'

'Tell the lady Colonel Ostroff is reconnoitring the enemy and that she is to come on with us.'

He waited while this exchange took place. It was clear from the Baroness's expression and attitude that she did not take orders from English sea-officers. Jago's interpretation confirmed this. 'She says, sir, that she wants to go back.'

'Very well.' Drinkwater passed the woman and scooped up the girl. 'Tell her,' he said over his shoulder as he strode away, 'she may do as she damned well pleases.' The girl writhed in his arms and a blow from her fist struck him across the nose just as her foot drove into his groin so sharply that he swore at her with ungallant ferocity. She froze in his arms, staring at him with such horror that he felt sick with hunger, pain and fear. He had no business to be here; he was too old for such quixotic adventures; such things were part of his youth. He stumbled on, fighting the nausea that her assault had caused. A few minutes later he had to pause again and looked back. Jago was following him with the Cossack. A hundred yards behind, the Baroness and her son had been arguing, but now they began to follow. Turning again, he stumbled on, the sand dragging at his feet. Then, looking up, he caught sight of the hard grey line of the sea-horizon.

'Now, Frey,' Drinkwater muttered as he paused and waited for the party to close ranks, 'it all depends upon you.'

As the expanse of sea opened before them, Drinkwater saw the cutter. Behind him he heard Jago telling the Baroness, for whom the sight of the limitless ocean was a profound shock, that their ship was in sight. So insubstantial a vessel as the little *Kestrel* scarcely mollified the poor woman, who had difficulty seeing it. Reduced by anxiety and exertion, she fainted. As for the Russian, he stood staring uncomprehendingly at the seascape before him.

'*Attendez-vous votre mere!*' Drinkwater snapped at the young boy as he set the wailing and struggling girl down and turned to Jago. 'Get some brushwood, anything to make a fire to attract Lieutenant Frey's attention!'

The cutter was some four or five miles to the north-east of them, presumably lying offshore not far from the point at which they had been landed. It was clear Frey had had to get under weigh and had been unable to remain at anchor all night so close inshore, but Drinkwater had anticipated that. Although *Kestrel* was apparently some way off, the tide, ebbing along the coast to the westward, would help Frey reach them, and the distance along the coast which he would have to cover was not as far as it looked. If only they could make themselves seen, they had a reasonable chance yet. Fire without smoke was what they required, for it was a certainty that Frey would be on the look-out for them.

Ignoring the groans from the unfortunate Baroness, Drinkwater bent to the task of building a fire as Jago brought in driftwood and detritus from the last spring high-tide line. The Cossack, seeing what they were doing, turned from the sea and joined Jago in the hunt for fuel. As Drinkwater worked at building the pile of combustible material, splitting kindling and laying a trail of gunpowder from his pistols into the heart of it, he was aware of the boy standing beside him.

'M'sieur,' the lad demanded. 'M'sieur . . .'

Drinkwater looked up and then, cutting short the boy's protests about the honour of his mother, explained in his poor French, 'M'sieur, regardez le bateau.' He pointed at the distant cutter, then at the heap of wood before him. 'Je désire faire un feu, eh? Comprenez?' He turned again to the cutter and made the gesture of a telescope to his eye. 'Le bateau regarde la côte. Eh bien! Embarquez!' Drinkwater made a gesture that embraced them all.

The boy looked at him coldly.

Drinkwater inclined his head with a smile and reached for his pistol just as Jago arrived with more fuel. 'Explain to the boy', he said, as he went on building the fire, 'that I heartily esteem his mother, she is a brave and courageous woman and his sensibilities do him credit, but we have no time to argue and scant time for courtesies. Tell him also, that many, many years ago, I rescued his father from a French beach near Cherbourg and that he may trust me to do my utmost for him and his family. And, when you have done all that, tell him to convey this to his mother and sister and ask them to do exactly as I say in the next hour. Impress upon him that I require their absolute trust and obedience. And tell him that if he is not satisfied, I shall be happy to exchange pistol shots with him when we reach England.'

Drinkwater looked up at the boy and smiled as Jago rattled off his translation. The expression on the boy's face metamorphosed several times and then he drew himself up and gave a short bow before withdrawing towards his mother and sobbing sister.

'What is your name, my boy?' Drinkwater called in English, and Jago obligingly translated.

'Charles.'

'Well, Charles, bonne chance!' Bending to the powder trail, Drinkwater pronated his wrist so that the pan and frizzen of the pistol lay over the tiny black heap, and pulled the trigger. There was a crack and flash, then a flaring as the powder caught and carried the sputtering fire into the heart of the pyramid of wood. A moment later a wild crackling was accompanied by small but growing flames licking up through the pile.

'Don't let us down, Frey, don't let us down,' Drinkwater intoned, raising his eyes to the distant *Kestrel*.

The fire flared up wonderfully, throwing out a welcome heat that drew the Baroness and her daughter towards it. Jago kept them away from the seaward side as Drinkwater stared at the cutter for the first sign that they had seen the fire and knew it for the beacon it was. He walked down the beach, detaching himself from it in the hope that they might see his figure.

For a long time, it seemed, nothing happened. *Kestrel* lay with her bowsprit to the north-north-east, stemming the tide, hove to on the starboard tack and standing offshore slightly, trying to maintain station. It was the worst aspect from which to attract attention. The fire began to die down, though Jago revived it with more driftwood. It died down a second time and Drinkwater was about to give up when he saw *Kestrel* swing round and curtsey to the incoming sea as she tacked and paid right off the wind which had now veered more to the eastwards. He hardly dared hope for what he so earnestly desired, but a few moments later she was headed southwestwards and Drinkwater saw a red spot mount upwards to the peak of the gaff.

'British colours!' he muttered to himself, and then he turned and walked back up the beach to the huddle of fugitives, unable to conceal his satisfaction.

'They have seen us,' he announced. And as they watched, sunlight flooded the scene, turning the grey sea to a kindlier colour and chasing away the fears of the night.

Chapter Twelve

Escape

Drinkwater hurriedly kicked the fire out. '*Allons!*' he said and began to lead off down the beach. The sight of *Kestrel* running along the coast towards them relieved him sufficiently to spare a thought for Edward. If his brother had encountered trouble, there was little he could do to help. If not, then Edward must by now, with the coming of the sunrise, have realized that the party could not lie alongside the high road and that Drinkwater would quite naturally gravitate towards the sea. In either case, Edward's salvation lay in his own hands. At the worst they could cruise offshore until, somehow, he re-established contact.

The five of them had reached the damp sand which marked the most recent high water and stood waiting patiently while *Kestrel* worked down towards them, looking increasingly substantial as she approached beyond the line of breakers. Drinkwater took Jago to one side as they assessed the size of the incoming waves.

'This isn't going to be easy, Jago.'

'No, sir.'

'They're frightened and they're hungry. Trying to get them to clamber into the boat is going to prove impossible, so I want you to take the girl and I'll take the Baroness. We will lift them over the gunwale and I want you to go off first. I'll follow with the boy. Don't come back for me. Stay aboard . . .'

'But sir . . .'

'Jago, you're a good fellow and you've done more than necessary tonight, but don't disobey orders.'

'Aye, aye, sir.' Jago paused, then asked, 'What about that bearded fellow, sir? Who is he?'

'He's Colonel Ostroff's Cossack servant and God knows how we are going to get him into the boat. Perhaps we shall just put a line round him and drag him out to the yacht.' Drinkwater turned and looked along the beach. The vast expanse of strand stretched for miles and remained deserted. 'So far, so good,' he said, 'but I don't know how long our luck will last.'

'No, sir.'

'Now go and pick up the girl, for the boat's coming.'

Frey had not wasted time. He had towed the boat astern and now sent it in on its line, a single man at the oars as instructed, to work it inshore across the tide. Drinkwater ran back up the beach and saw a figure sitting at *Kestrel*'s cross-trees. Watching the bobbing and rolling approach of the boat he waited until she was in the breakers and then flung up his hands and waved his arms frantically above his head. The figure in the cutter's rigging waved back and, somewhere out of sight of Drinkwater, beyond the curling wave-crests, they ceased paying out the line and the boat jerked responsively. The tide had taken the thing down the coast a little but the wind was just sufficiently onshore to drive it into the shallows with a little assistance from the oarsman. Hurrying back to the waiting fugitives, Drinkwater nodded to Jago. The seaman turned to the boy and commanded him to stay put, then he scooped up the girl and began to wade into the sea.

'*Madame, s'il vous plait . . .*' and without further ceremony, Drinkwater lifted the Baroness and followed Jago, leaving the Cossack to shift for himself. At once a wave almost knocked him over. The woman screamed as she took the brunt of it, stiffening in his arms. The sudden shock of the cold water and the spasm of the Baroness caused him to stumble and he fought to keep his balance as he lugged the greater weight of her sodden clothing. The mangled muscles of his wounded shoulder cracked painfully, but he managed to keep his footing. Jago, ahead of him, was now up to his armpits in the water but was able to lift the terrified girl above his head and deliver her roughly into the keeping of the oarsman.

Drinkwater struggled forward, the water alternately washing him back and forth, tugging at his legs one second, then climbing his body to thrust at his chest. It swirled about his burden so that he half-floated, half-floundered, while the frightened woman clutched him and averted her face. Jago was splashing back towards him, giving him an arm as he shuffled, bracing himself as every successive wave washed up to him. Then he was in the breakers, close to the boat, and Jago and he had the woman between them. The boat seemed to come close, then a wave rolled in and the boat soared into the sky. Drinkwater felt the insupportable weight of the wave knock him over. He fell backwards, oddly cushioned by the water, but with the gasping Baroness fighting free and both of them lying in the receding wave, undignified in their extreme discomfiture as they fought for their footing.

Jago had also been knocked down, but the two men, soaked and now shivering, grabbed the Baroness and helped her to her feet. In the wake of the steep breaker, the sea fell away and in the brief lull Drinkwater was yelling: 'Now, Jago! Now!'

The two men struggled together, clasped their arms beneath the protesting woman's rump and hove her up. The boat loomed again, then fell and was suddenly, obligingly close to them, offering them an instant of opportunity. They pitched the woman in with a huge, unceremonious heave as the oarsman trimmed the craft. The Baroness cried out with the impact and the hurt, while a moment later Drinkwater was flat on his back, fighting for breath as he dashed the water from his eyes. Ten yards away the transom of the boat flew up into the air with Jago clinging to it, kicking with his feet.

The oarsman was pointing and shouting, but Drinkwater, struggling to his feet, waved for them to get out, shrieking the order and then turning to make his sodden way back to the shore and the others. Wiping his eyes, he hoped that the ordeal of the Baroness had not completely unnerved her son.

As he waded through the shallows, he saw the young boy watching the departing boat as the line from *Kestrel* plucked it out into deeper water. Alongside him, his face obscured by his beard, Khudoznik stared expressionlessly. Drinkwater tried to smile reassuringly, but the smile froze on his lips, for beyond the boy, a line of horsemen spread out across the sand.

They were some way off and Drinkwater spun round to try and gauge how long it would be before the boat came in again. It would take some time to get the Baroness and her daughter aboard *Kestrel* and perhaps they had not yet seen the approaching cavalry in their preoccupation. *Kestrel* was, after all, only a yacht and had but a handful of men as her crew who would be occupied in dispositions they had made on the assumption that this evacuation would take place in the dark, uninterrupted by the intervention of any enemy.

He ran a little way up the beach in an attempt to gain some elevation to see what was happening, but *Kestrel*'s waterline remained out of sight behind the cresting breakers, though a dark cluster of men amidships could be seen actively engrossed in some task. He looked over his shoulder. The cavalry were quite distinct now, advancing at a gallop, and he felt the knot of panic wring his guts. His pistols were soaked and empty, his sword his only defence. He hurried back to the boy who, in turning to follow him, had seen the cavalry. So had the Russian.

'*M'sieur, regardez!*'

Drinkwater nodded at the boy. 'Where in the name of Hades is that boat?' he muttered, hurrying back. Suddenly he saw the transom on top of a wave and Jago's face above it waving the oars as he back-watered furiously.

'Come on, son!' Drinkwater cried, holding out his fist and splashing forward, waving at Khudoznik to follow. He felt the boy's hand take his and the two of them splashed forward, first up to their knees in the water and then, suddenly, to their waists, then their breasts.

Faint cries came from behind. Drinkwater thanked heaven for fine soft sand – horses could get through the stuff no quicker than humans – but his moment of congratulation was short-lived. Out of the corner of his eye Drinkwater could see that off to the right, half a dozen horsemen had ridden directly down to the firm wet sand and were thundering towards them at full gallop. Jago drifted closer and Drinkwater thrust the boy forward.

'Tell him to hold on, Jago! Don't try and get us aboard!'

'Aye, aye, sir.'

The boy understood. The two of them splashed and kicked and grasped the gunwale of the boat and then they succumbed to the feeling of being drawn through the water as the line was hauled in. After what seemed an eternity Drinkwater felt them bump alongside *Kestrel*. He called for a rope with a bowline to be dropped down and, passing his arm round the boy's waist, got him to put his head and shoulders through the bight as he spat water and kicked with his feet.

'*Courage, mon brave!*' he shouted in his ear. The boy was shivering uncontrollably but above him he could see the white face of his mother. Blood ran down her cheek from a gash on her forehead but she had extended her hand in a gesture of supplication and she wore an expression of such eloquent encouragement and bravery that Drinkwater fought back his emotions. 'Haul away!' he bellowed harshly as he waited his own turn, watching the boy's spindle shanks lifted out of the sea above his own bobbing head.

'Welcome back, sir,' Frey called down to him. 'Where's the Colonel?'

'We lost contact,' Drinkwater said, but then Frey looked away as the first ball flew overhead.

'Here, sir!' The bowline dropped alongside Drinkwater. He let go of the boat and struggled into the loop. The next second the line was cutting excruciatingly into his back and under his armpits as he was drawn high out of the sea. For a moment he stared at the cutter's wildly pitching deck and the great quadrilateral of her slatting mainsail, then as he descended he span slowly round. The beach looked suddenly very close and there in the surf was the Cossack Khudoznik running alongside a single horseman and pursued by a semi-circle of hussars.

One hussar had lost his shako and another was already dead on the sand. A second fell as Khudoznik ran in among the horse's legs, grabbed a boot and swiftly detached it from the stirrup, pitching the trooper off his horse which he then mounted with consummate agility. Alongside him the single horseman tossed aside his pistols and drew a sword. It was Edward.

A moment later Drinkwater was lowered to the deck.

'That's the Colonel, sir!' shouted Frey, pointing.

'I know!' Drinkwater turned to find Jago alongside. 'Get the Baroness and her brats below, Jago. Mr Frey, clear the left flank with one of the swivels.' But Frey was already pointing the after port swivel, and its sharp bark sprayed the beach with small shot.

Drinkwater threw his legs over the cutter's rail and dropped back into the boat. The swivel had struck one of the hussars from the saddle and hit a horse. Miraculously it had left both Edward and Khudoznik unscathed, but the following shot from the forward swivel was less partial. Edward's horse foundered beneath him and he threw himself clear as it staggered and sank to its knees with a piercing whinny. Khudoznik had whipped the pistols from the saddle holsters and was laying about him when a second shot from the after gun drove the hussars back. By now a frantic Drinkwater, his teeth chattering, was paddling backstroke towards the beach, shouting at Edward.

'Run into the sea, Ned! For God's sake don't stay there!'

A hussar bolder than the others, an officer by the look of his fur shabraque, spurred forward, intent on sabring the fugitive, but Edward still had his sword and cut wildly with it so that the officer's horse reared. At the same moment Khudoznik drove his own mount directly at the attacker. Just as Edward avoided the low thrust made by the hussar officer under his mount's neck, horse and rider crashed to the sand under the impact of the Cossack's terrified horse. With its bit sawing into its mouth, it reared above the dismounted hussar and its wildly pawing hooves struck the unfortunate man.

Edward staggered back and saw for the first time that it was Khudoznik looming above him. He shouted at him in Russian, but the next second the Cossack lurched sideways as a carbine ball struck him in the side of the skull. Khudoznik slipped from the saddle and landed heavily on the wet sand. Edward took a single glance at him, then turned and ran into the sea.

No more than ten yards separated them now, then Drinkwater felt the boat strike the bottom with a jarring thud that made his own teeth snap together. Edward seemed to tower over him before the next wave passed under the boat and then he had his arms over the transom and Drinkwater was jerking the painter and saw it rise dripping from the water as the hands aboard *Kestrel* lay back on it. As they began to draw out through the surf followed by a few balls from the hussars' carbines, Drinkwater met his brother's eyes as Edward gasped for breath.

'Where the hell did you get to?' Drinkwater asked.

'The devil . . .' Edward retorted, but his explanation was cut short. Drinkwater felt the ball strike the boat through the body of his brother. Over Edward's shoulder, he saw a hussar lower his carbine and reload.

Now that the boat was clear of their field of fire, the swivels aboard *Kestrel* opened up again behind them, the shot buzzing past overhead as Drinkwater lunged aft to grab Edward.

'Hold on, Ned! Hold on!' A thick red stream ran astern of the boat.

'Too late, Nat. My back's shot through.' He looked up and Drinkwater saw the last flicker of the departing soul. 'No trouble . . . to you now . . .' he gasped as he relinquished his grasp upon the boat and upon life itself. Drinkwater tenaciously clung on to his brother as he was once more pulled alongside *Kestrel*. Ned was dead before they reached the cutter's side, but they dragged his body aboard and laid him in the scuppers.

'Are you all right, sir?' Frey asked as Drinkwater almost fell over *Kestrel*'s low gunwale on to the deck, while a last carbine ball whined overhead.

'Yes, yes.' He looked down at Edward. The eyes were already glazed, opaque. 'Poor fellow,' he sighed, as he bent down and closed the lids. Then he stood and looked at Frey. 'Do you get under weigh now, Mr Frey.'

'Those devils have given up now,' Frey said matter-of-factly, jerking his head at the shore. Drinkwater turned to see the hussars tugging their mounts' heads round and turning away. Several of the horses had bodies slung over their saddles. One, that of the Cossack nicknamed Khudoznik, lay exposed by the retreating tide.

'You need to dry yourself, sir,' Frey advised, 'you look blue with cold.'

'What's that? Oh ... oh, yes, I suppose I am a trifle ...' Drinkwater realized he was chilled to the marrow and quite done in. He stared again at Edward's body, reluctant to leave it. 'We'll take him home and bury him,' he said to Frey, as he moved on shaky legs towards the companionway.

'It's a long way from Russia,' Frey remarked.

'Yes. But perhaps that does not matter too much.'

Chapter Thirteen *April 1815*

The Chase

'Out of the frying pan, Mr Frey,' Drinkwater said, lowering the glass. Astern of them, the sharply angled sail of a lugger broke the line of the horizon with a jagged irregularity as the French *chasse marée* came up, carrying the wind with her. Seven miles further north *Kestrel* experienced nothing more than a light breeze. 'Almost the only circumstances', Drinkwater muttered angrily, 'which could place us at a real disadvantage.'

Frey turned from his place by the tiller as Drinkwater looked aloft, but they had every stitch of canvas set and no amount of tweaking at the sheets would improve their speed. Drinkwater cast about him. 'They must have slipped past *Adder*. At any other time we might have expected a British cruiser in the offing but all we have in sight at the moment are a couple of fishermen . . .'

He raised his glass again. It was damnably uncanny. The lugger was carrying the wind with her, sweeping up from the south, and would be quite close before they felt the benefit of it themselves. He looked at Frey. A brief glance was enough to tell him that he was seething at their ill-fortune. He would be dog-tired now after a sleepless night, as were the rest of them, Drinkwater himself included. Poor Frey, *Kestrel* was a pathetic enough command; to lose her to the enemy like this would be a worse blow to his pride than the loss of the yacht to Drinkwater!

Perhaps there was something they might do, though.

'I'm going below for a few moments, Mr Frey.'

'Aye, aye, sir.'

In the cabin the Baroness and her daughter were fast asleep, wrapped in blankets while their outer garments dried in the rigging above. The boy Charles lay on the settee awake, his face pale with seasickness, his eyes huge and tired. Drinkwater smiled, trying to convey reassurance to the young lad. He smiled wanly back at him. 'That's the spirit,' Drinkwater said, helping himself to some cheese, biscuits and wine as he drew out a chart and studied it. 'Help yourself,' he offered, indicating the wine and biscuits and hoping the lad would remain below and not get wind of their pursuer.

After about ten minutes of plying dividers and rules, Drinkwater stuffed the chart away, pulled his hat down over his head and went up on deck. Striding aft he relieved Frey.

'Go and try to get some sleep, there's a good fellow. You need it and we may have work to do in an hour or two.'

'I don't give much for our chances, sir. At the very least he'll have twice our numbers, and we made enough of a display of ourselves outside Calais to call down the vengeance of heaven. I don't suppose the deaths of half a dozen cavalrymen endeared us to them either.'

'Very well put, Mr Frey. Now do as I ask while I try and devise a stratagem.'

'Do you think . . .?'

'Don't ask me.'

Reluctantly Frey handed over the tiller and the course. Drinkwater leaned his weight against the heavy wooden bar. 'I'm going to alter a little to the westwards. Now do you go below for an hour. I shall call you well before things get too lively. Stand half the men down too.'

Frey went forward and some of the men on deck drifted below. *Kestrel* was just feeling the wind picking up and began to slip through the water with increasing speed, as though she felt a tremor of fear at the approach of the large, three-masted lugger coming up astern.

Drinkwater steadied the cutter on her new course and settled himself to concentrate upon his task. The satisfactions in steering were profound. The sense of being in control of something almost living struck him and he recalled that he had forgotten so much of what had once been familiar as he had risen to the lonely peak of command. He made a resolution not to look astern for half an hour. It was difficult at first, but the glances of the others on deck, increasing in frequency and length, told him the lugger was gaining on them so that, when the thirty minutes had passed, he turned, expecting to see the lugger's bowsprit almost over their stern. Though she was still some way off, two miles distant perhaps, she was no longer alone. Now he could see a second lugger behind her, five miles away or maybe more, but close enough to spell disaster if his half-germinated plan miscarried. He resolved to wait twenty minutes before he looked again and set himself to reworking the hurried and imperfect calculations he had made below.

He now discovered a greater anxiety, that of wishing to see the chart, to re-measure the distances and make the tidal estimates again. It was easy enough to make a silly error, to rely upon a misunderstanding only to find that the stratagem, which was shaky enough as it was, would misfire and carry them to disaster. And then, with a forceful irony, a thought struck him. *Kestrel* was his own property and he might do with her as he pleased. He would not have to answer at his peril and so was free of one constraint at least, thank heavens!

He began to stare ahead and study the surface of the sea, to try and discern the almost invisible signs of the shoals, where the tide ran in a different direction and at a slower speed. The mewing gulls had a good view of these natural seamarks and he looked up to see the herring gulls gliding alongside, their cruel yellow beaks and beady eyes evidence of their predatory instincts. But they were lazy hunters; he was looking for more active birds fishing on the edge of the bank ahead.

He saw the first tern almost immediately, flying along with a sprat or some small fry silver in its red beak, and then another diving to starboard of them, under the foot of the mainsail. He craned his neck and stared intently over the port bow. As he did so a man forward rose and peered ahead, aware of Drinkwater's concern. A moment later more terns could be seen and then his experienced eye made out the troubled water along the submarine ledge.

'Sommat ahead, sir, looks like a bank . . .'

'It's the Longsand! Take a cast of the lead.'

Alongside the rushing hull the sea ran dark and grey, dulled by the cloud sweeping up and over the blue of the sky. The sounding lead yielded seven fathoms and then suddenly it was only three and they passed through a strip of white foam, dead in the water like the cast from a mill race seen some few hundred yards downstream. As suddenly as it had appeared, the white filigree was gone and the water was brown and smooth, as though whale oil had been cast upon it. Drinkwater knew they were running over the Longsand Head. He counted the seconds as *Kestrel* raced on, her pace seemingly swifter through the dead water on top of the bank.

'By the mark, two!'

Drinkwater felt the keen thrill of exhilaration, his heart fluttering the adrenalin pouring into his bloodstream. At any moment their keel might strike the sand, and at this speed the impact must toss the mast overboard, but he held on, pitching the risk against the result, until the man in the chains called out 'Three . . . By the deep four . . . By the mark five!' and they were over the bank and ahead of them they could just see the low stump of the brick tower daymark on the Naze of Essex. Drinkwater, his knees knocking uncomfortably, altered course a touch and looked astern. His plan had almost worked, but the big lugger had seen the trap just in time and bore away, to run north, round the extremity of the bank, losing ground to the escaping cutter. It was not so very remarkable, for the commander of so large a lugger would know these waters far better than Drinkwater, who was relying upon knowledge learned thirty years earlier in the buoy-yachts of the Trinity House. Nevertheless, they had increased their lead and every mile brought them nearer the English coast and the presence of a British man-o'-war out of Harwich to the north-west of them.

The wind had steadied now, a topsail breeze which, in the lee of the Longsand, drove *Kestrel* homewards with inspiriting speed. Drinkwater forgot his exhaustion in the joy of handling the little cutter and for a few moments scarcely thought about her pursuers until the anxious looks of the men on deck again drew his attention to them. He turned and looked over his shoulder.

The two enemy luggers were closer together now and were setting more sail, clear evidence that they were determined to overhaul *Kestrel* before she made it into Harwich harbour.

'They must know of the quality of our passengers,' he muttered grimly, for this was surely no mere retribution for the death of a handful of hussars or British insolence in the entrance to Calais. And then he recalled the man who had watched them from the extremity of the Calais jetty, and wondered who or what he was and whether he had anything to do with this determined pursuit.

Drinkwater had hoped that he might lure the larger of the two luggers over the Longsand so that she ran aground, and in doing so he had let *Kestrel* sag off to the west a little. With the flood tide now running into the Thames estuary from the north, he had to regain that deliberately sacrificed northing, sailing across the tide while the French luggers already had that advantage from their forced diversion round the seawards extremity of the shoal. There was, however, a further obstacle behind which he would feel safe. If he could lure the luggers on to the Stone Banks, to the east of the Naze, he could shoot north into Harwich through the Medusa Channel.

The idea filled him with fresh hope and he laid a course for the Sunk alarm vessel, lying to her great chain mooring and flying the red ensign of the Trinity House. She lay ahead, with her bow canted slightly across the tide under the influence of the strong southerly breeze. She was a fortuitous seamark and one which the Frenchmen might even attack if they were frustrated in their pursuit of *Kestrel*.

For another twenty minutes they ran on, the luggers still gaining slowly, though now heeled under a vast press of canvas. As the range closed, Drinkwater called the crew to their stations for action and Frey, blear-eyed and looking far worse than if he had never slept, staggered out on deck, followed by the boy Charles.

'Send the lad below,' Drinkwater began, but it was too late. The boy had seen the luggers and glimpsed the large tricolours, and his face betrayed his fear.

'It's to be a damned close-run thing, Frey. We might make it into the Medusa Channel, we might not, but I think you had better . . .'

'You keep the helm, sir, now you have it. I'll send two men aft to trim sheets, then I'll fight the ship,' and without another word Frey swung away to see to the loading of the swivels and the mustering of the men with their small arms.

Drinkwater leaned on the tiller and, as Jago and a man named Cornford came aft, he ordered a little weight taken in on the mainsheet. *Kestrel* dashed through the water and a gleam of sun came through the clouds to turn to silver the spray driving away from the lee bow, making a brief rainbow with its appearance. Looking astern, terns dipped unconcernedly in their wake, while a fulmar quartered the sea in a single swoop. The fulmar caught Drinkwater's eye, swept down and upwards, away across the dark, predatory shape of the luggers' sails, absorbed only in its ceaseless quest for food and quite unaware of the grim game of life and death being played by the men in the three vessels below.

The nearer and larger of the two luggers was driving a bow wave before her that rose almost under her gammon iron. Her sails were stiff as boards and, even at the distance of a mile, Drinkwater could see the three great yards which spread her sails bending under the strain. If only, he thought, if only one would carry away . . .

But they stood, as did the lighter topsail yards above them, and the Frenchman loomed ever larger as the distance between them shrank and their courses converged. Drinkwater stared forward again and saw the tall lantern mast of the Sunk alarm vessel also growing in size as they rapidly closed the distance. He was aiming *Kestrel*'s bowsprit for the bow of the anchored vessel, hoping to draw his pursuer in close enough for him to lose his nerve and bear away again as the tide swept them down on to the alarm vessel. It was an old trick, learned, like so much else he had used recently, in the buoy-yachts a lifetime ago, to determine the position of the alarm vessel's anchor by sailing up-tide of her, when any prudent mariner would pass down-tide, under her stern.

Forward, Frey turned and stared aft, suddenly alert to the danger into which they stood. Seeing Drinkwater confidently aware of how close they were going to pass the alarm vessel, he relaxed and made some remark to the hands who looked aft and laughed. But Drinkwater was too tense even to notice. Every muscle he could command was strained with the business of holding *Kestrel* on her course without deviation, gauging the exact strength of the lateral shift of the racing hull under the influence of the tide, yet making allowances for the quartering sea which created a gentle see-sawing yaw. He could see the hull of the Sunk now and the men lining her rail as the three vessels closed, and at that moment, the first gun was fired. The shot passed across *Kestrel*'s deck, right under the boom and out over the port side, to be lost somewhere in the choppy seas on their port beam.

'God's bones!' Drinkwater blasphemed, as the wind of the shot's passing distracted him. The next second he was aware of a ragged cheer from the crew of the alarm vessel and the rush of a red hull and slimy green weed along a waterline that passed in a blur as the cutter dashed across the tide and was suddenly under the Sunk's high bow. Then there seemed a number of cries of alarm, of crashes and the thud of another gun, of a great rushing to starboard and more shots, of pistols and the starboard swivels all barking at once in a moment of packed incident in which he took no part, rooted as he was to the heavy tiller. All he saw as they tore past the alarm vessel was the great iron chain of the Sunk stretching down to the anchor in the seabed below them. Then they had run beyond the Sunk's bow and he relaxed, looking round to watch the strength of the tide as it bore them sideways and as the apparent motion made the alarm vessel seem to cross their own stern. He looked round for their nearer pursuer. She had been unable to pass up-tide of the alarm vessel and had been compelled to haul her wind and duck under the Sunk's stern. In doing so she had passed so close that she had exposed herself to one of the alarm vessel's carronades, mounted as a warning gun but loaded with an extempore charge of debris. The discharge of old nails and broken glass tore through the lugger's straining foresail as she bore up too much. As a consequence, her stern brushed the alarm vessel's hull and her mizen snagged it. Her after rigging was torn away, dragging the whole mizen, mast, sail and yard with it. As she broke away from the Sunk, the lugger left white canvas fluttering from the stern of the alarm vessel and with it her tricoloured ensign. Of the second lugger, all that could be seen was the peak of her sails to the southeast as she reached across the wind, anxiously watching the fate of her consort.

'Harden in those sheets!' Drinkwater roared, pushing the tiller with all his might. 'Stand by to tack ship!'

Instantly Frey divined Drinkwater's intentions. 'Prepare those starboard swivels! Get those port swivels mounted over here!'

Kestrel dipped into the wind with a flogging of her sails and paid off on the other tack. Runners were set up and let go, the sheets shifted and slackened as *Kestrel* spun to port, swung off the wind and ran back towards her late tormentor. Confusion reigned on the deck of the *chasse marée* as *Kestrel* passed on the opposite tack, spattering her with small-arms fire and raking her with the swivels.

'Here, Jago!' Drinkwater tossed the seaman one of his pistols and Jago aimed and fired it into the throng of men struggling to bring their lugger under command again. Seeing the pitiful sight and the execution done to the lugger's decks, Drinkwater noted the mainsail had ripped badly so that she was almost immobilized.

'How I wish we had one decent gun,' he lamented to himself, but Frey had had all four swivels discharge into the enemy as they passed and the carnage was bad enough. The second lugger was a mile away now, and stood steadily south-eastwards. Drinkwater pursued her for a while and had the satisfaction of chasing her from the field before he turned back towards their erstwhile enemy. The larger *chasse marée* was a sorry sight, her mainsail down on deck. And though the main topsail was being hoisted and she might yet run off before the wind, it appeared she was *hors de combat*. Inspiration struck Drinkwater. 'Where's young Charles, Jago?'

Jago called out in French and Drinkwater saw the lad raise his head from beside the boat on her chocks amidships where he had been huddled, watching the action.

'Tell him to find out this fellow's name, Jago, and then ask if he surrenders.' Drinkwater raised his voice. 'The rest of you prepare to fire and to scandalize the mainsail and heave to.'

As they came dancing up under the overcast and pointed their little guns at the lugger, the boy called upon her to surrender. The response was a torrent of French at which the lad stiffened and Jago merely laughed.

'Well, damn you, what does the bugger say?' Drinkwater prompted Jago, who addressed a few words to Charles.

'*Elle est la* Mathilde Drouot *de Calais, M'sieur. Le maître est mort, et . . .*' The boy shrugged and looked appealingly at Jago.

'She's the *Mathilde Drouot* of Calais, sir, the master is killed and her mate says he is compelled to surrender to pig-butchers. He has had five men killed besides the master, and eight wounded. One is very bad and he asked if we had a surgeon.'

Drinkwater pulled a face. 'That is unfortunate, I had no idea the swivels were so effective . . .'

Jago shook his head. 'I don't think it was our swivels, sir. I reckon it was the men on the alarm vessel firing broken glass bottles at 'em from a large-bore carronade mounted on the quarter.'

'I see. We may take the prize, but not the credit.'

'Aye, I reckon so, sir. 'Tis against the laws of war, the Frog yonder says, sir.'

Drinkwater ignored the objection. 'Tell the *Mathilde Drouot* to pitch all his ramrods overboard, then head for Harwich. Tell him to stay in close contact under my guns. If he tries to make a run for it,

I shall sweep his decks with glass bottles myself. I think we have a few down below, don't we, Mr Frey?'

'A few, sir, but not many.'

'Then let us hope the matter is not put to the test, eh?'

Captain Scanderbeg was somewhat ruffled to be woken early next morning by a lieutenant demanding accommodation for prisoners-of-war in the town bridewell.

'And who, sir, are you, pray?' he asked, emerging dishevelled from his chamber in the Three Cups.

'Lieutenant Frey, sir, of the hired cutter *Kestrel*. I have some twenty-seven prisoners and several need a surgeon, sir.'

Scanderbeg frowned. '*Kestrel*, she's Captain Drinkwater's yacht, ain't she?'

'Yes, sir, under my command. We fought an engagement off the Sunk yesterday afternoon and took a French National lugger, sir. We anchored last night on the southern end of the Shelf and . . .'

'And here you are disturbing me, Lieutenant . . .'

'Frey, sir.'

Scanderbeg sighed, then said mildly, 'I recall you now. Well, damn you, sir, you shall wait until I have shaved and broken my fast and then perhaps we shall find somewhere for your confounded prisoners. Don't you know I have an army to embark?'

'So I see, sir,' said Frey politely, withdrawing. 'I do beg your pardon. I had no idea it took quite so long.'

Scanderbeg stared at the retreating young man, then he scratched his head and burst out laughing. 'By God, sir, neither did I!'

PART THREE
Ebb Tide

It is said that of all deaths, drowning is the least unpleasant.

The Oar

Captain Poulter leaned over the railing at the port extremity of his bridge. His agitation was extreme, though he fought to conceal it as he waited patiently for the wreckage of the boat to be recovered, along with the survivors clinging on to it.

He counted the bobbing heads; two remained missing. One was almost certainly old Sir Nathaniel and he half-hoped the other might be Drew, but he could see the Elder Brother now and realized the other was Mr Quier, *Vestal*'s second mate.

Poulter willed Forester to hasten the recovery, though he knew full well that the mate and his boat's crew were doing their utmost. When at last the matter was concluded, he shouted for half speed ahead.

'We have everyone except Sir Nathaniel and Peter Quier, sir,' Forester reported when he eventually came up on the bridge.

'Yes, I know.' The two men looked at each other. They were both thinking their luck had run out, but neither wished to voice the apprehension. 'We must keep on searching, Mr Forester.'

'Aye, aye, sir.'

'Quier has a chance, I suppose . . .'

'Let us hope so.'

Drinkwater was not so cold now and thought he had stopped shivering. It did not seem to matter that the water rose above his head. There was a simple inevitability about things; an acceptance. All would be well, and all would be well . . .

It was almost a disappointment when, without effort, almost in spite of himself, he encountered the oar again and found that he was breathing, his head clear of the water with the arch of the sky above him. But now it hurt to breathe; almost as much as it hurt not to . . .

Last Casts of the Dice

Edward was buried next to Hortense in the grounds of the old priory and with him Drinkwater consigned a great anxiety. Once he might have relied upon the protection of Lord Dungarth, but after the Earl's death, had Ostroff's true identity or past crime of murder been exposed, along with his own part in Edward's escape, he scarcely dared to think what would have happened to Elizabeth and the children. That Edward had rendered signal service to the British Crown at Tilsit might not have weighed in his favour so long after the event, and now, in any case, the war had finally ended and with it those expedient measures behind which wrongs were obscured.

Nine weeks after the return of *Kestrel* from the French coast, England learned of the débâcle of Waterloo, the quondam Emperor's flight to the west coast of France and his surrender to Captain Maitland of the *Bellerophon*. Thereafter, the presence of Napoleon aboard ship in Torbay attracted widespread interest before he was transferred into the *Northumberland* and carried south, to exile on distant St Helena. In the months that followed, Elizabeth persuaded her husband to fill in those gaps in his personal history that the loss of his early diaries during the sinking of the *Royal George* had caused by writing down his memoirs. She considered her husband's service to be of some interest to their children and, while she expected him to be deliberately reticent concerning some of the incidents in his life, she knew sufficient to want his sacrifices, and by implication her own, not to go unknown by their family. There was also a more practical consideration, and in initiating her husband's task, Elizabeth demonstrated the depth of her own understanding.

For Drinkwater the process brought back many memories. So daily an accompaniment of his life had the war become that the absence of it seemed to remove the main purpose of existence itself, and yet he learned that for Elizabeth and his household, the war had been but a distant backdrop to their own lives, lives which were more intimately connected with the ebb and flow of the seasons than the tides, of ploughing and planting, of reaping and harrowing, of tending livestock and mending fences, of buying and selling, of butter-making and fruit-bottling. Drinkwater was at first suspicious of Elizabeth's motives, suspecting her of wanting him occupied and not interfering in the business of the estate, but he quickly realized that he was guilty of a mean misjudgement. Elizabeth was only too acutely aware that the end of the war and the end of active service would confront Drinkwater himself with numerous regrets and frustrations, and that while he might say he wished to be left in peace, indeed he might desire it most sincerely, nevertheless such a desire would in time wane and, in the manner of all ageing men, he would wish for the excitements of youth and maturity. A period of reflection and evaluation would, she astutely hoped, reconcile him to a gentler, less tempestuous life.

In the first year of peace, Drinkwater bent to his task and found that it did indeed ease his transition from active command to the life of a country gentleman. He had no knowledge of either livestock or agriculture and eschewed the company of farming men, not out of snobbery but out of ignorance of their ways and their conversation. They were as great an oddity to him as was he to them. There were fewer expressions more accurate or appropriate than that of being a fish out of water. Rather than try, as many of his naval contemporaries did, to join the squirearchy, he retained the habit of command, was content with his own company and, when in need of male companionship, sought that of his friend Frey. Frey's expectation of advancement had terminated with the sudden end of the war and he had returned to painting, enjoying a continuing success. A solicitous husband, he nevertheless slipped away from time to time to laze afloat aboard *Kestrel* for a day or two. It seemed impossible that on these very decks had once lain the body of a mysterious Russian officer, or that they had carried off the Baroness and her children from the teeth of a French hussar detachment in the very yacht that lay at anchor beneath the hanging woods on the River Orwell.

Drinkwater received an occasional letter, written in painful and stilted English, from the young Charles Montholon. He had acquired a certain importance because his uncle, General Montholon, had been appointed to the small suite which accompanied to St Helena the man the British cabinet had meanly insisted was to be known as 'General Bonaparte'. This tenuous connection had, despite the young man's fugitive situation during the Hundred Days, encouraged an ambition to join the French army on the assumption that the glories of the past might be replicated in the future. Drinkwater sincerely hoped they would not; a world riven by battles of Napoleonic proportions was not one that he wished his own son to inhabit, but reading Charles Montholon's correspondence, it occurred to Drinkwater that his own generation had lived their lives in an extraordinary period which, seen through the younger man's eyes, was already vested with a vast and romantic significance. Not the least thread in the fabric of this great myth was the distant exile of the dispossessed emperor.

While Napoleon languished on his rock, Drinkwater completed his journals and enjoyed his quiet excursions under sail. Occasionally he and Frey would undertake a little surveying of the bar of the River Ore, or Drinkwater would submit a report on some matter of minor hydrographical detail. These, finding their way to the Court of Trinity House, in due course resulted in his being invited to become a Younger Brother of the Corporation and this, in turn, led him to accompany a party of Elder Brethren in the Corporation's yacht on an inspection of the lights in the Dover Strait. Thus, one night in the summer of 1820, anchored in The Downs close to the *Severn*, a fifty-gun guardship attached to the Sentinel Service, Drinkwater found himself at dinner with a Captain McCullough, commander of the *Severn*, who had been invited to join the Brethren at dinner.

The after cabin of the Trinity yacht was as sumptuous as it was small, boasting the miniature appointments of a first-rate. The meal began with the customary stilted exchanges of men with an unfamiliar guest in their midst. McCullough, who had joined Drinkwater and the two embarked Elder Brethren, Captain Isaac Robinson and Captain James Moring, by way of his own gig, was quizzed about his naval career and his present service.

'I made the mistake', he admitted, smiling ironically, 'of suggesting that the revival of smuggling might be countered by several detachments of naval officers and men posted along the coasts most exposed to the evil. Their Lordships took me at my word and offered me the appointment of organizing the task. The command of *Severn* came, as it were, as a by-blow of their decision, for she acts as storeship and headquarters of the force.'

'And as a visible deterrent, I daresay,' observed Captain Moring, who had recently relinquished command of an East Indiaman.

'I believe that to be the case, yes.'

'How many men do you command?' asked Captain Robinson.

'The whole force amounts to only about eighty men who occupy the old Martello towers along the shore. Each division, of which there are three in Kent, is commanded by a lieutenant, with midshipmen and master's mates in charge of the local detachments. A similar arrangement pertains to the westward in Sussex. Each post has a pulling galley at its disposal, so we are an amphibious force.'

'You take your posts at night, I imagine,' Drinkwater said, 'and enjoy some success thereby.'

'As an active counter-action to the nefarious doings of the free-trading fraternity, we have enjoyed a certain advantage, yes, though this has not been achieved without loss.'

'You suffer deaths and injuries then?' Drinkwater asked.

'Oh yes, severely on occasion. The smugglers are a ruthless lot and will stop at nothing in their attempts to run their damnable cargoes.'

'Well, I confess that the odd bottle of contraband brandy has passed my lips in the past, but with the peace and the present difficulties the country faces, the losses to the revenue must be stopped,' Captain Moring put in.

'Indeed,' went on McCullough, nodding, 'and the problem lies in the widespread condonation that exists, partly due to the laxities practised during the late war, but also due to the material advantage accruing to the individual in avoiding duty.'

There was a brief and awkward silence, then Captain Robinson raised his glass and remarked, 'Well, sir, I give you the Sentinel Service . . .' and they drank a toast to McCullough's brainchild.

'Perhaps,' Drinkwater added, 'one might consign the magistracy to some minor purgatory. I gather that when the Preventive Waterguard were formed, what, twenty years ago now, they often threw out of court actions brought against well-known smugglers.'

'That is true,' went on McCullough, warming to his subject with the enthusiasm of the zealot, 'for the justices were usually the chief beneficiaries and how else does a man get rich in England but by cheating the revenue? But they are less able to try the trick on naval men, and besides, there was some mitigation during the war when continental trade was made difficult and it was in our interest to encourage it. The paradox no longer exists, therefore the matter is simpler in its argument. Its resolution, however, remains as difficult as ever.'

'The risks are high for those caught,' said Moring.

'Indeed. I should not wish to face transportation or the gallows, but the profits are encouraging enough and the risks of apprehension, despite our best efforts, are probably not so terrifying.'

'No,' put in Drinkwater. 'And it is not entirely to be wondered at that fellows made bold by the experiences of war and who find no employment in peace, yet see about them evidence of wealth and luxury, should turn to such methods to support their families.'

'That is true, sir,' replied McCullough, 'and there is a certain irony in seeing victims of the press remaining at sea for their private gain . . .'

'That is not so very ironic, McCullough,' Drinkwater responded, 'when you take into account the fact that the men who oppose you and the revenue officers are by birth and situation bred to the sea and find it the only way to earn their daily crust. I am certainly not sympathetic to their law-breaking, merely to their situation. It seems to me that an amelioration of their circumstances would remove many of the motives that drive them to break the law.'

'You mean measures should be taken by government', Robinson asked incredulously, 'to *regulate* society?'

'I think that is a necessary function of good government, yes.'

'Government regulation gave us the confounded income tax,' protested Moring.

'Well,' said Drinkwater, 'I think the present government can give us little . . .'

'You are a reformer, sir!' said Moring accusingly.

Drinkwater smiled. 'Perhaps, yes. There can be very little wrong in promoting the welfare of others. I seem to recall something of the sort in the gospels . . .'

'Damned dangerous notions . . .'

'Revolutionary . . .'

'Come, gentlemen, keep a sense of proportion,' argued Drinkwater. 'We cannot entirely ignore events either over the strait or, for that matter, on the other side of the Atlantic . . .'

'I doubt our present Master', remarked Moring, referring to the Corporation's senior officer who, as Lord Liverpool, was also the Prime Minister, 'would agree with you.'

'I hope, sir,' said Drinkwater, with an edge to his voice, 'that you are not implying disloyalty on my part by my expressing my free and candid opinion? One may surely disagree with the opinions of another without the risk of retribution? After all, it is a hallmark of civilization.'

There was a moment's awkward silence, then McCullough said, 'The present state of the country is a matter for concern, I admit, but this should not condone law-breaking.'

'I do not condone law-breaking, Captain McCullough. I have already said so. The present woes of our country, with trouble in our unrepresented industrial towns, unemployment in our countryside and difficulties in trade, are matters close to all our hearts,' Drinkwater persisted. 'My case is simply that the solution lies either with government or in revolution, for there are limits to the toleration of even the most passive and compliant people. I have spent my life in fighting to contain the latter and see that the wise solution must therefore lie with the former. Was Lord Liverpool here this evening, I am certain he would agree with me that something must be done. But the problem seems to lie in what exactly one does to ameliorate dissatisfactions. One can hope something will turn up, but this seems to me damned foolish and most unreliable. The unhappy experience of France is that one cannot throw over the cart without losing the contents and that to do so runs the risk of bringing down a tyranny greater than the one formerly endured. On the other hand simply to obstruct all progress upon the principle of exclusion seems to me to be both dangerous and foolish.'

'What policy of what you are pleased to call *improvement*', sneered Moring, 'do you advocate then, Drinkwater?'

'Since you ask,' Drinkwater replied, smiling wryly, 'a policy of slow but steady reform, a policy which would be perceptible to men of every condition, but which would allow due controls to be exerted. It is my experience that neither coercion nor bribery produce loyalty, though both may produce results, whereas some moderating policy would be wiser than sending in light dragoons to cut up political meetings that can have no voice other than in open fields.'

'Well, I ain't so damned sure,' said Moring, motioning the steward to refill his glass as he dabbed at his mouth with a napkin.

'Of course you're not,' Drinkwater said quickly, 'for it is your certainties you must sacrifice . . .'

'Gamble with, more like,' put in Robinson.

'Indeed. But you have spent your professional life gambling, Captain Robinson, pitting your wits against wind and sea, bringing your cargoes safely home against considerable odds, wouldn't you say?'

Robinson nodded with lugubrious acquiescence, apparently defeated by this line of argument.

Moring was less easily subdued. 'But that doesn't alter the fact that by conferring liberties upon the masses, disorder and chaos might result,' he persisted.

'True, but so they might if we leave Parliament unreformed and half the veterans from the Peninsula wandering our streets as beggars, and half the pressed seamen returned to common lands they find enclosed, or consigned to those stinking factories that are no better than the worst men-of-war commissioned under Lord Sandwich's regime in the American War. God forbid that the English disease of snobbery should set a real revolution alight! Imagine what the men who raped and pillaged their way through Badajoz might do to London!'

'But Drinkwater, to enable a government to function in the way you so passionately advocate, it must needs garner its revenue,' argued McCullough, a note of vexed desperation in his voice.

'Unquestionably, McCullough. Gentlemen, I apologize for ruining your evening,' said Drinkwater, temporizing, 'I am in no wise opposed to Captain McCullough's Sentinel Service and had we not drunk to it already I should have proposed a toast to it now . . .'

But Drinkwater was interrupted by a loud knocking at the door and the sudden appearance of the yacht's second mate.

'Begging your pardon, gentlemen, but there's a message come for Captain McCullough. Your tender's just arrived, sir, with word of a movement along the coast, and they're awaiting orders.'

McCullough rose, a somewhat relieved expression crossing his face. 'I'll be up directly,' he said to the second mate and, turning to the others, apologized. 'Gentlemen, forgive me. It has been a most stimulating evening, but I must leave at once. My tender, the *Flying*

Fish, was not expected to return until tomorrow, so this news means something considerable is under weigh . . .'

Robinson waved aside McCullough's explanation. 'Now, Drinkwater, here's an opportunity for us all to do our duty! Will you accept our services as volunteers, McCullough? You will? Good man! Gentlemen, to our duty . . .'

And with that Robinson rose and went to his small cabin, muttering about priming pistols. 'Will you have us, sir?' Drinkwater asked, rising slowly to his feet. 'Antique and libertarian as we may seem, we are not wholly without experience in these matters.'

McCullough shrugged. '*Your* reputation is solid, sir, but I am not so certain how strong a *trade*-wind blows . . .'

'Come, sir,' Moring snapped as he leapt to his feet, 'that remark is of dubious propriety. Let us show *you* how strong a trade-wind may blow, damn it!'

And so the uncongenial occasion broke up in petty rivalry, and Drinkwater went reluctantly to shift his coat and shoes, and buckle on his hanger.

It was a moonless night of pitchy darkness and a light but steady southerly wind, a night made for the running of tubs on to the beaches of Dungeness, and the *Flying Fish* slipped southwestwards under a press of canvas. The comparison with *Kestrel*, thought Drinkwater, as he squatted on one of the tender's six carronade slides, ended with the similarity of the tender's rig. Thereafter all was different, for *Flying Fish* was stuffed with men, and the dull and sinister gleam of cutlasses being made ready was accompanied by the snick of pistol frizzens as the men prepared for action. What precise intelligence initiated this purposeful response, Drinkwater had only the haziest notion. Treachery and envy loosened tongues the world over, and word of mouth was a deadly weapon when employed deliberately. But patient observation, infiltration and careful analysis of facts could, as Drinkwater well knew from his brief tenure of command of the Admiralty's Secret Department, yield strong inferences of intended doings.

In truth his curiosity was little aroused by the matter; he felt he had exhausted his own interest in such affairs years ago. It was, like the command of *Kestrel*, something he was quite content to give up to a younger and more eager man. Every dog had his day, ran the old saw, and he had had his. If the evening's evidence was anything to go by, he was out of step with the temper of the times. Younger men, men like Moring, Robinson and McCullough, had made their own world and he was too rooted in the past to do more than offer his unwanted comments upon it. Nevertheless, it seemed that with the past something good had been lost. He supposed his perception was inevitable and that the hard-won experience and wisdom of existence was perpetually squandered as part of the excessive bounty of nature. These men would learn in their turn, but it seemed an odd way for providence to proceed.

Such considerations were terminated by McCullough summoning them all aft. Stiffly Drinkwater rose and joined the others about the tiller. A master's mate had gone forward and joined to brief the hands, and Drinkwater stood listening to McCullough while watching the pale, bubbling line of the wake draw out from under the *Flying Fish*'s low counter, creating a dull gleam of phosphorescence at the cutwater of the boat towing astern.

'Two of our pulling galleys reported a long-boat from Rye run across to France a couple of nights ago,' McCullough was saying. 'Information has reached us that the contraband cargo will be transferred to three fishing-boats which will return independently to their home ports. The long-boat will come in empty, apart, I expect, from a few fish.

'The rendezvous is to be made on the Varne Bank, near the buoy of the Varne. It is my intention that we shall interrupt this. I want prisoners and I want evidence. From you, gentlemen,' McCullough said, turning to his three volunteers, 'I want witnesses, not heroics.'

As Moring spluttered his protest, Drinkwater smiled in the darkness. At least Elizabeth would approve of him being a witness; he was otherwise less certain of her enthusiasm for his joining this mad jape.

'And now, gentlemen,' McCullough concluded, 'I must insist upon the most perfect silence.'

For another hour they squatted about the deck, wrapped in their cloaks against the night's damp. The low cloud was breaking a little, but a veil persisted over the upper atmosphere, blurring the few stars visible and preserving the darkness.

But it was never entirely dark at sea; the eyes could always discern something, and intelligence filled in details, so that it was possible, while one remained awake, to half-see, half-sense what was going on. The quiet shuffling between bow and helm, accompanied as it was by whispers, told of the transmission of information from the lookouts, and in due course McCullough himself discernible from the shape of his cocked hat and a tiny gleam on the brass of his night glass, went forward himself and remained there for some time. Drinkwater had, in fact, almost dozed off when something like a voltaic shock ran along the deck as men touched their neighbours' shoulders and the company rose to its feet.

After the long wait, the speed with which events now accelerated was astonishing. The preservation of surprise had compelled McCullough to keep his hand hidden until the last moment and now he demonstrated the skill of both his interception and his seamanship, for though their course had been altered several times in the final moments, it seemed that *Flying Fish* suddenly ran in among several craft to the accompaniment of shouts of alarm and bumps of her intruding hull.

The drilling of her company was impeccable. On a single order, her mainsail was scandalized and the gaff dropped, the staysail fluttered to the deck with the thrum of hanks on the stay, and men seemed to drop over the side as they invaded the rafted boats which, until that moment, had been busy with the transfer of casks and bundles of contraband.

For a brief moment, it seemed to the observing Drinkwater that the deterrent waving of dimly perceived cutlass blades would subdue the smugglers, but suddenly riot broke out. Cries of surprise rose in reactive alarm, the clash of blade meeting blade filled the night, and the grunt of effort and the flash and report of the first pistol opened an action of primitive ferocity. Beside Drinkwater, Moring was jumping about the deck with the undignified and frustrated enthusiasm of a schoolboy witnessing his first prize-fight, while all about them the scene of struggle had a contrived, almost theatrical appearance, for the pistol flashes threw up sharp images in the darkness and these stayed on the retina, accompanied by a more general perception of men stumbling about in the surrounding boats, grappling and hacking at each other in a grim and terrible struggle for mastery.

This state of affairs had been going on for no more than two or three minutes with neither side apparently prevailing, though shouts of execration filled the air along with the cries of the hurt and the occasional bellowed order or demand for surrender. Suddenly matters took a turn for the worse.

The ship-keeper, left at the helm of the *Flying Fish*, added his own voice to the general uproar. 'To me! Help! Astern here!'

Drinkwater turned to see the flash of a pistol and the ship-keeper fall dead. A moment later a group of smugglers came over the *Flying Fish*'s stern and rushed the deck. He lugged out his hanger just in time, shouting the alarm to Moring and Robinson, and struck with a swift cut at the nearest attacker.

He felt the sword-blade bite and slashed at a face. It pulled back and, in the gloom, the pale oval passed briefly across the dim light from the *Flying Fish*'s shrouded binnacle. For a moment, Drinkwater thought he recognized the man but he swiftly dismissed the thought as a figure loomed to his left and he thrust hard, driving his very fist into another man's belly as his sword-blade ran his victim through.

Drinkwater felt something strike his own shoulder as he twisted his wrist to wrench the sword-blade clear and half staggered, barking his shin painfully against a carronade slide as he broke free of his dying assailant. After the first moment of shock and the reactive thunder of his accelerating heart, he found the cool analytical anodyne to this horrible work. He seemed to be able to see better, despite the darkness, and he breathed with a violent and stertorous effort, snorting through distorted nostrils as he hacked at the invaders, slashing with a terrible effect, and twisting his wrist with a savage energy that tore at the very tendons with its violence. He was a butcher of such ferocity that he had cleared the deck and fought his way to the very stern over which the last of his opponents jumped, when he heard Robinson cry out, 'Turn, sir! Turn!'

It was the smuggler he had first seen and whom he thought he had struck down, the man whose face had been briefly illuminated by the binnacle light. Now he recognized him, and by some strange telepathy, he himself was recognized.

'Jago!'

'Stand aside, Captain, or I'll not answer . . .'

'You damned fool!'

'Stand aside, I say!'

For a moment they confronted each other in silence as Drinkwater raised his sword. His madness cooled and then, through teeth clenched ready for reaction, he muttered, 'Go over the side, man, or I must strike you . . . Go!'

But Jago did not jump. Instead, the sword of another ran him through from the rear and he stood transfixed, staring at Drinkwater as he fell, first to his knees and then full length, snapping the sword-blade and revealing his executioner as Captain Moring, a broken sword in his hand.

'That, sir,' Moring said, his eyes agleam, 'is how strong a trade-wind may blow!'

Chapter Fifteen

The Knight Commander

Drinkwater drew off his gloves, threw them on to the table and took the glass stopper from the decanter.

'There are some strange ironies in life, are there not, my dear?' he asked, pouring two glasses and handing one to Elizabeth. 'To be thus honoured as an act of spite against a foreign power for something done years ago seems too ridiculous.'

Accepting the glass, Elizabeth sank into a chair, kicked off her shoes and wriggled her toes ecstatically. 'Thank you, *Sir* Nathaniel,' she said, smiling up at him.

'I hope that is a jest and does not become a custom,' Drinkwater replied, sitting opposite and raising his glass in a silent toast to his wife.

'Is that a command, Sir Nathaniel?'

'It most decidedly is, my dear, or else I shall have to call you *Milady* and refer to you as *Her Ladyship* . . .'

'*Leddyship*, surely, my dear. '

'Well at least we agree about that being fatuous.'

'I was referred to in that way sufficiently today to last me the remainder of my life. But tell me', Elizabeth said, after sipping her wine, 'what you mean by annoying foreign powers. It all sounds rather serious and sinister, this matter of spite.'

'It's also damned ironic, but I had no idea until that fellow, what was his name, the cove who looked after us at the levée . . .?'

'Ponsonby, I think.'

'That's the fellow! Must have spent half his life bowing and scraping. What a damned tedious time he seems to have had of it too . . .'

'Took us both for a pair of country tree-sparrows and I'm not surprised, this gown must be at least three years out of fashion . . .'

'You looked perfect, my dear, even the King said so.'

Elizabeth clucked a laugh. 'Bless him,' she purred, 'he reminded me of a rather over-grown midshipman in his enthusiasm. He seemed to have a soft spot for you too.'

'Yes, odd that. I think 'tis because we both commanded the frigate *Andromeda* at one time or another and he still believes I took the *Suvorov* when I commanded her. Well,' Drinkwater said with a sigh, "'tis too late to disabuse him now that I'm dubbed knight for my trouble.'

'Knight Commander of the Bath,' his wife corrected, laughing, 'that is surely better than being an *Elder* Brother of the Trinity House.' She made a face. 'But you haven't told me of this spiteful snub to France.'

'Not France, my dear. Russia is the target of the Government's displeasure. The diplomatic vacillations of St Petersburg have, as Ponsonby put it, to be "disapproved of" and this disapproval has to be signalled by subtle means . . .'

'La, sir, and you are a "subtle means", are you? Well,' she burst out laughing, ' 'tis as ludicrous as being a Knight of the Bath or an Elder Brother . . .'

'And I never commanded a ship-of-the-line,' he laughed with her, adding ruefully, 'nor hoisted a flag, though I managed a broad pendant but once.'

'My dear Nathaniel, the King is not quite the fool he looks. Your services were more subtle than the means by which your knight-hood is to be used against the Russians, and the King knows sufficient of you to be aware that of all the post-captains on the list your name is the most deserving . . .'

'Oh come, my dear, that simply isn't true.' Drinkwater splut-tered a modest protest only slightly tinged with hypocrisy.

'Well I think so, anyway.'

'I approve of your partiality.' Drinkwater smiled and looked about the room. They had hardly changed a thing since the house had been left to him as a legacy by Lord Dungarth. It had appar-ently been the only asset in Dungarth's estate that had not been sold to satisfy his creditors. It was a modest place, set in a terrace in Lord North Street, and it had been Dungarth's intention that Drinkwater should use it when he succeeded the Earl as head of the Admiralty's Secret Department. In the event Drinkwater's tenure of that office had been short-lived and the house had merely become a convenience for Drinkwater and Elizabeth when they were in London. They had discussed selling it now that the war was over and they had purchased Gantley Hall, but Elizabeth, knowing the modest but secure state of their finances, had demurred. Now, with her husband's knighthood, it had proved a wise decision. She was already contemplating a visit or two to a dress-making establishment near Bond Street in anticipation of the coming season.

'I thought His Majesty paid you a singular compliment in speaking to you for so long,' she said, echoing his mood of satisfaction.

Drinkwater laughed. 'Whatever King William's shortcomings,' he said, 'he does not lack the loquacity or enthusiasm of an old sailor.'

'They say he knew Nelson.'

'They say he doted on Nelson,' Drinkwater added, 'and certainly he admired Nelson greatly, but poor Pineapple Poll had not a shred of Nelson's qualities . . .'

Drinkwater refilled their glasses and they sat in silence for a while. He thought of the glittering occasion from which they had just returned, the brilliance of the ladies' dresses and the uniforms of the men, the sparkling of the glass chandeliers and mirrors, the powdered immobility of the bewigged servants and the ducking, bobbing obsequiousness of the professional courtiers.

Among such surroundings, the pop-eyed, red-faced, white-haired King seemed almost homely, dressed as he had been in his admiral's uniform, leading in Queen Adelaide who had, after years of open scandal, replaced Mrs Jordan, the actress. The King's eyes had actually lit up when he caught sight of Drinkwater's uniform, and after the ceremony of the investiture, he had asked how high Drinkwater's name stood upon the list of post-captains.

'I am not certain, Your Majesty,' Drinkwater had confessed.

'Not certain! Not certain, sir! Why damme, you must be the only officer in the service who don't know, 'pon my soul! Confess it, sir, confess it!'

'Willingly, sir, but it is perhaps too late to expect an honour greater than that done me today.'

'Well said, sir! Well said!' The King had turned to Elizabeth. ' 'Pon my soul, ma'am, your husband makes a damned fine diplomat, don't he, eh?'

Elizabeth dropped a curtsey. 'Your Majesty is too kind.'

'Perhaps he ain't always quite so diplomatic, eh?' The King laughed. 'Well, let that be, eh? But permit me to say, ma'am, that he is a lucky man in having you beside him, a damned lucky man. I speak plain, ma'am, as an old sailor.' The King looked at Drinkwater. 'Charming, sir, charming. I hope you won't keep her in the country all the year.'

'As Your Majesty commands.'

The King had dropped his voice. 'I purposed your knighthood years ago, Sir Nathaniel, d'ye recall it?'

'Of course, sir, you were most kind in writing to me . . .'

'Stuff and nonsense. You might have confounded Boney, and saved Wellington and all those brave fellows the trouble of Waterloo. Damned funny thing, providence; pulls one up, sets another down, don't you know . . . Ah, Lady Callender . . .'

'What are you laughing about?'

Elizabeth's question brought him back to the present. 'Oh, the King's notion that I might have saved Wellington the trouble of fighting Waterloo. It was absolute nonsense, of course. I could only have done that had the Congress at Vienna decided to send Napoleon to the Azores rather than Elba. His Majesty has, it seems, a rather loose grasp of detail.'

'But he recollected that promise to make you a knight.'

'Remarkably yes, but I think it had more to do with taking a revenge upon the Admiralty, of putting Their Lordships in their places, than with upsetting the Russians, as Ponsonby suggested.'

'Why so? *Had* Their Lordships at the Admiralty upset him?'

'Indeed, yes. They had, you may recall, prevented him from commanding anything after *Andromeda* on account of the harshness with which he ruled his ship . . . except, of course, the squadron that took King Louis back to France, and then he had Blackwood to hold his hand. I think he felt the humiliation keenly, though I have equally little doubt but that Their Lordships acted correctly.'

'I had forgotten . . .'

'We have so much to forget, Elizabeth. Our lives have been rich in incident, I often think.'

'Well, my dear, you have all that heart could desire now,' Elizabeth said.

'Indeed I have. I can think of nothing else except a lasting peace that our children may enjoy.'

'I do not think even *your* knighthood will annoy the Russians to the extent of spoiling that, Nathaniel,' Elizabeth said, laughing

'Indeed I hope not,' her husband agreed. 'Here's to you, Lady Drinkwater, and the luck of Midshipman Drinkwater who found you in an apple orchard.'

'And to you, my darling Sir Nathaniel.'

'May I speak?'

'Of course, sir,' said Frey, glaring at the immobile Drinkwater as he stood in a futile attempt to look impressively relaxed. Frey's attention shifted from his model to his canvas as he worked for some moments, his face intense, his eyes flickering constantly from his image to his subject. Periodically he paused to recharge his brush from his palette or mix more colour.

'This reminds me of standing on deck for hours in bad weather, or in chase of the enemy. One is obliged to be there but one has nothing to do, relying upon others to work the ship. Consequently one passes into a state of suspended animation.'

'Yet,' Frey said, placing his brush between his teeth while he turned to his side table to replenish his dipper with turpentine, 'yet you always seemed to be aware of something going wrong, or some detail needing attention, I recall.'

'Oh yes, I was not asleep, though I have once or twice fallen asleep on my feet. But under the cataleptic conditions I speak of, I had, as it were, retreated into myself. All my professional instincts were alert but my mind was passive, not actively engaged in the process of actually thinking.'

'And you are not thinking now?' asked Frey almost absently, as he worked at the coils of bullion that fell from Drinkwater's shoulders.

'Well I'm thinking *now*, of course,' Drinkwater said, with a hint of exasperation which he instantly suppressed, 'but a moment ago I felt almost disembodied, as though I was recalled from elsewhere.'

'Ah, then your soul was about to take flight from your body . . .'

'And how the deuce d'you know that?'

'I don't know it. I just think it might be an explanation,' Frey said simply, looking at Drinkwater but not catching his eye and immediately returning to his canvas.

'You don't think it might be that I was just about to fall asleep?'

'You said yourself', said Frey, working his brush vigorously,

484

'that it reminded you of how you felt when you stood on deck. Presumably you weren't about to go to sleep then? In fact I supposed it to be a natural state to enable you to remain thus for many hours.' He paused, then added, 'My remark about the soul may have been a little facetious.'

'You wish to concentrate upon your work. I shall remain quiet.'

Frey straightened up, relaxed and looked directly at his sitter. 'Not at all, sir. Please don't misunderstand . . .'

'My dear Frey, I am not deliberately misunderstanding you. But I have never thought you had the capacity for facetiousness. I think you believed what you said, but you have no means of justifying it on scientific principles and so you abandon it rather than have me ravage it with my sceptical ridicule.'

Frey smiled. 'You were always very perceptive, Sir Nathaniel, it was one of the more unnerving things about serving under you.'

'Was I?' Drinkwater asked, his curiosity aroused. 'Well, well. I suppose as you are engaged in painting my portrait it would not be inappropriate to quiz you a little on your subject.'

Frey laughed. 'Not at all inappropriate, Sir Nathaniel, but immodest in the extreme.'

'Nevertheless,' persisted Drinkwater with a grin, 'my curiosity quite naturally overwhelms my modesty.'

'Well that is not unusual, but it is rather disappointing in so unusual a character as yourself, sir.'

'Ah, now you are just baiting me and I'm not certain I should rise to it.'

'Perhaps that is truly my intention.' Frey resumed work, dipping his brush in the turpentine, filling it with a dark colour and applying it to his canvas with those quick, almost indecently furtive glances at his subject that Drinkwater found strangely unnerving.

'What? To put me off pursuing this line of conversation?'

'Just so, sir. To embarrass you into silence.'

'Do your sitters always want to talk?'

Frey shrugged. 'Some do and some don't. Most that do soon get bored. I am apt to reply monosyllabically or occasionally not at all, and then, depending upon my sitter's station and person, I am obliged to apologize.'

'But I can quite understand the concentration necessary to execute . . . By the by, why does an artist "execute" a portrait?'

'I really have no idea, sir.'

'Anyway, the concentration necessary to do your work must of necessity abstract you from gossip.' Drinkwater paused, then went on, 'So some of your sitters are difficult?'

'Many regard me as no more than a servant or at best a clever craftsman. The example of successful artists like Sir Joshua Reynolds counts for little here in the country, and wherever the gentry pay, they believe they own . . .'

'There is more than a hint of bitterness in your voice, Frey.' Drinkwater sighed. 'I am sorry I did not do more for your advancement in the Service. I can see it must irk you to be painting me in sash and star . . .'

'That is not what I meant, Sir Nathaniel!' Frey protested, lowering brush and palette, and emerging fully from behind his easel, no longer looking at Drinkwater as a subject for his brush.

'I know, I know, my dear fellow, of course it isn't what you meant, but I know it is what you feel and it is perfectly natural . . .'

'No, sir, you read me wrongly. I am aware that you did what you could for those of us who regarded ourselves as being of your "family", but the death of poor James Quilhampton, though providing me with the opportunity of happiness with Catriona, set an incongruously high price upon so-called advancement. Believe me, I have no regrets. Indeed, sir, you will not know that, upon your recommendation, I was asked to accompany Buchan's Arctic voyage in 1818. I rejected the appointment because I did not wish Catriona to be left alone again; she had suffered too much in the past.'

'I had no idea you might have gone north with Buchan,' Drinkwater said. 'Well, well. But you are a kind fellow, Frey, I have long thought you such.'

'No more than the next man, sir,' Frey said, colouring, and then he looked down at his palette, refilled his brush and resumed work.

For a moment the two men's private thoughts occupied them and silence returned to the studio. Drinkwater thought of his own Arctic voyage and the strange missionary named Singleton whom he had left among the Innuit people. And then, as he was stirred by an uncomfortable memory, the door opened and Catriona entered bearing a tray. Instinctively Drinkwater moved, before realizing the enormity of his crime.

'My dear Frey, I beg your pardon.'

Frey laid down his gear, wiped his hands on a rag and smiled at his wife. 'Please do break the pose, Sir Nathaniel. Let us enjoy Catriona's chocolate while it is hot.'

'He will keep you sitting there until your blood runs cold, Sir Nathaniel,' she said knowingly, guying her husband, her tawny eyebrows raised in disapproval. 'A've told him about the circulation of the blood, but he takes no notice of good Scottish science.'

'Thank you, my dear,' Drinkwater said, smiling and taking the cup and saucer. 'I am sure this will restore my circulation satisfactorily.'

Drinkwater looked at Catriona's pleasant, open face. She was no beauty, but he had seen a portrait of her by her husband which had the curious effect of both looking like her to the life yet investing her with a quite haunting loveliness. Elizabeth, who had also seen the painting, had remarked upon it, attributing this synthesis to a combination of Frey's technical skill and his personal devotion.

'It is', Elizabeth had explained in their carriage going home, 'what makes of a commonplace portrait, a work of art.'

He thought of that now as Catriona placed Frey's cup of chocolate upon his work table, and he saw the small gesture of gratitude Frey made as they smiled at each other. He envied them this completeness. His own contentment with Elizabeth was quite different. He acknowledged his own deficiencies and was reminded of the uncomfortable thought that had entered his head with Catriona's appearance.

'Will you take tea with us, Sir Nathaniel, when he has finished with you?'

'That is most kind, my dear. If I am not an inconvenience.'

'You will be most welcome.' She stood beside her husband, looking from the portrait to Drinkwater who, by agreement, was not to see the work until Frey judged it complete.

'I shall finish all but the detail of the background today,' Frey said.

'I shall be glad. When I am under such scrutiny I feel like an object.'

'That is what he sees you as,' Catriona threw in. 'However,' she added, putting her head to one side and looking at the portrait, 'I think you will be tolerably pleased.' And with that pronouncement she gathered up her skirts and swept from the room.

Frey and Drinkwater exchanged glances, the former's eyes twinkling. 'She is my harshest critic.'

'And yet the picture you painted of her is outstanding.'

'Oh that. She will not let me hang it. Since that day I showed it to you and Lady Drinkwater, it has stood facing the wall. I think when I am dead, Catriona will burn it,' he said, laughing and gathering up his brushes and palette again. 'They are strange creatures, women . . .'

And yet, thought Drinkwater, resuming his seat and the pose, you understand them infinitely better than I do myself.

'A little more to the left, sir . . . No, no, just the trunk of the body . . .'

Again they fell silent. Drinkwater knew the uncomfortable thought could not be excluded from his mind, and that it must needs be uttered. He had never enjoyed complete intimacy with any other human being, not even Elizabeth, for there had always been that vast gulf created by his profession, his long absences and his ignorance of most of her life ashore. There had been the brief and torrid physical passion with the American widow, a moment of intimate joy so exquisite that its aftermath was a long and lingering guilt. The effect was to have prohibited a more destructive lust with Hortense Santhonax, for she had infected him with another sickness, that of discontent and wild longing. He had, by chance, captured a portrait of her when he took her husband's ship *Antigone* in the Red Sea, and it had lain like a guilty, reproachful secret in the bottom of his seachest for years until he had burnt it. It was ironic that she, perhaps the most beautiful of the women whom he had known, now lay under the ruined flint arch of the priory at Gantley Hall, alongside his wild and ungovernable brother Ned.

But perhaps men, at least that majority of men in his situation and from which Frey was excluded, never got close to women. It demanded the most noble sacrifice upon Elizabeth's part for her to comprehend all the complex workings of his seaman's mind. God knew she was a marvel and had done her best! That he was unable to understand her in her entirety was, he concluded, one of those imperfections in life that were profoundly regrettable, but equally profoundly unavoidable. The enigma resided in the eternal question as to why mankind troubled itself with the unattainable. He sighed. Providence had regulated the matter very ill, but that is why many men, he supposed, were often easier in the company of their own sex. He had been close to young Quilhampton and had counted him a friend. After James's death, for which he still held himself accountable, he had grown very friendly with Frey. That last escapade upon the coast of France had left them with more than the bond of shared experience, and he thought that the thing had coalesced when Frey had said that if Drinkwater handled *Kestrel*, he himself would fight her. In that odd moment of decision, they had become one, divining each other's thoughts as they engaged in their horrible profession of execution.

And so, in the circumambulatory nature of thoughts, he was returned to the central theme of his anxiety and unconsciously uttered a deep sigh.

'You seem to be in some distress, Sir Nathaniel. Is it the pose?'

'What?'

'Are you all right, sir?'

'No, if I am honest, I am far from being all right . . .'

Frey lowered his brush and stepped forward. 'Please relax, sir,' he said, alarmed. 'Pray invigorate yourself!'

Drinkwater smiled. 'No, no, my dear fellow, do not concern yourself. I am merely troubled by conscience. Invigorating myself at such a moment might prove fatal!'

Frey gave his sitter a steady, contentious look; what they had between them come to call, with reference to Catriona, 'a Scotch glare'.

'No, really. I am quite content to sit still a little longer.'

Frey stepped back behind the easel and resumed work. 'I cannot imagine why your conscience should trouble you, sir. I have not known another person with your sense of duty.'

'That is kind of you, Frey, but it may be the essence of the problem. Duty is a cold calling. It induces men to murder, giving them licence without consolation. Have you any idea how many men I have killed?'

'Well no, sir.' Frey looked up, astonished at the candour of the question.

'No,' replied Drinkwater bleakly, 'neither have I.'

'But . . .' Frey began, but Drinkwater pressed on.

'One remembers only a few of them and they were almost all friends! James, for example . . .'

'You did not kill James!' Frey protested.

'There were others, Frey . . .'

'I cannot believe . . .'

'You do not have to. It is only I who need to know. And I don't . . .'

'But you once said to me that you did not believe in God, Sir Nathaniel, that matters were moved by great but providential forces. Providence has been good to you. This portrait, for example,' Frey said, stepping back and waving his brush at the canvas, 'is evidence of that. Surely the reward is to be enjoyed . . . To be appreciated . . .'

'You are probably right, my dear fellow. I was always a prey to the blue-devils. We drag these deadweights through our lives, and the megrims have been a private curse of mine for many years.'

'You have been lonely, sir,' Frey said reasonably. 'Perhaps it is the penalty for bearing responsibility.' He paused and worked for a moment of furious concentration. 'Perhaps it is the fee you must pay to achieve what you have achieved, a kind of blood-money.'

Drinkwater grinned and nodded. 'You are a great consolation, Frey, and I thank you for it. Alas,' he added sardonically, 'I think there may yet be unnamed tortures still awaiting me.'

'Apart from your rheumaticks, d'you mean?' Frey replied, returning the smile, pleased to see the lugubrious mood lifting.

'Oh yes, far worse than mere rheumaticks.'

For a further fifteen minutes, silence fell companionably between them and then Frey stepped back, laid down his brushes and palette, and picked up a rag. Vigorously wiping his hands he said, 'There, that is all I shall need you for. I think perhaps you had better pass verdict, Sir Nathaniel. Though I say so myself,' he added, grinning with self-satisfaction, 'I do believe 'tis you to the life.'

Chapter Sixteen

The Rescue

The spectral faces of the dead came near him now, touching him with their cold breath. If he expected vengeful reproaches, there was only a feeling of acceptance, that all things came to this, and that this was all there was and would ever be. His mind filled with regrets and great sadnesses, too complex and profound for him to recognize in their particulars, and in these too he felt touched by the unity of creation, reached through the uniqueness of his own existence.

In his dying, providence made one last demand upon him.

There was someone near him, someone tugging at the oar with a frantic desperation which seemed quite unnecessary.

'Oh, God!' the man spluttered, thrashing wildly. 'Oh, thank God!'

Dimly it was borne in upon Drinkwater that clinging with him on the oar was Mr Quier.

'Sir Nathaniel . . . 'Tis you . . .' The oar sank beneath their combined weight. 'It's me, Sir Nathaniel . . . Quier, sir, Second Mate . . .'

Odd that he should have known two men whose names began with that curious letter of the alphabet. Odder still that he should make the comparison now, in this extremity, a last habitual shred of rational thought. But he was feeling much warmer and he had seen Quilhampton a little while ago, he was sure of it. Or perhaps it was Frey . . . Frey and Catriona, yes, that was it, the presence of Catriona had confused him.

'The oar', he said with a slow deliberation, 'will not sustain us both . . .'

Drinkwater felt the oar suddenly buoyant again, relieved of the young man's weight. Mr Quier, it appeared, had relinquished it and kicked away.

This was wrong. It was not what he had meant by his remark,

but it was so difficult to talk, for his jaw was stiffened against the task. With a tremendous effort of will, Drinkwater hailed Quier.

'Mr Quier, don't let go, I beseech you!'

Quier headed back, gasping and spitting water, fighting his sodden clothing in his effort to stay afloat. He suddenly grasped the oar loom again with a desperate lunge just as Drinkwater let go.

'Hold on, my boy,' he whispered, 'they're sure to find you . . .'

It was Mr Forester who saw the man in the water waving. He shouted the news to Captain Poulter without taking his eyes off the distant speck as, every few seconds, it disappeared behind a wave only to reappear bobbing over the passing crest.

'Six points off the port bow, sir! Man waving!'

Poulter called out, 'Hard a-port! Stop port paddle!' He heard with relief the order passed below via the chain of men and was gratified when *Vestal* swung in a tight turn. Poulter was sodden with the perspiration of anxiety, yet his mouth was bone dry and he felt a stickiness at the corners of his lips.

'Come on, come on,' he muttered as he willed the ship to turn faster.

'Three points . . . Two!' *Vestal* came round with ponderous slowness.

''Midships! Steadeeee . . .'

'Coming right ahead!' Forester bellowed, his voice cracking with urgency.

'Meet her!' Poulter ordered. 'Steady as she goes!'

'Steady as she goes, sir. East by south, a quarter south, sir.'

'Aye, aye. Make it so. Both paddles, dead slow ahead!'

Vestal responded and Poulter, seeing Forester's arm pointing right ahead, ordered Potts to bring the ship's head back to starboard a few degrees, to open the bearing of the man in the water whom he himself could see now.

'Steer east by south a half south.' He turned aft from the bridge wing to check the men were still at their stations, ready to lower the boat once more. Reassured, he noted they were only awaiting the word of command. Poulter swung forward again and watched as they approached the man in the water. Poulter could see it was Quier, the second mate, who maintained himself by means of his arms hanging over the loom of one of the smashed boat's oars.

'Thank God for small mercies,' Poulter breathed to himself, then, raising his voice, he ordered: 'Stop engines! Half astern!'

Beneath him, hidden under the box and sponson, the paddle-wheels churned into reverse. Slowly Quier drifted into full view almost alongside them, some twenty yards away on the port beam. As *Vestal* came to a stop, he looked up at them. He was quite exhausted, his face a white mask devoid of any emotion, bereft of either relief or joy. Quier's expression reminded Poulter of a blank sheet of paper on which he might write 'Lost at sea', 'Drowned' or 'Rescued'.

'Stop her!' he called out, then, leaning over the rail, shouted, 'Boat away!'

So close was Quier that it seemed almost superfluous to lower the boat. It looked as if he might be hooked neatly with the long boathook and hove on board like a gaffed fish, but Poulter knew the second officer's life was not saved yet, that considerable effort had still to be expended by the boat's crew to haul the helpless, sodden man out of the sea and into the boat. Poulter turned to the able-seaman stationed on the port bridge wing as lookout.

'Run down to the officers' steward and tell him to bring hot blankets from the boiler room up to the boat-deck right away.'

'Aye, aye, sir.' The man abandoned his post for a moment and disappeared below. Poulter envied the sailor the opportunity to run about, for he found such moments of inactivity irksome in the extreme. He was impatient now. Locating a man was so damnably difficult and the weather was not going to last. The glass was already falling and the sky to the westwards looked increasingly threatening

Poulter frowned; where there was one, there might also be another. Carefully he scanned the heaving surface of the grey-blue sea surrounding the ship for a further sign of life, but could see nothing. He made himself repeat the process twice, working outwards in a circle of ever-increasing diameter, surveying the scene slowly so that he reckoned to cover every few square feet as the sea writhed and undulated beneath his patient scrutiny. He held in his head a mental chart of the search pattern he had carried out. Although he knew how, from a single central point, a combination of wind, tide and the frantic efforts men might make under duress could spread the debris from a capsized boat, he was as certain as he could be that *Vestal* had quartered the area in which they might reasonably expect to find the upset crew. Indeed, they had not been unsuccessful, for with Quier they had now found everyone but Sir Nathaniel Drinkwater.

Sadly, the evidence, or lack of it, seemed conclusive, and by now Poulter privately held out no hope for the elderly captain. The shock alone must have dispatched him long since. Poulter's ruminations were brought to an end as a cheer went up from the men waiting at the davit falls on the boat-deck. Quier was being taken aboard the boat, and a moment later the crew had their oars out again and were vigorously plying them as they pulled back towards the waiting ship. Putting the tiller hard over, the coxswain skilfully spun the boat in under the suspended blocks and his crew hooked on to the falls. Seldom had Poulter seen it done smarter. The boat fairly flew upwards as the falls were hove in, plucking her out of the water.

'Mr Forester!'

'Sir?'

'I don't suppose Quier knows anything of Captain Drinkwater, but ask.'

'Aye, aye, sir!'

Potts was waiting at the wheel as Poulter called out, 'Steady as you go! Half speed ahead!' *Vestal* gathered way and recommenced her search. The lookout had returned from his errand and a moment later Forester joined Poulter on the bridge.

'Sir! Don't go too far away, Quier says Drinkwater was with him a little while ago and that he insisted on leaving the oar to Quier. Apparently it would not support them both.'

'Does Quier think . . .?'

Forester shook his head. 'I don't think Quier can think of anything very much, sir. He has no idea how long he has been in the water and certainly not of how long he has been hanging on to that oar. But it seems Drinkwater was definitely alive not so very long ago.'

'Very well.' With a sinking heart Poulter was convinced he already knew the worst: old man or not, Captain Drinkwater had been lost at sea in an unfortunate accident. 'We shall continue the search, Mr Forester,' he said formally. 'Tell the lookouts to remain sharp-eyed. We don't give up until there is no hope at all, d'you understand?'

'Yes, of course, sir.'

*

Two hundred yards away, one cable's length or one-tenth of a nautical mile distant from the *Vestal*, Captain Sir Nathaniel Drinkwater caught a last glimpse of the ship. It was a dark mark upon his fading, no more. It meant nothing to him, for he was disembodied and might have been at Gantley Hall, walking on the soft, rabbit-cropped grass that he always thought of as a luxurious carpet. Elizabeth was there too, and somewhere about the ruins of the priory were the laughing voices of Richard and Charlotte Amelia. He remembered that he hardly knew their children and tried to tell Elizabeth how much he regretted the fact, but somehow he was unable to, although she was beside him and he could see her face quite clearly in the swiftly gathering dusk. He was certain he was holding her hand, but the children had gone.

They had often walked beneath the ruined arch of the priory in the long years they were granted together. Gantley Hall was a modest house, but the ivy-covered remnant in the grounds gave the place a fashionably Gothick aura and had proved a fitting resting-place for Hortense and Edward, two spirits who had never, it seemed to Drinkwater, had anywhere to call their own.

Frey had been right, as Frey so often was, in saying that providence had been good to him.

Providence had been kind to his family too. Charlotte Amelia had married, and had had children, though he could not recall her married name. It bothered him and it bothered him too that he could not remember how many children she had had, or what their names were. Had not one died? Yes, the little boy, the third child. He could ask Elizabeth, but she would think him an old fool for not knowing about his grandchildren. And what had happened to Richard? He had not married, had he?

It was almost dark now and they had turned back towards the house. He felt Elizabeth's hand dissolve from his own and she moved on ahead of him. He wanted to ask her the answers to these terrible questions. She would know and it no longer mattered what she would think of him for having forgotten. Elizabeth would help him, he felt sure, but she was walking away from him and growing smaller and smaller with the distance that seemed to grow inexorably between them . . .

He tried to call her name . . .

'There is no need for you to be on the bridge, Mr Quier,' Poulter said as the Second Officer appeared, wrapped in warm blankets. He was deathly pale and still shaking with cold. 'You should go below; you will catch your death of cold, sir!'

'I'm all right, sir, it's Sir Nathaniel, sir . . .'

'What about him?'

'We were together, sir. Right up to the end.'

Poulter frowned. 'Mr Quier, while we lay alongside you getting you inboard, I searched the surrounding sea meticulously. I could see nothing.'

'But he gave me the oar, sir. Insisted I had it, though he was clinging to it first. He saved my life, sir.'

'Mr Quier,' Poulter said kindly, 'you are still feeling the effects of your ordeal. You had been in the water for well over an hour. Pray go below and remain there until later. I do assure you we shall continue to look for him, but I fear we are already too late. Console yourself. In due time you will simply recall Sir Nathaniel's last act as one of great selflessness.'

'I thought perhaps the gulls might have found him and have given us a clue,' Poulter said, 'but the wind is getting up again and we will have a full gale by the end of the afternoon.' He raised his voice. 'Hard astarboard and steady on sou' sou' west.'

Vestal rolled heavily as she turned and the three men on the bridge wing steadied themselves by grasping the rail, their faces stung by a light shower that skittered across the sea.

'I think, Captain Poulter, that we must regretfully conclude that Sir Nathaniel has drowned.' Captain Drew turned and looked aft, raising his eyes to the ensign. 'We had better half-mast the colours.'

'I'll see to it, sir,' Forester said, and he crossed the bridge to where one of the lookouts still stared out over the heaving grey waste of the Atlantic Ocean.

'I shall give it another hour, sir,' Poulter said firmly.

'You are wasting your time. Stand the additional lookouts down now, Captain Poulter,' Drew said, watching Forester dispatch the able-seaman aft to tend the ensign halliards. 'I think we have done all that we can.'

'I command the ship, Captain Drew, and I ran the boat down, God forgive me. The responsibility is mine . . .'

'Forester told me the telegraph chain parted. It is what is to be expected from so newfangled a contraption. It was not your fault and I shall not say that it was, if that is what is concerning you.' Drew's tone was testy. 'He was an old man, Captain Poulter. Infirm. Rheumaticky. The shock of immersion has killed him long since. Quier's notions of the passage of time have been distorted by his ordeal. Sir Nathaniel could not possibly have survived for very long.'

'That is probable, Captain Drew, but it would have been better if, after so many distinguished years' service, he had died in his bed.'

Drew gave Poulter a long look, sensing the reproach in his voice. 'You do not think we should have attempted the landing, eh? Is that it?'

Poulter sighed. 'I have observed that such so-called misfortunes often follow a single mistake or misjudgement. The fault seems compounded by fate. An error swiftly becomes a disaster.'

'And you think', Drew persisted, 'that we should not have made the attempt?'

'I shall always regret that I did not dissuade you, sir, yes.'

'And you therefore blame me?' Drew asked indignantly.

'I said, sir,' Poulter replied quietly, 'that I shall always regret that I failed to dissuade you from leaving the ship and making the attempt.'

'That verges on the insolent, Captain Poulter,' Drew said, stiffening.

'As you wish, Captain Drew . . .'

For a moment Drew seemed about to leave the bridge, then he hesitated and thought better of it. Poulter turned away and stared about him again, dismissing Drew from his mind. There would inevitably be some unpleasantness in the aftermath of this unfortunate affair, but no good would come of moping over it while there was still a task to be done, no matter how hopeless. There was a definite bite to the wind now and the rain came again in a longer squall that hissed across the sea. The day was dissolving in a monotonous grey that belied the high summer of the season. He had almost forgotten Captain Drew when the Elder Brother cleared his throat, reclaiming Poulter's attention.

'Let us say no more of the matter now, Captain Poulter,' Drew said. 'Sir Nathaniel died doing his duty and he was a sea-officer of impeccable rectitude.'

'Indeed he was, sir,' Poulter said coolly. 'Let us hope his widow finds that a sufficient consolation.'

Two miles away Nathaniel Drinkwater gave up the ghost. The faults and follies of his life, the joys and sorrows, finally faded from his consciousness. In his last moments he felt an overwhelming panic, but then the pain ebbed from his body and he became subsumed by a light of such blinding intensity that it seemed he must cry out for fear of it, and yet it did not seem uncomfortable, nor the end so very terrible.

The Yellow Admiral

The arrival of mail at Gantley Hall was sufficiently unusual to arouse a certain curiosity upon the morning of 20 July 1843. The post-boy was met by Billy Cue who had heard the horse and skidded out on his board to see if his services were required. The legless Billy had acquired his name from the line-of-battle ship *Belliqueux*, aboard which he had been conceived, but he had long since converted himself from the sea-urchin he had been born to a general handyman in the Drinkwater household. Susan Tregembo had originally put him to work scrubbing the flags in her kitchen, a task for which she felt him fitted, but Billy's good nature was undaunted by this practical approach and, by degrees, he made himself indispensable. He had grown into a good-looking man and was said to cut a dash among the more soft-hearted of the local farm girls, so that, upon the death of her husband, it was rumoured that Susan Tregembo allowed Billy into more than her kitchen.

He made up for his lack of mobility by skating about on a board fitted with castors, driven by his powerful arms which wielded a short pair of crutches. With these contrivances, he was able to get around with remarkable agility. He had also acquired a considerable skill as a carpenter, working on a bench set one foot above the level of his workshop floor. Here he had made a number of stools, steps and low tables, and these permitted him to carry out a multitude of tasks, the most remarkable of which was the care and grooming of Drinkwater's horses. Though Drinkwater was no lover of horse-flesh, the demands of household and farm had required the maintenance of four or five patient beasts who could pull a small carriage or trap, or act as hack when their master or mistress required a mount. Thus, while he might black boots, scrub floors and polish silver, it was in the stables of Gantley Hall that Billy Cue reigned as king.

'You are an ingenious fellow, Billy,' Captain Drinkwater had said when he had first seen the arrangement his protégé had made in one of the stalls to enable him to curry-comb the horses.

'Got the notion from the graving dock in Portsmouth, sir. A set of catwalks at shoulder height lets me get right up to the beasts,' Billy had said from his elevated station.

'Are you fond of horses then, Billy?' Drinkwater had asked.

'Aye, sir, mightily,' Billy had replied, his eyes shining enthusiastically.

'But you've never ridden one?'

'Not with me stumps, sir, no.'

'Then you had better make such use of the trap as you wish. 'Tis no good having a first-class groom who cannot get about the countryside.'

Billy's gratitude had resulted in daily offers of the trap being at Elizabeth's command and an increase in errands into Woodbridge or even Ipswich, notwithstanding the most inclement weather, while any horse arriving at Gantley Hall drew an immediate reaction from Billy. Thus, when the post-boy arrived on that fateful morning, it was Billy who took delivery of the letters and brought them to Susan.

'Two letters,' he announced, 'one from the Admiralty and one from, er . . .' He scrutinized the post-mark, but was unable to make head or tail of it and Susan swiftly took both from him with a little snort of irritation, indicating that Billy was trespassing upon preserves forbidden him by the proprieties of life. Susan cast her own eyes over the superscriptions and sniffed.

'Her Ladyship's gone for a walk,' Billy offered helpfully. 'The usual place, d'you want me to . . .?'

'You mind your horses, my lad,' Susan scolded, 'I'll see to these,' and gathering her skirts up, she swept from the kitchen, leaving a grinning Billy in her wake.

'You're a curious woman, Susie,' he muttered, chuckling to himself as he watched her run off in pursuit of her mistress. She had never ceased nagging him as if he were a boy when they met about their duties, which was a strange and incomprehensible contradiction to her behaviour towards him as a man.

Susan Tregembo was a woman for whom idleness was a sin and for whom keeping busy had at first been a necessary solace and later became a habit. But though she manifested an unconscious irritation when she discovered idleness in others, those who knew her well forgave her brusque manner, for much of her activity was directed at the comfort of others, and in her devotion to 'the Captain' and his wife she was selfless. Neither had been bred to servants and they never took this devotion for granted, least of all Elizabeth who, in her heart of hearts, would many a time in the loneliness of her isolation have welcomed Susan as an equal. But her husband's rank made such things impossible and with his successes, culminating in his retirement and knighthood, had come the irreversible constraints of social conformity. For Susan, the matter was never in doubt. Elizabeth was of the quality because she possessed all the natural advantages of birth and education. Her Ladyship's penurious upbringing, her struggle to cope with the demands of running the household of a poor country parson and of maintaining some semblance of social standing in the face of the ill-concealed condescension of almost all with whom she was obliged to come into contact, was not a matter that troubled Susan. She had married a man who had claimed that his future lay with Nathaniel Drinkwater, and she had fallen into step with his decision. It never occurred to Susan Tregembo that the same Nathaniel Drinkwater had had a hand in her husband's death. As she tripped across the grass towards the great ruined arch of the priory where she knew her mistress would be found, she was only conscious of being, in her own way, a fortunate creature, rescued from the harsh life of the waterfront with all its pitfalls and temptations by 'the Captain' and his lovely wife.

On warm summer mornings, it was Elizabeth's invariable habit to take a short walk in the grounds of the Hall. Since she had learned that on the east coast of Suffolk any change in the weather would not arrive until about an hour before noon, a fine morning beckoned. The grounds of the Hall were not extensive, bounded by a road, a stream and the farmland rented to Henry Vane, but they included the jagged ruins of the old priory and these, broken down though they were, anchored her to her ecclesiastical past, reminding her of her father more than her maker. Chiefly, however, they performed the function of a private retreat where she was able to escape the demands of the house and sit in the warm, windless sunshine, content with a book, her correspondence, or simply her own thoughts. Her husband had been much in her mind of late.

She had had difficulty reconciling herself to his absences on account of the Trinity House. She thought him too old for such duties and the jokes about his appointment as an 'Elder' Brother had seemed somewhat too near the mark for wit. Though he cited the appointments of octogenarian admirals to posts of the highest importance during the late war, claiming that the responsibilities of Barham and St Vincent far outweighed those of a mere 'Trinity Brother', her husband's assurances failed to mollify Elizabeth. She had long nurtured a chilling conviction that Nathaniel would not be spared to die in his bed like any common country gentleman, and for several days past she had slept uneasily, troubled by dreams.

In the daylight she had chided herself for a fool, rationalizing the irrational with the reflection that she simply missed him, that she herself was old and that with age came the ineluctable fear of the future. And as she sat beneath the great arch, its flint edge jagged on one side, overgrown with ivy and populated by the buzzing of bees, its inner curve smooth with the masonry of its elegant coping, she was mesmerized by a single cloud which, pushed by a light breeze, moved against the sky and made it look as though the masonry was toppling upon her.

She was almost asleep when she heard the rustle of Susan approaching through the bushes which, she noted, needed trimming back to clear the path. Susan's appearance started a fluttering in Elizabeth's heart which increased as she saw the hastening nature of her housekeeper's approach and the letters in her hand.

'What is it, Susan?' Elizabeth asked anxiously, sitting up and pulling her spectacles from her reticule.

'Billy's just brought in two letters, your Ladyship, one's from the Admiralty . . .'

'The Admiralty?' Elizabeth frowned. 'What on earth does the Admiralty want?' She looked up at Susan as she took the two letters and then read the superscriptions.

'The other is to you, ma'am.'

'So I see. I suppose I had better open that first. Thank you, Susan.'

'Thank you, ma'am. ' Susan bobbed a curtsey and retreated, looking back as she passed through the bushes to where Elizabeth was opening the first letter. She read it with a cold and terrible certainty clutching at her heart. Unconsciously she rose to her feet as though the act might put back the clock and arrest the news. Captain Drew had been sparing of the details, wrapping the event up in the contrived platitudes of the day, expressing his deepest regrets and ending with a solicitous wish that Lady Drinkwater could take consolation from the fact that her husband had died gallantly for the sake of others. Exactly what Captain Drew meant by this assertion was not quite clear, nor did his phraseology soothe Elizabeth in any way. Distraught as she was, Elizabeth was not beyond detecting in Captain Drew's words both condescension and a poor command of self-expression.

But as she sat again, her tears coming readily, her down-turned mouth muttering, 'Oh, no, oh no, it should not have been like this', she thought something stirred beyond the arch. It was a man, but her tears half-blinded her. For a moment or two the certainty that it was her husband grew swiftly upon her, but the shadow length-ened and turned into Mr Frey.

'Lady Drinkwater, good morning. I do hope I didn't startle you. Forgive me for taking the liberty of entering through the farm . . . My dear Lady Drinkwater, what is the matter?'

'He's dead,' she said, looking up at the younger man. 'My hus-band's dead, drowned in a boating accident, at sea . . .' She held out Drew's letter for Frey to read.

'My dear, I'm so sorry . . .'

Overcome, Frey sat beside her and hurriedly whipped out his handkerchief, reading the letter with a trembling hand. After he had digested its contents he looked at Elizabeth. She shook her head. 'It had to happen,' she said as she began to cry inconsolably, 'but why at sea? Why not here, amongst his family?'

Frey put his arm round her and, when her sobbing had sub-sided to a weeping, she rose and he assisted her into the house.

It was Henry Vane who, much later, walking through from the farm to offer his condolences, found the second letter lying on the grass. Frey was still with Elizabeth and had sent Billy Cue into Woodbridge to summon Catriona and bring her out in the trap to stay with Elizabeth overnight. Vane presented himself and the lost letter.

'It seems to be from the Admiralty,' Vane said, handing it to Frey who, having taken a look at the embossed wafer, agreed.

'Thank you, Henry. I think it can be of little consequence now, but I suppose I should let Her Ladyship know.'

'How is she?' asked Vane, his open face betraying his concern.

'Inconsolable at the moment.'

'Would you present my condolences?'

Frey shook his head. 'No, no, my dear sir, you are of the family and have as much right as me to be here, come in, come in.'

Frey announced Vane and left him with Elizabeth for a few moments, joining them after an interval. Vane sat alongside her, holding her hand, and Frey noticed she seemed more composed.

'There was a second letter, Elizabeth,' Frey said softly. 'Vane found it; you must have dropped it.' He held it out towards her. 'It has an Admiralty seal.'

'Please open it. It cannot be of much importance now.' She smiled up at him and he slit the wafer and unfolded the letter. For a moment he studied it and then, lowering it, he said with a sigh, 'Sir Nathaniel attained flag rank on the 14th. He has been gazetted rear-admiral, Lady Drinkwater.'

'They are rather late, are they not?' Elizabeth said, with a hint of returning spirit.

'I think Sir Nathaniel would rather have died a post-captain than a yellow admiral,' Frey said with his engaging smile.

Elizabeth reached out her other hand and took Frey's. 'I am sure you are right, my dear,' she said, shaking her head, 'and I am sure he would rather have died at sea than in his bed, painful though that is for me to acknowledge. Do you not think so?'

Frey nodded and gently squeezed Elizabeth's hand. 'I rather think I do, my dear.'

It took some months for Elizabeth to feel her loss less acutely, but her husband's absences during the long term of their marriage had, despite their last years of intimacy, in some ways prepared her for widowhood.

'It seems to me', Catriona had once said to her, after the untimely death of her own first husband and before she had married Frey, 'that a sea-officer's wife lives in an unnaturally prolonged state of temporary widowhood in preparation for the actual event.' It was a sentiment with which Elizabeth perforce agreed. She was an old woman and her lot, compared with Catriona's for instance, had been a far easier one.

If she regretted anything, it was that she had not known her husband well until both of them were advanced in age. Now, that sweet pleasure, and it seemed very sweet in retrospect, was forever denied her. It was at this point that she recalled the task she had given him: that of recording his memoirs. About twelve weeks after the news of Drinkwater's death had arrived at Gantley Hall; after his body which had been washed up on the beach of Croyde Bay was sent home in its lead coffin; after the visits of their children and the renewed weeping that accompanied the funeral rites; and after Sir Nathaniel Drinkwater had been laid with due pomp and ceremony beside his brother Edward and the mysterious Hortense, it occurred to Elizabeth to go through her husband's papers more thoroughly than she had at first done.

She was familiar with most of what she found, though she had not read the pages of penned memories earlier, merely flicked through them. Nor did she now intend to read them in their entirety, but her eye was caught by this phrase or that, and as she dipped into them so the hours passed and she felt a curious contact with him as she sat in silence. Regretfully reaching the end of the document which had no real conclusion, but simply mentioned his continuing connection with the sea through the Trinity House, she was about to lay it down when a loose leaf of paper, folded in half and stuck in amid the rest, fluttered to the floor. She bent and picked it up, unfolding it as she did so.

It seemed to be a draft, separate from the main body of the memoirs and written with less certainty, for it contained several erasures and corrections. At the top right-hand corner was scribbled a date. With a fluttering heart, she noted it had been written on the eve of his departure to join the *Vestal*, and it struck her that he might have had some premonition of his death. It was not so curious a fancy, she thought, given his age and the exertions of the duty he was about to undertake. She had to wipe her eyes before the script swam into focus.

In Concluding these ~~Memoirs~~ Recollections, Drinkwater had written, *I am ~~almost~~ Compelled almost, to Review my Life, to Weigh the Balance of Profit and Loss, not in terms of Success, for Providence, as Frey reminded me, has been Materially Kind to me, but in terms of Usefulness. My Actions will have caused Grief in Quarters /quite unknown to me, and in Quarters known to me but not to Those whom I have Offended and this Troubles me. Such a Pricking of Conscience may be but an Indulgence, perhaps a Punishment in Itself for those whom I dispatched from Life had no such Period for ~~Contemplation~~ Reflection or Regret.*

Yet I was Compelled by Duty and I am left Wondering whether I am thereby Exculpated and whether Anyone takes Ultimate Responsibility? The King, perhaps? In whose Name and under whose Authority a Sea-Officer conducts himself and Who was Mad? Or is All Ordered by Providence? And is it therefore beyond our Comprehension?

If it were so, it would be a great burden lifted from my Soul.

~~I think that~~ ~~It seems that~~ ~~I can only conclude~~

In the end, the Complex <u>must</u> be rendered Simple, and our Understanding kept Imperfect.

Elizabeth laid the sheet of paper in her lap and stared out of the window. Grey clouds were sweeping in from the west and she would need a candle if she intended reading any more, but there was nothing else to read. Her husband had found a kind of peace, she thought, rising. As Frey said, providence had been very kind to him.

Author's Note

In this, the fourteenth and last in a series of novels which form the 'biography' of Nathaniel Drinkwater, I have taken some liberties with the patience of my readers. For this I must crave an indulgence. For twenty years I have accompanied Drinkwater and, from time to time, our lives have enjoyed curious parallels. His capture of the *Santa Teresa* and heady anticipation of prize money coincided with my own part in the salvage of a cargo ship in the North Sea which, at first sight, seemed to hold the promise of a small fortune; his incarceration in an attic office at the Admiralty happened when I myself relinquished sea-going command in exchange for an office desk. It was no accident that he assisted me in escaping my confinement, just as I engineered his own. There have been other, more technical comparisons, but they would be tedious to enumerate and, in this last novel, he has, at least at the time of writing, preceded me over the final threshold.

In the invention of Drinkwater and his adventures, I have worked through an obsessive fascination with the period in which he lived. Beyond the basic concept and a handful of historical facts, I started each story with no particular idea of what exactly would happen to the main protagonist. For me the process of writing was to find out, and to that extent Drinkwater's life was not entirely my own conscious creation. I have consequently derived much fun from the stimulation which this form of exploration produces, but one thing I resolved upon, that where what appeared to be expedient invention threw up a train of events, I must follow the train of cause and effect to its conclusion. To this end, this fourteenth book concludes several yarns, bringing together storylines begun in the earlier novels. It is for this that I ask my readers' indulgence, in the hope that they, like me, wanted to know what happened to Hortense, or Edward or Mr Frey, or why for years poor Nathaniel endured the recurring and horrible nightmare of the white lady.

As to the manner of Drinkwater's death, it is expected nowadays that a novelist must most assiduously research his subject. Some years ago, I came across an account by an eighteenth-century seaman who had only narrowly escaped drowning. It was powerfully written and made an impression on me, thus sowing the seed of an idea. Furthermore, by a series of personal misadventures, I have myself been three times helpless in the sea. On one of these rather desperate occasions, I did not expect to live.

For those who wish to know upon what historical hook the substance of this last tale is hung, the Trinity House Steamer *Vestal* did indeed run her own boat down on 14 July 1843 after abandoning an attempt to land at the foot of the cliffs at Hartland Point. Also drawn from life are Captain McCullough and the Sentinel Service, a little known part of the Royal Navy's rich history. As for the two troopers aboard *Cyclops* in 1780, it is matter of fact that in that year two men were dismissed from the 7th Queen's Own Light Dragoons and sent to serve in the Royal Navy as a punishment. Moreover, cheese issued by the royal dockyards was often of such age and consistency that sailors fashioned it into boxes and worked it like wood, and there is a record of a cheese being fashioned into a mast-truck, fitted with flag halliard sheaves and shipped atop a warship's mast where it remained for the duration of her commission. Such are the happy gleanings of assiduous research!

As for more seminal inspiration, whilst still a teenager I came across six battered volumes of William James's monumental *Naval History of Great Britain*, which records in meticulous and largely accurate detail every action fought by the Royal Navy during the wars of the French Revolution and Empire. I parted with my pocket money of half-a-crown, a sum which now sounds as archaic as the age of the books themselves, though they had been published a century before my own birth. Astonishingly, most of the pages were uncut. This purchase was to create a lifelong interest in maritime history and to result ultimately in the 'biography' of Nathaniel Drinkwater.

I am aware that when coming to the end of a much-enjoyed book, the reader is often assailed by a sense of regret. Something of the same tristesse hangs over me now as I tap out the last words of the saga. I have immensely enjoyed writing the series, but every voyage has its ending and Drinkwater exceeded his allotted three score years and ten to die not ignobly. To those of my readers who have shared something of this enjoyment, may I simply express my gratitude. Your support meant the whole tale could be told, and while your precise image of Nathaniel Drinkwater may differ slightly from my own, the substance of his invention is common to us both.

The Night Attack

This short story about Nathaniel Drinkwater was specially written for the second edition of *The Mammoth Book of Men o' War*. Set in August 1801 it fits chronologically between the fourth and fifth books of the fourteen titles in the Drinkwater series, following *The Bomb Vessel*, which ends with the newly promoted Commander Drinkwater returning from the Baltic where he was present at the Battle of Copenhagen, and takes place before Drinkwater's departure for the Arctic as Master and Commander of the sloop *Melusine*, described in *The Corvette*. There is a reference in an early chapter of *The Corvette* to Drinkwater having acquired a second wound as a result of taking part in Lord Nelson's abortive attack on French invasion forces assembling at Boulogne. Drinkwater had sustained an earlier wound in the right arm as a result of a sword-fight with Edouard Santhonax in an alleyway in Sheerness related in *A King's Cutter*. Although this second compounding disfigurement is alluded to on several occasions in the subsequent novels, the action in which Nathaniel Drinkwater received it is here related for the first time.

Chapter One

The Cutter

Commander Nathaniel Drinkwater stood poised expectantly in the stern of the cutter. He closed his watch as the first flowery plumes of smoke rose from the waists of the bomb-vessels anchored to the west of him and fished in his tail pocket for his Dollond glass. He caught sight of the thin line of one of the shell's trajectories as it rose overhead, culminated and then descended somewhere amid the forest of masts crowded in Boulogne Harbour. The brief orange glow of explosions told where the shells burst, throwing up clouds of grey and, Drinkwater fancied as he focused the telescope, the small and distant evidence of destruction.

'Give way if you please.'

Beside him Midshipman James Quilhampton marked the drift of the cutter by the altering transit of his shore marks. The coxswain, a man named Hathaway, ordered the seamen to ply their oars, maintaining station in advance of Vice-Admiral Lord Nelson's squadron in an attempt to mark the fall of the shells. As the thunderous booms of the ten and thirteen-inch mortars rolled across the rippled sea, Drinkwater felt a distinct lack of enthusiasm for his task. A better vantage point was to be had from the tops and mastheads of almost any one of Lord Nelson's men-of-war, including his own sixteen-gun brig-sloop *Wolf*, which lay at anchor offshore beyond the bomb-vessels. But Drinkwater, obedient to his lordship's command conveyed by a letter signed by Nelson's flag-captain, John Gore, had boarded the cutter sent from the flagship, taking Midshipman Quilhampton with him. Hence he now occupied his advanced station closest to the target of the mortars: the huge assembly of flat-boats, barges, peniches, radeaux, corvettes, luggers, gundalows and God knew what besides, assembled by General Bonaparte for the invasion of England. With peace between France and Austria, the war on the European continent had been won by the French. Great Britain was now isolated, the only hostile obstacle to the ambitions of Revolutionary France.

The tone of Gore's note reflected the hurried, piecemeal assembly of the so-called 'Anti-Invasion Flotilla'. It was under this grandiloquent name that the Admiralty had scratched together an opposing collection of frigates, sloops, bomb-vessels, gun-brigs and gun-boats. Their instructions to harry and deter the French forces had been issued by the First Lord of the Admiralty, Earl St Vincent, orders intended to assuage the extreme public anxiety caused by the collapse of Britain's last continental ally, Austria, as much as furnish a rampart against the French armies. St Vincent had placed his favourite, Lord Nelson, in command of the flotilla partly to pacify his own political critics, but also to dissipate Nelson's immoral notoriety, acquired by his continuing scandalous liaison with Emma Hamilton. St Vincent's true strategic appreciation had been summed up in the House of Lords when the old man had risen to his feet to reassure their Lordships that he did not say that the French would not invade, only that they would not invade by sea.

This witty remark was held in many quarters to be too clever a sophistry. Only the appointment of Nelson, the victorious hero of the battles of the Nile and Copenhagen, satisfied those that considered all that could be done, should be done.

As for Commander Drinkwater, he was not at all sure that the appointment of Nelson to the command of this odd assembly of men-of-war was entirely wise. While he shared St Vincent's conviction that an attempt by the French to throw a vanguard of 40,000 soldiers across the Channel to effect a beach-head was far more difficult than Bonaparte and his staff appreciated, Drinkwater was anxious about Nelson's own intentions. Although there was nothing wrong with throwing explosive carcasses into a crowded anchorage as a means of interfering with whatever preparations the French had in train, Drinkwater, in common with most of the officers in the squadron, guessed that this was only a prelude to what Nelson had in mind. The entire British flotilla knew the admiral was a glory-hunter, often careless of the men he commanded in his ruthless desire to annihilate the enemy and, it was rumoured, add another star to those glistening on his undress uniform coat. Everyone had heard of the disastrous boat attack made on Tenerife one dark and blustery night four years earlier. Nelson himself had lost an arm in the affray, and this severe wound had somehow caught the sympathy of the public, obscuring the serious losses of other men and conveniently burying the accusations of foolhardiness and even bungling that were whispered in certain heretical corners.

Drinkwater was no coward, but was worried about this present enterprise against the invasion fleet of the French. After the careful, comprehensively plodding preparations and the final painstaking execution of the attack on Copenhagen earlier in the year, this new operation had all the hallmarks of hurried expediency. Were there not other flag-officers charged with the defence of the shores of Kent, Sussex and the Thames Estuary? Graeme commanded at The Nore and Lutwidge was in The Downs not fifteen miles away. It seemed clear that the fire-brand Nelson had hoisted his flag at the main truck of the frigate *Medusa* with one objective in mind: to make a quick and major attack upon Bonaparte's invasion fleet at any cost. This haste was echoed in Drinkwater's own appointment to the *Wolf*, an order to transfer his crew from the bomb-vessel *Virago* to the brig-sloop and to commission her 'with all despatch'. Initially he had embraced the order with his customary energy, for the *Wolf* was bound upon 'a Particular Service' which seemed to hold the promise of personal opportunity, but the process of disillusionment had begun when he had set eyes upon the dismantled *Wolf*. Months earlier the appearance of *Virago* laid up in Ordinary had been depressing enough, but that of *Wolf* had been far worse. Even now she bore all the marks of neglect about her hull and only her rigging displayed the diligence of men hard-pressed to get her fit for war.

Perhaps there would be more time after this Particular Service had been executed to complete her paintwork and better organise her interior arrangements. Fortunately the Viragos were well acquainted with the business of storing and stowage, their old ship having been in her original form nothing more prestigious than a bomb-tender, but Drinkwater would have liked to make his debut as a sloop commander in a vessel in which he could have taken a little more pride. Not that the *Wolf* was not a smart enough craft under her patina of neglect; on the contrary, she had been French-built only four years previously, a privateer of sixteen six-pounder guns fitted-out for an *armateur* of Nantes. But since being captured

517

by the British frigate *Magnanime* she had been languishing in the Medway with a few scandalously idle hands assigned to maintain her.

'Very well . . .'

Quilhampton's voice brought Drinkwater back to the present with a jerk. He had been about to embark on another train of thought, that of his wife's new pregnancy, but threw aside his anxieties on Elizabeth's behalf. That too was clouding his judgement these days, and he could not admit so personal an intrusion into the afternoon's business. He coughed to clear his mind as much as his throat, lowering his glass and turning to stare down at the midshipmen in the stern.

Mr Quilhampton looked up expectantly. The young man's gangling figure with its incongruous wooden fist in which he held a writing tablet, seemed oddly out of sorts with the popular image of the Royal Navy's midshipmites. The boy next to Quilhampton was more in keeping with the public notion, a small blond child whose parents should be horse-whipped for sending so young and delicate a creature aboard a man-of-war. He, like the cutter, her coxswain and her oarsmen, belonged to *Medusa*, though unlike them he looked sadly inexperienced on this warm August afternoon. Drinkwater smiled at the boy.

'Mr, er . . .?'

'Fitzwilliam, sir,' the boy squeaked nervously as he eyed the standing figure with the scarred cheek, the long queue down his back and the odd blue marks on one eyelid. Mr Fitzwilliam was as yet unable to stand up in a boat; as for the figure of the strange commander with his single epaulette, it seemed to the boy that the remote persons who bore such gold embellishments were an odd, disfigured breed. This Commander Drinkwater, though not quite so knocked about as Admiral Lord Nelson, seemed to have something wrong with his right arm. As for the timber fist of his adjacent colleague, Midshipman Quilhampton, poor Mr Fitzwilliam could not bring himself to look at so horrible a thing! The wretched boy kept his eyes steadfastly on the commander and thought he did not look so forbidding when he smiled.

'Mr Fitzwilliam,' Drinkwater was saying kindly, 'I desire that you take the cutter in a little closer. I fear we are going to disappoint his Lordship at this remove.'

Drinkwater nodded encouragingly. The greenhorn midshipman

had been told to repeat all orders so that they were known to be comprehended by both parties and he did so now with a certain diffidence.

'T-take the cutter in a little closer, sir. Aye, aye.'

Next Fitzwilliam turned to the grizzled coxswain who, Drinkwater guessed, had been appointed by Gore or his first luff, to be sea-daddy to the tow-haired infant.

'Hathaway, take the cutter in a little closer, if you please.'

'Aye, aye, sir,' Hathaway responded with a dry and solemn dignity, unmoved by any thought of the incongruity of taking orders from a child. 'Stand by!' he commanded. The oarsmen leaned forward and their oarblades flashed in the sunshine as they held them poised above the glassy surface of the Strait. 'Give way . . . tooo-gether!' At Hathaway's last syllable they stabbed at the water, the grunting seamen leaning back while the cutter laid her clinker strakes to the tide and sent the water chuckling away from her cutwater.

'Keep her on this transit, Mr Q,' Drinkwater said to his own acolyte as he braced himself against the sudden surge of the boat, 'oh, and you had better explain to Mr Fitzwilliam what a transit is and how he will need to crab across this damned tide to maintain it.'

'Aye, aye, sir.'

Drinkwater raised his glass again, satisfied with Quilhampton's explanation as the older midshipman coached the younger in the business of allowing for the set of the tide, pointing out the two marks they had selected to keep in line as they swept in closer to the French anchorage.

Chapter Two

Lord Nelson

'I think, my Lord, that we certainly hit several of their lugger-rigged gundalows, and we may have sunk two or three of 'em. One was most positively driven ashore, for I did see a shell explode forward and shortly afterwards noted her drifting out of the line—' Drinkwater ceased speaking as Lord Nelson cut him short.

'Thank you. So, out of the two dozen corvettes, gundalows and a schooner, we sank two or three, and perhaps drove another ashore.' The admiral stared around the group of officers gathered in the *Medusa*'s stern cabin which did duty as his headquarters. The candlelight sparkled on their gilt buttons and their single epaulettes, for all except Gore, *Medusa*'s captain, were mere masters and commanders. The admiral's good eye raked each in turn, his wide mouth mobile with his suppressed disappointment.

'I saw a brig-corvette in trouble, my Lord, at the tail of the line . . .'

'Did anyone else other than Captain Cotgrave witness a corvette in trouble?'

'Yes, my Lord,' confirmed Commander Somerville, 'I did, though my first lieutenant initially spotted her predicament. I think she too drifted out of the line and may have got ashore.'

'You did not see this from your advanced position, Captain Drinkwater?'

Drinkwater shook his head. 'I did not, my Lord, but it seems quite possible since she could have been obscured, my horizon being somewhat limited by my height of eye and the arrangement of the French line.'

'Quite so. Then we must have effected some damage within the pier, judging by the amount of shells thrown into the place and the crowded state of the anchorage. Confound it, we lost three men ourselves as a consequence of a mere handful of shells the enemy fired back at us!' The admiral's tone of voice made the lilt of his Norfolk accent rise as he expressed his exasperation. 'I think therefore that ten is a not impossible number by way of losses of flat-boats and the like, but I had hoped for more, damn it!' Nelson stared down at the table where a sheet of notes lay over a chart of the Strait of Dover. After a moment he looked up and his whole body stiffened with resolve, the movement making the stars upon his breast glitter in the candlelight and drawing attention to the empty, gilt-braided cuff pinned across his chest. 'Well, gentlemen, it ain't much of a haul for the expenditure of powder and shells! Over nine hundred carcasses were thrown at the enemy, but it shall have to suffice for the moment.'

'It has proved useful as a reconnaissance, my Lord,' enthused the young Edward Parker, catching the admiral's mood.

'That may be so, Ned, but if we have but tapped at the door, they will be the readier when we next pay them a call.'

A low murmur of assent greeted this remark. Drinkwater, waiting in silence as behove the most junior commander, felt the worm of anxiety uncoil in his belly. There was something vaguely posturing about the gallant admiral, and something disturbing about the response it evoked among the young officers surrounding him as he assiduously plied them all with the courtesy title of 'captain'.

'And might we know when that might be, my Lord?' Parker asked, presuming on his friendship with the admiral, but asking the question that was almost palpably springing up all around the table.

'Well, I shall need to consult the almanac, gentlemen, but I can tell you now that it will be a night attack.'

'We should be concentrating against Flushing,' Lieutenant Rogers said firmly. He and Drinkwater paced the *Wolf*'s tiny quarterdeck as the brig-of-war lay under her topsails, stemming the ebb as it ran fast through the Strait of Dover. 'That is where the greater number of flat-boats lie.'

'I heard aboard *Medusa* that Nelson is all for striking Flushing but that we lack the resources or the time for such a move. Moreover, St Vincent is the more eager for a blow against Boulogne.'

Drinkwater broke off and cast a glance about the horizon. To the north-west, dark against the afterglow of the sunset, the cliffs of Dover stood sharp against the sky. To the east only a smear of grey marked the cape of that name, as Cap Gris Nez faded into the night, so insubstantial that it seemed impossible that a few miles inland an army massed to invade England. But then in the twilight even Rogers' face was growing indistinct as Drinkwater and his first lieutenant discussed the situation.

'I presume St Vincent wants to strike directly at France, hence his desire to attack Boulogne,' Drinkwater went on after satisfying himself no hostile sail was in sight.

'Aye,' added Rogers, "tis the nearest port and that from which the first assault would come.'

'Perhaps,' responded Drinkwater, unconvinced. 'Anyway,' he added, 'we shall have to wait a day or two, I suppose. His Lordship has gone to Harwich, though for what purpose I do not know.'

'To throw one arm and both legs about La Belle Hamilton, I'd say,' Rogers said in his coarse way.

Drinkwater ignored the crude reference to Nelson's mistress. 'Well, if it is to be Boulogne again, I think we shall find the French have not been idle. They were active enough this afternoon.'

'Quilhampton said that you thought they were laying out chain moorings . . .'

'No doubt about it,' Drinkwater said promptly, 'I have done the same myself sufficient times to know what they were up to,' he said. 'They have clearly protected the invasion-craft in the inner harbour with that cordon of moored vessels outside the mole. Such a boom constructed by mooring their corvettes and outer gundalows head-and-stern with chain will prove most effective. The Elder Brethren of the Trinity House have long had such a contingency in mind for blocking the Thames. If the French stuff those outer vessels full of infantrymen and marines as well as their regular seamen, then cover the cordon with fire from batteries ashore, we shall have as warm a reception as met his Lordship's last such assault on Tenerife.'

'Good God Almighty, I had forgot that fiasco!' Rogers exclaimed.

'And you should recall the strength of the tides hereabouts,' Drinkwater added gloomily. 'I fear Lord Nelson with his greatest triumphs in the Mediterranean and the Baltic, has too little appreciation of the tides.'

It was a conviction that had been growing for some time in Drinkwater's mind. He was familiar with these waters, for it had been here that he had cut his teeth as a young man in the buoy-yachts of Trinity House when, after the American War, the Royal Navy had had no use for him. And here too, not so very long ago when the Revolution convulsed France and first precipitated war with Britain, Drinkwater had rejoined the Royal Navy and, as master's mate aboard the man-of-war cutter *Kestrel*, had carried out the cloak-and-dagger orders of the Admiralty's Secret Department. He knew well that operations conducted in these waters had to be precisely planned, that delays compromised success and that it was better to abandon an enterprise rather than have it miscarry to the enemy's advantage. The bombardment of the invasion-craft at Boulogne on the fourth August had been a lacklustre affair, and any repetition seemed doomed now that the French had had due warning. It was inconceivable that they had not reinforced their defences.

On the fourteenth a lugger appeared, recalling to the admiral's anchorage in The Downs the *Wolf* and the two hired revenue cutters left to watch Boulogne. That evening Drinkwater found himself again in *Medusa*'s great cabin as the extempore flagship swung to her best bower, under the lee of the Kent coast. As he listened to Nelson summing up his plan and impressing upon the assembled commanders the necessity of keeping in close contact, Drinkwater felt his gloomiest forebodings coming true, for Nelson proposed nothing less than a grand cutting-out expedition. The boats of the squadron, supported by howitzer-armed launches, were to seize all the craft lying at anchor outside the pier of Boulogne, cut them loose from their moorings, and bring them out under the guns of the frigates *Medusa* and *Leyden*, the sloops and the gun-brigs.

During the discussion, Drinkwater had emphasised his belief that the enemy had formed a defensive cordon of their own vessels anchored not by rope cables, but moored head-and-stern by chains. Somerville, who would lead the first division of boats in his capacity as senior commander, buried any anxieties under a cheerful response. He had some reason for this, for if he succeeded and survived, he would as senior commander undoubtedly be promoted to post-captain.

'Well,' Somerville had concluded to Nelson's obvious approval, 'once we have taken their decks, we shall be put to the trouble of casting them off from these chain moorings you so apprehend Captain Drinkwater. However, I think this will prove but a trifle.' Nelson agreed with Somerville, and Drinkwater felt stung by the admiral's quick glance in his own direction. He coloured accordingly and was still flushed as the commanders took their written orders from Nelson's secretary and walked out onto *Medusa*'s twilit quarterdeck, unaware that there was any concern in the minds of others until John Conn, a man whom Drinkwater did not know and under whom Drinkwater would serve with a division of howitzer boats, plucked his sleeve and drew him to one side.

'Drinkwater,' Conn began, 'you clearly perceive the difficulties of this night's work.'

'Indeed, I do, and it runs to more than mere anxiety about the strength of the enemy's moorings. I am very concerned about the ability of the boats to act in concert, for the tides are devilish strong and at night separation is all too likely.'

'Perhaps, but the admiral is determined. Besides, who are we to question the affair until our blood is spilled in sufficient quantity to appease the public appetite for gore? No pun is intended, I assure you, but it strikes me that our roll of giving covering fire may place us in a position of attracting more attention than we warrant. However, I want to assure you that I shall support Somerville to my utmost and that I shall expect you to be of similar mind.'

'What precisely are you saying, Commander Conn?' A horrified Drinkwater, aware that he had misunderstood Conn, confronted his colleague. 'That you share Lord Nelson's doubt as to my courage because I report a strengthening of the French defences?' Drinkwater's blood ran icily cold now. He felt his fists clenching and he longed for the mad catharsis of action to put an end to this shilly-shallying. 'Have a care, sir,' he said as he turned on his heel and went to seek his boat.

The Mortar Boat

A little over twenty-four hours later, at half past eleven on the evening of the fifteenth August 1801, the assembled fleet of boats bobbed in the darkness alongside the *Medusa*. The squadron lay all around them in mid-Channel, well to the east of the Varne shoal and about a league off Boulogne. The night was moonless and dark, with a light breeze from the east and a low swell from the west, the one bringing the pleasant scent of the land, the other warning of a gale far out in the Atlantic. The tide was flooding, running north-east past Boulogne, with a greater strength on the French coast than on the opposite English shore.

Somerville's division led off, his boats loosely roped together, followed by those of Parker, Cotgrave and Jones. Conn and Drinkwater's howitzer boats, consisting of launches from Chatham and Sheerness dockyards, each of which bore a small mortar, departed last.

'Keep close up with Somerville, Captain Conn, and good luck to you.' Drinkwater heard Nelson's East Anglian accent cut the night air with its characteristically slightly high-pitched diction.

'Aye, aye, my Lord, and thank you,' Conn responded. No word of encouragement or instruction came from *Medusa*'s rail for the last division to leave. Commander Nathaniel Drinkwater felt the omission keenly; it was as if his part in this night's enterprise was of no consequence, and that he was already forgotten.

Sitting in the stern of the big launch Drinkwater brooded on his misfortune. Not to have reported the strengthening of the French line would have been a dereliction of duty, so the attracting of vague suggestions of cowardice were unjust. But the inner conviction that matters augured ill had undoubtedly engendered a lack of enthusiasm, and he regretted revealing this to Conn. The man's odd turn of phrase had misled him into thinking he shared

Drinkwater's misgivings, but there was nothing he could do about it now, except avoid any further possibility of such accusations during the attack, which meant he must now thrust himself forward to avoid the slightest chance of such a charge. To this end he had sent Quilhampton forward, to keep an eye on the boats ahead, taking a seat in the stern-sheets beside Tregembo and alongside the artillery bombardier and two artillerymen who would man the mortar when they closed in on the enemy. Following astern of Drinkwater's launch came the other four boats in his division, but the night was so dark that already there was no sign of *Medusa* or her consorts, though they could not yet be far away.

'This is likely to go very ill with us,' Drinkwater muttered, lowering his glass and sitting down in the stern-sheets and instantly regretting giving voice to his apprehensions.

'Do you know where we are, sir?' a voice asked in the darkness and Drinkwater made out the face of the bombardier, who was clearly mystified as to how they knew their way over the black water. The man's nervous curiosity drew a brittle laugh from Drinkwater, but he said nothing to assuage the fellow's anxiety, merely bending to uncover the shuttered lantern so that, for a brief moment, the candlelight fell upon the boxed compass lying on the bottom-boards.

'Ahhh,' the bombardier sighed at the revelation, but really was none the wiser.

'Can you see the next ahead, Mr Q?' Drinkwater called.

'Just about, sir.'

Drinkwater grunted and looked astern to where a faint white feather showed the second boat in his own division. The rhythmic sway of the oarsmen and gentle knocking of the muffled oar-looms on their thole pins was accompanied by the faint grunts of their labour. From time to time the bright glow of phosphorescence was stirred up by the dipping-blades and with every stroke those in the stern swayed forward and back in a curious motion that induced a state of somnolence in those not actively employed. Drinkwater's mind wandered obsessively back to the council aboard *Medusa*.

Had Nelson really glared at him, or had he imagined it? True, he had got off to a bad start with his lordship months earlier when they had met in Great Yarmouth, but the misunderstanding had been cleared up, and he had been in no doubt that his conduct under fire at Copenhagen had attracted Nelson's notice. Moreover, the little one-armed admiral had commended him to the Commander-in-Chief for promotion. But Conn's unpleasant comment seemed to lend credence to Drinkwater's view that his own assessment of the French preparations had been taken, not as a professional judgement, but as an indication of his lack of personal courage.

Many men lost their appetite for danger if they did not lose their nerve altogether and, it occurred to Drinkwater, he was the oldest among the commanders, a fact emphasised by his unfashionable queue, his shabby uniform and his several disfigurements. This would not be lost on his younger colleagues. Conn, Parker, Somerville and the rest were as eager as puppies, and he would have to put up with his present circumstances as with so much else in this unfair and unfathomable life. At this point in his philosophical deliberations Quilhampton's voice jerked him back to reality.

'Sir! I can't see the boat ahead!'

'God's bones!' Drinkwater blasphemed and bent to uncover the lantern and check their course. They were two points to starboard of it. Why the devil had he fallen prey to foolish daydreaming? 'Come to larboard, Tregembo!'

'Larboard hellum, sir,' Drinkwater's own coxswain acknowledged the order and the boat heeled slightly as she swung.

Again Drinkwater looked astern. It was bad enough losing touch with Conn, but to lose contact with his own boats would be unforgivable! The white feather was still behind them and he saw it follow them round as they adjusted their course.

'Steady,' Drinkwater said, relieved. 'Steady as you go . . .'

The launch drove on and Drinkwater relaxed a few minutes later when Quilhampton called out that he could see something ahead, then confirmed it as the transom of a boat. Drinkwater's relief was short-lived, for they rapidly overhauled the stranger and found her lying on her oars, all alone.

'What boat is that?' Drinkwater called out in a low voice.

'Number Three in Captain Somerville's division, who are you . . . sir?' The voice was adolescent and uncertain, but the strange boat got under way again, keeping pace with them as the midshipman in charge answered.

'You say you are with Somerville?' Drinkwater asked, astonished.

'Is that Captain Drinkwater?'

'It is. Is that Mr Fitzwilliam?'

'Yes, sir.'

'Have you lost touch with your next ahead, Mr Fitzwilliam?'

'Er, yes sir; I think I have. Our line parted,' the boy was obviously terrified at the consequences of his failure.

'Very well, Mr Fitzwilliam, maintain station on my starboard beam.'

'On your starboard beam, sir, aye, aye,' responded the relieved and faultlessly obedient midshipman.

They pulled on, Drinkwater leaving the compass uncovered and consulting his watch. Another quarter of an hour dragged by and then, quite suddenly all the uncertainty ended when about seven cables length ahead they saw a bright flash light up the night. This was followed by smaller, surrounding points of twinkling fire as first the howitzers and then the small arms of what Drinkwater presumed to be Conn's and Parker's divisions encountered the line of anchored French vessels. The boom and crackle of the discharges rolled over the water towards them, accompanied by the flash of the defending gunfire which was startling in its furious concentration. Against the individual flashes of Conn's howitzers and a pair of twelve-pounder boat-carronades in Parker's craft, the low line of a score of cannon stabbed the night with brilliant points of fire. Before the concussion of the French response reached Drinkwater, the whine of shot and even the splash and curious whizzing noise made by a ricochet flew past them.

'Steadeeee my lads,' Drinkwater growled. 'Keep the stroke my boys, keep it going together; that's the way, that's the way.' He coaxed them along, keeping their minds on their laborious task.

They could hear the shouting now, and Drinkwater could see intermittently in stark images that lingered on the retinae, brief vignettes of the struggle as they drew closer. Conn's boats lay on their oars firing their mortars, while what he assumed were Parker's were already clustered alongside the elegant sheer of a corvette and her flanking neighbours. He could see figures reaching up in an attempt to gain the corvette's decks, saw men clustered on the channels, thrusting inboard with pikes and cutlasses. Among them the sparkle of fire-locks was less intense as men grappled hand-to-hand, and then the ordered discharge of a volley of musketry betrayed the presence of French infantry or marines.

'Up forrard!' Drinkwater ordered the bombardier and his artillerymen as he motioned Tregembo to ease the stroke and then to hold water. The launch lost way and then Quilhampton clambered aft and acted as co-ordinator, ordering the oars plied to swing the boat onto target. Like Conn's, Drinkwater's boats were to hold off and throw their shells over the boat-attack made on the enemy's cordon largely to intimidate reinforcement from the shore, but also to do whatever execution they could. They were already late getting to their station, a fact that would doubtless be held against him if the night's work went according to Drinkwater's doom-laden prognostications.

A moment later the bombardier expressed himself satisfied and with a great roar and a bucking of the launch, the howitzer threw its first charged carcass high into the air. A faint trail of red soared up as the shell's fuse rose on its high trajectory before it fell beyond the flashing fire-fight of the main assault.

After the sudden momentary blindness that followed the flash of the howitzer's discharge, Drinkwater became aware of Fitzwilliam's adjacent boat. As the artillerymen carefully prepared the next shell, he raised his voice and pointed ahead.

'Mr Fitzwilliam! There is where you should be! Do you go forward directly and lend your support!'

The midshipman's response was drowned in the boom as the next howitzer boat in Drinkwater's own division fired her own mortar, and one by one the rest of his craft reached their positions to bombard the French. Watching Fitzwilliam's boat pull forward, vividly if erratically silhouetted against the gunfire ahead, Drinkwater raised his glass and took stock of the situation. He was aware that Quilhampton had continuously to order the boat's crew to ply their oars, for the north-easterly flood tide was as strong as Drinkwater had predicted and in order to fire the howitzers they had to lie athwart the stream. Their own rate of fire was therefore necessarily slow. Moreover, as a result of this constant manoeuvring the tide was setting them obliquely towards the action. Drinkwater's heavy launch was by now drawing close to a brig-corvette, around which a number of the British boats had clustered. It was clear that the attackers had thus far been unsuccessful in gaining command of her deck, for Drinkwater could see not only a spirited defence being put up by the musketry of soldiers and marines, but the occasional shot from broadside guns still punched the night with flame and fire. Drinkwater observed, amid the shouts, screams, oaths, sputter of small arms, and the general clash of hand-to-hand fighting, the presence of taut boarding nettings leading up from the corvette's rails to her lower yard-arms. The attackers were unable to penetrate this defensive web. As he waited for his own howitzer to fire again, Drinkwater watched horrified as Mr Fitzwilliam's boat was swept by an iron hail. He saw the craft slew round, a mess of splintered oars and planking, the scream of its wounded piercing the night before it drifted inexorably north. God's bones, he had ordered that child into an inferno!

An instant later the air round them too was full of the lethal buzz and whine of projectiles. His own launch shuddered under the impact of shot, while grape and langridge spattered viciously into the water all around them.

'God *damn* the French!' a seaman cried, clapping one hand to his useless arm and relinquishing his hold on his oar loom. The loss of the oar was only averted by Quilhampton grabbing it while the wounded oarsman, his arm smashed, sobbed in a kind of pathetic rage at his bloody misfortune.

'God's bones!' Drinkwater blasphemed again, as the bottom-boards beneath his feet bucked with the discharge of their own howitzer, then darkened as water ran over them. 'Clap a pledget on that man, Mr Q, and tell him to keep his mouth shut! Look for leaks under your feet men, and stuff your kerchiefs into 'em. Come, look lively!'

As the boat slewed round, her crew bent and checked the planking about them, tearing off their neckerchiefs where a black roil betrayed the ingress of water. Drinkwater looked to the right and the left. He could see a struggle similar to that engulfing the corvette taking place alongside other craft to the north; to the south a further attack was being made, though on what Drinkwater could not see as the tide bore them away. Further gunfire flashes were intermittently visible elsewhere, but these were disembodied and confused, lacking the cohesion so essential to the achievement of Nelson's objective. As he stared through his glass, Drinkwater was convinced that this was not the mass attack that the admiral had intended; on the contrary, it had all the appearance of going off

530

at half-cock. Where in God's name were the remainder of the British boats?

A rumbling of oaths came from near at hand and Drinkwater lowered his glass. 'What's amiss?' he growled.

'Mortar's split, sir.' It was the bombardier's voice. 'We've fired our last shot, I'm afraid.'

'Well thank God for that,' Drinkwater said, shutting his glass with a snap. 'Now we may be able to do something useful.' Aware that Quilhampton had clambered forward and was now working his way aft checking on the stopping of the leaks, Drinkwater asked, 'well are we fit for further duty?'

'No doubt about it, sir,' said Quilhampton, 'though we've a man dead forward, as well as Bellings being wounded.'

'Whose gone forward?'

' 'Tis Jameson, sir,' someone piped up, 'shall I pitch him over the side?'

'Aye, if you please, and Bellings, do you move aft and let Mr Q have a look at your wound.'

'I'm all right, sir . . .'

'Do as you're told,' Drinkwater snapped.

'Aye, aye, sir.'

As this reorganisation took place, Drinkwater peered to the north. Something caught his eye and a quixotic hope leapt in his heart as the oars were once more manned and the boat's crew settled to their wearying task. He ordered Tregembo to give way. 'Put the helm over hard a-larboard, Tregembo,' he added, conning the boat away from the fight.

Within five minutes they had come up with Fitzwilliam's boat as it lay wallowing, half-submerged, its oars wrecked, its crew badly shattered by the full force of two bags of grape shot. Even in the darkness Drinkwater could see a cold pallor on the features of the young midshipman as he was almost tenderly passed across into Drinkwater's boat and laid down on the wet boards of the stern-sheets. Only five or six fit men were able to clamber after their young chief as, leaving the remaining wounded with orders to pull the boat as best they could into the tide, Drinkwater swung his own launch round again.

'Now put your backs into it!' he ordered sharply. 'Tregembo, lay me alongside that bloody corvette, and you spare hands change the priming and charges in your pieces.'

Fitzwilliam's boat had been intended for the assault and the handful of armed men they had taken out of her might prove useful additions to Drinkwater's own. Ordering the three now unemployed artillerymen to prepare to use their short swords, Drinkwater warned his oarsmen that they should be ready to support their colleagues once they had joined the fray. It took them twenty minutes to regain their position against the tide, during which they spoke with the rest of their division which still threw their howitzer shells at the enemy. Gathering these boats about him, Drinkwater headed directly for the nearest French vessel which now seemed the centre of the fight in their immediate locality.

'I intend to attempt to carry her,' he declared with a defiance he was far from feeling as he bowed to the stern demands of duty.

Chapter Four

August 1801

Cold Steel

As they approached, it was clear that the attack had failed utterly. Conn's launches had become separated, though they still threw their shells over the cordon of gun-boats and corvettes that lay moored outside the head of Boulogne Mole. Those boats of Parker's division, which had been in the thick of it, lay in complete disarray. They passed through several of these as they drifted aimlessly, a few exhausted and wounded men collapsed within them, the odd figure stoically plying half-heartedly at an oar. A few men splashed through the water, calling out for assistance and moving Drinkwater to order one of his following launches to veer aside and pick up as many of these wretched creatures as possible. Drinkwater pressed forward himself to where a few boats still lay alongside a large ship-corvette and, he could see clearly now, a large *chasse marée* astern of her.

It was quite obvious that the preparedness and fury of the defence had overwhelmed the attack, for at the first sign of Drinkwater's approaching launches, the *qui vive* went up with a shout and a fusillade of musketry burst all along the corvette's sheer. This was followed by a broadside which, though it left Drinkwater's launch unscathed, landed a round shot squarely into the bow of his third boat, smashing in the bow and sending her to the bottom in a matter of minutes. It seemed to Drinkwater that those British craft remaining alongside the corvette were filled with dead or wounded, such had been the intensity of the French fire.

It was now equally clear that little advantage could be wrung from pressing the attack further. Their only duty now lay with recovering the wounded. As the French reloaded, Drinkwater stood and shouted to Quilhampton.

'Put her about, James!'

Bracing himself he cupped his hands, and as they swept across the bows of the following launches, he ordered them each to fire their howitzers and small arms and then withdraw, rendering assistance wherever possible. There was sufficient confusion in the night to strangle any vain-glorious desire to send them to a certain death. Drinkwater was quite unaware that in the diverting approach of his handful of launches, the few survivors in Parker's boats had cast themselves adrift and made good their escape. As the tide bore them away, Drinkwater's own crew were dragging the survivors of the stove boat over their own gunwhale. All about them the French musket balls pitched, while round shot whined overhead, making them gasp, half-winded by their passing. But the tide was now their ally, so that they attracted only occasional fire from the rest of the French vessels as they were carried along the moored cordon.

Drinkwater's launch was now dangerously overloaded. He was hauling a man out of the water when Quilhampton roared out, 'Sir! Under the stern of the lugger!'

At the urgent cry of alarm, Drinkwater twisted round and relinquished his hold on the sodden seaman. The abandoned fellow slithered across his lap to lie gasping in the bottom of the launch alongside Fitzwilliam.

At that moment they were sweeping past a large *chasse marée*. Her topsides were so close that Drinkwater could see the ironwork strapping her wide channels to her topsides, and the deadeyes and lanyards of her shrouds as they vanished upwards into the impenetrable night. It was the appreciation of an instant, for the next thing he was aware of was the flurry of water at the bow of a wide flat-boat and the faint gleam of vigorously plied oar-blades: a counter-attack, by God!

'Watch there, my lads!' he bellowed, 'the enemy are upon us!'

The words had scarcely left him before there was a succession of shouts, a splintering of oars as the colliding flat-boat sheered them off and then her solid bow caught the launch a glancing blow. A moment later the two craft crashed together, bow to stern, the launch heeling under the impact. Drinkwater and his men were suddenly fighting for their lives.

In the struggle to get men out of the water Drinkwater's sword-belt had slipped behind him and he had no time to reach his hanger before a boarding-pike was thrust at him. He twisted away and fell backwards, crashing into Tregembo as the coxswain drew the tiller from the rudder stock and used it as an extempore weapon, reaching over Drinkwater to catch his commander's assailant a glancing blow on the foremost fist with which the French seaman held the weapon.

As the Frenchman lost his grasp on the boarding-pike with the agony of a smashed hand, Drinkwater twisted sideways and extricated himself. He rose with a tremendous effort as the launch rocked wildly under the assault of at least a dozen of the leaping enemy. He drew his hanger. The rasp of the blade against the gilded brass ferrule of the scabbard filled him with a savage determination. He drove the blade into the flank of the French sailor, twisted and withdrew it, leaving the wretch to writhe in agony underfoot. As the man fell, the brief flash of a pistol close by momentarily blinded Drinkwater.

'Watch the young gennelman, zur,' Tregembo shouted as Drinkwater unwittingly kicked the small, still form of Fitzwilliam lying at his feet half under the stern-sheet benches.

'Hela!'

Drinkwater spun round, his eyes clearing. A French officer was poised on the higher gunwhale of the flat-boat. Even in the darkness his posture was truculently triumphant, his sword blade a grey wisp at which Drinkwater struck with a cold and pre-emptive fury. The jar of the contact told him his opponent was a practised swordsman: the enemy's blade wavered not an inch. Then the Frenchman extended and Drinkwater felt his right shoulder pinked by his opponent's blade. He ducked as the French officer's sword-point tore through the fabric of his coat, then he thrust upwards with all his might before his enemy recovered his guard. But the French officer was too quick for him and, with a shout of triumph, drew swiftly back as the boats rocked and bumped together.

The launch seemed a seething mass of struggling men; their grunts were punctuated by oaths and howls and sobs and screams, and Drinkwater had not the faintest notion of who, if anyone, was gaining the upper hand.

Where was Quilhampton? Where was Tregembo? Where in God's name were his other boats? For a fraction of time Drinkwater hesitated, his concentration divided between his personal survival and his responsibility as a sea-officer in charge of a division of howitzer launches. In that instant he lost the cold concentration of his fighting instincts; he saw instead the justification of his misgivings, the consequences of Nelson's rashness and his own see-saw relationship with the admiral. He saw too his own successes and failures; the smooth curve of his wife's pregnant belly, the pale face of the wounded Fitzwilliam, and again the utter craziness of this night's foolhardy attack.

Then, alerted by some nervous imperative, he was recalled to the dangerous present. The French officer, having caught his own breath and recovered his footing, renewed his attack and flung himself down from his flat-boat's side in a wildly determined lunge intended to kill Drinkwater and destroy with him the spirit of the British boat's crew. Drinkwater sensed the descending loom of the man and swung to defend himself. He was too late: the French officer's sword blade stabbed Drinkwater a second time on his right shoulder, passing right through it up to its hilt.

All Drinkwater could do as the French officer fell upon him was to hold his own blade for as long as his right hand did as it was bid. He fell backwards with a sickening jar, his enemy falling on top of him, their common descent broken by a body sprawled over the opposite gunwhale. Drinkwater felt the breath driven out of his lungs and gasped at the fire in his shoulder. As the shock and pain robbed him of consciousness, Drinkwater beheld in the gloom his own blade emerging from the small of his enemy's back.

Chapter Five

The Wound

'Well sir, I see at last that you are cognizant of my presence. May I impress upon you, how fortunate a man you are to have fallen into my clutches at last,' said Mr Lettsom. Then, giving way to his muse, the *Wolf*'s surgeon declaimed:

> 'When people's ill, they come to I,
> I physics, bleeds and sweats 'em;
> Sometimes they live, sometimes they die,
> What's that to I? I let's 'em.'

'Lettsom? Is that you?'

'Of course it is I, sir. Who else would it be?'

'Where . . .? How long have I been . . .?'

'It is the eighteenth day of September, the year is the first of the new century, though there are those who debate this assertion. You are aboard the brig-sloop *Wolf* of which you are somewhat notionally in command and the said brig is lying off the dockyard of Sheerness into which anchorage she was rather creditably carried by Lieutenant Rogers. I refused to allow you ashore into the hospital on the grounds that you were too ill to move and were better left in my care. Fortunately their Lordships, having no immediate employment for the *Wolf*, have not seen fit to issue any orders regarding her movement, other than that she is to remain at anchor pending perhaps the outcome of what appear might be peace negotiations—'

'Peace?' Drinkwater interrupted. Then, half sitting up, he asked '*What* did you say the date was?'

'The eighteenth of September, sir.'

'Then I have been—'

'In a fever for a month and while Mr Q was convinced you were about to expire, I managed to prevent him alarming your wife. In short, sir, as far as the outside world is concerned, you are recovering from a wound received in hand-to-hand service, as the vicious boat-work such as you were sent upon is so euphemistically called by the powers-that-be . . . or should it be, that-are? Well, well, never mind. You are going to recover now, though it will be some time before you will be waving a sword again.' The surgeon smiled, adding, 'but then, if rumours of peace come to pass, you will not need to.'

Drinkwater was no longer listening. He was trying to recollect the events of that frightful night. He recalled the confusion, the strong, ineluctable sweep of the tide and the terrifying looming nemesis of the French officer. Then, as Lettsom's words made sense to him he remembered Quilhampton. 'Then James is all right?'

'Indeed he is, though his wooden arm took more knocks than it could stand.'

'And Tregembo?'

'Indestructible as ever.'

'And I have been in a fever for a month?'

'More or less; you enjoyed a few lucid moments.'

'And my report? Who wrote my report to Lord Nelson?' Drinkwater struggled to sit up.

'Your young friend James Quilhampton submitted his report, countersigned by Samuel Rogers, to Captain Conn. Word came back from the *Medusa* that his Lordship was well pleased with the conduct of all the officers and men employed upon that dangerous and regrettably unsuccessful attack. However, all had acquitted themselves as befitted British seamen and were rightly deserving of his Lordship's approbation. In short, my dear sir, it was a disaster. There, let's finish this damned catechising?'

Drinkwater lay back. He felt very weak, though his head was clear now, clearer than it had been for a very long time, he realised.

'It seems I owe my life to you, Mr Lettsom.'

Lettsom smiled, then said:

> 'No sword have I, no bayonet,
> No Frenchmen do I slaughter,
> I serve, dear sir, with my curette,
> With sutures, rum and water . . .'

538

'And my shoulder?'

'Ahh. Something of a mess, I am afraid. The French officer whom you impaled, spitted you rather well in return and although you will not lose the articulation of the enarthroidal joint itself, since it is intact, damage to the coraco-humeral ligament is sufficient to render you significantly weaker and you will suffer a consequent loss of power in your right arm. The scapula was badly chipped and the surrounding muscles lacerated but I have debrided the wound, removed the debris and,' Lettsom shrugged, 'your constitution has fought off the effects of the ensuing fever.'

'You almost inspire me with the notion you know your business, Mr Lettsom,' Drinkwater said with a wan smile, 'I am most grateful to you.'

Lettsom inclined his head. 'Thank you, sir, you are most kind. It would not, I think, be considered too overweening of me to assume that I knew my business better than his Lordship.'

'Nelson, d'you mean?' Drinkwater asked. Lettsom nodded. 'Then there is talk of what? A bungling?'

'No, not of that, but of an unlucky defeat. Mind you, 'twould have been a bungling had anyone else been its instigator. Nelson continues to ride a popular chariot, but the butcher's bill was high; too damned high, if you ask me. It included young Parker who was wounded and which circumstance has mortified his Lordship, I gather.' Lettsom paused, then added with a detached disdain for the technicalities of seamanship, 'they tell me quite half the boats did not come into action at all on account of the tide.'

'It does not surprise me . . .' Drinkwater said reflectively. 'I tried to warn his Lordship of the dangers inherent in a night attack in those waters, but—' Drinkwater broke off with a groan and an oath. 'God's bones, Lettsom, that fellow's sword-blade still bites like the very devil,' he gasped.

Lettsom smiled and bent over him. 'You should not attempt to shrug your shoulders, my dear sir. 'Tis such a very *Gallic* gesture!'

Chapter Six

The Omission

A week later His Britannic Majesty's brig-sloop *Wolf* lay moored in the trots off Chatham Dockyard. Drinkwater, his right arm in a sling, his face pallidly anaemic, dictated to James Quilhampton as he prepared to leave the little man-of-war. A knock at the door diverted their attention from the Navy Board's bureaucratic demands.

'Come in!' Drinkwater called, expecting Samuel Rogers, his first lieutenant. Instead a small, thin figure dressed in the uniform of a midshipman entered *Wolf*'s cabin, removing his hat and making a short, courteous bow. The youth had all the hallmarks of coming from a flag-ship, an admiral's protégé.

Quilhampton recognised the young man before his commander. 'Good heavens, Mr Fitzwilliam, how good to see you!' Quilhampton rose and impetuously held out his right hand. Seeing it was of flesh and blood, Fitzwilliam took it with a shy smile.

'Fitzwilliam . . .?' Drinkwater frowned, and then Quilhampton reminded him. 'Good God, I thought you were dead!' Drinkwater said with a grin as the youngster smiled and shook his head.

'No sir, thanks to you I am not yet dead.'

'I am damned glad to hear it, young fellow. Did you suffer much?'

'Nothing worse than a severe contusion. I was knocked senseless but, as you see, sir, otherwise unscathed.'

'Well, well. I'll be damned if I didn't think you trampled under our feet. Tell me, what brings you aboard the *Wolf*?'

'I, er, I wished to express my gratitude sir, and I am charged to pass a message to you from Lord Nelson.'

'Oh?'

'His Lordship wishes me to tell you, to tell you personally, sir, that he omitted your name from the list of commanders engaged,

540

and that he is most regretful that it slipped his mind but he was most uncommonly disturbed and distressed by the numbers of officers and men killed and wounded in the attack. He wishes me in particular to say that he was well aware that you not only supported my own boat after it was damaged, but that by pressing on and leading a second attack after the first had failed, you distracted the enemy sufficiently for most of Captain Parker's boats to get away in the confusion. Captain Parker owes his life to you, sir, and if his Lordship can be of service to you, Captain Drinkwater, he wishes only to be reminded of it in the future.'

'That is most kind of his Lordship,' Drinkwater replied, a feeling of relief filling him. 'Please tell him as much when you next wait upon him. Perhaps, Mr Q, you will see that our young Mercury has something to eat and drink before he returns. That is enough letter writing for this morning.'

After the two midshipmen had gone Drinkwater rose unsteadily and poured himself a glass of wine. Staring astern through the windows of the cabin he meditated on the news. It was a damnably unfortunate oversight that Nelson had not mentioned him in his report. On the other hand perhaps, Drinkwater supposed, the admiral was sensible that he had done Drinkwater a double injustice and had at least taken the trouble to admit the fact and send young Fitzwilliam to make amends. Drinkwater smiled wryly; it was typical of Nelson to offer his own influence in the belief that it was of more use to a wretched tarpaulin officer like Drinkwater than a supplementary note to the Admiralty!

Drinkwater shook his head. How could he ever remind Nelson of such an error, let alone seek advancement thereby on some conjectural future encounter? He could never bring himself do such a self-seeking thing. Although Nelson would not have hesitated to do it for himself, Nathaniel Drinkwater was an entirely different kettle of fish! Drinkwater dismissed the idea as a chimera. It was a kind but misguided notion and, Drinkwater concluded, palliative enough. He finished his glass of wine as he stared out over the grey waters of the Medway, watching the young flood tide swirl upstream under the *Wolf*'s transom. There was a dangerous energy in it, he thought ruefully.

He tossed off the glass and rose to his feet. Anyway, damn it, if there was talk of peace he would far rather be meeting Elizabeth than Lord Nelson.

The Steeple Rock

This short story, written originally for an anthology of sea-stories and here slightly modified, tells of an incident in Drinkwater's life that occurred in 1788. Readers familiar with the series will realise it falls chronologically, between the end of *An Eye of the Fleet* and the beginning of *A King's Cutter*, following the employment of the young Drinkwater by Trinity House, alluded to several times in the early novels and in a retrospective passage in the last book in the series, *Ebb Tide*.

Steeple rocks are notoriously difficult to locate and can fall between the lines of soundings run by even the most modern hydrographical surveying techniques; they thus evade detection until they make themselves manifest by other means. In the course of my professional seafaring life working on the British coast, I have discovered two such hitherto unknown obstructions, and therefore they have a quality of personal fascination. It seemed appropriate that Nathaniel Drinkwater should also encounter one.

Chapter One

The Surveying Party

'Well, Mr Drinkwater, behold the Cornish shore with all its rocky marvels. It looks benign enough today, and I hope it will suit our purposes and remain so for a further sennight . . .' Captain Judd's voice tailed off as he turned his head away from the land and stared to the westward. His expression grew apprehensive. The line of the horizon had a peculiar sharpness to it, as though acknowledging its business as the threshold to the vast Atlantic Ocean that lay beyond its rim. Above, the sky was a pale grey, overcast lying like a sheet and obscuring any discernible signs or portents of the weather to come. The sight seemed to rob Judd of any further speech and Drinkwater suppressed a smile. Captain Judd, a man of fifty-odd years of age, did not like his present task; he was an east-coast man, happiest when dodging among the shoals that lay in profusion between the South Foreland and the Dudgeon, sniffing and examining the lead's arming and pronouncing with a confidence that was absolute, that they were off the Haisbro' Tail, or the Outer Gabbard. Drinkwater had learned to admire the consummate skill of the man, not only in the matter of cabotage, but in his ability to handle his big cutter, for the *Argus* was a Trinity House buoy-yacht, a heavy, if somewhat ornate vessel, intended to maintain the increasing number of buoys, beacons and offshore lighthouses that came under the management of the Court of Elder Brethren of the Trinity House in London. She was a maid-of-all-work, with comfortable quarters aft for the Brethren when they chose to go to sea on one of their tours of inspection; amidships a pair of heavy working boats were stowed upon chocks. On her foredeck a heavy, pawled windlass spoke of her more robust function: overhauling the moorings of seamarks. Additional evidence of this appeared on her topsides, where sheets of copper protected her planking and a hefty baulk of oak extended outboard in the form of a davit; and aloft, where her stout mast supported an equally stout derrick with its outfit of topping lift, guys and fall.

The usual station of the buoy-yacht *Argus* was the River Thames. From her moorings at Deptford, she worked to seaward, down stream to the wide expanse of the dangerous Estuary, where she laboured amid the buoys and beacons of the Swin, the King's and the Knob Channels as they threaded through the maze of banks and shoals. She was commonly seen in Harwich, and ventured farther north to assist her sister buoy-tender based at Great Yarmouth, or rounded the North Foreland to anchor in the Downs and service the buoys placed off the Goodwin Sands. But she rarely ventured far to the westward, for there was only the Eddystone lighthouse off Plymouth, and that was attended by its own vessel, and the isolated lights on the Caskets, which were served from Alderney. Apart from the lighthouses at St Agnes, in the Isles of Scilly, and a few isolated places on the Welsh coast, much of the west coast of England still lay in primitive darkness, dangerous to seamen as they sought the entrance to the Bristol and St George's Channels after long passages across the Atlantic when overcast weather had made the determination of their latitude uncertain.

Captain Judd, a master of coastal arcana, was instinctively uneasy about his vessel's situation, the more so since a new buoy-yacht was about to be launched from the yard of Randall and Brent at Rotherhithe, and Judd nursed the ambition to command her. He did not want anything to go wrong, to foul up his chances of promotion, and the loss of Mr Drinkwater, his competent young mate, even if only for a week, meant he had to linger on this accursed and treacherous coast. It was true that he had a full cargo of coals for St Agnes, but he knew that the road off St Mary's was not the best holding ground for a ship's anchor, and the anxiety gnawed at his entrails. He was used to the glutinous ooze of the Thames, in which an anchor's palms embedded themselves with satisfying security, and mistrusted an anchorage prone to the swells of the Atlantic. Judd returned his attention to the shore, now only a league away. Even St Mary's Road would be preferable to the narrow estuary off which they now lay. He turned to his second mate who stood expectantly by the tiller.

'Very well, Mr Carslake, don't start the heads'l sheets but lay her

548

on the other tack and heave her to.' Then he turned to the man beside him. 'You have everything ready?'

Nathaniel Drinkwater suppressed a smile. Judd was a fretful fellow, possessed of a demon of anxiety. Drinkwater had had the starboard boat loaded and ready since mid-forenoon. 'I do, sir.'

'You do have two compasses?'

'I have two boat compasses, sir, and they agree. I worked six azimuths yesterday . . .'

'And sufficient paper . . .'

'I have sufficient paper and pencils, pen and ink, and a sextant.' Drinkwater adjusted his footing as *Argus* changed her trim, rolling as she came up into the light southerly breeze which blew across the almost westerly swell. 'There is one thing, though, Captain Judd.'

'What? What is that?'

'I shall need some money, sir, for our—'

'Yes, yes, of course, for your subsistence,' Judd interrupted. 'I have it ready in the cabin. Come below . . . Mr Carslake, you have the deck, as soon as she is steady, swing the starboard gig out.'

'Aye, aye, sir.'

Judd moved towards the companionway and disappeared below. Waiting for him to descend, Drinkwater caught Carslake's eye and the man winked at him. Drinkwater smiled. Both of the yacht's officers liked Judd, but privately they referred to him as 'Fusspot'.

Drinkwater stepped from the gloom of the tiny space at the base of the companionway into the after cabin. It was lit through a row of stern-lights which would not have disgraced a sloop-of-war. He removed his tricorne, stooping his shoulders as he ducked after Judd. The yacht's master took a key from his pocket, opened a small locker secured to the bulkhead and took out a purse and a scrap of paper, motioning Drinkwater to sit at his desk. Drinkwater unclipped the inkwell, dipped the shortened goose-quill and scribbled his signature on the receipt.

'I have provided you with seven guineas, Mr Drinkwater. I think it superior to your needs, but you must have sufficient funds to carry out your task. However, I shall require that you account for every penny, *every* penny, mark you, that you disburse upon this duty.'

'I understand, sir.'

'And you are conversant with the task.'

'Perfectly sir,' Drinkwater replied, adding with what he hoped was a perfect suppression of exasperation at Fusspot's endless concern, 'we have gone over the problem sufficiently.'

'That is as well, it remains that you discover the matter.'

'Indeed, sir. Let us hope that, as you say, the weather holds. If it does not . . .'

'Then you shall travel overland to Falmouth and rejoin me there.'

'But what about the gig?'

'Leave it in the charge of some responsible person, the parish priest will do. I can return for the boat, but I don't want you and your men absent for longer than is absolutely necessary.' Judd held out his hand. 'Good luck.'

The two men shook hands. 'You may think me anxious, Mr Drinkwater, but in due course, I hope, you will understand the concerns that beset a commander. You are yourself embarking on detached service in command of a boat. I am aware of your previous service in His Majesty's navy and value that highly, but do you guard against *all* the dangers hereabouts. They might not all be quite as obvious as you think. You will have to be quartered in a tavern, but beware the dangers of drink, not for yourself, but the men. Mead and Foster have a liking for the stuff, but they are also good men in a boat—'

'Captain Judd,' Drinkwater broke in, smiling the lopsided grin that charmed through its absence of insolence, wrinkling the pale line of the sabre cut on his cheek, 'I am aware of all the dangers of the land, believe me. I shall see you in a week here or in Falmouth and with my commission executed to the best of my ability.'

'Very well, Mr Drinkwater, very well.' It was Judd's turn to smile. A spare man of middling-height, he ran his hand over the thinning hair that was drawn into a tight queue at his nape. It was a gesture of dismissal, and Drinkwater was relieved to see it. He turned and, pocketing the purse, picked up his hat. Briefly ducking into his own tiny cabin to pick up his gear, he found it already absent. He smiled at the small watercolour on the bulkhead, a painting done years ago by Elizabeth, long before she became his wife. It showed the former American schooner *Algonquin*, lying in Falmouth, a prize to the frigate *Cyclops*. He kissed his fingertips and touched it for good luck.

A moment later Drinkwater emerged on deck and turned forward. Amidships, in the starboard waist and hanging onto the heavy double-burton of the running backstay, Carslake made him a mock bow.

'Your chariot hawaits, Mister Mate.' Drinkwater stared down into the boat lying alongside. 'For Gawd's sake don't *you* start fussing, Nat. I've 'ad hall your dunnage put in the boat.' Carslake held up his hand. 'No, no, I ain't forgotten nuffink; yer bleedin' tin tubes, yer watercolours, the whole festerin' lot's in the boat. There's nuffink else to do but be off wiv you. 'Ere you are.'

'Thank you Mr Carslake,' Drinkwater responded with mock formality, taking the proffered boat-cloak and throwing it about his shoulders as he grinned into Carslake's broad red face. A raw cockney raised in the stews of Wapping, between, as he himself boasted, low tide and Trinity High Water, Carslake had first shipped forward. Sheer ability and intelligence had, by the time he was thirty, gained him a place amid the yacht's small afterguard and he rather enjoyed such vulgar banter with a former naval midshipman, who had briefly held an acting commission as lieutenant.

Drinkwater clambered over the rail, waited his moment, and jumped down into the gig. Settling himself in the stern with the boat-cloak about him, he tucked the tiller under his arm and looked along the thwarts. Six men had been detailed to attend him and, each with his small, round bag of kit, now sat expectantly.

'Toss oars,' he ordered. 'Let go forward.' The painter was cast off onboard *Argus* and coiled down in the gig's bow. The bowman shoved the boat clear of the big cutter's side and Drinkwater gave a wave.

'Heads'l sheets there! Midships the hellum!' Judd's voice shouted and Drinkwater saw the backed staysail and jib suddenly released. For a moment they flogged before the lee sheets tamed them. *Argus* drew swiftly ahead as the gap between the buoy-yacht and her boat widened. Then, as he drew past, Judd's face looked down on them. 'In a week then, Mr Drinkwater.'

'Aye, aye, sir,' Drinkwater replied and then called out: 'Down oars! Stand by! Give way together!' Putting the tiller over he turned the gig for the shore and when he looked back, the big cutter, the huge red Trinity ensign flapping languidly above the end of her boom, was already diminishing with distance. 'Very well, lads, a nice easy stroke. We've about five miles to pull.'

The estuary of the River Carrow debouched into the Atlantic between two granite headlands. The northernmost fell almost sheer to the sea before a great buttress of rock seemed to lean upon it, so that it extended in a series of low steps down to the tideline and beyond. The short spur thus formed, was hidden by the surface of the water, though betrayed by the swirling disruption it caused to both the flood and ebb tides visible on a calm day. On the southern side the headland was grander, splendid enough to be named Pen Carrow. A great grey cliff, seamed with cracks and fissures, some so large that the locals called them 'zawns', and criss-crossed with tiny ledges upon which nested thousands of seabirds, white kittiwakes, black guillemots, dark brown razorbills and the charming little sea-parrots called puffins. The screams of these birds grew louder as the gig approached, the extent of their habitations exposed as the boat drew past a series of isolated rocks, remnants of the ancient extension of the southern headland long since destroyed by the sea's attrition. Drinkwater regarded them with interest, for he believed they might hold the key to his task. They would have names, he thought, given by the local fishermen, though they were shown as mere dots upon the imperfect chart he had brought with him.

He felt the boat lift beneath him and looked astern. They had pulled in almost between the two headlands, and as he stared over his shoulder he saw the low swell humping up so that it obscured the horizon. Foster, the man pulling stroke oar, nodded at the approaching swell. 'It be the bar,' he said flatly, as he tugged on his oar.

Drinkwater nodded. Here the Atlantic drove the sand of the seabed into the river mouth, while the river, contrariwise, tried to push its way out to sea. The depth would be much less here due to the submarine ledge of the bar, hence the steepening of the swell. It would break violently in an onshore wind, even at high water, and must have caused agonies to Captain Poynton when his ship was caught on this lee shore. Drinkwater looked about him. Poynton must have been driven across this very bar on that wild winter forenoon last January. Had it not been for Poynton's unfortunate experience, together with his influence with the Court of Trinity

House, Drinkwater thought it unlikely that he and his boat's crew would have been dumped here for a week.

'What's all this for then, Mr Drinkwater?' asked Foster, the man's question chiming with his own thoughts. Grunts of curiosity came from the other oarsmen as the gig passed under the shadow of Pen Carrow. Drinkwater recalled they had been told only that they were to gather dunnage for a week's absence from the *Argus*, to be sent upon a surveying expedition. Such temporary detachment was not unusual, but it was time he told them what the specific purpose of their absence was.

'Well, lads,' he said, raising his voice so that they could all hear, 'last January the slaver *Montrose*, bound from the West Indies to her home port of Liverpool, made her landfall hereabouts. Half a gale was blowing from the west and the weather was thick. The master, Captain Edward Poynton, let both anchors go when he found the land under his lee. As the weather cleared, he discovered he had fetched up to seaward of the bar we have just crossed. His anchors were holding and the lead showed him he was in about twelve fathoms with a fine sandy bottom. All seemed well, and despite the proximity of the land, they thought they could ride the gale out, but if the worst came to the worst, they might make a run through here.' Drinkwater gestured about him at the towering slopes that formed the entrance to the river.

'Bit narrow,' said Foster, staring up at the beetling cliffs as he threw his weight back on his oar-loom. 'You'd need a deal of nerve to drive a ship through here with a following gale.'

'That,' Drinkwater went on, silently agreeing with Foster, 'was what Poynton deposed. Anyway, the wind shifted three or four points and the weather cleared as the gale increased. The wind-rode *Montrose* swung to the change of wind and then, quite suddenly, both anchor cables parted and the ship drove over the bar and fetched up under the Head there. Poynton and four others escaped with their lives. Of the rest, and the *Montrose* herself, there was not a trace the following day. Poynton had his fortune sunk in the ship, moreover, he swore that the cables were in good condition and that something other than the violence of the wind caused them to part. He made representations to the Trinity House to discover if any wreck was known to exist in the area, upon which his cables might have fouled, but none was known of, nor rumoured.' Drinkwater paused, and then concluded his summary of the loss of the slaver. 'At all events, this Captain Poynton is a determined man and petitioned the Brethren. Now we are come to try and discover the cause of his loss.'

'This guineaman, she was underwritten at some value then, sir?' queried Ross over Foster's shoulder. A slim, wiry man, Ross's ability to read and write assured his presence in any surveying party.

'Indeed, Ross, at some considerable value, I understand.'

The men seemed content with the explanation. Judd had confided in Drinkwater that he had heard that Poynton had promised a substantial bequest to the Trinity House if an effort was made to determine the cause of the loss of the *Montrose* and the realisation of her insured value. 'Wheels within wheels,' Judd had concluded obliquely.

The headlands fell astern and the gig emerged into the broad estuary of the River Carrow beyond. The transition was remarkable – the sea retreated, a narrow grey sleeve glimpsed between the capes, while on either side grass and woodland spread out, the small town of Porthcarrow nestling on the southern bank in the lee of Pen Carrow, behind a small stone breakwater. Drinkwater tugged on the tiller and headed the gig for the cluster of stone cottages which scrambled up the hillside about the square grey tower of a church. It looked an idyllic spot to quarter oneself for a week.

Chapter Two

Porthcarrow

'I don't have a room and you'll not find one, Mister, not here, nor in the Plough in Upper Town.'

'There would be the finding of two meals a day, and I have six men to feed and accommodate,' Drinkwater persisted.

'The answer would be the same – No.'

Drinkwater frowned. He had not expected such open hostility from the landlord of the Anchor and Hope. It was an ironically named tavern, given his situation and his mission. He stared about him. There were three or four elderly men in the low-ceilinged taproom and they stared at him from their benches, clay-pipes poised as though his presence had suspended their conversation.

'We are not the press.'

'We know that, mister. You'm from Lunnon ... the Trinity House, no doubt. We had Cap'n Poynton down here a month or two back, askin' about rocks and wrecks and suchlike, and swearing black murder about wreckin'. That were false witness, mister and we don't like such things, particular' when the Cap'n knew full well that his cables parted ... Maybe,' the landlord added with a grin, 'the mermaids cut them.'

The company roared with laughter at this witticism.

'That's as maybe,' Drinkwater broke in, 'but it has nothing to do with me. I have a simple task to carry out and I'd be obliged if ...' he turned and stared back at the circle of old men. '... If any of you would care to put up myself and six seamen for a few days. I shall pay well,' he added, certain that the inducement would arouse someone's cupidity. For an instant he thought he detected a flicker of interest in the eyes of the old fishermen, but then they turned away and, murmuring amongst themselves, resumed their interrupted game of cribbage.

Drinkwater swung back to the landlord and took his departure.

As he lifted the latch on the door, the landlord called after him. 'You can sleep on the strand, mister, near your boat,' and the advice was accompanied by another rumble of laughter from the cribbage players.

Outside, the Trinity seamen were sitting on benches, their backs to the tavern wall, their faces uplifted to the late-afternoon sunshine. They had gathered about them a knot of curious children and earned the glances of the townsfolk as they went about their business. Drinkwater was nonplussed. For a moment he stood uncertainly as his men looked up at him, expecting some instructions. Then an idea struck him and, just as Foster opened his mouth to enquire after his plans, Drinkwater said, 'Stay here, I shall be about half an hour.'

He found the rectory without difficulty, a fine house set back from the lane which rose up the back of Pen Carrow, and knocked upon the door, recalling his first encounter with Elizabeth in similar circumstances. A plain, severely dressed woman appeared in the doorway and Drinkwater removed his hat.

'I wish to see the incumbent, ma'am. Upon a matter of some urgency and importance,' he added as the woman hesitated. It was clear she was a servant, not, as he had briefly thought, the mistress of the house.

'What name?' she asked curtly.

'Nathaniel Drinkwater. I am an officer of the Trinity House.'

'*The Trinity?*' she asked with some astonishment.

Suppressing his amusement, Drinkwater seized the advantage. 'The Trinity,' he confirmed. He noticed the atmosphere of the house was stale, redolent of cooking and unemptied chamber pots, and did not resent being left upon the doorstep. The rector might be, as Judd had put it, a person of some importance, but he was clearly not a man insistent upon the quality most next to Godliness.

The woman reappeared, a man accompanying her. He was unwigged, dressed in waistcoat and breeches, both of which were stained with snuff and his neck-linen was none too clean. He brought with him the sweet smell of old sweat and had the appearance of a man aroused from sleep.

'Well, sir, who are you?'

Drinkwater smelt brandy upon the rector's breath as he repeated his name. 'I seek accommodation for myself and six men and I am refused at the Anchor and Hope. I am on official duty on behalf of the Trinity House, London—'

'He ain't from the bishop, Mary,' the rector said sharply, and the woman melted away, rebuked. 'Damned fool,' the rector muttered, then he addressed Drinkwater. 'What is your business here?'

Drinkwater tried to explain, but was cut short. 'So, you act in behalf of that troublesome fellow Poynton . . .'

'He lost his ship, sir. He has, er, a natural anxiety to determine the cause—'

'The cause I hear, Mister Drink . . .'

'Drinkwater.'

'Quite so. The cause was well known to be the failure of his anchor cables.'

'He does not believe so . . .'

'And what do you believe?'

'I have an open mind, sir. I am not his creature. I am on official duty with orders to execute and, at the moment, I seek lodgings.'

'And there is no room at the inn, eh?' The rector smiled, a peculiarly unpleasant grimace revealing an intermittent row of stained teeth.

'I was hoping,' Drinkwater began, though the prospect of sleeping under the rector's roof was most displeasing, 'that you would be able to help me . . .'

'*Help you*? You mean accommodate yourself and your sailors here?' The idea of Christian charity seemed entirely foreign to the rector.

'I should pay, sir,' Drinkwater said sharply.

'I should insist upon it, sir. But the matter's quite impossible.' The rector put a finger in his ear, waggled it and removed it, examining the yellow adhesion to its extremity. Then he looked at Drinkwater and shrugged.

'Very well, I am sorry to have troubled you.' Drinkwater turned away, exasperated. The rector's attitude, added to that of the landlord of the Anchor and Hope, boded ill. It was clear that this was not just a lack of local hospitality – this was hostility. Drinkwater could not imagine what Captain Poynton had done to upset the inhabitants of Porthcarrow, but whatever it was, it was going to prevent him finding lodgings for his men, and already the shadows were lengthening.

'Where are you going?' the rector called boorishly after him.

Drinkwater turned his head without arresting his retreat. 'To rig a sail and sleep under my boat on the beach, damn it.'

'Wait!'

Drinkwater stopped and turned. The rector came out under the porch and cupping his hands, bellowed, '*Billy!*' A moment later a small, ragged boy appeared, and the rector bent to chuck his cheek and give him some instruction after which the boy ran off. Straightening up, the rector announced, 'Mr Goodhart has the farm at the end of the lane. I've told him to take you and your men in at half a sovereign a night . . .'

'Have you, sir. That is most kind of you,' Drinkwater responded ironically, but the rector had turned away, and Drinkwater finished his sentence addressing the rectory's slammed door.

The barn was at least plentifully supplied with straw and the farmer's wife gave them a hearty breakfast. Drinkwater had been unable to negotiate a lesser charge than the exorbitant rate arranged by the rector, and Mr Goodhart had belied his name. Nevertheless, the morning promised well, with no trace of either the previous day's overcast or wind. As they pulled out through the heads, an ebb tide sweeping them seawards, Drinkwater, putting the unpleasantness of Porthcarrow behind him, considered the day's work ahead. Mead, Foster and two others, named Thorn and Kerr, manned the oars, while in the bow Wynn, having got out the boat anchor, made the lead ready, a large pot of tallow on the bottom-boards beside him. In the stern-sheets with Drinkwater, the literate Ross prepared pencils and note-tablet, while Drinkwater readied his compasses, pegged a large sheet of paper on his drawing board and tucked his precious sextant under the after thwart.

'We've a good position from Poynton showing where the *Montrose* lay after the shift of wind. We know the direction of the gale and the scope of cable she had veered. So,' Drinkwater explained to the gig's crew, 'that will be our datum point.'

'Have you any idea what we are looking for, Mr Drinkwater?' Ross asked, looking up.

'Yes,' Drinkwater said with a confident grin. 'I think I have. It's called a steeple rock.'

The Steeple Rock

The phenomenon of the steeple rock was one well known to the officers of the Trinity House. The most famous of them lay off the Land's End and was called the Wolf Rock. It had defied all attempts to mark it with a beacon, for only its peak broke the surface of the sea, and it was constantly swept by the monstrous swells of the Atlantic Ocean. This made it the most dangerous of the known hazards off the coast of Southern England, for the only warning of its presence was a swirl of white foam at low tide, and an occasional ominous howl as air compressed in its fissures vented and gave the rock its name. Close to the rock there was deep water, so the danger manifested itself as a needle of hard granite, somewhat like the steeple of a church, upthrust from the bed of the sea far below.

More complex reefs, composed of several rocks, like the Eddystone, could often be seen by vigilant lookouts even at night, or in stormy weather. The very name 'eddystone' indicated the means by which the reef made its presence known. Moreover such reefs could support a lighthouse, as had been established at both the Eddystone and the Caskets, but steeple rocks presented an insuperable danger. Furthermore, a steeple rock could lurk unknown below the surface of the sea, ready to catch the bottom of a vessel passing overhead at low tide and in the trough of a great wave perhaps, or simply to rend a straining anchor cable snagged about its jagged flanks. That, at least on the basis of Poynton's account, was what Judd and Drinkwater had concluded had occurred to the unfortunate *Montrose*.

Drinkwater had no reason to disbelieve Poynton's account, for it had been sworn before a notary. On the other hand, the references to the *Montrose*'s master he had encountered in Porthcarrow began to shake this simple viewpoint, and the loss of certainty increased as the day dragged by and they found nothing. The second day was no more successful and the grins of the fishermen of Porthcarrow, as they passed the Trinity House gig engaged on their own business, were infuriating. On the evening of the third fruitless day, Drinkwater brought the gig into Porthcarrow in their company. The local fishing boats consisted of line and pot boats along with larger luggers. Although they had seen much of these boats, they had had no contact with them, for it was clear the fishermen were deliberately ignoring the interlopers.

'Sent us to bleedin' Coventry, the whores'ns.' Foster succinctly put it.

As they pulled the gig inside the breakwater and made its painter fast to a ring in the wall, Drinkwater caught the eye of a young man in an adjacent line-boat.

'I wish to hire your boat tomorrow,' he said. 'I will pay you five shillings.'

He saw the gleam in the fisherman's eye. Five shillings was a huge sum of hard money, well worth a day off his grounds. Drinkwater's generosity provoked a sharp interest among his own crew, but the young man turned away without a word, busying himself with the coiling down of a line.

'I addressed you, sir, in a perfectly respectful tone.' Drinkwater made a second attempt. 'I am offering you five shillings for the hire of your boat . . .'

The young fisherman looked up. 'No! My boat's not for hire, bugger you.' Scrambling forward, the fisherman grabbed his painter, hauled his boat alongside the quay wall and climbed a rope hanging down it. Drinkwater sighed and Ross caught his eye.

'He were upset, Mr Drinkwater. It hurt him to turn down five shillings . . .'

'It'd hurt me,' put in Foster, to a chorus of agreement.

'Follow him, Ross. Find out where he lives. He'll have a wife or a mother who might be more pliant. Go with Ross, Foster – make it look casual. Just find out where he lives.'

'We might need a drink sir, if he goes in a tavern . . .'

Drinkwater fished a coin out of his pocket. 'Here's thruppence, now get on with it.'

'Aye, aye, sir,' Foster grinned and winked at his disconsolate fellows.

'They're a bloody rum lot hereabouts,' said Mead as they began to take the gear out of the boat. 'Suspicious as Frenchmen . . .'

'What d'you want his boat for, sir?' asked Kerr.

'I want to make a sweep. To stretch a weighted line between two boats and drag it along the bottom. It's going to be the only way to locate this damned rock. I thought it would be quite large. Now, I'm not so sure.'

'There's somefink Ross said, Mister Drinkwa'er,' put in Mead.

'What's that?'

'Well, sir. If this rock cut fru the *Mon'rose*'s cables, couldn't them bleedin' cables have broke the rock . . .'

Drinkwater stared incredulously at Mead. It was certainly possible . . .

'Ross found an old carrot in that barn, d'you see, sir, an' 'e hexplained it to me, like. The carrot broke . . .'

'Yes, of course, that's quite possible. D'you know that never occurred to me.'

Irritated that it had not occurred to him before, Drinkwater ruminated on this possibility. It was obvious when he thought about it. The weight of a ship under the impulse of a strong wind, even with her topmasts sent down and her lower yards a-portlast, was considerable. Add the additional strain conferred by the surge of the breaking seas, and the thing was not only possible, it was quite likely. Drinkwater felt certainty oozing back into him, along with the realisation that he had been foolish in making too many assumptions.

'That don't explain the unfriendliness of these poxy fisherfolk,' said Thorn, adding as he indicated the sextant and compasses, 'I suppose we've got to hump this lot back up to the barn, Mr Drinkwater?'

'I'm afraid you have, Thorn. Do you be getting on with it, and see what Mrs Goodhart has got for us to eat this evening.'

After two days, Mrs Goodhart seemed not to share the hostility of the rest of the inhabitants of Porthcarrow, perhaps because she was a farmer's wife and not one of the bigoted fisherfolk, perhaps because half a sovereign a day put several shillings into her own purse. She and her husband, Drinkwater had gleaned, worked land owned, if not by the rector, then by the squire in whose gift the rector's parish lay.

They had eaten Mrs Goodhart's stew before Foster and Ross appeared in the farmhouse's kitchen. The two men were amiably drunk and pitched into their portions of stew before Ross edged up to Drinkwater, whose position as officer-in-charge gave him the privilege of the only spare upright chair in the room. It had been another long day and Drinkwater was soporific with food and the warmth of the kitchen. He leaned back and drowsily asked, 'Well, Ross? What news?'

'Found his home, sir. Lives with a handsome young bint and their babe near the quay.'

'Very well.' Drinkwater roused himself. 'You can show me when you've eaten.'

An hour later the two men descended to the town. It was almost dark under the shadow of Pen Carrow, which rose dark and sharp against the twilight. Lights were appearing here and there, and the narrow streets were almost deserted. An old woman shuffled past them muttering to herself, a young man and a girl drew back into an alleyway, and a dog urinated against a doorpost. The town smelt of rotting fish, for piles of nets were lying outside the doorways awaiting repair by the women.

Ross quickly led Drinkwater to a tarred black door outside which stood a pair of boots, a pair of oars and a coil of light line, left in readiness for the morning.

'This is the place, sir.'

Drinkwater knocked on the door, lifted the latch and gently eased it open. The hinges had dropped and it scraped on the flag-stones. The young fisherman lay slumped at a table, head forward, asleep on his crossed arms. At the opposite end, a young woman looked up from the basin of water in which she was scouring her pots. The astonishment in her eyes rapidly turned to alarm at Drinkwater's uniform coat, and she called 'John!' so that the young man stirred.

'Don't be alarmed, ma'am. You clearly know who I am, but you may not know that your husband refused to hire me his boat . . .'

'John!' she called again, and this time a wail came from a crib beside the fire.

'Did you know I offered him five shillings?' Drinkwater persisted, gesturing to the baby. 'It would have bought some comforts for you and your child.'

Drinkwater saw the fact strike her, but she was too frightened to say more than, 'John, wake up!' The alarm woke the baby whose squalling filled the room and the fisherman lifted his head from the table. The intruders swam into focus and the legs of his chair squealed against the flagstones as he rose, unsteady with drink, food and fatigue.

'What the hell do you want?'

'I only want to know why you won't let me hire your boat tomorrow.'

'Get out of my house!'

'Name your price, man. You owe it to your wife and child.'

'What 'ave you said to 'im?' he said to his wife with a sudden ferocity.

She had scooped up the child and swayed from side to side, patting its head as the wailing subsided. 'Nothing, John, they just bursted in . . .'

'Five shillings . . .'

'I don't want your five shilling, damn you . . .'

'John, think—'

'Hold your tongue, woman. As for you,' the fisherman pushed himself clear of the table and confronted Drinkwater, 'we don't want you round here! Not you no more'n Poynton. Take my advice and get out while you can. I don't know what the bloody rector be doing encouraging you to stay, damn his drunken soul. Just get out of my house!'

'I don't think we are doing—' Ross began, but Drinkwater had already come to the same conclusion.

'I am sorry to have troubled you,' he said to the woman and backed out into the street.

'There's something not right,' remarked Ross as they walked down the dark street and turned uphill towards the church.

Drinkwater woke early. The sun had yet to rise, and although the air was filled with birdsong it failed to raise his spirits, for he was greatly troubled by the apparent impossibility of his task, the unpleasantness of the previous evening and the knowledge that he was running out of time. The conviction that Ross might be right, and the *Montrose*'s cables had demolished the steeple rock even as the cables were cut through, was less strong as he lay in the straw listening to the snoring of the seamen about him. It was just too much of a coincidence, however attractive it might seem after a long, unsuccessful day. If the rock remained in existence he simply *had* to find it, and the thought prevented him from falling asleep again. Then it occurred to him there *was* something he could do, something simple. Brushing the straw from his person he pulled on his shoes, picked up his coat and stumbled out into the yard. Dishevelled and sticky from sleep he set off up the damp flank of Pen Carrow.

An hour later he arrived at the summit, his legs aching. Like most seamen, although capable of keeping his balance in difficult circumstances, he found walking arduous, and the rising sun, though low, was already warm on his back. As soon as he had gained the vantage point he sought, he settled himself on an outcrop of rock high above the river mouth. From here he could see the swirl of the river as it ran into the sea, its stream adding to the ebbing tide. Delicate filigrees of foam formed necklaces about the rocks below him off the foot of Pen Carrow, while the continuing windless conditions ensured there was no sea running. The water's surface was not even ruffled in the prevailing calm. A low swell, perhaps left over from some long dead gale, perhaps presaging a blow far out in the Atlantic to the westward, seemed to make the ocean breathe with a slow, languid undulation. Drinkwater realised he could expect no more perfect conditions for his observations.

Carefully, he scrutinised the scene below. Almost at once he detected something interesting. About the rocks were set the tiny dan buoys of the fishermen. These small stakes, each with a weft of torn cloth to distinguish it, were anchored to a crab or lobster pot on the seabed. They were mostly tucked close in to the rocks, the habitat favoured by the lobsters. But while there was a sprinkling across the estuary marking lesser outcrops, in one place there were three or four clustered about a single spot. Could that be the location of the steeple rock? Drinkwater felt his heartbeat quicken. Wondering why he had neither noticed nor thought of this before, he pulled his notebook from his pocket. Of course, he thought, quickly thumbing through the leaves, everything looked quite different at sea-level, but the position was some considerable distance from the one Poynton had given which they had been so unsuccessfully searching.

He found Poynton's bearings and regarded the scene before him. The *Montrose*'s master had given a bearing to the north-east which was incontrovertible. Moreover, it ran right through the cluster of dan buoys. Drinkwater broke out in a sweat of anticipation. The second bearing ran to 'a sharp rock', and he realised that Poynton had not laid his compass upon the slab of granite he himself knew as the Mewstone, but at a lesser, more pointed rock, which at sea level lay directly in line with the Mewstone when erroneously viewed from the *assumed* position. Interpretation of the bearing was therefore anomalous at sea level and, Drinkwater thought, chiding himself, he had made a false assumption. On the morning that he had first located the supposed position, these two rocks had been in the eye of the sun and he had assumed the Mewstone to be the 'sharp rock' to which Poynton, in the extremity of his situation, had referred. Both revised bearings crossed over the cluster of pots, but, if he had it aright, the third remained stubbornly obdurate. Poynton had written simply, *S° Headland SE¼E*, and there seemed no way that a bearing of South East a Quarter-point East could be made to pass through anything other than the rock outcrop on the summit of Pen Carrow, the very spot upon which Drinkwater now sat.

He tried visually transferring the bearing through the dan buoys and then he smote his head, berating himself for a silly fool. Just behind him, hidden by a fold in the cropped grass to an observer in a small boat, rose another peak. From the quarter-deck of a ship, it would, he thought, appear as the summit of the south headland! Drinkwater had fallen into the simple but effective trap of making erroneous assumptions – had he acted with less impetuous certainty, it would have saved him much time and labour.

'God's bones,' he swore, thrusting himself to his feet. 'What a callow numbskull I've been!' He began to run back to the farm, not noticing the line of cloud gathering on the western horizon, or the gently increasing undulation in the smooth Atlantic.

As he ran gasping into the yard, he met Ross. Anxiety was plain on the seaman's face.

'Where've you been, sir? We've been looking everywhere for you.'

'Why, what's the matter?'

'We went down to the boat, sir, thinking you were down there, and the buggers have stove it!

Chapter Four

The Matter of a Boat

The gig had been removed from its mooring off the breakwater and dragged up the beach a quarter of a mile upstream. Here an axe had been taken to its bottom and a dozen ribs had been chopped through; the garboard on both sides of the hog were split and, for good measure, several adjacent planks on either side had been beaten in.

Drinkwater's blood ran cold at the sight. Outrage at the act combined with a furious frustration that he was now so close to his objective and had been deprived of the means to achieve it. His only consolation was that their instruments remained safe. For a moment he strode up and down in a lather of conflicting emotions and then he decided what he should do. Appealing to the justices, one of which was almost certainly the rector, was likely to avail him nothing. He must get a boat and finish his task in defiance of local opposition. Then perhaps he could contemplate what action he should take against these fisherfolk who nursed so intense a hatred of strangers that they would commit such an act as deliberate wrecking. Making up his mind, he turned to his men who stood awaiting his decision.

'Well, they've done their best to dissuade us, but I've been out this morning and I wish to make another attempt to locate this rock.' He looked at the men and tried to gauge their mood; it was clear they were waiting for him to finish. 'Foster and Mead, you've both served in the navy, haven't you?'

'Aye, sir.' The two men shifted their feet in the sand and a buzz of flies rose from the dried bladderwrack they disturbed.

'So have I, sir,' said Wynn.

'Good,' Drinkwater replied. 'I intend to commandeer one of the inshore boats. I would rather none of these people were hurt, because if they are we'll not get back ashore alive, but if we employ a little subterfuge, I think we may be lucky. Now, Ross, Thorn and Kerr, are you game for this?'

'Aye, sir, of course.'

'That's as well. Now, this is what we are going to do.'

The men responsible for wrecking the *Argus*'s gig had broken its oars into several pieces. The looms of these had been recovered by Drinkwater's men as they clustered about the smashed boat, and then hidden up their sleeves before they shuffled disconsolately back through the little town with a demoralised air.

'Not a word,' Drinkwater had ordered. 'Not a scowl at a single soul. You may kick a dog out of your way, but you must appear defeated. We are going to retire from this place . . .'

It was clear from the number of men lounging in doorways, that many of them had deferred putting to sea that morning in order to be available if a show of force was put up by the Trinity House party. Judging by their state of penury, it was clear that few could afford a day off in such fine weather – a fact that increased Drinkwater's suspicions. But Drinkwater was gambling on their going to sea as soon as they were certain that he and his men had gone. In this he obliged them by leading his party out of the village before the church clock struck nine, amused to find that two boys had been sent to trail them as they set out inland along the single track which climbed uphill towards Bodmin.

Long before noon the boys grew bored and turned back. Determined to maintain his deception, Drinkwater trudged on so that to anyone watching with a glass, he and his men would be seen crossing the moor and vanishing over the horizon. As they marched, the men speculated on the reason behind the hostility of the fisherfolk of Porthcarrow. Their opinions varied; most regarded the villagers as retarded primitives, suspicious of any outsiders. Ross, on the other hand, claimed that there was another more sinister cause.

'They're wreckers,' he said firmly. 'The place is stuffed with the booty from wrecked ships, *that's* why they didn't want Poynton sniffing around, and that's why they don't want us snooping about.'

Drinkwater paid little attention to the idle discourse of the men. They seemed able to shrug off the events of the morning with ease. Ross, Drinkwater considered, might well be correct, but then he did not have to take responsibility for the smashed gig or the discovery of that damned steeple rock.

They had bought a loaf and a flagon of cider from Mrs Goodhart before their departure and ate and drank once they were over the brow of the hill. After a short rest, they began to work their way back towards Porthcarrow off the beaten track, finding a small spinney to hole up in until late afternoon. As the sun began to wester amid a riot of cloud which presaged a change in the weather, Drinkwater gave his final instructions.

It was almost dark when they set off again. Drinkwater was anxious not to return to Porthcarrow until the fishing boats had come in and the menfolk were dozing about their hearths, so the church clock was again chiming nine as they reached the first cottage on what they knew was called Church Street. But if they had thought to find the tiny harbour deserted, they were mistaken, for a group of men were manning a large lugger and Drinkwater was compelled to retire to the churchyard, hide among the tomb-stones and revise his plans.

He left the men crouching amid the graves and set off to watch the harbour, only to find that in the interim the lugger had sailed and the quay was now deserted. Staring out across the river, he saw the jagged outline of the lugger's sails as she moved out into the tide, heading for the open sea beyond the twin headlands. Drinkwater went back to the churchyard and waved his men on. The moon had yet to rise, and they moved swiftly onto the stone quay. After the tension of the day, the ease with which they stole the young fisherman's boat was a relief. Before casting off, Drinkwater opened the lay of the standing boatrope fastened to the iron ring on the quay wall, and through the splayed strands he inserted a folded leaf of his pocket-book. It was a promise to pay five shillings for the hire of the boat on his return.

He kept the boat inshore as they edged out between the headlands. He could still see the lugger, but thought it most unlikely that anything of the following boat, creeping under the massive shadow of Pen Carrow, was visible from seaward. What concerned him more was the steepening swell and the fresh breeze that met them as they emerged from the shelter of the land.

He had intended that they should lay off the Mewstone to await daylight, then locate the rock before the hue and cry caught up with them. He had left the promissory note to distract the boat's owner, so confident was he now of finding the steeple rock. But the deterioration in the weather, which could only worsen, meant they must start at once. Fortunately, there was sufficient light to see the dark masses of the two headlands and the rocks, and it would not take them long to work their way onto the position. Fortunately too, the boat contained a tub of light line, well furnished with hooks but terminating at one end in a small boat-anchor, or killick. This would simplify matters considerably and, armed with his new knowledge of the dan buoys, Drinkwater headed the boat further to the south than hitherto.

Despite the wind, which was from the south-west, they were also lucky in that its direction threw the assumed position of the unlocated rock in the lee of the Mewstone. They must take advantage of the shelter and, as the boat's crew bent to the oars, Drinkwater explained his reasons for making this last effort and was gratified to hear grunts of approval.

'It'll make all our trials and tribulations worthwhile,' said Ross as he shipped his oar and prepared to assist Drinkwater.

'We might even 'ave this boat back on its moorin's afore any of those daft buggers wake up!' put in Mead, and his fellow oarsmen laughed agreeably.

In the end the discovery of the steeple rock was almost ridiculously simple, though it took five attempts. The first three were disrupted by heavy swells which rolled down upon the wallowing boat at an inappropriate moment, and the fourth was abandoned when they ran foul of one of the fishermen's dan buoys. This and its attached crab-pot had to be lifted, but thanks to the long line left in its tub by the boat's owner, Drinkwater was able to perfect his technique and at the fifth sweep, the drag-line came up all standing.

'I think we have the thing,' he said, as the boat's head jerked round. 'Now just pull easily and take the weight of the boat off the line. Kerr you heave in and tell me when the line's up and down.'

Drinkwater had dropped the killick clear on the landward side of the estimated position of the steeple rock. He had then taken the boat in a wide sweep around the assumed location, with Ross carefully paying out the line over the boat's transom. From time to time Ross had sworn as the hooks caught him, and the four false starts tested all their patience, but the fifth went smoothly, despite the slop of the waves and the spatter of spray that made them curse the chill. By encircling the rock with the anchored rope, they were able to pass a bight of the fishing line about it, girding and thus effectively 'capturing' it. The critical moment came as the loop was completed and tugged the boat's head round so that she was moored to the killick with the line about the rock, almost replicating the situation Poynton's *Montrose* had been in the previous January.

By gently pulling the boat forward until the line led vertically down into the sea, they would bring her over the very spot beneath which lurked the dangerous outcrop. As they did so, Kerr, in the bow, dipped his lead repeatedly, while Drinkwater, his sextant held horizontally and lining up two of the three objects he had selected for the best triangulation, prepared to fix the position of the steeple rock for posterity.

Kerr seemed to be dibbing over the bow for an eternity, and Drinkwater was almost praying as he shook with the effort of trying to retain the images in both sextant mirrors. But at last, just as it seemed he could retain the posture no longer, Kerr shouted with triumph.

'Rock, sir, no doubt! Hard as flint and two, no two-and-a-half fathoms off the soft sand about it!'

'Well done,' Drinkwater called. 'Now maintain station boys, don't lose the bugger . . .' As the men dipped with their oars and kept Kerr's lead bumping on the steeple rock below them, Drinkwater frantically took his first set of angles, then bent double, he ducked into the bottom of the boat where Ross had the boat's lamp alight. Carefully Drinkwater read the angle off the silvered arc, his eyes streaming with the effort. He dictated them to Ross who wrote them down, then he stood again. 'Still holding, Kerr?'

'Bouncing right a-top the bugger, sir.'

'Hold it another moment, then . . .' Drinkwater struggled with the second angle. The two angles bisected adjacent chords of two circles, the left extreme of the right-hand angle resting on the vertical cliff where Pen Carrow fell into the estuary, which in turn became the right extreme of the left-hand angle. The Euclidean solution to this plane triangulation – that the angle subtending a chord at the circumference of a circle was half that subtended at the centre – was simple on paper, but resolving it in practice, in a wildly dancing boat and in the semi-darkness, was beset by practical difficulties. Strained though Drinkwater's skill and patience were, he sat down with a grunt of triumph, having captured the second angle, and read it off to Ross by the light of the lamp. The two angles gave the intersection of the two circles, and immediately beneath that geometric certainty, lay the elusive steeple rock.

For a further half an hour they pulled about the site, roughly establishing the extent of the rock and finding it was indeed a steeple, no more than two or three feet across, yet rising from the seabed some fifteen feet; a sheer needle of granite, and one, it seemed, quite capable of severing a pair of heavy rope cables if they were sawed across its striated surface for a short length of time. Concentrating thus upon their task, it was only when they began to consider that it was complete, that Mead remarked that 'it was blowing a bit now.'

Drinkwater looked up. The lee of the Mewstone in which they had been working had been perfect, but beyond it, the wind had already kicked up a vicious sea. Astern of them the bar was now covered with heavy breaking waves, grey white in the growing light of dawn. They were another quarter of an hour recovering the fisherman's line and killick, which Drinkwater insisted they should not cut loose, by which time the wind was not only freshening, but was veering, blowing ever more directly into the estuary of the Carrow. When the killick had been lifted, Drinkwater set the boat's head towards the bar.

'Give way, my lads.'

There were only four oars in the boat, so the unoccupied men sat shivering, ready to relieve their companions as they pulled for the wild barrier of breaking waves that bestrode the hidden obstruction of the submerged sand-bar. The noise of the breakers mingled horribly with the howl of the rising gale. Drinkwater fought the kick of the tiller as the boat tried to swing round under the impetus of the following seas. The eyes of the crew were astern, where the crests of each succeeding wave rose higher and higher above them, while Drinkwater stared ahead, constantly checking the boat's inclination to broach. The surface of the sea steepened as they ran into shallower water until, with a savage roar, one broke above them and, lifting the boat and flinging it forward, roared past on either side in a welter of white water.

As the crest passed under them, the boat dragged on the reverse slope of the onrushing wave. Drinkwater roared, *'You idlers! Prepare to bale! We may not be so lucky next time!'*

Then they were in the wind-shadow of the next crest, feeling the indifferent mass of it raising them as the boat was accelerated again, feeling the slam of it against the broad transom, and then the dip of the bow and the surging rise of the cartwheeling stern. 'Hold on!' bellowed Drinkwater, as the sudden chilling shock of cold sea water seemed to fill the whole world.

Chapter Five

A Warm Welcome

The wave passed swiftly beneath them before they pitch-poled and the boat fell back on an even keel. It was filled to the thwarts with water, but they were through the worst, and although the wind blew strongly onshore, they had passed the bar into calmer water.

The 'idlers' needed no second bidding and baled frantically, Kerr with his bonnet, Ross with his cupped hands until Drinkwater, securing the sextant and boat compass in their wooden boxes, threw him his own tricorne hat. Once they were between the headlands the oarsmen ran their oar-looms across the boat and they too joined their baling mates. Swamping a boat, while not a common occurrence, was a not unfamiliar predicament to the seamen of Trinity House. The most dangerous aspect of their situation was the long, hook-infested line of the boat's rightful owner. No one escaped its vicious barbs as they mastered their plight, but in due course, cold, wet and hungry, their hands bleeding from the fishing-hooks, they plied their oars again and headed for the grey breakwater.

'Looks like they've discovered the missing boat, sir,' Kerr called from forward.

It was now daylight and Drinkwater could see the figures gathering on the quay.

'Have any of you still got your broken oar-looms,' Drinkwater asked, 'or were they all washed away?'

'I've got mine,' responded Foster, 'jammed it under bottom boards.'

'And I've mine . . .'

'And me . . .'

'Looks as though you might need them,' Drinkwater said, standing up in the stern, retrieving his sodden tricorne from Ross and clapping it on his head. 'Now a nice clip of a stroke there, Foster. Let's show these cod-heads we know what's what, eh?'

Drinkwater put on a bold front as the boat was pulled smartly round the end of the breakwater into the smooth pool within its compass.

'Oars!' he commanded. 'Hold water larboard!' The boat spun round, its stem heading for the ringbolt and its standing boatrope by which it was moored. Kerr was ready in the bows. 'Hold water all!' The boat came to a stop and Kerr picked up the rope. As he did so, Drinkwater, still standing in the stern-sheets, looked up at the fishermen lining the quay and staring down at them. The young fisherman he knew simply as 'John' was there and in his hand a slip of white paper fluttered. So he was aware of the five shillings owing for the hire of his boat. Drinkwater swept the wet hat from his head and made a small bow from the waist.

'Good morning, gentlemen,' he said, then turning to the young fisherman, added, 'I'm obliged to you for the use of your boat, John, and see, it is returned to you early enough for you to go fishing, if you'll risk your neck out there in this weather . . .'

'Why, you damned trickster—' an older man began, but Drinkwater was in no mood for repartee and continued addressing John.

'Your fellow fishermen wantonly destroyed the *Argus*'s gig, and I had, perforce, to avail myself of your kind offer to hire me your own boat for five shillings.'

'Oi made no such offer,' protested John as an exchange of mistrustful glances passed among his mates on the quay.

'Did you not? Well your wife seemed to indicate something of the sort when we visited you the other evening.'

'That's a damn lie!'

Having precipitated an immediate altercation between the unfortunate John and his colleagues, and thus diverted attention from themselves, Drinkwater gathered up his sextant box. 'Disembark nice and quietly, lads, no pushing or shoving.'

'You'd better go first, Mr Drinkwater,' Mead offered.

'Well, if you insist . . .' Drinkwater stepped the length of the boat over the thwarts and, clambering up the rope found a pair of leather boots confronting him as he raised his eyes over the edge. He looked up. 'If you are thinking of kicking me in the teeth, sir, I

574

should think again. If I choose to take proceedings against you, rather than claim my boat was damaged on rocks and that I lost it, I shall have at least one of you hanged. As it is I've completed my business and can truly go to Falmouth without further delay . . . Now, let me up, if you please . . .'

After a moment the crowd fell back with a buzz of comment at the news. Drinkwater disembarked, recovered the sextant box from Kerr and waited for his crew to muster on the quay. Turning to the crowd about him he remarked pleasantly, 'You have a fine steeple rock in the approaches to Porthcarrow, gentlemen, but I guess you already knew that, and could have saved me a deal of labour and anxiety, had you chosen to.'

'We mean you no harm, mister,' said the man with whose boots Drinkwater had been confronted. 'But the sooner you're out of here the better for all of us.' The announcement was greeted with a chorus of assent.

'Well then,' Drinkwater said, 'you had better arrange for that ruffian at the Anchor and Hope to serve us a breakfast, and allow us to dry our clothes there . . .'

'You've half an hour to get out of town . . .'

'Breakfast, sir, before I do another damned thing . . .'

But this argument was scotched before it proceeded further. Attention was demanded by a cry from the bottom of Church Street. Drinkwater could not make out what was said, but suddenly the crowd was moving away, shouting at the man standing in the narrow gap between the houses which marked Church Street's junction with the quayside. Suddenly they were almost alone; only John lingered uncertainly, looking anxiously after his fellows but clearly reluctant to relinquish his chance of claiming five shillings.

'Here, fellow,' Drinkwater said, beckoning him back and reaching into his pocket. 'The five shillings is yours if you'll just put a word in for us in the Anchor and Hope.'

'Why you're a bad wicked man, sir, and that's the truth.' John came hesitantly back toward them, holding his hand out.

'The Anchor and Hope, John,' Drinkwater insisted. 'Then the five bob's yours.' He turned to his men. 'Come lads, breakfast.'

They had to beat upon the tavern door, but when the landlord appeared, Drinkwater stood quietly and let John explain their needs in a low voice. He caught the words, 'hurry up' and 'the alarm's been raised', which turned the landlord from anger at being roused, to obvious compliance. John turned to Drinkwater. ' 'Tis fixed,' he said shortly and held out his hand.

'Come, Landlord, some rum punch for my lads, and then a hearty breakfast of whatever your wife has to hand. We've been up all night and have a King's appetite, eh lads?'

'My money,' demanded the fisherman.

Drinkwater began counting it out into the man's grubby, split hand. 'What's all the hurry, John? Come, stay and have a drink . . .' Drinkwater saw the man hesitate. 'Join us in a bite. I don't imagine,' he added dryly, 'that it will be long in coming.'

'Oi, er, oi'd, er . . .'

'You know there's no hurry, John. You know as well as I do that you'll not get a ship over that bar until high water and that's four hours away. By then,' Drinkwater continued, taking the proffered rum from Kerr and offering it to the fisherman, 'the weather'll make it impossible. You were expecting her yesterday, that's why you wanted us out of town isn't it, eh?'

'How the devil . . .?' John stopped himself, but he had already given the game away and it fell silent in the taproom. Drinkwater motioned the young man to take the rum punch. Having served them, the landlord had disappeared to raise his wife and cook up the demanded breakfast. John found himself surrounded by the Trinity seamen.

'You bastards are wrecking,' Ross said accusingly.

'No, no, we ain't wrecking,' John protested vehemently.

'No, they're not wrecking,' Drinkwater explained, 'but they are expecting contraband. They're smuggling, and a full cargo, if I'm not mistaken.'

'How d'you know—?' John began, alarm written across his pleasant, guileless face, but at that instant the door crashed open and three men with clubs came in, seized the wretched fisherman and dragged him out into the street, where they began belabouring him.

'I think we need those oar-looms, lads,' said Drinkwater, fisting his pewter tankard and slamming it down on the head of one of John's assailants. The fight was short-lived. With one of their number knocked bleeding and unconscious to the ground, the other two men ran off. Unusually solicitous, Kerr and Wynn helped John to his feet. Blood poured down the young fisherman's face from a gash to his head and he was ashen.

576

'Ross,' Drinkwater said sharply, 'do you run to his cottage and get his wife. Those bastards have concussed the poor devil.'

'Aye, the bloody landlord had a hand in it,' Foster said.

'Seen our bloody breakfast off, then, the bugger!'

'Ow d'you know about this 'ere, smugglin' then, sir?'

'I guessed,' replied Drinkwater. 'Ross gave me the lead, but these men aren't deliberate wreckers. Oh, certainly they'd plunder a wreck if they had the chance. I think they'd have had a go at Poynton's *Montrose* if there was any of it left and maybe they've been dragging the site in the hope of some plate, but smuggling's a different matter. The rector's in it up to his breeches, and probably the squire, but we haven't had the pleasure of *his* acquaintance.'

'So what do we do now, sir?'

'Break our fasts and then . . . Well, I can't see Captain Judd working the *Argus* round the Land's End for a week, so we had better make our rendezvous in Falmouth.'

'That's a fair march from here, sir,' Foster said, regarding his empty pot ruefully. 'And we was up all last night after marching all day yesterday.'

'An' our clothes is intol'rably wet, sir.'

Drinkwater looked round the circle of faces and grinned. 'We could stay here until tomorrow if one or two of you could persuade the landlord of the fact. I don't suppose there are too many to argue the point just at the moment.' Foster agreed, as did Mead and Wynn. 'This fellow still looks grim,' Drinkwater added, regarding the fisherman stretched upon the adjacent bench.

At this point the door opened again and Ross led the man's wife into the taproom. 'Help the lady home with her husband,' Drinkwater said wearily.

After the fisherman's wife had been calmed, told what had happened and seen home, they settled to a belated and resentfully served breakfast. Following this, Drinkwater and his men dozed as their outer garments dried before the fire. It was late morning before any of the Trinity men stirred, but when a gust of wind blew the taproom door open and a swirl of rain flew in, Drinkwater woke with a start, then stretched and felt the agony of returning circulation to his cramped and numbed limbs. Slowly he recalled his circumstances, and then, thinking of the injured fisherman and the hours of idleness before he could lead his men out of this benighted place, he decided to see how the wretched fellow was.

Stepping out into the narrow street Drinkwater was almost swept off his feet by a gust of wind. Having struggled to John's house he knocked and went in, removing his hat as he did so. The young man was conscious, his head bandaged with a clean rag and his wife was peeling potatoes. He stirred from his seat, his face puffing with anger at the intrusion, but Drinkwater held up his hand.

'I'm sorry about your injury, John,' he said, 'but it was your own people who hit you. At least you are no longer concussed.'

John subsided and shook his head. 'There's trouble. Mister, an' there'll be more afore this is all over. Reckon you owes me more than five shillings.'

Drinkwater ignored the last remark. 'I know there's trouble, but what is it?'

'It's nowt to do with you, sir, and I'd keep out of it.'

Drinkwater nodded. In his pocket he found a shilling and, leaning forward, he placed it on the blanket covering the sleeping child in his crib. 'Fine baby,' he said, smiling at the woman.

'John, like his father,' she said, smiling back at him. 'You married, sir?' He nodded. 'But no children?'

'No, no children. Tell me, is Big John involved with this smuggling . . .?'

She looked across at her husband. 'Be silent, woman,' he said. 'There's trouble enough already.'

'What *is* this trouble?' Drinkwater persisted.

'There's a damned ship due. She's late like you said an' now they've got her anchored off the bar . . .'

'Just like the *Montrose*, eh?'

'Aye, jus' like the bloody *Montrose*! An' just like the *Montrose* she'll go all to pieces an' we'll lose her an' the cargo, an' then that poor little bastard,' John nodded at the child, 'will have to drag himself to sea like his father an' his gran'father . . .'

'Don't talk like that . . .' his wife cut in, but Drinkwater was already leaving them to their domestic misery, glad at least that the poor young fellow was alive.

When he returned to the Anchor and Hope, Drinkwater made an announcement. 'You're welcome to remain here, but I'm going up on Pen Carrow head. I think we might have a wreck on our hands by darkness.' The door slammed behind him.

'On *our* bloody hands,' Foster protested, 'what's a wreck got to do with us?'

'He's like a bloody bulldog,' Ross remarked, half-admiringly.

Chapter Six

Rescue

The scene from Pen Carrow was stupefying. The fishermen of Porthcarrow were scattered about the slope of the headland, huddled in impotent little groups, like flotsam, Drinkwater thought, washed hither and thither from the quay to this lonely, wind-scoured spot by the circumstances from which they wrested their existence. He felt sorry for them, standing there, watching the small brig as she snubbed at her cable. Whatever the brig's cargo, the attempt to evade duty was a determined and well-planned operation, only spoiled by the weather. Drinkwater could not imagine why they had let her get so close inshore, but concluded those responsible must have decided to cross the bar before the weather precluded it altogether. One thing was certain, the brig could not linger offshore. Every day's delay increased the likelihood of word of her presence reaching Bodmin or Launceston precipitating the arrival of the Excisemen. Now they stood watching any chance of landing their precious cargo ebb away.

'*You* could get her in, sir.' Drinkwater turned to find Ross beside him. 'We could get aboard and you could get her in . . .'

'What the hell are you suggesting, Ross?' Drinkwater frowned at the able seaman. 'You know what Foster said, the entrance is too narrow.'

'*Foster* said it was too narrow . . .' Ross left the sentence hanging for a moment. 'Look, sir,' he went on, 'none of these fishermen is used to handling a brig of that tonnage. They're cod-heads, good at their trade, but ignorant. On the other hand the crew of the brig probably don't fancy lying this close inshore on an unfamiliar coast. She ain't registered in Porthcarrow, is she? And I don't suppose anything much larger than a lugger is, but we . . . you, me, Wynn, Mead, even Foster and the others, we're used to working inshore. You'd not lose your nerve, sir.'

'Wouldn't I? How the deuce d'you know that?'

' 'Cause I've seen you.'

'You don't want to leave the brig to her fate, do you Ross?' Drinkwater asked.

'Doesn't seem right, somehow, sir.' Ross paused.

'Well that's true . . .' The mad idea gathered momentum in Drinkwater's active mind. 'Very well. We'd better ask these villains for the loan of one of their boats again.' And with that, Drinkwater located the fisherman whose boots he had become acquainted with earlier that day, and walked down the hill toward him.

'We've put a pilot aboard,' said the villainous man, whom Drinkwater now knew as Jacob. 'He's a fishermen like ourselves, but he was a prisoner in France during the American War and he speaks the lingo.'

'She's a French vessel, then?'

Jacob turned and looked at him. 'Aye, as you'll find out if you gets aboard her.' They sat in the stern-sheets of the lugger as eight oarsmen pulled her out to sea against the wind and the swell that now, near the top of the tide, swept in between the headlands.

'Your pilot went out in the lugger this morning, then,' Drinkwater said.

'Aye. This lugger.' Jacob smacked the rail beside him. 'She came back in while you were at the inn.'

They sat in silence. It was increasingly difficult to talk as the wind howled about them. The big lugger bucked into the sea and sheets of spray shot aft, stinging their faces and inducing the painful wind-ache that followed. After a few minutes, Jacob turned to Drinkwater. 'Why are you doing this, mister? So's you can turn us all over to the Riding Officers?'

Drinkwater grinned. 'No, Jacob. I know nothing beyond the fact that there's a vessel in distress off Pen Carrow. It is our duty to assist, if it is humanly possible. But let's get her inside the heads and lying to an anchor in the stream first. It brings ill luck to count your chickens before they're hatched.'

The seas on the bar were less violent now the tide had risen, but the state of the sea beyond was wild in the extreme. So strong had the wind become that the crests had ceased to break, but were torn off and shredded instead, their disintegrating spray streaming to lee-ward with the force of buckshot. Pulling directly to windward, they could do little except inch the big lugger forward with tedious, back-breaking slowness. The oarsmen had fallen into a numbing rhythm, and Drinkwater admired their stout fortitude as they swayed back and forth in faultless unison in spite of the shrieking wind and the thrashing seas that pounded the adjacent cliffs with a ceaseless roar.

Ahead of the lugger's stem Drinkwater could now see the brig, her bow rising high out of the water as she breasted the incoming seas, her single cable stretching tightly and leading steeply down into the water. Their own progress was barely discernible, but over a period of half an hour, the brig was noticeably closer.

'The tide's turned.' Drinkwater now had to shout to make Jacob hear. 'We're being carried to seaward by the ebb.'

While this would afford them some assistance in getting out to the brig, it increased the danger of bringing the vessel in, since not only would the strength of the tide grow inexorably against them – something which the power of the wind would easily overcome – but with the wind and tide in opposition, even steeper seas would run in the estuary and, worse still, across the bar itself. Whilst it may have been possible to pass the bar at a lower state of the tide in good weather, to do so in these condi-tions could result in the brig striking the bottom. If that were to happen she might quickly break up. It was not a prospect Drinkwater wished to dwell upon. Besides, they were running out of time.

Then they began to get a little shelter from the plunging hull and, shielded from the worst of the wind, they made better progress, watched by half a dozen heads peering over the brig's rail.

'Keep going, lads, not far now.' Drinkwater turned to Jacob. 'I want all my men aboard. You may have to make several approaches, but do your damnedest.'

'Aye, aye, sir.'

Something about the way Jacob responded led Drinkwater to ask, 'have you ever served in the navy?' Jacob nodded and spat to leeward. 'So have I, Jacob.'

'You, mister?'

'Aye, Jacob. As Acting Lieutenant.'

'*Acting* Lieutenant? Then you were a midshipmite.'

Drinkwater nodded and, despite his precarious situation, grinned. 'We all suffer bad luck, Jacob, but *especially* if you're a midshipmite in His Britannic Majesty's Navy.'

'*Were* a midshipmite, mister,' Jacob growled, and spat again. 'You're bugger all now.'

A moment later the brig, yawing and sawing at her cable, loomed above the lugger as it surged up and down by her dun-coloured starboard side. A short pilot's ladder had been flung over the side and, as the boat rose, Drinkwater made a leap for it. The instant both his feet felt the rungs, he scrambled upwards, for fear the lugger should rise behind him and catch his ankles against the brig's side. Clambering over the rail he jumped down on the deck and cast about him.

Drinkwater recognised the fisherman-cum-pilot, and the worried-looking master. He bowed. '*M'sieur.*' He struck his breast and said, 'Drinkwater *à votre service. Attendez-vous votre,* er . . .' he pointed aloft to the foremast, '*hunier,*' he finished, recalling the French for 'topsail'.

'*Pourquoi?*'

Drinkwater turned and indicated that the brig would proceed through the heads. The master violently shook his head, countering with equal insistence that they should remain at anchor. Drinkwater held out his right arm and sawed it across his left fist, then pointed downward before flattening his hands and waving them laterally in a universal gesture of failure. Realising the master did not comprehend, he turned to the fisherman and asked him to explain his concerns. 'Tell him there's a steeple rock in this area, that the *Montrose* was lost here with two cables down, that he doesn't have a hope in hell unless he gets under way without more delay. Tell him the tide's on the ebb and I haven't come out here to argue with him. Tell him to have his men ready to loose his fore topsail, cut his cable and be ready to give her a stern board and cast her head to starboard.'

Drinkwater turned to his own men, the last of which was Foster. 'I want you men on the forebraces. Except you, Foster. You get forward with that knife of yours and start cutting the cable.' He addressed the master again. 'Captain, get that festering *hunier* ready, stand by the bloody clewlines!'

The unfortunate Frenchman stood uncertainly for a moment,

then a tremor ran through the whole fabric of the brig. From forward a cry of alarm was raised as the cable began to part and the French master bawled his orders.

'*Get forrard, my lads!*' Drinkwater shouted, '*Let fly the starboard and heave aft the larboard forebraces!*' He turned aft to the heavy tiller by which the brig was steered and threw his weight on it, forcing it over to starboard. Even before the brig's crew had let go the fore topsail's clew and buntlines, with a second tremor and helped by Foster's knife, the cable parted. The brig gathered sternway and, with the rudder hard a-port, her head fell off to starboard. With a slam aloft, the half-sheeted topsail slatted aback against the foremast.

Drinkwater stared intently astern, watching Poynton's 'sharp rock' draw closer, aware that the French master was beside him, muttering anxiously. '*M'sieur, m'sieur, regardez . . .*'

But Drinkwater needed no bidding. The fore topsail was now all a-tremble as the wind caught the weather luff. '*Let go and haul!*' he shouted, adding to the French master, '*Capitaine, m'aider!*'

Both men threw themselves on the tiller and, in defiance of the brig's momentum astern, forced it right across the deck so that as the gale caught the after side of the topsail, the stern board was arrested, the brig's bow continued its starboard swing and she slowly gathered headway. But a moment later the vessel was spinning round, her bowsprit appearing to rake the northern headland as Drinkwater and the French captain steadied her for the centre of the channel and the tumbling mass of breakers thundering across the bar.

From their standing start, they seemed now to have gained the speed of an arrow as they raced towards the fearful sight. The topsail had been sheeted home and, as the brig steadied on the entrance to the Carrow, the foreyards were squared. They were committed to the narrow vent through which the river funnelled to meet and mingle with the ocean. Drinkwater felt his knees knock with sudden, terrifying panic. This was sheer madness! He could not believe the self-conceit that had led him to harken to Ross's flattery. He felt certain that, in a few minutes, as they passed into that hideous welter of green, grey and white water, he would feel the fatal impact of the keel on hard sand, see the masts whip and hear the shrouds part with the twang of fiddle strings.

'*Mon Dieu!*' Beside him, the Frenchman blasphemed as the bowsprit stabbed upwards at the sky above Pen Carrow. Drinkwater felt the stern fall into the trough of the following sea, heard again the sudden hush as a wave reared over their stern, and then felt the stern lift, lift with such sudden violence that he could feel the compression acting on his legs and spine. The bowsprit drove downwards and even the topsail seemed to shiver in the lee of the breaker.

Now, now would be the instant the brig drove her forefoot into the sand bar and the masts would go by the board as they cartwheeled, broached and became a helpless wreck. The French master continued to pour out a torrent of invective, but the two men worked like one at the tiller.

There was no impact; instead the bow seemed to lift with an astonishingly graceful majesty. Riding up, the brig was borne forward in triumph on the crest of the wave as it broke beneath them and foamed on beyond the quivering hull. There was a second, less terrifying pitch, exhilarating after the first, and then they were through, the headlands rising on either side. It seemed for a moment that the lower yardarms would scrape the cliffs, but they sped past, sailing in across the placid waters of the estuary. Behind the brig, the lugger, under a scrap of sail, followed in their wake.

Fifteen minutes later the brig, the *Rozelle* of Quimper, lay at her second bower anchor off Porthcarrow and Drinkwater was shaking the hand of the French master who, eyes ablaze with the exhilaration of their triumph, insisted on planting a kiss of gratitude on each of his burning cheeks.

As Drinkwater gathered his men and gear together on the quayside, he was aware that a crowd was assembling at the foot of Church Street.

'Looks like trouble, Mr Drinkwater,' Foster said.

As the Trinity House men approached, the fishermen spread out, barring their exit from the breakwater. Jacob stood truculently at their head and Drinkwater walked straight up to him.

'Come now, Jacob, stand aside. There has been enough bother.'

'Why did you help us, mister?' The question was accompanied by a rumble of agreement. 'Aye, why?' 'Why?' 'Tell us!'

'Why?' Drinkwater set down his bundle and faced Jacob. 'Because I must explain the loss of a fine gig, damn you, Jacob. As you and your fine friends hereabouts all well know, she was lost as I boarded the brig *Rozelle* to render assistance . . .' He turned to the men standing in a semi-circle behind him. 'Wasn't she, lads?' he asked them with a wink.

Ross caught on quicker than the others. 'Aye, sir, lost she was, rendering assistance to the brig *Rozelle*.'

It clearly took a moment longer for Drinkwater's subterfuge to sink in among the fishermen. The subtlety seemed to occur to someone in the crowd after a moment, and the word was whispered to Jacob who remained suspicious, his eyes fixed on Drinkwater.

'And what of the brig *Rozelle*, mister?'

'I shall report her arrival here when I reach the Custom House at Falmouth, Jacob.'

Jacob squinted at the young officer, convinced he was being outwitted. 'That'll be tomorrow, then?' a man next to Jacob asked, his intelligent eyes picking up Drinkwater's intention.

'Perhaps the day after if we can find decent lodgings in Porthcarrow,' Drinkwater responded quickly. 'We have been up all night,' he added, gesturing at the men about him, 'and,' he made a mock yawn, 'I'm deuced tired.'

'We could find you a decent berth, mister,' said the man.

'Not at Mrs Goodhart's,' chipped in Foster. 'She don't serve no ale.'

'No, not at Mrs Goodhart's, Jacob,' Drinkwater added grinning, 'The Anchor and Hope will do very well, if you please.'

The man whispered into Jacob's ear and he nodded reluctantly, still half-bemused at his good fortune.

'I'll slit your gizzard if you've tricked me, mister.'

'Stand aside, man. I've a steeple rock to mark on a chart, a report to write and some sleep to catch up on. I'm too tired to trick a monkey.'

At Jacob's order the fishermen fell back and, slinging their dunnage over their shoulders, the Trinity House men headed for the tavern.

'I told you you could do it, Mister Drinkwater,' Ross said, falling into step beside the mate of the *Argus*. 'But did you really do it to explain the loss of the gig?'

'Don't ask me, Ross. As I said, I'm tired . . .'

Drinkwater wondered if the explanation would really satisfy

old 'Fusspot' Judd. Perhaps, he reflected, he should have paid more attention to Judd's advice to avoid *all* the dangers hereabouts. Well, it was too late now.

But it was true, that young fisherman's wife was a damned handsome young woman.

On Nathaniel Drinkwater

A Valedictory Essay

Each of the fourteen stories of the Nathaniel Drinkwater series has been accompanied by an Author's Note. The first was a self-exculpation, offered to any reader my tyro novel might attract, explaining why I sought to add another runner to what one reviewer of *An Eye of the Fleet* called 'the Hornblower stakes'. But what began as an act of diffidence became, if something of an indulgence, an important part of each book, for I considered it necessary to establish that Drinkwater was a rank outsider in the Hornblower stakes. By way of my Author's Note, I was able to express precisely what I hoped made my new sea-warrior different from his fictional contemporaries. This difference sprang in part from my desire to truly reflect the reality of the sea-life of the period, and not some romanticised version of it, but also from a strong urge to insert my imaginary naval protagonist into the very fabric of recorded history. That is what I believed an historical novel should attempt and, insofar as Hornblower was concerned, what C. S. Forester failed to achieve convincingly. Drinkwater's character emerged from my disillusion with Hornblower after I had discovered that poor Forester, the victim of his own success, had been boxed into a corner, and that a mid-shipman of Hornblower's background, sailing with Edward Pellew in the frigate *Indefatigable* in the early 1790s could not possibly have been a Commodore of the maturity suggested in the novel of that name by the year 1812. Other questions that arose in my adolescent mind as my reading of the period widened also diminished Hornblower's power over my imagination, and while I have been accused of choosing in 'Drinkwater' a name too similar to that of Forester's hero, I can only point to the synonymity between our surnames as well. Is that providence or merely a coincidence?

As a child, I was fortunate enough to attend a small village primary school, perched upon the very edge of the then sacrosanct Green Belt girding greater London, where, incredibly, a class of only three boys and nine girls were coached for the eleven-plus. I was already determined upon a career at sea, and was lucky in having a teacher whose brother had served at sea and whose strenuous efforts and encouragement secured me a place at a good grammar school. Alas, I proved a poor pupil and recall very little of those miserable years beyond the sardonic smile of Sir Peter Lely's portrait of King Charles II – one of the benefactors of the four poor schools from which ours claimed descent – who gazed down upon our assemblies. Only the long tube journey there and back enabled me to escape my torture and to read what I chose. Books on history and books about the sea fed my insatiable appetite for fact and credible fiction. History was the passion of my ascetic father; as for the sea, I can only suppose that my mother's suppressed but romantic tendencies (on those painful parent's evenings when my academic failure was discussed, she loved to see Lely's portrait of the wicked Charles) exposed me to the lure of adventure.

But in a London still bearing the marks of the Blitz, I was confused by inherited notions of national grandeur and achievement, and the ancient ties of events, which were at odds with the changing world about me. Current affairs and politics were not in the curriculum, but they were not off the agenda either. The retreat from empire, the Korean War and the disturbances in Kenya, Indo-China, China and Malaya all impinged upon my primary school days and the threat of recall to the colours disturbed my parents' post-war tranquillity at least once. But receiving my education a stone's throw from Buckingham Palace, the Palace of Westminster and both the great Abbey and the Roman Catholic Cathedral; being able to see the Royal Standard flying above the royal residence from the school's art-room windows and eating my lunch in St James's Park, all sharpened my appreciation of the affairs of state and heightened an impressionable imagination with notions of politics and power. In those days state visits by foreign leaders began not at Heathrow, but at Victoria station, and a procession of broughams with a couple of clattering squadrons of troopers of the Household Cavalry were almost a commonplace just beyond the school gates.

Along with this education by osmosis came negative influences:

the debacle of Suez, the prevailing culture of rejection of my parents' generation's values, anti-establishment mockery and rock and roll. These were followed by acts of adolescent rebellion on my part – a refusal to wear the school cap, smoking cigarettes and falling hopelessly in love with a girl travelling home on the Northern Line. Thanks largely to the distance between my home and school, I managed to keep my personal revolt secret. Not being the type to join the Combined Cadet Force, I instead discovered in the Sea Scouts a means to get afloat. On the Thames I encountered the indifferent brutality of the tides and, having mastered oared whalers and gigs, graduated to sailing dinghies. It is still one of my proud boasts that I did my first chart-work and learned to use a sextant aboard Scott's *Discovery* in the days when she lay at Charing Cross Stairs. Ships became my obsession: I made models of them, went aboard any ship or boat I could gain access to and sent some pocket money to Frank Court's appeal for the preservation of the *Cutty Sark* in 1956.

Alongside my minor nautical experiences in the scouts, ran my passion for reading and, when I could afford it, book buying. Most significantly, the fund-raising efforts of my scout troop in the form of jumble sales, yielded me a complete set of William James's *A Naval History of Great Britain* for the price of half-a-crown – a week's pocket money in those austere days. The cloth bindings of the six volumes were in poor condition, but they dated from 1847 and were the second edition, which unlike the first, included the events of the American War of 1812–14. However, the chief magic of my acquisition lay in the fact that almost all of the pages were uncut, and I formed the curious conceit that I would be the first person to read them!

As I slit the folds to turn and read this 'undiscovered' narrative, I gained my first impression of the real nature of those long years of war before the apotheosis of Nelson – upon which we had over-dosed at school – and the weary ten years of merciless attrition after Trafalgar. James's work is not great literature, for it is necessarily repetitive; nor is it objective, as he is a shameless and unreasonable nationalist; nor is it entirely comprehensive, a few incidents having been omitted. Despite these limitations, however, its merit lies in its author's meticulous attention to detail and his desire to record everything about the remarkable achievements of the Royal Navy which fell within his compass. That the work is an encomium is a given; James never touches upon the horrors or inequities of Georgian life, but then, why should he? He was an establishment supporter, a Tory gentleman, a proctor of the Vice-Admiralty court in Jamaica who was taken prisoner in America upon the outbreak of the war in 1812 and who later escaped to Halifax, Nova Scotia. His work may be no more than a long chronological account of encounters and engagements, but at twelve years of age, who was I to mind? I was swept up by the cracking thrill of it all.

My own small triumph came four years later when I walked out of my last GCE examination, picked up my bags and went to Waterloo station. That evening I was bound for Norway in a very large yawl, to participate in the Oslo to Ostend Sail-Training Race of 1960. I had escaped school at last – and in a sailing vessel!

By that same autumn I was a midshipman indentured to Alfred Holt and Company of Liverpool, bound to serve them for four years while they turned me into a ship's officer, and it was at this point that I began my second apprenticeship: as a writer. In addition to the letters that were then the only way of keeping in contact with home, my employers insisted we midshipmen kept a journal. To my colleagues it was a boring chore, to me it was a joy from which sprang in due course the idea of turning to writing as a serious pursuit. For the time being, it bred a daily discipline to write something down. Years later these embarrassing adolescent memoirs were an invaluable aid to recalling those halcyon days, and inspired me to write *Voyage East*, an 'autobiographical novel' telling of a commonplace voyage in a cargo-liner which was published by John Murray in 1988.

The moments of leisure afforded by the routine of a sea-going life continued to encourage my reading, and developed in me both critical faculties and wild enthusiasms. These centred on historical themes, and I devoured and began to collect any book about the Anglo-French wars of 1793–1815. Stumbling across Sir Arthur Conan Doyle's *Brigadier Gerard Stories* gave me a greater familiarity with the battlefields of Europe, exposing me to the other side of the Nelson coin – the side inhabited by the enemy. Forester's *Death to the French*, arguably his best historical novel, had long before expanded my imaginary horizons beyond the quarterdeck of a British frigate, and I now began to pursue the writings of real participants of those old wars which, before 1914, had been called

'The Great War'. I tramped across Spain with Wellington's weary Peninsula infantry courtesy of Sir William Napier; rode across Europe with Major Marbot and his *chasseurs-à-cheval*, and marched to Moscow with Sergeant Bourgogne of Napoleon's elite Imperial Guard.

By the time I had completed a circumnavigation at the age of eighteen, I had already twice harried the French out of Mother Russia alongside Petya Rostow, and this introduction to real characters in a drama inseminated a modest desire to ape the great Tolstoy as well as C. S. Forester. It was a presumption that at first seemed unrealisable until I read three of Kenneth Roberts's fine novels, *North West Passage*, *Rabble in Arms* and *Oliver Wiswell*, which shifted my historical perception back a generation and sparked an interest in the Colonial Wars in North America. I found the wonderful books of Francis Parkman and devoured them with enthusiasm, after which I sought a one-volume history of the American War of Independence and could find little to cart off to sea.

Soon I was serving in home waters; a married man with a mortgage, a serious career and the prospect of slow promotion. Whilst my work was demanding, responsible and spiced with the occasional excitement, I felt the irksome constraints of 'maturity'. I was also cursed with a wild imagination and infected with the creative bug. In a rash moment I began to write a history of the War of American Independence, carting off my reference books and notes to sea where in off-duty moments I bashed away at a portable typewriter thoughtfully bought for me by my wife. I felt inspired. Not only did the buzz from recreating the past satisfy my disturbing desire to escape from the present, but I thought in my self-conceit that not only would I get the work into print but my timing would be irresistible to any publisher, for the American bicentenary was imminent. Moreover, in working on my reconstruction I stumbled across a young midshipman, Edward Pellew, fighting the Yankee rebels on Lake Champlain. Here, it dawned upon me, was where the real Hornblower stakes could have had their starting point; here, amid the fury of a civil rebellion and a British *defeat*. Here, the *failure* of the Royal Navy had secured French domination of the American east coast and thus delivered success to George Washington and Rochambeau at Yorktown. My interest in sea-power was rekindled, and my thoughts led inexorably towards the bugging question: what happened next?

What happened next to me personally was in fact post-creative depression. While my typescript was being considered, I found I missed the occupation of writing and missed it badly. My commanding officer, having inured himself to my hitherto isolationist tendencies, noticed the difference in me, while my next-door neighbour, the ship's chief engineer, unwittingly suggested a simple cure for my thoroughly nautical complaint of the blue-devils: 'You've done all the research,' he said in an exasperated moment, 'now write a novel about the period!'

I went on leave and thought about it. Back at sea a few weeks later we went to the assistance of a ship in distress. She was aground on a shoal in the North Sea, her engine-cooling system was full of sand and gale warnings were in force. The stranded vessel was immobilised, her crew cold and miserable. As First Officer I was sent aboard to assess the prospect of salvage and a few hours later we had her off the Haisbrough Sand, under tow and with a Lloyd's Open Salvage Agreement between our two masters. I remained aboard the refloated ship for forty hours as we dragged her painstakingly through a freezing North Westerly Force 9 gale – for it was early February – and into the River Humber. She was our prize but there was a drawback. Under the terms of the Lloyd's Open Agreement, it was a case of no cure, no pay. The task of bringing the stricken vessel into a safe haven demanded the skill of an accomplished crew, and when I returned exhausted to my own vessel after seeing the salved ship secure in Immingham docks, it was to a transformed ship's company. Success had lit the fire of cupidity in every eye.

As I showered wearily it occurred to me that men of the eighteenth-century navy must have felt a similar thrill after having taken a prize of war. This, combined with my colleague's notion of my writing a novel, was instrumental in Nathaniel Drinkwater's conception. There was also to be a further strangely apt connection in this incident, for later, as we waited to be called into the Court of Admiralty where our salvage claim was subject to due process of civil law, the German master of the salvaged ship told me that he was a descendant of a Hanoverian major of infantry in the King's German Legion who had fought under Wellington. Despite the fact that we would be on opposite sides of the dispute in court, we chatted amicably about history and he even asked me for directions to Apsley House!

Many other connections between the past and the present were occurring to me. The specialised work I was now doing consisted of complex operations and some very old-fashioned seamanship; I was constantly involved in difficult cabotage, and life was dominated by wind and tide. This bore more than a strong parallel with an earlier period of history, and was much more than artificial replication, for links of usage and practice had not then been displaced by technology and the fanatical rationalisation of postmodern reformers. In short, my nautical roots not only drew nourishment from the past through my writing and research, but also from this very traditional steeping in the art of seamanship which continued to inform my ability to recreate it. Out of this dual experience came my fictional hero in embryo.

But what was I to call this embryonic protagonist? His Christian name, Nathaniel, leapt unbidden into my mind. During the writing of my so-called 'history' of the American rebellion I had conceived a great admiration for the American General, Nathaniel Greene. He seemed not only a more accessible figure than the remote George Washington, but also a more successful soldier. That he fought and beat the tenacious Cornwallis, a man I felt had been let down but who bore his humiliation with some dignity, only added to Greene's lustre. While I admired Cornwallis to a degree, I was not automatically impressed by either his Britishness, or his aristocracy. Greene seemed of sound middle-class stock and, at least at the moment of rebellion, a Brit as well, just as were most of the makers of the revolution at its outset. But perhaps most importantly, history has afforded him little credit for his achievements. It is incontrovertible that Admiral De Grasse's triumph over Admiral Thomas Graves off the Chesapeake in September 1781 secured victory for the Franco-American Alliance and independence for the Thirteen Colonies, but it was Greene who drove Cornwallis into the redouts and trenches of Yorktown where his isolation could be encircled by General Washington and his French ally, the Comte de Rochambeau.

I was attracted to the unsung heroism of Nathaniel Greene: perhaps my own hero would also prove a modest, unsung mover and shaker? The idea was appealing. I thought too, of those odd mysteries and backwaters of history where the record is obscure and the real protagonists unknown, of the vague presence of multitudes of unknown men. I had been much impressed by Showell Styles's Michael Fitton stories. Fitton had really existed and Styles had clothed the few known facts with a personality and a life. And if I placed my Nathaniel in this earlier war, this British defeat in which all the later veterans of the war against the French Revolution and Empire were blooded, I would have a fine opportunity to develop him as a person who for me would become not merely real, but a friend.

But what else was I to call him? Much rests upon a surname and some quality of the age in which he lived had to be implicit in it. Quite clearly I could not steal a surname from a real sea-officer, nor did I want my hero's handle to suggest the slightest whiff of aristocracy or gentility. I simply wanted something respectable, with all that that would have connoted in the latter half of the eighteenth century. To be candid, it never occurred to me at the time that there was any similarity to the name 'Hornblower' when I settled on 'Drinkwater'. I saw it on a refuse skip and I thought therefore that it had an honest ring about it. Perhaps it sounded a little pious, but then I recalled a certain Colonel John Drinkwater had written an account of the Siege of Gibraltar. When I referred to my copy of this book, I discovered within it a pencil portrait of him showing him to have been a man of not unpleasing looks. The fact that his son was much later commissioned into the Royal Navy added a possible 'family' link, but I never made it. My Drinkwater was from a much lower social strata than Colonel John, and his family might have had a rather less exalted station in life as indicated by the appearance of their name on a rubbish skip. Nevertheless, this 'connection' seemed to authenticate the rightness of the surname for the period and it went well with Nathaniel; I even tried out a signature, which meant it was too late for second thoughts. I had the strange sensation of a shadow forming at my shoulder – a shadow that began to haunt me: Nathaniel Drinkwater had been born.

The name of Drinkwater's first ship, the frigate *Cyclops*, was the name of the Blue Funnel cargo-liner of which I was once the senior midshipman, but it was a happy accident that this one-eyed monster chimed so well with the first novel's name: *An Eye of the Fleet*. It was to have been called something else, but the original title clashed with that of another book about to be published, and so after some panicky brain-storming, my editor and I took the notion of the fleet's lookout frigates from a quotation of Nelson's.

Another source of delight to me was that my hardback publisher, John Murray, could scarcely have been more appropriate for my book. The architecture of their premises in Albemarle Street was headily redolent of the Age of Reason and, as they had been Byron's publisher, there was a connection to the Romantics too. John Barrow and John Wilson Croker, both intimately connected to the Admiralty of the day, had been familiar faces at No. 50 as well, so not only did it seem fitting that John Murray should publish Drinkwater, but also its historic links to the period I was writing about somehow authenticated Nathaniel's 'existence'.

Murray had sensibly rejected my history of the American War, but they had not done so offhandedly. Indeed they had done me the courtesy of sending me the reader's report and asked if I had written anything else. I am not sure whether they expected a response so quickly or so comprehensively, but they had received the typescript of Drinkwater's first adventure by return of post. At the time they were publishing the last of Professor Northcote Parkinson's De Lancey novels. Northcote Parkinson's stature as a serious naval historian has been rather eclipsed by his eponymous law, for which he is better known, but his work is well worth reading, giving valuable insights into the whole of the maritime world of the late eighteenth century and his *The Life and Times of Horatio Hornblower* had already become an indispensable complementary volume to Forester's own *'Hornblower' Companion*.

Hornblower and De Lancey had long since been joined by Alexander Kent's Richard Bolitho, Dudley Pope's Ramage and Patrick O'Brian's Jack Aubrey. Upon the launch of Nathaniel Drinkwater one reviewer posed the question of whether 'another naval hero' was required. Even after writing fourteen Drinkwater stories, I am not certain.

Perhaps it was rather that I needed to create him.

Drinkwater's first ship had, of course, to be a frigate. I had become intimate with frigates with Jack Easy, in Captain Marryat's novel *Mr Midshipman Easy*. Marryat had served in *Impérieuse* as a midshipman under Captain Lord Cochrane and I delight in his books to this day, for he is an undervalued author with a keen eye for detail and possessing a mordant wit. With a father at Lloyd's,

Marryat knew a great deal about the merchant service – indeed as part of his remarkable achievements he developed a code of signals for the mercantile marine – and his novels thus encompass the whole spectrum of the maritime life of his time. But Drinkwater's *Cyclops* is no clone of Marryat's *Impérieuse*, nor is Drinkwater's first captain anything remotely resembling Cochrane.

Drinkwater began his naval life in 1779, older than was customary for a midshipman. This maturity enabled him to avoid much of the hell of long apprenticeship and, once he was noticed as being able and active, meant he could obtain an acting commission quickly. But it also allowed him to suffer a greater disappointment when his expectations were in due course dashed. I did not wish to have him languishing overlong in the obscurity of the midshipman's berth aboard *Cyclops*, nor, on the other hand, have him leaping up the ladder of promotion with the ease of a Nelson. *Cyclops* was initially employed on routine fleet business, which enabled me to blood my hero at the Moonlight Battle of January 1780 that was fought between Cape St Vincent and Cape Trafalgar, the sites of later British triumphs, and a remarkable, pell-mell fight, full of action and, for Drinkwater, opportunity. The *Cyclops*'s acquisition of a prize, the Spanish frigate *Santa Teresa* was, I felt after my experience of salvage, something I could readily imagine. It was aboard *Cyclops* that Drinkwater was befriended by the Cornish seaman Tregembo and he in turn befriended a younger, better-heeled midshipman named Richard White. Drinkwater also attracts the notice of the first lieutenant, the Honourable John Devaux, who as Lord Dungarth, is later to become his patron.

It is aboard *Cyclops* that Drinkwater acquires his first wounds, serves as a prize-master and meets the young woman destined to become his wife. Like almost all the women of her time, Elizabeth's history is obscure, overshadowed by that of her husband. Her fidelity is undisputed, but assumed; I felt more able to live with the assumptions made by Drinkwater himself, than to confuse our joint endeavours with too many troublesome worries. After all, I wrote most of these stories at sea and knew how he felt.

The original draft of *An Eye of the Fleet* submitted to John Murray had a different ending, which had been added when I had considered submitting the story for a competition. When my publisher accepted the typescript I was asked to axe this, and finish the story at the point where coincidentally I had first intended it to end. Keen to make any sacrifice that ensured publication, I complied, but in doing so, had to lose some scenes that seemed, to me, indispensable to the history of Nathaniel Drinkwater. In fact they were the basis of much of the second novel, called *The Run of the Tide*, and it came as a shock when this material was rejected, particularly as my editor had intimated that the acceptance of *An Eye of the Fleet* was more or less conditional upon it being the first of a series. My confidence was badly shaken, but I was not dismissed and, instead was asked to go away and think about it. On reflection, *The Run of the Tide*, set in the period following the Peace of Paris and the end of the War of American Independence, lacked action and had degenerated into a rather simpering love story. In something akin to desperation, I dumped the lot, both baby and bathwater, and shifted my chronology several years on, by which time Drinkwater was a father, the French Revolution had taken place, Louis XVI had been executed, and Britain and France were once more at war.

Many years later, unwilling to entirely relinquish the early part of Drinkwater's relationship with Elizabeth and the sinking of the line-of-battleship *Royal George* at her anchorage at Spithead, I did resurrect and rewrite some of *The Run of the Tide*. These events, which are otherwise omitted from the saga, appear as part of the memories that assail Drinkwater in his death throes. They are related in *Ebb Tide* and appear in this fifth and final omnibus. Another yarn arising from this period in Drinkwater's life, though not connected with *The Run of the Tide* and written much later in 1999, is *The Steeple Rock* which is also contained in these pages.

My second novel, *A King's Cutter*, was first published in 1982. I had long been fascinated by these small vessels, the smallest 'cruizers' in the Royal Navy of the period. I had become a small-ship sea-officer myself, and Drinkwater first saw the light of day in the First Officer's cabin of an elderly 1,000 ton lighthouse tender called the *Patricia*. Moreover, I owned a small and largely rotten little Victorian gaff-cutter at the time called *Kestrel*, and it was only natural that Drinkwater's cutter should have the same name. I transferred a few characters from *An Eye of the Fleet* and, as I had myself been promoted to Commander of a vessel with a largely Welsh crew by the time I was writing *A King's Cutter*, I made the *Kestrel*'s lieutenant-in-command a Welshman, Madoc Griffiths. By good fortune my ship's cook, with whom I had sailed before, was himself of a literary bent, being an admirer of the French naval officer-turned-writer, Eugene Sue. He was also a Welsh speaker and proved a willing helper by supplying some Welsh phrases for Griffiths. Aboard *Kestrel* Drinkwater maintains his acquaintance-ship with Lord Dungarth and meets the beautiful Hortense with whom he is to be fatefully linked. The pace of this short novel is fast and Drinkwater finds himself peripherally involved in the Mutiny at the Nore in 1797. Drinkwater's near fatal encounter in the alley in Sheerness with Edouard Santhonax initiates an enmity which is to be of profound consequence to the two men. Where Drinkwater stands for the dogged persistence of British sea-power, Santhonax reflects some of the glory of Napoleonic France, a nod perhaps to Marbot and Bourgogne.

My main purpose in locating *Kestrel* near the Thames Estuary was, however, to enable Drinkwater to take part in the Battle of Camperdown in October 1797, which gave the story a fitting climax with Drinkwater finally getting his commission as lieu-tenant.

At that stage, insofar as envisaging the series running on to a third book, I had only two themes in mind. One was the repetitive dream of the white lady that Drinkwater has in moments of crisis and the purpose of which is made clear in the final story, *Ebb Tide*. The other was the notion that Drinkwater needed patronage and that Lord Dungarth must provide it. Dungarth therefore became a shadowy figure, in charge of the Admiralty's even more umbral Secret Department. It was this that provided the main source of inspiration for the succeeding novels, for Dungarth had his ear to what was going on and was able to facilitate the movement of both anti-revolutionary and British agents, like Major Brown. Dungarth was also able to provide Drinkwater with challenging tasks, making the latter's actions important and, by their subtle influ-ence, pivotal to the outcome of great events.

Despite these definite ideas, *A King's Cutter* proved the most difficult of the entire series to write owing largely to its shaky start. I was uncertain of my ability to produce a succession of novels and I nursed no great ambitions to become a novelist. Besides, I had a career at sea to pursue. Since I was now in command myself, I was not sure I needed Drinkwater's vicarious experiences to trou-ble my sleep; my own life seemed busy and complex enough, full of anxieties and excitements. I felt that I ought to put sticks and canvas behind me. After all, a helicopter regularly operated off the quarterdeck of my own ship; what on earth was I mucking about with Nathaniel Drinkwater for?

I had not counted on the persistence of my hero's shadow nor the qualities of his colleagues. Madoc Griffiths might have been down at the end of *A King's Cutter*, but he was not out and he proved irrepressible as the commander of the *Hellebore* in *A Brig of War*, which was published in 1984. The Royal Navy's minor part operating in the Red Sea during the French invasion of Egypt in 1798–9 is not well known, and it seemed a good opportunity for Drinkwater to add to the lustre of his reputation. At the same time as baulking his old enemy Santhonax he is able to capture the French captain's frigate as a prize. In due course *Antigone* becomes a British cruiser and later Drinkwater's own command. Morris, the sodomitical bully whose tyranny of the midshipman's berth Drinkwater opposed in *An Eye of the Fleet*, also appears in *A Brig of War*, as does Richard White, though by now he has been elevated to post-rank and he has only one further role to play in support of his old mess-mate.

It had been my original idea to progress Drinkwater through all the different types of vessel from a frigate to a cutter, then to a brig. So when I was considering the Battle of Copenhagen as a suitable event in which Drinkwater might figure in some way, I hit upon the idea of making him part of the bomb-vessel flotilla that proved decisive in forcing the Danes to comes to terms in 1801. By leaving the anchored bomb-vessels with their mortars trained on the city as he withdrew his main squadron after the action, Nelson provided an insurance policy for later, should the enemy prove difficult. The truth was that Copenhagen was one of the most insecure of Nelson's three great victories; the Danes were in no mood to submit and very nearly refused. Victory at Copenhagen therefore rested in part on Nelson's odd diplomacy and also on the sight of the little bomb-vessels with their destructive mortars anchored on the far side of the King's Deep, just off the Middle Ground. Writing *The Bomb Vessel* proved a most enjoyable experience, for not only did it include the reading of Dudley Pope's fine book *The Great Gamble*, but it enabled me to deploy much of my own knowledge of buoyage and surveying, something in which I was intimately involved. Moreover I was able to offer another vignette of Nelson, along with other well-known naval officers of his day.

Reconstructing a great fleet action and the details impinging upon the chief protagonists was a thrilling experience. Absorption in such a task can often persuade one that in another life you were not merely a distant witness, but a participant, for working in my cabin late at night I often felt that Drinkwater was whispering his own memoirs into my ear. In such a state of mind it was easy to share Nelson's enthusiasm in promoting Drinkwater to Master and Commander. Less easy was the short-term fate of Edward Drinkwater (Nathaniel's brother), whose purpose was, at this stage in the series, planned but latent. Soon after Copenhagen Nelson was appointed to the anti-invasion squadron stationed in the Strait of Dover and went on to bombard Boulogne. Then, shortly afterwards, the so-called Peace of Amiens halted hostilities for a while.

At the beginning of the fifth book, *The Corvette*, which was first published in the spring of 1985, there is an allusion to Drinkwater having acquired a second shoulder wound to add to the one inflicted by Santhonax in 1797. This was received during Nelson's bombardment of Boulogne and was only alluded to in the novels. However this incident is fully related in *The Night Attack*, written much later in 2000 and appearing in this omnibus.

In *The Corvette* Drinkwater finally gains a command, being ordered aboard the former French corvette *Melusine* as a 'Job-Captain', temporarily replacing the ship's real commander while that officer recovered from the effects of a duel. Drinkwater's *Melusine* was beset by problems: the first lieutenant had the clap, the vessel was bound on a seemingly hopeless mission to protect the whaling fleet in the Arctic, and she had a missionary on board. I have a great interest in the British Arctic whale-fishery and am an ardent admirer of William Scoresby, a notable practitioner of the hunt for the bowhead and Greenland right-whale, but also an intellectual and a Godly man. Some of his characteristics appear in the persons of the whale-ship commanders, many of whom were attached to the Trinity House at Kingston-upon-Hull whose real-life Elder Brethren were once kind and generous hosts to me personally, hence their appearance along with their rush-strewn court room in the story. Also given a cameo role is the Admiralty clerk Templeton; he is of some significance because he resurfaces in *Beneath the Aurora*, set some few years later.

On completion of *The Corvette*, I was conscious of the looming 180th anniversary of the Battle of Trafalgar in October 1985. I had not thought to incorporate Trafalgar into the Drinkwater story because the great battle was so much Lord Nelson's territory that to insert my own man might be thought a presumption – as indeed some reviewers later thought it was. Moreover, my principle was only to involve Drinkwater in an historical event in which it might actually have been possible for him to have participated, and the extensive documentation about Trafalgar seemed to deny me any such opportunity. Then I recalled that two of Nelson's fleet, *Ajax* and *Thunderer*, had been commanded by their first lieutenants during the battle. This was because their captains had been recalled to stand as witnesses at the court-martial of Admiral Sir Robert Calder. Now clearly I could not alter history and deny these two first lieutenants their rightful place but, I asked myself, might not Nelson have wanted a post-captain in at least one of those two ships? And if he had had such a man available, might he not have given orders to transfer him into either *Ajax* or *Thunderer*? I felt the answer was almost certainly 'yes'. So with Drinkwater a newly appointed post-captain not far away in the frigate *Antigone*, it seemed logical that Nelson should consider his presence in *Thunderer* highly desirable. Drinkwater was already 'known' to Nelson and his Lordship might have felt some lingering obligation to him since not only had Drinkwater been badly wounded in the night attack on Boulogne, but Nelson had omitted his name from his report of proceedings. Thus I imagined that both personal and pragmatic influences might well have induced Nelson to write his order for Drinkwater to leave his frigate, in which he had been watching the French coasts since the summer of 1804 and which was then near Gibraltar, and after handing over to his first lieutenant, to make his way in a local boat to join the seventy-four-gun *Thunderer* with the fleet off Cadiz. It was to be the closest Drinkwater would ever get to the command of a line-of-battle-ship, for fate was to intervene. Drinkwater was taken prisoner, and ended up at Cadiz being interviewed by the Commander-in-Chief of the Combined Fleets of France and Spain.

Obscured by the heroic shadow of Nelson is his overlooked opponent Vice Admiral Pierre Sylvestre de Villeneuve. Villeneuve deserves more attention than he receives, for though he has been cast in the role of a defeatist who was beaten before he had begun, the truth is more complex. The Commander-in-Chief of the

Combined Fleets laboured under huge difficulties, not least an imperial master who did not understand naval warfare, a naval establishment too ruled by politics, and a fleet which, although brimful of courage and commanded by a number of gallant officers, nevertheless lacked real sea experience despite its recent crossing of the Atlantic. Several reviewers thought my fascination with Villeneuve smacked of treason and that I sought to belittle Nelson's achievement! These cavilers also considered having Drinkwater present at the battle was too far-fetched. But as a matter of fact, Cochrane was present as a prisoner at the battle of Algeçiras, so the notion was not entirely without precedent.

These critics misunderstood my purpose, seeing only an attempt to tarnish some of the incomparable Nelson's lustre by paying excessive attention to Villeneuve. But if the hero is worthy of study, then his enemy must surely be of some interest too. After all, Achilles gained greater glory from his slaughter of the noble warrior Hector. Be that as it may, the ghost whispering in my ear insisted that my hero had been there, and so the captive Drinkwater gained Villeneuve's confidence and was able to persuade him to sail. Edouard Santhonax also played a part, roughly that of General Lauriston in real life, but thereby increased his personal enmity for Drinkwater. There was another reason for observing the battle from a French perspective. In the aftermath of Trafalgar much occurred that is lost in those accounts which end the battle with the death of Nelson and a great victory gained: the gale, the loss of many British prizes, the wreckage and death all along the coast, and the sally of Don Enrique O'Donnell from Cadiz in the Spanish line-of-battleship *Rayo* – all these are part of the story too.

As a compliment to Forester having made Hornblower the officer responsible for the funeral of Lord Nelson, I made the released Drinkwater responsible for repatriating Villeneuve on the admiral's exchange. The wretched admiral was said to have committed suicide at Rennes, though how anyone could stab their own heart six times remains a mystery.

Despite my having to pore over charts and read the accounts of the surviving French officers – on one ship the senior surviving officer was a mere midshipman – the book had to be delivered in double-quick time to make publication on 21 October 1985 possible.

This was achieved by a whisker and *1805* made it onto the shelves for the Trafalgar anniversary.

Some years earlier than 1805, I had purposefully landed Nathaniel's ne'er-do-well brother Edward on the coast of Jutland in *The Bomb Vessel*. The mystery of how the British government learned of the secret clauses of the Treaty of Tilsit, agreed between Napoleon and Tsar Alexander of Russia on a raft in the middle of the River Nieman in 1807, had long fascinated me. An unfounded rumour suggested that a British agent concealed himself within the flotation chambers of the raft and afterwards escaped with information crucial to Britain. These secret clauses agreed that Denmark and Portugal would be invaded and their fleets added to those of the new allies, thus securing an overwhelming naval superiority over Great Britain. Gleaning these facts enabled the British to take pre-emptive action: the Portuguese fleet was escorted out of harm's way to Brazil, while the Danish fleet was destroyed at the second Battle of Copenhagen. Acquisition of these fleets by the French and her allies, among which Tsar Alexander now counted, would have materially altered the balance of naval forces for, Trafalgar notwithstanding, France and her allies still had formidable battle squadrons and were constantly adding men-of-war to their strength. Despite these imperatives for British action, the unprovoked attack on Copenhagen still rankles with the Danes, made as it was without a formal declaration of war, and interestingly it formed a precedent for the Japanese attack on Pearl Harbour in 1941.

The precise circumstances of the passing of the secret of Tilsit from the banks of the Niemen to those of the Thames remains a mystery. Or rather it did until it was revealed in *Baltic Mission*, the seventh book in the Drinkwater series published in 1986.

By 1807 Lord Dungarth's Secret Department at the Admiralty had employed Edward Drinkwater as an agent. At this time Nathaniel's naval service is closely attached to 'special' or 'particular' service. Several naval officers were in fact engaged in such missions, which often combined espionage, the running of agents and specific diplomatic functions. The best known of these is Sir Sidney Smith whose protégé John Wesley Wright was also an active agent up to his capture and subsequent death in captivity on 28 October 1805. These two officers were largely engaged as part of the efforts of the British Foreign Office to destabilise the revolutionary governments of France. Up to the Peace of Amiens their endeavours favoured various royalist conspiracies against the successive administrations, including those of the Directors and finally First Consul Bonaparte. The breaking of the various rings and cells, the defeat of the Chouans and the assertion of power by Bonaparte largely put an end to these attempts at a counter-coup. Wright was captured and imprisoned in the Temple in Paris where he was said to have cut his own throat. However, the razor 'found' in his hand was closed, and his alleged suicide, though strenuously asserted by Napoleon ever afterwards, has always been suspect. He was a danger to many in Paris at that uncertain time for he knew too much. Suicide was the 'explanation' advanced for the death of Pichegru, a French conspirator, though evidence exists that he was in fact put to death. Both Wright's and Villeneuve's ends similarly bear the hallmarks of political murder, and seem particularly suspicious after the naval humiliation of Trafalgar; indeed, some historians claim Wright's death was not unconnected with the British victory.

The activities of Smith and Wright, sanctioned and funded by the Foreign Office, greatly angered flag-officers like Admiral Lord Keith, in whose areas of command they took place. They also upset Earl St Vincent while he was at the Admiralty, since Smith in particular took on the character of a maverick and seemed outside the chain of command that was so sacrosanct to St Vincent. These senior admirals complained of the Foreign Office's behaviour, but nevertheless such activities persisted after the renewal of war in 1803. Other examples of naval officers on such duties are Captain Sir Edward Owen, who served in the Channel on the French coast for a long time, and Captain Sir Home Popham, whose exploits, like those of Smith, extended the length and breadth of Europe. These were colourful men; officers aware of their own powers and upon whom the constraints of Admiralty control and command fell lightly. They were impervious to the fulminations of flag-officers and as a consequence their names have not been lost to history. Nathaniel Drinkwater is a different kettle of fish. St Vincent's anger with the Foreign Office may have been, at least in part, due to the fact that its actions could run counter, or even compromise, those of the Admiralty's own Secret Department.

At the height of British pre-eminence at sea the Admiralty

commanded a little under one thousand men-of-war, achieving this with a mere eighty clerks and other proto-civil servants. A proliferation of departments and directorates would have been inimical to this administrative economy, yet it seemed not improbable to me that Lord Dungarth might have occupied a modest office under the lead and copper roof of the building in Whitehall, just below the Semaphore Telegraph office. Supported by a brace of clerks, the impoverished earl maintained his connections with the denizens of the Foreign Office and the Cabinet, moving easily among men of rank and power, yet with his naval experience also enabling him to influence and communicate with the Admiralty Board. Dungarth's Francophobia was due to the defilement of his wife's body by revolutionaries when he was travelling through France at the outbreak of the revolution. This event had historical precedent, for it also occurred to General Sir Thomas Graham's wife. Lord Dungarth's Secret Department, briefly presided over by Captain Nathaniel Drinkwater after the earl's death, left no records and was wound up towards the end of the war. There is, however, ample evidence of its activities.

To return to the events of 1807. In the aftermath of Russian defeats by the French at Eylau and Friedland, Drinkwater sailed to the Baltic to do what he could to prevent the Tsar changing sides. In this he fails, but an intercepted message transforms this incursion into a personal mission of extreme danger in which both Santhonax and Edward Drinkwater are involved.

Raking together all the various accounts, hints, rumours and anecdotes relating to the story of the man under the raft, I constructed my own version of this incident. The actual outcome proves that the secret clauses were betrayed or overheard – the method does not now matter much, but it is one of the most exciting true spy stories in history and it seemed fitting for Drinkwater to play his part in it. Not that it did him much good, of course, though he finally kills Edouard Santhonax to preserve the secret. Drinkwater's path was never to be easy, for too much approbation from high places risked him being sent to a line-of-battleship and by this stage of the war that would usually mean enduring the worrying boredom of the close blockade, and being constantly under the eye of an admiral, a circumstance which must have irked active post-captains. Drinkwater had always to remain something of the outsider; the reliable but slightly maverick officer whom Dungarth, in part for his own purposes, keeps in biddable thrall.

The dangerous knowledge acquired by Drinkwater during his role in the affair of Tilsit almost guarantees his temporary oblivion, and so in a new ship, the big frigate *Patrician* – a play on the name of my own ship, for I was then in command of the relatively new 2,500-tonne *Patricia*, and a replacement of her much smaller namesake – Drinkwater was sent into the Pacific where he endured more of fate's vicissitudes. *In Distant Waters*, published in March 1988, took its tone from the temper of the times. After Trafalgar the British naval effort consisted of the blockade and containment of Napoleonic ambitions, the maintenance of constant pressure upon France's allies, the destruction of her trade and the protection of Britain's own. British cruisers like *Patrician* were despatched to the ends of the earth. *In Distant Waters* touches on that curious extension of the Russian Empire into parts of North America at a time when 'ownership' of the Pacific coast was disputed between the Russians, Spanish, Americans and the British. The story of the Russian Rezanov and the beautiful daughter of the Spanish *Commandante* of San Francisco is true and, had it been consummated, might have altered the course of history. In the event its only lasting effect has been to inspire a rather unusual Russian rock-opera. So much for incidentals; the *Patrician* festered with mutinous souls anxious for the war to be over so that they, men of no prospects unlike their officers, could return to their lovers, wives and families. A weary, dispirited Drinkwater was beset by troubles and nearly failed; only his remoteness aided his recovery, for desperate circumstances engender desperate measures. That he was thereby made relatively wealthy was an irony which he cannot share with another soul. In this story, old Hill, his sailing master died. As the war drags on, death is a familiar visitor, depriving Drinkwater of many of his friends.

At the conclusion of the ninth novel, *A Private Revenge*, which was published in May 1989, Drinkwater lost Tregembo amid the mangrove swamps of the Borneo coast. The death of Drinkwater's faithful coxswain and servant so much affected one reader that he complained bitterly, but the revenge of the title concerns Drinkwater's *bête noire*, the obnoxious Morris, last heard of in *A Brig of War*. He was too vile a character not to receive his final comeuppance, and his reappearance allowed me the indulgence of an historical diversion: Admiral Drury's extraordinary attack on the Chinese at Canton. The incident was long considered a significant victory by the Chinese, and with some justification, but it is an event largely ignored by mainstream Napoleonic historians and viewed as being attached more to mercantile than naval history, though of course the two are indivisible.

Such minor events always attracted me as potential settings for Drinkwater's adventures, their sidelining guaranteeing the obscurity of my hero, but also attesting to his 'existence'. The economic blockade by which each side attempted the strangulation of the other was most effectively pressed by the British, with their sea-power and access to all European markets but those under French control. In fact they achieved deep penetration into these too, largely by diplomacy, the corruption of Napoleon's administration and a complicated but effective system of licensing foreign merchant ships. This dimension of the war seemed not to attract my 'competitors' in the Hornblower stakes, but I found it an interesting issue, and one which played a vital part in the war of attrition that took place in the decade between Nelson's victory at Trafalgar and the first abdication of Napoleon at Fontainebleau in 1814. The most significant location in this economical outmanoeuvring was the island of Helgoland, close to the estuary of the Elbe and the old free city of Hamburg; close too to the coast of Hanover whose ruling prince was still King George III of Great Britain and which provided the manpower for the King's German Legion then about to fight with Wellington in Spain. The island had been taken from the Danes in 1807 as a side-show of the major operation of seizing the Danish fleet at Copenhagen and remained a British possession for almost a century. I discovered a file in the Public Records Office which revealed that numerous merchants established warehouses on the island and that a small squadron of minor men-of-war guarded Helgoland and patrolled the adjacent coast. I even discovered that an attack was made on the neighbouring island of Neuwerk which neither William James, nor Sir William Laird Clowes mention in their comprehensive histories of the Royal Navy. There was even a reference to 'special service'. It was a perfect cover for Captain Nathaniel Drinkwater, now fully seconded to the Admiralty's Secret Department and therefore clear of any prospect of being sent to a line-of-battleship. Ageing, trustworthy and dependable, Drinkwater had made himself almost indispensible to the British war effort. Not quite the gentleman, he is nevertheless more than a tarpaulin officer. At home his devotion to Elizabeth and their children, and the quiet personal satisfaction of his wealth are sufficient to assuage his ambition; well, almost. The start of the tenth novel, published in May 1991 as *Under False Colours*, had him in a brooding black mood, caught up in a plan to expose the secret commercial dealings of the Russians with their British enemy and so bring about a rupture between Napoleon and his fickle new ally, Tsar Alexander. The mission naturally miscarried, involving Drinkwater in a dangerous adventure into Hamburg and an encounter with Marshal Davout, the 'Iron' Marshal, who is one of the least likeable but most militarily able of Napoleon's satraps. Here Drinkwater again encounters the bewitching Hortense Santhonax, whose husband he has killed, and in an encounter on the frozen Elbe he fights the horse-chasseur officer Dieudonné. It is a flight of fancy permitted to historical authors to include the minor as well as the major figures in history. *Under False Colours* has several 'real' people in it, as is explained in the Author's Note, and Dieudonné's role is minimal but significant, for we know what he looked like. Years earlier at school, a lunchtime spent illegally in the art-room had revealed to me a wonderful portrait, Theodore Géricault's painting of *An Officer of the Imperial Guard*. The picture shows a cavalryman on a rearing horse. His sabre is drawn, his scarlet hussar-style pelisse flies from his left shoulder and he glares back over his shoulder, his grey's rump covered with its gorgeous leopard-skin shabraque. His red and green plumed busby reveals his regiment as the Chasseurs-à-Cheval of the Imperial Guard, whose undress colonel's uniform Napoleon frequently wore, and four of whose troopers attended the Emperor everywhere he went, even mounting a quadrilateral guard when he urinated. I had read somewhere that the real model for this finely executed portrait of a fiercely moustachioed Napoleonic hero was a Lieutenant Dieudonné – a veteran soldier probably commissioned from the ranks who died in the Russian campaign. I had tucked the fact away until the occasion arose when I needed such a character. I recall typing the name with a flourish, if one can do such a thing. Dieudonné – what a name for a soldier of the *Grande Armée*! – had been real, ergo his encounter with Drinkwater made Drinkwater 'real'. It was all very satisfying creatively.

Drinkwater's continuing involvement with the Secret Department ensured his employment was never dull, and a year later the publication of *The Flying Squadron* introduced the possibility of the dark event that overshadowed the triumph of British sea power over Napoleon's European Empire: a war with America. At the beginning of the book Richard White makes a brief if retrospective appearance, for he is instrumental in enabling Drinkwater to acquire a modest house and a parcel of land in a remote corner of Suffolk. Gantley Hall is not far from the sea and is based on a real house. The ruined priory that lies within its grounds are, in fact, a little distance off and it is a location to which the reader returns in *Ebb Tide*.

The Flying Squadron also dealt with Drinkwater's unfortunate feet of clay. His affair with Arabella Shaw brought several protests. The hero had slipped in the moral quagmire of his 'real' life. To several readers it was unforgivable for him to be unfaithful to Elizabeth. These protesters ignored the amorality of Drinkwater's core business – that of war; they subscribed to the notion that it was all right for a man to be licensed by the state to commit murder of the state's enemies, but reprehensible for him to submit to physical passion. Reprehensible it might have been, but realistic it certainly was. I was interested in the effect a lifetime of licensed murder might have had on the soul of the man himself. Drinkwater received no counselling and bore his various traumas pretty well. Besides, I had another motive in this act of infidelity and Drinkwater carried away from his short *affaire* a mighty burden of guilt.

The Flying Squadron tells of an attempt by the Americans to coordinate the use of privateers – for they had insufficient men-of-war – to disrupt British trade, and the timely measures Drinkwater employs to thwart them. It also sees the end of Lord Dungarth who dies in the company of Lord Moira, a soldier I much admired in his younger days as Francis, Lord Rawdon, and whose defence of Fort Ninety-Six is a minor epic of the last days of the War of Independence. The minor cameo part was a small tribute to a man who subsequently threw his life away by joining the coterie of the Prince of Wales. Moira's presence at Dungarth's death-bed is also an indication of the high circles in which Dungarth had moved and, by definition, the influence he wielded. Moreover, Moira himself appears to have inhabited the edges of covert diplomacy. One consequence of Dungarth's death is that Drinkwater 'inherits' the Admiralty's Secret Department and its clerk Templeton, who had made a brief appearance at the beginning of *The Corvette*.

Napoleon's defeat in Russia shook his supporters, especially the marshalate, who had much to lose if its patron was destroyed and whose members began to seek fall-back positions. Bernadotte was in the process of changing sides and metamorphosing into the Crown Prince of Sweden, while Napoleon's brother-in-law, the extravagantly flamboyant Marshal Murat, who had already usurped the Neapolitan half of the kingdom of 'the Two Sicilies', was anxious not to lose power if his imperial brother-in-law, Napoleon, was defeated. The British actually signed a treaty with him, though they had little intention of honouring it if push came to shove. For the time being it sufficed to deprive Napoleon of the wholehearted support of Murat and his Neapolitan army, much of which had, like other French allied forces, marched among the columns of the *Grande Armée* into the horrors of a Russian winter. Not so many had marched out again and Murat would do almost anything to ingratiate himself with the British, including augment his betrayal of Napoleon to keep his usurped kingdom. Thus, when by way of a quid pro quo a Neapolitan officer brings news to London of a secret concordat between the Americans and the French, it is Drinkwater whose Secret Department intercepts the intelligence and Drinkwater who finds himself at sea once more.

Drinkwater's brief stint at a desk coincided with my own much longer sojourn in similar circumstances. Promoted and living ashore I found myself feeling like a fish out of water. Happily, I escaped to the fjords of Norway in Drinkwater's company, aboard the frigate *Andromeda*, once commanded by Captain Prince William Henry, Duke of Clarence, and afterwards King William IV. His Royal Highness had not proved a good captain, having been too harsh on his crew, and had been quietly removed by a sensitive Admiralty, though ashore he continued to climb through the naval ranks with the ease afforded princes. Why did I choose this ship? Well, it was another indulgence; mythical names had often been used for frigates as they also were for the Blue Funnel liners in which I had cut my professional teeth; moreover I had bought a small, five-ton gaff-cutter of the same name, my own little *Kestrel* finally having fallen apart.

Beneath the Aurora was published in April 1995. There had been an hiatus of three years since *Under False Colours* due to the fact that John Murray had bravely commissioned me to write a history of convoys to Russia during the Second World War. Writing of these harsh voyages in arctic waters led me to set the new Drinkwater story in a northern theatre.

The spectacular fjords of the Norwegian coast, which I had first visited as a sail trainee in 1960, had indeed been penetrated by British men-of-war, for after 1807 in the wake of the 'Rape of Copenhagen, Denmark – whose territory Norway then was – had become a savage and implacable enemy. In what they themselves still call 'The English War', the Danes fought bitterly to strangle Britain's vital Baltic trade; a trade in naval supplies that was made the more acute by the outbreak of war with America, the loss of American supplies and American interdiction of Canadian resources. It was a struggle in which the Danes enjoyed some success, and while today the Americans might have more or less forgiven us for burning Washington, the Danes have most certainly not done so for our destruction of their own capital city. Sadly, while Nelson's battle of Copenhagen is known of, few in the United Kingdom have even heard of the second battle of 1807, though at Waterloo Wellington rode a horse acquired in that short campaign and named after the Danish city.

In its conclusion, *Beneath the Aurora* revealed Drinkwater's softening nature. He was older and wiser, war-weariness had laid siege to him and he was pricked by grief and bad conscience. He was devastated by the loss of his great friend James Quilhampton, Mr Q, whose companionship he had greatly valued. He felt this acutely and in some way it explained his odd behaviour in dealing with Templeton. He was by now a man who dragged a burdensome past with him. But the residual guilt left from his *affaire* with Arabella Shaw was sufficiently potent to prevent him succumbing to the charms of Hortense Santhonax when she throws herself at his feet in the aftermath of Napoleon's downfall in the opening chapters of *The Shadow of the Eagle*.

The association of *Andromeda* with the Duke of Clarence, along with her availability at the time, ensured that Drinkwater's frigate was part of the Allied Squadron that conveyed fat King Louis XVIII back to France in 1814. The squadron was commanded by Clarence, who had by this time become an Admiral of the Fleet and who was entrusted with this short task. I had some fun with this event, which also included two of the yachts of Trinity House, with which Drinkwater soon renews his association as an Elder Brother, and in due course Drinkwater will receive his knighthood, though long after this first encounter with royalty. There is a painting by Nicholas Pocock that was exhibited in London in 1815, and which now hangs in the Old Royal Naval College at Greenwich. It shows this flamboyant squadron, with its British, Bourbon French and Russian escorts, surrounding the British royal yacht, the *Royal Sovereign*.

But this is only the start of the penultimate Drinkwater story (first published in 1997) for Hortense arrives to trade security for information and our hero is off again – this time to thwart a plot to spirit the defeated Napoleon to the United States in order to mastermind an invasion of Canada and the establishment of a new, Napoleonic state in that former French colony. This was to be facilitated from the Azores, which in 1814 was being considered as Napoleon's final place of exile by the delegates attending the Congress of Vienna. The quondam Emperor's father-in-law, Emperor Francis of Austria, objected to Napoleon being left on Elba, an island too close to Europe in general and the Austrian provinces in northern Italy in particular. As the Congress danced and debated, all sorts of mad schemes and intrigues were underway as attempts were made to settle that delicate balance of power in Europe upon which the only prospect of peace lay. In the event, the impositions of the restored Louis XVIII and his exiled court, who behaved as if the Revolution had not occurred, made conditions favourable for Napoleon when he tossed his hat back into the ring, escaped from Elba and marched on Paris, initially with only one thousand men. As a consequence the Azores were eventually dropped as a place of exile for the man who had now, according to the furious delegates, placed himself outside the law, in favour of the remoter and less accessible island of St Helena.

Some of the confusion of this brief but electric period was evident on the broad and indifferent bosom of the Atlantic where Drinkwater fought a sharp action with his enemies. Though he could not prevent the so-called 'Hundred Days' of Napoleon's last gamble, he successfully upheld the power of Britain at sea.

Returning home, Drinkwater too was caught up in one final adventure linked to the Waterloo campaign, though scarcely a part of it. *Ebb Tide*, as has been intimated earlier, is a compound story of flashbacks centred upon the last days of Drinkwater's life, and sees the end of Hortense and of Drinkwater's brother Edward. The disaster of running down her own boat by the Trinity House steamer *Vestal* in 1843 is based on a real event about which I had known for many years and kept in store for the purpose of despatching Drinkwater. His life, I felt, should not end in bed, nor should he be allowed to die in his wife's arms. That final deprivation was part of his dutiful life and spiced with the irony of his just-too-late promotion to flag-rank as a retired, or 'yellow', admiral. He had long lived with the premonition of his death, brought to him periodically in the dream of the white lady who eventually turns out to be neither the succubus he had once thought, nor the transfigured Hortense, but the angel of death in the form of *Vestal*'s virginal figurehead. It was, I think, a fitting end for an old sea-warrior. He had made his pile, achieved his knighthood and continued to serve his country as an Elder Brother of Trinity House. I also played a final card of my own in *Ebb Tide*. I too was once The First Officer of a Trinity House Vessel, and I wanted a walk-on part in Drinkwater's world. Recalling that fortuitous synonymous coincidence, The First Officer of the *Vestal* is therefore named Forester; he is myself in a previous life, and thus I claimed a passing acquaintanceship at the very least with the principle character of these stories.

Drinkwater's last act was not so much heroic as sensible. He was an old man, he was injured, his time had come, so he relinquished the oar that supported him, giving it up to another, younger man. His sense of responsibility was over-developed, the habit of command excoriated the inner man.

In a sense I mourned his passing, even though I had played God with him for over twenty years. I am uncertain of his position in 'the Hornblower stakes'. Is he as different from his colleagues and competitors as I wished him to be? Only you, the reader, can say. As to whether he will survive, who knows? All I can say is that fundamental to all my writing is the fact that for the greater portion of my working life I myself have *been at sea*. Its influence on me in all its moods has been profound. I have earned my living on it and by it, been seduced by its beauty, terrified by its power, overwhelmed by its elemental quality. I have dodged its worst moments and twice cheated it of drowning me, though it may yet succeed. Now I am, as it were, on half-pay ashore. I cannot live without being in sight of the sea and I spend my leisure hours pottering about on it like the Water Rat, messing about in boats.

If the stories of Nathaniel Drinkwater have any purpose, apart from whiling away the captive hours of their creator, it is simply to entertain. If, however, they engender an enthusiasm for maritime matters and naval history, they will have exceeded their remit and gratified their author. And if the reader has struggled to the end of these ramblings with a faint air of exasperation, I offer the consolation of a quotation of D. H. Lawrence. Lawrence wrote that one should 'not listen to the didactic statements of the author, but to the low, calling cries of the characters, as they wander in the dark woods of their destiny'.

Perhaps I might substitute 'quarterdeck' for 'woods' and leave the reader to the faint echoes of the past, real and recreated.